Melissa K. Roehrich is a dark fantasy romance author that loves coffee, dragons, and constantly rearranging her bookshelves. She spends her time writing, reading, and homeschooling her three boys in the Middle-of-Nowhere, North Dakota, where she lives with her boys, husband, three dogs, multiple barn cats, and chickens on a small farmstead. She is constantly trying to convince her husband they need to add goats and ducks to the mix, and one day, she'll succeed.

LADY OF DARKNESS SERIES
Lady of Darkness
Lady of Shadows
Lady of Ashes
Lady of Embers
The Reaper (novella)
Lady of Starfire

THE LEGACY SERIES
Rain of Shadows and Endings
Storm of Secrets and Sorrow
Tempest of Wrath and Vengeance

Lady of Ashes

Melissa K. Roehrich

BOOK THREE

ONE PLACE. MANY STORIES

This novel is entirely a work of fiction. The names, characters and incidents portrayed in it are the work of the author's imagination. Any resemblance to actual persons, living or dead, events or localities is entirely coincidental.

HQ
An imprint of HarperCollins*Publishers* Ltd
1 London Bridge Street
London SE1 9GF

www.harpercollins.co.uk

HarperCollins*Publishers*
Macken House, 39/40 Mayor Street Upper,
Dublin 1, D01 C9W8, Ireland
This edition 2025

4

First published in Great Britain by
Melissa K. Roehrich 2022

Copyright © Melissa K. Roehrich 2022

Initial cover and map design: Melissa K. Roehrich

Melissa K. Roehrich asserts the moral right to be
identified as the author of this work.
A catalogue record for this book is
available from the British Library.

ISBN: 9780008719418

Set in Goudy Oldstyle Std by HarperCollins*Publishers* India

Printed and bound in the UK using 100% Renewable
Electricity at CPI Group (UK) Ltd

All rights reserved. No part of this publication may be reproduced, stored in a retrieval system, or transmitted, in any form or by any means, electronic, mechanical, photocopying, recording or otherwise, without the prior permission of the publishers.

Without limiting the exclusive rights of any author, contributor or the publisher of this publication, any unauthorised use of this publication to train generative artificial intelligence (AI) technologies is expressly prohibited. HarperCollins also exercise their rights under Article 4(3) of the Digital Single Market Directive 2019/790 and expressly reserve this publication from the text and data mining exception.

To everyone who took a chance on Lady of Darkness,
To everyone who fell in love with
Scarlett, Sorin, and crew,
To everyone who has taken the time to message me,
fill my cup, and make my world a better place—
This is for you.

Map

- Chateau
- Solembra
- Fiera Moutains
- Fire Court
- Tana River
- To Avonleya ←---
- Windonelle
- Baylorin
- Water Court

White Halls
Wind Court
Shira Cliffs
relarion
Forest
eon
Dresden Forest
Toreall
Witch Kingdoms
Earth Court
ack
alls
Night Children
Shifters
ra

Playlist

Music is powerful. When I write I have music blasting in my earbuds, and many asked for a playlist. I adore when books come with playlists that follow along with the story. You feel everything more. It immerses you more. It brings everything to life. If you find this to be true for you too, here you go! Enjoy!

Spotify link:

If you don't have Spotify, the full Playlist can also be found on my website: https://www.melissakroehrich.com

A Lady of Darkness Reference Guide

Having a little trouble remembering all the people, gods, and who fits where? With this quick and easy reference guide, you'll have all the information you need at your fingertips.

THE TWO BIG ONES

Scarlett Monrhoe: Scar-let Mon-roe
Our heroine, Death's Maiden,
Fae Queen of the Western Courts

Sorin Aditya: Sore-in Ah-deet-yah
Your new book boyfriend,
Prince of the Fire Court,
King of the Western Courts,
formerly known as Ryker Renwell

BAYLORIN CHARACTERS

Callan Solgard: Cal-in Soul-guard
Crown Prince of Windonelle

Cassius Redding: Cas-ee-us Red-ing
A member of the Assassin Fellowship,
Scarlett's personal guard,
Commander in Windonelle army

Nuri Halloway: Noor-ee Hal-o-way
Death's Shadow, Night Child

Juliette: Jewel-ee-et
Death Incarnate, Witch, Oracle

Mikale Lairwood: Mi-kay-l Lār-wood
Dirty bastard, Successor Hand to the King

Veda Lairwood: Vā-duh Lār-wood
Mikale's sister, Conniving bitch

Tava Tyndell: Tā-vah Tin-del
Daughter of Lord Tyndell

Drake Tyndell: Dr-ache Tin-del
Son of Lord Tyndell

Lord Balam Tyndell: Lord Bay-lum Tin-del Leads the Windonelle armies

Alaric: Ah-lār-ick
Assassin Lord

Sloan: Sl-own
One of Prince Callan's personal guards

Finn: Fin
One of Prince Callan's personal guards

PLACES

Baylorin: Bay-lore-in
Rydeon: Ride-ee-on
Solembra: Soul-em-bruh
Xylon Forest: Zy-lon For-est
Jonaraja Forest: Jon-uh-raj-uh Fore-est
Avonleya: Av-on-lay-uh
Aelyndee: Ā-lin-dee
Tykese River: Tie-key-s Riv-er

Windonelle: Win-dun-el
Toreall: Tore-ee-all
Threlarion: Thruh-lair-ee-on
Dresden Forest: Drez-den For-est
Shira Forest: Sheer-uh For-est
Maara: Mar-uh
Edria Sea: Ed-ree-uh See
Siofra: See-ō-fruh

A Lady of Darkness Reference Guide

FAE CHARACTERS

Talwyn Semiria: Tal-win Si-meer-ee-uh
Fae Queen of the Eastern Courts

Eliné Semiria: Ell-ee-nay Si-meer-ee-uh
Former Queen of the Western Courts

Henna Semiria: Hen-uh Si-meer-ee-uh
Former Queen of the Eastern Courts

FIRE COURT

Cyrus: Sigh-russ
Second-in-Command of the Fire Court

Rayner: Rā-nir
Third-in-Command of the Fire Court

Eliza: Ee-lie-za
General of the Fire Court

Beatrix: Bee-a-trix
Fire Court Healer

WATER COURT

Briar Drayce: Br-eye-er Dr-ace
Prince of the Water Court

Sawyer Drayce: Soy-ur Dr-ace
Second-in-Command of the Water Court

Neve: Neh-vā
Third-in-Command of the Water Court

Nakoa: Nuh-kō-ah
Commander of Water Court armies

EARTH COURT

Azrael Luan: Az-ree-ehl Lou-on
Prince of the Earth Court

WIND COURT

Ashtine: Ash-tin
Princess of the Wind Court

OTHER CHARACTERS OF NOTE

Deimas: Day-i-mas
Former King of Mortal Lands

Esmeray: Ez-mer-ā
Former Queen of Mortal Lands

Hazel Hecate: Hay-zl Heh-ka-tay
High Witch

Rosalyn: Roz-uh-lyn
Night Child Contessa

Stellan: Stel-on
Shifter Alpha

Arianna: Are-ee-on-uh
Shifter Beta

Auberon: Aw-bur-on
Rosalyn's Second, Night Child

Tarek: Tār-ik
Talwyn's twin flame, Fae

A Lady of Darkness Reference Guide

THE GODS

Anala: Ah-nall-ah
Goddess of Sun/Day/Fire

Saylah: Say-luh
Goddess of Shadows/Night

Celeste: Sell-esst
Goddess of the Moon/Sky

Sefarina: Sef-uh-ree-nuh
Goddess of Wind

Silas: Sigh-lus
God of Earth/Land/Forests

Anahita: Ah-nuh-hee-tuh
God of Sea/Water/Ice

Reselda: Ruh-zel-duh
Goddess of Healing/Health

Falein: Fae-leen
Goddess of Wisdom/Cleverness

Arius: Ar-ee-us
God of Death/Darkness

Serafina: Sair-uh-fee-nuh
Goddess of Dreams/Stars

Temural: Tem-oor-all
God of the Wild/Untamed/Adventure

Sargon: Sar-gone
God of War/Protection/Courage

THE SPIRIT ANIMALS

Amaré: Ah-mār-ā
Phoenix, Bonded to Sorin

Shirina: Shi-ree-nuh
Panther, Bonded to Scarlett

Maliq: Mal-eek
Wolf, Bonded to Talwyn

Nasima: Naw-seem-uh
Silver Hawk, bonded to Ashtine

Rinji: Rin-gee
Red Stag, bonded to Azrael

Abrax: Uh-brax
Water horse, bonded to Briar

Celene: Suh-leen
White Fox

Paju: Paw-juh
Golden Owl, previously bonded to Eliné

Ejder: Edge-der
Dragon

Kilo: Kee-low
White Python

Altaria: All-tar-ee-uh
Black eagle

Ranvir: Ran-ver
Dragon

LITTLE WHIRLWIND & THE PRINCE

The girl clapped her hands over her mouth to quiet her breathing. Her knees were drawn into her chest as she huddled under the sofa table in the drawing room. The navy and gold embroidered decorative covering hid her from view.

She sniffed the air, scenting him in the room.

"I know you are in here," came his voice. She felt a flicker of power spearing out into the room. She couldn't hear his footsteps even with her Fae hearing, but then again, when a Fae warrior was hunting you, he knew how to move without a sound.

She focused on steadying her breathing like she'd been practicing, willing those winds that flowed around her to calm and keep that covering from moving even an inch. That other power flowed around her, and she felt it scrape a flaming claw down her cheek. She flung her shields up, but it was too late.

"Got you!" The covering was flung up as flames surrounded her, and a male peered under the table at her, his dark hair falling over his forehead into his eyes.

The girl screamed.

The male's laughter filled the room as the girl giggled with delight. "You calmed your wind, but forgot about your shields, Little Whirlwind."

"I know, I know," the girl huffed. "There is so much to remember."

The male's golden eyes twinkled. He gave the girl a wink as he said, "Extinguish the flames around you, and I will sneak you some frozen cream before your aunt returns." Then he added, "Blowing them out with your breath is cheating."

The girl narrowed her jade green eyes at the male. In a whiny voice she said, "Why can I not just blow them out?"

"Because you need to learn to use your power with your mind, not just with your hands and mouth. So either put them out by sucking the air from them, or you will be stuck under there all day while I eat frozen cream by myself," he answered.

The girl had a pout on her lips, but she closed her eyes. In and out. In and out. She steadied her breathing just like he had taught her to do, pulling from her pool of winds and air.

"Easy, Talwyn," the male said softly. "You control it. It does not control you."

"I know. I know," Talwyn muttered. She reached into that pool of swirling wind, trying to pull up just a small amount of air current, when something else caught her attention. There were flowers and sand and leaves amongst her winds. Where had those come from? The flowers were beautiful. Tiny purple lavender and white dogwood blooms. She reached towards those now, swirling in her whirls of air, and as she touched one—

A gust of wind blew through the room. The flames around her roared to life. She could feel the heat but knew they would not burn her. Sorin would never let harm come to her.

"You blew flowers in from the gardens, Little Whirlwind," Sorin said, flicking her nose as he extinguished the flames that surrounded her. Talwyn took his hand, and he helped her from beneath the sofa table. Her turquoise dress swished on the floor as her mahogany brown hair flowed on the phantom winds around her.

"Ashtine never does that. She has more control than I do, and she is younger than me," Talwyn complained as Sorin led her to the door.

"Lady Ashtine is nine. She is only a year younger than you," Sorin answered with a soft smile.

"And she is a Wind Walker. It is not fair," Talwyn said.

"What is not fair?" came a feminine voice from the hall. Her aunt swept in, graceful and perfect as always. Her dark brown hair was swept into a loose knot at the nape of her neck, and her icy blue eyes were soft when they landed on Talwyn. Talwyn let go of Sorin's hand and ran to her. "Hello, little queen," her aunt said, crouching down to peer into her eyes and stroking her cheek. "Now tell me. What is not fair?"

Talwyn sighed, blowing a piece of her hair out of her face. "Ashtine has better control over her magic, and she's a Wind Walker."

"You will master your power, Talwyn. You have only just started

your magic lessons. Because she is a Wind Walker, her powers emerged sooner. Your magic will grow as you grow," her aunt replied gently. "How did your lesson go today?"

Her aunt had straightened, taking her hand and leading her from the sitting room. Sorin, as always, was to her right as they walked along the corridors of the Black Halls. "It was fine," Talwyn answered. "Except that I blew flowers in from the gardens."

"Did you now?" her aunt said with a laugh. "The violets or the roses?" "They were little white and purple flowers," Talwyn answered.

Her aunt halted. "We do not have such flowers around the Black Halls."

"She probably blew them in from across the Courts, Eliné. It was quite the gust," Sorin said from beside her.

"Of course," Eliné replied, resuming their walk down the corridor, but something had changed. Talwyn couldn't quite put her finger on it. "Are we off to get frozen cream?"

"She figured out our secret plan again," Sorin said to Talwyn conspiratorially. Talwyn giggled. "It is not really a secret if we do it every day, Sorin."

Sorin feigned shock. "Shh, Little Whirlwind. She will hear you." Talwyn giggled again as a swirl of leaves appeared beside her aunt's head. Eliné reached up a slender hand and plucked a message from the leaves that disappeared as suddenly as they'd appeared.

Sorin instantly went rigid. "What does Luan want?"

Eliné gave him a pointed look. "Prince Azrael is responding to a question of my own, Sorin." She placed Talwyn's hand into his. "I need to speak with him quickly. I shall meet you both in the kitchens." Tweaking Talwyn's nose, she said, "Leave me a scoop of strawberry frozen cream please."

"I should go with you," Sorin said, his focus on his queen.

"It is a quick inquiry, Sorin," her aunt said, running her hands down her sea blue skirts. "I will be fine."

"Eliné—"

"I will be fine, Sorin," Eliné said, cutting him off. Her eyes flared brightly. Talwyn stood still, looking between her aunt and her closest advisor. She rarely saw them upset with each other.

Sorin was giving her aunt a contemplative look as he said, "Something is wrong." It was a statement, not a question. As if he knew her aunt so well, he could tell such a thing just by looking at her. It was these moments, these glimpses into her aunt's world as queen, that made her pray to the Fates that Sorin would be able to remain her Second when she had to take up her role as Queen of the Eastern Courts.

When her aunt did not reply, Sorin said, "Ten minutes, Eliné. Then I will come to you if you have not returned."

Her aunt sighed. "Someday, Prince of Fire, we need to revisit the chain of command here." She lifted her hand, her palm flat, and blew across it, splashing water into Sorin's face.

Talwyn laughed delightedly, and her aunt threw her a wink before she disappeared into the air. Concern still lined Sorin's face, but when he noticed Talwyn studying him, it morphed into a smile. "Well, Little Whirlwind, what kind of frozen cream shall it be today?"

"Chocolate!" she cried. "It is always chocolate."

"You know you will need to extinguish some flames before it melts into chocolate soup, right?" he asked, rolling small balls of fire between his fingers.

Talwyn groaned. "I bet Ashtine doesn't have to do this."

Sorin smiled, sending one of those flames dancing down her arm. "Lady Ashtine is not going to be a queen someday."

"Do you think I will be as wonderful as my mother was?" she asked, while Sorin pushed open the doors to one of the bustling kitchens. One of the cooks saw them and immediately went to the ice boxes.

"Little Whirlwind," Sorin said, lifting her off her feet and setting her onto the counter. "You will be one of the greatest queens this world has ever seen."

Talwyn's heart filled with pride at the look Sorin gave her. So proud. So adoring. "You will be with me too, right?

"As long as I am still on this side of the Veil, I will be by your side," he said, giving her long hair an affectionate tug.

"Aunt Eliné doesn't like me sitting on the counters, you know," she said, the cook handing her a bowl of chocolate frozen cream.

"We will call it another one of our little secrets," Sorin said with a wink, as he took a bite of his vanilla dessert. "Now hurry, before you are drinking your frozen cream instead."

Talwyn felt her bowl warm in her hands, and she focused on wrapping her icy winds around the bowl to keep her frozen cream from melting.

PART ONE
OF SECRETS & BETRAYALS

CHAPTER 1
TALWYN

Talwyn Semiria opened her eyes. She was in her large four-poster bed in her chambers at the White Halls. Books were scattered beside her across the comforter. She slid out from under the covers, grabbed a navy blue silk robe and slipped her arms into it. The moon still hung high in the sky, telling her it was the middle of the night. She breathed air into the embers still smoldering in the hearth, and they flickered to life. As she stood before the window, she opened her palm. Small purple lavender and white dogwood flowers appeared in her palm.

Ashtine was gone, flitting amongst the winds. She had been more distant than usual since Scarlett had mentioned the Maraan Lords. Azrael was at his Desert Alcazar tending to some inner court matters. Sorin and Briar were with their queen preparing for a trip to the mortal kingdoms.

And she was alone. Utterly alone.

She closed her fist, crushing those little flowers in her palm. As she did, she shoved the memory she'd just relived down to the depths of her soul.

Little Whirlwind.

Then she threw the window open and tossed the crushed flowers, sending them flying on a gust of wind.

She was climbing back into bed to try to sleep a few more hours, when a breeze that was not hers blew through the room, and Ashtine, Princess of the Wind Court, stepped from the winds.

"Good. You are awake," the female lilted. Her silver hair was flowing around her on her own winds. She stood looking out the window Talwyn had just vacated.

"I find sleep hard to come by these days," Talwyn sighed, getting back out of the bed and crossing to her closet. "To what do I owe the pleasure this night?"

Ashtine was silent while Talwyn slipped on a pair of loose pants and a shirt and re-emerged.

"I thought you would be more upset," Ashtine mused. Talwyn froze. "Why would I be upset?"

"Queen Scarlett is missing," she said simply.

Talwyn checked her temper, knowing her friend wouldn't react to it anyway. "What do you mean Scarlett is missing?"

"I mean no one knows where she is," Ashtine said, as Nasima, the spirit animal of the goddess of the winds, flew through the still open window. The silver hawk came to rest on Ashtine's shoulder. Ashtine turned and fixed Talwyn with her sky-blue eyes. "You did not know?"

"No, I did not know," Talwyn snapped. She drew an earth message in the air, sending it off in a whirl of leaves. "How did this happen? Did Shirina come for her?"

"Perhaps. The winds do not know."

The winds might not know, but Talwyn had a good idea of someone who would.

"How long has she been missing?" Talwyn demanded, beginning to pace her bedroom.

"The West Court Princes were confronting the Night Children at their borders a few days ago, when she disappeared," Ashtine said, gracefully lowering to a chaise by the window.

A few days ago?

Talwyn clenched her jaw. "Why were they doing that?"

"Because the Night Children demanded to speak with them."

"Why were we not informed?"

"Why would they inform us?" Ashtine asked as she stroked Nasima's head.

"I am the Fae Queen. Sorin should have told me," Talwyn said tightly.

"You are not *their* Fae Queen any longer." Ashtine's eyes were fixed on her in question, her head tilted to the side.

"So I am simply no longer informed of anything regarding their Courts?"

"One would assume you would be told what Queen Scarlett deems necessary, and since she is currently unavailable . . ." Ashtine trailed off as Azrael Luan, Prince of the Earth Court, stepped from the air.

"What?" he demanded.

Talwyn's brows rose at his address. "Rough night, Az?"

"It has been a rough few days when there is a fucking fight just north of my border, and I find ten dead Night Children there. Or what was left of them anyway," Azrael said, crossing his arms over his chest.

"Why is it suddenly a godsdamned trend not to inform me of anything?" Talwyn snarled.

Lightning flashed across the sky outside. Azrael's hard stare was assessing her now as she continued her pacing, a vortex of wind at her fingertips.

"Talwyn," he said slowly, "what has happened?"

"The world is going to shit, apparently. That is what has happened."

Azrael must have looked to Ashtine because the princess said, "She is upset that the Western Courts no longer answer to her."

"That is *not*—" Talwyn sighed, running a hand over her face. "I am upset that my cousin has apparently gone missing. *Again*. And I was not immediately informed that a queen is nowhere to be found. However, now I cannot deal with that because we need to do damage control at the Earth Court border."

"The border is under control," Azrael said sharply.

"You know who killed the Night Children?" Ashtine asked.

Talwyn met Azrael's hesitant gaze. "There were ashes and bodies that were frozen and shattered. Others with no apparent cause of death."

"You think it was Scarlett? Why?" Talwyn asked, finally ceasing her pacing to study her Second.

"I think the one who may hold those answers, likely holds the answers you seek as well," Azrael ground out.

"Let me change," Talwyn sighed. "Then we will pay a visit to the Fire Court."

She turned to speak to Ashtine, but she was already gone, vanished on a wind.

Talwyn stripped off her top as she entered her closet once again and called out to Azrael, "So, when were you planning to tell me about the issues at the border?"

"In the morning. After you had actually slept. Which apparently was not happening anyway," he retorted.

She reemerged to find him still brooding, and leaning against a wall. His features were taut, his entire body rigid. Talwyn bent down to lace up her boots. "What else do you need to tell me?"

"I crossed the border to examine everything," Azrael answered. "There was another scent woven amongst everything. It was buried and muted, but it was there."

"What was it? Scarlett?" she asked, standing and reaching for her weapons to begin strapping them to her leathers.

"No. It was not hers. It smelled of . . . Earth Court descent," Azrael finally admitted.

Talwyn slid daggers into her boots. "You think you have a traitor in your Court, Prince?"

Azrael crossed the room and grabbed her cloak from near the door, handing it to her. "I think there are many possibilities for that, starting with mere coincidence and ending with the new queen not being who she appears to be."

Talwyn's fingers froze on the clasp of her cloak. She slowly brought her eyes to his dark brown ones. "I told you what the Oracle showed me. We will need her, Az."

"The Oracle is known for saying something and not revealing how that knowledge should be used," Azrael snorted, crossing his arms once more. "The Oracle is worse than Ashtine."

Talwyn rolled her eyes as she resumed clasping her cloak. "You are just upset that you do not intimidate Scarlett."

Azrael scowled at her. "That is rich coming from you, your Majesty."

"Are you ready?" Talwyn asked, holding out her hand to the Earth Prince and ignoring his comment.

"To go verbally spar with Aditya and Drayce? Not particularly. They are no longer under your rule. They were insubordinate before Queen Scarlett showed up on the scene. Now they are going to be impossible, especially with Aditya's wife and twin flame missing," Azrael pointed out, his arms still firmly crossed.

"Maybe she is not missing. Maybe there is a perfectly rational explanation. Let's go," Talwyn said, motioning for him to take her hand so she could Travel them to the Fire Court.

"Too many things are not adding up, Talwyn," Azrael replied, pointedly ignoring her outstretched hand. "We should sort through these things before we charge into a Court that is no longer ours."

"For the love of Celeste, there is not time," Talwyn said, her temper beginning to rise. "Those fools might already be doing something incredibly idiotic to get her back. Either take my hand or I am going alone."

"This will not end well," he muttered, finally taking her hand.

"It never does with Sorin," Talwyn replied, as they disappeared into the air.

CHAPTER 2
SORIN

Sorin Aditya stared at the map of the mortal kingdoms before him. They were in his personal study at the Fiera Palace; his Inner Court and Briar's Inner Court were debating amongst themselves where she could be. The same thing they had been doing for the last two days. Nakoa, Commander of the Water Court armies, had been left in charge of the Water Court border, and Neve, Prince Briar's Third, had been stationed at the Fire Court border. Sorin's own entire Inner Court would be accompanying him whenever they decided where they were going. The problem was, they had no idea where to even begin to look. She'd left no clues or indications of where she was going, and then she'd blocked their twin flame bond.

The most obvious place was the mortal lands, but there was no concrete evidence that that was where she had gone. Sorin could only assume she had gone to Mikale Lairwood, despite him adamantly refusing that being an option. They had never finished the argument though, and she would do whatever was necessary to protect those in her charge.

He had known something was wrong. Unease had filled him with each step he'd taken away from her. He should have sent Eliza and Cyrus over the border to speak with the vampyres. He should have stayed behind and watched with her until she had been ready to tell him everything she'd figured out; but she had already blocked him out by that point. She had already put some type of resistance on their bond, before she'd somehow enacted that Blood Mark in the dirt, her blood splashed across it, obstructing their bond.

Scarlett. Scarlett. Scarlett.

He kept throwing her name down the bridge between their souls, kept feeling his words slam into an ancient wall. One glimmer. That's all he wanted. One flicker that she was all right. One glimpse to get an idea of where she had gone.

Sorin glanced down at the twin flame Mark that flowed over the back of his hand, down his thumb and first two fingers, showing that they'd completed three of the five Twin Flame Trials. It was still there. She had to still be living. Cyrus's Mark had faded when Thia, his twin flame, had been killed. Talwyn's had done the same when Tarek had died. Although hers had taken longer to disappear. He assumed it had been because they had still been in the Trials that needed to be completed to become fully bonded twin flames. If Scarlett was—

No. That was not a possibility. He would know. He would know if she were gone from this world.

And if she was, he'd rip apart everyone involved before he tore down every realm in existence to find her beyond the Veil.

The entire room fell silent as the lit braziers roared higher, and Sorin clenched his jaw, reining in everything that was coursing through him. His hands were flat on the table beside the map he was staring straight through. Embers rolled off of him, and he knew there were likely flames flickering in his eyes.

"Sorin," Cyrus said calmly, placing a hand on his shoulder. "We will find her. You'd know . . ." He swallowed thickly. "You'd know if she were somewhere you could not follow."

"There is nowhere she can go that I will not follow," Sorin snarled. Before Cyrus could reply, a breeze fluttered through the room and Princess Ashtine stood before them all. She bowed to Sorin. "I apologize for coming unannounced and uninvited, Prince of Fire."

Sorin blinked at the show of respect. Ashtine had always been incredibly considerate, but he could count on one hand the number of times he'd interacted with her without Talwyn present. Briar was striding for her, and it took Sorin a moment to remember that the Water Prince and the Wind Princess were involved. He glanced to his Court and found the same recollection crossing their faces. Sawyer Drayce, Briar's brother and Second, however, was still focused on the maps before them. Clearly seeing his brother with Ashtine was not a rare occurrence for him.

"Ashtine," Briar said, stopping in front of her. He reached up and stroked Nasima's head, and Ashtine closed her eyes to the touch as if she could feel it herself. When his fingers moved from her hawk to her cheek, her sky-blue eyes opened to meet his icy blue ones. "Something has happened?"

"You do not know that your queen is missing?" she asked with a tilt of her head, her gaze flitting around the room.

"Yes, my dear, we know this well," he said softly. "Do the winds speak of where she has gone?"

"I do not know where she currently sits, but I know where she Traveled to when she left these lands."

"Baylorin?" Eliza asked sharply.

Ashtine's gaze fell on her with that piercing intensity. "No. She was seen closer to your other homeland."

"The Earth Court?" Sorin growled. "Why?"

"The winds do not know why your wife traveled there, but Prince Azrael reports that she took on and defeated many Night Children in Toreall near the border. He and Talwyn will arrive shortly. I do not know what they plan to reveal to you." She spoke swiftly and softly. Nasima clicked her beak, and Ashtine's head tilted, listening.

Sorin glanced at his Ash Rider. Rayner nodded and disappeared in the smoke of the braziers, understanding the silent order to go and investigate the border himself.

"Did the winds reveal anything else, Ashtine?" Briar asked.

Ashtine stepped closer to him. "The winds have all changed, my heart," she whispered. "They speak . . ." She shook her head, and Nasima's feathers ruffled. "They speak differently. I cannot walk among them as easily."

Sorin could only stare at the princess. The odd female who never showed emotion. The princess who spoke in quirky riddles and vague references. She was visibly trembling as Briar's arms came around her and pulled her into his chest. Her cheek rested lightly against his chest, and this time the room fell silent at what stood before them.

Sawyer looked up from the map, a grim expression on his face. "The last time she spoke like this was right before we learned of Eliné's death," he said quietly.

"She is not a Seer. She cannot possibly know such things," Eliza snapped, stepping to Sorin's side. A snarl that Sorin rarely heard from the male rippled from Briar, and Eliza's brows shot up at the ferocity of the sound. Sawyer opened his mouth to say more, but another voice spoke first.

"She may not be a Seer, but I am."

Everyone turned to see a young woman who appeared to be around Scarlett's age. If she had gone through her Staying, however, who knew how old she actually was. She had long, red-brown hair that was half up. She wore gray pants and a white top that laced up the front, and was barefoot as she stood in the study that had quickly become far too overcrowded with people. But beside the woman stood Shirina, the goddess Saylah's panther, her tail switching back and forth and her silver eyes pinned on Sorin. Every Fae in the room bowed deeply to the panther.

"Who are you, and how did you enter these walls?" Eliza asked, stepping in front of Sorin and Cyrus. Briar and Sawyer had moved in front of Ashtine, but she seemed unconcerned.

"I am many things to many people," the woman answered, stroking the panther's fur.

"But to you," Ashtine said, stepping around her lover and his Second and dropping to a knee before the woman, "she is an Oracle outside of her cave."

Sorin knew then as he sank to his own knee. Juliette.

A hand came to her slender hip. "Normally I am incredibly formal when it comes to things like this, but since you have been dealing with my sister, who is anything but formal, I am hoping this can be a rather casual affair." Sorin's head snapped up, meeting her eyes. She gave him a soft smile as she continued. "And please, for the love of Reselda, do not tell her you all just bowed before me. I would never hear the end of it."

As one, the Fae all rose to their feet, and Sorin stepped forward. "I have heard much about you," he said. "She misses you greatly."

"I know, Prince," Juliette replied softly. "And I wish we had more time to discuss such things, but I cannot stay long. Shirina brought me here because she cannot get to her."

"What do you mean she cannot get to her? She is her spirit animal," Briar cut in, stepping to Sorin's side.

"You are correct in your thinking that she has learned to read and interpret the ancient magic, Prince of Fire," Juliette went on, ignoring Briar's question. "You are also learning that she will go to extreme lengths for those she views as in her care. Those she claims as her own. She saw that moment as a way to save many, to save all of you, but she did not understand the cost."

"There is always a great cost for that magic," Sorin replied.

"Indeed. She thought she knew it. She thought *you* would be the cost. That she would have to sacrifice her bond with you. But she was willing to do so to save your Courts. However, the cost was greater than she anticipated."

Sorin stepped closer to the Oracle. "What was it? What was the cost?" Juliette shook her head. "I cannot tell you more than that Prince of Fire. I can tell you, though, that you will need more than the people in this room to get her out. And that when you find her, she will not be the same as when she left."

Sorin reached to grab her hand, but Shirina gave a snarl of warning, and he dropped his hand back to his side. "Can you tell me where she is? Does Mikale have her?"

"At this moment? No. Will she be turned over to him once more? Even I have not seen."

"Lord Tyndell or the Assassin Lord?" Sorin asked.

"Act quickly. Time is not on your side," Juliette replied.

There was a flash of soft light, and she and Shirina were gone a moment before Talwyn and Prince Luan stepped into the room from the air.

"Princess Ashtine," Talwyn said curtly when she spotted her near Briar. "You beat us here."

"I anticipated you would be here sooner," Ashtine replied, her voice having returned to its usual lilt.

"And what have you told our Western Court friends?"

"Little that they did not already know," she answered.

Talwyn studied the princess for a moment while Luan's eyes swept the room with distaste.

Eliza and Cyrus were immediately flanking Sorin once more, but he gave Talwyn and Luan a mocking smirk as he drawled, "I am glad you are both here. We are in need of your assistance."

Every head in the room whipped to him. "Come again?" Cyrus asked.

But Talwyn spoke before Sorin could say more. "Were you planning to ask us for help before or after you informed us that Scarlett had gone missing again?"

"Since she went missing after defending the Earth Court border,

I figured the least you can do is help us get her back," he answered, casually strolling behind his desk and lowering into his chair, leaning back.

"Excuse me?" Luan growled.

"My queen went to aid your border, did she not?" Sorin asked with a raise of his brow.

"We did not request her aid."

"We were monitoring the situation just fine," Talwyn said, stepping to the edge of the desk, bracing her hands and leaning over it. "Perhaps if you had taught my cousin the proper procedures and politics of our Courts, this could have been avoided."

"My queen does things her own way. Something you should be familiar with Talwyn," he quipped, holding her gaze as he laced his hands behind his head. "Proper procedures aside, you were right, Little Whirlwind. We have found ourselves planted on the same side."

Talwyn had gone still as death at her childhood nickname, and fury poured off of her. "That is not the way to gain my assistance, Prince of Fire," she whispered with lethal calm. "I suggest you try a different tactic."

Lightning flashed across the sky outside, and Sorin glanced at it, a bored expression on his face. "Someday you will learn to control that temper, Talwyn."

"Be very careful with your next words, Sorin."

Sorin unlaced his hands and leaned forward, bracing his palms against the desk before him. "Through our own resources, we have narrowed down her whereabouts to Baylorin. Most likely in one of two places." He waved his hand across the map on the desk. A swirl of smoke had it morphing to a map of the capital of Windonelle. "The problem is that I cannot simply walk into either of them. Due to the little quest you sent me on, I am fairly well acquainted with both establishments. I will be expected and not welcome."

"And how exactly can we help with that?" Talwyn asked through gritted teeth.

"*You* can help by giving Luan use of your ring to Travel us in and back out once we have her. I will not risk another queen of the Courts going into the mortal lands until we know what we are up against."

"That does not explain how exactly you are going to get to her,"

Luan cut in, studying the map before them. His dark shoulder-length hair swaying around him.

"I do not need to explain the full scope of my plans to you. Not any longer," Sorin answered, maintaining his bored air.

Talwyn snorted. "How happy you must have been to finally be rid of me, hmm, Sorin?"

Sorin studied her jade green eyes and mahogany hair braided down her back. And for the briefest of moments, he saw the child she had been. He saw them in the gardens of the Black Halls working on controlling her magic. He saw her picking flowers to bring back to Eliné. He saw her sipping hot chocolate in his Fiera Palace after playing in the snow all afternoon, while Eliné had been away on a trip to another Court or territory.

And he found himself saying quietly, "No, Talwyn. I have never once been happy to not be on the same side as you."

Talwyn pulled back from the desk, straightening. Her tone had softened almost imperceptibly when she said, "We will help in whatever way we can to get her back, so that we can proceed with finding the keys."

Sorin nodded. "I need to finalize a few things. Be ready to depart tonight. We will go in under the cover of darkness."

Everyone was quiet while Talwyn held Sorin's stare. "Do not lose another one of mine, Sorin," she said quietly.

"I swear to you on my life, Little Whirlwind. He will come back to you."

CHAPTER 3
SCARLETT

Scarlett.

Scarlett. Scarlett.

Her name was a faint knocking at the back of her mind. A voice she could almost make out. A voice that pulled at her soul. A voice that was sometimes echoed by a growl. But then it would become silent once more. Kept just out of reach.

Tarek had slapped shirastone shackles to her wrists and ankles and hauled her atop a horse. There was nothing she could do. She was too weak and drained. She had slipped in and out of consciousness as they'd ridden well into the night.

Until a voice that made her entire body tremble spoke out of that night.

"Death's Maiden. I have missed you."

Darkness swallowed her whole and when she woke again, she found herself still in shackles, her wrists chained to the wall above her head. At least she was able to sit on the floor; though her ankles were still shackled as well. Her lips were wet, and the taste of blood filled her senses as she slowly cracked her eyes open.

She took in the room around her and immediately recognized it as the Assassin Lord's dungeon study. She still wore her witch-suit and witch-leathers. All the weapons had, of course, been removed. She twisted her wrists and winced slightly as shirastone dug into her skin.

Shirastone to hold Fae and block their magic. Shirastone to hold her. She tried to summon her shadows, but there was nothing. No fire or water or ice.

Footsteps outside the door had her gaze swiveling to it as the

Assassin Lord entered. He paused for a moment upon seeing her awake, but she couldn't see his face. His hood was in place as always. She'd never seen it off.

"My Darkest Maiden. You wake," he said with harsh pleasantry.

Scarlett said nothing, waiting to see what kind of mood he was in. The man had basically raised her and overseen all of her training. His mood would determine how she would interact with him.

"Come now," he said, walking closer to her but staying out of range of her chained feet. "No greeting after we have been separated for months?"

"How long have you been working with Tarek?" she rasped, her throat dry and hoarse from disuse.

The Assassin Lord walked to a nearby table and poured a glass of water. "How do you think I learned the identity of the Fire Prince?"

"You knew. The whole time he was with me. When I brought him to the Syndicate," she croaked out.

"Yes, Scarlett," he answered, crossing back to her. "I knew who he was. Tarek informed me he had entered the city shortly after he arrived three years ago." He stooped down beside her, bringing the glass of water to her lips. Scarlett twisted her head to the side. "It is only water, Scarlett. You will not accept a drink from me?"

Scarlett huffed out a gravelly laugh. "Only water? I'm sure that's all it is. There's not a tonic mixed in there to drug me and quell my magic?"

"I was not the one who started your tonic. Your mother was. She did not want your magic manifesting in the mortal lands. I simply continued it because there was no way to train you in your power here," he answered, reaching over and placing a finger under her chin to turn her head back to him. "Furthermore, your magic is wide awake now. I believe the only way to force it to slumber once more would be to force you to do the same. I would rather not do that. You are of no use to me asleep. Now drink."

He brought the glass back to her lips and tipped it up. The water was cool against her parched throat, and she gulped it down greedily, draining the entire glass. The Assassin Lord rose and strode to the pitcher once more, refilling the glass.

"What's your plan, then?" she drawled. "Keep me chained in shirastone so I cannot access it? What use to you am I in that way?"

He crossed back to her, crouching down once more. "The shirastone will keep your fire and water contained until we come to an understanding," he answered, bringing the glass to her lips. She again drank the entire glass down, leaning her head against the wall behind her when she was done. "Is your thirst quenched, or do you need another glass?"

Scarlett closed her eyes. So incredibly . . . familiar. The Assassin Lord had brutally trained her, yes. He had denied her retribution for Juliette's death. He had punished her and caged her and tried to break her. But he had also raised her, after her mother had been murdered. He had also cared for her. Just as he was doing now.

When she did not answer, he stood and crossed to his desk. It was smaller than the one upstairs in his much grander main study. There were no chains on the walls in that study.

He perched on the edge of the desk, and Scarlett opened her eyes, feeling his piercing gaze on her from beneath that hood. "Tarek tells me you figured out a number of things during your time away."

Scarlett gritted her teeth. She would wait him out. Force him to reveal his hand first.

The Assassin Lord chuckled. "I taught you well, Death's Maiden." He ran his fingers along the edge of the desk. "I know that physical punishment will be of no use with you."

Scarlett stiffened at what he implied, but immediately forced herself to relax. They were all safe. The orphans. Nuri. Cassius. They were all safe behind wards that they could not penetrate.

That the Maraan Lords could not penetrate.

But did the Assassin Lord know where they were?

She kept her face neutral, a mask of carefully trained boredom as she held the Lord's gaze beneath his hood. He folded his hands and placed them in his lap, and Scarlett worked to control her breathing. That was a mannerism she'd seen him make numerous times. When he was about to reveal exactly what her punishment was to be.

It often involved hurting Cassius or one of the others in front of her and refusing to allow her to tend to them. She had been chained in this very spot numerous times, for hours, with Cassius unconscious before her. "I am surprised that your Fire Prince has not yet attempted to come for you," he said casually.

Scarlett's heart constricted with fear and longing. "You are keeping me as bait? For him?"

"Do not be ridiculous," the Assassin Lord said harshly. "I am keeping you because you are powerful. Him coming to attempt to rescue you will simply be a bonus. But alas, he has yet to do so."

"How long have I been out?" Scarlett demanded.

"You have been in and out of consciousness for several hours."

"That's impossible. We could not have traveled all the way here from the far edges of Toreall in just a few hours. It would have taken at least two weeks and that's riding with very few stops," Scarlett argued.

"True," the Lord replied. "But you did not ride. You were Traveled back here."

"Tarek is a Traveler? How did he do so in the mortal lands?"

The Lord laughed softly. "No, Scarlett. Tarek is not a Traveler. Tell me, do you know where the Traveling gift came from?"

"I would assume from the Avonleyans like the other Fae gifts," she ground out, drawing her knees to her chest. The chains on the shackles scraped along the floor.

"Very good," the Lord replied. "But they are not the only ones who possess such gifts."

"Let me guess," she drawled. "The Maraans?"

The head beneath the hood nodded. "The Maraans are even more powerful than the Avonleyans were when it comes to Traveling," he answered.

"That doesn't explain how they accessed their magic in these lands."

"You can access your magic here, can you not?"

"Not currently," she muttered, wriggling her wrists and causing her chains to rattle once more in emphasis.

"Yes, well, can you really blame me there?" he asked with a shrug.

"Scared of a little fire and ice and darkness?" Scarlett crooned.

"The fire and ice, yes. The darkness, however . . . We have not given you enough to restore the depths of *that* magic."

Scarlett bit the inside of her cheek, unsure how to respond to that. A game. The Assassin Lord was playing a game, dangling information in front of her. She knew if she were to ask what he meant, there would be a price for the answer.

When she didn't say anything, he went on. "However, I do believe that the little bit we are giving you is also the reason the Fire Prince has not been able to find you yet. If I were to let you weaken to such a state that the Blood Magic Mark you enacted were to wear off, a certain bond may be reestablished."

For all her years of training, Scarlett could not hide the shock that came over her face.

"I finally have your full attention," the Assassin Lord mocked as he rose from the desk. He came to stoop before her once more. "While I am not entirely surprised that you learned how to interpret and use Blood Magic so quickly, I am amused that you did so without understanding the costs of such things."

"I know the cost I paid," she spat at him.

The Assassin Lord reached out and stroked fingers down her cheek. She jerked her head away from him, but had nowhere to go. "You really do not. I am guessing you had no idea that when you enacted that particular Mark to block your twin flame bond, you also blocked all bonds to you, including the bond with your spirit animal."

Shirina. Scarlett had not even thought of the panther. He was right. She'd had no idea. The thought had not even crossed her mind.

"Did you not wonder why she did not come to your aid in Tore-all? Or here?"

Scarlett swallowed. She didn't know what to say as she processed what he was revealing to her.

"Not only did you stifle those two incredibly important bonds," he continued, "but you blocked the bond to your Guardian."

"My what?"

"Your Guardian. I am not sure when or how she did it, but your mother bonded you to another as your Guardian. That is ancient magic of the gods, but I have seen the Mark on both of you at various times over the years," he said bitterly. "She bonded you, and then a Witch cast a spell to make you both forget the encounter."

And the dream came flooding back to her. The memory of her mother taking her to the beach where they met the strange woman with silver hair. She had drawn on her and Cassius and made them drink a mixture of their blood. She had told her of a kingdom where people were bonded as Guardians and where they danced under the stars.

"So you see, Scarlett, the cost of that Mark was blocking every single bond put in place to keep you safe. To keep you from the Maraan Lords."

"How do you know all of this?" she whispered to the Assassin Lord.

A soft chuckle escaped from underneath that hood. "I know plenty about Blood Magic, Scarlett. For example, I know that is how you obtained your powers of fire and ice."

"My mother's magic was fire and ice. I inherited them from her," Scarlett snarled.

"No, child," he said with a shake of his head. "Those were Eliné's gifts. Not your mother's."

"That doesn't make any sense," Scarlett said with a shake of her head, as if to clear her thoughts.

"Your mother's gifts were of shadows and night, Scarlett, not fire and ice." And Scarlett couldn't decipher the Assassin Lord's tone. It wasn't gentle, but it wasn't harsh either. It was just . . . factual. "Your mother is also the one who could have done the Blood Magic to transfer Eliné's gifts to you, since she did not have an heir of her own."

"You're lying," she whispered. Tears were burning in the back of her eyes, but she refused to let the Assassin Lord see them.

And with no small amount of shock, Scarlett watched as the Assassin Lord reached up and wrapped his long fingers around the edges of his hood and pulled it back. Long onyx black hair was tied back at the nape of his neck, and eyes just as black were fixed on her. He had a long, handsome face with thin lips that were pressed together and pointed ears arching up into his hair. "I do not think you will believe me unless you can look into my eyes," he explained.

Scarlett couldn't say anything. She had lived with this man for over half her life, had trained with him even longer, and had never seen his face. Not once.

"I am not lying about your mother. Your mother is the one who bonded you to Cassius, and she is the one who linked Eliné's gifts to your own," he said. There was nothing soft in his features. Only a calculating stillness as he watched her take in the information.

"I don't believe you," she finally managed to say to him.

His brows rose in surprise. "Tell me, Scarlett, did Prince Aditya tell you that the Fae cannot practice Blood Magic? Nor can the Witches? In fact, there are only two bloodlines in this world who can practice such magic."

"Which ones?" Scarlett whispered, closing her eyes. She knew.

She knew in her gut that whatever the answer to this was, it was going to crush her in some way. Because if what he was saying was true, then that meant the woman from the memory, the woman with the silver hair who had called her Starfire and who had told her she loved the night and the dark and the stars, was her real mother. That meant that she had been standing on that beach under the night sky with her mother.

The Assassin Lord seemed to know what she was figuring out, because now his features were morphing. They were becoming the face of the Assassin Lord that she had always imagined, as a cruel grin came across his lips and lined his sharp features. "The Avonleyans and the Maraans," he finally said.

Scarlett felt the air whoosh from her lungs, but she managed to get out, "And how exactly do you know all this?"

"Because before my father was defeated, he made sure I knew our people's history," the Assassin Lord said coldly, his eyes boring into hers.

Any air she had managed to get down was ripped from her lungs once more as she gasped, "Deimas was your father? And Esmeray your mother? You are a Maraan Lord?"

"I am a Maraan Prince," the Assassin Lord corrected as he stood. "You, however, are not Maraan, and perhaps now you finally understand why you have been kept under constant watch and caged."

"You . . . You were keeping me as a weapon. Not just to kill the Fae, but . . ." She trailed off as her eyes came back to the black eyes of the Assassin Lord.

No. Of Alaric. The Maraan Prince.

"You plan to use me to break the wards and enchantments around Avonleya."

CHAPTER 4
CALLAN

Crown Prince Callan was lying on his bed in their guest suite, staring at the ceiling as the morning sun streamed in the window. It had to be nearing midday by this point. He didn't care. Books were scattered around him, but it was all for nothing now. She was gone. She had married him. She was his twin flame. She was his. All his. No longer his own.

He had been a fool. An idiotic, lovesick fool to think he could keep up with her wildness. But that was why he'd clung to her, wasn't it? She was unknown and untamed. He never knew what she was going to say or do next, and she utterly fascinated him. Scarlett had shown him a side of the kingdom he hadn't known existed. She had shown him the ones who lurked in the shadows. She had shown him the ones who fended for themselves, who did not look to a king or nobility to take care of them, but made their own justice. The ones who recognized no one was coming for them, and that they needed to take care of themselves. Needed to save themselves.

She had made him believe that he could actually do something about it. That with his knowledge of the crown and her knowledge of the Syndicate, they could truly make a difference. He did not want her chained to a throne in his shadow, but serving the people of Windonelle at his side.

Teaching him how to do just that, not as a woman with a crown on her head, but as someone who grew up as one of them.

Scarlett had never once looked at him with the awe-struck eyes of the Court Ladies or the vindictive desires of those wanting to move up in their noble positions. He was never seen by her as a prize to be ensnared or a prince to be worshiped. From the very first note she'd left for him, she had mocked him for falling asleep in the middle of a clearing while reading. He would never forget her teasingly calling him 'princeling' the first time they danced at the Samhain Ball. She had thought he'd been offended, but he had been relieved. She had been a breath of fresh air, the first rain of spring after a long, cold winter. He had been relieved to have found someone who didn't feel the need to flatter him or wear a mask around him.

Until he'd learned just how many masks she wore.

Until he'd learned that perhaps the only person who had ever truly seen her for what she was, was the Fae Prince who now held her heart.

Callan had watched them these months here. He had watched how the Fire Prince had weathered every storm she went through. He had watched as he coaxed smiles from her when she seemed unreachable. He had watched as Sorin had fought his way past her shadows over and over and over. He had watched as they were drawn to one another as if unable to help themselves. Every smile. Every stolen glance. Every silent conversation. He had watched as she had slowly realized what he'd feared since the day they had surprised them at Sorin's apartment in Baylorin. That her heart belonged to the Fire Prince. She was his, and he was hers.

Callan knew they were a better fit. He knew Sorin could help her and serve her and love her in ways he would never be able to. He knew that what they had would change this world.

It didn't make the ache in his chest any easier to endure. It didn't ease the emptiness he now felt. Now he would be going home without her at his side. The loneliness he had so often felt, before she'd swept into his life on a dark wind, was already pressing down on him.

He heard a knock on the main door but didn't bother to get up. Sloan or Finn could get it. He'd be shoved back into his world of polite manners and duty in a few days' time anyway, assuming they were still returning. Rayner had come to him a few nights ago and told him their travels had been delayed, but he had heard nothing since. Scarlett hadn't even bothered to tell him herself. Not that he could really blame her, he supposed. Their last conversation hadn't exactly ended in pleasantries.

The knock came on his bedroom door this time.

Callan sighed, rising to his bare feet, and opened the door. He expected Sloan or Finn, but instead he stood face-to-face with Eliza.

"Mortal Prince," she said grimly.

"I am not in a particularly chatty mood today, Eliza," Callan gritted out. "Say what you have come to say."

Eliza straightened and the face of the Fire Court General took over her features. "Pack your things. We leave in the dead of night."

"What?" Callan asked, unable to keep the shock from his voice.

"Was something I said unclear? Did you not say no small talk?" Eliza asked with a raise of her brow.

"I was told travels were delayed."

He could see Sloan and Finn watching and listening to the conversation from where they sat at the dining table.

"They were. Now they are not. Be in the main foyer by nightfall and decide if you'll be staying in Baylorin or returning with us once we've recovered our queen," Eliza said, turning to leave the suite.

Callan reached out and gripped her arm without thinking of who he was grabbing. Eliza had spun, broken his hold, had his arm restrained behind his back, and a blade at his throat faster than he could blink. Sloan and Finn were on their feet, but flames encircled their throats and they froze.

"This is not the time to test any of us, Mortal Prince," she hissed. "We are all on edge and had I been anyone else, this blade would likely have gone through your neck without a second thought."

Callan swallowed before saying slowly, "Release Finn and Sloan."

Eliza lowered her blade, stepping back from him, the flames vanishing from around his friends' necks. "Get your things in order and be ready to go. I have things to prepare."

She was once more striding for the door, and Callan fell into step behind her. He waved off Finn and Sloan as he followed her into the hall. "Tell me what has happened," he demanded.

"I do not answer to you, Princeling, nor do I have the time to fill you in on everything that has occurred." Her tone was short as she made her way toward the bridges.

"What did you mean by 'once you have recovered the queen'?"

"None of us are sure what happened, but she is being held in the mortal lands, likely in Baylorin," Eliza answered.

"Does Mikale—"

"We don't know."

"Can Sorin not find her? Like he did when we came here?"

"No, he cannot," she snarled.

"Why not? Is this like the time they had that fight?"

Eliza whirled on him, and for the first time ever, he saw panic and terror on the general's face. "We do not know!" she hissed. "We do not know where she is or how she got there. We do not know what is happening to her. There is ancient magic at work here. There are secrets being unearthed and dark forces awakening. And my damn queen, my *friend*, is in the middle of it all, and we cannot get to her."

Callan's eyes were wide at the general's loss of control. "Eliza, I . . ." He didn't know what to say, what to do.

And the general seemed to sense his uncertainty. "What you can do to help right now, Callan, is pack and be ready to go. This will be nothing like last time. There will be no riding on horses through the woods. This is the Fae coming for what is theirs. We will be aided by Witches and Shifters. This is a Court coming for their queen. This is a twin flame coming for his mate. There will be death and bloodshed, and you must decide on which side you will stand."

"I will help in whatever way I can," Callan said swiftly, taking a step towards her.

"Then you will find yourself planted against your own kingdom and your own people," she spat, her grey eyes wild with challenge and bloodlust.

Callan went rigid at the words. "My people have nothing to do with this."

"Your people may not, but your crown does, Princeling," she sneered.

"You are blaming my throne for the actions of a few men who desire power? My family, my people, are innocent in this," Callan argued, feeling anger rising in his veins.

"Sorin will not care," Eliza hissed. "Sorin will not stop until his queen and wife and mate are back at his side. He will rip this entire godsdamn world apart to find her, and we will help him do it."

"Then you are truly the savage Fae bastards we all believe you to be," Callan spat back. Eliza bared her teeth at him and had him shoved against a wall in the next breath. And Callan found himself not afraid at all of those elongated canines so close to his throat or the deadly female that had him pinned to stone. Not as that fury that had been slowly making its way to the surface burst forth.

"My people are innocent," he snarled at her. "Those who are involved in this? Yes, punish them, General. Make them suffer in ways only the Fae can do. Get Scarlett out and save those children in the Black Syndicate, but you touch any of my innocent people, and I will use the secrets I have learned in my months here. You will find armies at your doorstep making you pay for every single innocent life you take, even if it takes my bloodline centuries to accomplish it."

Eliza's breathing was ragged as she stepped back from him. Callan straightened his tunic, staring down the general. "Tell the Fire Prince that how this is handled will determine whether we are allies with Queen Scarlett or enemies. As for my decision about where I will stay when she is out of my kingdom, I will be staying with my people."

Callan did not wait for Eliza's response as he turned from her to stalk back to his suite, but he found Sloan and Finn waiting for him several yards away. Their faces were unreadable as he approached, but they both straightened.

"What?" he demanded, coming to a halt in front of them.

A long silence fell between them, until Sloan bowed at his waist before him. "Well done, your Majesty."

"I am not the king," Callan snarled at him, fury still burning through him.

"That was not a Crown Prince who just tore into a general of the Fire Court," Finn said quietly. "That was a King."

Callan looked his friends in their eyes, his rage beginning to subside. "Let's go pack," he finally replied. "We are going home tonight."

CHAPTER 5
SORIN

Sorin stepped through a fire portal into the receiving area of the desert palace in Siofra, the capital of the Shifters territory. Gauzy curtains lined the open terrace walls as waterfalls cascaded among the rocky dunes surrounding the building. The palace sat in an oasis in the middle of the desert lands that they'd been sequestered to. The sun glared down brightly outside, and he watched as various animals moved about the grounds. With so many of them, it made it difficult to discern which were actual animals and which were Shifters in their animal forms.

He had come alone, leaving the others to pack and prepare for their departure tonight. He would not need backup in Siofra. Not with her. Not with their history.

He'd sent Eliza to deal with Callan and prepare him to return home. He didn't have the time or the patience to coddle the mortal prince right now. Although, now that he was thinking about it, perhaps Rayner would have been the better one for that task. He had never witnessed his general so on edge. But Rayner was off doing some final scouting before they left for the mortal lands, and Cyrus was getting other things together and finalized.

"My, my," a sultry voice purred from behind him, a hand landing on his shoulder. "This is a very pleasant surprise. The Prince of Fire again in my company."

That hand trailed along his sculpted back lower and lower, stopping just before it grazed across the upper swells of his ass. Sorin turned to address the owner of that voice, but a golden cobra was now winding its way up his leg. It slithered around his torso and along his chest. It stopped near his neck, hissing, and its forked tongue brushed the area beneath his ear. It continued moving across the back of his shoulders, winding down his other arm. Until it stopped and lifted its head when it reached his left wrist.

The cobra hissed again before there was a flash of soft golden light and a woman stood before him. She possessed effortless beauty with her dark skin and olive, almond-shaped eyes. Her long, black hair was braided into several small braids and gold beads adorned the ends of all of them. The thin, gold, silk dress she wore sported a plunging neckline, reaching nearly to her navel, and the slits up the sides revealed ample amounts of her long legs. She reached for his left hand, the gold bangles at her wrists tinkling against each other.

"You have a marriage band on your finger, Prince." She brought her eyes to his. "You have a wife."

"I do," Sorin replied. "That has only been the case for a few days."

"You have also started the Trials. Wife and twin flame then," she continued, her gaze back on his hand.

"Yes," Sorin answered, a small smile playing on his lips.

The woman dropped his hand, a pout forming on her full lips. "Pity," she said. But then those lips tilted up sensuously. "Unless she is with you, and you are both here for fun?"

Those olive eyes scanned the room, presumably looking for his wife.

Sorin cleared his throat. "She is not here, Arianna. She is also not one to share."

Arianna brought her eyes back to his, as she asked coyly, "She is not one to share, or *you* are not one to share, Prince?"

"I think the feeling is mutual, my Lady," he answered with a slight bow, "and that is no slight to you."

"My dear prince," Arianna said as she sauntered over to a low, coral-colored settee. "I know well that you enjoy everything I have ever had to offer." She sat, bringing one foot to the cushion beside her. Her other foot dangled to the floor, her dress revealing all too much as it hung between her legs.

A giant tiger prowled through one of the curtains to the right and padded to her. She ran her fingers through its fur as it rubbed against her leg.

"Jamahl," Sorin said with a nod of his head.

The tiger gave a nod of its own before sprawling onto the ground before Arianna's feet.

"You could bring your new bride, and I could bring Jamahl, and we could all have some fun," Arianna suggested, tilting her head back against the settee. Sorin opened his mouth to decline once more, but she spoke again before he could. "Maybe you should ask her before you speak for her, Prince."

Sorin crossed the distance between them and sat on the other end of the settee. A woman immediately appeared with a tray of iced tea and red grapes, setting it on the low table before them.

"If you are not here for pleasure, Prince, does my brother need to be summoned for this little meeting?" Arianna asked, picking up a grape and biting it in half.

"Not unless you desire him here," Sorin answered, filling a glass of iced tea and handing it to her.

She scoffed, taking the glass from his hand. "I do not even know where he is. The ports maybe? Or visiting a neighboring town? Alpha business, I am sure."

"Alpha business but not Beta business?" Sorin asked with a raised brow, pouring himself his own glass of iced tea.

"I do enough business in this territory. Stellan would run me ragged if I did not push back against him," she said with a frown. A large brown wolf had come stalking in, shifting in a flash of light to his human form, and begun massaging her shoulders. She groaned softly as he worked a knot from her neck.

"I need your help, Arianna," Sorin said quietly, setting down his glass of iced tea.

"What kind of help?"

"The posing as another person kind of help," Sorin answered grimly.

Arianna sat up straight at the words, brushing the hands of the Shifter away from her neck. "Outside of this territory?"

"Yes. In the mortal lands," Sorin answered. "To get my wife and queen out."

"You, a full-blooded, all-powerful Fae Prince of Fire, need my help to get your wife and twin flame away from humans?" The doubt and suspicion were stark on Arianna's beautiful face. "What aren't you telling me, Sorin?"

Sorin launched into the short, abridged version of who Scarlett was, where she'd been hidden, her new role as queen, how she'd been taken, and what he needed from Arianna.

"You seem to forget I cannot shift in the mortal lands," Arianna said gravely. "How I enter the mortal lands is how I will stay."

"You can shift with this," Sorin said, holding up his hand with the Semiria ring on it. "Prince Azrael will be wearing Talwyn's to Travel us all out once we have her, if she cannot do so herself."

He didn't want to think about what state she might be in. If Mikale had her, her mental state would be shredded. If the Assassin Lord had her, she might not be physically able to do anything. He had no idea what she'd been enduring since she blocked their bond.

Home.

He needed to get her home. When she was whole and fine again, they'd have a long discussion about this blocking the bond shit.

"Do you know how long it has been since I have been out of these lands?" Arianna asked, sipping from her iced tea. "Stellan usually takes care of the tasks that require us to go outside of our own lands."

"Would you prefer I ask Stellan instead?"

"Gods, no," she cried. "I would do just about anything, or anyone for that matter, to get out of here, even for just a few hours."

"We will likely be gone for more than a few hours. I am hoping for no more than a few days, but it could be longer," Sorin replied grimly.

"Even better," she said, standing from the settee.

"This is not a vacation, Arianna," Sorin warned, standing as well. "Those who hold her are not mere mortals. Night Children were involved in her capture."

A dark look crossed her face, her lip curling up from her teeth. "Do I need to remind you, Prince of Fire, that I was killing alongside the Fae while you were still suckling at your mother's tit?"

"You do not, Lady," Sorin said. "I simply do not want you to be unprepared."

She snapped her fingers, and the tiger at her feet shifted. Jamahl stood in his human form. Tall and muscled and as dark-skinned as his Beta. "Keep an eye on him while I pack a few things," Arianna ordered.

"Yes, my Lady," Jamahl answered with a bow of his head.

There was a flash of light, and Arianna had shifted into a red falcon soaring out of one of the terrace openings.

Sorin sat back on the settee, sipping his iced tea and going over his plan in his head again and again. Arianna Renatus agreeing to help him was the first step of many. He hadn't been worried. She was always eager to leave her lands, and her brother often kept her sequestered here while he handled other affairs. He knew she would leap at an opportunity to leave, and he knew coming directly to her and by-passing Stellan only aided his cause in convincing her to help him. The Alpha wouldn't be happy with him, but he'd deal with that later.

Ten minutes later, the falcon flew back in through the same terrace opening, and in another flash of light, Arianna stood before him, a small pack dangling from her fingers. She had changed out of her thin silk dress and now wore loose pants that cuffed at the ankles. Her top was the same coral color as the settee, and the sheer sleeves cuffed at the wrists.

"You do know I live in the mountains and that the mortal kingdoms are in the winter months?" Sorin asked, his lips tilting up slightly in amusement. He knew she wouldn't care. He'd spent enough time with the Beta to know her intimately in more ways than one.

"I assume you can keep your palace plenty warm, Prince," she answered. "As for the mortal lands, it sounds as if I will rarely be in my own skin." She turned to face Jamahl. "I have left a note for Stellan, but I am sure he will be unhappy I have gone without consulting him. You know what to do."

"Of course, my Lady," Jamahl said, bowing his head once more.

"Good."

Sorin opened a portal and gestured with his hand. "After you."

Arianna threw him a sensuous look as she stepped through the fire portal, Sorin a step behind.

CHAPTER 6
TALWYN

"I do not like this, Az," Talwyn said as she paced in the private quarters of his Desert Alcazar. Azrael was putting two sets of clothes in a pack, along with a few other necessities. "I do not like that we do not know the plans. I do not like that we are not more involved in the particulars."

"It is a mission, Talwyn. Nothing more," Azrael said, ever the warrior, as he buckled more daggers and weapons to his body.

"It is not just a mission."

"How is it not? Your cousin was compromised defending my Court. We owe them this debt," he said. Striding for his desk, he took something from a drawer and put it in his pocket.

"We owe them nothing," Talwyn snarled.

Azrael glanced at her briefly before crossing the room once more to get something else. She wasn't paying attention any more to what he was packing. "You are the queen, Talwyn. Do not let your emotions cloud your judgment. Aiding them with this will strengthen relations with your cousin. It will get us closer to our end goal."

She paused her pacing then, turning to face him. Politics and tactical moves. That's where Azrael's head always was. The best moves for their Courts, for her as a queen.

He was bent over his desk once more, writing on several pieces of paper.

"What are you doing?"

"Instructions for Orestes," he replied. "Things that need to be taken care of in my absence." His charcoal continued to scratch across the parchment.

"I will still be here, you know," she said dryly. "I can take care of things in the Earth Court."

"You are already pacing like a child," he said in response, unfazed by her tone. "You will not be focused enough to tend to my inter-court matters."

"Do not speak to me like I am a little girl, Azrael Luan," she spat, crossing to him and ripping the charcoal from his hand. "I am your queen."

"Then begin acting like one, your Majesty." Azrael rose to his full height. He was several inches taller than her, and his granite hewn features were hard and sharp. His earthy brown eyes met hers.

"I am thinking like a queen. I am thinking that it is stupid to ask you to do this when we could send another warrior who is just as capable. You could deliver them and wait for a message to go and retrieve them. You do not need to stay. Why are we sending another Prince of the Courts into this madness?"

Azrael studied her face, and she made herself withstand his scrutinizing glare. "You are sending me because I am your greatest resource in this matter, Talwyn." His tone had softened just a touch. "You are sending me because I will be your eyes among the Courts we are no longer part of. We cannot trust them to share everything they will see and hear while they are there. Do not feel guilty for asking this of me and utilizing me."

Talwyn didn't know what to say as he stepped around her once more to continue his preparations. He was right. She knew he was right. Even Ashtine had been unable to find out vital information from the winds. She did need eyes and ears on the inside if Sorin and his new queen were unwilling to share them with her.

"You will . . ." She swallowed, looking out the window of his rooms at the sky that was quickly losing sunlight. They were to meet at the Fiera Palace at sundown. "You will keep me informed of things? So that I know when to expect you home."

"I will send updates as I am able," he confirmed, hefting his pack onto a shoulder.

"That is not a good enough answer, Prince," she retorted.

Azrael stilled once more and slowly set his pack back down on his bed. "What is this really about, Talwyn?"

"It is about making sure one of the few people in my life I can depend on is returned to me in one fucking piece," she snarled, locking eyes with him once more.

Azrael was silent for a long moment before he said, "This is very different from ten years ago, Talwyn."

"Is it? Is it not a mission led by Sorin to retrieve someone important to him, no matter who is lost in the process?"

"Talwyn." He said her name with a thoughtful sadness that had her turning away from him.

"Forget it. Just forget it."

She turned, striding for the door out to his living area. "Talwyn."

"I said forget it, Az. We need to go. Grab your pack."

She wrenched the door open and crossed the sitting room straight out to the terrace, gulping down the cool night air. She glanced down at her left hand where a Mark had once stood stark against her skin. A Mark that had faded over time. A hawk soared across the sky, and she tracked it as it dove to the earth after some prey or another.

She scented him, soil and forest and fir, before she heard him come out onto the terrace. She knew if she glanced over her shoulder he'd be leaning against the doorway, his arms crossed over his chest. Her hair was blowing on the winds she was siphoning off, releasing her emotions that were making her magic roar up inside her. The hawk reemerged, and with her Fae sight, she could make out a shape dangling from its talons.

She felt a tickling sensation at her wrist, and she looked down to find a piece of ivy growing, tiny purple wisteria blooming along it. A peace offering from the Earth Prince. Still, she did not turn to look back at him.

This was no place for emotions. He was right. This was a mission like any other. They needed information. They needed to retrieve the Fae Queen of the Western Courts. Without Scarlett, they could not track down these keys. She could not move forward with her plans without those keys.

Taking a steadying breath, she finally turned to face Azrael. His pack was on the ground beside him. "Are you ready?" she asked. Her tone was frank and cold. The voice of the Fae Queen.

"I did not consider how you would feel about this undertaking, Talwyn," he replied, his hard voice softened in a way he only spoke to her.

"Feelings have no place in this undertaking," she said, closing the distance between them and looking pointedly at his pack. "If you are ready, let's go. I want to talk to Sorin more before you all leave."

"Aditya will not make the same mistakes, Talwyn. His entire Court journeys with us. He knows the lands we are going to. He knows the people who have her, and he knows allies." He was watching her carefully as she reached down and picked up his pack, extending it towards him.

"Good. Then you should not be gone long. Is there anything else you need to grab, or can we go?"

"Talwyn."

"What?" she snapped, finally meeting his gaze once more.

"I swear to you that I will come back to you," he replied, holding her stare. "Nothing there will keep me from returning to your side."

There was a beat of silence before she said, "Good. Building relations with a new prince would be annoying, and I doubt his distractions would be as effective."

The corner of his mouth twitched, as if a smile were about to form, but it never did. Smiles rarely found their way to his harsh face. He took the pack from her fingers where she held it out to him and set it back on the ground. Then he took that outstretched hand and pulled her towards him.

"I will send Rinji with updates as often as I can, and will Travel to you whenever possible," he said, tilting her face up towards his.

"It is fine, Prince Luan. Whenever you can be spared will be fine. I appreciate your willingness to do this."

His ever-present scowl deepened. "Do not do that, Talwyn."

"We need to go," Talwyn said, trying to work her way out of his grip. "They will be waiting for us."

"Talwyn," Azrael growled at her, tightening his hold.

"Az, it is fine," she bit out, the earth below her rumbling slightly. "Let's go."

She wrenched herself from his grasp, grabbing his pack. Before he could say anything else, she snatched his hand and Traveled to the Fire Court. They landed outside the Fiera Palace gates. She dropped his hand, shoving his pack into his arms, and strode through the gates without a backwards glance. She knew Azrael wouldn't push this here. Not in front of the other Courts. They were always a united front in the presence of others.

She also knew he'd bring it up later. Even if later meant weeks from now. She could feel his eyes boring into her back as she breathed deep to calm her temper and magic. A sentry opened the main door for her, bowing slightly. When she stepped into the entrance hall, a few of the staff were rushing about here and there, and her eyes fell on the mortal prince and his guards. His hazel eyes locked onto hers. There was something different about him. Something harder, more imposing.

She smirked at him as she said, "Good evening, Crown Prince."

"Queen Talwyn," he said with a slight bow. "I was unaware you were accompanying us on this journey." His two guards had come to his sides, hands casually on their swords, as if they thought they could do anything to her with them.

"I am not joining you, but Prince Azrael is," she answered, gesturing behind her.

"Do you know the plan, then?" Callan inquired, shifting his gaze to the prince.

"Likely little more than you do," Azrael replied.

"Glad to know it is not just me being kept in the dark then," Callan muttered, and Talwyn almost laughed out loud at his musings.

"Where is Sorin?" she asked.

"Preparing I assume," Callan replied with a stiff shrug.

Talwyn studied the mortal prince with a tilt of her head. Despite his best attempts to hide it, she could see his anxiousness underneath. He was ready to return home, likely to get away from Sorin and Scarlett.

"And are you prepared for what awaits you upon your return home, Crown Prince?" Talwyn voiced now.

Callan's hazel eyes dragged back to hers and held a steely resolve. "I am prepared to serve and protect my people from whatever . . . threats may be in store. Their wellbeing is a higher priority than my own."

"Spoken like a true prince," drawled a female voice. They all turned to find Eliza striding towards them. She was bedecked in her usual attire, although she had more weapons than usual. She carried a pack on her shoulder, along with a bag in her hand.

"Where is Sorin and the rest of his cabal?" Talwyn said when Eliza came to a stop before them. She detested all of Sorin's Inner Court, but Eliza was by far the worst with her insufferable arrogance and smart mouth.

"Cabal?" Eliza questioned. "Such interesting names you have for us, Majesty."

There was a slight rustling of smoke near the braziers, and Rayner stepped into view. "Do not stir things up, Eliza," he chastised quietly. "We have enough to worry about right now." His gaze shifted to Talwyn and Azrael, and he bowed slightly in greeting. He had his own weapons adorning him and a pack gripped in his hand as well. Talwyn still couldn't believe Sorin's entire Inner Court was going to the mortal lands. Such utter stupidity.

Of the three of them, Rayner was the only member of Sorin's Inner Court who she could stand to be around for longer than a few minutes. Probably because he rarely spoke. When he did speak, though, he was respectful and tried to keep the peace. Not that she was fooled by his seeming aloofness. He was as deadly as the rest of them. She'd only seen him unleashed a handful of times, and while she'd never admit it to anyone else, he'd been terrifying.

"Rayner," she greeted in response. "One of you needs to fill me in on the plan."

Eliza opened her mouth to snap a reply, but Rayner cut her off. "The prince will be here shortly."

"We both know Sorin will not tell me everything," Talwyn retorted.

"It is not my place to reveal his plans, your Majesty."

There was almost a note of regret in his voice that sent Talwyn's nerves into overdrive. She glanced sidelong at Azrael, who was watching her, before she quickly averted her gaze once more.

"Since two of the three parts of this little party are not aware of the plan, maybe it would be best to share before everyone jumps into the unknown," Talwyn stated, crossing her arms in front of her.

Prince Callan stepped forward at her words. "I am in agreement with that idea."

Eliza smirked at both of them. "Too bad you two don't really get a say in the matter. This isn't a majority rules situation."

"I damn well get a say if you are taking my Second and my ring," Talwyn snarled in return.

"Sorin is on his way down. He will be here in moments," Rayner interjected.

He had barely finished speaking when footsteps echoed from the hall. They all turned to find Sorin, Cyrus, and Arianna Renatus. What the hell was the Shifter doing here? And if she was here, where was Stellan?

Talwyn did a quick scan of the entry looking for the Shifter

Alpha but didn't see any sign of him, at least not in his natural form. The three came to a stop in front of them all, and Arianna propped a hand on her hip, a vixen's smile on her lips.

"Sorin dearest, you did not tell me we would be traveling with such delicious company," she said in her sultry tone, her eyes drinking in the Crown Prince before moving on to Azrael.

"Arianna," Talwyn said tightly, with a nod of her head to the Beta. "A pleasure, as always."

"Of course, your Majesty," she returned with a bow of her own. Then she moved closer to Callan, sliding a hand up his arm and around his shoulders as she circled behind him. Callan stiffened at the liberal touches, looking as uncomfortable as a virgin in a brothel.

Sorin cleared his throat, a grin of amusement playing around his lips as he watched. "Arianna, this is Crown Prince Callan Solgard of Windonelle. Callan, meet Arianna Renatus. She is the Beta of the Shifters."

"A pleasure to meet you, Lady," Callan said awkwardly, attempting to step from her reach.

"Oh no, Prince. The pleasure is indeed all mine," she replied with a flirtatious grin, moving into his personal space once more and sidling right into his side.

Callan threw a pleading look around for someone to take pity on him, and Talwyn huffed a sigh. "Lady Arianna, the Crown Prince is not used to such affection. Perhaps you should give him some space?"

Her relations with the Shifters were the best alliance she had. Granted, she preferred to work with Stellan, but she'd had plenty of interactions with Arianna as well. They were both Power Shifters, able to shift into any animal or human form, and she did everything she could to remain on good terms with the siblings. They were invaluable when it came to power plays, and while they enjoyed their share of roguery and promiscuity, they were incredibly cunning and powerful. Stellan was also very protective of his sister, which made it all the more concerning that he wasn't present.

Arianna's grin became one of mischief at Talwyn's suggestion. "Maybe he would find he likes my type of affection," she replied, nuzzling into his neck.

"I am sure he would adore your affection, Lady, but perhaps another time would be more conducive," Talwyn replied, with a pointed look at Sorin.

A pout formed on Arianna's full lips as Sorin held out a hand to the Shifter. "I am afraid Queen Talwyn is right, Lady. You know we are short on time as it is."

Arianna sighed, slipping her hand into his waiting palm. "Of course, kitten," she conceded. "But you will be sure to tell him how much he will enjoy my company, won't you?"

Her olive eyes were wide with an innocence the Shifter in no way possessed, and a wry smile pulled at Sorin's mouth. "I will be sure the Crown Prince knows exactly how good you would make him feel, my Lady."

Seemingly satisfied, Arianna stepped away from Callan and back to Sorin's side, who smoothly passed her off to Cyrus when she tried to cling to him. Cyrus snaked an arm around her waist, tucking her in tight against him and whispering something into her ear that had her grinning a feline grin and running her fingers along his jaw.

"Does everyone have everything they need?" Sorin asked, shouldering his pack. Cyrus stooped to pick up his pack along with another bag Talwyn assumed was Arianna's.

"I am in need of an explanation of the plan, Prince," Talwyn bit out from between clenched teeth.

Rayner and Eliza came to Sorin's side as he met her glare. "I have as much of a plan in place as possible, Talwyn, but I do not know in what state we will find Baylorin. Our most pressing matter upon arriving will be to find our allies."

There was a swirl of ashes near Rayner, and he pulled a map from them, passing the parchment to Sorin. Sorin gestured for Azrael to come over, and Talwyn moved with him, his arm brushing against hers.

Azrael and Rayner each took a side of the parchment, and Sorin pointed to the castle. "Obviously, this is where the king resides. Mikale's father, Lord Lairwood, is the hand-to-the-king. This is his estate." He moved his finger to another area. "This is where all the unmarried soldiers reside for the most part, including much of the king's High Force."

"Do you think that is where she is being held?" Azrael inquired, rubbing his jaw in thought.

There was a low snarl from beyond them. "My father is not keeping her prisoner," Callan said tightly.

"No offense, Princeling, but if he has learned what she is, he may indeed have arrested her," Eliza replied flippantly.

"No," Callan insisted. "She is not there."

"While Eliza has a point, I do not believe that is where she is," Sorin cut in. He pointed to an estate a short distance from the castle grounds. "This is the Tyndell Estate. This is where she resided for a year before I brought her here. Lord Tyndell is in charge of the king's armies and was my superior while I was there. He is working with Mikale and . . ." Sorin paused for a moment, seeming to debate something internally, before he took a breath and added, "Scarlett believes Lord Tyndell is one of the Maraan Lords."

Talwyn's eyes snapped to him at that. "And who exactly are these Maraan Lords?" she asked in a dangerous tone. They had been mentioned a few times now by Scarlett and Ashtine, yet no one had bothered to fill her in on this threat.

"I am not entirely sure," Sorin admitted. "Scarlett knows far more than I do, and before she could tell me everything, we had to deal with the Night Children at the borders. She believes that Deimas was, in fact, a Maraan King. She had several theories as to why he entered into a union with Esmeray, but couldn't say for sure."

"So who are the Maraan Lords, then? What are they doing here?" Azrael asked. Talwyn could see him calculating all of this new information.

"Scarlett believes they are after the same thing they coveted in the Great War. Something in Avonleya. She thinks they are trying to find a way through the Avonleyan wards using Blood Magic," Sorin answered. "She does not know how many Maraan Lords are here. According to her research, there are seven Lords in total. She and the other Wraiths of Death supposedly killed one a few years ago. She also believes Mikale to be one. Who the rest are, she does not know. If she has inklings, she did not share them."

"You believe she is at the Tyndell Estate then?" Talwyn asked, her eyes returning to the map before them.

"No," Sorin countered once again.

Talwyn released a frustrated huff. "For the love of Celeste, Sorin. Where the fuck is she then?"

"Our best guess is that she is either being held by Mikale here at the Lairwood Estate," Sorin answered, indicating the sprawling estate even bigger than the Tyndell property. "If that is the case, we already know the general layout of the house; as that is where we had to break her out of before we returned home."

"And if she is not there?" Azrael intoned.

Talwyn watched a muscle feather in Sorin's jaw, and a small part of her that used to be attached to him ached deep in the recesses of her soul. She knew his tells, his small ticks. It was taking every ounce of self-control to keep his emotions in check right now. Before her stood her aunt's Second. The Fae who took control and got results. The Fae who would become as callous and as wicked as necessary to achieve an end he desired.

"If she is not with Mikale, she is likely with the Assassin Lord, her old master. In which case, she is likely being held deep in the Black Syndicate, and we will need to rely on our allies there. They will intimately know the layout," Sorin answered.

"We are going into the Black Syndicate then?" Azrael asked, violence tangible in the aura around him.

"We will not get within a mile of the Syndicate before we find ourselves either dead or captured, which is why we need to find Cassius and Nuri as soon as possible," Sorin explained. He pointed to an area of the map near the docks. "I do not know how similar Traveling is to portaling, Luan, but this is where I need you to Travel us to. Or as close to this location as possible. It is far from the Black Syndicate, but it is where we have close to a hundred orphans hidden. In the last correspondence we had from Cassius, he told us Nuri has not left the area since we left Baylorin. I am hoping that is still the case, and she will find us swiftly."

"We are going to rely on her finding us?" Azrael asked. "Why not track them down?"

A grim smile hooked up the corner of Sorin's mouth. "You will find, Luan, that you do not track down Death's Shadow. She finds you."

Azrael didn't show any reaction to learning that one of their allies would be a Wraith of Death. Talwyn, however, voiced her own concern. "And what of the other Wraiths of Death? Do they know their companion has betrayed them?"

Sorin's eyes darkened, but it was Prince Callan who answered her question. "One of them is dead, and the other is whom you seek to rescue."

Talwyn couldn't keep the surprise from her face. "Scarlett is a Wraith of Death?"

"Your cousin bears many titles and wears many masks," Callan replied, with a surprising amount of bitterness for the woman he claimed to love.

She turned her eyes to Sorin, seeking confirmation.

"Yes, Talwyn. Scarlett is Death's Maiden. The other, Death Incarnate, was killed a year and a half ago." Silence fell for a few moments while Talwyn tried to process all this new information before Sorin cleared his throat. "We have no more time for questions or explanations. We need to arrive in Baylorin undetected, which means the cover of night will be the best. We need as much time in the dark as possible to track down Cassius or Nuri. Luan, how close do you think you can get us?"

Azrael studied the map a moment longer. "I have never Traveled to Windonelle, but from the map, I should be able to get us close. It would be wiser to aim for the outskirts of the capital to avoid arriving at an inconvenient location. Will it be difficult to enter the city on foot?"

Sorin rubbed the back of his neck in thought. He pointed to an area in the north of the city near the coast. "I think if you can get us to this area, near the docks and cliffs, we'd stand the best chance." He turned his attention to Callan's guards. "Would you agree?"

The two sentries exchanged a look and a glance at Callan, who gave a nod. "If he can get us in that general vicinity, there are secret tunnels that lead into the city. They are in place to get the royalty out in case of an attack," the shorter of the two revealed. "It branches off in various places throughout the city."

Sorin's brows rose in surprise. "Are these the tunnels they used to get in and out of the castle when she would come to Callan?"

"They are a section of them, yes," the guard confirmed. "Although the Black Syndicate residents seem to know more about the tunnel system than we do."

The taller guard snorted behind them, clearly not happy about that fact.

"That is where we go then," Sorin said, taking the map and rolling it up.

Everyone turned and gathered their things, and Azrael came to Talwyn's side, checking all the weapons buckled to him one final time. "Orestes will take care of things in the Earth Court. Stay close to Ashtine. Send Maliq if you need me. You are my priority, Talwyn. Not the Fae Queen of the Western Courts," he said in a low voice. The same ivy and wisteria he'd wrapped around her wrist coiled there once more.

Talwyn slid the Semiria ring from her finger and held it out to him. He took it, subtly brushing his fingers along hers. He slid it onto his little finger, the magic of the ring stretching to accommodate his larger hand.

"Do not inconvenience me by dying, Prince," Talwyn replied coolly.

Azrael nodded his head once in acknowledgment, before he moved to stand beside Sorin. Sorin's Inner Court all gathered around him, touching an arm or shoulder. Cyrus still had Arianna tucked into his side, and Eliza held Callan's hand in her own. The mortal prince's two sentries each had a hand on his shoulder. As Sorin reached for Azrael's shoulder, his eyes met Talwyn's. She stared at him and let her walls down for a moment. She let him see everything she couldn't say.

Sorin bowed his head. It was a small movement, barely noticeable, but she saw it for what it was. A thank you for letting them take Azrael and a promise to bring him home.

If he broke that promise, there would be no more chances. They would no longer just be rulers who often disagreed. He would become her enemy, and she'd enjoy plotting his downfall along with all those he loved.

Just like she would enjoy taking down the Avonleyans when they retrieved those fucking keys.

CHAPTER 7
SCARLETT

There was warm water being brushed down her arms, along her neck, her face. Her head pounded as she tried to blink her eyes open. It took a few tries, but Scarlett finally managed to pry them open and blinked against the light. It wasn't overly bright in the dungeon study, but her head hurt so much that the light from the braziers was enough to cause her to grimace.

Before her was a woman who had to be in her late forties. She wore a cream-colored dress, and her light brown hair was tied back in a knot at the nape of her neck, while she continued to gently clean Scarlett's skin. Scarlett tried to jerk back, but her arms were still shackled above her head to the wall so all she could do was pull her knees to her chest, the chains scraping along the floor. The woman paused and pulled her hands back, glancing over her shoulder.

"Relax, Wraith," came the Assassin Lord's voice. He was seated at his desk and didn't bother to look up as he spoke to her. "This is Inez. She is simply helping you clean up."

"One could let me have a bath," Scarlett retorted hoarsely. "That would surely be a better alternative."

Alaric chuckled softly from beneath his hood. "It likely would be, but we have not discussed what such a privilege would require yet."

Privilege. Everything always had to be earned with the Assassin Lord.

What would be required of her to take a godsdamn bath?

Scarlett leaned her head back against the wall and closed her eyes while Inez finished her sponge bath. The woman also finger combed her hair for her before braiding it into a loose plait over one of her shoulders. As she was finishing, there was a knock on the door and another servant pushed a cart into the room. The cart contained covered dishes.

Food.

She hadn't eaten since she'd arrived here. Alaric had only given her water. She pulled her knees back to her chest to stifle the ache in her stomach. What would be required of her to get food?

"Thank you, Inez," Alaric said in dismissal, as he stood at the arrival of the food. "That will be all."

Inez bowed slightly before following the other servant out of the room, the door clicking shut behind them.

"Are you hungry, Death's Maiden?" he asked, rounding his desk. Once the door was securely closed, he pulled his hood back, allowing Scarlett to once again see his face. He pulled one of the silver covers off one of the platters, and the smell wafted over to her. He tilted the plate slightly to show her the contents— toast, eggs, and a ration of bacon. "Well? Are you hungry?"

Scarlett gritted her teeth as he stood waiting for her reply. A trace of a smile ghosted over his lips, his cold black eyes boring into hers. "Yes," she finally answered.

The Assassin Lord slowly made his way to her and crouched before her. Using a fork, he cut off a piece of toast and stabbed it along with some egg and bacon. He brought the bite to her mouth, and Scarlett had to stifle the moan that crept up her throat at the taste.

Then her heart sank as he set the plate aside and sat, propping one leg up and resting his arm on it. "Let's discuss what shall be required to earn the rest of that food and any future meals, shall we?"

"It doesn't appear I have much of a choice, does it?" she retorted.

"On the contrary, my dear. You always get a choice. You know this," he answered.

Scarlett snorted. Oh yes, she was sure there would be a choice. Do what he wanted or choose a punishment for disobedience. The Assassin Lord picked up a piece of bacon and ate it while he studied her. She held his gaze, not moving an inch. "Always so stubborn," he murmured, wiping bacon grease from his fingers on a napkin. Then he reached out to stroke his knuckles down her cheek, but she turned her head, jerking away from him. Alaric sighed as he gripped her chin, turning her back to face him once more. "My dear Scarlett, in your time away you seem to have forgotten whose you are." His voice had turned icy and cold. A voice she was all too familiar with. "Who do you belong to, Scarlett?"

I am yours, and you are mine.

The words drifted through her mind. What a fool she had been. The idea that she could ever possibly be someone else's. The idea that she could ever choose to give herself to another so completely. Of course Alaric would always own some part of her.

As if he could sense where her thoughts had gone, a hiss escaped from the Assassin Lord's lips. "You are not *his*." Scarlett swallowed hard as his grip on her chin tightened. "We will address *that* later, but first, your choices today."

He stood once more, leaving the plate of food on the floor out of her reach. She tried her hardest, but she glanced at it anyway, and he didn't miss it. A faint, cruel smile graced his lips. "Hunger can sometimes cause us to see things so clearly, but it is so much worse when your power reserves are empty, isn't it?" He strode back to the cart and picked up another plate, extending it out, and for the first time, Scarlett realized there was someone else in the room. Tarek took the plate from Alaric with a slight nod of his head and a smirk at Scarlett.

Had he been here this whole time?

Alaric took the final plate to his desk, where he leaned against the front of it, taking a bite of egg and toast while watching her carefully. She was used to all of this. Used to his games. Used to his power plays.

Used to submission in the end, even if that submission took a year to achieve.

He took a few more bites before he finally set his plate aside and braced his hands on the desk behind him. "You can finish that plate of food beside you after you have made your choice."

"And my options are?" Scarlett asked through gritted teeth.

"Tell me where you have hidden Prince Callan."

Scarlett couldn't mask her blink of surprise. "I didn't hide Prince Callan anywhere."

"Semantics," Alaric sneered. "You may not have hidden him away, but you know where he is. I know you, Death's Maiden. You care too much for him to not make sure he is safe and protected."

"What do you want with Callan?"

"Lady Veda misses him so," Alaric said with mock sympathy.

"That is not what I asked," Scarlett replied. "What do *you* want with Callan?"

"What does it matter to you? It appears you have given yourself to another, have you not? You seem to think you belong to someone else." He gave a pointed glance at her left hand.

Could he see the Mark? "And my second option?"

"Ah. The second option is the one I would prefer you choose," he answered, arms folding across his chest. "Swear loyalty to me and the other Maraan Lords. I will release you. Allow your powers to refuel to their full strength. Teach you the depths you have yet to fully embrace. All it takes is submission on the deepest levels, my Wraith."

"How would you ensure such a thing?"

The slight smile on the Assassin Lord's face widened. "You are right, Death's Maiden. I would not trust your word. However, there is a way to make sure your end of the agreement is upheld." He gestured to Tarek, and the Fae held up his right hand. In the center of his palm stood a Blood Mark, stark against his dark, golden skin.

"What did you do?" she whispered in horror to the Fae. Tarek smiled. "It's a Blood Bond, your *Majesty*."

"Similar to the vow your Guardian took to you," Alaric cut in. "The Blood Bond is a promise of submission . . . with a magical guarantee."

"You mean it is magical enslavement," Scarlett countered.

The Assassin Lord shrugged nonchalantly. "Or merely a symbol of loyalty. It is all about perception, I suppose."

"This is hardly a choice," Scarlett spat. "If I choose option two, you shall simply require option one from me once I have accepted the Blood Bond. Either way, you get Callan's whereabouts from me."

Alaric said nothing. He just stared at her expectantly, waiting for her to make her choice, apparently. After several minutes of silence, he sighed. "I will give you some time to decide, Scarlett. But should you not make a choice by the time I return, there will be a consequence."

He bent down and scooped the plate of food from the floor, tossing it back onto the cart with a clatter. Raising his hood and motioning for Tarek to follow, he strode out of the study, closing the door behind them.

Scarlett was left alone in complete silence. She rotated her wrists. She was numb to the constant bite of the shirastone by now, and hardly noticed the stinging on her skin. Her shoulders ached from her arms being suspended above her head for hours, and her tailbone was sore from sitting on the stone floor.

She really didn't know how long she had been down here, drifting in and out of sleep. With no windows and no clock, she also didn't know what time of the day it was. Based on the food selection, one would venture to guess it was morning and that was breakfast, but Alaric enjoyed his games. Part of his control was trying to control your reality. He decided if it was morning, noon, or night in her world right now. Not some piece of mechanics or even the godsdamned sun. He controlled it all.

Scarlett rested her head back against the wall and tried to mentally prepare herself for whatever consequence the Assassin Lord was going to see fit to bestow upon her when he returned. She would rather die than choose either of those two options. Alaric surely knew that, and whatever hell he had thought up was going to be designed to break her on the basest of levels.

The smell of the forgotten food on the tray wafted over to her, and she tried to think of anything to distract her from the ache in her stomach. She'd survived longer without food. At least, she thought she had. Without knowing exactly how long she had been down here, she couldn't really say for sure.

She tried not to let it, but her mind drifted to Sorin. Her husband. Her mate. Her twin flame. She closed her eyes at the memories, picturing his face in her mind.

She had been happy. Not right away. When she had first arrived in the Fire Court, she had walked about in a daze, going through the motions and trying not to drown on dry land. But walking the path back to *wanting* to live had been beautiful in the end, with him by her side, and she had truly been happy. Her heart had been full, and she had felt loved for who she was. No masks. No demands placed on her for affection and acceptance.

She wondered if she'd ever see him again. She had known she would block their twin flame bond when she'd enacted that Blood Mark. She'd watched him cross that border knowing it could very well be the last time she'd lay eyes on him.

Scarlett, I love you like the stars love the night. All the way through the darkness.

His words floated back to her, and she fought the tears that burned at the back of her eyes. She could do this. She could make this sacrifice to ensure that Sorin and Cyrus and Eliza and Rayner and everyone she loved wouldn't have to live through the darkness the Maraan Lords would surely rain down upon them. She would do whatever was necessary to make sure they didn't find the keys and make their way into Avonleya. Her family was safe. That was all that mattered. Sorin would come for her. He promised he would always find her, and even if he didn't, as long as he was safe, the sacrifice was worth it. He was worth it.

She didn't know how much time had passed before footsteps sounded outside the door, and the Assassin Lord came back into his dungeon study. He had a covered platter in his hands and when his eyes met hers, he pulled the lid back, revealing the chunk of roast meat smothered in gravy with potatoes, bread, and glazed carrots. Her stomach growled as the smell accosted her.

"As soon as you tell me your decision, this is yours, my dear." He dragged a piece of meat through the potatoes and brought the forkful with him as he crouched before her, holding it in the air, poised at her lips. "Well?"

"I will take your consequences before I see harm come to Callan or any of the other people I love," she sneered, her face a snide mask of cruelty.

Alaric heaved a sigh of disappointment. "I cannot say I am surprised. I was, of course, expecting some resistance, especially after how you held out the year after Juliette's death."

"Do not speak her name," Scarlett spat, jerking against her restraints in an attempt to get to him. The action drew his attention to her wrists, though, and his eyes narrowed in annoyance at her left hand.

The Assassin Lord pursed his lips. "I was not planning on addressing *that* issue until tomorrow, but it appears it needs to be discussed now." He stood, tossing the fork on the plate forcefully before he leaned against his desk and crossed his arms over his chest. "You do not belong to him, Death's Maiden. I am the one who trained you. I am the one who raised you. I am the one who made sure you were fed and well and cared for. I did not invest all of that time and interest in you just to have you think you can give yourself to a fucking Fae Prince."

"I am not some investment for you to order around and dictate," she snarled in reply, holding his stare. "I have always resisted your cages, and I always will."

"That's where you are wrong, my dear," he said, too quietly, as he rounded his desk. He sat and grabbed a quill, writing something onto a piece of parchment. He pulled his hood into place before summoning a servant into the room and sending him off with the paper.

When the servant had gone, he removed the hood once more, clearly no longer feeling the need to keep his face hidden from her, and poured himself a glass of liquor. He came to her again and raised the glass to her lips. Scarlett pressed them firmly together, refusing to let a drop of the liquid onto her tongue.

"Come now, my dear. I know you are thirsty," he chided, taking a sip himself.

"For water, you ass. Not for liquor."

The sting from the slap across her face was sharp, and she tasted blood in her mouth where she'd bitten the inside of her cheek at the impact.

"That godsdamn mouth," Alaric muttered, sipping at his drink again. He reached out and gripped her chin, forcing her to look at him once more. "I do not know how to make things any clearer to you, Scarlett. You are *mine*. You have been mine since I took you in after Eliné was killed; before that even. I decide your future. I decide what you eat. I decide what you wear. I decide who you bed. I decide who's future children you will grow in your womb. I decide who you will serve."

"No," she bit back through clenched teeth. "I am not a piece of property that you own."

The fingers gripping her chin squeezed tight enough to bruise. "You are my property, Scarlett Monrhoe. I own you. No one else, and certainly not some Fae piece of shit. I do not care if he is your twin flame. I do not care if you have married him, as I suspect you have. None of that matters. You are still mine to do with as I please." He shoved her head back against the wall as he pushed himself to his feet, knocking back the entire glass of remaining alcohol. "I was lenient with you after Juliette died. I let you get away with more than I should have, but I let you mourn. I let you throw your tantrum like a child."

"You let her be murdered! You invested just as much in her," Scarlett cried. It didn't matter that she knew Juliette still lived.

It didn't matter that she knew she had a higher purpose and was now fulfilling it. That year had been utter hell. The things she had endured because of that death would haunt her for the rest of her immortal life.

Alaric snorted in disgust. "Juliette and Nuri were trained to make sure you were kept safe. You were never told. An enchantment was used to ensure they never breathed a word of it to you. *Everyone* I brought into your life was for the sole purpose of making sure you survived."

"You lie," Scarlett seethed, but even as she said it, she knew he wasn't lying. Everything he'd said made sense and was like puzzle pieces slotting into place. She'd been kept hidden and locked away from the world for nearly ten years. Only Cassius, Juliette, Nuri, and their personal guards interacted with her and knew who she was. Alaric had orchestrated it all. Almost everything in her life, he had planned as if he truly did decide her future. But if that were true . . .

Her eyes flew to his. "*You*. You arranged for my mother's— For Eliné's death."

A cruel and cunning smile tilted up on his lips, and he cocked his head as he looked down at her. "She needed to be eliminated to keep you safe. I had thought the Fae princes had long since given up on her, but I was wrong. When I received word that the Fire Prince and his Court had tried to come for her, I knew it was only a matter of time before they got close enough to find you. So, yes. I hired Dracon to kill her. In fact, I was in the alley with him when he did it. I later learned she was planning to take the three of you to the Fae lands when your magic became too much for your tonic. So really, it was something that would have had to be done eventually," he said with a shrug.

"You fucking asshole," Scarlett cried, a few tears running down her cheeks as he talked about her mother so cavalierly. She knew Eliné wasn't her blood mother, but she was the woman who had raised her and cared for her. She was the woman who had loved her like a mother. She was someone else the Assassin Lord had taken from her so brutally.

There was a knock on the door, and Alaric crossed the room to answer it. When he pushed the door open, Mikale Lairwood walked in, a smug grin on his face. The Assassin Lord turned and came back to her. Crouching before her, he said, "I will do whatever is necessary to break you, Scarlett Monrhoe. I will do whatever it takes for you to learn that you are, in fact, my property. I own you. Every hair on your head and every drop of Avonleyan blood in your veins. And if I need to keep you in a cage to keep you under control, I will do so."

Alaric stood and took a key from his pocket, unlocking the padlock that secured the chains of her wrist shackles to the bar above her head. Despite herself, Scarlett grimaced at the ache in her shoulders as he allowed her to lower her arms, keeping the chain firm in his grip. He tugged her to her feet by the chain, and when her legs gave out from being stationary for so long, he steadied her, looping his arm around her waist and holding her up.

Scarlett tried to jerk from his hold, but she was too weak from the sitting and lack of food and water to do much. "Don't be idiotic," Alaric scolded.

"What do you care?" she bit back, slowly rotating her ankles to get used to bearing her weight again.

"I care about my investments and take care of my property," he said softly into her ear. "You are both, and while I need your spirit broken, I need your physical body intact." He passed the chain over to Mikale before handing her body over to him as well. "Should you make a decision before morning, let Mikale know, and he will immediately bring you to me."

Alaric turned his back on them and took a seat behind his desk, pulling some paperwork towards himself and beginning to read it over and make notes in the margins.

"Come, my pet," Mikale purred, tucking her into his side and tightening his arm around her waist.

Scarlett said nothing as he pulled her to the door. But before they exited the room, Alaric spoke again.

"Oh, and Mikale?"

Mikale paused, looking over his shoulder.

"Do not let her out of your sight," Alaric said, his tone low and dangerous. "Should you lose her again, you can consider your claim on her relinquished."

Fury flitted across Mikale's face at the words. "You cannot do that," he hissed. "I have already fucked her. I have already claimed her. You cannot rescind a claim that has been consecrated. That is the law of our people." Alaric leaned back in his chair, his hands coming to rest on the armrests. "You may have claimed her, but you forget it is I who gave her to you in the first place. Do not make the mistake of thinking she is now yours, Mikale. Balam has had to secure her for you twice now. Should it be required a third time, I shall make sure the claim is indeed relinquished by whatever means necessary, which in this case, would be your death."

Scarlett's pulse increased at that nugget of information. She may not be able to get free of Alaric, but if she could escape Mikale, Alaric would take care of him for her. Of course, she had to be able to fucking walk on her own first, but that was beside the point.

Mikale was seething in anger at the Assassin Lord's words. "I will have her back in the morning as you ordered," he replied through clenched teeth.

"That would be wise," Alaric answered darkly, leaning over his papers once more.

Mikale tugged her roughly out of the study, slamming the door behind them. He didn't say anything as he dragged her down the hall to the stairwell. Scarlett knew where they were. She had walked these halls more times than she could count. She stumbled up the stairs to the private wing of the Fellowship, struggling to keep up, to Mikale's utter annoyance.

"One would think if he valued you so much, he would keep you better nourished," he muttered under his breath, scooping her up to carry her up the stairs. They passed Nuri's room, then her own, with Cassius's across from it. To her horror, he came to a stop in front of Juliette's room and placed her on her feet. Her legs almost gave out for a completely different reason.

"No," she whispered, swallowing thickly. She didn't care if Juliette still lived in the Witch Kingdoms as an Oracle. Too much trauma lurked beyond that door.

Mikale paused, unlocking the door and looked over his shoulder. "Have you made a choice then, my pet? Do I need to return you to the Assassin Lord so soon?"

"I can stay in another room," she ground out, finding her voice.

"You are right. We can." He turned to fully face her. "Once you have accepted that Blood Bond, you can come home with me where you will reside for the time being. This can all be remedied immediately." Scarlett stood silent, unable to fully comprehend she was back in this situation, back to having no choices whatsoever, throwing herself pointlessly against the bars of a cage. "What will it be, my pet?"

"Unlock the door," she whispered, taking a deep breath and closing her eyes as she heard the lock click.

Mikale jerked the chain to beckon her forward and into the room. She and Nuri had personally cleared all of Juliette's personal effects from it, as punishment for allowing Juliette's death. It was just a standard bedroom suite now, but memories lurked here. Memories of the three of them sprawled across her enormous bed, going through job requests or reading books. Memories of late night talks and laughter. Memories of fears spoken and dreams shared.

When Mikale started towing her towards the bathing room, she dug in her heels. "What are you doing?"

"You may be the Assassin Lord's property, but you will be my wife. Pretty Fae marriage customs mean nothing to us. You are still to be mine, and I like my pets in their best health possible; which includes not smelling like last week's garbage," Mikale answered, leaning over the tub and turning the cold tap on. "However, I have been instructed to keep you . . . uncomfortable until you begin making better choices."

Scarlett was silent as the tub filled with cold water, Mikale keeping a firm grasp on the chain of her wrist shackles as he began unbuckling the witch-leathers that still adorned her body. When the tub was almost full, a servant appeared with various soaps and towels. She then came forward with a pair of shears.

Scarlett jerked back. "Absolutely not," she said, backing directly into Mikale's chest.

The servant paused with her eyes lowered to the ground, waiting for instruction from Mikale. He leaned down to speak into Scarlett's ear, the hand not holding the chain wrapping around her front, pressing her ass into his crotch. "My pet, I will not be removing these chains from your wrists or ankles so there is no other way to remove . . . whatever it is you are wearing. You can either let her remove it, or I can take you back out to the bedroom and find much more creative ways to take it off your body."

Scarlett growled but stepped forward to the servant once more. "As it appears you are not in fact needed for this, you can shut the door on your way out," she sneered while the servant began to cut apart her precious witch-suit. It was slow going as the material was designed to withstand sword and dagger slices, so a pair of shears wasn't making much headway.

Mikale snorted. "Were you not listening when the Assassin

Lord said I was not to let you out of my sight? I will not make that mistake again." His tone turned dark and foreboding as he said that, and Scarlett glanced over her shoulder to see the ire in his dark eyes.

"Poor little lordling," she crooned. "Did someone get in trouble for my escape?"

Mikale stared back with disdain. "Careful, my pet. I decide how *uncomfortable* your night shall be."

Silence filled the bathing room as the servant continued to slowly cut the witch-suit from her body. After several long minutes, the final cut was made, and she stood bare before them, trying to cover herself as much as possible. Mikale stepped forward, scooping her into his arms to lower her into the tub. With the ankle shackles, she wouldn't have been able to lift her leg over the side of the tub herself. She immediately began shivering in the freezing water as the servant began to wash her body. The metal of the shirastone against her skin added another freezing bite. Her teeth were chattering when she came back up from submerging her head to rinse the soap from her hair.

The servant stood to make way for Mikale to lift her from the tub and set her on her feet, then she toweled her off, squeezing the water from her hair. She was forced to stand naked while the servant proceeded to brush her long hair out before braiding it down her back.

"What exactly is the plan here, then? How will I get clothes back on?" Scarlett managed to get out between her chattering teeth.

"The Assassin Lord thought of that," Mikale said with a nod towards a folded black garment that had been resting beneath the stack of towels. "As much as I would prefer to take you to bed like that, I have been told I am not allowed to fuck you again until you have accepted the Blood Bond." Scarlett smirked at that information. "Do not look so smug, my pet. Touching was not deemed off limits."

The smug grin fell from her lips as the servant grabbed the black garment and unfolded it. Mikale held her steady, and she stepped into the black fabric. The servant pulled it up her body where it tied at her shoulders, creating two straps. The gown hung nearly to the floor, and the straps created a neckline that showed ample amounts of her chest. The fabric itself was thin and partially sheer.

She would have preferred to remain dirty and smelling atrocious in her witch-suit.

When she finished, the servant gave a small bow to Mikale before leaving the bathing room. Mikale tugged her chain to pull her out to Juliette's bedroom and led her to a small table near the window. She looked out at the familiar view. Their rooms had faced the front of the Fellowship overlooking one of the main streets of the Syndicate. Despite it apparently being the middle of the night, the street was still busy. Sin and wickedness thrived in the dark after all.

Her attention was drawn back to Mikale as he poured a small glass of water and held it out to her. She reached for it tentatively, glaring at him suspiciously.

"It is just water, my pet. As the Assassin Lord has told you, we do not want your magic suppressed. We never did."

She kept her eyes locked on his as she greedily drank the water down, already aching for more. The water pitcher was still practically full, and Mikale smiled mockingly, noticing when she glanced at it. "You know what you need to do to get more."

She scowled, handing the cup back to him in clear refusal, her hand shaking from the cold. There was a small fire burning in the hearth, but it wasn't nearly large enough to heat the space.

Mikale sighed in disappointment. "You will not win, my pet. He always wins."

"I will die before he wins," she spat back.

"No, you will not. Because he wants you alive," Mikale said simply, leading her to the bed.

He pulled the covers back and motioned for her to get in. She almost groaned at the soft mattress beneath her ass. She pulled her legs up and laid back, savoring the feel of the pillow beneath her head. After sitting on a stone floor for who knew how many days, this was pure bliss.

Until Mikale climbed over top of her to lie beside her, that damn chain still firmly in his grasp.

"No," she barked in horror. "I'm not sharing a bed with you."

"You do not get a choice in the matter," Mikale replied, pulling the covers up.

She wanted to argue, but the warmth of the blankets quelled her tongue. And when Mikale wrapped an arm around her and tugged her into the cradle of his hips to tuck her in close, she couldn't bring herself to pull away from his warmth either.

She knew this for what it was. The Assassin Lord excelled at making you so miserable that you started giving in on little things. You began making small concessions and tiny exceptions so that when the big request came, you'd already given up so many things that the last leap didn't seem so big any more. He was a master at manipulation.

But he had also trained her in that manipulation, so now it would come down to a battle of wills. And as her limbs soaked in the warmth surrounding her, she vowed she would win and kill him before the end. For now, though, she closed her eyes and welcomed the darkness where she could see the stars.

CHAPTER 8
SORIN

Sorin found himself surrounded by trees in a forest as Luan pulled them all through a rip in the world. The moon filtered through the leaves, glaring off the light layer of snow and illuminating some of their surroundings. He turned in a slow circle, trying to figure out where exactly they were.

"Eliza," he called, summoning his general to his side. "Do you recognize where we are?"

She came stumbling over to him, and he gripped her arm to keep her standing.

Fuck.

He'd forgotten they would all be reeling from the loss of their magic here.

He glanced around at the others. Cyrus was doubled over and appeared to be doing his best not to vomit. Rayner was leaning against a tree. He would still be able to move among the smoke and ashes here, but he wouldn't be able to wield them, and he would weaken faster. He was pale, and his breathing was uneven. Luan had his arm looped around Arianna's waist, supporting all the Lady's weight as her head fell forward against his shoulder, and she tugged her cloak tightly around herself. The Earth Prince met his gaze, his lips forming a grim line.

"You are all right?" Sorin asked him.

He nodded once. "We need to get everyone behind the wards. Perhaps the mortals know where we are."

"Sloan and I will scout ahead and figure out how far from the tunnel system we are. That will give you all time to . . . adjust," Finn said.

Sorin nodded in agreement as he led Eliza over to another tree, helping her lower to the ground atop her pack to keep the snow from soaking into her cloak. "Even knowing this was coming, I wasn't prepared," she muttered.

Sorin could say nothing in response. He remembered when he'd first come to the mortal lands nearly four years ago. He had spent the first five days violently sick in a cave in Toreall, adjusting to not having his magic at his fingertips. It was like having a piece of your soul inaccessible to you. Being able to wield their magic was as essential as eating and breathing for Fae. Not siphoning it off throughout the day in the Courts would drive the power to seek a different outlet, making a Fae volatile, much like Scarlett's had done when she was on her tonic. Not having access to one's magic at all was a different kind of torture in and of itself.

"Once we find Cassius, he can brew a potion for you all to have access to your magic if you want it," Sorin said into the night.

"Fuck that," Cyrus hissed. "You said the High Witch brewed some for you to bring with."

"She did," Sorin confirmed. "But they are for emergencies."

"This seems like a pretty big emergency. We aren't going to be able to walk anywhere right now," Cyrus retorted, finally giving in and dropping to his knees.

"Cassius will brew some when we get there, but you need to think long and hard about taking it. You did not see what Scarlett went through when she had to detox from her tonic. Hazel said it would be worse than that, and take less time to become addicted to one that grants you access to your magic than one that suppresses it," Sorin warned.

"Fuck you, Sorin. You have that damn ring on your hand," Cyrus bit back bitterly.

"I lived without my magic for three years, Cyrus. I know exactly what you are going through."

"Enough," Luan cut in. "You are Fae warriors. Start acting like it."

"Says another with a ring on his finger," Cyrus spat at him.

"Will it make you feel better to wear it, Faeling?" Luan taunted him. "Is it too uncomfortable for you?"

"Fuck you, too, Luan," Cyrus snarled, lurching to his feet and clearly planning to take a shot at the prince.

Sorin grabbed his arm, pulling him to a halt. "Save your energy,

Cyrus. When Cassius brews the potion, you can decide then if you will take it and how often. I am not your keeper, but you need to suck it up until we get there."

Cyrus jerked his arm out of Sorin's grip and stalked to a tree near Eliza, sliding down to the ground atop his own pack. Silence descended among them. The only sounds were the trees rustling in a light breeze and a hooting owl here and there. Sorin stood guard along with Luan and Callan, while the other immortals tried to get their extreme discomfort under control. He started a few small fires near them all to keep them warm and sporadically sent waves of warmth through Arianna as well. She had insisted on wearing that ridiculous lightweight outfit, but it was the perfect excuse to release some of the magical tension growing in his veins.

Nearly a half hour later, the sound of twigs snapping and brush rustling had Sorin and Luan calling on their magic. Flames danced at Sorin's fingertips while a long, thick vine grew in Luan's hand, a whip waiting to strike. Finn and Sloan came into view a moment later.

"There's a tunnel about half a mile from here," Finn explained, coming to a stop at Callan's side. "Can you guys make it?" He looked at the Fae seated on the ground with concern.

"Once we make it to the tunnel, how far to the safe house?" Luan asked, helping Arianna to her feet. The Shifter swayed slightly but managed to stay standing on her own. Luan still kept a supporting arm around her, though. The gods help them if something happened to the Beta. Stellan wouldn't stop until everyone involved with the death of his sister was dead. Sorin was surely already in enough shit with the Shifter Alpha for asking Arianna to help him behind his back.

"Hard to say," Finn answered, rubbing the back of his neck. "I can count on one hand how many times we've been in this section of the tunnels."

Sloan snorted a derisive laugh next to him. "I'm pretty sure the only time we've been in this section of the tunnels was when we were trying to figure out how she was getting into the godsdamn castle undetected."

"Let's just get moving," Eliza said from where she sat at the base of the tree. "We need to be in that warehouse before the sun rises. We're wasting darkness."

Sorin couldn't agree more as he crossed the clearing to help her to her feet. He left her leaning against Rayner, and he moved over to Cyrus and extended a hand. "You got this?" he asked the male quietly when he pulled him up.

"This is nothing like when we cross near our border," Cyrus replied, his jaw clenching.

It was true. The closer they were to Fae territory, the less they noticed the strain of their magic being suppressed. When they had crossed to converse with the Night Children, it had hardly registered. But here? Miles from any Fae border?

"I can't believe you did this for three whole years," Cyrus gritted out.

"It gets easier, but the first week kicks your ass," Sorin agreed grimly, clapping him on the shoulder.

Finn, Sloan, and Callan led the way into the thick of the trees. Luan and Arianna were behind them in case the Earth Prince's magic was needed to protect the Crown Prince. Sorin made his Inner Court go in front of him while he brought up the rear, making sure no one got left behind.

It took them double the time it had taken Finn and Sloan to get to the tunnel, having to move slower due to the incapacitated Fae in the group. Sorin and Luan may have maintained their magic, but their Fae senses had still become muted here with the shift to mortal forms. They moved cautiously, straining their hearing and eyesight for any sign of being hunted or followed. When they slipped into the darkness of the underground passage, Sorin lit a few balls of soft, glowing flame to help guide them through. The tunnel continued straight for quite a ways, until it branched off into three separate directions.

"Which way?" Arianna asked, seeming to be adjusting to her lack of gifts faster than his Court. It made sense. She was older than any of them here, having had more decades to learn to adjust quickly to not having access to her gifts.

"Well, we need to head west towards the sea," Sorin reasoned. "I would think we would need to either continue straight or take the passage to the right."

Murmurs of agreement came from the group, and in the end, Sorin made the executive decision to take the right passageway. If they kept going west, they'd have to reach the docks eventually.

They had only been in the passageway a few minutes when he scented her, but before he could say anything, Sorin was thrown face first against the rocky wall, a cut being gouged along his cheek, and a dagger was pressed to his spine.

"Now this scene is awfully familiar, Son of Fire," a voice of silk and honey purred into his ear. "Me sneaking up on an unsuspecting Fae bastard."

"No one fucking move," Sorin snarled to his companions, as he heard weapons being drawn from their sheaths.

"Why the fuck are we not running this bitch through?" Cyrus demanded.

"Because that is Nuri," Eliza replied, stepping from Rayner's side and sliding her blade back into the sheath at her back. "She is Death's Shadow."

"I told you when you returned that you and I would have some fun," Nuri crooned into Sorin's ear, sliding the dagger up the side of his throat.

"That you did, Nuri dear, but you seem to have failed to notice my back-up," Sorin taunted in reply.

Nuri only huffed a laugh. "You mean the back-up you brought because you knew you wouldn't be able to best me on your own?"

Sorin growled at the implication and challenge. "We will have to test that theory another time, Daughter of Night. We are here for Scarlett."

Sorin felt the dagger leave his throat as Nuri released her hold on him. "Is she not with you?" She glanced around at his companions, clearly searching for that head of silver hair.

Sorin shook his head. "No. She was taken from us. A few days ago." Nuri reached up and yanked her hood back. The soft glow of the flames allowed him to make out the fury dancing in her honey-colored eyes. "You had one task, you asshole. What the fuck happened?"

"Maybe the explanations and hair braiding can wait until we are behind some wards and the Witch has brewed us a potion to give us back our godsdamn magic?" came Cyrus's irritated voice from down the tunnel.

"Who the fuck are you?" Nuri asked, her tone saying she really didn't care, as she whirled to face Cyrus.

"Someone not in the mood to listen to your bitching at the moment," he snarled back.

Nuri's lip peeled back and her fangs lengthened. "Careful, Fae bastard, I've developed quite the taste for your type of blood."

Cyrus just smirked at her. "Sweetheart, you'd have to take it by force."

"For fuck's sake," Luan muttered from his position near the mortals. "Can we just get to the damn safe house? Now that she is here, I am assuming she knows the way so we can meet our other allies? Get moving, vampyre."

Nuri dragged her eyes up and down the Earth Prince. The mannerism was so similar to one that Scarlett would have made, that Sorin's chest tightened at the action. A wicked grin tilted up the corners of her mouth, and she tilted her head to the side. "I don't know who the fuck you are, and I couldn't care less. What I do know is that should you try to give me an order again, I will taste your blood and cut off body parts while I do so."

Luan sneered at her. "I do not have time for petty Night Child egos. I am here to do one thing, and it is my understanding you are essential to completing our task. So fall in line or—"

"Fucking hell," Sorin said in exasperation. He knew that Cyrus and Nuri meeting would be a nightmare. He had not accounted for Nuri and Luan clashing. He stepped between the Earth Prince and Death's Shadow. "Nuri, we need to be safely behind wards before the sun begins to rise. I can only assume you know the tunnels better than Callan's guards, seeing as you snuck up on us. For Scarlett's sake, can you please get us to the safe house where we can meet up with Cassius and figure out how to get my godsdamn wife back?"

Nuri sucked in a breath at the word, a gloved hand grabbing his left hand where his black-gold marriage band adorned his finger. "Just wife or . . . ?"

"We both bear the twin flame Mark as well," he confirmed. "We have one Trial left to complete and the bond can be Anointed."

A wide grin spread across Nuri's face at that, and she let out a sharp whistle. A boy appeared behind them from the way they had come. Sorin instantly recognized him as Malachi, a young boy with a chip on his shoulder that he had met when Scarlett had taken him to meet the orphans in the Black Syndicate. His younger brother was one of the orphans who had gone missing, likely dead and likely because they were pure-blooded Night Children, just like Nuri.

"We're taking this lot back with us, Malachi," Nuri said. "Bring up the rear. You know what to do."

The boy nodded as Nuri jerked her head for Sorin to follow her, going back the way they had come. Sorin moved to her side, looking over his shoulder to make sure everyone was accounted for. When they reached the area where the passageways split, Nuri made to follow the one that went straight, but before they stepped into the tunnel, Luan called out to them to halt. He moved to Sorin's side and said, "Get out your map, Aditya. I need to see in what general vicinity we are located."

Nuri gave him another once over. "I really do need to know who this is, Sorin."

"Meet Azrael Luan. He is of the Earth Court," Sorin replied, summoning the map from a pocket of flame.

Understanding flared through Nuri's eyes at what he meant. He was unable to come right out and say that Luan was the Earth Prince, courtesy of the enchantment that kept all Fae from identifying Fae Royalty in the mortal lands.

"He is also a Traveler and by knowing exactly where we are, he can be prepared to move us back to this place should we need it," Sorin continued, unrolling the map.

Nuri took an edge in her hand and pointed to a section north of the main docks. "We will take the tunnel before us for another mile or so, then we will turn west. We should be at the warehouse within the hour, assuming there are no surprises along the way, but as we have people patrolling this section of the tunnels at all times, we should be fine."

Luan gave a nod before gesturing for them to continue along. They moved as quickly as they could and met no one as Nuri led them along the tunnel system. When the tunnel emptied out onto a beach from the side of a cavern, Nuri informed them the warehouse was ten minutes from their location.

Sorin's Court was waning when they finally reached the safe house. It was just as Sorin had remembered it from when he'd helped Nuri get the children here all those months ago. An abandoned warehouse, the four-story brick building loomed before them. The wards Cassius had created made it look far more decrepit than it actually was and made it appear it was seconds from collapsing. In reality, however, save for some broken windows and the garbage and junk that had littered all the floors, the warehouse was in pretty decent shape. The first floor was one wide open space, and they left it that way for the most part in case anyone did manage to make it inside. The second floor held a kitchen, so it was converted into the mess hall and general congregating area. The third and fourth floors were office spaces that they converted into bedrooms that everyone shared.

As they came to the entrance, Nuri stopped before one of the men on guard. "Send word to Cassius to get here as quickly as possible. Tell him they've returned." She paused, then added, "And if we can get a message to the Tyndell heirs, that'd be best as well."

The man took his leave, disappearing in the shadows of the night, and Nuri led them inside and up to the second floor. A young woman with lightly tanned skin and brown hair braided down her back, met them at the top of the stairs. She gave a small smile to Sorin.

"Lynnea," he greeted warmly. "Good to see you again."

"And you," she answered with a small nod of her head. She shifted her gaze to Nuri. "Take them to the kitchen. I will get some soup and bread warmed up."

"Thank you," Sorin said, following Nuri once more. She led them into the moderate kitchen space, and the Fae all collapsed onto chairs around the small table to the left of the space. Lynnea immediately moved to the stove and began adding various vegetables and some meat to a large stock pot, before getting out two loaves of bread and slicing it for them.

"When do you expect Cassius to be here?" Sorin asked Nuri, while she removed her cloak and draped it over a stool. She left her gloves and weapons in place.

"I'm hoping sooner rather than later. I think the message that you've returned will hasten his return," she replied.

Sorin nodded. "Let's wait until he arrives to fill you in on our side of things. Why don't you catch me up while we eat, and hopefully Cassius and the Tyndells will be here by then."

Nuri agreed and proceeded to tell him of how Cassius had continued to work tirelessly to constantly reinforce the wards. He had apparently found some new upgrades in the books Sorin had given to him when he had visited the Fire Court. The secret of the warehouse location had been kept quiet by everyone. They hadn't even revealed it to the Assassin Lord, which is why Nuri hadn't reported to the Fellowship since Scarlett and Sorin had left the kingdom. Lord Tyndell apparently kept Cassius from the Assassin

Lord's wrath somehow, but they were all conscious of how quickly that could change.

Sorin was finishing his second bowl of soup when a man with shoulder-length brown hair and rich brown eyes came rushing into the room, followed closely by a man and woman who had matching golden-blonde hair and ocean-blue eyes. Cassius Redding and Drake and Tava Tyndell. Cassius's eyes scanned over everyone, pausing on Sorin briefly before continuing to look around the kitchen wildly. "Where is she?" he demanded.

Sorin stood from his place at the table. "She is not with us, Commander."

"Where the hell is she?"

"We have reason to believe she is in Baylorin, but her exact whereabouts are unknown to us."

Cassius's entire body went rigid as he turned to face Sorin. "What do you mean her whereabouts are unknown to you?"

"She was taken. After she defeated several Night Children in Toreall near the Earth Court border."

"Taken by who?" Violence and rage radiated off the Commander as he held Sorin in his gaze.

"We do not know. We were told Mikale does not currently have her, but we do not know for how long that will remain true," Sorin answered, swallowing thickly.

"How did you let this happen?" Cassius demanded. "I left her in your care, believing she would be safe with you!"

"She was safe with me," Sorin retorted. "You know you cannot control her. You know she does things of her own mind, often refusing to let others know her plans until she is in the thick of them."

Cassius stalked towards Sorin and gripped the front of his tunic in his fist, and Sorin readied himself to take the hit from the Commander. He was Scarlett's personal guard, assigned to her in the Black Syndicate. He was so protective of her, Sorin had thought they might be lovers when he'd first met her. He wasn't surprised by his rage, and he'd allow this hit for failing in his promise to keep her safe.

But the blow never came. Drake and Nuri were behind Cassius, pulling him off of Sorin as he tried to jerk free of their holds.

"For the love of Anala," Cyrus barked, standing and coming between Cassius and Sorin. "Everyone needs to calm the fuck down. He is the Witch, yes?"

Sorin nodded in confirmation. "Yes, he has Witch blood along with the girl who fed us."

"Great. Get them what they need to get started. While they're brewing the potion, we can fill them in on everything that has happened. After they have heard it all, if they still deem you worthy of having your ass kicked, we will let that happen," Cyrus said.

Sorin clenched his teeth, turning to Cassius. "Is that agreeable to you?"

Cassius nodded curtly. "I haven't done much with potions. I do not know how much help I will be."

"You will be able to do it," Sorin replied, knowing exactly whose Witch-blood ran through the Commander's veins.

"Then let's move to the fourth floor. There is a small kitchenette on that level to make sure things aren't disturbed."

Everyone gathered their things and climbed the stairs once more, Cassius and Sorin walking side-by-side. "Since I left her last, I've been experiencing these . . . episodes," Cassius said quietly to Sorin.

"What kind of episodes?" He glanced side-long at the Commander.

"I don't know how to describe it. One time, I had excruciating pain in my arm and along my ribs, like they'd been broken. Other times it's minor, fleeting scratches, as if I were sparring. But it all stopped suddenly, a few days ago, which is when you said Scarlett was taken. It can't be coincidence, can it?" Cassius asked, clearly hoping Sorin had an answer for him.

"Scarlett broke her arm and some ribs in an attack a few months ago," Sorin answered. "I do not know how you would be able to sense that. None of what you just told me makes any sense."

"It has to be related, though, right?" Cassius pressed, pushing open a door into a small room that had a tall, wooden table, ice box, hearth, and wash basin.

"It would certainly seem so," Sorin answered, running a hand down his face. "So much has happened, Cassius. Let's get these potions going, and we will tell you everything. Hopefully, when it is all said and done, we can come up with a plan to figure out where the hell she is and get her back."

CHAPTER 9
SCARLETT

Scarlett was jolted awake from her soft cocoon of warmth when the blankets were ripped from her body. She whimpered as her arms were dragged above her head and her stiff shoulders screamed in protest. The chain of her shackles was clipped to a hook in the headboard that had not been there the night before. She looked around blearily, trying to get her bearings as her ankle shackles were hooked onto something at her feet, rendering her immobile.

Mikale stood at the end of the bed, a maniacal grin on his face. He was dressed in pants and a thick tunic. The small fire in the hearth had been extinguished, and the window was open, letting in gusts of winter wind. Her skin had broken out into gooseflesh the moment the blankets had been stripped from her, and in the thin gown she was wearing, her body was already beginning to shiver from the chill.

Mikale began walking towards her, and she plunged into the darkness within her soul as deeply and as quickly as she possibly could. She knew what was coming. Some type of punishment and she wasn't mentally prepared to handle it yet. She wasn't in the right headspace as she plummeted deeper and deeper, racing towards that place where it didn't matter what happened to her.

This was how the Assassin Lord worked. He tortured you, then he cared for you. He made you ache, then he made it better. Over and over again until he got what he wanted.

One of her punishments had once involved withholding food from her for days. She had been chained in the same spot in his dungeon study, and it had been day five of no food and minimal water. Alaric had come in with a small feast of meats, breads, and vegetables. She'd known it was a trap. She'd known she'd regret it, but survival came first, and she'd needed food. She'd needed sustenance. So she'd devoured what he laid before her, only to learn within an hour or so that everything had been laced with minute doses of columbine that left her with abdominal pain and violent vomiting for nearly two days. It was during the second day that Alaric had gently unchained her and carried her up to her room himself. He'd sat by her bed, pressing a cold cloth to her forehead and holding her hair back when she vomited, until she'd finally fallen asleep and the fever broke.

Mikale straddled Scarlett at the waist and looked down at her, pure desire flaring in his dark eyes. His hands roamed over her hips and up her sides until one gripped her jaw, forcing her to meet his eyes. She said nothing as they stared at each other, but a look of confusion passed over his features before he was able to school them back into neutrality. He broke the stare first and his eyes flashed to her arms above her head. He leaned over her, running his thumb along the silver Mark on her forearm, then dragging his hand down the length of her arm and over her shoulder.

"That Mark would not stop me," he murmured to himself, his eyes following his hand.

"Stop you from doing what?" she rasped, trying to move her arms into a position to put less strain on her shoulders, but it was useless.

Mikale suddenly stilled over her, his eyes going wide. Scarlett stilled too at the rage that filled his face. He yanked the tie of the strap over her right shoulder and pulled the fabric aside, exposing half of her chest to the freezing room.

"What are you doing?" she cried, but the sound was cut short when his hand wrapped around her throat, squeezing tight enough to cut off her air.

"When did you get this?" Mikale snarled, his fingers brushing along the length of the right side of her collarbone.

"Get what?" she gasped, writhing beneath him to try to loosen his grip.

He only squeezed tighter, bringing his face close to hers. "This Mark?" he spat. "When did you get it? How did he do this?"

He loosened his fingers enough for her to speak, and Scarlett gulped down the little air that she could. "I don't know what you're talking about," she rasped out, and his fingers tightened once more.

"Liar," he spat. His fingers ran over the Mark again. It was the Mark the beautiful man had given her when she and Talwyn had been taken to that rip in the plane. Mikale's fingers dragged down farther and cupped her right breast, squeezing. He groaned, tilting his head back and closing his eyes briefly.

When he opened them once more and looked back at her, lust mixed with the ire in his gaze. "Alaric will not be pleased with this development, my pet. Maybe he will let me have you after all." A cruel smile tilted on his lips as he finally released her throat and reached to retie the strap of her gown.

Scarlett panted out a string of curse words at him, gulping down breath after breath. Mikale only chuckled as he refastened the tie and climbed off of her, unhooking first her ankle shackles and then her wrists. He yanked her from the bed, and she fell to her knees before him.

Mikale reached out and gripped her hair, yanking her head back. "See, my pet, this is how you should always be. On your knees, that fucking mouth quiet for once, and waiting to serve me."

Scarlett wanted to spit at him, but her mouth was so dry there wasn't anything to spit. So instead, she spat words laced with venom. "Fuck you, Mikale."

Mikale only smiled at her, like he knew a secret that she didn't. "You will learn soon enough, my pet." He reached down and grabbed her elbow, pulling her to her feet. He tugged her to the door and began leading her down the hallway. She stumbled along down the stairs, trying to keep her head from spinning. She was dehydrated. Combined with the lack of food and hunger pains, she was fighting dizziness and nausea.

More than once Mikale had to steady her and keep her on her feet, but he didn't slow his pace.

He didn't bother to knock before he burst into the Assassin Lord's dungeon study, and Scarlett dropped to her knees as the nausea finally overtook her. With nothing in her stomach to vomit up, she dry heaved as Mikale held the chain in his hands.

"We have a problem," he snarled.

Scarlett couldn't focus on the two men in the room. Her vision was blurring, and there was a sharp burning along her left hand.

"Sorin," she gasped out, heaving up nothing again.

Alaric had surged to his feet when they'd burst into the office, but now he was storming around his desk. "I'll say we have a problem!" he roared. "What part of do not let her get too weak did you not understand?"

"What?" Mikale bit back in obvious shock. "I took care of her, just as you ordered. She was bathed and given water, and she slept soundly on a soft bed beneath blankets. That is not the issue—"

"It is the only issue that matters right now," Alaric barked.

Scarlett!

The voice was so faint in her mind Scarlett was sure she hadn't actually heard it. It had to be the dehydration causing some sort of delirium, but she didn't care at this point. She needed to hear him, even if it was all in her head.

"Sorin," she rasped again.

"No!" Alaric snarled, dropping to his knees in front of her. "Go and get Tarek. Now!" he barked at Mikale. If she hadn't been half-conscious, Scarlett likely would have marveled at the idea of the Assassin Lord being on his knees in a panic before her.

Scarlett! Love, where are you?

"This is hardly my fault," Mikale was arguing with Alaric.

"She is so weak that her magic is taking over to keep her alive. Soon she will be weak enough that her Blood Magic will shatter. It is already cracking," Alaric snapped. "Go and get Tarek!"

Mikale turned and stalked for the door, but Scarlett couldn't even lift her head to watch him go.

"Sorin."

Mikale had dropped the chain for her wrist shackles to the floor, and Scarlett curled in on herself, her stomach aching from dry heaving, and her head throbbing.

"Scarlett, open your eyes," Alaric demanded.

I am here, Love. I'm here. Tell me where you are.

So much desperation in the words swirling in her mind. She tried to form a thought to answer him, but someone was shaking her shoulders, moving her body.

"Open your eyes, dammit," Alaric snarled again. "Now."

Scarlett cracked her eyes open, seeing two of the Assassin Lord before her as her vision continued to blur. He was cradling her in his lap. "Good. Good, Scarlett," he praised, a look of relief passing over his face. "Drink." A glass was pressed to her lips, and she tried to turn her head from it.

She attempted to crawl from his lap, but Alaric held her firm. "It is water, Scarlett. Drink," he ordered again.

She shook her head, trying to clear her thoughts, but the movement just made the nausea rise again. She lurched forward, convulsing once more.

"That useless son of a bitch," Alaric muttered under his breath. When she was done heaving, he pulled her back into his lap. "This could all be avoided if you would just make a decision, Scarlett." He brought the glass of water back to her mouth, tipping it up so it wet her dry lips. "Drink."

But Scarlett pressed her lips into a firm line. She'd learned a long time ago that if he was acting this way, it was a ruse. Something much worse than what she was currently enduring was to follow. She closed her eyes, breathing in deep. Darkness reached for her, and she sighed at the familiarity of it.

I am coming for you, Love. We are coming for you. Tell me where you are.

"No." Alaric's sharp command reached through the fog in her mind. "Stay awake, Scarlett. Look at me."

But she didn't want to. Here in the darkness she could hear him. She could almost see his face.

"More," she whispered to the darkness.

"No!" Alaric bellowed. She felt the glass press to her lips again, but she still refused.

Scarlett, please. One word, Love. That's all I need.

There was yelling and cursing around her, but she couldn't process what was being said or who was saying it. Something warm and sticky was pressed to her mouth, but she clamped her lips shut tighter.

There was clanging and more cursing as the warmth withdrew from her mouth.

"Scarlett, open your damn eyes!"

Come on, Scarlett. One word. Just one. Please.

"Alaric," she gasped, and when she said it, something was shoved into her mouth, forcing liquid down the back of her throat. It tasted of copper and metal, and her mouth was forced closed before she could spit it out.

"Swallow, Scarlett. Drink it down." Alaric's voice was low and coaxing in her ear. She fought against his hold and new hands gripped her, holding her down. She had no choice but to swallow whatever it was they'd given her.

"That's good. Good, Scarlett," the Assassin Lord praised, as though she were indeed a prized pet.

Something smooth was pressed into her mouth again, more liquid shooting down her throat, forcing her to swallow it again. Two more times of the same before she was finally able to crack her eyes open and the room didn't spin around her.

She was still held in Alaric's lap, and he looked frantic, sweat beading at his brow. Mikale was above her, holding her shoulders down. Above them both stood Tarek, blood leaking down his arm for whatever reason.

A look from Alaric had Mikale releasing her shoulders, and the Assassin Lord helped her slowly sit up. He gently smoothed her hair back. She was so weak she couldn't even raise her arms with the heavy shirastone shackles on her wrists.

"Get her some water, Tarek," Alaric ordered calmly. "Mikale, go get her some food."

A moment later, a glass was being handed to Alaric, and he brought it to her lips. "Drink or we force it down again, Scarlett," he commanded, tipping the glass up. She took a small sip, then a big gulp as the cool water rinsed the coppery taste from her mouth. He pulled the glass back before she could take another gulp.

"Small sips, or it all comes back up," he chided, setting the glass on the floor. She followed it with her eyes and saw a metal syringe beside it.

"What did you give me?" she rasped at the sight of it.

What fresh hell would await her now?

"It is nothing that will harm you, Scarlett," Alaric answered, adjusting the fabric of the black gown she was wearing, as if he actually cared about her propriety after he'd *given* her to Mikale.

"Bullshit," she breathed, trying to free herself from his hold once more.

The Assassin Lord chuckled low in his throat as Mikale came back into the room with a covered platter. He placed it down on the floor, removing the lid to reveal a small plate of eggs and toast.

Scarlett shook her head in refusal when Alaric began stabbing pieces of egg with the fork. He sighed, bringing the fork to her mouth. "You will eat, Scarlett. While I require your submission, I also require you healthy and well." When she still refused the food, he calmly set the fork back down. "Very well, Death's Maiden. We will do this the hard way."

He stood, bringing Scarlett with him and carrying her to the wall where he could hook her chains to the wall. As he secured the shackles once more, he said over his shoulder to Tarek, "Send a message to Balam to come here immediately."

When he stood, Mikale cleared his throat. "Balam will be needed for more than one reason."

"I am assuming you are referencing the Mark along her collarbone?" Alaric ground out, walking behind his desk. He braced his hands on it, leaning forward, his head hanging down.

"You knew?"

"I just saw it this morning," he admitted. "That suit she was wearing hid it from me the past few days."

"It is why I brought her down early this morning," Mikale supplied.

"It is a good thing you did. She is more powerful than I anticipated her to be at this point. She will need to be fed more often to keep it in check," Alaric answered, lifting his head. He looked over to Scarlett, a look of wariness about him.

Scarlett was too exhausted to care. She leaned her head back against the wall, closing her eyes once more. With the water and whatever it was they'd forced her to swallow, the delirium had lifted. Her head was quiet once more, and she found herself wishing it weren't. The hallucination of his voice had been comforting to her soul.

"I want extra security around the Fellowship and an extra guard stationed outside this room at all times, two more in the hall. When she goes up with you, the same. No one gets near her without us knowing about it," Alaric ordered.

"You already have three guards—"

"I know what security is already in place," Alaric said harshly. "You underestimated them once. I am not as foolish as you."

Mikale bristled at the insult but said nothing. He crossed to the sofa, taking a seat as Alaric lowered himself to his desk chair, rubbing his temples. Scarlett remained silent, trying to focus on the conversation happening around her, but her head was still spinning.

"Do not sleep, Scarlett. You need to be awake to eat."

"I'm not eating anything," she retorted, her voice gravelly and hoarse.

Mikale snorted in disbelief from the sofa, and her eyes dragged to him. "It is funny you think you have a choice in the matter," he sneered.

"Mikale," Alaric warned. "She will come around soon enough."

Nothing more was said for the next hour, until Lord Tyndell knocked and entered the office, Tarek filing in behind him.

"Good Morning, Alaric," he greeted cordially. "Mikale." Then his attention swiveled to Scarlett. If she didn't know he was a conniving bastard, she'd have thought his smile was genuine. "Scarlett, my dear, it is so wonderful to see you."

"I wish I could say the same, but I'm not a lying asshole like the rest of the people in this room," she spat back with as much of a sneer as she could muster.

Lord Tyndell let out a chuckle. "Your dinner conversation always did entertain me. And I am told you have begun to master your magic. How delightful."

Scarlett bared her teeth at him as she flipped him her middle finger.

Alaric stood at that, coming around to pick up the plate of eggs and toast. "She has refused to eat," he explained to Balam. "She has also acquired a new Mark."

"Has she now?" Lord Tyndell asked, a brow arching. "If only someone had not let her escape for a second time, that could have likely been avoided."

Mikale cursed under his breath from where he sat behind the two men who were clearly superiors to him, aside from the fact that the Assassin Lord was actually a Maraan Prince.

Lord Tyndell crossed the room, crouching down and reaching forward to touch her. Scarlett lurched back, pressing herself as much as possible against the wall. He tsked. "I am not going to hurt you, my dear," he chided, reaching forward again and brushing the strap of her gown aside so he could see the whole Mark lining her collarbone.

"How can you see it?" she breathed, while Lord Tyndell continued to study her skin.

"Now that your magic has emerged, your glamours are different from Fae since you are not, in fact, Fae," Lord Tyndell answered simply, his gaze staying fixed on the Mark.

"If I were Fae, you wouldn't be able to see it?"

"If you were Fae, I would not be able to see your Fae Marks. However, this is not a Fae Mark," he replied, pushing back to his feet. He turned to speak to Alaric. "Order her some fresh food. It will take some time, but I should be able to work around that. Getting her to eat, though, should not take too much."

"Thank you, Balam," Alaric said, nodding to Tarek to apparently fetch more food.

Lord Tyndell nodded and removed his cloak, moving to lay it across the sofa before coming back to crouch before Scarlett again. Alaric and Mikale came to stand behind him, and Scarlett stared at the three men before her.

No.

At the two Maraan Lords and a Maraan Prince.

"You need to eat, my dear," Balam said with fake gentleness.

"You need to go to hell," she bit back, drawing her knees to her chest.

A half grin tilted on the Lord's lips, and he reached out to grasp her chin between his thumb and forefinger, forcing her to meet his stare. "Now, now, my dear. If something happens to you, you would cause us to go after someone else you love. You do understand that, don't you?" Scarlett went utterly still. She tried to jerk her chin from Lord Tyndell, but he held firm. "Do you really want to be responsible for *another* death?"

Breathing suddenly became difficult as she found herself on the floor in the stone cell of the Lairwood House. Juliette was lying in her lap, blood pooling from her chest. Her own hand was curled around the dagger.

"No," Scarlett gasped, releasing the hilt from her hand. It clattered to the floor. "This wasn't my fault. Mikale made me do this."

"Did he?" came Lord Tyndell's voice. "If you had done things differently, everybody could have walked out of that cell that day. You should have negotiated better. You could have saved her, and you know it."

She shook her head at Juliette's vacant and lifeless eyes staring up at her. "No. This had to happen. It needed to. To set other events into motion," she answered firmly.

"And this death? Did this death need to happen too?"

Scarlett peered out of a hole in a rubbish bin as Dracon began cutting her mother into pieces. Eliné's screams were echoing off the alley walls.

"Stop!" Scarlett cried, slamming her hands over her ears. "Stop!" "Shh, Scarlett," Alaric soothed, his voice seeming to come from beside her. She felt a hand stroking through her hair. "You can make this all stop."

Scarlett opened eyes. She hadn't realized she had closed them. Her cheeks were wet from tears, and blood was running down her arms from the shackles biting into her wrists as she had yanked on them, trying to bring her hands to her ears outside the vision Lord Tyndell had somehow thrust her into. Her breathing was uneven, and she choked trying to draw air into her lungs that wouldn't expand. Lord Tyndell was sitting back on his heels, a faint smile on his lips.

"What did you do?" she managed to gasp, trying to even out her breathing.

In and out. In and out.

She repeated it over and over in her mind, trying to make her lungs obey.

"I did nothing, my dear," he replied, his tone ringing with innocence. "You are the one who causes so much death around you."

"Those were not my fault. *He* ordered my mother killed," she hissed, with a jerk of her chin to Alaric.

"Perhaps, but it was still because of you. If she had not taken you in, and agreed to act as your parental figure, she would still be living and breathing in the Fae lands. She was only in Baylorin because of you," Lord Tyndell said casually.

"That . . ." Scarlett trailed off as she contemplated those words. Then shook her head, clearing her thoughts. "No. Stop it. Those deaths were not my fault."

Lord Tyndell sat forward and gripped her chin once more, his dark eyes boring into hers. "You can spin it any way you want, my dear, but you know deep down that you are responsible for their deaths. It is their curse for simply knowing you. And should something happen to you, the next one will be your fault as well."

Scarlett suddenly found herself in the Fellowship dungeons, a man with shoulder-length brown hair lying in a pool of blood at her feet.

"Cassius!" she cried, dropping to her knees and frantically searching his body to figure out where the blood was coming from. Cassius gripped her hand, blood smearing over her fingers.

"Seastar," he rasped. He coughed and blood sprayed from his mouth. "Cassius, no," she sobbed, leaning over him.

"You can stop this, Seastar," he whispered, his chocolate-brown eyes so dull as he stared up at her.

"You're going to be fine. I'm not going to let anything happen to you," she promised, brushing her bloodied fingers along his brow. "You're going to be fine."

"Eat, Scarlett," Alaric purred into her ear as warm eggs were touched to her lips. "Eat, or what you are seeing will come to pass." There was a promise in his voice, and she knew he'd follow through. She knew what this monster was capable of. And she knew she'd do whatever was necessary to keep her family safe.

She opened her mouth and allowed that forkful to be fed to her. "Good," the Assassin Lord praised softly, brushing a tear from her cheek. "I knew you would see things my way eventually."

Scarlett swallowed the eggs, opening her eyes to look at him. Alaric speared some more eggs onto the fork and before she took another bite, she said, "I am going to kill you. You and all your Lords."

"Not before I have broken you so thoroughly, you will never contemplate leaving my side again. By the time I am done with you, you will call me Master and mean it. You will know who owns you, Scarlett. And when I claim my throne, you will be my greatest weapon to help me maintain it," he replied. "Now eat before I summon Cassius home."

Scarlett did as she was told, allowing Alaric to feed her the entire plate of eggs and two slices of toast. She would do this for now, but she would die before she'd allow him to use her for such a purpose. All that was left to do now was figure out how to eliminate herself from the equation.

CHAPTER 10
SORIN

"Dammit!" Sorin snarled, flames hovering in his palms and embers dancing in his vision.

"Sorin," Cyrus said cautiously. "I do not have my magic right now, brother."

The two were in the small bedroom they were sharing. Rayner was in a room with Luan next door, mainly because he was the quiet one, and the two could pretend the other wasn't there. Arianna and Eliza were across the hall, with Callan and his men in a room next to theirs.

They'd stayed up until nearly dawn going over what everyone knew and coming up with plans. The biggest issue was they didn't know where exactly Scarlett was. Their best guesses had been the Tyndell manor or the Lairwood estate, but Cassius said he hadn't felt anything different with the wards. They'd started making plans for areas to scout. Places to search. Ways to get into the castle to check the dungeons there.

They'd finally all had to go rest. The Fae who didn't have access to their magic had been exhausted. Cassius had managed to make a small batch of the tonic, and Sorin's Inner Court had all taken small doses to ease some of the discomfort. The few hours of sleep they had gotten were not nearly enough, when Sorin had been jolted from sleep, his left hand burning.

He could feel her. It was faint. So faint it was hardly there. But he could *feel* her. She was weak. Far too weak. And he *heard* her. He heard her say his name. His magic hummed at the sound of her voice in his mind, seeking its counterpart as much as he was seeking her physical being.

And he'd tried.

Gods, he'd tried to reach her. He'd begged her to tell him where she was. There was so much resistance down that bridge between their souls, hairline cracks fissuring along whatever barrier was there. He'd thrown flames against it, trying to weaken it further, all the while reaching for her, telling her he was coming. But he needed something. He needed a direction to go.

And just when he thought that wall blocking their bond was going to shatter apart, the cracks disappeared. It repaired itself, and a force seemed to emanate from the wall, shoving him back, away from her. But not before he heard her voice one final time, full of pain and pleading.

Alaric.

The Assassin Lord had her. Not Mikale.

Not Lord Tyndell.

This changed everything. They didn't need to scout anywhere or try to find a way into the castle. They needed to get into the Black Syndicate, into the heart of hell itself.

"Sorin!" Cyrus snapped. "Get it under control, or I'll be forced to get Luan."

Sorin glanced down to find the flames in his palms had grown, tendrils of fire snaking up his wrists and around his arms. And all he could think about as he watched his fire was how much it reminded him of Scarlett's shadows doing the same.

Why weren't her shadows helping her? They'd protected her from the Night Children all those months ago. They'd bit at him. They'd cocooned around her when she was at her darkest. They'd been there when he couldn't, so why wasn't she using them now?

"We will get her back, Sorin," Cyrus said, his voice low and tense as he watched his prince. "We will find her, but you need to remember that you are the Prince of Fire. There are innocent children in this building. Get it under control."

He inhaled deeply, but it didn't feel like enough air. Nothing felt like enough. Not without her here.

Cyrus was right. They would find her.

And then he'd burn every motherfucker who'd touched her until even the ashes were nothing.

"Get the others," Sorin said, his tone low and lethal as he strode for the door. "Meet me on the beach."

Without another word, he left the room. He was down the four flights of stairs and out the back door facing the docks within minutes. He finally stopped when his feet sank into wet sand, the waves lapping at his toes. He hadn't even bothered to put on boots when he'd left the warehouse, despite the winter weather. With a bellow full of every bit of rage and helplessness and longing building in his soul, he released a stream of flames across the water, steam rising and hissing.

He heard his Court come up behind him, but they said nothing. There was nothing to say. There had been nothing to say for four days. Their queen was missing. His wife had been taken. She was in the hands of perhaps the one person who was worse than Mikale. She was in the hands of the person who knew how to break her. She could handle Mikale. She could take every touch and every foul thing that man would do and say to her. The Assassin Lord, though? That man was a master manipulator. That man knew her inside and out. That man knew just how strong she was and exactly how to wreck that strength. That man knew how to break her in ways he didn't know that he could help her walk through twice.

When you find her, she will not be the same as when she left.

The Oracle's words had haunted him since she'd said them in his study two days ago. He'd tried not to assume the worst. An Oracle's words were often vague and misconstrued. The true meaning of them not becoming clear until the events had come to pass. But knowing she was in the hands of her former Master?

She will not be the same as when she left.

The only sound was the waves. A gull occasionally squawked as it flew overhead. He didn't know how long they stood there, his Court a solid presence at his back. He stared across that sea until he finally began registering the chill air against his skin. And when he turned to face his family, it was the Prince of the Fire Court who looked at them. It was the face of the Court that filled the nightmares of mortals; and the looks on the faces of his Inner Court told him they had gone to this place, too. They had come for what was theirs, and the gods help anyone who stood in their way.

"We need to find Nuri and Cassius," Sorin said, his voice low and lethal. "She is in the Black Syndicate. They will know the layout and what we need to do."

"You can feel her?" Rayner asked.

"For a brief moment. She is . . . not well," he answered, quelling the rage that immediately tried to surge up once more; the wet sand beneath him beginning to steam.

The faces of his family darkened even more, and they all turned and headed back into the warehouse. Sorin went to the room he shared with Cyrus and got dressed, stopping in a washroom to run some water over his face and hands. By the time he stepped into the first floor room, his Inner Court was there along with Luan, Arianna, and Nuri.

"Cassius is coming with Drake and Tava," Nuri said tightly. She had several knives in her hand and was hurling them into a wooden beam at the other end of the room. They landed nearly on top of each other. When she had thrown the last one and was stalking to retrieve them, she said, "You believe she is with Alaric."

It wasn't a question. It was a statement, and Sorin could hear the skepticism in her tone.

"I *know* she is with Alaric," Sorin corrected.

"I have eyes inside the Fellowship, *General*," she replied. "No one has said a word about her being there."

"She is there," Sorin ground out from between gritted teeth.

"All I am saying is that we shouldn't entirely abandon our other plans," Nuri argued, prowling back towards him, her knives in her hand. "Yes, we can investigate the Syndicate, but I think we should also still look into the Lairwood house—"

"There is no need," Sorin interrupted. "All of our efforts need to be focused on the Black Syndicate."

"And if you are wrong?" she snapped. "We could at least have other leads to follow if we still look into—"

"No," Sorin growled. "She is with your Master. She is in that hellhole you call home, where you knew what was happening to her for years and did nothing. You and Juliette let her—"

One of those knives in her hands was flying through the air in the next blink, and he barely managed to get a shield up to avoid it. His Court was instantly before him as Nuri prepared to hurl another knife at him.

"If you release that blade, you will regret it," Cyrus said, his voice low and full of warning.

A sinister grin twisted onto Nuri's features, and she let her fangs slide free. "I think you will find that you will be the one with regret, fire bastard," she retorted.

Sorin could feel her voice of silk and honey scraping down

his soul as she tapped into her entrancing abilities. Before Sorin could do anything, vines were snaking up Nuri's legs and torso, snagging her wrists and pinning them behind her back. She hissed in outrage, and Sorin turned to find Azrael leaning casually against the wall. His face was hard, and he looked bored out of his godsdamn mind.

"If you are not going to play fair, Nuri dear, neither are we," Sorin taunted with a mocking grin.

"Fuck you, Sorin," she spat. "You sit here and blame me for what Scarlett endured in the Black Syndicate? She was not the only one there. Juliette and I were trained just as harshly. We were treated just as brutally. In fact, I would say our training was even more vicious because everything was always about *her*. *She* had to be protected at all costs. *She* was the one that mattered above all else. *She* was the reason Juliette gave her life to begin with. So do not stand here, berating me for doing nothing, when *you* let her get taken from your own godsdamn Court, right from underneath your arrogant ass. Do not sit here and tell me how much she suffered for years at the hand of my *Master* when there was nothing I could do but endure the same beside her. She is not the only one who has made sacrifices."

"What the hell is going on in here?"

Cassius and the Tyndells stood in the doorway of the warehouse, the door clicking shut behind them. His eyes bounced from Nuri, restrained in vines, to Sorin, where fire simmered at his fingertips.

"Sorin wants to march into the Black Syndicate and take on the Assassin Lord," Nuri quipped with a sneer.

"That is not what I said," Sorin retorted, the fire at his fingertips flaring brighter.

"Sorin," Rayner said, in quiet warning.

"Why do we think he has her?" Cassius asked, stepping further into the room.

Drake and Tava stayed near the entrance.

"Because he had a super special feeling," Nuri sneered again.

A hand clamping onto his shoulder from behind had Sorin halting mid-step when he began to move towards the Night Child. He bared his teeth, Cyrus's fingers digging into his flesh.

"Sorin, you are riding a very dangerous edge right now. Maybe you should take the ring off for this conversation," he said, his voice low.

"Maybe we should be making plans to enter the Black Syndicate and find her, rather than arguing with a godsdamned vampyre," Sorin snarled in reply.

Nuri hissed again, but Cassius interrupted before she could say anything. "What did you learn and how?"

"I felt our bond briefly. She managed to tell me she was with Alaric. She is weak, Cassius. She is not—" Sorin paused, swallowing the smoke curling in his mouth and pushing it back down with the rage and worry and helplessness that were surging up once again. He would not be able to contain it much longer. They needed to come up with a plan and put it into action. Now. "She is there. Tell me what we need to do so we can get her the hell out."

Cassius blew out a deep breath, running his hand through his hair. "It will not be that simple, Aditya. We cannot just go into the Black Syndicate. It will take at least a couple days to plan and—"

"We do not have a couple days," Sorin spat, jerking free of Cyrus's grip and stalking forward. "Did you not hear what I said?"

"I heard you," Cassius replied, his voice even and strained. "I want to find her as badly as you do, but there are dozens of places he could have her. Even at that, the places that are most likely . . ." He ran his hand through his hair again, letting out another heavy breath. "They will be nearly impossible to get into undetected. This plan will need to be precise and intricate, and if we make one error, the consequences for her, for everyone involved, will be horrific. You think she is weak now? You think she is hurting now? Alaric is just getting started."

The room fell silent. Sorin's chest was heaving with every breath. He let the flames spring to life around him once more. "The Assassin Lord will not be an issue for two Fae with access to their magic, let alone if the others take the tonic you brewed to access theirs as well. The only thing we need to do is figure out where the fuck she is. Once that task is done, getting to her and getting her out should not be an issue."

Nuri snorted derisively, still bound by Luan's vines. "You think they do not expect you to come for her? I assure you, asshole, they are more than prepared for you and your fire tricks."

"She is right," Cassius said. "Also, I would release her. She has likely already planned fifty different forms of revenge."

Nuri's face twisted into a half-grin as her eyes narrowed on Luan. The Earth Prince glanced once at Sorin, and Sorin gave a jerk of his chin. The vines unwound, and Nuri slowly rolled her neck and shoulders, her honey-colored eyes closing. When they reopened, a Night Child stared back at them. Her face was cold, her eyes hard as they stared down Luan. She said nothing, that half-grin growing more wicked, and Cassius casually stepped between them.

"As we were saying," Cassius continued, his eyes fixed warily on Nuri, "figuring out where exactly she is being kept is likely the least complicated part of this. We are not going there today."

"The fuck we aren't," Sorin snarled.

"Sorin," Rayner warned, "we cannot risk it. We need to listen to them."

"It will take us several days, if not weeks, to figure out where she is. And even at that, we'll be lucky," Cassius said. He glanced at Nuri again. "I have a few suspicions about where she might be, but getting into them to see will be . . . difficult."

"So you send me in," the Shifter Beta interjected. She had been standing silently near Luan, observing everything taking place, listening and calculating. Everyone turned to look at the female, the beads on her braids clinking as she sauntered forward. "I will find her, and then we can make a plan to get her out."

"That would not be wise," Luan cut in. "Your brother would be very opposed to this idea."

"My brother is not here," she countered, her eyes shifting to Sorin. "Let me find your bride. That is why I am here, is it not?"

"This was not the part of the plan you were brought for, Lady," Sorin replied, but the Shifter had a point. She could get in and out of wherever they suspected Scarlett was, likely undetected . . . Unless there were wards.

"I have never been asked to put up wards in the Syndicate," Cassius said when Sorin posed the question. "Even if somehow there are wards, would he be able to tell the difference with Scarlett there? Or me? Or Nuri?"

"This is not a good idea, Sorin," Luan cut in again.

"It is the best option that has been proposed," Sorin retorted. "Unless you have another idea?"

"Do you really believe the two of us cannot handle a mortal assassin?" Luan countered, his doubt clear in his tone.

"He is not a mere mortal assassin. He runs the entire Black Syndicate," Sorin answered.

"Again, a district of mortals."

"Clearly not just mortals," Nuri countered with a wicked smirk, toying with her knives.

Luan glanced at her briefly. "That is a valid point, I suppose."

"Is the Assassin Lord mortal, then?" Tava asked, drawing attention to her and her brother for the first time since they'd arrived. Sorin had forgotten they were even here.

Cassius and Nuri glanced at each other, some form of silent communication passing between them.

"What?" Sorin demanded. "Do you know something?"

"No," Cassius answered, shaking his head. When Sorin continued to stare at him in expectation, he sighed. "It would not surprise me to learn that he is not mortal at all."

"You think he is what? A Night Child?" Sorin asked. Nuri shrugged. "Perhaps."

"But you have your suspicions," Sorin pressed. She shrugged again. "Perhaps."

Cyrus's hand was again on his shoulder, forcibly holding him back as he lurched towards Death's Shadow.

"*Perhaps*," Cyrus drawled, "you could share your suspicions so that we are better prepared when we go for our queen."

"This is not your domain, firestarter," Nuri replied lazily. "I do not answer to any of you."

"No," Sorin sneered back. "You answer to a master who has my wife, my twin flame, and my godsdamn queen."

"You forget that before she was any of those things she was my sister and his ward," she shot back, with a jerk of her chin towards Cassius. "We have not seen her in months, and we desire to have her back just as much as you do."

"Then why are you withholding information that could help us?" Sorin demanded.

"We are withholding nothing, Sorin," Nuri cried. "We have told you that storming in there unprepared will kill us all. We are trying to tell you that every detail needs to be planned out meticulously. We were raised here. We are the nightmares on these streets. Not you and your merry band of Fae. We know its secrets. It is you that keeps refusing to listen to us. It is you that keeps refusing to accept the fact that our knowledge is superior here."

Sorin ground his teeth together so hard it was a miracle he didn't crack molars. Cyrus still had a hand on his shoulder, but his grip had loosened, waiting to see what he was going to do. After several moments of silence, Sorin said, "What do you propose we do then?"

Nuri glanced at Cassius again before she said, "If we can get your Shifter into the Syndicate, she could scout it out. Cassius and I can draw a map of the Fellowship. The problem will be getting her in, and it'd be best if she did not go alone."

"The Lady is definitely not going into the Black Syndicate unaccompanied," Luan cut in.

The Beta's eyes flashed to his. "While I find it adorable that you are so protective of me, Azrael, do not forget that I have just as much power as my brother. You would be wise to fear my wrath as much as you appear to fear his."

"It is no slight to you, Arianna," Luan countered with a bow of his head. "We are facing unknown forces. It is simply not wise to send any one person in alone, let alone a leader of the realms."

"Whether or not she can handle herself is not the issue here," Nuri cut in. "We can only assume that Alaric has some sort of wards around the Fellowship. We cannot be foolish enough to think they are around the Tyndell and Lairwood estates and not around the Fellowship. Nor can we be foolish enough to think they are not all working together."

"No one said that," Cassius cut in quickly, glancing at Drake.

"It seems it was implied," Drake shot back.

"We are on your side, and Scarlett's side," Tava interrupted, her chin lifting slightly. "Our family matters will not interfere with our involvement here."

"How can they not, when your father is part of the issue?" Eliza countered.

"Is he? Do we not now believe that the Assassin Lord has her?" Drake retorted.

"Why are we arguing about this?" Sorin cut in. "At this point, we are going to assume Alaric knows of Lord Tyndell and Mikale. I agree that it would be foolish to think he doesn't know, since he clearly knew about Scarlett's heritage. As for the allegiance of Drake and Tava, until they prove otherwise, we trust them. They have done nothing but aid us from the very beginning, and nothing else will be said on the matter," Sorin added, as Eliza opened her mouth to argue. She pursed her lips, but lowered her eyes in acceptance.

"If we're not sending Arianna in by herself, how are we getting her in?

Who is going with her?" Cyrus asked.

"Assuming any wards around the Fellowship are like the ones Cassius put around the Tyndell manor, another immortal would need to go with her," Nuri answered.

"But the wards would still detect them," Cyrus countered.

Nuri rolled her eyes. "That's the point. They will assume whomever is accompanying her set off the wards, leaving her to move about freely."

"But what happens to the one that goes with her?" Rayner asked quietly.

"They would be caught, likely alerting the Assassin Lord to the fact that we are coming for her," Nuri answered.

"How is any of this helpful?" Sorin snapped.

"You didn't let me finish," Nuri replied casually, beginning to throw her knives at the beam across the room again. "If we go in ourselves, that would be the outcome. But if we could somehow orchestrate a member of the Fellowship to be summoned by the Assassin Lord, she could go in with him undetected."

"That's . . . brilliant," Cassius breathed, staring at Nuri. "Obviously," Nuri scoffed, throwing another knife.

"Gods, it's like talking to Scarlett," Cyrus muttered under his breath.

Sorin's chest tightened at the words. Because it was. She had always said she and Nuri were two sides of the same coin. Her mannerisms. Her arrogance. All of it was so damn similar to Scarlett.

"So we get Cassius summoned, and then what?" Sorin pushed. "Before we get that far, we need to make sure Arianna has the layout of the Fellowship memorized," Cassius said. "We don't want to risk having to send her in twice. This needs to be a one-time thing until we go back for Scarlett, if she is, in fact, there."

"And we will need to know which members are stationed where that day. We have a few people on the inside. It needs to be a day when they are patrolling the perimeter of the Syndicate," Nuri added casually, another knife leaving her gloved hand.

But it didn't embed itself into the beam across the room with the others she had thrown. No, this knife went flying at Luan's face. No one saw it coming, and the blade grazed a shallow cut along his cheekbone before sticking into the wall beside his head. She had another knife already posed as Luan let out a growl, a whip of thorny vines appearing in his hand.

"Bind me again in your pretty plants, earth prick, and my next blade will be aimed lower and won't just give you a little scratch," Nuri sneered with a pointed look between his legs, her face a cold mask of wickedness.

A drop of blood was sliding down the Earth Prince's cheek, everyone holding their breath as he stared down Death's Shadow. Sorin wasn't sure if he should interfere or not, and he honestly didn't really care at this point. He didn't want to be focusing on a petty squabble between Luan and Nuri. He wanted to be focusing on getting to Scarlett.

"Sorry to interrupt."

Everyone turned to find Lynnea standing in the stairway. Her cheeks flushed slightly at the sudden attention, and some of the tension in the air dissipated. She tucked some stray hair behind her ear. "I made a meal for you all. If you're hungry."

The last thing on his mind was food, but before Sorin could politely decline, Eliza was already striding for the stairwell.

"Thanks, Anala," the general groused. "I'm starving."

Sorin sighed. A hungry Eliza was a cranky Eliza, and he didn't need to deal with an unruly general right now. He turned and began to follow everyone across the room, and Rayner fell into step beside him.

"This is good, Sorin," he said quietly. "We are getting a plan together."

Sorin only nodded, not looking at his Third, but Rayner grabbed his arm, tugging him to a stop. Cyrus glanced over his shoulder at them before nodding to Rayner and trudging up the stairs, leaving Rayner and Sorin alone.

Rayner released his arm, sliding his hands into his pockets. His swirling grey eyes were pinned on Sorin as he waited for him to speak.

Sorin swallowed thickly, his eyes roaming around the now empty room, before he finally found the courage to say the words he hadn't wanted to voice. The words that had been haunting him since he found her marriage band floating on a bed of shadows.

"What if we are too late?"

"You would know, Sorin. You would know if she were gone," Rayner answered.

When you find her, she will not be the same as when she left.

"What if . . ." Sorin swallowed again, dragging a hand down his face. "What if the Oracle is right? What if she is not the same?"

"She will be different, Sorin," Rayner answered. "We do not know what she has been experiencing, but no matter what it is, it will have left its mark."

"What if I do not know how to help her, Rayner? What if I cannot be what she needs when we find her?"

Because at the heart of it, that was what scared him most. What if the mark left on her by this, by her former Master, was so deep, was so raw and brutal, he couldn't help her? What if he was no longer what she needed? What if he could no longer help her find the stars in the darkness? What if she was so lost to her shadows that he couldn't reach her? What if there was no way out?

Rayner was quiet for a long moment, staring out a dust- and grime-covered window. "I think that if there is anyone who will be able to be what she needs, it will be the one who has always seen her for exactly what she is. I think she will need the one who has never once given up on her, even when she wanted to give up on herself. I think that the Fates gave her exactly who she needed, and I think the Fates gave you exactly who you needed, and this will not change that."

"And if it is not enough?" Sorin asked, meeting Rayner's eyes.

Rayner shrugged. "Will you give up? Will you ever stop trying to be what she needs?"

"Of course not."

"If she is so different you hardly recognize her, will you walk away from her? Will you help her find someone else to fulfill what she needs?"

"No," Sorin growled, the mere idea of that making thoughts of violence rise to the surface. "She is mine, and I am hers."

"Then there is your answer, Sorin. Be hers, and you will be exactly what she needs, just as you were always meant to be."

They stood in silence for a few more minutes before Rayner said, "Are you ready to go eat?"

Sorin nodded, following his Third to the stairwell and climbing the stairs to the second floor. The sound of chattering and laughter reached him through the door when they came to the landing. Rayner reached for the door handle, pulling it open and leading the way through the converted mess hall. They would eat in the kitchens, at the private tables set up where they'd all congregated last night.

They were halfway across the room when a delighted squeal reached Sorin's ears, making him pause and turn to the source.

"Sorin!"

A little girl with blonde curls was sprinting across the room. He hardly had time to open his arms to catch the child as she flung herself at him.

"I got you this," she squealed again excitedly, shoving something into his face.

He leaned back, trying to see what was in her hand, and burst out laughing when he realized she was holding a cookie. He took a bite of the treat, giving her a wide smile in return.

"Little Tula, I think you have grown since I last saw you," he said, shifting her slightly in his arms.

The little girl nodded seriously, her baby blue eyes wide as she replied, "I had my birthday. I am so big now that Nuri started teaching me how to fight."

"Has she now?" Sorin asked, his brow arching at that.

She nodded seriously again. "She made me a sword out of wood for my birthday, and she practices with me. Do you want to see it?"

"I do, but I need to eat first," Sorin answered.

"Do you want to sit with me?" Tula asked, her little head tilting to the side with her question, as she fiddled with the collar of his tunic.

"I need to eat with my friends this time, but I promise to eat dinner with you," Sorin added quickly, when a frown pulled at her mouth.

Tula glanced over his shoulder, and her eyes widened again when they fell on Rayner. "Does he need a treat, too?" she asked. "I can get another cookie. Lynnea has more in the kitchen."

Sorin huffed a laugh. "Rayner will give you smiles for free, Little Tula. Just ask."

Tula glanced back at Rayner in suspicion. "Why are your eyes like that?" she asked the Ash Rider.

Rayner's lips tilted up at the frankness. "So that I can see in the dark."

"Really?" Tula asked, her eyes widening with amazement this time.

"Sort of," Rayner answered with a deep chuckle.

"Tula, this is Rayner. Rayner, meet Tula," Sorin said, turning slightly so they could face each other properly.

"It is a pleasure to meet you, Tula," Rayner said, holding out his hand to shake hers.

"Do you know Scarlett, too?" Tula asked when she put her little hand in his big palm.

Rayner glanced at Sorin before looking back at the little girl. "I do know Scarlett."

"Is she here?" Tula asked, looking around the room again. "I want her to see my sword, too!"

Sorin swallowed, the smile slipping from his face. "She is not here yet," he answered.

"But she will be soon," Rayner added.

"Scarlett is the one who told me Sorin's secret," she whispered loudly to Rayner.

"What secret is that?" Rayner asked in amusement, another smile hooking up on his lips.

"That treats make him smile," she answered, squirming to make Sorin set her down. She reached up and grabbed his hand, tugging him towards the kitchens. "But I figured out his other secret all by myself."

"Oh?" Rayner questioned, falling into step beside her. "Mhmm," she hummed. "He smiles biggest when he sees her."

CHAPTER 11
TALWYN

Talwyn sat at the desk in her room at the White Halls. Rinji had just vanished in a flash of soft, green light. He'd arrived in the same way, a scroll tied lightly around his neck with a vine of Azrael's earth magic securing it, purple wisteria blooming along the greenery.

She'd read his note. They'd all arrived fine, although adjusting to not having their magic was affecting the magic wielders who didn't bear Semiria rings. They had found the allies they were seeking in the mortal lands, and then apparently Sorin had nearly lost his godsdamn mind when he had somehow managed to hear from Scarlett down their twin flame bond. He'd wanted to storm into the Black Syndicate and burn everything to the ground to find her. Brash and impulsive, as he had always been. When she was younger, she had admired his confidence and surety. Now it annoyed her to no end.

Talwyn stood and crossed to the window, facing south towards the mortal lands. She'd never experienced that crazed mania when she'd been in the Trials with Tarek. She had always assumed it was because she was so powerful she was able to withstand the pull, but deep down she'd wondered if it was more so because the bond wasn't strong enough. They had only completed the first Trial. It wasn't uncommon to take years to complete all the Trials. It had taken Cyrus and Thia nearly five years if memory served her correctly, so the fact that it had been three years and she and Tarek had still been waiting wasn't concerning. But she had often thought there should be *something*.

Finding one's twin flame was rare, so there wasn't much known about the bond and the path to Anointing it. Until Sorin and Scarlett, the only other twin flames she'd even known personally were Cyrus and Thia, and when she was going through her own Trials, she was already on rocky footing with the Fire Court. There wasn't a chance in hell she was going to seek advice from the Fire Court Second on her own twin flame bond.

But how could they not have had one Trial completed? Not even the Joining? They had certainly done plenty of that physically, but there was a power component to the Joining too, that much she knew. Their magic needed to join, needed to mix and bond just as much as their physical bodies did. It was deeply intimate and based on trust and unwavering faith and loyalty to the other. She had trusted Tarek with all that she was. She'd lain awake at night wondering how she could possibly prove she trusted him more. It had driven her mad. One would think the Joining Trial would be the easiest one.

Talwyn lifted her left hand, studying where the Mark had once adorned the back of her hand, winding down her thumb. When Tarek had died, she'd felt . . . nothing. She'd grieved for a male she'd loved, yes, but she'd felt nothing in her soul. She'd felt no fracturing of some essential bond. Not like Cyrus obviously had. If Sorin had lost his mind over merely not being able to feel Scarlett, it was nothing compared to Cyrus. Sorin had locked him up in his mountain chateau for nearly six months, paying out of his ass for the High Witch to put up wards and enchantments to keep Cyrus contained. The male had been a walking ghost for years whenever she'd seen him, as if a piece of him had truly died when his twin flame had crossed the Veil.

Talwyn had figured she didn't feel such a breaking because they were still in the Trials. Her Mark had taken another two years to fade entirely from her hand, but Cyrus's had disappeared the moment Thia had stopped breathing. She'd attributed that to her bond not having been Anointed as well.

Despite all of that, despite all the frustration and confusion of the twin flame bond and Trials, for those few years, Talwyn hadn't felt so alone. She'd had someone. Tarek had been by her side nearly every day from the moment they took that Mark. She'd met him on a trip to the Earth Court for some advanced earth magic training that she still did with Azrael on regular occasions. He'd been a part of Azrael's Inner Court as his Third, and when Azrael had needed to go deal with a Court matter, Tarek had offered to entertain her. He'd taken her to some desert caverns outside the capital city of the Earth Court, and they'd spent the entire day talking. She'd found herself telling him things she'd kept shoved down in her soul. Hurt over Sorin abandoning her. Grief she'd never processed over her aunt leaving without a word. Azrael had seemed irritated when he'd returned to find them out on a terrace of his Alcazar, iced tea in their hands, staring up at the night sky. He hadn't said a word, though. He'd remained her stoic Second, and Tarek had become someone that had made her feel wanted, for the first time in years.

Lightning crackled from her palm, drawing her from her memories.

Here she was, alone again. She was always alone, except for those few shining years with Tarek. Her parents had left her. Her aunt had left her. Sorin had left her. Everyone always left her. Even growing up, her only friend had been Ashtine. She couldn't count on Sorin. He was more than a century older than her and her aunt's Second, not to mention her personal tutor. If anything, he'd been more like an older brother.

Until he'd dropped her, like everyone else in her life seemed to do. "Ashtine," she said into the empty room, knowing the winds would take her summons to the Wind Princess.

Talwyn stepped through a rip in the world and Traveled down to the part of Xylon Forest that ran along the Tykese river in the Wind Court. A dozen wolves of varying colors and sizes immediately came to her, rubbing along her legs and nuzzling into her hand. This pack answered to her, but they were Maliq's pack. She was their alpha by default in a way, she supposed.

She ran her hands down their coats, soaking in their company. Her wolves didn't leave her. Her wolves didn't abandon her. Her wolves were there for her time and time again. She'd been told her mother could shift, that she preferred the form of a grey wolf. Talwyn, however, had never been able to do so. It had taken her years to get a handle on shifting energy. She'd never come close to shifting her physical form, not even her hair or eye color.

"For someone who prefers to be alone, you certainly spend a lot of time among pack animals," came Ashtine's lilting voice. Talwyn turned to find her standing in a small clearing, Nasima at her shoulder.

"Clearly I do not prefer to always be alone. I summoned you here," Talwyn retorted, her palm gliding along black fur.

Ashtine's head tilted, her blue eyes studying her in that eerie way she had, as though she could see into her very soul. "You are troubled today. Are you still upset about no longer ruling over the Western Courts?"

Talwyn sighed. "I was never upset about that."

"You seemed upset by that."

Talwyn sucked in a deep breath, exhaling slowly and reining in her temper to deal with Ashtine. "I was upset because no one informed me Scarlett was missing."

"I informed you."

"Days later. Sorin should have told me immediately."

"So you are upset because Sorin no longer answers to you?" Ashtine questioned, reaching to pet one of the wolves. Talwyn tracked the movement. She was the only other person her wolves let touch them.

"No," Talwyn replied through gritted teeth. Ashtine stared back at her expectantly, waiting.

"Have you learned anything new?" Talwyn finally asked, turning back to the wolves and continuing along the path she had been following.

"I have learned many new things," Ashtine replied, falling into step beside her. "Is there something in particular you are hoping I have learned?"

"About Avonleya. Have you learned anything new about Avonelya? Or these rips that we have been researching?"

Ashtine ran her hand along a brown wolf's back. "Avonleya houses many secrets. The winds would whisper of them at times, but they have gone silent since Queen Scarlett went missing."

"What do you mean they have gone silent?" Talwyn asked, halting her stride.

"They no longer speak of Avonleya. They no longer speak of the things long forgotten on this continent," Ashtine continued, her tone becoming hushed. "They are resistant to much these days."

"What does that mean?" Talwyn demanded.

Nasima startled at Ashtine's shoulder, and Ashtine reached up to calm her, casting a glare at Talwyn. It was rare for the Wind Princess to show any type of ire, except when it came to Nasima.

When she really thought about it, she'd never seen Ashtine angry. She was always calm and collected, her thoughts among the winds.

"I . . . apologize," Talwyn forced past her lips. "What do you mean the winds are resistant?"

"I mean they do not offer guidance like they once did. They do not allow me access to their secrets, and they often block my path these days," Ashtine answered, her tone colder than Talwyn had ever heard it.

"Ashtine?" Talwyn ventured, stepping closer to one of the only friends she had. "Are you all right?"

"No," Ashtine whispered. "Everything hangs in the balance, Talwyn. One wrong move and the scales will tip. One misstep and—" She stopped speaking, her head tilting to one side as Nasima clicked her beak. "Stellan is unhappy."

Talwyn sighed. She could only assume it had to do with his sister being recruited for a mission to the mortal lands without his permission.

"I will go to him in a moment," Talwyn replied. "Finish what you were saying."

Ashtine flashed her a soft smile, reaching up to stroke Nasima once more. "It was nothing. Just chatter," she answered.

"It was not nothing," Talwyn insisted. "You were speaking as if you were a Seer."

"I am not a Seer. I cannot glimpse what could be."

"I know that," Talwyn snapped before collecting herself once more. "I know you are not a Seer, but you are knowledgeable. And I need that knowledge to build the best defenses against Avonleya."

"I already told you the winds no longer speak of there," Ashtine replied. "Likely because they know of your plans."

"Are you saying the winds side with Avonleya?"

"I am saying the winds answer to what lies within Avonleya, and you plotting against them is not wise," Ashtine replied.

Talwyn stepped back as if Ashtine had hit her. "This is what we have been working towards from the beginning, since I took the throne. Since we were children. Are you saying you will no longer aid me in getting revenge against the people who led to our parents being slaughtered?"

"I am saying things may not be as we remember them," Ashtine returned.

"As we *remember* them?" Talwyn spat. "I do not *remember* them,

Ashtine. I was barely walking when my mother went to fight Esmeray. You were not even a month out of your mother's womb when your own parents were—"

"Enough, Talwyn." Ashtine's voice was a vicious whisper. "You asked of my knowledge of Avonleya, and I have told you what I know."

"You have told me nothing," Talwyn hissed.

Ashtine's eyes narrowed, her lips tilting up slightly. "I suggest going to see Stellan, your Majesty," she said coldly, stepping back from her.

"You will tell me what you know, Ashtine," Talwyn retorted.

Ashtine shook her head slightly. "I cannot aid you in this any more, Talwyn. It is no longer the best path."

"That is not your decision to make," Talwyn said, stepping toward her once more.

Nasima let out a cry, flapping from Ashtine's shoulder to circle around her, the wind picking up with each beat of her wings.

"I cannot be separated from the winds, Talwyn," Ashtine replied, her tone almost desperate. "I cannot go against them."

"No, Ashtine. You cannot go against *me*," Talwyn countered, the earth stirring beneath her feet.

Ashtine's eyes widened. Nasima let out another cry, disappearing in a flash of light, as a vortex of wind appeared at Ashtine's fingertips. "This is why you are alone, Talwyn," she said softly.

Talwyn scoffed. "I am alone because the Fates stopped giving a fuck long ago."

"That is not true," Ashtine replied, shaking her head. "The Fates set things in motion, but they cannot interfere once it is done."

"This is not done until Avonleya has paid for the lives they stole from us," Talwyn cried. "If it were not for them, I would not be alone."

"This is bigger than you and your revenge, Talwyn," Ashtine replied. "You must understand that."

"My revenge? Not a month ago, this was our revenge."

The wolves had scattered at the earth magic that Talwyn was struggling to keep under control. Yet Ashtine stood before her, perfectly composed, watching her carefully.

"You have nothing to say to that?" Talwyn demanded.

"Much changed when you sent the Fire Prince to find his twin flame," she finally answered, her feet coming off the path as she used her wind magic to lift herself from the shuttering ground. "In a way, Talwyn, *you* set this in motion."

Wind gusts radiated from Talwyn as she lost control completely. The magic was sucked into Ashtine's vortex, now swirling violently above her palm, reaching to the sky. She had risen higher, hovering several feet off the ground.

Before Talwyn could say anything else on the matter, a water portal appeared, the Water Prince stepping through with Nasima on his shoulder.

"What are you doing here uninvited?" Talwyn demanded.

"Nasima went for him," Ashtine replied from the air, her hair whipping out around her while she continued to work to contain the winds Talwyn had unleashed.

"Why would she do that?" Talwyn sneered.

"Because Nasima is bound to protect her, as Maliq is bound to protect you," Briar answered, striding to stand beneath Ashtine. He lifted a hand, reaching for her, and Ashtine slowly began lowering to the ground.

"I know that," Talwyn snapped. "Why did she come to you?"

Briar shrugged as Ashtine placed her hand in his, her feet landing on the earth once more. "One would assume because Prince Azrael is unavailable."

As if they had coordinated a dance, Briar raised her hand and spun her under his arm. With a long exhale, Ashtine released all the wind from her palm, blowing it away from them, before gracefully completing the spin to face Talwyn once more.

"I suggest taking a few moments to compose yourself before going to speak with Stellan." She tilted her head once more, before saying, "But I would not wait long. He is very upset."

Another water portal appeared, and Briar began leading the Wind Princess towards it, Nasima flitting back to her shoulder.

"Where are you going?" Talwyn asked.

"The Water Prince and I have some matters to discuss regarding imbuing some new weapons. We had a meeting planned for this afternoon," Ashtine replied, her tone returning to her usual lilt. "The winds will find me should you need me."

With that, she stepped through the portal to wherever she had been planning to meet with Briar, leaving Talwyn alone.

Again.

She'd given herself an hour. She'd Traveled to Jonaraja Forest and unleashed hell on those ancient trees, letting control slip entirely. When her winds had finally calmed and energy had stopped lighting up the sky, when the earth had stopped trembling; Talwyn had sat against one of the old trees, trying to catch her breath. Maliq had appeared then, coming to rest beside her, his head lying in her lap. She had idly scratched his ears as she'd regained her composure.

She couldn't believe what had happened. Since they were children, they had dreamt of getting revenge on Avonleya. They had lain beneath the skies in Ashtine's Wind Citadel in the Shira Cliffs. They had giggled as they'd used their wind magic to push in clouds and shape them into various pictures against the blue background. They had spoken of what their lives would have been like had they been raised by their parents rather than proxies. And as they had grown older, those talks had turned to what they could do when they had mastered their magic, when they were more powerful than their parents had been. They could go after those responsible. Not Deimas and Esmeray. They had disappeared shortly after the wards had gone up to separate the Fae lands from the mortals, once they had slaughtered the sitting Royals. Mortal history said they gave their lives to enact wards to keep the Fae and Avonleya contained. Fae history said the Fae enacted their own wards to keep Deimas and Esmeray out. And Avonleya?

Some accounts said they were banished. Others said they enacted the wards to hide behind, leaving their once allies to fend for themselves.

And die for a cause that was never theirs.

Deimas and Esmeray may have been directly responsible for the deaths of their parents, but this stemmed back farther than them. This was Avonleya. If they had not beseeched the Fae for help, neither she nor Ashtine would have grown up orphans. If Avonleya had fought their own godsdamn war, everything would have been different.

So they had plotted. Their daydreams had turned from fairy tales in the clouds, to how they could get revenge on an entire kingdom. Running and playing in the gardens turned into dueling with their magic as it grew stronger. It became training with swords and intense private tutoring. And when Ashtine finally mastered walking amongst the winds, she would bring back information for Talwyn, while Talwyn threw herself into her political lessons. She learned everything she could about running the Courts. Sorin taught her how to study people, how to watch for specific mannerisms that betrayed their emotions and to capitalize on them. Azrael taught her how to keep her emotions in check, how to keep a mask of cool indifference on her face at all times. Her aunt had been guiding her through dealing with the other territories.

And in the dark hours of the night, Ashtine would still come to her rooms on the winds, and they would discuss anything new either of them had learned. That was how Talwyn had learned that the physical war may have ended with Avonleya, but there was still a silent war brewing. She may not have known a thing about who was involved in it, but she knew the Avonleyans were causing some sort of unrest in her world. It only renewed her will to see justice brought against them. They simply couldn't leave well enough alone. They couldn't accept their defeat and just stay in their own lands across the sea.

Everything had seemed to be falling into place when the Oracle told her of Scarlett. She had an ally. She had a blood relative that possessed her aunt's powers. They would have all four elements at their disposal. More than that, her union with Sorin would unite the Courts once more.

It was one more step in the right direction, one step closer to bringing Avonleya to their knees. In the three years that Sorin had been gone, she had begun building up their defenses with Azrael's help, but Avonleya was frustratingly hard to find information on. So much of it had been buried or lost in the years since the Great War. Ashtine would show up at times with useful information, but it wasn't until Sorin had sent word asking Briar about the Semiria rings that the winds had really stirred. After that night, Ashtine had new information almost daily . . . until the day Scarlett claimed her throne. Since that day, Ashtine had seemed on edge, and now, apparently, she had decided that their lifelong quest for justice was no longer the "best path."

Talwyn swore as she pushed to her feet. In a swirl of magic, her usual weapons were in place, and she stepped through the world and into Siofra, just outside the Alpha's oasis home he shared with his sister. The guards at the entrance stiffened as she approached, bowing their heads.

"Is Stellan available?" Talwyn asked, keeping her tone as neutral as possible.

"Yes, your Majesty," one answered. "I can have Keenan escort you if you wish."

At his words, a tall male stepped from the gates. He wore a sleeveless tunic with linen pants, curved blades at his waist. His black hair was tied in a knot on the top of his head, and he bowed at the waist before turning and heading down a dusty road.

Talwyn followed his lead, already sweating in her leathers, as he led her around the various pools of water and past the cascading falls. They crossed a terrace before he stopped and gestured with an arm to a wide area where a huge lion was pacing back and forth in clear agitation. His large paws were leaving tracks in the sand, and his dark mane was tossed as he turned around and followed his own path. A jaguar was lying off to the side with a big, tawny-colored wolf sitting at attention. When she entered, the wolf was instantly on its feet, while the jaguar slowly curled up, stretching and yawning, leveling its golden-eyed stare on Talwyn. The wolf let out a low growl that had the lion halting its movements, a snarl emanating from his massive chest when he spotted her.

In a flash of golden light, a man was striding towards her. He was even taller than Keenan had been, his dark skin gleaming in the hot sun.

His black hair was cut short and close to his head, and dark tattoos spiraled down his arms. He wore loose linen pants, and his chest was bare. He didn't have any weapons on him, but he didn't need them. He could summon a lion's claws in his human form, and he could shift energy at will. His olive eyes matched his sister's, but where Arianna was flirty and cunning and tended to keep her enemies close, you knew exactly where you stood with the Shifter Alpha. He was harsh and commanding and just as cunning as his sister. He also gave Azrael a run for the title when it came to being a hard-ass prick.

Today was no exception. Rage was written on every line of his face, his square jaw clenched tight, and energy crackled around his knuckles as he clenched and unclenched his fists. He halted in front of her, and Talwyn didn't miss that he failed to bow. Instead, he barely inclined his head before he spoke in a low voice laced with ire, "Where is Arianna?"

She lifted her chin as she answered. "She is with Sorin in the mortal lands."

"On whose orders?" Stellan demanded.

"His."

The growl that emanated from his chest sounded like something that would come from the beast he had just shifted from. "Since when does he have the authority to order my sister to do anything?"

"Since he became the husband and Second to the Fae Queen of the Western Courts who is currently away. Thus, he has assumed command until she has returned," Talwyn replied sharply, wind rolling off of her and making the sand stir at their feet.

"Did you know of this?" he asked sharply. "Did you know the Fire Prince was going to require her assistance?"

"Of course not," she retorted. "You know I would have come to you first, and if for some reason it had to be Arianna, I would have discussed it with you." Stellan's eyes narrowed on her further as she continued, "Judging by your current mood, I am going to assume that Sorin did not give you such a courtesy."

Olive eyes bored into her jade ones a few more seconds, before he seemed to decide she was telling him the truth. He turned and began pacing again, just as he had been doing in his lion form.

"You need to take me to her," he said.

"I cannot," Talwyn answered. "Prince Luan has my ring to allow your sister to shift in the mortal kingdoms. I cannot Travel to the mortal lands without it."

Another low rumble came from the Alpha. "When will they return?"

"I do not know. Prince Luan is keeping me updated. His latest report told me they all arrived safely and were adjusting to not readily having access to their power. It is my understanding that the High Witch provided them with potions to access their gifts in the mortal lands should an emergency arise," she answered, fighting the urge to clench her fists.

"What are they doing there?"

Talwyn gritted her teeth. "Apparently, Queen Scarlett went missing.

They have gone to retrieve her."

"Went missing like Queen Eliné?" Stellan asked, pausing his pacing to look at her again.

"No," she replied with a shake of head. "She was taken."

"Why would he go to Arianna for this mission?" Stellan demanded, resuming his pacing once more.

"I am no longer privy to the Fire Prince's reasonings, but if I had to guess, I would assume it is because he has previous relations with your sister," Talwyn answered.

She hadn't thought anything of it when she was younger, but as she'd gotten older, she'd begun to notice the way Arianna would sidle up to Sorin, brushing her fingers along his arm. He would often return the touches, leaning in to whisper in her ear. When she'd assumed her throne, more than once she'd hear of him visiting Siofra and spending his night with the Beta. Those visits had all but stopped after Eliné left. She'd still hear of him visiting Arianna every once in a while, but those visits became few and far between, and they had stopped completely when they'd gotten word of Eliné's death.

"We have not even met the new queen, and my sister finds it appropriate to go off on a mission to search for her?" Stellan scoffed.

"She has not been a queen for long. I am sure Sorin would have had her come to formally meet you soon, but those plans were derailed by unforeseen events," Talwyn replied.

"We should have been invited to her coronation."

"She did not have a formal coronation," Talwyn said. "Queen Scarlett is . . . unconventional, but I understand why you feel slighted, Stellan."

He stopped his pacing, looking over his shoulder at her. He nodded once, before turning and beginning to walk into the desert palace. "Come, your Majesty. Since you are here, you may as well have dinner with me."

She did not particularly appreciate an order coming from him, but it wasn't as if she had anyone else to go home to. She would simply be returning to her empty chambers in the White Halls. She huffed out a small sigh before following the Alpha. The jaguar shifted beside her, a beautiful female with golden skin and dark brown hair that went just past her shoulders appeared instead. She wore loose silk pants that cuffed at the ankles, and her shirt of the same material stopped above her navel. The wolf stayed in its animal form, but Talwyn knew it was Ilyas. He and the female, Sariah, were Stellan's two personal guards and lovers.

"Your Majesty," Sariah greeted, bowing her head. "He is most agitated," she continued, her voice dropping to a whisper.

"I gathered that," Talwyn replied, stepping through the gauzy curtains into an open dining area. Servants were quickly setting another place at the table. Stellan was nowhere to be seen, and Ilyas padded past them, disappearing through an archway to the left. Talwyn glanced at Sariah in question.

"He will be right back," Sariah said with a dismissive wave of her hand, moving to a drink cart and pouring wine into a chalice. She handed it to Talwyn before pouring her own.

"Do I need to be worried about his loyalties?" Talwyn asked, taking a sip of the wine. It was tart to the point of almost being bitter.

Sariah's golden eyes swept up and down Talwyn's body. She took a sip of her own wine, before saying, "You know how the siblings are, your Majesty. Stay on their good side, and their loyalties stay with you as well."

"Yes, but, as you said, Stellan is agitated. And Sorin clearly chose Arianna's good side over Stellan's," Talwyn countered.

A slight smirk appeared on Sariah's lips. "I cannot speak for him, however, seeing as the new queen could not be bothered to formally meet him but has visited the High Witch not once, but twice, I would venture to guess you have nothing to worry about."

"Do I need to do anything to make sure it stays that way?"

"You seem very worried about losing his allegiance," Sariah said, taking another sip of her wine.

Talwyn pressed her lips together. She knew full well anything she said to the Shifter would be repeated to Stellan. "The Alpha and Beta are powerful leaders that I am honored to count among my allies. I simply wish to ensure there are no hard feelings between us due to misunderstandings."

Sariah nodded once, her gaze moving over Talwyn's shoulder. Talwyn turned to find Stellan entering the room, Ilyas beside him in his natural form. He wore a sleeveless tunic over his broad chest, and Stellan had donned a sleeveless tunic as well. Ilyas's black hair was nearly as long as Talwyn's and was tied back at the nape of his neck. His hazel eyes landed on her with a glare as he stalked to the wine cart. Sariah brushed past him, taking a chalice of wine to Stellan, brushing her fingers down his arm before she made her way to the table. When they had all taken their seats, their plates were filled with roasted lamb, rice, greens, and flatbread. "Thank you for inviting me to stay for dinner," Talwyn ventured, cutting off a piece of lamb.

Stellan merely nodded in acknowledgement, biting off a piece of his bread. Despite what Sariah had said, Talwyn wasn't so sure that she was still in his good graces, even though she'd had nothing to do with Sorin recruiting Arianna. But Stellan's protectiveness of his sister rivaled a twin flame's possessiveness. His agitation likely was not with her, but the fact that Arianna was not here.

After several more minutes of silence, Talwyn took a sip of her wine and cleared her throat. "May I ask you something, Stellan?"

He nodded, picking up his own chalice.

"Did you ever have dealings with the Avonleyans? Before they were sequestered across the sea?"

If Ashtine was going to refuse to supply her with information, she'd hunt it down herself.

The Shifters around the table all froze, Ilyas and Sariah looking at their Alpha.

"You know we fought in the Great War alongside the Fae against Deimas and Esmeray," Stellan answered, slowly setting his chalice down.

"Yes, but did you personally interact with any of the Avonleyans?"

"Queen Henna and Queen Eliné handled most of that. As you know, we were not granted our gifts until the Sorceress was detained. Avonleya was banished shortly after she was captured, so I did not get much interaction with any of them, no."

Talwyn nodded, stabbing some of her greens onto her fork. "Why did you fight with them?"

Stellan's brow furrowed. "I did not fight with them. I fought with the Fae Queens. It was why we were granted our gifts. To aid the Fae in the fight against Deimas and Esmeray."

"But you were alive for some of the fighting, before Avonleya was defeated, yes? Would you have sided with Avonleya if you'd been asked to fight in their war?" Talwyn pushed.

He sat back in his chair, his olive eyes studying her. She stared back, refusing to blink at his scrutiny.

"Why do you ask such questions this evening, your Majesty?"

"I have been studying the Great War and the repercussions of the event," Talwyn answered with a slight shrug. "I have obviously never met anyone from Avonleya. I am just curious about those who did have relations with the kingdom before they were banished."

"Some say they were not banished, but that they retreated themselves," Sariah said, swirling her chalice of wine.

Talwyn met her golden gaze. "I am not sure which would be worse. To have surrendered and accepted banishment as the cost for inciting an unnecessary war, or to have run back and locked themselves away, leaving the Fae to clean up their mess."

"You are bitter," Stellan observed, picking up his chalice again.

"It seems like it was a pointless war with many lives lost for no reason," Talwyn countered.

"You speak of your parents, of your mother," Stellan replied, understanding dawning in his eyes.

"They were not the only unnecessary casualties of that war," she ground out.

Stellan seemed to mull this over before he said, "Without that war, we would not have been given our gifts. Nor would the Witches."

Talwyn stilled.

"We fought with the Fae because the Fae Queens were the ones to gift us such power," Stellan continued. "We were given such a thing for the purpose of aiding your kind. The Fae were given their own gifts by the Avonleyans for the purpose of aiding them. Surely you know this."

"Of course I know my own history," Talwyn said.

"Do you?" Stellan countered. "Because based on the questions you have posed this evening, it would seem you do not know your full history. It also makes me truly question why you are suddenly seeking such answers."

He waited expectantly for her answer, and she had never felt more like a child. She had never felt so in over her head. Azrael was always with her for these types of discussions. She may have been on her throne for decades, but political power plays and politics amongst the territories were still something for which she relied heavily upon the Earth Prince. She had not anticipated the conversation going this way. She had merely wanted information on Avonleya. Now she appeared to be a queen who didn't completely grasp her world's own history.

None of those insecurities were allowed to play across her features, though. The cold mask of indifference Azrael had taught her to carefully craft stayed fixed in place as she met the Alpha's stare once more. She picked up her chalice, taking a long sip before saying, "There is a possibility that the new queen and I may have the opportunity to lift the magic keeping the Avonleyans sequestered." Stellan's eyes widened at that information, but Talwyn pressed forward before he could say anything in response. "As a fellow ruler, I am simply curious as to your opinion of the kingdom and its inhabitants. The war they incited seems pointless when studying history. Do we free a country that could incite such a thing again?"

"Do you punish the children for the sins of the fathers?" Stellan countered.

"They are as immortal as you and I are," Talwyn argued. "You were alive during that war. Surely, a good number of those who survived the war still live. I would even wager their king and queen still live and rule. Who is to say they have not spent those centuries plotting revenge?"

"Who is to say the daughter of a slaughtered Fae Queen has not done the same in her decades of life?" Stellan asked, his brows arching in knowing.

Talwyn pressed her tongue to her cheek.

Stellan pushed his plate back, leaning forward and bracing his muscled forearms on the table. Sariah and Ilyas hadn't said a word during this entire exchange, but both of the Shifters had stopped eating, watching it all with interest.

"You are young, your Majesty," Stellan began.

"Do not patronize me, Stellan," Talwyn interrupted, her tone laced with warning.

"Ask me what you wish to know, then. Quit dancing around it," he challenged.

"If the Avonleyans would be freed, would your loyalty reside with them, or would it remain with the Fae?" Talwyn asked.

"They were on the same side. Why would I be required to choose?" Stellan replied, maintaining his piercing stare.

"You are required to answer the question," she snapped.

"Are you planning to be at odds with them, that you require such an answer from me?" he asked, ignoring her command.

Talwyn pushed her chair back from the table, the wood scraping against the stone floor as she got to her feet. Ilyas was on his feet at the same moment, but Sariah simply swirled her chalice once more, her golden eyes fixed on Talwyn. Stellan didn't move, just stared at the queen. "Thank you for dinner," Talwyn ground out. "I will send word when I receive updates from Prince Luan."

She needed to get out of here before she did something that would put further strain on her relationship with the Shifters. If she were going to go up against Avonleya, she would need their support. She would come back and discuss this with Azrael at her side. She would come back when Arianna was home and when Stellan wasn't so on edge.

She turned and began walking to the terrace, preparing to Travel as soon as she was outside, but she paused when Stellan called out to her.

"Queen Talwyn."

She glanced back over her shoulder, lightning flashing across the darkening sky.

"You would do well to remember that your own gifts come from the Avonleyans. What was given can be taken away," Stellan said stoically, still bracing himself on his forearms.

"Perhaps you should take your own advice, considering the Fae granted you your gifts," Talwyn shot back with a sneer.

"The Fae may have deemed us worthy of such power, but they did not bestow it upon us. They do not hold that kind of power."

She turned back to face him fully. "Explain."

He stood now, striding to the archway he had come from before dinner. "You were on your way out, your Majesty. Perhaps another time. I look forward to your updates on my sister. Good evening."

"Stellan!" she snarled, the ground shuddering, the dishes of unfinished food on the table rattling. She took a step towards him, but she didn't get any father as a jaguar leapt over the table, landing between her and the Alpha, a warning growl rumbling from the feline.

Talwyn stood and watched as, for the second time in the same day, one of her closest allies walked away from her.

She stepped through a rip in the world, feeling more isolated than ever before.

All of this over a locked away kingdom that stole everything from her. All of this over Avonleya.

CHAPTER 12
SCARLETT

"Scarlett."

She was wrapped in blankets in that bed she slept in with Mikale. True to his word, Alaric had made sure she was taken care of. Physically, at least. She was still chained to the wall in his dungeon study every day, but she received three small meals a day that Alaric himself fed to her. He refused to let anyone else do so, ensuring he was associated with her receiving food. Every day at varying hours, Mikale hauled her to Juliette's old room to sleep. Sometimes it was night. Sometimes the sun was shining through the windows. The dungeon study was located near the stairwell that led to Alaric's private wing of the Fellowship. Some were given the "honor" of having their rooms in his wing. The Wraiths and Cassius were some of those gifted such an honor. But with the dungeon study just outside his private wing, there was no one else in the hallways other than the guards Alaric had ordered to be on duty at all times. She didn't recognize any of them, which meant they likely didn't know who she was either. There was no one else to see that she was here. No one to recognize she was back. No one to let it slip in a passing conversation where she was. No way to get word to Cassius and Nuri. No way to tell Sorin.

But here, in the depths of sleep, she could pretend. She could pretend it was his body pressed to hers. She could pretend she was in a palace in the mountains instead of some extravagant manor in the heart of the Black Syndicate. She could pretend she wasn't alone in the darkness. She could pretend the stars still shone in all their brilliance. She could pretend she could truly hear his voice, and this wasn't all a dream.

But now she was beginning to wake. She was slowly coming up out of that slumber, and she clung to it with desperation. She needed to hear his voice one more time. Just one more time before she had to face another day without him.

"Scarlett."

But her soul didn't sigh in relief at his voice. She didn't feel the comfort that usually came from his slight accent skittering along her bones.

"Scarlett."

But that was his voice, and she was no longer in the depths of sleep. "Scarlett. Wake up. I am here. We need to go."

She felt her shoulders gently being shaken, fingers skating down her cheek.

"Scarlett, please wake up. We need to go before we are discovered." Her breath caught in her chest, and she slowly cracked her eyes open.

The room was dark, but in the glow of the fire in the hearth she could make out piercing, golden eyes staring down at her. Raven black hair fell across his forehead and into his eyes that were full of urgency. She didn't dare move. Because this? This wasn't possible. There is no way he could have gotten into the Fellowship undetected.

"Come, Scarlett," he whispered, reaching for her and helping her to a sitting position, her legs hanging over the side of the bed. He ran his hands down her arms, his fingers skimming the shirastone at her wrists before clasping her hands in his. "Are you going to say anything?"

She opened her mouth, but nothing came out. Because this didn't feel right. Something was off. Something was wrong. She just couldn't put her finger on what exactly.

He crouched down before her, looking up into her face. "We really do need to go, Scarlett. Prince Callan is in danger. Are you well enough to walk?" He glanced down at her bare feet.

"Where is Mikale?" she finally managed to ask.

His eyes came back to hers, and he reached to tuck her hair behind her ear. "He is being distracted for the moment, but not for long. We need to get back to Prince Callan."

"Where is he?" Scarlett asked, scooting to the edge of the bed.

"Where you left him."

Her brows pinched together in confusion. "How is he in danger if he is in the Fire Court?"

His lips pressed together, forming a thin line as though he was displeased with what she had asked. He pulled a key from his pocket and reached for the shackles on her ankles.

But Alaric was the only person with a key, so how had he gotten it? "Sorin?" she asked tentatively. He paused, looking back up at her in question. "Where did you get that key?"

His eyes dipped to the key in question. "That is not important right now. We need to go, my dear."

Scarlett's eyes went wide, and she jerked back from him, drawing her knees to her chest.

"How did you get that key?" she asked again, her voice nothing more than a whisper.

"Scarlett, we need to go," he repeated, rising to his feet and reaching for her once more.

She shook her head, swallowing down the lump in her throat. This wasn't him. He wouldn't call her "dear." His touch wasn't the same. He didn't *feel* the same.

"I told you this wouldn't work." Mikale's voice floated in from somewhere beyond.

"She was speaking to him. She said where Callan is," another voice argued.

Lord Tyndell.

A vision. He had trapped her in a vision again. He'd been doing this randomly over the last several days, and she was finding it increasingly difficult to differentiate between his visions and reality.

She closed her eyes, not wanting to see the image of Sorin before her. Her chest was rising and falling rapidly as she tried to suck down air, her heart hammering. He wasn't here. It hadn't been real. He wasn't real.

"Open your eyes, Scarlett." Alaric's voice filled her ears, and she shook her head, pressing her lips together. She could feel the shackles against her wrists, her hands suspended above her head. She was in the study, still chained to the wall. "You need to breathe, Scarlett," he soothed. "Open your eyes."

"This was fruitless," Mikale snarled. "We already figured Callan was in the Fire Court with her. We learned nothing."

"Stop speaking until she is under control," Alaric ordered, his tone cold.

Something was pressed to her mouth, that same metallic syringe they used to force some kind of tonic down her throat. She still hadn't figured out what it did. A glass of water followed.

"Look at me, Scarlett," Alaric demanded. She felt a finger under her chin, tilting her face up, and she finally opened her eyes. Depthless, black orbs stared back at her. He seemed to search her face, for what she had no idea. She'd been waiting for the other shoe to drop. She'd been waiting for him to reveal his next punishment for disobeying him, but it had been days since he'd held her in his lap in a panic. She didn't know how many days. Maybe it had been weeks. She'd long stopped trying to keep track.

Mikale and Lord Tyndell stood nearby, their eyes fixed on her, as Alaric said, "I need you to tell me where in the Fire Court Prince Callan is, Scarlett. Was he in Solembra with you?"

She pressed her lips together, turning her head and looking towards the wall in clear refusal.

Alaric sighed. "I can only assume he stayed close to you. You did let him fall so hopelessly in love with you, after all."

She was focused on her breathing, trying to shut out his words.

"The king is very upset he has been gone for so long, Scarlett," Alaric continued. "In fact, he has decided that young Callan is showing a great lack of responsibility and is feeling the need to rectify the situation."

Scarlett slowly opened her eyes, turning her head to meet his gaze once more. She still said nothing, waiting for him to volunteer information.

Alaric reached over, smoothing down her hair, his fingers dragging along her jaw. "He has decided that Callan needs to take a bride, hoping that having a family will make him stop . . . wandering off and shirking his duties."

Her eyes widened. Callan would hate that. He would be furious. He would . . . blame her. For more than he already did.

"An arrangement has already been agreed to," Mikale cut in smoothly, a cruel smile curling on his lips. "Veda is so very excited."

Scarlett's head whipped to him, and she let out a hollow huff of laughter. "How very unbecoming of her," she rasped out. "She couldn't hold his attention herself, so she went above him to the crown."

Mikale's face darkened with rage, but Lord Tyndell cut in. "It was the king's idea, my dear. After a little push in that direction, of course."

"Why would you care if Callan married Veda? What does that possibly matter to you?" she demanded, her gaze bouncing from Lord Tyndell to Alaric.

"My Dark Maiden," Alaric sighed, patting her cheek patronizingly. "We have been moving pieces into place for a very long time. This is simply another move that needs to be made." He braced his hands on his knees, pushing himself to his feet. "But that is neither here nor there. We need Callan to come home, even if that means we must retrieve him ourselves. Where is he?"

His tone had grown harsh and commanding, the voice of the Assassin Lord. He glared down at her, his hands clasping behind his back. When she merely glared back, his lips thinned. The room was quiet for a long moment before he said evenly, "So be it, Scarlett. I am out of time and out of patience. I know how much you like your choices, so it is time to make one. Tell us where Callan is and how to bring him home, or you can watch Cassius suffer. Slowly. Over several days. I will make sure he is alive for all of it. Feels every single thing we do to him. And then I will let you watch while he slowly fades over hours. You will find you feel the death of your Guardian on a very deep level, even if you cannot currently access that bond."

Her eyes widened in horror, and Mikale let out a chuckle. She couldn't think of a word to say. She couldn't think at all. Not at what was being presented to her again.

"Isn't this scene familiar, my pet?" Mikale asked cruelly, leaning down to stroke her hair. "Will you choose to save one you so deeply care for, or an innocent? Whom shall you sacrifice this time?"

"I will give you some time to think about it," Alaric said, turning and striding to his desk. He quickly wrote a note, folding the paper in half. "When I return with some food, be prepared to make your choice." He passed the note to Lord Tyndell as he continued, "I will make sure Cassius is here so that the repercussions of your decision can begin immediately. It would be very unfortunate for you to not make a choice at all." He swung his cloak over his shoulders, pulling the hood up and over his head, once again hiding his features from view, as he swept from the room.

Lord Tyndell followed Alaric from the room, and Scarlett peered back up at Mikale who stood over her. His malicious grin of victory, that she had witnessed so often when she had been held in his house, was back on his face as he stared down at her.

How was this happening again? How was she again faced with the choice of saving her family or protecting someone simply caught in the cross-fire? Granted, Callan wouldn't be dead. He would just be forced into a marriage that would slowly suffocate him. But wasn't that always a possibility anyway? He was the Crown Prince. The likelihood of him ever marrying for love was practically non-existent to begin with. His marriage was always destined to be a political move.

Mikale slowly lowered to a crouch before her, reaching out to cup her chin in his hand. "This isn't really that hard of a decision, is it, my pet? Would you really sacrifice Cassius to keep Callan from my sister?"

"Why are you so desperate to have her marry him? Simply so she can be queen? I cannot believe it is that simple. I cannot believe that there is not more to it. Everything Alaric does has motive behind it. If he is involved with this, I have no doubt that is the case," she spat back at him, her voice hoarse and raspy.

Mikale released her chin, pushing back to his feet. He strode to the water pitcher, returning with a glass of water. He brought it to her lips, and she drank, having stopped resisting this particular offering a while ago. "And what of our own arrangement, my pet? We had an agreement," Mikale said, placing the glass on a nearby table. He lowered into a chair, his arms coming to rest on the armrests.

"Fuck off, Mikale," she snapped. "That is never happening."

"Never?" he repeated, his head cocking to the side as his dark eyes slid over her. He let out an exaggerated sigh. "Then I suppose I shall have to fulfill my end of that bargain. You remember the cost of refusing, do you not?"

"You cannot touch them," Scarlett sneered, her lip curling. "They are hidden away and protected from all of you."

Mikale's smile widened. His hand came up, and he propped his head on his fist, continuing to study her. "I am well aware that they are currently inaccessible. After the matter of Callan is settled, they are next, my pet. The children and Death's Shadow are next on his agenda with you."

Scarlett leaned her head back against the wall, shifting to ease the ever-present ache in her tailbone from sitting on a hard floor. "Then he shall die waiting."

Mikale clicked his tongue. "We both know that is not true. I may have failed to break you, but he will not. He does not fail."

Scarlett closed her eyes, trying to tune him out. Trying not to let his words burrow their way into her mind. Trying not to let their truth settle into her soul. Trying not to let her world crash in around her. Grasping for the stars. Grappling for the hope that threatened to ebb away a little more every day.

She heard Mikale shift in his chair as he spoke again. His tone was low, almost consoling. "This is your opportunity to make it hurt a little less, my pet. This is your chance to stop it all before it begins. You know the more you resist him, the harder the fallout is going to be."

And she did. Alaric was biding his time, yes, but the longer he took to come at her, the more it was going to hurt. He was formulating the best way to bring her to heel. She had endured so much suffering at his hands, but nothing would compare to what he was preparing to do to her this time. It would be ten times worse. It would not be a drawn out game of who would break first. He was growing impatient. She had messed with his plans when she'd fled to the Fire Court. When he struck this time, it would be swift, and it would be designed not just to break her, but to crush any sense of hope. Any type of resistance. He would be coming to ensure that she would not stand against him again.

And she did not know if she would be able to endure it.

Her days were spent appealing to the Fates that she did not believe in. Praying that she could hold out long enough to end her own existence before he could use it against those she loved. If she were out of play, if her power were gone from this world, if the ability to find these godsdamn keys and get into Avonleya was no longer an option . . . It would at least give the others more time to figure out a way to defeat the Maraan Lords before they could formulate a new plan.

A hand brushed down her hair a few times, and Scarlett ground her teeth together, enduring Mikale's touch and how wrong it felt.

"I have no doubt that you are willing to sacrifice your own wellbeing to keep innocents safe, to keep your dear friends from harm, but think of all those who will get caught in the crossfire, Scarlett. Think of all those like Cassius and Callan and Nuri. Think of those children who will be used, who will be hurt, who will suffer, because you choose to stand against him."

She pressed her lips together, her throat burning as tears welled behind her closed lids. She felt him lean closer, felt his hot breath against her cheek as he whispered into her ear, "He is not coming, Scarlett. And if he does, we are prepared. You have experienced a fraction of what Balam can do. You have seen some of what I can do, but you have yet to experience *his* power. You are not the Fire Prince's. You are not even mine. You are *his*. Just as you always have been."

She heard his boots on the stone floor, heard the door slide shut, the lock click into place. Then he was gone.

She swallowed, forcing down the sob that wanted to fall from her lips. She would die before she gave those children up to the Assassin Lord. The sacrifice would be her own life. And she was okay with that. She was okay with giving up her own life for theirs. She hoped she could end it before they came for her. She knew they would. She knew Sorin would tear the Syndicate apart to get to her once he figured out where she was. She hoped she was gone before he could face whatever they had lying in wait for him, that she could give him that one final gift.

But she wished she could have seen him one last time. She wished she could have tasted his lips just once more. She wished she could feel safe, feel *home*, one final time in her life.

She let two tears slip down her face. They were the only two she allowed to escape. She breathed in deep, allowing air to fill her lungs, calming her racing heart.

In and out. In and out. In and out.

A tiny squeaking sound had her opening her eyes to see a little brown field mouse scurrying along beside her ankle shackles. Scarlett tilted her head to the side. She had never, in all her time at the Fellowship, seen any type of rodent in the building. Certainly not in one of Alaric's rooms, even if it was a dungeon study.

The mouse cautiously stretched towards her, its whiskers twitching while it sniffed in her direction, squeaking once more.

"You are a brave little thing," she murmured as it crept forward, its tiny claws scratching on the stone floor. It skittered over her bare feet, and she cringed back at the feeling of it. "That wasn't an invitation to come closer," she muttered, shaking her foot out and sending it flying a few feet away from her.

The mouse seemed to squeak indignantly before it came scurrying back towards her, slipping behind her just as the click of the lock sounded again. Scarlett's gaze shot to the door.

No. Alaric couldn't be back yet. He hadn't even been gone an hour. There hadn't been enough time to think about what she was going to do. Not when Mikale had hung around, trying to sow seeds of doubt in her mind.

But Alaric indeed walked back into the room, a covered plate in his hand. He was alone, and when the door had shut behind him, he reached up and pulled his hood back. He set the plate down on his desk then slowly removed his cloak, draping it over the arm of the sofa. He walked to the water pitcher, pouring her another glass of water before picking up the plate and coming to stand before her. He lowered himself to the floor like he had every other time he brought her a meal. He set the plate off to the side, his eyes coming to settle on her. He bent his knee, resting his arm on it again, leaning back on his other hand.

"It occurred to me," he said, "that perhaps if you were allowed to ask questions, if you were able to understand a few things, you may be more amicable."

Scarlett gave him a dry look, her brow arching. "I don't think we will ever see eye-to-eye on things."

"Perhaps not, but it would be worth the effort to try, would it not?" he countered.

"What do you want in Avonleya?"

Alaric chuckled. "Jumping right into it then, are we?" He reached for the plate, lifting the lid and letting the smell of roasted vegetables and meat waft towards her. He picked up a piece of bread, bringing it to her lips. She bit off a bite as he said, "Did you know the Avonleyans weren't always what they are now?"

"You were in charge of my education," she replied drolly around the food. "You know the lies I was taught to believe."

Alaric tilted his head, appearing to contemplate her words. He cut a piece of venison, bringing it to her mouth. "The Avonleyans are called something different in other worlds."

She chewed the meat, swallowing before she said, "I do not care what they are called in other worlds. I do not care what they are called on other planes. I do not care what they were before. I care about what you want there. I care about the innocent children you are slaughtering to get to them."

"They are called Legacy in other worlds," Alaric continued, as though she hadn't spoken at all, bringing another piece of meat to her mouth. "Have you come across that term in the research you have obviously been doing?"

She shook her head while she chewed, and he stared at her expectantly, knowing he wouldn't continue until she answered him.

"That is a pity," he said with mock sympathy. "It would really tell you so much more about yourself. We can go over that history another day, but circling back to your original question, the Avonleyans have something hidden on their continent that we were sent to retrieve a long time ago. They are what drew us to this world in the first place. So really, our presence here is their fault in the end."

"Sent by who?" Scarlett asked, shifting on the floor again, stretching her legs out before her.

Alaric noted the movement, reaching out to bring a bite of vegetables to her mouth. "You can ask them that question when we enter Avonleya, my Wraith."

"If your plans depend on me getting you into Avonleya, then you are going to be sorely disappointed," she replied. "Even if I had the slightest desire to help you, I cannot do so chained to a fucking wall."

"A temporary setback," he agreed, bringing her another bite. "One that shall be rectified soon."

"Doubtful."

A small smile curled on his lips. "We shall see, Death's Maiden."

He fed her the rest of her meal in silence. She had just finished the glass of water when there was a sharp knock on the door and Tarek came in. He held one of those metal syringes in his hand, and Alaric pushed to his feet.

"Perfect timing," he said, striding to Tarek and taking the syringe from him.

"Redding was just reported to be entering the Syndicate as well, my Lord," Tarek replied, moving to settle into his usual place on the sofa.

"Excellent," Alaric answered, coming back to Scarlett's side. "When he gets here, I will be ready for your decision." He gripped her chin, bringing the tonic to her mouth. She jerked as she felt the mouse move behind her back. She'd forgotten about the rodent in her conversation with Alaric, so focused on the information he was allowing her to hear.

Alaric sighed. "Must we do this every time?" he asked, taking her movement as resistance. He tipped her head back, forcing the tonic into her mouth and down her throat.

She didn't fight, though. Because Cassius was almost here. She was going to see him for the first time in months, and she was chained to a wall. She would not be able to go to him. He would not be able to come to her. His fate was hanging in the balance. His fate was in her hands. And while it shouldn't be much of a choice— his life was worth Callan having to suffer through a marriage for political purposes— she knew there was more to it. She *knew* that a marriage to Veda, a Maraan Lady if she was truly Mikale's sister, was more than that. Was Cassius's life worth potentially putting an entire kingdom in jeopardy? An entire country of innocent people?

Time seemed to speed up as the seconds ticked by, and far too soon, the door opened again. Lord Tyndell strode in with Cassius following behind, and the color drained from his face when his brown eyes landed on Scarlett.

"Seastar," he breathed, lurching for her, but Alaric's voice rang out in order.

"Not so fast, Cassius." The Assassin Lord was leaning against his desk, his cloak on and hood up. "Death's Maiden has something she needs to say before you can go to her."

All eyes came to rest on her, and she began shaking her head, forcing back the tears burning at the back of her eyes. "Please, don't," she whispered, her eyes locked on Cassius. "Please, Alaric."

She knew it would do nothing. She knew her pleas were falling on deaf ears.

"Are you ready to receive a Mark, then, my Wraith?" Alaric asked.

She shook her head again, knowing she couldn't do that, not even to save Cassius from this.

"Then you know what choice lies before you. Choose. Cassius or Callan's whereabouts," he demanded.

"Callan is back," Cassius interrupted. "Callan has returned. He will be arriving at the castle later this evening."

The entire room went still, and Scarlett's eyes widened. Sorin wouldn't have sent Callan back without some sort of plan to keep him safe. But did he come with him? Did Cyrus? Did Eliza and Rayner?

"If that is the choice you are facing, Seastar, then it has been made for you. Callan has returned. This is not your burden to bear," Cassius continued, his eyes fixed on hers.

Alaric pushed off his desk, striding for him. "Stop speaking, Cassius. You are not here to counsel or console her. Where is Callan?"

"All I have heard is that he is set to arrive at the castle this evening. The king has been notified, and Princess Eva is very excited," Cassius explained, trying to peer around him to see Scarlett again. She craned her neck, trying to do the same.

"How have you heard this news and I have not?" Lord Tyndell demanded. The gentler tone he used with Scarlett was gone, replaced by the Commander of a kingdom's armies. "How am I unaware that the Crown Prince has returned? Why were additional men not sent to meet him?"

"I do not know, my Lord. I do not know how his guards communicated with the crown."

"And how did you come across this information, Cassius?" Alaric asked slowly, repeating Lord Tyndell's question.

"I heard it being spoken of among the castle guards," Cassius replied smoothly. "I assumed it was common knowledge."

Scarlett squirmed, biting down on her cry of surprise as that damn mouse scuttled out from behind her along the wall. It would meet its death if any of the men saw it, but they were all focused on Cassius.

Except Tarek.

His eyes were set on her, a slight smirk on his lips.

"You are not to leave the Fellowship until this has been confirmed. If you are lying, boy, expect consequences," Alaric snarled, striding for the door. "And you are not to enter this room. Tarek, stay with her. You know what to do if she shows signs of weakening."

Mikale and Lord Tyndell followed him out of the office, Cassius trailing after them, glancing back at her over his shoulder. She could see the longing in his eyes. She was sure they were a mirror of her own.

"How do you always seem to pull babysitting duty?" Scarlett asked when the door was closed and locked once more, her gaze shifting to Tarek.

"The Assassin Lord trusts me to ensure his property is properly cared for," Tarek answered. His fucking dagger was back in his hand, and he was idly flipping it again, just like he had that day he took her from Toreall.

"He trusts a Fae over his Maraan Lords?" Scarlett questioned, her head tilting to the side.

"Did you forget his mother was Fae?" Tarek countered. He stretched his long legs before him, crossing them at the ankles.

"And what did he promise you, Tarek?" she asked instead. "What made you turn your back on your entire race of people? What was so great, so irresistible, that you sacrificed your *twin flame?*"

"You act as though we are so different, your Majesty," he replied, a light amusement flickering in his pale, green eyes.

"We are nothing alike," she said, leaning her head back against the wall. She had a constant headache these days, the dull throbbing never seeming to cease.

"No?" She could hear the inflection in his tone. "Did you not sacrifice your own twin flame that day you came to meet the Night Children at the Earth Court border?"

"That is different. I did that to save him, to protect him," she argued, glancing at the Mark on her left hand.

"I did not realize you knew my motives," he retorted harshly.

She slid her gaze back to his, blinking slowly. "Are you saying you have let Talwyn think you are dead all this time to protect her?"

He stopped flipping the dagger at her name. A sneer curled onto his lips. "Tell me, your Majesty, does the Fae Queen not have another in her bed these days?"

"She believes you are *dead*," Scarlett replied incredulously. "Since you are not, how did the twin flame Mark fade?"

His sneer morphed into that slight smirk once more, and he resumed the flipping of his dagger. "So many questions today."

Scarlett rolled her eyes, leaning her head back against the wall once more and closing her eyes, assuming the conversation was over. But he spoke again.

"Did Aditya ever tell you why there is such conflict between the Fire and Earth Courts?"

"No," Scarlett sighed, keeping her eyes closed. The throbbing in her temples was growing again.

"He likely doesn't know what truly started it all. Relations were not always strained. In fact, the two Courts got along fine until my family was challenged for the Royal title, long before either of us were born into this world," Tarek said.

She opened her eyes at that. "Why would the Fire Court care if the Earth Prince was challenged? Isn't that how the Fae work? The most powerful takes the throne?"

"I suppose so," Tarek answered, his dagger flips becoming more forceful.

"And do you believe yourself more powerful than the current Earth Prince?" Scarlett asked. "If that is the case, challenge him for his place. It's not that complicated, is it?"

Tarek's teeth clenched. "Here I was, trying to have a pleasant conversation, and you had to become nasty."

"That happens when you're chained to a wall for days on end," Scarlett replied, shifting again, her shoulders aching.

"And *that* happens when you refuse to recognize the greater power."

"Says the disgruntled wanna-be Fae Prince," Scarlett scoffed.

A growl emanated from Tarek's chest that had Scarlett fighting the urge to stiffen. Alaric would punish him if he hurt her without permission, but she could tell she was pushing him to an edge.

"You're just as powerless here as you are there, Tarek," she sighed. "If you can't see that Alaric is merely using you as a means to an end, then it's probably a good thing Talwyn believes you to be dead. You would be useless at her side."

"Enough." Tarek's tone had dropped, low and dangerous. Gone was the smirk. Gone was the slight amusement. He was up and striding across the room towards her. The tip of his dagger was under her chin, forcing her head up to meet his gaze where violence glimmered. Her lips curled into a small antagonizing grin.

"When you finally learn what he has planned, when you finally realize what you are truly here for, you will see who is being used as a means to an end, your Majesty. Here's a hint: It is not me." He leaned forward, that dagger sliding along her jaw before moving down her neck.

"I know what I am here for," she replied, swallowing as the blade grazed along the hollow of her throat.

Then he leaned in close to whisper into her ear. "Getting into Avonleya is just the beginning. In the end, it will not matter who is by Talwyn's side. It will not matter who is by your side. In the end, there will only be one side."

CHAPTER 13
CALLAN

Callan was in the converted mess hall eating his midday meal with all the Black Syndicate orphans. He could eat in the kitchens where the Fae preferred to eat, he supposed, but then he'd have to actually converse with them. Something he was doing as little as possible.

They'd been back in Baylorin for nearly three weeks. He hadn't been outside of this warehouse since he'd entered it in the dark of night. The Fae kept insisting they didn't want him to return to the castle until Mikale was under control, and Scarlett had been retrieved. The first few days, he had tried to convince them that he could handle his own affairs. Sloan and Finn were siding with the Fae, though. *Sloan* was siding with the godsdamned Fae. The guard who despised Scarlett thought it was safer for him to remain here until the Fire Prince deemed it safe to return.

Rayner, Cyrus, and Eliza had taken to keeping an eye on him to make sure he didn't try to return on his own. So here he sat. At a table with children who didn't know who he was. He had taken to helping wherever he could. He assisted the young woman in the kitchens with prepping meals. Although he was pretty sure she knew who he was. She rarely met his eyes, and while she didn't call him Highness, she was very formal when she spoke to him. He spent some of his time playing games with the younger children as a way to simply keep himself busy, and sometimes he'd accompany Finn and Sloan to the small training areas that had been set up for the older children. Once most in the building were sleeping, Drake and Tava Tyndell would arrive, sneaking out of their manor at night. They would meet with the Fae, Cassius, and Nuri in the kitchens to brainstorm and plan.

He didn't want any part in that, though. At this point, he figured he'd be told what he needed to know when he needed to know it. No one seemed to notice he wasn't there anyway.

Lady Tava was kind enough to bring him books to read when she came, along with papers so he could catch up on everything that had been happening in the months he'd been gone. Drake had tried to keep him informed, but despite his father being the overseer of the kingdom's armies, the Tyndell heir was kept in the dark about much of what was going on behind closed doors at the castle.

Callan sighed, pushing the beans that remained on his plate around with a fork. He really needed to get home. His father was going to be irate as it was, and he missed his mother and little sister. He didn't know if or when he'd be returning, when he'd followed Scarlett to the Fire Court. He also thought that if he did, she would be at his side. He didn't know how he was going to convince the Fire Prince that he needed to return, though. Sorin's sole focus was Scarlett. If it could somehow affect her in a negative way, it was immediately dismissed. Callan supposed his best bet was likely trying to convince Eliza and having her talk to Sorin, but the general had hardly spoken to him since they'd arrived.

"Good day, young prince."

Arianna dropped down onto the bench beside him. Her hand landed on his arm, and her fingers began brushing back and forth along his skin. He was starting to get used to her liberal touches... Sort of.

He turned slightly, pulling his arm from beneath her hand. "Hello, Lady. I was not aware you had returned."

He knew that Cassius had been summoned by the Assassin Lord early that morning. They had apparently been waiting for such an opportunity to get the Shifter inside the Black Syndicate, and they had departed shortly after breakfast.

Arianna nodded, leaning back against the table and resting her elbows behind her. She was as informal as Scarlett was. "I have just returned. I have not even seen Sorin yet."

Callan arched a brow at that. "Was your time away fruitful?"

"Quite," she confirmed, bringing one of her hands up in front of her. Some type of fine silver mist was glimmering above her hand. It looked like a cloud of shimmering dust.

"What is that?" he asked, leaning forward to study it a bit more. Arianna glanced at him out of the corner of her eye. "It is energy."

"It is what?"

"Energy," she answered, the mass of dust beginning to slow, becoming a crackling swirl in her palm. Some of the younger children had taken notice and were beginning to draw closer, attracted by something shiny.

"I can shift the energy and matter around me just as I can shift my physical form," Arianna said. "Although, admittedly, shifting energy takes a much bigger toll on my power reserves, so I do not do it often."

"You cannot touch energy," Callan said skeptically.

"It is magic," she replied with a shrug.

"You cannot touch magic," Callan muttered, but, of course, she heard him. She had hearing as exceptional as the Fae.

"No?" Arianna questioned, arching a brow with a half-grin. "Magic is everywhere. It is all around you, at all times. One could argue that a child being formed in a womb and born into the world is magic. With a skilled partner, one could say fucking is magic. When more than one is involved, it is most certainly magic. And I assure you, there is plenty of touching in *that* magic." Callan choked on the water he had just taken a sip of, but he stiffened at her next words. "One could say the act of falling in love is magic." Arianna didn't seem to notice his change in posture. "One could also say that a young prince stepping into his destiny is . . . magic," she said, meeting his gaze.

She threw the energy into the air, and it drifted down like sparkling snow. The children squealed with delight as they attempted to catch it, but it seemed to evaporate as soon as they touched it.

"I do not know what you are implying," Callan said slowly when the last of the energy had vanished, and the children were wandering back to their games and lessons.

"Tell me, young prince, are you ready to marry?"

"What?" Callan balked at the sudden change of subject. "No."

"No?" Arianna repeated. "It was my understanding that you wished to marry Queen Scarlett."

"Well, yes, but that was . . . different," he answered, stumbling over his words.

"Because you love her?" she asked.

"Yes," Callan answered hesitantly. "Because I loved her."

"Loved or love?"

"Does it matter?" he countered bitterly. He was rather annoyed at the fact that she seemed to know so much about his relationship with Scarlett. "Not to me," Arianna answered. There was a crackling sound, and this time the Shifter had lightning buzzing about her knuckles, a ring like Scarlett's nestled onto her middle finger. "Your new bride may want to know the answer to that question, though."

"That is not something that I need to worry about for quite some time," he replied, unsure as to why he was talking about this with a woman who he would likely never see again once she returned to her territory. He planned to have as little interaction as possible with the magical territories. His focus would stay on the humans in his charge.

"Do you know a woman named Veda?" Arianna asked, and Callan stilled.

"How do you know that name?"

"Do you believe in the Fates?" Arianna asked instead.

"I have never really thought about it," Callan answered, still stuck on how she knew Veda's name.

"The gods then?"

"I suppose so."

Arianna nodded. "I saw the queen today on my visit to the Black Syndicate." She said it so casually, as if she were telling Callan of something she saw at a shop in the markets.

"I am sure Sorin will be glad to hear that," Callan said. "What does Veda have to do with this?"

"While I was studying the chains that keep her bound, there were several men there, and you were mentioned. They are seeking your whereabouts," Arianna answered. "They threatened the queen with Cassius's life unless she revealed your whereabouts."

Callan felt the blood drain from his face. He started to get to his feet, to go find Sorin, but the Shifter placed her hand on his arm, pulling him back down onto the bench. "I am not finished, young prince. I think you will want to know what I learned before we get the Fire Prince involved."

Callan nodded at her to continue, lowering back down onto the bench.

"Your father is unhappy you have been gone so long and has

apparently decided it is time for you to marry. They said he seems to think it will make you settle down and take your responsibilities more seriously."

Callan could not believe what he was hearing. He had left to keep Scarlett's secrets, to be with a woman who ended up choosing someone else, and he was returning to a forced marriage? But Arianna was not done.

"This Veda person. An agreement has already been made between her family and your father," she said, her olive eyes watching him closely.

He had followed Scarlett to the Fae Courts to avoid this exact situation. He knew Veda desired to be his queen. She had made her motives clear on more than one occasion, and it had been made more clear by the events that had unfolded the year after Scarlett had stopped coming to him.

"Do you wish to marry her?" Arianna asked.

"No," Callan said, his objection at the idea clear in his tone.

"So what will you do about it?" she pushed.

"I suppose we will go tell Sorin what you learned and see what he thinks we should do," Callan said, beginning to stand once more.

"And what will you do when you are king, Callan? Will you wait for someone else to fix things for you?"

Callan stared incredulously at the Shifter Beta. "Forgive my rudeness, Lady, but you really know nothing of what you are talking about."

"I have lived for centuries, young prince. I was born in the midst of the Great War. I was a child when my kind was given our gifts. I know more than you could ever imagine. I have seen mortal kings rise and fall. I have outlived Fae Queens and High Witches and Contessas alike," Arianna said, something in her eyes turning fierce.

"My family has ruled Windonelle since the kingdom was founded," Callan countered.

"Yes, but Windonelle was not always its own kingdom, was it? The three mortal kingdoms were once ruled by one."

"I do not know what you are trying to tell me, Arianna," Callan said, failing to hide his irritation.

Arianna pushed to her feet, stretching her arms above her head. Then she reached out and cupped his cheek as she said, "There may be three separate kings on three separate thrones, but they all follow the same path. I am merely suggesting that perhaps your destiny is another path, but it is not one that can be chosen for you. You must choose it yourself."

"My path was chosen for me the moment I was conceived," Callan replied, pulling away from the Shifter's touch.

"And yet you were willing to forgo that path if Scarlett had accepted your proposal," Arianna countered.

Callan pressed his tongue to his cheek at that, his eyes darting to the door as Tava entered, carrying an armful of books and papers. What was she doing here in the middle of the day? She caught Callan's eye, and she bowed her head slightly, leaning back against the wall and clearly waiting for him to finish his conversation.

Arianna had straightened and taken a step back from him. "I will give you a few hours to figure things out before I find Sorin and tell him what I learned."

Callan started at that. "You are not going to tell Sorin right now?"

"This is your fate, not his," Arianna replied, her gaze catching on a guard and a coy glimmer entering her eyes. "I am sure I can find some way to make myself scarce to give you some time." She glanced back to Callan one final time as she said, "I have learned many things in my many years, young prince, but something I learned early on is that my feet decide which path I take. No one else's."

"I am not sure I am afforded such a luxury," Callan muttered under his breath.

A cunning smirk curled up on her lips. "You misunderstand me, your Highness. Many have tried to direct my path. That was their mistake."

With those parting words, she set off toward the guard she had been watching, her hips swaying. When she reached him, the guard stiffened as she pushed up onto her tiptoes, whispering into his ear. A wide grin spread across his face and that was when Callan turned his attention back to Lady Tava.

She had started walking towards him, and he met her halfway. Her eyes were full of worry as she held out the books and papers in her hand.

"Your Highness," she greeted with a slight bow.

Callan sighed. "Lady Tava, I think at this point you can call me Callan."

"That would be most inappropriate," she replied, her cheeks flushing slightly.

Callan arched a brow. "More inappropriate than me leaving my kingdom for months and then hiding away in a warehouse with the children of the wicked when I do finally return?"

Tava huffed a soft laugh. "Fair enough . . . Callan. But then I must insist you simply call me Tava."

"Agreed," Callan said with a small smile. He set the books aside on a table and began rifling through the papers she had brought to him. "I am surprised you are here during the day."

"Yes, well, something has happened," she replied, and he glanced up to find her biting her lip nervously.

"I am going to hazard a guess that it has to do with your father learning of my return?"

"You know?" Tava asked in surprise.

"I was just informed," he answered grimly. "Apparently, I am also to take a wife because I have been shirking my duties, according to my father." She winced slightly at the words, quickly schooling the expression from her face.

"I am sorry, Callan," she said.

"Why?" he asked, returning his attention to the papers in his hands. "It will be of no surprise to anyone. It is something my father has been pushing for the last few years."

"Yes, but . . ."

He glanced back up at her hesitation, waiting for her to continue.

She sighed, all pretenses seeming to disappear when she spoke again. "I know you loved her, Callan. I can only assume you are not ready to devote yourself to another so soon after everything that you have been through these last few months."

"Everything I have been through?" he repeated.

"Going with Scarlett to escape a threat on your life. Having to watch the woman you love fall in love with someone else. Coming home and not being able to actually go home . . ." she explained, trailing off when he just continued to stare at her.

He had forgotten how observant the Lady was. He had forgotten how clever she was. Admittedly, he spent most of his time with Drake when in the company of the Tyndells, so he didn't know her well, but he remembered her brilliance at the dinner with Mikale and Veda months ago.

"I apologize if I am overstepping," Tava said in a rush, her eyes falling to the floor and a blush entering her cheeks once more.

"No, you aren't. Overstepping, I mean," he said quickly. "I just forgot how nice it is to converse with someone who isn't . . . Fae or some other immortal being. A human conversation is refreshing."

Tava met his gaze once more, her head tilting slightly to the side. "Your guards were with you. They are mortal."

"You spend months with the same two people, and you will find you are craving some new company from time-to-time," he answered with a small smile.

She smiled at that and gave a slight nod. "Well, I am sure you will have plenty of options when you return to court."

Callan's smile slipped from his face. "Apparently, that has already been decided for me as well. I have learned that my father has made an arrangement with Lord Lairwood."

Tava audibly gasped, her hand coming to cover her mouth at the sound. The same horror he felt at the idea was in her eyes. "He is not giving you a choice?" she asked.

"It would appear not, but I suppose we will see when I actually return."

"Will you agree to such a thing?"

Callan was quiet for several long moments, Tava patiently waiting for his answer, before he finally said, "I do not know. I do not know what I will do."

✦

"You went to the mortal prince before you came to me?" Sorin demanded when Arianna finished explaining what she had discovered at the Fellowship.

Apparently Sorin had learned of her return soon after she'd come back, but true to her word, she'd been "preoccupied" for the last few hours, sending the Fire Prince into a rage at having to wait for her. As soon as she'd emerged from her room— the guard she'd brought with her sneaking out behind her with his head ducked down— she'd come to collect Callan before following Sorin up to the fourth floor. His Inner Court was already there, along with Nuri and the Earth Prince.

"Why would I come to you with information that directly affects his Highness?" Arianna asked, clearly unconcerned as she lounged back in one of the chairs, her legs crossed one over the other.

Callan watched with no small amount of amusement as Sorin swallowed, sucking his teeth and clearly reining in a temper. "Because I brought you here for a specific purpose, Arianna, and you learned things that directly affect my *wife*."

"I just told you everything I learned," she replied, brushing her long braids over her shoulder and proceeding to inspect her nails.

"Arianna," Sorin growled, but his tone had the Lady snapping her head up.

"Do not, for one second, think I answer to you, Sorin Aditya," she hissed, her tone dark and deadly.

The Fire Court all sat up a little straighter, hands sliding into casual reach of their weapons as flames flickered in Sorin's eyes.

"This is not the time nor the place, Aditya," Prince Azrael cut in.

"No one asked you for your input, Luan," Sorin retorted, his eyes still fixed on the Shifter.

"Does it really matter at this point?" Tava asked. "What's done is done. Can we figure out what we are going to do? We are not really going to let Callan marry Veda, are we?"

Sorin dropped into a seat with a sigh, running a hand through his dark hair. "Scarlett would not be happy with that turn of events."

"I do not think it is Scarlett's happiness we should be concerning ourselves with here," Tava argued. "We can only assume Veda is one of these Maraan *things*, but even if she were not, Callan should not be forced into a marriage he does not want."

"That is often the life of royalty," Sorin countered.

"Sorin, you cannot be serious," Eliza hissed from where she sat between Cyrus and Nuri.

Callan had no idea why the general was jumping into the conversation at this particular point in time. He had no idea why any of them were coming to his aid in this. Sorin had a point. Marriages among royalty were rarely for love. He had been an idealist to dream of ever having something like that.

"The issue of Veda can be handled later. The main concern here is the fact that I need to go home. Tonight," Callan said. He glanced at Finn and Sloan. They were standing near the door, their arms crossed, looking grim.

"Not until this is figured out," Sorin replied, barely glancing at Callan before his eyes went back to Arianna.

Callan's jaw clenched at the obvious dismissal yet again. Sorin was saying something to Arianna, but the Shifter's eyes were on Callan, a small smile playing on her lips.

"Destiny is a fickle thing, isn't it?" Arianna said, interrupting whatever Sorin had been saying.

"This is not the time, Arianna," Sorin sighed, leaning forward and bracing his elbows on his knees, his head falling into his hands.

"Is it not?" she asked. "Maybe this is the queen's destiny," she continued with a shrug.

Sorin was on his feet, with Rayner and Cyrus jumping to their own in case they needed to restrain the prince. "Her *destiny* does not lie with *them*."

"And if the Fates have declared it so?"

"She will crawl into the space between the stars and use her darkness to give the Fates physical form for the sole purpose of cutting them apart piece by piece for even trying to dictate her path, and I will be by her side handing her the blades wreathed in flames to do so," Sorin snarled, his chest heaving. "Mention leaving her to this *fate* again, Arianna, and your assistance here will no longer be needed."

"Defying the Fates is never easy," Arianna said, unfazed.

"It is when you have every reason to defy them," Sorin snapped in reply.

"Indeed," was Arianna's only response as she leveled her gaze on Callan yet again.

And he didn't know what she wanted from him. What would fighting against Sorin accomplish? He was a fire-wielding Fae prince with an entire Court of Fae backing him, not to mention a Witch and vampyre. What would he possibly be able to do against that?

"Prince Callan needs to go back tonight, Sorin," Tava cut in. "Cassius's life clearly depends on it. Scarlett will never forgive you if something happens to Cassius."

"She will also never forgive me if I let Callan willingly walk into danger and enter into a union with a Maraan Lady," Sorin countered, slumping back into his seat, his hands going through his hair again.

"So we do not send him back alone," Tava said slowly.

"He won't be alone," Sloan chimed in from the doorway. "We'd be with him, but the two of us against the king and his Lords . . . That does nothing against Lady Veda." He trailed off, clearly thinking what everyone else was.

Everyone else except Tava.

"So he goes back committed to another," she continued. "Committed to another who has Maraan blood and is of nobility. Someone who would be acceptable and difficult to argue against."

The room fell completely still at what she was suggesting. No one said anything for a full minute.

"I appreciate your loyalty to Scarlett, Tava. Really I do, but—" Sorin started.

"I do not offer this out of loyalty to Scarlett," Tava interrupted, her lips pursing slightly. "I do this out of loyalty to my own kingdom. I do this out of loyalty to the children I have spent the last six months serving and protecting in any way I could. I do this because everyone should have a choice about their destiny, not just Fae Queens and Princes."

Callan could only stare at this Lady who was willing to risk her own well-being for him.

No, not for him.

For innocent children. For her kingdom.

And some form of guilt and shame slithered down his spine as he admitted to himself he had been sitting idle and stagnant these last few years. For his entire life if he was being completely honest. The entirety of his life had been someone else deciding his every movement. From his father's grooming to one day rule, to his mother's constant pushing to meet every Lady in the kingdom to find a bride. Even Scarlett taking him to the Fire Court for his safety, had been someone else deciding for him. He'd been sitting back. Letting it all happen to him. Content to just . . . let it. Content to let everyone else make the decisions. Content to wait for someone else to fix things, to tell him what to do. Of course he was eager and willing to help in any way he could, but, despite once telling Scarlett his greatest desire was to take care of those already in their charge, what had he done to make any sort of difference? What had he ever done to prove to anyone that he meant those words and sentiments?

And what will you do when you are king, Callan? Will you wait for someone else to fix things for you?

What would he do when he sat on the throne? When he was the one responsible for making the decisions? When thousands of people were looking to him to lead them?

Maybe the more important question to be asking, though, was what had he ever done as their Crown Prince to prove he deserved to be sitting on that throne and leading them to begin with?

His gaze settled back on Tava, and he couldn't help but think back to their dinner months ago. When she had sat next to Veda, cunning and witty, helping get information to Scarlett. Aiding Cassius and Drake to get her out and intercepting Veda at every turn. And he realized she could do this. She had always been in the background, in her brother's shadow, but from there she could see everything. And she had. No one would ever suspect sweet, quiet Lady Tyndell to be a threat, to know anything. But as that scene at the Lairwood house played again and again in his mind, he realized she was a threat. She knew things. He was willing to bet she knew secrets people would kill to keep quiet. Secrets that would be incredibly useful if they were going to outwit Mikale, Veda, and her own father.

He took a step towards her. He could tell she wanted to step back, but she held her ground. "You are willing to do this? To appear to be courting? To put yourself in Veda's path? Mikale's? The king's?"

She swallowed, her slender throat bobbing with the motion. "If it will buy us time, if it will buy *you* time, yes."

"Maybe we should run this by Drake before . . ." Nuri started, but trailed off before she finished her thought.

Tava was already shaking her head, turning to look at Death's Shadow. "If you manage to get her out, I can only assume she will want to come after them. The Assassin Lord. Mikale. My father." She paused for a moment, her gaze darting to a window before going back to Nuri. "You will need people on the inside. Who better than the Crown Prince himself?"

"This will be dangerous," Sorin said. "Scarlett would not like—"

"Scarlett is not here, nor does she have any say in this," Callan cut in, moving another step closer to Tava. "If Lady Tava is willing to risk her safety for her kingdom, who are we to deny her that choice? And who am I to not be willing to do the same for the people I am to one day lead?"

Tava's face flushed for the hundredth time that day at once again being the center of attention. She didn't back down, though Callan could see her trembling slightly.

"You will need to be . . . convincing," Nuri said tentatively. "Mikale and Veda are crafty and vicious. Their weapons are not swords and daggers, but power plays and prowess. They excel at manipulation."

"We are not seriously discussing this right now," Sorin said in disbelief.

"She has a point, Sorin," Nuri said. "We could use people on the inside. That was the whole reason Scarlett began seeing—" She cut herself off, glancing quickly at Callan.

"I was a means to an end," Callan supplied. "I am well aware of what I was to Death's Maiden," he added bitterly. "But that is neither here nor there. There is a threat against my people, and I will do what is necessary to stand against it. I will not, however, force Lady Tava into this if she is not certain."

"I can do this," Tava said, her ocean blue eyes sparking with determination. "I can play the part until we figure something else out."

"No," Sorin said, pushing back to his feet. "This is not happening until every possible outcome has been explored. If this negatively impacts Scarlett in any way—"

"This is about more than your wife," Callan snarled, stepping towards the Fire Prince. "This is about *my* people. This is about *my* kingdom that has been caught in the crossfire of a battle between immortal beings, and your queen is at the center of it all. My concern is not for how this will affect the Fae Queen but for how it will affect the children in this building and the people on my streets." Sorin opened his mouth to argue further, but Callan pushed on. "You have no say in this matter. Not here. This is not your Court. This is *mine*."

A muscle feathered in Sorin's jaw, embers dancing in his golden irises. Without another word, he turned on a heel and left the room. Rayner and Cyrus exchanged glances before Rayner slipped out to follow him.

"So what is your plan then, Princeling?" Eliza drawled, from where she still sat.

Callan glanced at Finn and Sloan before looking back at Tava. "It would appear I will not be going home alone tonight."

Arianna pushed to her feet as she said, "You best be on your way. It was stated you would be arriving this evening, and the sun is nearly set." She started walking the way Sorin and Rayner had gone, but stopped beside Callan. With a slight smirk, she winked at him. "Destiny is a fickle thing, isn't it?"

CHAPTER 14
SORIN

He couldn't stand to be in that room anymore. He couldn't stand to hear them all talking about the mortal prince and what they needed to do to help him. Maybe that made him a selfish prick, but he didn't give a fuck. Not when it involved Scarlett. The rest of the world could go to hell for all he cared at this point, because his entire world was chained to a wall in some private study where everything he feared was coming true. Alaric had her, was breaking her in ways far worse than physical torture. And now he'd brought Cassius into this, knowing exactly what kind of leverage he now held over her.

He was down on the first floor of the warehouse, debating if he could safely burn some of the scattered crates to ash to release some of the tension in his veins. Rayner was standing near the stairwell, watching and waiting. What he wouldn't give to feel her down that bond again, just another glimpse to know she was still fighting, still reaching for him as adamantly as he was reaching for her.

Scarlett.

But the word was met with the same resistance it had been since she had left him at the border. There were no cracks in that wall this time. No weaknesses to hurl flames at. No fissures to exploit to try to bring that wall crashing down.

Footfalls sounded on the stairs, and a moment later, Arianna stepped into the room, followed by Eliza, Cyrus, and Luan. Of course, it was Luan who opened his mouth first.

"We cannot meddle in the affairs of mortals, Aditya. That is not what we are here for," he said, his tone holding a slight chiding tone to it.

Sorin snorted a hollow laugh. "Of course you would say something as foolish as that."

"Foolish? What is foolish is you getting into an argument with a mortal prince when we could be focusing on getting your wife and queen out. He wants to go back to his castle and walk into some kind of trap? That is his choice to make. Leave him to it, and focus on what we came here to do," Luan retorted.

"I would not expect you to understand any of this, Luan," Sorin sneered. "Your motives have always been purely about gaining the upper hand for the Earth Court any way you can."

"Of course it is," Luan drawled. "They are who I answer to. They are who I am responsible for. They *expect* me to fight for them, to go after whatever advantages we can."

"At the expense of the wellbeing of others?"

"As if you and your Court are any different," Luan countered. "Tell me, Aditya, who were you thinking about when you dragged a small unit across the border to *rescue* Eliné? Was that for you, your Court, or the good of the world? Were those lost worth the sacrifice you asked them to make?"

Sorin snarled, lurching towards him, but Rayner got there first, casually drawing his short sword with a dark grin.

"Oh, Luan," Eliza sighed from behind them. "When will you learn not to spout off when we're all present?"

"When will you all learn that I am not concerned by your little threats and pretty blades?" he returned, the dirt beginning to swirl at his feet.

"Sometimes I forget how young and petty you all are," Arianna cut in, sauntering to the center of the room. She held out her palm where a piece of iron sat. Where she had found it, Sorin had no idea. "Which one of you is going to give me what I need?" she asked, glancing between the princes.

Luan crossed his arms in clear refusal of giving Arianna his Semiria ring when Sorin didn't need his. Sorin gritted his teeth, sliding Scarlett's ring from his finger and feeling his fire magic stutter out in his veins. He handed it to Arianna. She slipped it on and her attention turned to the iron in her palm. It immediately began shifting, shrinking and thinning out, into a long, small key.

Her olive eyes landed back on him, and they had softened a touch, some form of sympathy looking back at him. "This key will unlock her chain anchors," she explained. "She wouldn't let me close enough to look at the actual manacles."

Sorin snorted a small laugh at the thought of Scarlett kicking the Beta Shifter off her foot, even if the Beta was in the form of a small mouse, but the laugh died in his throat as quickly as it had come. He swallowed thickly before locking eyes with Arianna again. "She is chained? To a wall?" he asked, the Beta's words on constant replay in his mind.

Cassius had carried her into the Fellowship in his pocket. While he had been intercepted and questioned, before apparently being taken directly to Scarlett, Arianna had slipped from him and made her way along the halls and rooms. She'd spent hours the last few weeks studying the maps Cassius and Nuri had drawn, learning everything she could about the Fellowship and memorizing the places Scarlett might be held.

When Arianna said she had found her, laid eyes on her, and heard her speaking, Sorin had been ready to charge into the Black Syndicate immediately. Of course, he knew Nuri and Cassius were right. This plan was multifaceted and figuring out where she was at was only one of many, many steps. Besides, who was to say she was always held there? Was she constantly moved to throw them off? Or had she been chained to that stone wall since she'd fallen back into the Assassin Lord's hands? Had she once again been sleeping on a stone floor? Had they been withholding food? Giving her water? Had he been letting Mikale have her?

Fury, hot and acidic, flooded him at that last thought, and he was suddenly grateful he didn't have that ring on his finger. He was certain something would be on fire if he did. His eyes fell to the ring on his left hand though. His marriage band. His only mark of their union in this land. His only connection to her here. Another wave of fury washed through him at the thought of her blocking their bond. That anger was nearly as potent as the rage he felt about Mikale laying a single finger on her.

"Yes, Sorin," Arianna replied. "Shirastone shackles adorn her wrists and ankles. While her wrists are anchored above her head, her feet are not secured to the floor. This key should unlock the anchor. If another key needs to be made once we have her out, I can do so here."

"Why can you not just make another key there?" Eliza asked. She was leaning against the far wall, her face calculating and grim.

The face of his general, going over battle plans and strategies. "If she can have access to her magic, it will certainly aid us in getting her out."

"Because there are wards around that place," Arianna answered, her face going dark. "They are wards like I have never felt, that block my abilities, even with a Semiria ring on my finger." At the mention of the ring, she slipped it off her finger, handing it back to Sorin.

"You have met Cassius. He is very powerful," Sorin countered, feeling his flames spring back to life with the ring back in place.

"Those were not Witch wards, Sorin," Arianna said.

"Cassius also stated he's never been asked to put wards around the Fellowship," Rayner supplied.

"Then we can only assume that these wards will affect us when we go in to get her," Cyrus chimed in.

"I will not need my magic to get to her. My blades and my own hands will be enough," Sorin said darkly. "When I come for her, she will walk out of that cesspit with me, or I will stay there with her. There will be no in between. There will be no middle ground."

"Your blades and your hands will be enough in a house and district full of lethally trained assassins, thieves, and mercenaries? I think not, fire prick," Nuri drawled from a shadowy corner.

Where the hell had she come from?

"Would you care to test that theory, Daughter of Night?" Sorin answered with a dark grin.

"You take that ring off and tell your lackeys not to interfere, Sorin, and I will certainly be willing to make you bleed," she answered with a wicked grin of her own.

"If you need a drink, Nuri dear, you only need to ask," Sorin taunted. Nuri hissed at him, her fangs snapping out. "Every time I start to think you're not as bad as I remember, you prove just how big of a dick you truly are."

"Let's just focus on getting her out," Rayner cut in again, but his low voice was dark and tense, and it snapped Sorin's attention back to where it should be. Rayner was always so stoic, always so impassive, that when some sort of emotion did make its way to the surface, you took notice. Mainly because if his Third lost control, there would be more than blood littering the floor of this warehouse, and his tone said he was riding an edge Sorin had been on for weeks now.

"How far out did you feel these wards?" Luan asked, his eyes fixed on Nuri, watching her every move.

"Not until outside the grounds of the Fellowship," the Beta answered. "As much as we're going to want to go in and kill everyone we come across, I think it's going to be best if we can get in and out undetected. Can we go in disguised somehow? As servants, like I did for so long at the Tyndell estate?" Eliza asked.

"You'd be better off trying to go in disguised as assassins," Nuri said. "If the Assassin Lord's attention is focused on Scarlett right now, there is a chance you could get in. You'd be cloaked and hooded, your faces hidden. I can only assume his most trusted are guarding her so the others may not instantly recognize an outsider."

"What if we were with one of his most trusted?" Sorin asked slowly. "I can't go there, Sorin," Nuri answered.

"Not you," Sorin said, shaking his head. His gaze swung back to Arianna. "You said Mikale was in that room while you were there. And Lord Tyndell."

"Yes, along with another and the Assassin Lord," Arianna confirmed. "Did you see them, specifically Mikale, well enough to shift into him?"

Eliza pushed off the wall she was leaning against. "You want her to impersonate Mikale and go in for Scarlett? Scarlett would never believe he had come to rescue her."

"No," Sorin said, shaking his head again. "I want her to impersonate Mikale so that when I enter as an underling assassin, no one will question it. Then, when I find Scarlett, I can explain who Arianna is. If Mikale is with me, who will question us moving her about?"

Nuri had a knife in her gloved hand, playing with the blade as she thought over everything he'd said. "It could work," she said thoughtfully. "Before all of this happened, if I had entered with an outsider, no one but Alaric would have questioned me. If he is distracted, his awareness of your presence would likely be delayed." She fell quiet again, clearly running over different outcomes in her mind. Everyone stayed quiet, letting her think, recognizing that she was the expert here. As much as he hated it, she'd been right when she had yelled at him, reminding him that her knowledge was superior to his here.

"This will probably be our best shot," Nuri finally conceded. "And now that he has Cassius too—"

"What do you mean he has Cassius too?" Cyrus interrupted. "I thought he was only keeping the commander if he was lying about the mortal prince? That has been taken care of."

Nuri huffed out a hollow laugh. "If you think the Assassin Lord is going to release the greatest leverage he has against Scarlett, you are sorely mistaken. Cassius will be used against her until he has gotten everything he wants from her, and even then, he will likely be kept as collateral, to keep her under control."

"So you are saying when we go in for Scarlett, we will need to get him as well?" Rayner asked, the smoke swirling in his eyes seeming to thicken.

"Yes," Nuri answered simply.

"Well, that's just great," Eliza muttered. "Because getting Scarlett out wasn't challenging enough, we now need to try to smuggle two people out."

"When?" Sorin demanded. "When can we go in?"

Nuri's honey eyes met his. "Give me a few days, Sorin." Her tone had softened, like it often did when he glimpsed her conversing with the younger children. "Let me make sure that we have as many of our people on duty as possible when we go in. It will give us the best chances."

Sorin nodded, not liking having to wait even another hour, let alone a few days, but what else could he do? If those few days were what it took to avoid losing their advantage, then he'd suffer through them.

They all dispersed, agreeing to meet again later tonight as usual to discuss things further, after Nuri had some time to get in touch with her contacts. Eliza went to speak with Callan and make sure they were as prepared as possible for returning to the castle. Sorin didn't know if the mortal prince would even speak to her, but he didn't care any more. The mortal prince could do what he wanted.

He found himself slipping out the side door, his feet carrying him back to the beach. This was where he normally ended up in the afternoons, staring out across a sea so vast and endless, yet it felt minuscule compared to the abyss separating him from his twin flame.

Hold on, Love. Just a little longer. I am coming.

CHAPTER 15
CALLAN

"You are sure you are ready for this?" Callan asked, glancing sidelong at Tava.

She sat beside him in a carriage as it made its way to the castle. They had decided this would be the best way to arrive and make their story look convincing. He would tell his father and the others that he simply hadn't been able to wait to see her as soon as he arrived back in Baylorin, and she had accompanied him to the castle to see her father.

"I do not think it matters much if I am ready or not, your Highness," Tava replied, her hands folded and resting in her lap, ever the Lady.

Callan drummed his fingers against his thigh, his knee bouncing with nerves. "If it is to be believed we are courting, you really do need to call me Callan instead of your Highness."

"Noted."

"And we should probably establish some . . . boundaries or something," he added.

"Boundaries?" she asked, turning to face him in confusion.

"Yes, boundaries. What is acceptable to you? What makes you uncomfortable? If we are courting, it will be expected that we are at least somewhat affectionate with each other, I suppose," he answered, his fingers drumming on his fidgeting leg once more. He turned to look out the window. They were only a few blocks from the castle now.

"Hmm," she mused. "I suppose hand-holding, whispering sweet nothings, and soft kisses to the hand and cheek would be acceptable, but perhaps we keep the more passionate displays for when we are alone?"

Callan's head whipped back around, his eyes wide. But when they landed on Tava, he found a small smile gracing her lips and a teasing glimmer in her eyes. Her hand landed gently on his knee, ceasing the incessant bouncing. "Relax, Callan. I was raised in this society, just as you were. I know what will be expected of us. I know how to play a part."

"I know," he murmured back, his eyes fixed on her hand still resting on his knee. "This is just . . . dangerous. I do not feel right letting you risk your safety for me."

"I have been at risk since the moment I helped Drake and Cassius bring Scarlett into our home over a year ago, Callan," she said softly. "I am at risk each time I sneak away to that warehouse to care for children or bring you news." She pulled her fingers from his knee, and he instantly felt the loss of heat from her hand. She grasped the spirit amulet at her neck, sliding the three interlocked circles back and forth along the chain, her eyes going to the window.

Callan ran a hand through his hair. "I know you can handle this, Tava," he said. "I watched you with Veda at that dinner." She slowly brought her eyes back to him as he spoke. "But I would feel better about this whole situation if we have some sort of signal or sign that you use if you are uncomfortable or feeling unsafe."

"All right, Callan," she answered with a small nod of her head. "If that will ease your nerves."

"It will," he confirmed, forcing his knee to still once more when he realized he'd started bouncing it again.

"If I am uncomfortable or would like to end our arrangement, I will make a comment about how much I love hot summer days."

"How is that a signal?" he asked in confusion.

"Because I *hate* summer," she answered with a note of disgust, and an unexpected chuckle burst from Callan at just how passionately she felt about a season. "The only person who would find my comment out of character for me is Drake. He will understand the signal without needing to be told."

"So you prefer the winter months, then?" Callan asked, as the carriage began its trek up the long drive from the castle gates.

"Very much so," she confirmed, still fiddling with the amulet at her neck. It was the only sign she was showing of her own nerves.

He brought his hand to her elbow, and she stilled at his touch, meeting his eyes once more. "Thank you for this, Tava," he said softly. "You did not have to do this."

"Yes, I did," she answered, her voice quiet, almost a whisper. "I love Windonelle, and if my father is part of something that is jeopardizing our kingdom, hurting innocent children . . ." She trailed off, her lips pressing into a thin line.

Callan waited for her to go on, but she never did, and a moment later, they were pulling to a stop in front of the castle. The carriage door opened, Finn's face appearing. "Are you ready for this?"

"As ready as we can be," Callan answered, moving to step out of the coach. His boots crunched on the cobblestones, and he looked up the steps to find Mikale Lairwood himself waiting for him. He had a wide smile on his face that, up until now, Callan had always thought was sincere. I guess we'd see how well he maintained that farce when Tava stood beside him.

Tearing his eyes from Mikale, he turned back to the door, holding up his hand to help Tava out of the carriage. Delicate fingers landed in his palm, and his own wrapped around them, squeezing gently as she descended the two small steps to the ground. She gave him a shy smile, already playing the part, and maneuvered her fingers so they intertwined with his.

"Mikale is waiting for us," Callan murmured, his tone tense.

"I am well aware, Callan," she answered, not a trace of nerves or unease to be found in her voice. "Take a breath, tuck my hair behind my ear, and when you are ready, lead me up the steps."

Callan studied her for a moment, taking in her fierce determination, before he did just what she said. He took a deep breath, bracing himself to play this role, before he reached up and tucked a piece of golden hair behind her ear, letting his fingers brush along her jaw slightly. Her smile softened a touch, and he turned to face what was waiting for them.

Mikale watched them the entire way, his smile never faltering. When they were at the last few steps, he bowed as he said, "Welcome home, your Highness. We are very glad to have you back."

"It is good to be home," Callan answered, pulling Tava forward gently.

"Lady Tava," Mikale said with a small nod of his head. "What an unexpected surprise this evening."

"It seems the night is full of those," Tava replied. "Callan surprised me at my home. I did not know he was returning today." She glanced up at Callan from beneath her lashes.

"Callan," Mikale repeated slowly, his smile seeming more forced as he noted Tava using his name so casually. "You stopped at the Tyndell manor before returning home?"

"I did," Callan confirmed, moving forward and brushing past Mikale. The doors were opened for them, and he breathed a deep sigh at being home. Everything might be going to hell here, but he was still happy to be home, back where he belonged. Where fire magic and shadows didn't lurk around every damn corner. He was fairly certain he'd rather face Mikale and whatever magic a Maraan Lord possessed, than have to live amongst Scarlett, Sorin, and the Fire Court another day.

"Everyone is gathered in the dining hall," Mikale was saying. "A small feast has been prepared to dine over while you tell everyone what you have been up to."

The implication was subtle, but there. His father would be demanding an explanation for his prolonged absence. Finn and Sloan's footsteps sounded behind them as they rounded a corner. He could hear talking, and he heard Eva's laughter. The doors were opened, and he had taken all of two steps into the hall when Eva squealed, damn near tripping over her skirts as she ran to Callan, leaping into his arms.

"Hello, Eva," he said warmly into her light brown hair.

"I missed you so much, Callan," she replied, her small arms wrapping around his neck.

"I missed you, too," he answered, lowering her back to her feet. His mother was standing there, waiting for him, and he stepped forward, pressing a kiss to her cheek. "Hello, Mother."

Queen Meredith pushed up on to her toes to wrap Callan in a hug. "Thank the gods you are finally home," she said, smoothing her hand down the arms of his tunic as she pulled back. "Although you look dreadful. Where have you been sleeping? Shacks along the road?" She laughed at her own joke, and Callan forced a chuckle. If she only knew he'd been sleeping in a rundown warehouse for the last few weeks.

"The downfall of traveling on horseback for days on end, I am afraid," he answered, glancing around the room at the rest of those present. His father was sitting at the head of the table. He hadn't bothered to rise to greet him. He had a gold chalice in his hand, his eyes narrowed slightly at Callan. Lord Tyndell was here, along with Drake. Lord Lairwood stood next to his father, watching everything with interest.

"Your Highness, how lovely to have you home once more."

Her voice made the hair on the back of his neck stand on end, and he turned to find Lady Veda a few feet away. She wore a deep blue gown cinched so tightly around her waist he truly wondered how she could breathe. Her brown hair was woven into an intricate coronet atop her head.

"Lady Veda, it is nice to see you," he said, trying to keep his tone neutral. He glanced over his shoulder to find Tava murmuring something to Drake, whose eyes kept bouncing to him, then back to his sister.

"Come and sit, Callan," his father called from the table, his deep tone commanding. "We have much to discuss."

"Of course, Father," Callan said, turning and extending a hand to Tava. She somehow made her cheeks flush slightly as she stepped to his side, and he placed a hand on her lower back to guide her towards the seats. He rounded the table, stopping at his chair directly to his father's right. Lord Lairwood usually sat on the other side of Callan, but he was already a seat farther down the table, leaving a chair between them. He pulled the chair out, motioning for Tava to sit.

"Callan, I couldn't possibly," she said softly, shaking her head slightly, her eyes going to the floor.

"Yes, Veda had requested to sit next to you tonight," Mikale cut in. "She is eager to hear tales of your travels."

"And I will be delighted to share them," Callan replied. "But she will be able to hear them just as well from another seat. Lady Tava will sit next to me."

"Why did my daughter arrive at the castle with you, your Highness?" Lord Tyndell asked, taking a seat down the table between Eva and Drake. Tava glanced at Callan demurely again while she lowered herself into the seat, and Callan sank into his own chair. He gave her a soft smile, his eyes fixed on hers when he answered, "I simply could not wait to see her when I arrived home."

"You could not wait to see *her*?" Veda demanded harshly, and heads turned in her direction. The look of disdain was quickly wiped from her face, and a pinched sort of smile appeared on her lips. "I mean, I did not realize you and Lady Tava were . . . close."

Callan reached for Tava's hand, bringing it up and pressing his lips to the back of it. "There is something to be said for exchanging letters and getting to know each other via ink and paper rather than monitored conversations and touches."

Tava's cheeks darkened further, and he had to wonder if that was all a complete farce. He kept her hand in his when he brought his gaze back to Veda. Her mouth was slightly agape in obvious shock as she stood frozen in place.

Mikale cleared his throat from down the table. "When did all of this . . . develop?"

Callan released Tava's hand to pour her a glass of wine as he said, "Interestingly enough, the evening of your engagement dinner to Miss Monrhoe. Where is she, by the way? I thought she would be with you."

Tava stiffened beside him. They had discussed how to spin their relationship, but bringing Scarlett into the conversation had never been brought up. She glanced at her brother across the table, taking the wine glass when Callan extended it to her.

"Our wedding was unfortunately delayed," Mikale said smoothly. "Her illness took a turn for the worse, and she is away seeking a treatment that will hopefully cure her of having to rely on that dreadful tonic."

"That would be wonderful," Tava cut in, taking a sip of her wine. "I do hope she finds what she's looking for on her travels."

Mikale's gaze slid to her, and the look he gave her had Callan tensing. He shot a look at Drake, who was glaring at Mikale from across the table.

"Do you mean to tell me that you have finally found someone, Callan?" his mother asked, her voice filled with hope. His mother had been trying to set him up with court Ladies for the last three years, constantly giving him lists of potential brides that would make for suitable partners. Before he could respond, she had turned to his father. "Isn't this wonderful, Theo?"

King Theodore was studying Callan closely, his chalice still in his hand, swirling the contents. "It will be wonderful news if he tells me they are betrothed," he finally answered.

"What?" Callan balked, his eyes going wide. Drake's glass

landed on the table a little harder than necessary, causing a slight thunking sound, and Tava had inhaled sharply.

"There was an agreement made," Mikale interjected, his fist slamming onto the table.

"Calm yourself, Mikale," Lord Tyndell chided from across the table. "I am going to assume they are not betrothed considering Tava is *my daughter*, and I was not asked for her hand."

"How could he when he has been off doing the gods-know-what all over the damn continent?" his father said tightly.

"I know you have questions about where I was and what I have been doing," Callan started, "but perhaps this can be discussed tomorrow, and not the moment I have returned."

"This will be discussed tonight, Callan," his father said, his deep voice rising, and his chalice banging down onto the table, wine sloshing over the side. "You have been gone for months, neglecting your responsibilities. I received correspondence once a week if I was lucky, and I still have no godsdamn idea what the fuck you were off doing!"

"Theodore!" his mother exclaimed. "Mind your tongue at the dinner table."

"Perhaps the women should take their leave so this can be discussed without your sensitivity then," the king snapped.

"Not until after we have eaten, Theo," his mother replied curtly, reaching for her own alcohol. "I have not seen my son in months. I will certainly be eating dinner with him and the Lady he is courting."

Silence wrought with thick tension settled in the room as servants entered with the first course of the evening. While plates were being placed in front of them, Callan felt a soft touch on his arm, and he turned to find Tava looking up at him. Her poise was perfect, but he could see the smallest glimmer of concern in her eyes. He gave her a tight smile, trying to reassure her, but he didn't know how this was going to play out. He'd thought his father would be pacified to simply know he was courting someone, but as he glanced at him from the corner of his eye, he knew that was not going to be the case. The king was livid.

Callan had only eaten a few spoonfuls of soup when Veda set her spoon down as she said into the tense quiet, "I am sorry to bring this back up again right now, but what exactly is happening here?"

Her eyes were narrowed on Tava, and Callan had the sudden urge to push Tava behind him and shield her from Veda's death glare. Tava, however, sat up a little straighter, dabbing at her mouth with her napkin before she said, "I really should be thanking you and Mikale for this actually."

"What?" Veda asked, her lips pursing.

"If it had not been for that engagement dinner for Mikale and Scarlett, this may have never happened. So really . . ." She glanced at Callan, giving him a shy smile before turning back to Veda and saying, "This is all because of you."

Callan had to fight the grin at the real meaning of those words, but he saw them hit home as Veda's features twisted into wrath. She had dark eyes naturally, but they seemed to go completely black as she stared back at Tava.

"I do not understand what you mean," Mikale ground out, and Tava leaned around Lord Lairwood to square off with Mikale now, too. Lord Lairwood was oddly silent, and Callan didn't know what to make of that. One would think he would be more upset about his daughter's chance at the throne being jeopardized, but he was watching his children warily, eating his soup.

"After you had to help Scarlett to her room that night, my brother was called away on some other business. Callan did not want me riding home alone. He insisted I ride with him in his carriage to make sure I arrived home safely. Quite silly of him, really, but who am I to deny a prince?"

She shrugged innocently, picking up her wine glass. "We had pleasant conversation and discovered a common love of books and preferring quiet over the bustle of daily life. Of course, he had to leave unexpectedly the next day, and I did not think anything of our time together, until his first letter arrived a week later. As more and more letters were exchanged, things just . . . happened."

She looked back at Callan, another smile gracing her lips. Her story had been so smooth, as if she'd rehearsed it for months, not merely discussed it with him a few hours ago.

"One could almost say it was fate," he added, picking up his own wine glass.

"One could say destiny is a fickle thing," she said with a small smile, echoing the Shifter's words from earlier that day. She was witty, this quiet, docile Lady.

"Did you know of this?" Lord Tyndell demanded, his attention fixed on Drake.

"I had no idea, Father," Drake answered, pushing his empty soup bowl back from him. "But I trust you are as excited as I am. I think they make a lovely match."

"Of course he is excited," Queen Meredith tittered, seemingly oblivious to the obvious tension around her, a servant refilling her chalice with wine. "His daughter is going to be the queen someday."

"It is settled then," the king said from the head of the table. "We can make an announcement first thing tomorrow."

"What? No," Callan said, unable to believe they were somehow back on him becoming engaged this very night.

"Enough!" his father barked, his fist slamming on to the table again. He lifted a finger, pointing it at Callan. "You have a responsibility to this kingdom, Callan."

"I know that!" Callan retorted, his own voice rising.

"Do you? Because the people of Windonelle just saw their Crown Prince disappear for months. We had to make up stories about your extended absence. How am I supposed to entrust you with the throne when you behave this way?"

"I can explain—"

"And you will," the king sneered. "But you will also start fulfilling your duties to this kingdom, and you will begin by taking a wife."

"Father, please," Callan said, gritting his teeth. "Let's discuss this further."

"Yes, let's discuss this further," Mikale ground out. "There was an agreement made regarding this matter."

"That was before my son returned with a potential bride," the king answered, picking up his soup spoon again.

"That voids your word?" Mikale demanded.

"Watch it, young Lord," the king snarled.

"Forgive me, your Majesty," Mikale said, his tone tight with restraint. "I am simply trying to understand to be better prepared to serve Callan as his Hand."

"A marriage will be much smoother if he has a say in the bride, Mikale," his father replied dismissively, reaching for a piece of bread from the basket before him. "Him returning already courting is far better than forcing him into a union."

"But you *are* forcing me into a union," Callan cut in.

"Would you rather I choose your bride then, Prince?" the king asked, his eyes cutting to him. "Would you rather we give you a princess for political purposes and power plays? Or you would like to continue courting the young woman sitting beside you?"

"I would like to continue courting her, yes, but that does not mean I am ready to ask for her hand," Callan countered.

"I am giving you the choice of who, not the choice of when," the king said. "An announcement will be made tomorrow morning either way. It is time to grow up, Callan. It is time to take your place in this kingdom."

Servants were silently clearing away dishes, preparing to bring out the next course, but Callan couldn't eat even if he'd wanted to. Asking Tava to pretend to be courting was one thing, but to ask this of her? They could have come up with a simple enough way to end a courtship, but an engagement?

"Balam, do something," Veda hissed from down the table, and her father's eyes snapped to her.

"Mind your manners, Veda," Lord Lairwood reprimanded. "You were raised better. You know your place."

"How are you not more upset by this?" Mikale demanded.

"I am sorry to interrupt, but I am failing to understand why Lord Mikale and Lady Veda are so upset by this demand," Tava cut in, her tone calm and collected, as though this wasn't turning into a colossal disaster. "It does not affect them nearly as much as it does myself and Prince Callan. Unless I am missing something?"

Callan caught a tiny smirk flit across Drake's face across the table before he quickly schooled his features back under control.

"You know damn well why we are upset," Veda spat, jabbing a finger in Tava's direction.

"Veda," Lord Lairwood admonished again. "Stop this nonsense at once, or you will be removed from this table."

"But Father—"

"Victor, are you concerned about the change of plans?" the king asked, as plates of meat and vegetables were placed in front of them. "Is there anything we need to discuss?"

"Of course not, your Majesty," Lord Lairwood replied, glaring at his daughter across the table. "I think your comments were wise regarding this union going smoother if Prince Callan has a say in the bride. He clearly already has an established relationship with Lady Tava, and her upbringing and bloodline are certainly suitable for the role of queen. A king happy in his marriage is better for the kingdom than one forced to endure the company of a woman he does not want."

"Father—" Veda tried again, but she was cut off by the king once more. "And you, Balam? Do you have an issue with your daughter becoming betrothed to Callan?"

A pointed smile spread across Lord Tyndell's face as he lifted his chalice. "It would be an honor," he said tightly.

Because what else could he say, Callan realized. It was not as if he could show how furious this made him. Why would a Lord be upset by his daughter being set on a path to become a queen? That was what every Lord dreamed of if they had a daughter. Saying he did not agree with this would open him up to more questions, and he clearly needed to regroup.

"Splendid," the king said tersely. "This matter is settled then, and there will be no more discussion of it this evening."

"That is it?" Callan demanded, his palms flattening on the table before him.

"Was I unclear with my wording, boy?" his father asked, his eyes narrowing on him.

Callan forced himself to bite his tongue on everything he wanted to say. Nothing he said right now was going to change his father's mind. That much was clear.

"No, sir," he answered tightly, pushing his chair back from the table. "But I do need a moment. Excuse me." He stood, striding for the doors, Finn and Sloan meeting his gaze with grim expressions.

"Sit back down, Callan," his father commanded, but another chair scraping sounded in the room. "You, too, Lady Tava."

"With all due respect, your Majesty, if you are going to force this union on us before we are ready, I am to be his wife, and it will be my duty to comfort him when he is upset. You will not keep me from going to him now, and you can give us a minute to adjust to the sudden demands placed upon us," Tava replied, strong and confident, her footsteps sounding as she made her way to him.

"Tava!" Lord Tyndell reprimanded.

But she didn't even glance at her father as she came to his side, slipping her arm around his. She pressed up on her tiptoes so she could speak into his ear. "Take me somewhere we can talk without prying ears, Callan."

Callan nodded, sliding his arm from hers to the small of her back. He led her up a set of stairs and down the hall where his rooms were at the end of it. He glanced at Finn, who nodded once, understanding the silent order that no one was to come near the door.

Pushing the door open, he stepped to the side to let Tava pass, following her in. He crossed to a window, pushing it open to feel the cold, winter air on his face, cooling his skin.

"That entire conversation I was waiting for you to comment about hot summer days," Callan said grimly, watching the snow fall, flakes glistening in the moonlight.

"Why? Those words are to be said when I want out or do not feel safe," she replied.

"How are you so calm about this?" Callan asked, running his hands through his hair.

"I am terrified, Callan," Tava answered. "You do not get brought into Scarlett's world of darkness without learning how to face monsters, but I am still not her. I am not as fearless as she is, even if I have learned how to keep my fear from showing."

"Perhaps if she were less fearless, things would be different. Perhaps if she feared *anything*, things would be different."

"She has fears."

"Do not defend her to me. Not when this is all because of her. Not when she is one of the monsters you speak of. She is what they want."

"I am not trying to defend her, Callan," Tava replied. "I am merely saying that, while she may be one of the monsters, she does not hide what she is. Not like they do."

"She wore so many masks. How could I possibly know what was real and what wasn't?" Callan retorted.

"She wears masks, yes, but knowing her, I can only assume she also gave you glimpses beyond them a time or two," Tava said gently.

Callan snorted bitterly. "I guess," he said, feeling Tava come up beside him. "She told me, over and over, I was not made for her darkness. That I was made to be in the light." Tava didn't say anything, letting him gather his thoughts. "If I had listened, perhaps we would not be in this mess."

"I think you and Scarlett meeting was necessary, even if it was brutal," Tava said softly. "We will need her."

"I do not need *her*," Callan snapped. Tava took a step back from him, her hand coming to her spirit amulet, her fingers twisting in the chain. "I am sorry," he said, turning to face the woman risking everything for . . . what? He didn't even know any more.

"No need to apologize."

"I certainly do need to apologize," he sighed. "I am taking things out on you that are not your fault."

"You are hurting, Callan," she said, her arms crossing and hands gripping her upper arms as she stepped towards the window. "Grief makes us say and do uncharacteristic things."

"I am not grieving anything," he said, trying to keep the bite from his tone.

Tava gave him a quick glance with a sad smile, but she didn't try to change his mind. Instead, she said, "My father is worried."

"That . . . is not how I gathered he was feeling," Callan replied, stepping to her side, his hands sliding into his pockets.

"No," she conceded, her head tilting to the side a little, golden hair slipping over her shoulder. "If you do not know what to look for, you would not know he is concerned."

"Concerned because of what my father is demanding?" Callan asked curiously.

Her lips pursed before she said, "I think it is more so concern for how their plans are being altered and affected. Not so much concern for me or our apparent engagement."

"Tava," Callan said, reaching for her elbow and gently turning her to face him. "If you do not want to do this, if you want an out, I understand. Finn and Sloan can get you out of here discreetly. I can try to talk to my father again . . ."

Another soft, sad smile lifted on her lips, making him trail off.

"While I was not anticipating this turn of events, our plan is working, Callan," she said. "My father and Mikale are nervous."

Nervous? Furious maybe, but he wasn't sure he'd say they were nervous. If anything, he felt as though they'd given them more of a reason to come after them. The way Veda had glared at Tava . . .

"I do not know that nervous is the right way to describe how they are feeling, Tava," he ventured.

"Their tempers may have been on display this evening, but they are shaken, Callan," she answered, turning back to the window, stretching a hand out over the sill into the night and letting flakes gather in her palm. They instantly melted against her warm skin.

"Can you explain why you think that?"

"My entire life I have been pushed to the outer edges of my father's world," she said with a slight shrug. "You see a lot of things when you are on the fringes of society. You watch people. You learn to read people, especially those you are closest to. When you are seen as quiet and meek, people tend to assume you are nothing to worry about." She shrugged again, as if everything she had just said was not a big deal.

But she'd just confirmed his earlier suspicions. The things she knew were more than just things that could ruin a person socially. She knew the small tells that betray when someone was lying. When someone was anxious. She knew their ticks, the little mannerisms, the slight facial expressions.

And that was arguably more dangerous than any secret.

"They want Veda at your side," she continued, when he didn't say anything. "For what reason? I do not know. I can only assume it is because she is Mikale's sister. They must think that if she were queen, she would have more control over the kingdom."

"What do they want control over Windonelle for? I thought they wanted Scarlett."

Ocean blue eyes settled back on his. "That is the question, isn't it?"

CHAPTER 16
SCARLETT

When she came up from the depths of slumber this time, she couldn't clear her head. It was fuzzy. Sound was muffled. Her vision was blurred when she tried to open her eyes. Her mouth was dry.

And she wasn't chained in the dungeon study.

Her ankle chains were anchored to the floor. Her wrists were still shackled, but they weren't suspended above her head. She could freely move her arms. She was lying on the floor, the stone cool against her cheek, and she sucked in a sharp breath as memories surged up.

She pried her eyes open, and then she couldn't breathe at all. The room around her came into focus, and she realized where she was. She was still in the dungeons of the Fellowship, but this room had a drain in the center. This room had manacles on the walls. A chair to be restrained in. A table to be strapped to. It had numerous devices to inflict immeasurable pain.

And chained to the wall across from her was Cassius.

Scarlett jerked upright, her head throbbing in pain. All she could hear was the rush of blood pulsing in her ears.

"No," she whispered, crawling across the floor as far as she could go.

Her knees split open through the thin gown as she struggled to get to him. "Cassius."

His eyes were fixed on her, wide and full of dread. He looked exhausted, as if he'd been struggling against his restraints for hours, yet he still let out a bellow of rage around the gag in his mouth as he watched her dragging herself across the floor to get to him. Not that it mattered. Her ankle chains stopped her, her fingers a foot from his bare feet.

This was a vision. It had to be. Lord Tyndell was doing this to her. She'd heard nothing from the Assassin Lord since he had left the study to verify Callan was back. That had been at least two days ago. Tarek or Mikale had been giving her the tonic they were forcing her to swallow along with small meals. Mikale never answered her when she asked about the status of Callan, and she'd stopped speaking to Tarek after their last conversation.

It's not real, she told herself over and over again. *It can't be real.*

"The Guardian bond is so much more powerful when the Guardian chooses it for himself, rather than being forced into it," came Alaric's cold voice from the corner of the room. She heard his footfalls on the stones, but her eyes stayed fixed on Cassius. He was pale, and she could see every ounce of apology and regret shining in his brown eyes.

She tried to swallow, but her throat was too dry. She felt the tears welling at the back of her eyes, as those footsteps came to a stop beside her. This was it. This was checkmate. This was what would break her. She didn't know what the choice would be, but she had no doubt it would end with Cassius losing his life.

Scarlett couldn't take her eyes off of Cassius, as she felt Alaric lower to a crouch beside her and slowly stroke her hair, as if trying to soothe her. His hood was down. Apparently, he had deemed Cassius worthy of knowing his identity before he killed him.

"His need to protect you goes beyond any magical bond enacted, when it is entered into willingly. He may not feel your physical pain like he once did, but he has been quite tortured seeing you lying here unconscious these last several hours."

Two tears slid free, and Cassius slowly shook his head. She knew he was trying to tell her not to cry, not to show weakness. She knew he was trying to convey how much this was not her fault. She knew if he could speak to her right now, he would tell her this sacrifice was worth it and not to blame herself or carry this guilt with her.

But none of that helped. None of that eased the splintering happening inside her chest.

"He was furious when I told him how I had Tarek drug you with your last meal," Alaric continued, reaching over and swiping the tears away with his thumb. "It was the . . . safest way to get things into place for this next bit of business."

He stood back up and walked to a low table, swiping up a dagger before coming to stand by Cassius. Scarlett saw Cassius's breathing increase, his chest rising and falling faster and faster as he mentally prepared for what he was about to endure.

"What he said was true," Alaric mused, studying the dagger in his hand. "Prince Callan has returned."

Scarlett's breath hitched at the words. She finally broke her gaze with Cassius, turning her head to look up at Alaric. His jaw was clenched tight, his shoulders tense. He seemed to be lost in thought as he tapped the tip of the dagger against his finger.

"If Callan has returned, then why is Cassius chained to the wall?" she demanded, her voice hoarse and raw.

His black eyes slowly came to hers, and Scarlett had to fight the urge to flinch back from him. "Callan has returned, but he returned betrothed to someone," he gritted out.

Her brows flew up, and her head whipped to Cassius, who looked as surprised as she was. He shook his head again to tell her he had no idea what Alaric was talking about.

"Yes, we were all quite surprised by it. Especially Balam," Alaric continued. "Considering he is betrothed to Tava Tyndell."

Scarlett couldn't help the bubble of hollow laughter that escaped from her lips. Somehow, some way, they had learned of the plans to force Callan into a marriage to Veda and had saved him from that fate.

And Tava. Brilliant godsdamn Tava.

Tava would be on the inside, next to a man who felt nothing but contempt for Scarlett these days. She would be a source of information for the others.

"I am failing to see the humor here, Death's Maiden," Alaric said coldly.

Another breath of laughter escaped her. "You've spent centuries putting things into motion, carefully laying plans, and then Lord Tyndell's own daughter derails them. The humor is the irony. One would think Lord Tyndell would be thrilled."

Without warning, that dagger in his hand went into Cassius's thigh, right atop the place he had been stabbed by Veda nearly two years ago. Cassius bellowed around the gag in his mouth, and

Scarlett screamed, lurching forward only to be halted violently by the chains.

"Stop!" she cried. "Stop!"

But he didn't. Instead, Alaric twisted that dagger in deeper. Cassius was jerking against his chains, the veins in his neck straining as he endured the pain.

Alaric left the dagger in his leg and dropped down to a crouch before her, taking her chin in his hand and tilting her face up to his. "I have given you time. I told you what the consequences of continued disobedience would be. This is your fault, Scarlett. *You* have caused this fate."

Scarlett tried to shake her head in denial. She tried to look at Cassius over Alaric's shoulder, but he refused to allow her such movement. "We will work around this thing with Tava and Callan. That is not a be-all, end-all issue. But while I am dealing with that, I need to know where the Black Syndicate orphans are." She tried to jerk back from him at the words, but his grip on her chin only tightened, becoming bruising. "You will tell me, Scarlett. I am through playing games. For every hour you do not tell me, you bestow more pain upon your Guardian."

Alaric shoved her away from him as he stood, and she fell back, catching herself on her elbows. He jerked the dagger roughly from Cassius's thigh, causing another bellow of pain. He pulled the gag from his mouth in the next breath.

"Maybe you can talk some sense into your charge," he snarled at Cassius. "Your life depends on it. I will be back in an hour."

Alaric wrenched the door open, stalking out, but before it swung closed, Tarek strolled in.

"What are you doing here?" Scarlett demanded.

Tarek tsked under his breath. "You didn't really think he would leave you two alone in here, did you?"

"We have never been alone, Scarlett," Cassius said from between gritted teeth, drawing her attention back to him. "Someone was always here while you were out."

"I am so sorry, Cassius," she whispered, her voice catching.

"Look at me, Seastar."

But she couldn't. She couldn't meet his gaze.

"Now, Scarlett," he commanded.

Blue eyes met brown ones brimming with intensity. "This is not your fault. Do you understand me?"

"This is Juliette all over again, Cass," she breathed. "I cannot do this. Losing you—" She swallowed down the sob that cracked her voice. "I will not come back from this, Cassius."

"You will, Scarlett. You will have Sorin and the others from—"

"They are not you!" she cried. "Yes, I love Sorin. Yes, he is my twin flame. But you are as much a part of me as he is. I will not survive this."

"You will, Scarlett," Cassius repeated. "You will survive this because you must. You will survive this because others depend on you. You will survive this because when it is all over, I know Sorin will give you a place to rest. To heal. To live. Hang on, Seastar. Hang on just a little longer. Promise me you will hang on."

She was shaking her head, tears streaming down her face.

"I will make the choice for you, Scarlett. You do not need to make it. I choose the innocents. I choose the children. Let me do this for them. Let *me* make this choice," he begged.

She reached for him again, wishing she could just fucking touch him. Blood continued to spread from the wound, soaking into his pants. "What difference will it make?" she asked. "When you are gone, he will just find another thing to threaten me with."

"You know he will not leave you behind, right? That he will come for you," Cassius said, his voice so quiet she almost didn't hear him. His features had softened slightly, and a small smile graced his lips as he looked down at her.

Scarlett pushed herself up, drawing her knees into her chest and looping her arms around them. She rested her chin atop them as she stared up at Cassius. "If the prick by the wall wasn't in here, I would have so much to tell you," she said.

That small smile tilted up a little more. "I'm sure there are other tales you could tell while we wait," he replied, shifting slightly and trying to hide his grimace.

So she did. She told him of the Fiera Mountains and the Tana River and the Twilight Wildfires. They reminisced over days past, of moving through the night and drinking more than anyone should. They talked about when they were younger and he would take her to pick pears in the groves. He teased her about how awful she was with a sword when he first started training her, and she teased him about how she'd surpassed his skill.

And when Alaric would return, every hour just as he promised, when he would ask where the orphans were and Scarlett would press her lips together in refusal, her eyes stayed on Cassius, lending him strength the only way she knew how. She did not cry for him. She did not beg on his behalf. She gave him this gift of letting his suffering not be for nothing. When he was gone, she would shatter so completely that not even Sorin would be able to reach her any more, but until then, she would give him this. She kept her eyes on him, to remind him he was not alone. She became his final star in the darkness.

CHAPTER 17
SORIN

Sorin stalked down the streets of Baylorin, cloak on and hood up, hiding his features. Beneath the cloak were his fighting leathers and every possible weapon he could carry. Eliza, Cyrus, and Luan prowled beside him, along with Arianna, who had shifted to look like Mikale.

Nuri had pouted incessantly about being left behind again, but they didn't have much of a choice. They hadn't heard from Cassius since he'd been summoned by the Assassin Lord three days ago. Sorin was hoping it was because he was with Scarlett, but he knew that was likely not the case. He also knew if the Commander was being held at the Fellowship as well, they couldn't leave without him either. He could only hope he was easy to find. They needed to be in and out as quickly and discreetly as possible. As much as he wanted to kill every motherfucker who had a part in this, they couldn't leave a trail of bodies in their wake.

Not tonight, anyway.

But Nuri had still been invaluable. She'd spent the last three days working to get as many people as she knew they could trust into place, putting them on the rooftops so they'd turn blind eyes as they approached the Black Syndicate. There weren't many who would dare to cross the Assassin Lord, but those who would apparently had their own grudges against the man and welcomed any excuse to go against him. Sorin hadn't questioned it further, trusting that Nuri knew who they could count on and who they couldn't. If they came into direct contact with any of the men on their side, Nuri had given them a codeword that would be said immediately. If they weren't close enough to say the word, they knew to get out of the way.

Because there would be no second chances this night. There would be no hesitation.

When he stepped foot in the Black Syndicate tonight, he would be leaving with his queen.

On top of that, Nuri had set up an elaborate diversion that she swore would draw out the Assassin Lord. She'd told Sorin not to worry about the details, just to trust that he would be occupied for a good amount of time. He didn't have it in him to push her further. If it would get Scarlett back to him, then he was on board with the plan.

As for Mikale and Lord Tyndell, they'd been trailing them and learning their routines. Mikale was usually gone from the Fellowship in the evenings to have dinner with his father and Veda before heading back to the Black Syndicate in the later hours of the night. Lord Tyndell's visits to the Black Syndicate seemed sporadic and only happened when he received word from a messenger. They had eyes on them tonight with plans in place to keep them occupied if needed as well.

"Archers on the rooftops," Eliza muttered beside him.

"I see them. It appears they are Nuri's," Sorin replied, a lethal calmness settling over him.

They rounded a corner and found themselves on the main road through the Syndicate. The last time he'd been here was in the light of day. Tonight they were under the cover of the waning moon.

He was immediately pulled into memories of Scarlett bringing him here the first time. Of watching her scale brick walls and flit along rooftops. Of dining at a little cafe in a back alley. Of watching her care for children.

Of watching the Assassin Lord hit her and force her to her knees before him.

"Easy, Sorin," Cyrus muttered from his left, and Sorin inhaled deeply through his nose, quieting the flames in his veins and sparks filling the edges of his vision. The Fellowship was just ahead, and as they drew closer, he could feel the faint hum of wards. He hadn't felt that before, but then again, Scarlet hadn't taken him this close to the Fellowship grounds either.

The plan was to leave Luan and Eliza outside the Fellowship.

They couldn't risk their only Traveler getting caught. They'd be waiting for them at the exact spot they could Travel from to get back to the warehouse. Arianna had said the wards took effect as soon as she'd crossed the gates to the grounds, and as they drew closer, two armed men stood, exactly as Nuri said they would be. She was going to try to have people in place, but she couldn't promise anything.

And Sorin really didn't give a fuck at this point. He stepped towards them, Eliza at his side. The men reached for weapons, but before they had a chance to draw them, they had hands clamped over their mouths and daggers in their hearts. Sorin would have preferred to slit their throats and listen to them drown in their own blood, but he supposed a blood trail would be just as problematic as a body trail.

Luan and Eliza would be posing as the guards they'd killed, waiting for him, Cyrus, and Arianna to return. Sorin and Cyrus helped drag the dead guards to the shadows where they wouldn't be seen, and Arianna led the way in as Luan and Eliza took up their posts.

Sorin and Cyrus tugged their hoods lower over their faces, double-checking weapons strapped beneath their cloaks. His flames instantly guttered when he walked through the gates, and a glance at Cyrus told him he'd felt it, too. Eliza, Cyrus, and Arianna had taken strong doses of the tonic to make sure they could access their magic tonight, but that meant nothing with these wards. He had to agree with the Shifter Beta. He'd never experienced wards like these.

Cyrus wrenched the main doors open, and they found an empty foyer, but they heard muffled voices from a corridor to the left. Arianna strode straight ahead, heading to a doorway behind the grand staircase that wound up to the levels above them. They passed a few men along the way, but they took one look at Arianna in Mikale's form and continued on, clearly unconcerned. No one spared him or Cyrus a second glance.

When they pushed open the door that led down to what he'd been told were the holding cells, a guard stepped into their path.

"Lord Lairwood," he said gruffly with a nod of his head. He had short, cropped blonde hair, and his light brown eyes shifted to Sorin and Cyrus. "Who've you got with you?"

"Is that any of your business?" Arianna growled, Mikale's voice low and threatening.

"Well . . . yeah," the man said, running a hand over his head. "There are only certain guards allowed down there right now. He said I'm supposed to make sure everyone has clearance so . . ." He trailed off, clearly uncomfortable with having to question who he thought was Mikale.

"They are with me. Is that not proof enough that they have permission to be down here?" Arianna demanded.

"Listen, my Lord, I'm just doing my job. I don't ask questions," he answered, lifting his palms placatingly. "But if someone gets down there who isn't supposed to be, it's my ass."

"You don't even know what you are guarding?" Sorin asked.

"Not my place to know," the man answered.

"What if he is doing horrendous things?" Sorin pushed.

The man snorted a laugh. "We're assassins. We were trained to do horrendous things."

"To innocent people?"

"Not my concern," he answered with a shrug. "My concern is who the fuck you are, and if you're allowed to be down there."

"That is no longer your only concern," Sorin said calmly. Between one breath and the next, the man had a dagger in the side of his head.

"Sorin," Cyrus sighed, bending down to drag the man to a corner where, hopefully, no one would stumble upon him until they were long gone. "We need a low body count."

"We had a problem. I took care of it," Sorin answered, wiping the dagger off on the dead man's shirt.

"We cannot kill every problem, Sorin," Cyrus said. "Not this time."

"We also do not have time to sit and debate this," Sorin answered, gesturing at Arianna to continue leading the way.

The dungeon halls were eerily empty. Every once in a while they passed a cell that was occupied, but that was it. The people in those cells, though? They were clearly being starved. Their eyes were hollow and sunk in. How long had they been down here? And why?

His thoughts turned back to Scarlett as he followed Arianna deeper and deeper into this underground network of halls and rooms. He didn't know what state she was going to be in. Arianna had said she was chained and seemed thin and weak, but she didn't have anything to compare her to. She'd never met Scarlett before.

Or he was trying to convince himself she wasn't in the state Arianna had described.

They continued down more halls, their footsteps seeming to echo off the walls no matter how much they tried to soften them.

"How much farther?" he asked in a low voice.

"Assuming she is in the same room, just around the corner," Arianna answered.

But when they reached what appeared to be a study of some sort, the room was empty. There were places to anchor shackles on the wall beside a large wooden desk. A sofa stood along the wall, and everything was neat and orderly. And her scent. Citrus and embers. Jasmine and lavender and night. It lingered in the room.

Arianna hesitated just inside the doorway. "This is where she was," she said, Mikale's voice sounding strained.

"Then we check the other rooms down here before we start searching the upper levels," Cyrus cut in before Sorin could lose his godsdamn mind.

They had planned for this. Nuri had given a list of the most likely places she would have been moved to, starting with the private dungeon rooms the Assassin Lord used for his personal business and moving progressively up through the other floors. His private wing would be the hardest section to gain access to, but was also a likely place she could be. They made quick work of the first few rooms. The doors were open and clearly empty as they passed, but as they rounded a corner and found three men standing outside a door, they'd obviously found the room they were looking for.

The men glanced at Mikale, but as soon as they saw Sorin and Cyrus, weapons were drawn as they approached.

"He said only you and—"

The man didn't get to finish what he was saying as a dagger left Cyrus's hand and lodged itself in his throat.

"What happened to not killing every problem?" Sorin asked with a smirk, drawing a sword to meet the other two men now running towards them. One didn't make it past Arianna as she drew a blade as fast as any Night Child, slicing it across his middle and then his throat when he dropped to his knees.

"I thought I'd follow the lead of my prince," Cyrus retorted.

Sorin swung his sword, slicing clean through the remaining man's neck, his head rolling in the opposite direction of his body. He could have used fire, he supposed, but they'd all agreed to save the small bit of power they might be able to access. Despite Arianna's claims and the wards he had felt, he could still feel his flames. He knew he could access them, likely because of the ring he wore. It was to be used only as a last resort inside the wards.

"Scarlett would be so proud," Sorin said mockingly.

Cyrus rolled his eyes. "She would have said fuck covertness, announced her arrival, and then made a competition out of who could make the most kills."

Sorin barked a laugh at the accuracy of that statement, but it quickly died in his throat as they stopped before the heavy wood door. He swallowed thickly before he reached for the handle. It wasn't locked. They'd apparently believed the various obstacles they'd put in place, along with the wards, to be enough. He stepped into the room, and then clamped down on the snarl that wanted to claw its way out of his chest.

She was here, sitting on the stone floor, her ankles and wrists in shackles, just as Arianna had said. Her wrists weren't anchored above her head though. Her arms were wrapped tightly around her knees that were curled to her chest. Her ankle chains were anchored to the floor, however, and her chin was resting on her knees. Silver hair hung limp around her shoulders, and she wore a black gown that, from what he could tell, was partially sheer.

He pushed his hood back, taking another step into the room. "Scarlett," he whispered.

But he stopped short when she lifted her head at her name. Her face was covered in grime and flecks of blood, tear-trails cutting a path through it all. Her eyes were a muted silvery-blue, and they were vacant, hollow.

More haunted than he had ever seen them.

When you find her, she will not be the same as when she left.

Her eyes moved up and down him warily before she returned her head to her knees.

Arianna's description had been true. She was pale. She was far too thin, but even without much food, she shouldn't be this thin. Not in only a few weeks. He could make out bruises and cuts along her wrists and ankles where the shirastone cut into her skin.

"Is she in—" Cyrus started, coming into the room behind him but stopping short at the sight of their queen.

Scarlett's head lifted again at the sound of Cyrus's voice, and her head tilted slightly to the side. Her brows knitted together, and her nose scrunched in confusion for a moment before her head went back to her knees once more.

"If that is Cassius..." Cyrus said slowly, and Sorin realized that Scarlett was staring at a figure on the floor a few feet from her. He had been so focused on finally laying eyes on her, he hadn't taken in the rest of the room.

It was indeed Cassius, just out of her reach. He was bleeding from multiple places, puddles of blood pooling beneath him. His leg was at an unnatural angle, and the bruises marring his face made him almost unrecognizable.

"Is he..." Sorin said softly, his eyes going back to his wife, where she stared unblinkingly at the motionless body. Sorin couldn't say the words aloud. He didn't want her to hear them, as if voicing them would make it more real for her.

Cyrus made his way to Cassius, lowering beside him and reaching to check for a pulse. A flicker of relief flashed in his golden eyes. "He's not. Not yet. But his breathing is shallow." He glanced quickly to Scarlett, then back to Sorin again before saying, "He doesn't have long."

Sorin nodded once and took a deep breath before moving to Scarlett. He slowly lowered down to his knees before her. He reached out to cup her cheek, just to fucking touch her after not having done so for weeks, but she lurched back from him. Her chains scraped along the stones, and Sorin froze at the sound, his eyes widening.

He held up his hands placatingly in front of him, showing her his palms. "Okay," he breathed. "Okay, Love. I will not touch you."

Her gaze snapped to his as he spoke, but he had no idea why as she looked him up and down again. He took another deep breath, trying to decide what the fuck to do, because he didn't know. He didn't know what she'd experienced. He didn't know what had been done to her. And he couldn't fucking feel her. He couldn't reach her. He couldn't speak into her mind because she'd blocked their damn bond.

"I will get Arianna. She can use the key, and we can go," Cyrus said quietly.

Sorin nodded, not even glancing at his Second, his eyes fixed on his twin flame. Her gaze bounced from him to Cyrus before settling back on Cassius. He slowly lowered his hands, wiping his palms along his leathers.

"Hey, Love," he said gently. "You are going to be okay."

She didn't look at him, didn't show any sign that she'd heard him.

Cyrus and Arianna came in the door, and Scarlett's eyes narrowed in suspicion as they approached her, before going back to Cassius, her head returning to her knees.

That was her only reaction to who she thought was Mikale entering the room?

Sorin ran a hand through his hair at a complete and utter loss. She hadn't said a godsdamn word. She hadn't made a godsdamn sound. Could she? Had Alaric done something to her so that she could no longer speak? Was she in too much shock? At least when she had retreated into her soul on the journey to the Fire Court, he could feel her. He could sense her, even if it was a muted bond. Here, with her Blood Mark in full effect, he didn't know what to do. He felt utterly helpless. He had failed her. He had been too late. They had waited too long.

He felt a hand on his shoulder. Cyrus stared down at him, concern and understanding on his features, knowing he was struggling. He jerked his chin to tell him to move aside. Sorin pushed to his feet, moving closer to Arianna and letting Cyrus take his place.

"Hi, Darling," Cyrus said softly, and Scarlett stiffened before dragging her eyes to his. "I know it looks like we're here with this bastard, but rest assured, if it were truly him, he would not be breathing. I would be laying his corpse at your feet as a gift."

Scarlett sucked in a breath, but she still said nothing.

"This is Arianna Renatus," he continued, gesturing to where she stood. "She is the Beta of the Shifters. Her wearing that fucker's skin is how we got in, and she is how we will get you out." Scarlett's gaze flickered once to Arianna before meeting Sorin's briefly.

"Scarlett," Cyrus said softly, reaching for the chain. She clearly interpreted it as him reaching for her, though, as she lurched back from him.

"Love," Sorin croaked, unable to keep himself from taking a step towards her. "Love, let us help you. Let us get you out," he begged. "Please."

"I'm not going to touch you," Cyrus said quietly. "And neither is she. But she studied your chains a few days ago, Scarlett. She was here before. I am told you kicked her little mouse butt off of your foot when she was trying to get closer to your ankle manacles."

At those words, her entire demeanor physically changed, and she began trembling. Her hands came to her mouth, stifling some sort of cry. Her chains rattled with her tremors as tears welled in her eyes.

"Gods, Scarlett," Sorin pleaded. "Please let me come to you." Seeing her like this was pure torture.

But she shook her head, denying him.

"Take these off," she rasped, her eyes going to Arianna. Her voice was raw and hoarse, but it was her voice, even if he recognized nothing else about her right now, and the sound of it still nearly brought him to his knees.

Arianna nodded, taking Cyrus's place before her. She pulled the iron she'd shaped into the key from her pocket. "I made this before we came," she explained, Mikale's voice spilling from the Shifter's lips. "There are wards around this building that prevent me from being able to shift anything inside them."

Scarlett's eyes narrowed, but she nodded for the Shifter to continue. Arianna slipped the key into the lock that was keeping her ankle chains secured to the floor. The moment it fell open, Scarlett was crawling across the floor. She didn't wait for the shirastone shackles to be removed. Her arms nearly gave out as she pulled herself across the stones until she was next to Cassius. Carefully, as if she knew exactly where each injury he had was located, she draped herself over him, nestling into his side. Blood soaked into her dress and added to the grime already on her skin as her head came to rest on his chest.

Arianna crept forward carefully, reaching tentatively for her ankle shackles. She fitted the key into them, and a frown formed on her lips. "These are different from the first lock," she said. "This key will not work. I can figure it out once we are away from these wards."

Scarlett buried her face in Cassius's bloody chest, clutching at his shredded tunic, her trembling increasing.

"We are going to get them off, Scarlett," Sorin said thickly, cautiously coming to her side again. "But we need to get you out of here first."

"How are we going to do this?" Cyrus asked from his side.

They had been prepared to possibly have to carry Scarlett from here if she was not well enough to walk out herself, but they had not anticipated having to carry the Commander out as well.

There was no way Scarlett was going to let them leave him here, even if he was likely to not make it out of the Fellowship still breathing.

"One of us needs to carry Cassius, the other needs to be free to access weapons," Cyrus continued. "Arianna, can you carry the queen?"

"Yes," the Shifter answered. "If she will allow such a thing."

Sorin hated the idea of anyone other than him carrying her out of this hellhole, but he nodded in agreement. "I will get her for you. It will likely look more believable if Mikale is carrying her out anyway. Cyrus, you grab Cassius. I will make sure our way out is clear."

Arianna nodded, stepping back to wait for the handoff, and Cyrus walked around to Cassius's other side, lowering down once more.

"Darling," he said softly, swallowing thickly when she didn't even lift her head. "Scarlett, we will bring him with us. You can say goodbye outside of here, without chains." She showed no reaction. No sign that she had heard them. Cyrus glanced up at Sorin, regret heavy in his gaze. "You're going to have to force her. We're lucky no one has come in since we've arrived the way it is. We need to get moving."

"Come, Scarlett," Sorin said, his tone firming and becoming a command. He reached for her, and the moment his fingers touched her shoulders to pull her off of Cassius's body, a snarl emanated from her. Her head whipped up, and her eyes were bright with rage.

"Where is Mikale?" she rasped. "Where are Alaric and Lord Tyndell and Tarek?"

"Tarek?" Cyrus asked, his eyes widening in horror. "Love," Sorin said slowly. "Who is Tarek?"

Her lip curled into a sneer, and it was Death's Maiden who peered out from those silvery-blue orbs. "A male whose days are numbered," she hissed. "Where are they?"

"We do not have time to go into all the details, Scarlett," Sorin answered, resisting the urge to reach out and tuck her hair back. "Nuri created a diversion of sorts, but they will likely figure it out soon if they have not already. We need to go."

"They already know you are here," she answered. "They would have felt you the moment you crossed the wards."

"All the more reason we need to go," Sorin said, moving to reach for her again, but her grip tightened on Cassius's shredded shirt. "Scarlett," he begged. "Please. We need to go."

"Go where?"

"Back to the warehouse, then home," he answered.

"How will we get there?"

"Eliza and Luan are waiting for us. He will Travel us if you cannot."

"Sorin," Cyrus gritted out, his tone conveying his warning that they needed to get moving.

"Come to me, Love," Sorin coaxed. "Cyrus will carry Cassius. Arianna can carry you."

"I will walk," she replied hoarsely, eyeing Cyrus as though she thought he might leave Cassius here, before she slowly eased her grip on the shredded fabric. Sorin reached for her, helping her to her feet. As soon as she was standing, she pulled away from him again, swaying slightly. She watched as Cyrus lifted Cassius over his shoulder as carefully as he could, and when she was satisfied, she turned to Arianna. "You need to act like you are escorting me. Mikale never carries me unless I physically cannot walk, and even then he prefers to drag me along behind him."

Sorin snarled at that, and Scarlett glanced at him, tilting her head once more as she studied him. Her eyes snagged on his hands, and she leaned forward slightly. "Let me see your ring," she demanded, her chains rattling as she held out her palm to him.

"I need your ring to access my magic, Love," he replied, his fist clenching.

"Not that one," she answered, hand still outstretched.

He looked down at his left hand, where his marriage band encircled his finger. He slowly pulled it off, placing it in her palm. She held it up before her, studying it intently, as she murmured so softly he barely heard her, "Do you still see the light?"

"Yes, my Love." He stepped closer to her. "There are still stars to fight for."

"Perhaps," she muttered, more to herself than to him, as she extended his ring back to him.

He took it from her, letting his fingers brush hers, and she sucked in a sharp breath.

"You are sure you can walk?" he asked, sliding the ring back onto his finger.

She looked dramatically down at her feet. "It would certainly appear so."

"And here I thought we had found a better use for your tongue," he retorted, relief flooding through him at the brief glimpse of her snark.

Her lips twitched slightly, and he thought she was going to smile, before she turned and began making her way to the door. "Grip my arm. Turn right when we exit," she said, stopping beside Arianna.

"But the way out is to the left," the Shifter argued, reaching out to take Scarlett's arm as instructed.

"The odds of us getting out of here are slim the way it is. Although if this is Lord Tyndell's doing again, I suppose it doesn't much matter," Scarlett answered, swaying on her feet again, and making Sorin lurch for her. "The point is, I know a more discreet path out."

They didn't have time to question her at this point, and Sorin pulled the door open, allowing Arianna and Scarlett out first. Scarlett glanced down at the dead guard outside the room, bending down to swipe a dagger from the corpse.

They made their way down the hall, Cyrus keeping pace beside Sorin as the Commander steadily dripped blood, leaving a trail behind them.

"We need to go left up ahead," Scarlett murmured when they approached the end of the hall. He watched her shift the dagger she held, hiding it as best she could in her gown. "There will be guards. They are beneath you. Should they try to stop you, tell them if they question you again, they will answer to the Lord himself. Be convincing."

They rounded the corner moments later, and sure enough, four guards stood at the end of the hall before a stairwell. They straightened as their group approached, two reaching for short swords. Sorin tensed, his hand going to his own weapon.

"Where do you think you are going?" one of the assassin guards sneered.

"I did not realize I answered to you," Arianna growled back, Mikale's voice hard and gruff, and Scarlett flinched. Sorin didn't know if it was an act or a natural reaction to his voice.

"No one is allowed up this stairwell without permission," the guard retorted, his eyes sweeping up and down Scarlett, making no attempt to hide his perusal of her body.

"You are questioning me?" Arianna demanded, twisting Mikale's features into rage.

"If it were just you, no, but all of you . . ." the guard replied hesitantly.

"If I turn around, trust I will return with the Lord, and you can explain to him why there is a delay in our plans," Arianna snarled, stepping forward and tugging Scarlett roughly along with her.

The guard glanced at his companions, and Arianna pulled a dagger from her cloak, bringing it to the guard's throat. "Let me rephrase that. The others will explain why we are delayed. *You* will be bleeding out at the base of these stairs."

The guard swallowed, nodding slightly as he stepped to the side, the others following his lead. They climbed the stairs, Scarlett stumbling and tripping several times, but Sorin didn't dare say anything in case they ran into others.

When they reached the next floor, Scarlett spoke between labored breaths. "We shouldn't run into anyone else. This is Alaric's private living wing. His closest are allowed in this wing. Some of us have rooms here. Up the stairs and down a hall, we would come to his private suite." She gestured to the stairs. "No one is ever allowed in there, but that way," she said, pointing down a hall to the right, "leads to a private exit. There will be guards outside in the yard. You will need to kill them or be killed," she finished simply.

"How many guards can we expect?" Sorin asked, stepping closer to her on the vacant landing. He brought a hand to her back to steady her, but she stepped from his touch.

"Normally, there are only a couple, but as I said, he's been expecting you. He already knows you are here. He could be waiting for you himself, and he is prepared for the fire you wield," she answered indifferently.

"What does that mean?" Cyrus demanded, his breathing heavy from carrying Cassius up the stairs.

"I do not know," she answered with a shrug, her chains rattling slightly. "He did not tell me that."

"Which side of the Fellowship will we come out on?" Sorin asked. "The south," Scarlett answered. "If we survive, there are paths leading both east and west. We can take whichever is necessary."

"We go out together," Sorin replied. "Cyrus, start heading east to Eliza and Luan immediately. Scarlett go with him. Arianna and I will handle the fighting."

"I have a dagger," Scarlett scoffed.

"You are in chains and can hardly stand," Sorin countered.

Scarlett's jaw clenched, and she averted her eyes, looking down at her bare feet. "I have faced so much worse. This is nothing." She inhaled deeply before lifting her head once more and heading off down the hall, leading the way.

Sorin fell into step beside her, Arianna falling back to guard Cyrus. He saw Scarlett glance at him out of the corner of her eye before she quickly fixed her gaze forward once more. She halted a few feet from a door, turning to face him. "This is likely Lord Tyndell messing with my mind again, but on the off chance it is not . . . please don't die."

Sorin smirked at her. "I will do my best, Princess."

Her lips twitched again, but the smile still didn't form. "There are not many stars left."

"You are my necessity," Sorin answered, the smirk falling from his lips. "I will always come for you."

He thought she might reach for him. He was praying to Anala she would, but instead she nodded once before turning back and going to the door. He watched as she rolled her shoulders back and breathed deep before she pushed the door open, and he moved to follow her out into the night.

He only had one foot over the threshold when she was swinging her dagger. She slammed it into the chest of a guard standing just outside the door. She'd clearly known he would be there, and he growled at the fact that she'd gone first instead of telling him.

Because of course she had.

She darted out into the darkness, tripping over her chains as she began to run on the path, catching herself with her hands. Her dagger skittered from her grasp. She was back up before Sorin could reach her, and he cursed under his breath that she wouldn't let him touch her, let alone help her.

He heard the arrow whizzing his way seconds before he caught the shaft of it in his hand. He snapped it in two, before pulling a knife from the bandolier across his chest, cocking his arm back, and throwing it at the assassin who'd aimed for him, striking true. He crumpled to the ground, the knife embedded deep in his skull.

Sorin whirled to look for Scarlett. She had her wrist chains around another guard's neck, struggling to pull him back against her to finish him, and Sorin ran for them. His short sword went into the man's gut as a knife went across his throat.

Scarlett brought her hand to her abdomen, pressing against a gash and breathing hard. She was scanning the yard, relief flashing in her eyes as Cyrus and Arianna ran past them down the path.

"Let me carry you, Scarlett," Sorin said, sheathing his sword and knife once more.

She shook her head. "You need your hands free to fight."

"There is no one else out here, and you are bleeding. We are almost out," he insisted.

But she shook her head again. "They are coming. They are waiting."

"Who, Scarlett? Who is coming?"

She looked around the yard again before jerking her chin to the path Cyrus and Arianna had gone down. "Let's get as far as we can," she said, setting off down the path, even slower than before.

"What should I be preparing for?" Sorin asked, scanning the yard, slowing his pace to match hers.

"I don't know," she said around a grimace, her legs nearly giving out again.

"Who are they?" he pressed, catching her elbow to keep her upright.

She stiffened, coming to a halt, but for once it wasn't a reaction to his touch.

"I was beginning to think you were not going to come for her."

Sorin shoved Scarlett behind him, cursing himself when he felt her stumble, and Mikale stepped into view not more than twenty feet away from them down the path. Sorin called flames to his fingertips, but Scarlett was back in front of him, pushing his hands down and forcing him to extinguish the fire.

"No!" she cried in terror, tripping over those damn chains at her feet yet again.

Sorin caught her before she could face plant onto the ground, and Mikale chuckled, taking a few steps towards them.

"You really are so damn clever, aren't you, my pet? That will be so incredibly useful." He took another few steps as a sneer curled up his lip. "But right now, it is causing quite the inconvenience for us all."

"Where is Tarek?" she demanded.

Tarek. That was the second time she had said that name. He and Cyrus had immediately thought of Tarek Ordos, Talwyn's twin flame. He had been killed alongside Thia, so it obviously wasn't the same male, but the name still dredged up memories that both he and his Second liked to keep buried.

"He is waiting for you to be returned," Mikale answered. "He has your tonic ready for you. You will be needing it after exerting so much energy. How careless of you."

The mention of a tonic had another snarl ripping from Sorin, and he pulled Scarlett possessively to his side. She fought him for a moment before she sagged against him. He brought his other hand up again, preparing to cast fire and burn this motherfucker to ash, but she reached for his arm again.

"No," she rasped, leaning into him so much now he was holding her up. "He wants you to use your magic. I told you. They are prepared for it."

A frustrated growl came from Mikale, and he began striding for them with more purpose. "You are not leaving here with her," he snarled, pulling his sword from his side. "I will not lose her again."

"She is not yours to claim," Sorin replied darkly, his grip on her tightening.

"We shall see," Mikale answered with a dark smile, continuing his advance.

He wanted to push her behind him and shield her, but he was fairly certain she wouldn't be able to stand. Tucking her in even closer, Sorin raised his sword. She was not leaving his side again. She clung to him, a soft whimper escaping her lips.

"Let me go so you can fight," she rasped.

"Not a chance in hell, Love," he replied. "I will never let you go."

His blade met with Mikale's a moment later, the resounding clang echoing in the otherwise empty yard. Mikale's lip curled up on one side as he brought his sword down again and again, pushing them back down the path and towards the Fellowship. He was trying to figure out a plan, but his focus was on keeping Scarlett up and beside him and avoiding the swipe of Mikale's blade.

He felt Scarlett pull a knife from his belt a moment before it was being shoved deep into Mikale's side. He let out a bellow of rage and pain, stumbling back, and Sorin planted a foot in his gut. Mikale fell backwards to the ground with a grunt, and Scarlett was lurching from Sorin's side before he realized what was happening. She fell to her knees beside Mikale, reaching for the knife and twisting it in his wound, making him scream again. Sorin stalked forward, placing his foot on Mikale's throat to hold him in place for his queen.

"That is not shirastone, my pet. It will not kill me," he panted out through gritted teeth.

"I am well aware," she rasped back, tugging the knife from his side, blood instantly beginning to pool beside him. Sorin reached for her as she leaned in closer, ready to intervene if Mikale made one move to grab her. "I want you to know that the next time you see my face, you will be looking upon your death."

Sorin couldn't help the dark smile that spread across his face as he watched his wife and queen make threats when she couldn't even stand. But the words that came from Mikale's lips next had confusion coursing through him.

"Do you know why you are so weakened right now, my pet?" he replied, a cruel, vindictive smile on his face. "You weaken as your Guardian fades."

"No," she rasped, shaking her head at those words. "That bond is blocked. All my bonds are blocked. That is what Alaric said."

Mikale laughed as much as he could around Sorin's foot at his neck. "He also said that because Cassius *chose* the Guardian bond, you would still feel it. You did not feel a thing as you watched us carve him up and make him scream, but now you are weakening. You know what that means, my pet."

"You are lying," she rasped, horror and panic coloring her tone. Her already labored breathing was becoming erratic.

"Breathe, Scarlett," Sorin ordered.

"She can't," Mikale taunted. "She cannot because her Guardian is on death's doorstep. He already has a foot beyond the Veil, and when he fully crosses, the pain will be excruciating."

"Scarlett, I do not know what this means," Sorin said, looking from Mikale to his wife as she fell back, drawing her knees to her chest.

"Tarek will ease the pain, my pet. The tonic we give you will ease this loss," Mikale continued, his voice slipping into a coaxing tone, smooth and entrancing. "You know what is required of you."

"Scarlett, I do not know what is going on here, but do not listen to him. Do you hear me?"

But she didn't hear him. Her hands were clamped over her ears, and her eyes were closed tight as she rocked back and forth. Tears were coursing down her cheeks, sobs racking her body, and a scream of anguish left her throat. He couldn't go to her. He couldn't reach her. He could do nothing for her right now, but he could kill the man beneath his boot.

With a snarl of rage, Sorin pulled a shirastone dagger from his belt, but as he raised it to bring it down on Mikale's chest, another voice cut through the night.

"I wouldn't do that, Aditya."

Sorin's head snapped up to find a hooded figure crouching beside Scarlett. Where had he come from? And why was his voice so familiar?

"Get away from her," Sorin ordered darkly, his dagger halted inches from Mikale's chest.

The hooded man tsked as he stroked down Scarlett's hair, brushing it back over her shoulder. "How can I help her if I step away from her?" he mocked, pulling a dagger from the folds of his cloak. "Here's how this is going to work. You are not going to kill him," he continued, gesturing to Mikale on the ground. "And I will help the female you love so deeply."

"Help her how?"

"Not until we have an agreement," he answered. "You can keep Mikale beneath your boot. I do not really give a fuck, but I, unfortunately, must insist you do not end his life."

Sorin watched as he continued to stroke Scarlett's hair while she rocked back and forth, lost to the depths of her darkness and pain. His chest tightened painfully when she screamed again in clear agony.

"Agreed," Sorin said tightly. "Help her. Now."

The man pushed the sleeve of his cloak up, bringing the dagger to his forearm and slicing a gash up the inside. Then he took Scarlett's hair loosely in his fist, tilting her head back before moving his arm to her mouth. She fought him, pressing her lips together.

Until he leaned forward and said something into her ear that made her scream again.

As soon as her mouth opened, he was pressing his forearm to her lips, his blood dripping down her throat.

"What the fuck are you doing?" Sorin demanded, and Mikale began chuckling beneath his boot once more.

"You desire her so deeply, yet you do not even know what she is," Mikale managed to get out, and Sorin was pressing his boot down harder to cut off his air supply.

But Scarlett was indeed calming. The hooded man had tipped her chin up, closing her mouth and forcing her to swallow. She blinked her eyes open and seemed to know who was beside her, because she lurched away from him, crawling a few feet down the path.

"Now, now, your Majesty. We've become so close these past few weeks. I am wounded," he chided, pushing to his feet and striding towards her.

He stretched out a hand. "Come with me, and he may let your beloved live."

"Where is he?" she asked. Her voice was still hoarse and rough, but it sounded stronger than it had moments ago.

"He is waiting for you in his study. He is unhappy," the man said.

"He is always unhappy," she retorted, pushing herself to her feet to stand unsteadily before the man.

"I assure you, once you finally meet his demands, he will be quite pleasant to be around," the man replied, his hand still outstretched to her. "Tell me, your Majesty, is your lover's life not worth it? Will you sacrifice yet another person you love?"

"What do you know of sacrifice?" she spat back. "Is that what you think you've been doing here?"

Mikale squirmed beneath his foot, but Sorin wasn't sure what to do here. He wasn't sure if he should be attempting to intervene or standing back as he was. He had no idea what was being discussed or who the cloaked man was.

"Careful, Majesty," the man warned, his voice going cold. "We have discussed this before. Do not pretend you know my motives in what I do."

"From what I've gathered, your motive is a Court you think was stolen from you. But in actuality, you are too much of a coward to challenge the sitting Royal for it, so you sought out someone to take it for you," she replied, stepping back from his outstretched hand.

What the actual fuck was going on here? Because the way Scarlett was talking to this hooded man made it sound like he was Fae. The terms she was using made it sound like this Fae desired one of the Courts, thought he was *owed* one of the Courts.

"I am going to enjoy watching his punishments for what you have done today," the man gritted out, beginning to stalk towards her.

"Scarlett," Sorin called out to her, but before he could say more, a deep bellowing had them all turning to look down the path.

Running towards them beneath the moonlight was a great red stag, and Azrael Luan was on his back.

"No!" Mikale roared, rolling suddenly and catching Sorin off guard. "Grab her, Tarek!"

But Sorin was already racing for her as she stumbled back from the man again. A shirastone dagger was flying from his hand and embedding in the man's shoulder. He didn't slow as he lunged for her, too, but then Rinji was leaping clear over the top of him and standing between the man and the queen.

Sorin was beside Scarlett a moment later, pulling her into him, and she pressed her forehead to his chest. He pressed a kiss to the top of her head, and she looked up at him.

"If we do not get out of here—"

"No," Sorin snarled, pulling her towards Rinji but keeping his arms wrapped tightly around her. "There will be no goodbyes, Scarlett. Never again for you and me."

"Help her up, Aditya," Luan said, reaching a hand down for her.

"*You*," the hooded man hissed in rage, and Luan whipped his head around to face him.

"I know your voice." When the man did not reply, Luan said, "Lower your hood."

"We do not have time for this," Sorin snapped. "Get us out of here, Luan."

The Earth Prince's attention returned to him. "I cannot Travel within the wards," he said, pulling Scarlett onto Rinji's back. She sat sideways in front of Luan, unable to straddle the animal with her chains on. A moment later, Luan was helping Sorin up behind him.

With another bellow, Rinji stamped its front hoof, and the ground shook beneath them.

"Stop them," Mikale hollered in rage.

"I cannot stop a spirit animal, you idiot," the cloaked man spat back.

"You are useless," Mikale sniped, prowling forward.

But Rinji lowered his head and ran down the path, both men jumping out of the way of the animal's antlers. Minutes later, they were skidding to a halt at the east gate. Cyrus was reaching up to help Scarlett down, and Sorin was leaping from the animal's back.

"Hi, Darling," Cyrus said, setting Scarlett on her feet.

"Hi," she answered, tilting her head back to look at him.

"He's waiting for you."

And she was passed into Sorin's arms. He gripped her face in his hands, smoothing hair back from her face. He couldn't find his voice as her silvery-blue eyes stared into his own, and emotion finally flickered in their depths.

"Take these chains off," she whispered.

"As soon as we are at the safe house," he answered.

"No. Now."

"Let's go, Aditya," Luan said, reaching for them, preparing to Travel, but Scarlett pulled free of his grasp.

"Take the chains off," she said again, louder this time.

"Scarlett," came Eliza's voice as she came to Sorin's side. "There is not time. If you want to say goodbye to Cassius, we need to go now."

"Take them off," she demanded again, as though she hadn't heard the general speak.

"Grab her, and let's go," Luan said. Arianna was beside him, one of her hands clasped in his. She had apparently shifted back into her natural form before giving Luan Talwyn's ring. She was crouched down, her other hand on Cassius's still form.

Scarlett turned to say something to him, but her gaze fell on the Shifter.

"We are outside the wards. You can make the key now, can you not?"

"Yes, your Majesty," Arianna answered. "However, I have to agree with your husband. We have barely managed to escape alive this night."

"I do not care who you agree with," Scarlett answered. "Take them off."

Sorin started to move towards her, but he caught Cyrus's eye as he silently circled behind her. Yelling and pounding footsteps told him they had seconds.

"Now!" Sorin yelled, reaching out and grasping Eliza's hand at the same time she gripped Luan's. Cyrus came from behind, his arms coming around Scarlett's waist and trapping her arms to her sides. He forced her forward. She screamed in fury, but the second Sorin's fingers touched her flesh, they were pulled through a rip in the world.

Cyrus kept her held tightly to him as he hauled her up the path to the warehouse. Sorin didn't dare try to take her from him. She was kicking and fighting and swearing at them, and he didn't know why. He had no idea what had set this off, what she had experienced to make her react like a feral animal.

"Scarlett," he pleaded. "I am sorry, Love. We needed to get you out."

"What the fuck happened?" came Nuri's voice as she rushed out of the warehouse and fell still at the scene before her.

"Let's get inside, and we can fill you in," Sorin ground out, brushing past her and leading the way into the warehouse. They all filed in, Luan carrying Cassius. As soon as the door was closed, he gestured to Arianna. "Make that key."

"I need to see the manacles," she answered.

Scarlett was still thrashing in Cyrus's arms, and Sorin didn't know how she even had the energy or strength to be doing so. It couldn't all be from that man's blood, could it?

"Scarlett." Her name was an order, and she stilled long enough to sneer at him. "Cyrus is going to let you go."

"I am?" he asked, his brow arching.

"Yes, you are," he answered. His eyes were fixed on Scarlett as he continued, "Since you are in a particularly delightful mood right now, for reasons I am incredibly interested to learn I might add, I suspect you are going to run and fight. But know that I will chase you, and I will fight you, and you will not win tonight." Flames began to twist up his arms, and Scarlett glared at him. He nodded at Cyrus, and he slowly unwound his arms from her.

Scarlett didn't move, but she continued to glare at him. He took a tentative step towards her, and when she still didn't move, he closed the distance between them. "Keep your eyes right here, Scarlett," he said, his voice a soft command. He motioned Arianna forward. No one made a sound as the Shifter lowered to study the locks on the ankle shackles.

"You know why her emotions are heightened right now, do you not?" Arianna asked casually, running her fingers over the manacles.

"I am assuming because she has been a prisoner for weeks, experiencing any number of countless horrors, and we just freed her?" Sorin drawled.

"She is feeling much right now," Arianna continued, ignoring his sarcasm. "She is obviously feeling relief at being rescued, but she is also feeling sorrow for Cassius. I would guess she is also feeling rage at what she has experienced." The Shifter pulled the key she had used earlier from her pocket. It began shifting in shape as she continued speaking. "I am assuming she has been in these shirastone manacles since she was taken. Her magic has replenished these last weeks but has had no outlet. She is over-sensitized, on edge, feeling everything intensely."

Sorin had not even considered that. When he was in the human lands, his magic had simply gone dormant. Her's would not have done that. Her's would have been demanding she use it. It would have been trying to break through just like it had when she'd been addicted to her tonic. When it couldn't physically manifest, it would have sought out other outlets— like rage and sorrow. She would have fallen back on old habits, retreating into herself to try to keep from feeling anything at all.

Arianna slid the key into the shackle around one ankle, and a moment later it popped open. Scarlett began trembling, but her eyes stayed on his. He didn't reach for her, understanding that even touching her right now could set her off again. But gods; the desire to touch her, feel her skin, her mouth. To drive that haunted look from her eyes.

He swallowed thickly. "It is almost done, Love," he said softly.

"I wanted to burn the Fellowship to the godsdamn ground," she whispered back. "That's why I wanted them off there."

"Then when you are ready, we will go back and do just that," he answered, the second ankle shackle falling to the ground. "If you want to set the entire godsdamn world on fire, my flames are yours to help you do so."

Arianna stood and began examining the wrist manacles. A few minutes later, they fell from Scarlett's wrists with a clang. She closed her eyes, breathing in deep. She spun to face the expanse of the warehouse. Flames ignited up her legs and down her arms, and then she was arcing those flames into the air above them. Embers and sparks were raining down to the ground, and Sorin snuffed them out before they could set anything alight.

"Sorin," Eliza warned, stepping forward, but he thrust out a hand to stop her.

"I am prepared to intervene. Just stay back."

His hand was raised, ready to take control of her flames if they got out of control, but as those red and gold and blue flames began to arc towards the ground, Scarlett raised one hand higher. Water flew from it, but instead of snuffing out the flames, she froze them in midair and let them crash to the stone floor of the warehouse.

Sorin created his own wall of flames to shield the others as the frozen shards of flame shattered and exploded outward. When he was finally able to lower that wall, he turned to find her striding to where Cassius lay, frosty footprints left in her wake.

"What did he do to him?" Nuri asked, her voice quiet and tense.

"Everything," Scarlett answered, dropping down and curling herself into him just as she had back at the Fellowship.

"He was still breathing when we got here," Eliza said quietly, coming to Sorin's side. "I don't know how, but he was."

"What do we do?" Cyrus asked.

"We let her say goodbye," Sorin answered.

CHAPTER 18
SCARLETT

She was out.

They had come for her.

Sorin had crossed borders and lands and torn the fucking realms apart to get to her.

She was out, but her world was still burning around her.

She clung to Cassius's still body, willing her own life into his. She'd just spent months without him. She'd just watched him be tortured to keep her from having to make a choice that would break her. But she was about to break anyway. She was about to shatter into nothing.

But she wasn't shattering without a final fight.

She had just spent those same months putting herself back together. She had clawed her way out of the darkness. She had found light where it didn't exist. She had created stars in the endless dark. She had fought for every single one of them, and she would fight for this one, too.

The Fates could not have him. Not now.

Not tomorrow. Not the day after.

Not until she was ready to go with him.

She could hear the others whispering behind her. She could hear them saying he would cross the Veil at any time, but she refused to accept this outcome. She refused to say goodbye. She refused to finally be back with him, only to watch him fade. He was her godsdamn Guardian. She needed him, and he was going to make good on the vow he made all those nights ago on a beach beneath the stars.

"You do not get to leave me here, Cassius. Do you hear me?" she cried into his bloody chest. "You do not get to abandon me after pledging to stay with me. We have revenge to seek and battles to win, and I cannot do that without you. You begged me to hang on, and now I am begging you. Hold on. Please." She was sobbing so hard she could hardly get her words out, couldn't get enough air down to breathe properly. "Please stay with me. I need you, Cass. *I need you.*"

"Scarlett." Nuri was kneeling on the other side of Cassius, gripping his hand in her gloved one. "He . . ." She swallowed, but Scarlett couldn't meet her gaze. She could tell by her tone she had already given up. "He cannot survive these wounds. That he has clung on this long is—"

"He has clung on this long because he is the calm to my storm, and if he leaves, the storm will rage and will never cease. Do not tell me he will not live. Do not tell me he cannot survive this," Scarlett hissed, lifting a hand and sending her flying back with a blast of water from her palm.

"Love."

She looked up to find Sorin standing over her, sorrow and pity in his golden eyes.

"Do not look at me like that. Do not look at me like he is already gone," she begged. "He's not gone, Sorin. He's not. His heart still beats. He can't be gone. He cannot leave me!"

He lowered to his knees beside her, reaching for her and pulling her into his chest. "Scarlett," he rasped, his tone ringing with heartache for her.

"I need him, Sorin. I need him. I am not strong enough to lose him. I will not survive this. I need him. I need him!" she sobbed in hysterics, her tears soaking his leathers. Releasing some of her magic had cleared her head, but it had also paved the way for this soul-crushing grief to press in on her from all sides. Now, instead of feeling every emotion so intensely she couldn't separate them, she could only feel one.

And she was not strong enough to endure it. Not a second time.

"Shh," Sorin soothed, holding her tightly to him. "I hear you, Scarlett." He leaned back from her just enough to see her face, bringing a hand up to cup her cheek. "Let's take him home. Beatrix can try. She will do whatever she can."

Beatrix.

A Healer.

They needed a Healer. But not just any Healer.

They needed the most powerful one. They needed the High Witch.

They needed Cassius's mother.

She pushed back from Sorin, her gaze swinging frantically to the Earth Prince. "How many can you Travel with, Azrael?"

The Earth Prince was watching her with wary apprehension. "I can easily Travel with all of us here if you cannot."

She glanced back at Sorin. He must have noticed that there were no shadows or white flames when she'd finally been able to release some of her magic. The truth was, she couldn't reach her shadows. She couldn't reach her darkness, and somehow, her ability to Travel was also blocked.

"But can you Travel with everyone in this building?" Scarlett pressed, because she would be damned if Cassius just endured all of that hell to leave the orphans here now. No. Everyone was coming with her. No one was staying here to be found by Alaric and face the same fate.

"Scarlett, we cannot take everyone," Sorin said tentatively.

"Why? Why can't we?" she insisted.

But he didn't say anything. He just stared at her like she was losing her damn mind. And maybe she was, but Alaric would not take one more godsdamn thing from her.

"I would be able to, but it would take several trips," Azrael finally answered. "I could not Travel with everyone at one time."

"Nuri, gather everyone together. We leave immediately. Take only what they need. I will make sure they are cared for upon arrival." Everyone just stared at her. "Why is no one moving?"

"Love, let's take a moment and—"

"We do not have a moment!" Scarlett cried, and she knew flames flickered in her eyes. The temperature in the warehouse plummeted, and she reached out a hand to flood Cassius with heat. "Send a fire message to Hazel. Tell her to meet us in Solembra."

"We are not prepared to house so many, Scarlett," Sorin tried again.

"The palace is huge, Sorin. We will figure it out. They are as much my responsibility as the Courts are." She could not believe he was arguing with her right now. "It is only a matter of time until Alaric and the other Lords find them."

"Alaric is a Maraan Lord?" Sorin demanded, his eyes widening.

Scarlett barked a hollow laugh. "No, Sorin, he is not a Maraan Lord. He is a Maraan Prince. He is the son of Deimas and Esmeray, and his need for vengeance is something we are unprepared for. But these children will bring him one step closer if he gets his hands on them."

"That is not possible. Deimas and Esmeray did not have any heirs," Sorin balked.

"I do not have the time to argue about this and try to convince you of its validity right now. Send a message to Hazel before Cassius is out of time."

He tried to keep the wince from his features, but she saw it. She saw how futile he thought this all was.

"She will not be able to enter the palace unescorted. I would have to retrieve her."

"Then send Briar to do so," Scarlett demanded. "Rayner can go to him and tell him I am in need of his services."

"If I may, your Majesty," Arianna interjected. "The High Witch can enter the Black Halls without an escort. She and Queen Eliné were very close, especially after the death of Eliné's consort."

"The Black Halls?" Her attention went back to Sorin. "Is there still staff there? Guards? People to receive the children?"

"There is a small staff that keeps the Black Halls in prime condition, and I am sure more help could be found quickly, but Scarlett—"

Her head whipped to Eliza. "Can you access your magic? Did you take a tonic today? Send a message to Hazel. Please," she begged. Tears still streaming down her face, she pleaded with someone to do as she was asking, cursing the fact she hadn't learned how to send such messages yet.

Eliza glanced from her to Sorin before shaking her head. "I want to, Scarlett, but we cannot send fire messages from the mortal lands. It does not work that way."

Her heart cracked further at no one moving. No one doing anything to help her. Her eyes landed on Rayner, his grey eyes swirling with ashes.

"Rayner," she choked out. "Please. Please go get Hazel."

Rayner held her eyes for a moment longer before he nodded his head once, disappearing into smoke.

She whirled back to Sorin. "If you will not help me, then get back," she snarled, wishing she could access her shadows to force him to do so.

"I am simply trying to understand, Scarlett," Sorin said, reaching for her once more.

"Can you not just trust me?" she demanded, knocking his hands away from her.

"The last time I just trusted you, you blocked our fucking bond and ended up here, Scarlett. Forgive me for trying to get a read on the situation before blindly following your requests once more," he shot back. He immediately closed his eyes, wincing as he pushed out a long breath. "I am sorry. I did not mean that the way it came out."

"I think you meant it exactly as you said it," she replied hollowly. She turned away from him, shoving down the surge of emotions that threatened to overwhelm her. She knew that fight would come. She knew this conversation would have to happen, but she did not have the time or the energy to devote to it now. Not with Cassius's life hanging in the balance.

"Take us first, Azrael," she ordered, stretching out a hand to him.

"Scarlett, why can you not Travel?" Sorin asked slowly. "Your magic should be fully replenished. You just froze fire."

"Again, something I do not currently have time to discuss. Are you coming with me or not?"

"You think I would let you out of my sight right now? When I cannot find you through our bond?" he growled, reaching out to lay a hand on her arm.

"I will stay behind and help get the orphans together," Nuri said. "I will come with the last of them."

"Thank you," Scarlett answered, holding her gaze for an extra moment. She nodded once, her expression unreadable. That reunion would come soon enough, too.

And then Azrael was pulling them through a rip in the world. She was still kneeling next to Cassius when they emerged in a suite of some sort. A plush rug across a stone floor was beneath her knees, but she hardly noticed her surroundings.

"This was my quarters when I would stay here," Sorin said, looking around the room.

"I figured here would be better than the queen's rooms," Azrael replied. "The layout is identical to the White Halls. I assumed these were once yours."

"Someone figure out where Hazel is and bring her here as soon as she arrives," Scarlett said, leaning over Cassius once more, pressing her fingers to his neck. His pulse was somehow still there, but so, so faint.

She felt a hand on her back, and then Sorin was speaking softly into her ear. "If he will hold on for anyone, it will be for you."

She swallowed against the tears building in her throat, refusing to let more come. Rayner appeared in a swirl of ashes, a water portal appearing a moment later. Briar stepped through and behind him came Beatrix. Rayner must have somehow alerted them while going to the High Witch.

"Move him to the bed, Prince," Beatrix ordered Sorin.

"No," Scarlett argued. "Don't move him again. Not until Hazel gets here."

"Scarlett, it would give him a better chance if Beatrix could start," Sorin said, gently trying to pull her from where she was clinging to Cassius.

"Don't take me from him, Sorin," she half-hissed, half-cried at him. "Love, I am trying to make sure he is not taken from you at all. Let us move him to the bed so Beatrix can try."

She reluctantly let him pull her back from Cassius, and Cyrus stepped forward to move him. Sorin tried to help her up, but she was already crawling over to the bed, climbing onto it and grasping Cassius's hand. It was cold and clammy in hers, and she pressed some of her fire magic into his body again. She felt Sorin come up behind her, but he didn't reach for her, didn't touch her again.

Beatrix's hands were hovering over Cassius, a faint white light emanating from her palms. Her eyes widened with a mixture of horror and sorrow.

"Just try, Beatrix," Sorin murmured. "Please."

Scarlett kept her eyes fixed on Cassius's face, where one eye was swollen shut from when Alaric had to have shattered his cheekbone with his fist after hitting him multiple times. That was better than his other eye though. It looked swollen shut as well, but Alaric had cut into his chocolate brown eye with a long, thin dagger, effectively blinding him. There were various other cuts and bruises along his face, dried blood beneath his nose and along his lips. He'd endured so much. Broken bones. Hits to his head. Stabs and burns. There was little Alaric had not done. She had sat and watched everything, never allowing tears to fall. Never allowing Alaric and Tarek to see her break. And when he hadn't regained consciousness for hours, when they couldn't wake him, Alaric had decided they'd done what they could. He'd chided at her that this was all her fault, that she had sat by and watched him be beaten and tortured, and now she would watch him die as he'd slid a shirastone dagger between his broken ribs. He'd pulled the dagger from his side, before ordering him removed from where he'd been chained to the wall. He'd been laid just out of her reach, leaving her to watch as his life bled from him, and she could do nothing.

"I am sorry, Sorin," she heard Beatrix murmur. "I can ease some of the pain, but there is too much . . ."

"I understand," Sorin replied. She felt him shift closer, as if preparing to intervene somehow.

"Where is Hazel?" Scarlett demanded, panic rising and edging into her tone. Beatrix was one of the best Healers in the realms. She'd hardly done a thing. Cassius didn't look any different. His chest was still barely rising and falling.

"I am sorry, your Majesty," she said softly. "There is too much internal injury, and I—"

"Where is Hazel?" Scarlett demanded again. She nestled into Cassius's side once more, praying to any god that would listen, praying to the god of death himself.

The room was silent. There was nothing anyone could do. There were no words that would offer any sort of comfort to her shattering world. There was no touch that would ease the grief she was adamantly shoving down.

"Move."

Scarlett let out a sob of relief at the High Witch's sharp tone. Her head snapped up, her gaze instantly landing on Hazel. Her normally golden-brown skin was leached of color, but other than that, she looked every bit like the stern High Witch that everyone found difficult to deal with. Her lips were set in a thin line, pursing as she came to a stop beside Beatrix.

"My Lady," Beatrix murmured, bowing her head. "The injuries are too numerous and too severe."

"He is not like others," Hazel replied, her violet eyes sweeping over Cassius. She brought a hand to his cheek, and Scarlett saw it tremble slightly.

"He was protecting children," Scarlett whispered, her voice

cracking as her last hope met her eyes. "He was keeping children safe, Hazel. Please. I need him."

"Tell me, your Majesty, have you learned of your mother?" Hazel asked, white light beginning to emit from her palm where it pressed against Cassius's cheek.

Scarlett's brows came together in confusion. She glanced at the room of gathered Fae, not understanding why this was relevant, when Cassius could take his last breath at any moment.

"Yes," Scarlett answered slowly.

"His father was one of you," Hazel replied.

"What?"

"His father was like your parents. His father was like you," she said again.

Scarlett shook her head. "I don't understand."

"You need to understand," Hazel insisted. "You need to set your grief and panic and fear aside for a moment and think about everything that you have learned and discovered. His life depends on it, and even then, I do not know that it will be enough."

"Can you not just tell me?" Scarlett cried, and Sorin's hand came to her shoulder, squeezing gently in warning. But she didn't give a fuck. She didn't care about the reputation of the Witches being ruthless and brutal. She didn't care that she was being disrespectful. She didn't care that the room was full of godsdamn royalty.

"I cannot," Hazel replied, her eyes narrowing. "Just as Eliné was sworn to secrecy, so was I." She pulled up the sleeve of her witch-suit where a Bargain Mark indeed stood out. "So listen very carefully, Scarlett. Do you know how your mother's kind replenished their power? Do you know the cost the Fae paid for their magic when it was bestowed upon them?"

"What? Why would that matter?"

"Because it is also how they can heal from fatal wounds," Hazel answered. "Do you know?"

Scarlett was shaking her head, trying to sift through memories of history she'd read and research she'd come across. She was trying to push down her panic and terror of Cassius dying, but she couldn't focus. She couldn't think straight. Because Cassius was dying. Cassius was going to leave her. Cassius was going to—

"Scarlett," Hazel said sharply, pulling her from her spiral into darkness. "They must have given you something to keep you from weakening," Hazel insisted, a slight pleading entering her voice.

And realization slammed into her. The tonic they had given her was always coppery and metallic tasting. Alaric summoning Tarek when she was weak. His arm bleeding. Tarek pressing his bleeding wound to her mouth in the yard earlier, not even an hour ago.

Tarek.

Who was Fae.

Sorin's words from all those months ago atop a horse as they traveled to the Fire Court came flooding back to her.

Avonleyans need Fae for magical sustenance. They feed on their magic for healing and strengthening their own powers.

Her eyes widened in understanding, and she whipped her head around, her eyes landing on Cyrus. He was standing near the end of the bed, his face solemn as he watched everything play out.

"Cyrus, I need you," Scarlett said, reaching for him.

"Scarlett?" Sorin questioned, but she ignored him, motioning for Cyrus to come to her side.

As soon as she could grab him, she gripped Cyrus's hand, pulling him towards her. "I need a dagger," she said, holding out her other hand.

"Scarlett, you need to tell us—" Sorin started, but Hazel was already pressing one into her hand. She was slashing it across Cyrus's forearm before anyone could make a move to stop her, and she tugged him towards Cassius's mouth. Pressing the bloody wound against his lips, she glanced back at Hazel.

"How will we know if it works?"

"With wounds this extensive, it will take days," Hazel answered, her eyes on her son. "But we should have some idea within a few hours."

"I cannot ask Cyrus to stand here for hours," Scarlett replied.

"Of course not," Hazel said. "As long as he still breathes, we give him more every couple hours." Her eyes flicked to Scarlett's. "You need to go rest."

"Not until I know if he will live," Scarlett answered, shaking her head in refusal, gripping on to Cassius.

"You will be of no use to anyone if you cannot even stand," Hazel retorted. "I can help you sleep if you wish."

"No," Scarlett snarled.

Hazel stiffened slightly before turning to Beatrix and beginning to speak with her in a low voice.

Scarlett felt a light touch to her lower back, and she looked up to find Sorin looking down at her, his features tight and wary. "Hazel is right, Scarlett. You need to rest."

"I am not leaving his side," she snarled again.

"I know, Love. I hear you," he answered, his tone softening slightly. "Sleep here. I swear no one will take you from this room. If something happens, I will wake you."

At his words, the fight she'd been prepared for slipped from her body. She nestled back into Cassius's side, and she felt Sorin gently rubbing her back, making a soothing path up and down her spine. The exhaustion she'd been adamantly ignoring took over, and she was asleep in minutes.

***

She woke off and on over the next several hours. Whenever she did, Sorin pressed a glass of water to her lips and tried to get her to eat something. Hazel made sure Cyrus was giving Cassius blood every few hours. They tried to question her about what she had learned and what was going on when she'd wake, but despite the rest, she was still weakening. She'd make sure Cassius was still breathing, drink a few sips of water to appease Sorin, and drift back to sleep.

When she rose from the depths of sleep this time, though, she was not nestled on a bed next to Cassius. There was a hand stroking down her hair, and she was being held tightly against a hard chest. She sighed deeply, her hand coming up to rest against the tunic that covered the broad muscles where her cheek rested. She felt lips press to the top of her head and a wave of heat swept through her tired limbs. She could hardly crack her eyes open, let alone lift her head.

"I need some answers, my Lady," Sorin was gritting out, whispering in an attempt to keep from waking her.

"You can get them from your queen when she is ready to tell you," Hazel replied shortly. "I would assume you know that I could not break a Bargain Mark even if I wanted to, and certainly not a Blood Mark."

"She speaks the truth, Fire Prince." It took a moment for Scarlett to place the voice of the Shifter Beta.

"And do you know of the queen's true mother?" Sorin asked, his tone rising slightly as he fought to keep his temper.

"I do not," Arianna answered.

"How is Cyrus's blood keeping Cassius from crossing the Veil?" Sorin asked, clearly trying a different tactic.

"The same way Fae blood kept the queen from weakening too much while she was held captive," Hazel answered.

"Are you saying that she is going to need to . . . do the same thing we are doing to Cassius?"

There was no answer, and Scarlett again tried to pry her eyes open. They cracked open a little bit, and she winced at the light that assaulted her.

Sorin began to say something else, but there was a rustling sound of some sort. His grip around her tightened slightly, and a low rumble emanated from his chest at whoever had entered. Scarlett sighed internally, realizing that his overbearing protectiveness was about to increase tenfold. She felt him stiffen even more, and then she felt fur and a cool nose nudging against her hand.

She forced herself to open her eyes further, and they landed on a black feline with silver eyes. Shock rippled through her, not that she had the energy to show it. Her fingers flexed in Shirina's fur. How was she here? The bond was blocked. She would need to go to the Fiera Palace and dig through her books to figure out how to fix this monumental disaster she'd created.

"For now, yes, she will need to replenish some of her magic this way."

Her eyes flew open at that voice, and she tried to push herself away from Sorin's chest.

Juliette was here.

"Scarlett," he murmured, his hold tightening to keep her in his lap.

She tried to speak, tried to say Juliette's name, but her tongue felt thick and her mouth was dry. A moment later, a glass of water was being pressed to her lips. She took a few sips, but it did nothing.

"What do you mean for now she will need to replenish some of her magic this way?" Sorin demanded, pulling her back against his chest once more. She tried to push away from him again, but it was futile. She hadn't felt this weak, this helpless, since that morning Alaric had panicked at her state of wellbeing.

"We can discuss that at a later time," Juliette replied, stepping into her line of sight. "Sister," she murmured, reaching out and squeezing her fingers that were still buried in Shirina's fur.

"What do I need to do then?" Sorin asked. "She needs blood, right? Fae blood?"

"Yes, but not yet," Juliette answered. "She needs to weaken completely."

"That is not happening," Sorin snarled, his fingers flexing against her skin and digging in.

Juliette released her hand, her features hardening. "Do you want your twin flame bond repaired or not, Prince of Fire?"

"Of course I do," Sorin answered.

"Then this is the fastest way to achieve such a thing," Juliette continued. "Although it will also be the most uncomfortable. But if we are to save her Guardian's life, it is the only way."

"He is still alive. We are doing everything the High Witch instructs us to do," Sorin argued. "Is making her suffer even more truly necessary? Has she not suffered enough at this point?"

Juliette ignored him completely, bending down so she was on eye-level with Scarlett.

"You did well, Sister," she said softly with a sad smile. "The children are here. You protected the innocent. You saved them."

"She is not in any shape to discuss that right now," Sorin interrupted, trying to shield Scarlett from Juliette somehow. "Let her godsdamn recover a bit before we start involving her in any of that."

The softness in Juliette's eyes shifted to wickedness, as Death Incarnate stared down the Fire Prince. "You and Cassius," she chided, "always so intent on shielding her from uncomfortable things."

"I am shielding her from nothing," Sorin bit back. "She was chained to the fucking floor watching Cassius die in front of her less than a day ago. You can give her a fucking minute before demanding more of her."

"They certainly do like to coddle her, don't they?" came a voice of silk and honey, and another snarl emanated from the Fae holding her.

"Get the fuck out," Sorin ground out. "Both of you."

"She is the Oracle, Prince," Hazel reprimanded.

"I do not give a single fuck."

There was a long-suffering sigh from Nuri before she said,

"Relax, fire prick, you're going to need us shortly. I suggest we move to another room."

"I gave her my word I would not take her from his side."

"If you do not do this, you will be taking him from her," Juliette retorted sharply.

Scarlett tried to say something, not wanting to be taken from Cassius, but searing pain erupted along her limbs, her veins, her very soul. She felt like she was being ripped apart. She tried to scream around the pain, but her throat was too dry. Nothing came out.

"Scarlett," Sorin cried, his hold tightening on her again as she writhed in his lap.

She could feel pure terror.

That was separate from the pain. That was Sorin.

That was her bond with him.

"Scarlett, look at me. Look at me, Love," Sorin said, his tone almost hysterical.

Panic was clawing its way along her spine, and she was pretty sure that was his, too, but it was nothing compared to the pain she was enduring.

She was no longer in his lap. He had moved her to the floor and was leaning over her, his hands on her cheeks, but she couldn't focus on him. Her vision was blurred, the ache in her head was pounding, and the pain. Oh gods. It was as if a piece of her very being was being ripped away, and she knew. She knew deep down this was what Alaric had been referencing when he said you feel the loss of your Guardian on a soul-deep level.

Cassius was dying.

And there was nothing she could do about it. She couldn't even be next to him when he crossed the Veil.

"Scarlett, keep your eyes open," Sorin begged. "Please, Love."

Then there was nothing.

CHAPTER 19
SORIN

"What is happening to her?" Sorin demanded as Scarlett's eyes fluttered shut, fear and panic flooding through him. How had he finally gotten her back just to have her lying unconscious on the floor before him?

"She is weakening," Juliette said simply. "Exactly as she needs to."

He had felt her. For a brief moment, he had felt excruciating pain like he had never felt before. That had ceased the moment she had slipped into unconsciousness, but their twin flame bond was there. It was faint, like it had been a few weeks ago when she'd managed to tell him she was with Alaric. Had this been the state she was in when that had happened? Had she been lying unconscious in a dungeon study while the Assassin Lord and Mikale, and whoever that cloaked stranger had been, looked on?

"This needs to be timed perfectly."

Sorin looked up to find Hazel standing beside the bed. She had only moved from Cassius's side a few times. The others had all gone to help Nuri with the children that had been brought here. Someone was finding additional staff for the Black Halls. Cyrus was returning every two hours to give Cassius more blood.

"It will be," Juliette answered, taking the dagger that Nuri was handing to her.

Sorin reached for it, too. Scarlett obviously needed Fae blood. That was what the cloaked male had given her. He'd thought about it the entire time he'd watched over her, but sitting in a chair beside that bed, holding her hand or rubbing her back simply hadn't been enough. He'd needed to hold her, needed to reassure himself that she was here, that she was back with him. When she'd finally loosened her grip enough on Cassius to be moved from his side, he had pulled her into his lap. He'd only had her there a few minutes when she had begun to stir awake and the Oracle had shown up.

She will not be the same as when she left.

Juliette's words had swirled in his head as he held her against his chest, felt her breathing naturally fall into sync with his own. He watched as Cyrus gave Cassius blood every few hours, his eyes on Sorin every time. He knew his Second had the same questions swirling in his mind. He could only assume by the High Witch's vague questions and references that Eliné was not truly Scarlett's mother, but then who was? The only bloodline that had needed Fae for magic replenishing and healing were the Avonleyans. Hazel had told them that Scarlett was born in the Witch Kingdoms, so how had an Avonelyan gotten here to birth a child? And where was she now? And what of Scarlett's father?

He shoved all those thoughts and questions aside, focusing on his wife. He tried to take the dagger from Juliette, but she did not offer it to him. Instead, she shook her head.

"Not yet, Prince."

"What do you mean not yet? She is unconscious. She was in horrendous pain," Sorin argued.

"You could feel her?" Juliette asked, her eyes widening slightly with what appeared to be anticipation. "Can you now?"

"I could for a brief moment. Now it is very muted. Faint, but there," Sorin answered, reaching for the dagger again.

"Patience, Fire Lord," Nuri drawled sarcastically, dropping to her knees at Scarlett's head. She was still in her full Death's Shadow gear, clearly not having taken any time to change since arriving with the children.

"No," Sorin snarled. "Tell me what the fuck is happening, or she gets my blood now, even if I have to rip my arm open with my teeth."

"She cannot," Hazel cut in. "She possesses a Mark of her own that prevents her from speaking of what she knows."

"But *she* can," he said with a jerk of his chin to Juliette.

"Trust the Fates, Sorin," Juliette said, her tone softening a touch. "This needs to happen."

"What exactly are we waiting for?" he demanded, his gaze fixed on Scarlett's face.

"Tell me when you can feel her as before. Tell me when her Mark is broken," Juliette said, beginning to pace back and forth beside Scarlett's still form. "They gave her enough to keep her from weakening completely. If they had let her, the Blood Mark she enacted would have shattered, the magic breaking. They gave her just enough to keep that from happening, but not enough to replenish any of her power."

"She threw fire and froze it," he muttered, smoothing hair back from her face. "I think they failed."

"Not that power," Juliette said, glancing over her shoulder at Hazel. "The problem is, when that Mark is broken, it will reestablish all her bonds, including the one with her Guardian. A Guardian is required to do whatever is necessary to ensure the survival of their charge, including using their own power to heal them, even at the cost of their own life. She will start pulling power from him because she is so weak physically and that could . . ."

"Kill him," Sorin finished. "If this kills him, if she knows that *she* essentially killed him by siphoning all his power . . . You know she will not recover from that, right?"

"Yes, but even with the bond blocked, she is still trying to draw power from him, especially when touching him. The physical connection . . . It is why he is not healing," Juliette replied, her eyes going back to Scarlett as her breathing changed, becoming more ragged.

"Get ready, Juliette," Nuri said, her gloved hands coming to Scarlett's shoulders, pressing down as if to restrain her.

"Let her go," Sorin snarled, reaching to shove her back, but Nuri hissed at him, her fangs sliding free.

"She will be feral when she wakes," Nuri snapped. "Her magic will have taken over. She will be in a state of survival."

"I can handle it," Sorin retorted.

"You fool," Nuri laughed coldly. "She will be at your throat before you have a chance to stop her."

"Are you saying she will be like a Night Child?" he asked, understanding trickling through him.

"Yes, but not always, Sorin," Juliette cut in. "There are other ways the Avonleyans siphon power. They banished feeding this way centuries ago. This is a last resort, only to be used when there is no other option."

"So she is an Avonleyan then?" he asked, seeking confirmation for what he already knew.

"That is something to discuss with your twin flame, Prince," Juliette replied. "Can you feel her?"

He refocused on Scarlett, reaching down their bond. The fissures in that wall blocking their bond were deepening. She was right there. Right on the other side.

"Call for her," Juliette whispered.

Scarlett.

He felt Juliette grasp his wrist, pulling his arm toward her. "Again."

And he felt the tip of the dagger gliding along his forearm, blood already welling and running down his skin.

Scarlett.

"She is close," he heard Hazel call from the bedside. "His heartbeat is faltering."

There were no other signs, though. Scarlett hadn't moved. What they were waiting for, he didn't know. His blood was dripping onto the flimsy black gown she still wore, mixing with her own dried blood and Cassius's. Beatrix had healed the wound on her abdomen while she'd slept.

"Again," Juliette ordered.

Scarlett.

Her eyes flew open, muted, icy-blue irises settling him. "Hey, Love," he said softly.

She didn't answer him, though. Her nostrils flared, and her eyes went to his arm, her pupils dilating so much, her eyes almost looked black.

"Now, Prince," Juliette said, shoving his arm towards Scarlett. "We will make sure she doesn't take too much."

Nuri's teeth were gritted as she struggled to hold Scarlett to the floor.

One would think if she was so weak, she wouldn't be able to struggle this much, but she was jerking and reaching for Sorin as if she were possessed by the spirit of Arius.

Juliette caught her wrists, pinning them to the floor at her sides, and Sorin brought his arm to her lips. Her teeth sank in savagely, and she gulped several times, pulling his life force into her mouth and down her throat.

"Easy, Love," he ground out, because fuck. It had been uncomfortable when Nuri had drank from him, but she had been somewhat nice about it. Scarlett was just as Nuri had said she would be. She was feral and drinking from him as if his blood was a drug she couldn't get enough of. Her teeth sank deeper and deeper into his skin, but the longer she drank, the more her limbs began to relax.

"Scarlett," he said hoarsely when she took another long pull from his arm. Her eyes met his, and they were glowing, bright and silver. Shadows swirled among them and began to seep from her skin, snaking along her torso, her arms, and winding their way down to him. They crept along his skin, wrapped loosely around his throat, swept along his cheek, his brow, as if her own fingers were caressing him.

"That's enough, Scarlett," Nuri said after several minutes, nodding at Sorin to pull his arm back, but those shadows latched onto him, holding his arm in place at her mouth. "Scarlett!" Nuri snapped, but the more Scarlett drank, the stronger she was becoming.

"Let her go," Sorin said, grimacing as she took another long pull.

"Sorin, she needs to stop," Nuri said. "She will drink until there is nothing left."

"I understand. Let her go," he repeated.

Juliette and Nuri glanced at each other before they both released her at once, and Scarlett surged forward, her fingers digging into his arm. Sorin looped his free arm around her waist and drew her to him, pulling her back into his chest. He slid his arm up until his hand settled loosely around her throat, feeling her swallow against his hand.

"Love, stop," he whispered into her ear. And he sent his flames to mix with her shadows. He held in the groan at the feeling of his magic mixing with hers, but she didn't. She moaned against his flesh, her head tipping back against his shoulder and her canines dragging his arm with her. He shifted the hand from her throat until he cupped her jaw. "Stop," he whispered again, increasing the pressure on her jaw to make her release him.

Her shadows latched onto his hand, but he sent more flames into them, feeling them shudder in pleasure, their magic continuing to tangle as he kept hers distracted. She gasped at the feeling, finally releasing his arm, and Hazel was instantly next to him, healing the cut on his arm.

"More," Scarlett rasped, her voice breathy and igniting a different kind of fire in his veins. And he didn't know what exactly she was begging for more of.

"No, Scarlett," he answered, his hand slipping from her jaw back down to her throat, holding her against him as she tried to twist around in his lap.

"More," she hissed again in demand, her shadows converging on the hand around her neck.

His arm around her waist tightened, tugging her against him more firmly. Then he wrapped flames around her shadows just as tightly. She groaned in clear ecstasy, her entire body relaxing into him, the fight going out of her. Her nails raked sensually along his arms, and gods, feeling her touch again . . .

He took a deep breath, forcing down the desire coursing through him. She was riding some kind of high. She wasn't in the right state of mind. He didn't know what she'd endured at the hands of Mikale and Alaric. He didn't know if she would be ready for anything like that any time soon.

And there were other people present, so fucking her on the floor with their magic swirling together probably wouldn't be the best choice at the moment.

"Enough, Scarlett," he ground out when her hands dropped to his thighs, fingers slowly dragging up. "You need to rest, and we have things to discuss."

"No," she breathed, shaking her head, pushing her ass back into him, grinding against his hardness.

"Scarlett."

"Please, Sorin," she begged, reaching back and looping a hand around the back of his neck, trying to pull him down to her. "Please. I need more."

He shook his head again, standing and bringing her with him. "No, Love. Not now." He kept her back to him, knowing if she got her mouth anywhere near his flesh, she'd sink her teeth back into it.

"Sorin!" She said his name half in rage and half in pleading.

Hazel stepped forward when Scarlett started thrashing in his arms again, her shadows raking down his face. "I can make her sleep."

"No!" Scarlett shrieked, her entire body locking up. "No! Please don't, Sorin! Please don't!"

"Scarlett, I'm sorry," he rasped. "Gods, I am so sorry."

She will not be the same as when she left.

He didn't recognize her. He hadn't recognized her since he'd laid eyes on her at the Fellowship. She had hardly spoken while they'd fought their way out. Then she had exploded with rage at not having her chains off. Grief and panic had dragged her under, and now this.

This wild, feral thing in his arms.

Tears fell from her face, dripping onto his hand still grasped around her throat, her shadows clawing at him, ripping open his flesh. The fresh scent of his blood making her even more crazed.

Scarlett!

"I need more," she wailed. "Sorin, please!"

Before he could reply, Hazel's hand landed on her cheek. It took longer than it usually did for a Healer to make someone sleep. He watched as the High Witch gritted her teeth in clear concentration, fighting against Scarlett's strength and power, but she finally went limp in his arms. The hand from her throat dropped, his arm looping behind her knees so he could cradle her to his chest.

"Take her to sleep somewhere," Hazel said sharply, going back to Cassius's side. "When she wakes, she will be calmer. In control."

"You are sure? She will be in control, I mean," he clarified, because he would do just about anything to be alone with her right now.

Hazel nodded. "You have seen Night Children when they are starving," she replied. "She will no longer be that."

Sorin nodded, glancing at Nuri and Juliette. The Oracle took a step towards him, seeming to hesitate. "I . . ." She stopped, clearly debating whether she should say something or not. She cleared her throat before saying, "I know you love her, Prince of Fire, but you cannot shield her from everything." She held up her hand before he could say anything. "You cannot shield her from what you are feeling, Sorin."

"I do not know what you are talking about," he bit back, holding her stare.

Her lips tilted in a sad smile. "You should rest, too. You should both be fully rested for what is to come."

Sorin didn't say anything. He simply turned and left the room. He knew these halls. He could find his way around with his eyes closed, even if he hadn't been here in nearly two decades. In a few short minutes, he had climbed a set of stairs and walked down a short corridor, pushing open the door to the queen's chambers with his shoulder. He crossed the space, refusing to notice how absolutely nothing had changed since Eliné had lived here.

He went straight through to the bedchamber, pulling the heavy quilt back, and laying Scarlett among the sheets and blankets. Then he crossed the room, spinning an armchair around to face the bed so he could watch over her while she slept.

Because despite saying he didn't know what the Oracle had been talking about, he did. Now that Scarlett was back with him, now that everything with Cassius seemed to be settling down, and now that it appeared she was going to be okay, his relief at finding her was shifting. It was morphing into something hot and acidic that had been overshadowed by his panic and terror for his wife.

She had blocked their godsdamn bond. She had kept things from him. Big things. After they'd had a lengthy discussion about not doing that exact thing. She had promised not to keep things from him like Eliné had. He had promised the same. They had promised things to each other.

She will not be the same as when she left.

And she wasn't. She wasn't the same in so many ways. He was sure there were other things he had yet to discover.

But she was also exactly the same. She still had secrets.

She still kept others out. She still kept him out.

She will not be the same as when she left.

The words were on repeat in his head while he watched her sleep. An omen that he couldn't turn off.

She will not be the same as when she left.

And she wasn't.

But neither were they and what they once were.

CHAPTER 20
TALWYN

Azrael was slumped in a chair beside her. Despite his best efforts, he looked exhausted and completely drained. He'd brought that final group of children here, along with Death's Shadow, and nearly collapsed. The only reason he hadn't was because Briar had been here and caught him, helping him to the chair he now occupied. His magic reserves were clearly entirely depleted.

Ashtine had sent word that he was returning to the Black Halls of all places, and Talwyn was more than interested to know why they were coming here when Scarlett so adamantly claimed the Fiera Palace was her *home*. She hadn't learned of the children until she had arrived to find the princess here with Briar.

Eleven trips.

It had taken eleven trips back and forth from Windonelle to get them all here. Traveling with that many so quickly . . . It was no wonder he could hardly stand.

"Where is Scarlett?" Talwyn demanded.

Briar glanced up from some quiet conversation he'd been having with Ashtine. "The queen is with Sorin and the High Witch, tending to a friend that was mortally wounded."

"She needs to get down here and explain what the hell is going on," Talwyn retorted. "Why are all these children here? I need a full report of everything that happened while she was held captive."

"I am sure your Second can give that to you," Briar said casually, with a glance at Azrael. "He was there."

"That is not what I mean, and you know it," Talwyn said. "What did Scarlett endure? What did she learn? Who held her captive? Why? Do they still live? Are they a threat we need to worry about? All of these things need to be addressed."

"And they will be," Briar answered, his icy-blue eyes hardening like chips of ice. "But right now, her husband is taking care of her. When she is ready, I am sure she will be more than willing to meet with you and discuss these matters."

Talwyn clicked her tongue. "Yes, I am sure she will be," she deadpanned.

"Her captors still live," Ashtine said airily, her gaze fixed on the room before them, her head tilting slightly to the side.

"The winds told you that?" Talwyn asked.

Ashtine spared her a brief glance before saying, "No. Prince Briar did."

"And what else has *Prince Briar* shared with you that he has not shared with me?" she ground out.

Ashtine's features hardened a little, clearly still upset about their argument from a few weeks ago. Talwyn had seen the princess only a handful of times since then and only when summoned. Her visits were brief and to the point. Talwyn had thought she would have moved on from it by now. But if she were being really honest, Ashtine had never been this upset with her. She didn't know how long Ashtine would harbor these feelings, or if she would eventually demand they discuss matters again.

But they definitely needed to be discussed again. She couldn't seriously be abandoning their plans they'd been perfecting for years. Decades. Talwyn simply could not accept that.

"What would you like to know?" Ashtine asked.

"Everything," Talwyn gritted out.

"The winds no longer speak to me, your Majesty. I have nothing to reveal to you," she replied, her tone void of any emotion. Briar looked more upset by this than Ashtine did. The prince's jaw was clenched, his shoulders tense and rigid, and his fingers were curling at his sides.

"What do you mean the winds no longer speak to you?" Azrael asked from where he sat. His eyes were closed, his head tipped back against the chair, and his breathing was fast and shallow, as if he still couldn't quite catch his breath.

"Queen Talwyn already knows this, Prince," Ashtine replied. "She can tell you what she wishes you to know."

Azrael's eyes slowly opened, earthy brown irises settling on her. "What the fuck happened while I was gone?"

"Do not speak to me like I am beneath you, Prince Luan," Talwyn answered.

"Have you told the Alpha his sister is back?" Ashtine asked in her silvery lilt, but before Talwyn had a chance to answer her, she had turned back to Briar. "Why is Rayner holding the hand of a child?"

Talwyn followed her gaze and found the Ash Rider indeed had a little girl's hand enveloped in his. She had golden curls that bounced with each step, and she was chatting merrily beside him as he made his way around the great hall they were all in. Tables had been set up, with food constantly being brought out to fill them. The children were eating as if they hadn't had proper meals in months. Eliza and Neve, along with some of the older children, were directing the younger ones to bathing rooms, and they would emerge in fresh clothing that actually fit them, rather than the ill-fitting garments they'd arrived in. Laughter and chatter filled the air, along with excited squeals and the endless patter of running feet, as they ran and played and explored. Despite the lack of food and proper clothing, they were obviously well cared for. Very few possessed the destitute and dispirited looks that often accompany poverty.

But that was not what struck Talwyn most. No. What assaulted her the most were the varying scents that accompanied the children. There were so many woven among them, she couldn't place where each one was coming from. Shifter blood. Witch blood. Night Children. Even Fae. All of them, in one way or another, had some form of magical bloodline flowing in their veins.

"I do not know," Briar was saying to Ashtine. "I can only assume he knows her from the last few weeks."

"One would think she would be afraid of a male whose eyes swirl with smoke and who can disappear among ashes," Talwyn commented, as the little girl continued to chatter away, telling him some kind of story. A slight smile tilted on the corner of the Ash Rider's normally stoic features.

"Children tend to see things far more simply than adults," Ashtine replied. "It is a shame we lose such clarity as we age."

Sawyer appeared at Briar's side, leaning in to speak into his brother's ear. Briar's eyes widened slightly before he nodded once. He turned to Ashtine as he said, "Sorin has requested my presence for an update on how things are progressing down here. Do you need anything before I take my leave?"

"I do not," Ashtine replied. "I shall send a note if I require you."

Briar nodded once, his lips forming a grim line, before he turned and left the hall, but Sawyer lingered next to the Wind Princess. Talwyn was about to ask if he needed something, when Azrael's voice came from behind them.

"Where is Nasima, Ashtine?"

Talwyn's gaze snapped back to the Wind Princess at the question. Indeed, the silver hawk was not in her usual place on Ashtine's shoulder. How had she missed that? When was the last time she had seen Nasima with her? It couldn't have been that day they'd argued, could it?

Ashtine's lips pursed for a moment before she said tightly, "I have already stated the winds no longer speak to me."

"What does that *mean*?" Talwyn demanded.

For the first time that day, Ashtine turned to face Talwyn fully. Winds swirled around her, and some of the children let out cries of fright, wide eyes turning to look at the Fae Princess. Her sky-blue eyes were hard, unforgiving. The female that stood before her had Azrael pushing to his feet and stumbling to Talwyn's side, a hand going to the sword at his waist.

"What is the meaning of this, Ashtine?" he barked.

But her eyes stayed pinned on Talwyn. "You forced me to choose," she whispered with a terrifying calm. "I told you. I warned you that the winds answer to what lies there. I begged you to walk a different path, but you did not turn. You forced me to choose, and I chose you, your Majesty. But the sacrifice of that choice has been arduous."

"I did not ask you to choose," Talwyn snarled.

"You are correct," Ashtine replied, her winds swirling faster around her. "I chose you of my own free will. A concept that is difficult for you to comprehend."

"You are bound to choose me," Talwyn retorted.

"I did not choose you out of any duty or vows of my Court, Talwyn. The choice would have been far easier, if that is what I could have based such a decision on."

"This is not the place for this conversation. We are not in our Halls, and there are listening ears everywhere," Azrael said, giving a pointed look in the direction of Eliza and Rayner, who were indeed watching them intently.

"May I escort you somewhere, Princess Ashtine?" Sawyer asked, stepping to her side.

"Yes, please," she answered, placing a hand in the crook of his elbow. As he began to lead her away, she looked back over her shoulder. "You best inform Stellan, your Majesty. You do not need any more strained relations at the moment."

Talwyn bristled at the slight, her back straightening and teeth clenching as she bit down on a reply.

"What did she mean by *that*?" Azrael ground out.

"Stellan was upset by Sorin going behind his back and taking Arianna on this mission. I went to visit him, and things became heated," Talwyn answered. She cast a side-long look at Azrael. "You should rest. Then I can fill you in on everything, and you can do the same."

"This sounds like something that needs to be discussed now, Talwyn. Let's go somewhere private," he replied. "You need to rest."

Azrael rubbed at his jaw, looking utterly exhausted. "I do, but there is something I need to tell you first."

Talwyn sucked on a tooth before nodding tightly and reaching for his hand. She Traveled them to her chambers in the White Halls, and Azrael immediately collapsed onto the sofa.

"What is it?" Talwyn demanded.

"It might not be anything, but . . ." He tilted his head back, closing his eyes.

"Spit it out, Az."

"Do you remember when I mentioned that there was another scent amongst the Night Child carnage at the border?"

Her brow arched. "You learned who it was?"

"Not exactly. But he appears to be working with those who took Queen Scarlett."

"You saw him?"

"He was hooded, and his scent was still very muted. Almost undetectable, especially in the mortal lands, but he is definitely Fae and definitely of the Earth Court," Azrael replied, his eyes opening to meet hers. "He spoke though. His voice was . . . familiar."

"You think you know him?" she asked, going still. If there was indeed a traitor in their Courts, it needed to be dealt with before anything else, and she had a lot of shit that needed dealing with at the moment. This moving to the top of that list was not ideal, but one traitorous Fae shouldn't be too much trouble. They'd just need to draw him out.

"Talwyn, he . . ." Azrael ran a hand down his face, then pushed out a heavy breath. "His voice sounded exactly like Ordos."

Talwyn lurched back from him, nearly tripping on the rug at her feet. "That is not possible."

"I know," Azrael said, forcing himself back to his feet and swaying slightly. "But I swear to Silas, Talwyn, he sounded just like him . . . and he seemed to know who I was."

"There is some other explanation for that," Talwyn said. "Tarek is dead. He has been dead for over ten years. He would not be hiding out in the mortal lands, leaving me to think otherwise."

"I understand, Talwyn," Azrael said with a sigh. "I understand how unlikely this seems. We can look into it after my reserves have refilled. I did not want you to hear it from someone else while I slept."

"If Scarlett was in his company these last few weeks, I am sure she will be able to tell us who it is," Talwyn replied, watching him make his way to her bed.

"I am sure you are right." He practically fell onto the bed. "Talwyn."

"What?" she snapped.

"Do not do anything brash until I wake."

She turned to snap a retort, but found him already asleep, his breathing deep and evening out. It would take at least a day to fully replenish his reserves with his deep wells entirely depleted. Perhaps longer.

He had to be mistaken. There was no possible way Tarek was alive and living in the mortal kingdoms of all places. In Windonelle. In Baylorin. Where Scarlett had been hidden all these years. Where Eliné had been hiding. She could not even entertain such a ludicrous idea because if that were true . . .

If that were true, he had betrayed her on so many levels. He would have betrayed his Court. He would have betrayed his queen. He would have betrayed their twin flame bond. He would have betrayed *her*.

He'd known of her plans. He had known how deeply she sought revenge against Avonleya, and he had sought the same. There were times she had even felt like his drive for revenge was greater than her own, although she had never really contemplated why. She had always assumed it was because he was that loyal to her, and loved her so thoroughly, that he wanted what she wanted. That was how she had felt about him.

Azrael had told her not to do anything brash, but it wasn't as if she could ask Scarlett right now. Sorin undoubtedly wouldn't let her anywhere near his wife at the moment, and his Court undoubtedly wouldn't let her anywhere near him. But she couldn't just sit here on her ass, waiting for Azrael to wake.

She left a quick note for him, for when he woke, then Traveled back to the Black Halls. The great hall was as chaotic as when she'd left. Eyes scanning the room, they landed on Arianna. She hadn't seen the Beta since they'd come back, and Talwyn immediately began making her way to the Shifter.

"Lady Arianna," she greeted curtly when she reached her side.

"Queen Talwyn," Arianna replied in her sultry tone. "I thought you would be with your prince."

"He is not my prince," Talwyn retorted.

"He is certainly no one else's," Arianna said with a dismissive shrug. "How can I be of service?"

"I am here to escort you home. Your brother will be glad to see you have returned," Talwyn answered, figuring she could at least fix one of her relationships while she waited for Azrael to wake. Bringing Arianna back to Siofra was sure to put her back in the good graces of the Alpha.

Arianna looked her up and down, a small smirk curving up on her full lips. "I am sure Prince Sorin will escort me home when he is able."

"He is clearly otherwise occupied at the moment."

"And I am enjoying my time away," Arianna replied coolly. "I do not wish to return to Siofra so quickly. Although if you wanted to go and fetch Jamahl for me, I would not object to that."

"Lady, I think it would be best if you returned. The Alpha was very unhappy that you were gone—"

"I am sure he was," Arianna interrupted, her olive eyes darkening a shade. "He prefers to keep me there while he goes on adventures. He forgets, your Majesty, that I have just as much experience in these matters as he does."

"I did not mean to offend you, Arianna," Talwyn said, trying and failing to keep her frustration from her tone.

"Then try harder not to do so," the Beta replied sharply.

"I have to tell him you have returned, Arianna," Talwyn said. "I gave him my word I would keep him informed of any news I learned of you and your whereabouts."

"Then send him a note," she answered, turning and beginning to walk away from her.

"Wait," Talwyn demanded, and the Beta paused, looking over her shoulder, beaded braids clinking as she waited for Talwyn to continue. Talwyn sighed. "Did you see who Scarlett's captor was? Do you know of him?"

"I was with when she was retrieved, and I was sent in beforehand to figure out where she was being held. There were several involved in her capture," Arianna answered.

"And do you know any of them? Did you hear their names?"

"I think you should ask Prince Sorin these questions."

"Yet I am asking you," Talwyn said.

"There were three that Sorin appeared the most concerned with. One of them was the Assassin Lord of the Black Syndicate where we retrieved her from," Arianna answered, her lips tightening at the clear order and demand for submission from Talwyn.

"Did you hear their names?" Talwyn repeated.

"Alaric, Mikale, and Lord Tyndell," she answered shortly.

"No others?"

"No."

Talwyn nodded.

"Anything else, your Majesty?"

There was enough venom in the words to let Talwyn know she had officially pissed off the Beta, and that was just fucking fantastic. Not only was she going to have to tell Stellan his sister was back from the mortal lands but refused to come home, she was also going to face his wrath at having angered his sister.

"I had dinner with Stellan while you were away. We discussed several matters, and I would like to get your input on some of them."

Because fuck it. She'd already lit this fire. She may as well fan the flames.

Arianna's brows rose. "My brother did not give you the information you were seeking?"

Talwyn pressed her tongue to her cheek. "Not exactly."

"Either he did or he didn't. Stellan does not do things partially," Arianna countered.

"It involved Avonleya."

Her brows rose higher at that. "What of it?"

"If there was a possibility of removing the wards that surround them, do you think they should be gifted such a thing?" Talwyn asked.

"I would think you should learn if they would even consider that a gift," Arianna answered.

"Why would they not want to be able to move about freely once more?" Talwyn countered.

Arianna shrugged indifferently. "The wards were put in place for a reason. Until that reason is dealt with, I would imagine they would like the wards left exactly as they are."

"The wards were put in place to keep them sequestered across the sea."

"Were they?" Arianna asked, arching a brow, her lips tilting up in knowing. "I suggest continuing this conversation with Queen Scarlett and Prince Sorin . . . After you report to my brother, of course."

With those parting words, she turned and walked out of the hall. Ire coursing through her, Talwyn went in the opposite direction, heading for a concealed passageway that would lead up to the queen's private wing, where she was sure Sorin and Scarlett were holed up. She'd spent much of her childhood here. That knowledge, along with the fact that these halls were identical to the White Halls, meant she knew all of the place's secrets.

Unfortunately, so did Sorin.

The moment she stepped foot on the staircase to make her way to the rooms, Eliza appeared.

"They are not to be disturbed, your Majesty," she said with a dark smile.

"Move, General," Talwyn said with a sneer.

"My orders come from my prince who has informed me no one, save for a select few, are allowed beyond this point for the time being," Eliza said.

And Talwyn knew this was useless. If she continued to push this, Eliza would summon Cyrus and Rayner and even Briar. They no longer answered to her. She didn't have the power to command them to do shit any more.

"When can I speak with them?" Talwyn gritted out.

"The queen is resting and recovering. I will let Sorin know you desire an audience when she is well," Eliza replied nonchalantly.

"See that you do."

CHAPTER 21
SCARLETT

There was no moon on this night.

There were just the stars and the dark.

She did not know where she was, as she stared up at the black sky. She was not in the Black Halls. She was not in the Fire Court. She was not in Baylorin. She was not in a forest.

She found she did not care.

In this place, she did not feel. She did not feel the crushing grief of not knowing if Cassius was going to live or die. She did not feel the guilt for blocking her twin flame bond without fully understanding the cost. She did not feel the pressure of Courts and kingdoms depending on her. She did not feel the insatiable craving that had driven her to sheer madness. She did not feel the pain, the fear, the agony.

She interlaced her fingers, placing her hands on her stomach. She was lying in grass of some sort. It was soft beneath her back. If it was winter here, the chill of the season did not touch her, did not sink into her bones.

Her shadows shuddered as they rose from beneath her skin, and she inhaled deeply at feeling them again. They seemed just as joyous to be with her once more. They swirled along her arms, her legs. They drifted among her hair and caressed her face. She lifted a hand in greeting, swiping her fingers through them, feeling them dance at her touch.

And when the cry of an eagle reached her ears, she did not need to look around to know who was coming. She did not even bother to sit up. Her eyes went back to the stars.

"Welcome back, Lady of Darkness," the beautiful man with the silver hair said, dropping down beside her. He bent a leg, his arm resting atop it, and a moment later, Altaria swooped down to perch on his forearm.

"You are blessed by Temural," she said. A statement, not a question.

"One could say that," he agreed.

"What else could one say?" she asked, sensing the moment Shirina entered this place, wherever she was.

"One could say I have missed seeing you," he answered.

"That Mark blocked your way to me, too?" she guessed.

"That Mark did many things," he said. "But, yes, it blocked my ability to communicate with you among them."

"Am I dreaming?"

"Yes."

"You can enter my dreams at will."

"When my power reserves are relatively full, yes."

Scarlett chewed on her lip for a moment before saying, "You have never been so willing to answer my questions."

"You have never asked the right ones."

She tsked in annoyance under her breath, and the man chuckled. She turned her head as Shirina came into view, her silver eyes bright in the dark.

"Your eyes match hers," she said, glancing at the man.

"So do yours."

"My eyes are blue."

"When your power reserves are not full they are, but when you are at your most powerful, they are silver."

She didn't know what to say to that, so she didn't say anything.

The two sat in silence for long moments before she said, "If I am a Lady of Darkness, then what are you?"

"A Lord of Night," he said without a moment's hesitation.

"Is it always night here?"

"No, but we cherish the darkness like other places covet the light."

"Where are we?"

"Home."

Scarlett only nodded, not that he could see her. A comfortable silence fell between them again.

"It seems rather unfair that you can come to me whenever you please, but I have no way to contact you," she mused, her fingers brushing along Shirina's coat where she had lain down beside her.

"Allow me to rectify that," he answered. Scarlett turned her head in time to see him raise a hand. Something she could only describe as night itself seeped from his palm. It was darkest black and seemed to suck any light into itself. It was nothing like her shadows, yet somehow exactly like them, too.

When it receded, a piece of stone sat in the center of his palm. It was just as dark as whatever power had bled from him, and she pushed herself up into a sitting position when he extended it to her.

"What is it?"

"It is nightstone."

"What am I supposed to do with it?" she asked, turning the thing over in her hand.

"Use it if you need to speak with me," he said, leaning back on his hands and tilting his face back up to the sky.

"What? Just speak to it?" she scoffed.

She could somehow make out his smile in the starlight. "Something like that."

"You're seriously not going to tell me? You're just going to give me a rock?"

"You're welcome," he answered.

"Oh my gods," Scarlett muttered.

She had nowhere to put the thing, still in that black gown Alaric had dressed her in.

But then again, this was a dream. How was she going to take a rock out of here?

"Your focus now needs to be on finding the keys," the man said eventually.

She sighed deeply. "I figured as much."

"You will find the keys have always been trying to get home."

Her eyes snapped back to his at the words. "And I suppose I need a lock, too?"

He chuckled. "One would assume so. Or what use is a key?"

"Profound," she deadpanned.

Another bird's cry broke the quiet of the dark, and a moment later, Amaré appeared, swooping down and landing on Scarlett's shoulder. As she reached up to stroke his feathers, the man said, "He waits for you to wake."

"How long have I been sleeping?"

"Long enough."

She nodded again at his non-answer.

"You need a Source," he said.

"A source of what?"

"A Source to keep your power reserves replenished."

"You mean a Fae I can . . . drink from?"

"No," he answered, shaking his head. "Replenishing your power that way is... There are better ways."

"Good. That was . . . not enjoyable," Scarlett said, her fingers coming to her lips as she remembered them fastened to Sorin's flesh. Coppery liquid sliding down her throat, tasting like he did. Honey and cloves and lush smokiness.

"The problem is that it is too enjoyable," the man countered, knowingly. "It is why it was outlawed, and why the Night Children were forbidden to feed from the Fae. That is history you should look into. I do not have time to teach you everything right now."

Scarlett nodded, glad he couldn't see her properly in the dark. She was pretty sure her cheeks were slightly flushed because he was right. Drinking Sorin's blood gave her a feeling she couldn't describe. It was fire and power and strength, and the high she got from it was unlike anything she had ever felt before. But the frenzy she had experienced, the complete loss of control, the utter madness? That had not been pleasant in the slightest.

"You need to practice with your shadows and white flames. Learn your limits, so that what happened with the vampyres does not happen again. Learn to recognize when you are low on power, when you need to replenish. Keep your Source close always," he said.

"How do I find a Source?"

"I suspect you will find you already have one."

"That's helpful," she replied sarcastically.

"I am glad you think so," he said with a smirk. She rolled her eyes. "Do you have a name?"

"I do."

"Care to share?"

"Soon, Lady of Darkness."

"That's vague."

The man chuckled again, pushing to his feet and reaching down to help her to her own.

"When night and darkness meet, when dreams and stars collide, when ashes meld with shadows, you will find me waiting, and the first words from my lips will be my name."

CHAPTER 22
SCARLETT

For the first time in weeks, Scarlett woke with shadows drifting around her. She hadn't opened her eyes yet, but she could feel them— brushing down her arms, her face, her soul.

And she could feel him. A steady presence. A burning essence intertwining with her own being.

Sorin.

She pried her eyes open. There was no hint of the dull headache she'd been suffering through the last few weeks. She didn't know where she was, but she also didn't care because he was here. She could feel him. And this was different from all the times Lord Tyndell had tried to make her believe he had come for her. She knew this wasn't a dream. She wasn't questioning reality in the slightest.

Scarlett pushed herself up into a sitting position and fell still when her eyes settled on him. He was sitting in an ornate armchair several feet away from her. The chair was facing the bed though, and he was sprawled in it like a godsdamn king, his legs wide and his head propped on his fist. His black hair was disheveled, falling over his brow. His golden eyes narrowed at her slightly when she met his gaze, and she sucked in a breath. She could feel his presence, yes, but she couldn't tell what he was feeling. She couldn't *feel* that part of him.

Had that part of the bond not been restored? Had she done something irreparable?

She reached up, pushing her hair back from her face, and he still didn't move.

He didn't say a word.

"Why did I wake up to you looking like you want to throttle me?" she rasped.

He still didn't say anything. He just nodded his head towards the bedside table, and she turned to find a glass of water sitting there. She reached over for it and took several large swallows, nearly draining the glass, before turning back to face Sorin once more.

His unreadable mask hadn't changed, but he finally spoke. "Do you need any healing?"

She shook her head, drawing her knees to her chest and cupping the water glass between her hands. She was still wearing the black, blood-stained gown she'd had on at the Fellowship.

Sorin nodded at her response. "Are you feeling weak in any form? Do you need blood?"

She swallowed thickly, that part of everything rushing back to her, and she felt her cheeks heat slightly.

"No," she whispered, her eyes falling to the water glass.

"Are you . . ."

Scarlett glanced up when he didn't finish his question and found him clenching his jaw, his fist on the armrest doing the same.

"Did he touch you?"

"No, Sorin," she answered softly. "I was not touched or hurt like that." He nodded, a fraction of the tension in his body seeming to release.

He stood then, swiping up a bundle of clothing and tossing it onto the bed.

"Change, Scarlett. Then I will take you to see Cassius. There is a bathing room through there if you want to wash up first," he added, nodding towards a doorway to the left.

"You don't want to . . . talk about everything?" she asked, setting the water glass back onto the bedside table.

"We will definitely be having a conversation about that shit you pulled at the border, Scarlett," he replied, his voice icy with suppressed emotion. "But that is a conversation I need your complete attention for, and I know you will not be able to focus on it until you have seen Cassius."

Scarlett swallowed again, nodding once as she flipped back the blankets she was nestled under. He stepped closer but didn't reach for her. She slid from the bed, grabbing the small pile of clothing, and made her way to the bathing room. He followed, keeping distance between them, and she didn't know if she should reach for him or not. She didn't know if he was too angry with her, or if she should try to have this conversation now, despite him saying it needed to wait. She didn't want it hanging over them.

But he was also right. The longer she was awake, the more her thoughts were pulled to Cassius. He had to be alive. Sorin would have told her if he wasn't. Was he awake? Was he speaking? Was Hazel able to heal him completely?

Thoughts swirling in her mind, she used a cloth to quickly wipe down her skin, getting the largest spots of dried blood. She'd worry about bathing later. There wasn't time right now.

She quickly tugged on the pants, pulling the tunic over her head as she emerged from the bathing room. She was working her hair into a loose plait, making her way to the door, when Sorin called from behind her.

"Shoes, Scarlett."

"What?"

He held up a pair of silk slippers. "You need shoes."

She quickly tied off her braid, swiping the slippers from his outstretched hand. While she tugged them on, he walked past and opened the door for her. She practically flew through it, skidding to a halt when she realized she had no idea where she was or where to go.

"This way," Sorin said, coming out behind her. His hands were in his pockets, and he nodded his head towards a set of stairs at the end of the corridor. He fell into step beside her, and she let her shadows free after being confined for so long. He glanced side-long at them before looking straight ahead again, a muscle feathering in his jaw.

"Are you . . . all right?" she asked tentatively as they started descending the steps.

"No," he answered tightly. "But we will discuss it after you have seen that Cassius is recovering."

"Is he awake?"

"No. His injuries were so extensive . . ." He trailed off, running a hand along his jaw before tucking it back into his pocket with a sigh. "They do not know how long it will be before he wakes, but they believe he will. As long as he continues to receive Fae blood."

Scarlett nodded, crossing her arms and running her hands up and down them. She wasn't cold, but something was wrong. She could feel Sorin, but not in the way she had been able to before everything that had happened. His emotions seemed muted, as if they were still blocked. She hadn't tried to speak to him down their bridge yet, and if she were honest with herself, she was too nervous to try now. What if that hadn't been fixed either? What if she had done something irreparable to their bond? What if it would never be like before? What if what she had done affected their Trials? Kept them from ever being Anointed?

She hadn't realized they had stopped, but she looked up to find Sorin staring down at her, waiting for her to collect herself. He always knew. Always knew when she was spiraling. Always knew when she needed a moment.

She gave him a weak smile, but he did not return it, so she nodded to tell him she was ready, and he pushed open the door. He let her pass before following her through. Cyrus was there, his gaze instantly landing on her. He stood from where he had been sitting by the hearth, and immediately began to make his way to her, but he froze at the snarl that rippled from Sorin.

Scarlett's head whipped around, her eyes wide as she took him in. He looked feral, his teeth bared.

She smirked at him. "The mother hen is still not your best look, Prince," she said sweetly. But he did not return the sentiment.

"Do not start with that, Scarlett," he ground out. "*No one* is going to touch you right now."

Her mouth fell open. "It is *Cyrus*."

"I do not give a fuck if it is Anala herself. I am barely keeping it together the way it is. No one else is touching you."

She opened her mouth to spout something in reply, but Cyrus cut her off. "Let this go, Scarlett. This has been . . ." Cyrus clenched his jaw. "He has not been okay. What you did to him, to your twin flame bond, to all of us, was not okay."

"Cyrus," Sorin warned, a clear order not to interfere, but Scarlett felt the verbal hit.

"I didn't—"

"Not now, Scarlett," Sorin said, cutting her off. "You are not here to defend your actions right now. You are here to see that Cassius is still breathing. Speak with the High Witch. Get your questions answered."

The implication was clear, though. She would need to defend her actions to them.

She glanced at Sorin, but when she found his eyes pinned on her, she quickly looked away, moving to the bedside. Hazel stood, rigid and formidable as always, her violet eyes never leaving Cassius.

"You let males speak to you in despicable ways," she said when Scarlett came to a stop beside her.

"I did despicable things," Scarlett answered quietly. "I deceived them. My actions put them in danger. Put others in danger." She gestured to Cassius's still form at the words. "I deserve the things they have to say to me." When Hazel didn't say anything in response to that, she asked, "How is he?"

"He lives," Hazel answered.

"Will he wake?"

"Yes, I believe he will. Being half-Witch, half—" She paused, waving her hand in Scarlett's direction. "He will wake. Most of his injuries will heal."

"Most?" Scarlett questioned, turning from Cassius to look up at the High Witch.

"They used different blades," Hazel said, her angular features seeming to sharpen, violet eyes going darker. "Some were regular blades, easily healed. Others, like the one used on his eye . . ."

"He will be blind," Scarlett whispered, reaching out to take his hand in hers.

"In that eye, yes," Hazel answered. "Some of the stab wounds did extensive internal damage as well. We will not know the full implications of those wounds until he wakes."

"How long? When do you think he will wake up?" she asked, stepping closer to the bed. She wanted nothing more than to climb up beside him again, be close to him, hear his heart beating beneath her ear.

But she had responsibilities to tend to. She'd brought over one hundred children here. She needed to find Nuri, find out what's been happening in Baylorin, learn what is going on with Callan and Tava.

"When he is ready," Hazel answered, bringing her hand to his cheek, white light emanating again.

It wasn't really the answer she was hoping for, but something in her chest had loosened at seeing him alive, seeing his chest steadily rise and fall. There was no labored breathing, no pools of blood. Even his facial features were returning to normal. They had stripped his dirty and torn clothes off, his torso tightly bound and wrapped. His leg that had been shattered was set into some type of splint, but many of the smaller cuts, burns, and wounds were nowhere to be found.

They stood in silence for several minutes. She could hear Cyrus and Sorin speaking quietly together across the room, but she couldn't bring herself to look at them, let alone attempt to listen in on what they were saying.

"I need to go check on a few things, see a few people," Scarlett finally said, her fingers tightening slightly around Cassius's hand. "I will be back frequently to check on him, but please send for me if there is even the slightest change."

Hazel nodded, glancing at her for the first time since Scarlett had come to her side. "You made a choice, young queen. Now you lift your chin and handle the consequences, whatever they may be. You do not look back, only forward."

Scarlett nodded several times, forcing back the stinging at the back of her eyes. She knew Sorin had drawn nearer when she had mentioned going to check on the others. She could feel his presence, knew when she turned around he would be mere feet from her.

Taking a deep breath, she turned and met his stare. "I need to check on the children and find Nuri."

"You can do that after you and I have spoken," Sorin answered.

"Just let me make sure they have everything they need for the children—"

"No, Scarlett. Now," Sorin interrupted, a fire portal appearing behind him.

"You still don't give me orders, Prince," she replied with faux sweetness.

Sorin stalked forward, his hands back in his pockets. He was visibly trembling, and she felt a flicker of emotion down their bond. Fury? Desperation? Something else? She couldn't get a read on it, before it was gone as quickly as it had appeared.

He stopped directly in front of her, bending down to speak into her ear. "This conversation is going to happen, Scarlett. Now."

Scarlett's lips pressed into a thin line, but she nodded once before stepping through the portal and finding herself in the mountain chateau. Sorin came through a moment later, the portal snapping shut. He crossed to the hearth, tossing a flame into it before turning to face her.

"Do you need to rest before we do this?" "No, but I—"

"You left me." His voice was low and tense and filled with an emotion she couldn't decipher.

"I did it to protect you," she said, her own tone pleading with him to understand. "I did it *for* you. For all of you."

Sorin shook his head. He'd stepped behind an armchair, and his fingers gripped the back of it, digging into the upholstery. "In what world is you *leaving* me behind *protecting* me, Scarlett? In what realm is you *blocking our godsdamn bond* in *my* best interest?"

"Sorin, I—" She took a step towards him, but a thin line of fire erupted before her. She could have easily stepped over it, but she paused, accepting the boundary he was drawing for now. She reached for him down that bond that was back and flowing between them again, but he shook his head once more.

"No. You do not get to use that bond right now. Not for this." His jaw was clenched, and she could tell it was taking everything he had to keep himself under control, to keep his temper from exploding.

She closed her eyes, taking a deep breath, her hands fisting at her sides. She planted her feet, bracing herself for what was about to come. Opening her eyes, she looked directly into golden ones filled with embers as she said with confidence she in no way felt, "I can take it, Sorin. I can take what you have to say to me."

Sorin studied her for a long moment, before she felt so many emotions flood down that bridge between their souls she staggered under it.

Terror. Denial. Disbelief. Sorrow. Fury.

Pain. Anger. Hurt. Betrayal.

Scarlett's hands flew to her chest, clenching into fists over her heart as she took it all in, every single thing he'd been feeling since she'd enacted that Blood Mark. Tears instantly cut a path down her face, but she held her ground. She held Sorin's stare.

"We made vows to each other, Scarlett Aditya Semiria. You get all of me, and I get all of you. We do not shut each other out. We do not tell each other to leave. You chose me, and I chose you. And yet, with that one act, you created a you and a me. Mere days after saying those vows."

Sorin's chest was heaving, and his fingers were digging into the fabric of the chair so deeply, she was certain he was about to puncture the upholstery. Or set it alight, which was probably more likely, considering the smoke unfurling beneath his hands. She didn't know if he was waiting for her to respond or if he was preparing himself for his next strike, so she didn't say anything.

"When did you figure it out?" he demanded. "How soon after Cyrus came to our rooms did you figure out what was really going on? How long did it take you to come up with a plan that excluded the rest of us? That put you in a position to be taken from me? To be used against your own Courts?" She swallowed thickly, her eyes falling to the plush rug under feet, but he called her out on that, too. "No, Scarlett, your eyes stay on me for this conversation. I need to see them to know if you are lying to me yet again or if you are telling me everything."

"You're one to talk, Sorin," she snapped, her eyes flashing back to his. "You lied to me for months when we met. Then you lied about me being your twin flame. Oh, excuse me," she drawled sarcastically. "You didn't lie. You *withheld information*. How was this any different?"

Sorin shook his head again, huffing a hollow laugh of disbelief. "And I spent so many more months proving myself to you. Over and over again. And you are right. I did withhold so much from you. Maybe you find you can never fully trust me because of it, and that is on me. But if you are going to hold that over me, if you are going to use that as an excuse for doing something like *this* when enemies are at our doors, we are never going to pass the Trials, Scarlett. What we are will not survive if we are going to keep score about who has wronged who most. If that is the case, tell me now, and we will figure something else out."

Scarlett lurched back as if he'd struck her in the gut. "You don't mean that."

"I cannot trust you, Scarlett! I cannot trust my wife, my queen, my *twin flame*. Do you have any idea what you did to me when I stepped back over that border and found your marriage band floating there? When I could not feel you? When I could not find you?" He had stepped from behind the armchair, taking a few steps towards her, embers sparking with each footfall. His voice had risen, lethal with anger and hurt. "This wasn't the first time, either. We agreed to no more secrets. You told me you would keep nothing from me, and the very next day, you led me down to a secret passageway in the library. And a mere few hours after that, you pulled this shit."

He had stopped a few feet from her, the trail of flames still drawing a line between them.

"Are you saying you don't . . ." She swallowed again, tears streaming down her face, but she forced herself to say the words. "Are you saying you don't want this any more? Are you saying you no longer choose us? Choose me?"

The line of flames between them flared up, and Scarlett flinched away on instinct. When she turned back, she found him standing directly on the other side of the fire, his eyes as bright as the flames separating them.

"You are my necessity, Scarlett. I do not know how I can make it any clearer to you. I am yours. I choose you, and I will always choose you."

"Then choose me, Sorin!" she cried. "Because it seems all you have done since I woke is pull away from me. You haven't touched me. You haven't—"

"I have not touched you because the moment I feel your flesh beneath my fingers again, it's over, Scarlett," he snarled, and her breath caught in her throat. "The moment I taste your lips, the second I have you in my arms, the last shred of self-control I am clinging to will come apart. Do not think that holding you against me while fighting our way out of the Black Syndicate did not affect me. Do not think that it was in any way easy for me to sit in that room with Cassius, you mere feet from me, and not haul you off to another room when I have not seen you, touched you, felt you in weeks. I do not know what all you endured while there. I do not know if you are ready to be touched. I do not know how you are feeling, because you blocked our fucking bond, and the moment I touch you, I will lose that control."

"Then lose control, Sorin!"

The words had barely left her lips when he had crossed that line of flames, his hands coming to her face and his lips landing on hers. It was a brutal, punishing kiss that had her knees instantly trembling. One of his hands slid from her face, wrapping around her waist, pulling her flush against him and holding her up. She gripped the fabric of his tunic, fisting the material in his hands, as his tongue plunged into her mouth in desperation. Cloves and honey and embers danced along her taste buds, and the hand on her cheek slid into her hair, tugging her head back roughly so he could deepen the kiss.

"You left me," he said roughly against her lips.

"I'm sorry," she gasped as his mouth slid along her jaw, down her neck.

"It's not good enough, Scarlett," he snarled, his canines biting into the sensitive skin where her neck and shoulder met.

"I know," she whispered, her hips bucking forward, feeling him press against her.

His hands slipped under the back of her thighs, lifting her off of her feet. She instantly wrapped her legs around his waist, kissing him back frantically when his lips found their way to hers again.

"Can you Travel?" he demanded, nipping at her bottom lip, hard enough to draw blood.

"Yes," she rasped, her fingers grasping at his hair, pulling herself closer to him. She needed to feel him. Skin on skin. All of him.

"Upstairs," was all he said as he began walking, and for once, she did as he ordered. Between one step and the next, they went from the sitting room to the large bedroom. He dropped her onto the bed, releasing her to slide her pants and undergarments down her legs, her slippers coming with them. He pulled his own tunic over his head, and Scarlett whimpered in need, reaching for him.

"I should make you wait," he said with a cold smirk, stepping between her legs where they hung over the end of the bed. His hands landed on either side of her waist, bracing his body over hers.

"You should," she agreed breathlessly, looping her arms around his neck and trying to pull him down onto her, but he didn't give in. Instead, he stood back up, pulling her with him so she sat before him. His hands skimmed up her sides, taking her tunic with them, and she let him pull it over her head. He dropped the tunic to the floor, his eyes glued to her bare skin. His hands came up and shoved her shoulders, pushing her back down onto the bed, but he didn't follow. He stood, standing over her, his gaze trailing down her body, lust and hunger filling his golden eyes. Her blood was on fire, and it wasn't from any type of fire magic, but then she felt his power sweep over her, searching for her own power, and she instantly sent her shadows and ice and white flames to wind with it.

Sorin groaned, his eyes closing and head falling back in clear pleasure, as their magic touched and connected in ways she was dying to do with their flesh. His breathing was heavy as he held himself back.

"Sorin," she whispered. "Please."

His eyes snapped back open at the word. "I find it interesting that your manners only appear when they suit your needs, Princess."

She opened her mouth to snap a reply, but then his fingers brushed against her thighs, and she sucked in a breath. It was a whisper of a touch. Fingertips barely connecting with skin, and it wasn't enough. Not nearly enough as they slowly went higher and higher, his body coming over her as he went. They skated over her hips, up her sides, under her breasts. She arched into them, seeking out any other contact he would give her.

Then it was just a single finger sliding down her torso, over her navel, to her center, his eyes tracking the movement. Her hands were fisting in the bedding at her sides, knowing if she reached for him again, he would continue toying with her, teasing her, making her wait. He met her gaze, a slight cruel tilt of his lips telling her he knew exactly what she was feeling and thinking, before he plunged that finger into her.

She moaned at finally feeling him inside her again, even if it was just a finger. He pulled it back, adding a second one before diving back in, curling them against her inner walls as his thumb came down on that perfect spot between her thighs, making her writhe against his hand. He moved onto the bed beside her, continuing to thrust his fingers, his thumb making slow, tight circles against her.

"You left me," he growled again into her ear, his other hand slipping into hair and pulling, more strands coming out of her plait.

"I know," she panted, her back arching at the pull of her hair. "I'm sorry, Sorin. I'm sorry."

"Still not good enough," he snarled, his lips coming down onto hers as if he couldn't hold himself back any more, even if he wanted to.

"I love you," she breathed into his mouth. "I love you, and I choose you. Always you."

He pulled back, his hand stilling, fingers still inside her, and she whimpered at the loss of movement.

"You did not choose me when you left me," he said, his tone bordering on vicious.

"I did, Sorin," she insisted. "I chose your life over mine. I chose—"

He pulled his fingers from her, sliding on top of her, straddling her hips as his hands slammed into the bed beside her head, caging her in. His dark hair fell forward across his brow, his golden eyes glowing like hot coals. "How do you still not understand this, Scarlett?"

She froze at the violence and rage glimmering in his eyes. She was a mess of need and want. He'd brought her to the edge of pleasure, and she tried to push that down as she stared into the face of raw fury.

"I do not want a life without you in it. If the choice is a life without you or death at your side, I choose death, Scarlett. I choose wherever you are. If that means we are ashes in the voids between stars, then that is what I choose because I am *with you*. I am giving you my life. Let me give that to you," he begged. "Choose that. Choose doing this *together*. That is what I want you to choose."

"Okay," she breathed, reaching up to run her fingers down the side of his face, along his jaw, feeling a couple days' worth of stubble under her fingertips. Her thumb brushed along his lower lip, feeling his harsh breaths as he exhaled. Her hand slipped around to the nape of his neck, and she pulled herself up, her lips meeting his. She kissed each corner of his mouth, and a soft groan fell from his lips as she began sliding her mouth down his throat, his breathing ragged. Her hands slid to his shoulders, and she pushed, nudging him onto his back and pressing him down onto the bed.

Her mouth went lower, her tongue tracing ridges of hard muscles, as her hands found buttons on his pants and pulled him free. Her eyes on his, she lowered her mouth, swirling her tongue around his tip. He jerked against her, a curse falling from his lips, as his fingers found their way into her hair yet again. One of her hands wrapped around his base as she drew him back farther into her mouth and down her throat, and he groaned again, his fingers fisting tight around her strands as he began guiding her movements. The saltiness of him mixed with the honey and cloves of his kisses.

It wasn't long before he was pulling her off of him, though, flipping her back underneath him. He shoved his pants off the rest of the way and settled between her thighs. "That," he whispered into her ear, his breath hot against her skin and making her hair flutter, "is a much better use for your tongue."

Before she could reply, he thrust into her in one hard stroke, and she cried out at the feel of him filling her. Tears stung at the back of her eyes, and his face softened as he brushed his thumb along her cheek. He pulled almost all the way out, pushing back in slower.

"I'm sorry, Sorin," she whispered, her throat thick as she held back her tears.

"I know, Love," he replied, pushing hair out of her eyes and smoothing it back.

"I love you, and I hear you," she breathed while he continued to move inside of her, slowly picking up his pace, the arm he'd worked under her shoulders holding her tightly to him.

"I love you, Scarlett. I am yours. Always."

He pressed his lips to her forehead, and his movements became harder, faster, making her moan into his neck, her nails digging into his back. Within moments, she was tumbling over the edge of pleasure, gasping his name, and he was right behind her, with a few final thrusts before he was groaning her name, raining kisses along the top of her head.

They clung to each other, breathing ragged as they came down from their highs together, before he gently pulled out of her and rolled to his back. She went with him, resting her head on his chest, his arm curled around her waist and locking her to his side. He inhaled deeply, his other hand making long strokes up and down her arm.

She could feel some of his emotions down the bond, but it was still muted. There was a sort of contentment, but there was still a simmering anger underneath it. She released some of her shadows, letting them brush along his face, and she felt his flames rush up to meet them.

"Sorin?" she asked with uncertainty.

"Yeah, Love?" he hummed, and she glanced up to find his eyes closed, but his features taut with tension.

"Can you . . . I mean, our bond . . ."

His eyes opened as she stumbled over her words, and he waited patiently for her to finish her thoughts, his hand coming up behind his head.

"I can't feel you like I used to," she finally said in a rush. "I mean, our bond is there, but I can't feel your emotions as easily. As if there is still a block. Did I . . ." She blew out another long breath. "Did I do something irreparable? Can you feel me? Like before?"

"I can feel you, Scarlett, just as I always have been able to when the bond was not blocked," he answered, his long fingers beginning to make idle circles along her hip.

Relief flooded through her at his words, but then . . .

"Why can I not feel you like I did before?"

He sighed, his eyes going to the window over the tub across the room. "Just because I choose you, just because I need you in ways I cannot put into words, just because I am yours, does not mean you get my unwavering trust, Scarlett. It does not mean I will blindly believe what you say or do. It does not mean I will not question your motives. Not right now."

She stiffened against him, ice seeming to fill her veins, but he continued the soothing movements on her skin despite the temperature in the room dropping. "So because you don't trust me, the bond is not as strong for me?" she asked quietly.

"It is not that it is not as strong," he replied with another sigh. "The distrust is some of the resistance, yes, but I can shield against the bond to a certain extent."

Scarlett sat up at that, his arm slipping from her body, and he turned his head to meet her stare. "You are keeping me out?"

A muscle feathered in his jaw, and he pressed his tongue to his cheek. "To an extent, yes," he finally answered.

"How?" she demanded.

"There are mental shields we learn when we are young, to protect against entrancing mainly, among other things. I would have taught you how to use them, but we haven't had time with everything else going on," he said.

"You have been giving me hell for blocking our bond, and yet you are doing that exact thing?" she asked, trying not to let her voice rise.

His features twisted into ire in a heartbeat, and he pushed himself up to a sitting position, bringing his face close to hers. "This is not even close to the same thing, Scarlett. You can still sense me. You can still feel my physical presence. You could still find me if I were taken captive somewhere," he snarled. "That is not something you can block with a mental shield, or any type of shield for that matter. I didn't think anything could fully block the bond actually, but you certainly proved me wrong."

Scarlett reached for a blanket at the end of the bed, wrapping it around her shoulders and tugging it tight. She tried to will some heat into her body, but it didn't seem to make a difference as goosebumps rose across her skin. She felt Sorin try to push some warmth into her too, but she pushed back, letting her shadows latch onto his magic and keep it from touching her. He didn't say anything at the obvious rejection, letting her sort through things as he always had.

"So where does that leave us?" she finally asked, unable to bring herself to meet his eyes.

But he didn't let that slide either. She felt his fingers grip her chin, tipping her head up. "I am yours, and you are mine, Scarlett Semiria. That has not changed."

"It feels like everything has changed," she countered.

"You are not the same as when you left," he answered. "And neither am I."

"Then what do we do?"

"No one said this would be easy, Scarlett. It is not a choice you make once. It is a choice we must make every day. Over and over again. Even on the hard days. Even on the days we want to throttle each other."

"I don't know what else I can say or do, Sorin," she said, reaching up and swiping a lone tear from her face.

"It will take time, Love," he answered gently, his hand resting on her knee. "It took you time to trust me again, did it not?" She swallowed thickly again, and Sorin released her chin. "Let's rest, Scarlett. Take a proper bath if you want to. This conversation is not over. You still need to explain many things, but right now, just . . . rest."

She nodded but didn't move as he climbed off the bed, grabbing his pants and slipping them back on. He bent over her, cupping her cheek and pressing a kiss to the top of her head before he left the room. And of all things, Alaric's words flitted back to her while she sat alone, naked and wrapped in a blanket.

I am amused that you did so without understanding the costs of such things.

More tears slid down her cheeks. She hadn't known.

She hadn't known the costs.

And Alaric had trained her this way. He had trained her to trust no one. He had trained her to depend on herself, to do things on her own, to take matters into her own hands. All the while, he subconsciously taught her to rely on him. He provided her food, provided her shelter, provided her training, provided her with a family. And in the end, old habits die hard. In the end, he had still won. She may be free of his physical presence. They may have come for her and successfully extracted her from the Fellowship, but he had still won. Her relationships were all fractured. Cassius still had not woken. Cyrus was disappointed with her. She could only assume Eliza and Rayner and Briar, everyone else really, felt the same. Talwyn had been right. She didn't fully understand everything at play here.

And Sorin? She had never seen him so angry. So withdrawn. So hurt.

And that was on her. She had hurt him worse than he had hurt her when they had fought on the front porch here months ago. And he was right. It had taken her months to let him back in fully. She still hadn't. Not completely. That was why they were in this mess to begin with.

She heard his footsteps on the stairs, but she didn't look up when he came back into the room. She heard him pause, then he crossed the room and began filling the large tub. While the water was running, he came back to her. He pulled the tie from her braid and unwound what was left of the plait before he gently tugged the blanket from her grip.

"Come, Love," he said softly, reaching for her. "Have a bath and then we will sleep."

She lifted her chin, looking at him through teary lashes. "How can you even think of taking care of me right now? After everything?"

He took her face in his hands, pressing his forehead to hers. "Just because things are tense between us right now does not mean I love you any less, Scarlett. You are still mine. I will still sit with you in the dark, and together we will find the stars."

"You promise?" she whispered.

"I promise I will not leave you alone in the darkness. Not now. Not ever."

She nodded, and he pressed a soft kiss to her lips before saying, "Go bathe. You smell."

She huffed a small laugh as he helped her from the bed. "That certainly didn't stop you earlier," she retorted with a small mocking grin.

Sorin clicked his tongue, watching her walk to the tub. "Careful, Love, or I will put that tongue to better use . . . again."

Scarlett felt her cheeks flare slightly at his words, but she didn't say anything back as she climbed into the tub and slid beneath the steaming water, letting it wash away all the grime.

Her thoughts wandered as she sat under the water. She would fix this. Cassius would be all right. They would keep the orphans safe, find the keys, and kill the Maraan Lords. She needed to master her magic more. She needed to figure out ways to safeguard against Blood Marks, wards, and fucking shirastone. There had to be a way to overcome the effects of it. Right?

Maybe then, after all of that was taken care of, she could breathe again. Maybe after all of that, she wouldn't feel like she was suffocating, drowning on dry land. Maybe then—

She felt fingers brushing the top of her head, combing through her hair, and she pushed back above the surface of the water to find Sorin bent over the tub, his face full of concern.

"Love, I know Briar said you can breathe underwater, but I really need you to stop going under for minutes at a time," he said, pushing her wet hair back and off her face.

"I didn't realize— Wait, I can breathe underwater?"

A half smile curled up on his lips. "According to Briar, yes."

"How?" she asked, her eyes widening

Sorin lowered to his knees, reaching for a bottle of hair tonic and beginning to wash her hair for her. "I do not know. I imagine if I did, I wouldn't feel so uneasy when you go under for extended periods of time."

"I didn't mean to worry you," she answered softly, her fingers sweeping through the water.

"I know," he sighed. "You never do."

She didn't know if he meant it to be a verbal jab, but it certainly hit like one. She didn't reply as he finished washing her hair. She slid beneath the water, quickly rinsing it so she wasn't under very long. When she resurfaced, she scrubbed at her skin, and when she finally felt clean again, he was waiting to wrap her in a towel. He dried her hair for her with his magic as he walked to the armoire, returning with a sleeveless nightgown and sliding it over her head. The silky garment fell nearly to her ankles.

He cupped her jaw, tilting her face up. "I did not mean that as an insult, Scarlett."

She just nodded, her eyes looking anywhere but at him. He pressed another soft kiss to her brow and led her to the bed. When they were both settled, and he had tugged her back into his chest, his hand splaying across her torso, he said softly into her ear, "Never again, Scarlett. We never leave each other again."

She nodded, swallowing back tears, before she whispered, "Never again."

PART TWO
OF TRUTHS & PROMISES

CHAPTER 23
SCARLETT

When she woke, there was no male body beside her, and she shot upright in a panic.

"I am here, Love."

Relief instantly flooded through her at the sight of him. He was standing in front of the hearth, his back to her, already dressed for the day. He had on his usual dark-charcoal pants and red tunic. A black jacket was laying across the back of a chair.

She slid from the bed, her bare feet sinking into the plush rug as she made her way to him. When she reached his side, he wordlessly passed her a cup of tea, steam instantly beginning to rise from it.

"Thank you," she said softly.

He only nodded, his gaze fixed on the flickering flames. Black hair fell across his forehead, and she reached up tentatively to brush it back. When he didn't pull away from her, she ran her fingers gently along the side of his face. His eyes fell closed, and he sighed, the sound somehow both pleasure and wariness all at once.

As she withdrew her hand, he pulled a note from his pocket, passing it to her.

"It appears Talwyn is demanding to meet with you."

Scarlett glanced at the quickly scrawled message before incinerating it in her palm and tossing the ashes into the hearth. "Is Prince Azrael all right? I know I asked a lot of him."

"I have not heard," Sorin answered. "My focus has been rather singular for a while now."

She nodded, taking a sip of her tea.

"The others will be wanting to see you as well," Sorin continued after the silence stretched on.

"And hear my explanations for my actions, I am sure," she replied somewhat bitterly.

"Yes," he confirmed. "And that. You will . . ." He pushed out another long breath, raking his hand through his hair, those same strands she'd brushed away falling back onto his brow. "After this, Scarlett, you will need to prove yourself to them."

"I seem to remember you telling Talwyn I did not need to prove myself," she said.

"They trusted you without question once. It will not happen again. Not after everything that happened. Now you do need to prove yourself to them," Sorin replied.

She pursed her lips, calling shadows to her fingertips and letting them drift along her palm, drawing comfort from their darkness. She didn't say anything to that because what was there to say? Would it make any difference when they heard her explanations and reasonings? Sorin still hadn't let her fully explain her actions, and she knew even once she did, it still wouldn't repair any of the chasm that had formed between them.

"I think you should meet with my Inner Court, Briar, and the Water Court first. Deal with them. Give them time to react, so that when we meet with the Eastern Courts, you are not feeling attacked from all directions," Sorin said tightly, his hands sliding into his pockets.

"Attacked?"

He finally turned to meet her eyes. "They are angry, Scarlett. They are hurt. They feel betrayed by their queen. I told you they needed to know you trust them. You basically told them you do not."

His eyes went back to the fire, and she heard what he didn't voice: you basically told *me* you do not trust me.

"What things would you like to know before we go back?" she asked quietly, fiddling with the teacup just to keep her hands busy.

"When did you figure it out? What those Night Children were really doing at the border?"

"I had been trying to figure out their angle since I saw the reports at the meeting with Talwyn. The day I came for you," she answered.

"When did you figure it out?" he repeated.

"When Briar confirmed there were only three Night Children at his border, I knew for sure."

"So before I stepped foot over the border to speak with them, you already knew you were going to leave," he confirmed.

Her eyes fell to her tea. "Yes."

"What happened at the border?"

"There were several Night Children there. And the High Force. I fought."

She felt his gaze swivel to her. "You fought against the High Force? Alone? The force I trained?"

Scarlett shook her head. "When the leader of the Night Children realized who I was, he instructed the High Force to fall back. So he and the other Night Children could have room to detain me."

"You took on an entire clan of Night Children? By yourself?"

"Took on and defeated," she answered.

"Clearly not defeated, Scarlett. You were taken captive."

"I was not captured by Night Children, Sorin."

"Alaric was there?" he asked, and she could feel his eyes burning into her.

She lifted her chin to meet golden irises as she said, "No. Tarek is the one who captured me. I had used all my magic. I was weak, and I couldn't fight back."

"Scarlett," he said slowly, "who is Tarek?"

"Talwyn's twin flame. He was there waiting for her. They were expecting Talwyn to show up at the border," she answered.

"Tarek Ordos is dead. He died with Thia on that mission. It could not possibly be *that* Tarek," Sorin said.

Scarlett shook her head. "It is him, Sorin. He said he is the rightful heir to the Earth Court. He believes he should rule that Court. He told me the story of how his family lost their Royal seat to the Luans."

"I saw his corpse in that cave beside Thia," Sorin insisted. "It could not possibly be him."

"I don't know what to say, Sorin. It all fits. I could scent earth magic on him. He appears to know Talwyn very well. He knew who you were. Who Azrael was. He even knows Talwyn and Azrael are lovers now. His blood is how they kept me from weakening too much—"

"Who is your mother?" Sorin interrupted. Her eyes went wide.

"I do not know."

"Scarlett." Sorin said her name in a clear warning, as though he suspected she was lying.

He probably did.

"I swear I do not know who she is," Scarlett answered. "But I know what she looks like, and I know she is Avonleyan. I know my father was Avonleyan. Whether they still live, I do not know. The last time I saw her, that I can remember, was when I was five, and she made Cassius my Guardian."

"What is that? What does it mean that Cassius is your Guardian?" Sorin asked, turning to face her fully.

"I don't completely understand it," Scarlett admitted. "It was a blood ritual. Our blood was mixed, and we both drank. We were both Marked, and—"

"Where?" Sorin demanded.

"On our backs. Alaric said he has seen the Mark at various times over the years. He didn't know how she did it, but said a Witch cast some sort of spell to make us forget it."

Sorin was already reaching for her, his hands on her shoulders, spinning her gently and lifting her nightgown. "I have seen every inch of your skin, Scarlett. There is no Mark," he said, the cool air pebbling her exposed flesh.

"But you also cannot see the one on my arm," she replied. "Or the one on my collarbone."

He dropped the fabric of her nightgown, spinning her back and reaching for her left arm, running his thumb along her forearm. "You tried to tell me," he murmured. His gaze moving to her clavicle before landing on her eyes.

"Your eyes are silver."

"So I hear." When he just held her stare, she sighed. "The man I see in my dreams sometimes. He is the one who gave me the other two Marks . . . And told me my eyes are silver now."

"You saw him again? How often do you see him, Scarlett?" Sorin asked, his grip on her arm tightening.

"My connection to him was blocked by my Mark, just like my bonds to you and Cassius and Shirina were. I hadn't seen him since Talwyn and I saw him together. Not until after . . . You know," she said, trailing off, her eyes darting back to the hearth.

"Until after you drank from me," Sorin finished for her. She nodded.

"You are Avonleyan," he breathed, his hand coming up to cup her cheek.

"I am," she agreed.

"And Cassius?"

"Is half-Avonleyan, half-Witch," Scarlett confirmed, finally meeting his stare once more.

"And you will need to feed from Fae? To replenish your Avonleyan powers?" Sorin asked, his eyes searching hers.

"No. I mean, yes. For now. If it's needed again, but apparently that is not the best way. The man in my dream told me I need to find a Source."

"What does that mean?" he asked, his hand moving to tuck her hair behind her ear.

Scarlett sighed. "I don't know. He's about as helpful as the Oracle. He just said the way I . . . fed from you is apparently outlawed? I suppose I'll need to venture beneath the library in Solembra and see what I can find. Along with the keys. And a lock. And he mentioned training with my shadows and white flames more."

"There is so much to go into here, Scarlett. So much you need to explain," Sorin said with a shake of his head.

"Where do you want to start?" she asked, biting her lip. She would start with whatever he felt was most important, but she was also itching to go check on Cassius. She hadn't anticipated sleeping until the next day, when Sorin had brought her here yesterday afternoon.

"You should start with getting dressed and then you need to eat," he said knowingly. As if on cue, her stomach grumbled loudly, and she scowled at him. He chuckled, turning her towards the armoire. "Get dressed, Love. I will meet you in the kitchen. You can grab something to bring with us."

She dressed quickly in black pants and a white tunic, tugging her boots on before she descended the stairs. Sorin was waiting for her, holding out a pear in one hand and a pastry in the other.

"Ready?" he asked.

But she wasn't. She knew she had to face everyone, but her stomach dropped at actually having to do so now.

"We can go see Cassius first," Sorin said gently.

"And I need to check on the children."

"Yes, but I think it would be best to see everyone else first. I don't want you to run into any of them in front of the children . . ." Sorin trailed off.

"It's going to be that bad?" she asked quietly, glancing at the food in her hands. She suddenly wasn't hungry at all.

"It will be fine. I will be there with you. Always together," he replied, and she felt the heat of a fire portal open behind her.

She took a deep breath, straightened her shoulders, and stepped through into the room Cassius was sleeping in. Hazel was standing exactly where she had been when Scarlett had left yesterday. She set her food down on a nearby table before coming to her side, immediately taking Cassius's hand. It was no longer cold to the touch, but warm as it should be, and she let out a long breath of relief.

"You are feeling better?" Hazel asked with a sidelong glance.

"Very much so," Scarlett answered. "How is he today?"

"He is progressing," she said.

"Are you still giving him blood every two hours?"

"It does not need to be as frequent. Three or four times a day should suffice," Hazel answered.

"But if we continued with every two hours, would it speed things up?" Scarlett pushed, looking up and meeting her violet stare.

Hazel shook her head. "Now that you are not trying to draw power from him, it will be more than enough."

She felt Sorin come up behind her, and a moment later his arm slipped around her, the pear in his palm. "Eat, Love," he whispered into her ear. "I cannot imagine they fed you much these last weeks."

She looked at him and gave him a slight grimace. "I really don't think I can eat right now, Sorin."

He pulled the pear back and nodded once. "Let's get this over with then. You need to eat."

With another glance back at Cassius, she followed Sorin out and down a hallway.

"This is the queen's private wing of the Black Halls," Sorin said, interlacing his fingers with hers.

"The whole wing? Like the Fiera Palace?"

"Yes," he confirmed. "There are several private quarters. The one Cassius is in was mine."

"And where are we going now?" she asked as he led her down a winding set of stone steps.

"One of the council rooms."

"Everyone is already there?"

"Yes," he answered. "I sent fire messages this morning, after you agreed to meet with them before seeing Talwyn."

She nodded again and focused on her breathing. In and out. In and out. In and out.

They came to a stop outside of a set of double wood doors intricately carved with fire and water elements. She could hear muffled voices on the other side. Sorin turned to face her, his hands coming to rest on her shoulders.

"You can do this, Scarlett."

"I know," she replied. "If I can face the wrath of the Fire Prince, I can surely handle his Court and a Water Prince. Right?"

A soft smile tilted up the corners of his lips. "Right, Princess." He brushed his knuckles along her cheekbone as he said, "Ready?"

She took another deep breath, blowing it out harshly. She felt his fire magic brush along her skin as he turned and pushed one of the doors open. He stepped in and held the door open for her. Scarlett followed behind him, all the chatter coming to a halt the moment the door had opened. She scanned the room to find Eliza, Rayner, and Cyrus seated at the large round table occupying the center of the room. Briar and Sawyer stood nearby at a tall table along the wall. She was relieved to see Nakoa wasn't present.

All eyes watched her every movement as she crossed the room and sank unceremoniously into a chair at the table. Her fingers curled around the ends of the armrests, and she was unable to keep the shadows back that seeped from her skin, hovering around her like a black mist. Sorin pulled the chair out beside her, and before he took his seat, he bent down and pressed a soft kiss to her cheek.

I love you like the stars love the night, Scarlett. All the way through the darkness.

It was the first time he had spoken to her down their bond since it had been repaired, and the relief that flooded through her chest had her shadows receding and her breathing evening out.

He took his seat, an elbow on the table and his chin propped on his fist. His other rested on the surface, too, his fingers drumming a few times as he stared down his Court. She and Sorin may have their own issues right now, but at this moment, he was her Second. Her husband. King of the Western Courts.

Briar and Sawyer had silently made their way to the table and taken seats. There was so much tension in the air, Scarlett could have cut it with a knife.

"So who wants to go first?" she finally asked. When no one said a word, she locked eyes with the general. "Eliza? Surely you want to lay into me?" Her gaze moved to Cyrus. "How about you, Darling? I know you have much to say. You made that clear yesterday."

The Fire Court Second and the general glanced at each other, but to Scarlett's shock, neither of them were the first to speak.

"You deceived us all," Rayner said, his low voice dark and cold.

Scarlett's focus swiveled to him, landing on eyes swirling with smoke and ashes. "I did," she agreed.

"You went to another border. Alone. When you knew there were threats gathering at all the Court borders," he continued.

"I did," she said again. "I had suspicions about a few things and did not have the time to go through endless meetings and correspondence and debate about whether or not it was worth the risk."

"Then you send me in," Rayner said darkly. "You send in someone who can move among the ashes. You let me gather that information for you using the dozens of spies I have in place all over the godsdamn continent. You are the *queen*."

Scarlett had never seen Rayner display such emotion, and it was honestly terrifying. Her fingers tightened around the ends of the armrests further, but she kept her chin high. "I understand, Rayner. I am not used to being able to rely on others so thoroughly. I understand what my actions cost."

"And you considered the cost an acceptable price?" Sawyer asked.

Scarlett met his icy blue eyes, mirrors of her own when they weren't bright silver. "I thought I knew what the cost would be." She glanced at Sorin out of the corner of her eye, where he had stiffened slightly. "Did I consider the safety of these Courts to be worth the cost of my life? Yes. Did I fully understand what the cost of my actions would be? No. Do I understand what they have cost me now? Yes."

"Perhaps you can explain to us what you were investigating," Briar cut in. When she met his gaze, she didn't find the anger of the others. He gave her an encouraging smile as he asked, "How did you figure out what was going on at the borders?"

Scarlett repeated everything she'd told Sorin this morning about her suspicions after seeing the reports and finding a clan of Night Children there.

"Was your deception at least fruitful?" Eliza sneered when she had finished.

Scarlett shrugged. "Did I learn information about my own history and plans to kill the Contessa? Yes. Did I learn that Alaric is a Maraan Prince and the son of Deimas and Esmeray? Yes. Was it worth my capture, being chained to a wall for days on end with little food and water, being forced to sleep next to Mikale, and watching Cassius be tortured nearly to death? I guess that remains to be seen. Do I regret my actions? Yes."

Sorin's head slowly turned to her. "I believe you failed to mention the sleeping next to Mikale part during our various conversations," he gritted out.

"Yes, well, when you've kept so many secrets and spoken so many lies, I am sure it is hard to keep them all straight," Eliza said bitterly.

"Watch it, General," Sorin snarled, his head snapping towards her. Eliza rolled her eyes, crossing her arms and leveling him with a glare.

"Her actions put all of us in danger. She says she did this to keep our Courts safe? We just spent weeks away from our Court and risked our lives to get her out."

Scarlett opened her mouth to say something, but Eliza wasn't done. "You knew something was wrong," she said, still speaking to Sorin and not to her. "We all did. You tried to get her to tell you, but she just sat there drawing that fucking Mark in the dirt." Her grey eyes came back to hers, and Scarlett sucked in a breath to find tears glimmering there. "You just needed to say something! We would have listened, Scarlett. We would have helped you!"

"I'm sorry," Scarlett said softly. She wanted to look away from the general, but she forced herself to keep her eyes locked on hers. "I do not know what else I can say. None of my explanations are to serve as excuses, because there are not any excuses I can offer that will make what I did acceptable. I am sorry."

"This will not work if you cannot trust us, Scarlett," Briar said gently. "If you are going to insist on doing everything on your own—"

"I'm not," Scarlett interrupted. "I know my track record says otherwise at this moment, but it was never my plan to intentionally exclude you. It was not some calculated plan to sneak away from you all, to block my twin flame bond, to face a clan of Night Children on my own. It was a spur-of-the-moment decision, and it was the wrong one. I made the wrong choice, and I am sorry."

A heavy silence descended on the room, the tension still just as thick. "Is there anything in particular you would like kept from Queen Talwyn when we meet with her later today?" Briar asked, lifting a glass of water and taking a drink. Scarlett could only assume that while Nakoa and Neve were not here, they were watching on the other side of a water mirror.

"She needs to know about the Maraan Lords and their plans to kill the Contessa." She glanced at Sorin real quick before she continued and said, "And she needs to know Tarek lives and is working with them."

"Scarlett, we have discussed this. It cannot be her twin flame. There has to be another explanation for it," Sorin said.

"I know you think that, Sorin, but I think you're wrong. He flat out told me he is her twin flame. The things he told me . . ."

"Then he is lying. Just like Alaric and Lord Tyndell have done to you your entire life," Sorin argued.

Scarlett sat back, crossing her arms. "I guess we will have to wait and see, but I think you need to be prepared for the possibility of it being him. *Talwyn* needs to be prepared for that."

Her gaze caught on Cyrus who hadn't uttered a single word since she'd arrived here, and the thought suddenly occurred to her that if Tarek was alive, then . . .

"If it's true," she said slowly, "could that mean that Thia might—" "No," Cyrus said shortly.

"But no one thinks Tarek could be alive either and—"

"She does not live, Scarlett," Cyrus replied, his tone low and dark. "You do not feel your soul ripping apart the way I did at her death if half of it is not being torn away from you."

Scarlett's eyes had fallen to the table as he spoke, but they snapped back to his when he continued. "*Nothing* could compare to the terror and pain and grief that I felt when I knew Thia was gone, when I knew she had been taken from me. But learning my queen had been captured, not knowing what you were enduring? Seeing my prince go nearly feral at not being able to find you? To feel you? Gods, Scarlett! What the fuck were you thinking? Because it certainly did not have a godsdamn thing to do with our safety or the safety of these Courts."

"Cyrus," Sorin warned, but Scarlett held up her hand to silence him.

"Do you really not trust any of us that much? Me? Eliza? Briar? Your *godsdamn twin flame?*" Cyrus demanded. "You had every opportunity to say something. Fuck, you could have said something long before that day. You could have said something the day you found that chamber beneath the library that Sorin had to tell us about. You could have said something in any of the weeks between that night and the day you stood at our border and effectively told us all to fuck off." He was on his feet now, bracing his hands on the table and leaning towards her. "We claimed you as one of our own. From the moment Sorin carried you across that border, we claimed you. You were ours just as much as you were his. Not when you became queen. Not when you accepted your place. That very day we risked our lives without question to see you enter the Fire Court with him. We claimed you, and you could give all of two fucks about it. If you had simply said something, *anything*, while we were all discussing these matters at the border, this entire situation could have been avoided."

Tears were coursing down her face, and her hand was over her mouth to stifle the sob that was clawing its way up her throat. She was shaking her head at his words because they weren't true. They weren't true in the slightest. He was her family. They all were.

"Cyrus," she rasped. "Cyrus, I am sorry."

But he said nothing. He glanced once at Sorin before pushing off the table and stalking from the room, the door banging shut behind him.

Give him a little time, Love.

She nodded, swallowing back more tears, her gaze dropping to the table.

"Let's take a break," Sorin said to the room. "She hasn't eaten since she got here, and she wants to check on the children. Everyone take some time to cool down, and then we can meet again this afternoon."

The room emptied out, until it was only her and Sorin left sitting at the table. She heard him slide from his chair and turned her own away from the table. He crouched before her, looking up into her face. He reached up and swiped tears away with his thumb.

"Hey, Love."

"Gods, I am so sorry, Sorin," she said, more tears sliding free. "I told you I was not made for this. I told you I wasn't made to sit on a throne. I should have listened to my instincts."

"No," he replied, shaking his head. "I do not believe that for one second. I do not know what Alaric said or did to you while you were there to make you doubt yourself like this, but you are strong enough to face this. Mistakes were made. You made a bad call. What's done is done. Now you get to decide how to move on from here. But first . . ." He stood, taking her hand and tugging her to her feet with him. "You are going to eat."

"So demanding," she murmured, swiping at her face yet again.

He tucked her into his side, pressing a kiss to her hair as he guided her to the doors. "Love, you'll discover just how demanding I can be later tonight."

CHAPTER 24
SORIN

"I swear to Saylah, Sorin, if you make me eat one more bite of food . . ." Scarlett trailed off as she flopped onto her back on the grey sofa she was sitting on, her hair bright against the upholstery.

When they had left the council room, Sorin had led her back to the queen's private wing to a small den. It had a fireplace, the sofa she was currently sprawled across, a couple of cream-colored, high-backed armchairs, and a small table for six off to the side. A few floor-to-ceiling windows ran along one wall, letting in the warmth and sunlight of the day. He had opened one to let in the air off the water the Black Halls were built against, knowing simply being able to smell the saltwater would ease some of Scarlett's nerves. It was cozy and intimate and reserved for the queen and king of the Western Courts.

After he had sent messages to his Court and Briar that morning while she had still slept, he had also asked Rayner to have some sort of meal prepared for them and sent here to be waiting. He'd known the conversations with his Inner Court would be intense, and he'd also known she'd need this time to breathe.

And eat.

She needed to fucking eat.

So when they'd entered this room, he had immediately gone to the table that was laden with fruits and breads and cheeses and meats, piling her a full plate. He'd sat beside her on that sofa and made sure she ate the whole damn thing.

"Are you sure you got enough to eat?" he asked, putting more meat and bread onto the plate as he spoke.

"Yes, Sorin," she sighed. "They did feed me. I mean, not at first. But once they realized how quickly I could weaken, Alaric made sure I had regular meals. Small, but regular."

"Care to tell me more about this whole sleeping next to Mikale bit?" he ground out, dropping the plate to the table a little harder than he'd intended. "You told me he didn't—"

"He didn't, Sorin," she interrupted, and he turned to find her sitting back up. Her arms were folded across the back of the sofa, her head resting on them as she looked up at him. "I wasn't forced to do anything like that, but Alaric was trying to make me as uncomfortable as possible, while making sure I didn't weaken enough to break the Blood Mark. So I was given a bed to sleep in, but Mikale shared that bed. I was bathed in cold water with Mikale watching over me the entire time. He dressed me, and he took some liberties with his hands—"

Fire flared in his vision. Sorin was standing before her before she could utter another word, pulling her up onto her knees and slamming his mouth onto hers. She let out a surprised gasp, and he sank his tongue into her mouth, too. His arm snaked around her waist, forcing her to arch her back as he bent forward over the back of the sofa.

"Tonight," he growled onto her lips, "you will tell me every place he took *liberties* with you."

Her hand came up, brushing a lock of hair from his brow. "I am yours, Sorin," she said softly. "Only yours."

He pressed another kiss to her lips before releasing her and going back to the food. He filled the plate with more food despite her protests, setting it on the low table before the sofa. She'd sprawled back onto the cushions, and he lifted her head slightly as he took a seat, lowering it back onto his lap.

She stared up at him, playing with the shadows that she had released to flow around her, and she sent one to curl around his ear.

"Do you think we should tell Talwyn that I am Avonleyan?" she asked.

Sorin sighed. "I think it will come out eventually, and knowing her, it would be better if it came from us, rather than her discovering it on her own."

She nodded her head once. "Is there a library here?"

"Of course," he answered, running his fingers along her face.

"Can you take me there? After . . . everything is finished today."

"Yes," he said, twirling a piece of her hair around a finger. "Anything in particular we are looking for?"

He said it as casually as he could, but if she was seeking out books, she had ideas swirling in her mind. She was looking to research something.

"I need to figure out this Source thing," she sighed. "I can't do anything about Mikale or Alaric until I can use this magic and replenish it without..."

"Drinking my blood?" he supplied.

"Drinking any Fae blood," she replied.

His finger stilled, and he tugged sharply on the lock of hair wrapped around it. "Let me be very clear about this: If you need to do that before we figure this Source thing out, you come to me."

Scarlett rolled her eyes. "I'm not sure why you think you can give me orders lately."

He flicked her nose. "You and this godsdamn tongue," he muttered.

They'd sat in that den for another hour, just him and her, and he finally felt like he could breathe fully. After having her last night, sleeping beside her, having her close all day, sitting and casually conversing, the tension in his limbs had greatly abated, and he felt like he could focus on something other than her. He wasn't letting her out of his sight anytime soon, but he wasn't wrapped up in finding her, seeing her, consuming her.

He'd sent word to Talwyn that they would meet with her tomorrow. Scarlett would need a break from having to defend herself and dealing with her own Courts all day. Talwyn had been surprisingly amenable to waiting another day.

Now they were making their way down a back passageway to the great hall that had become the main room for all the children. He'd been told they'd all been given rooms, dividing the children into pairs. Some of the older ones, like Lynnea and Malachi, were given their own rooms. It was likely the first time they'd ever had such a thing.

He pulled open the door for her and let her step through. They emerged at the far end of the room, the door blending in with the stonework to look just like the wall. She stood still, looking around the room.

"They've found food and clothing and—"

"They have everything they need, Love," Sorin said, cutting her off. "If they don't, the help finds it for them."

She looked up at him. "I know you didn't think we should bring them all . . ."

She trailed off as he started shaking his head. "My sole focus these last few weeks was you. Nothing else mattered to me, Scarlett. I wanted to get you out of there. Taking the time to move all these children was delaying that. I know it was selfish and made me look like a prick for not caring, but I *didn't* care. I needed you out. I needed you safe. The gods know I was an uncooperative dick these last few weeks, but I don't care. I needed you and that was it."

"That's oddly . . . charismatic," she quipped, her head tilting to the side. "In a completely insane, over-possessive, mother hen sort of way."

"I swear to the Fates, Scarlett," he muttered as she turned away from him and began making her way into the room, stopping to greet several of the children along her way.

He started to follow after her, when his name was called out into the hall.

"Prince Aditya."

Sorin turned to see a tall, dark-skinned male striding through the sea of children. His olive-green eyes were narrowed and set on him. A golden-skinned female was trailing him, along with a light brown wolf. He reached him in a few more long strides, and faster than Sorin could brace for it, a fist slammed into his jaw.

"Sorin!" Scarlett cried, beside him in an instant with a hand raised and shadows leaping from her fingertips.

"It is fine, Love," Sorin said, rubbing at his jaw with his hand. "I deserved that."

"You deserve more than that," the Alpha growled, his fist drawing back again.

And then Scarlett was stepping in front of him, her shadows morphing into white flames as her head tilted up, and she locked eyes with the Shifter. "I'm going to need to at least know your name before you set about trying to throw down with my husband," she said sweetly, shadows pooling around her feet and twisting into snakes poised to strike.

"Relax, Love," Sorin said, reaching out and pushing her hand down. "This is Stellan Renatus. Alpha of the Shifters and Arianna's brother. Stellan, meet Queen Scarlett, my wife and twin flame."

Scarlett looked back over her shoulder at him, her brows arching in surprise. "And why does the Alpha deserve to punch you in your face?"

"Because he went behind my back to recruit my sister for his little rescue mission," Stellan cut in.

"Of course he did," came Arianna's sultry drawl as she sauntered up behind her brother. "Temural knows you would never have let me go otherwise," she added. Her gaze shifted to Scarlett. "It is wonderful to see you up and about, your Majesty."

"I owe you a debt, my Lady," Scarlett answered with a bow of her head. "I am sure without your aide I would still be chained to a wall, and Cassius would be dead. Thank you will never be nearly enough."

Arianna's gaze slid to Sorin's, and a coy smile made its way on to her lips. "Have you asked her yet, Prince?"

"We have had much to discuss, my Lady, but as I mentioned weeks ago, she is not one to share," he replied, knowing exactly what she was referencing.

"She may surprise you," Arianna countered, glancing at Scarlett. "People change. After all, you used to enjoy partaking in our group activities in Siofra. Jamahl and I can be very convincing."

"I am well aware of how convincing you can be, Arianna," Sorin said. "Hold on," Scarlett said, stepping back so she could look between Arianna and Sorin. "You two used to . . . With another? Who is Jamahl?" "Jamahl is my personal guard," Arianna supplied.

"Mhmm," Scarlett said. "And?"

"And the Beta does not like to limit herself to one partner," Sorin explained. "She also enjoys group activities."

Scarlett's eyes went wide. "And you've participated in these group activities?"

Sorin ran a hand down his face, his hand pausing over his mouth, hiding the grin curling on the corner of his lips. "I have lived many years, Scarlett, and I have experienced many things in those years."

Scarlett barked a laugh, her silver eyes bright and twinkling with amusement. "I would love to hear of these *experiences*, Prince."

"Or you could experience them for yourself," Arianna interjected, her hand coming up and fingers dragging sensually along her arm.

Sorin couldn't stop the possessive snarl that rumbled from his chest, and Scarlett fell into a fit of laughter. "I think I will let my ancient husband's *experiences* be enough for both of us," she said. "And he is correct. I do not like to share."

Arianna's full lip pushed out in a pout. "That's a shame," she sighed. "If you ever change your mind though..."

"You shall be the first to know, Lady," Scarlett replied with an amused grin.

"Back to the matter at hand," Stellan cut in, and Arianna rolled her eyes, huffing an exaggerated sigh.

"You have my deepest apologies, Stellan," Sorin said. "But I was working with limited time. I did not necessarily have the time to go through the proper channels and meetings."

Scarlett was slowly turning her head to face him. "Just to clarify here, Prince. You are saying you did not have the time to properly inform everyone of your plans and needed to make a quick decision?"

Scarlett, this is not the same thing, and certainly not the time to be discussing it, he sent down the bond in warning.

Her lips curled up into a smirk, but she waved her hand dramatically in a motion for him to continue.

"As I was saying, you were not in Siofra when I came to ask Arianna, and time was of the essence," he finished.

"You were gone for weeks," Stellan snarled. "And you had a Traveler with you. I am sure at some point in that time you could have made a quick trip to me to explain."

"By the gods," Arianna cut in. "His *twin flame* was being held prisoner, Stellan. You were the last person on his mind, I assure you."

Stellan whirled on his sister, and the two siblings began to argue, seeming to forget anyone else was near. Sorin reached for Scarlett's hand and gave her a wink as he tugged her away from them.

"We can have a more formal meeting and introduction to the Shifters another time," he said. "In fact, knowing Stellan, I am sure he will insist on it."

"Yes," she mused, "you seem to know the Shifters *very* well."

"Only Arianna, you wicked thing," he retorted, tugging her into his side and pinching her waist.

"And Jamahl," she teased as she batted his hand away. Then, "Is that Tula sitting on Rayner's lap?"

"They met in Baylorin," Sorin said, his eyes settling on the pair across the room. "She has taken quite the liking to him."

They were several feet away when the little girl's eyes landed on Scarlett and widened to the size of saucers before an excited scream fell from her lips.

"Scarlett!"

Rayner smiled affectionately as he lowered her to the floor and the girl was racing toward them. Scarlett was already lowered to her knees, arms open wide to catch her.

"Hello, Tula Bug," she murmured as her arms wrapped tightly around the little girl. "I've missed you so much."

"I kept waiting for you at the other place," she said. Then her voice dropped to a serious whisper. "Did you know they used magic to get us here?"

Scarlett smiled in amusement. "I did. Did you know I can do magic?"

"Show me," Tula demanded.

Scarlett raised a hand and white flames danced there. Tula gasped, and Scarlett's smile widened as she sent her shadows among them. Then she lifted her other hand and blew across it, small snowflakes flying into Tula's face. Her giggles filled the air, and Scarlett began showing her a few other things.

"Briar is here with Ashtine," Rayner said, and Sorin looked up from the pair to find Rayner had crossed the distance to them. A moment later, Briar and Ashtine entered the hall, making their way over. Tula had plopped herself onto the floor, watching Scarlett with wide eyes, and a few other children had made their way over to watch, too. She clearly hadn't noticed the other two Royals arriving.

"How is she?" Briar asked quietly.

"She is . . . surviving," Sorin answered, not liking that 'surviving' was the word he had to use to describe her right now. "She is enjoying these quiet moments before having to go behind closed doors with everyone again."

"Why does the child have a necklace of skystone?" Ashtine asked, seemingly oblivious to their conversation.

Sorin's eyes darted to Tula, and, sure enough, a thick chain had slipped from beneath the shirt she wore. A symbol that could only be described as a tangled knot hung from the chain. Temural's symbol, the god of the wild and untamed. The amulet itself was made of some black metal or stone. The chain it hung from was ivory with silver threaded through it, but it wasn't skystone itself. Skystone was brilliantly white with silver whorls running through it. This was too muted to be skystone. The necklace looked similar to any other spirit amulet.

Scarlett looked up at Ashtine's question, her silver eyes bright with the use of her magic. "What is skystone?"

"Stone only found in the Shira Cliffs in the Wind Court," Briar answered.

"On our highest cliffs that sit amongst the clouds," Ashtine said, her tone full of curiosity. "It is said that Sefarina herself touches those stones. That they are wind-kissed."

"What?" Scarlett asked, pushing suddenly to her feet. "What did you just say?"

Ashtine's head tilted as she studied Scarlett. "You have heard that term before."

"Is it rare?" Scarlett asked. "This skystone."

"Very," Briar answered. "I have only seen true skystone a handful of times in my life."

"I do not think that is skystone, Asthine," Sorin ventured. "I think it just looks incredibly similar."

"That is skystone," Ashtine said. "If Nasima were here, the silver visible on that chain would move like the winds."

"Where is Nasima?" Scarlett asked, and Ashtine stiffened, stepping back from her.

"That is a topic for another time," Briar said firmly.

Scarlett glanced between the two of them before she nodded. "You are sure that is skystone?"

"I am," Ashtine replied, then she turned to Briar. "I am going to go for a walk."

"I will come with you," he answered, concern clouding his normally twinkling eyes. "Send a message when you are ready to meet again," he added, before falling into step beside Ashtine.

Sorin turned back to find Scarlett crouched before Tula, her fingers running over the child's necklace. "Tula, where did you get this?"

"It's mine," the little girl replied defensively, trying to tug the necklace free from Scarlett's hand.

"But where did you get it?" Scarlett pressed.

"I found it," she mumbled, her baby blue eyes going to the floor. She clearly thought she was about to be reprimanded.

"Yes, but where, Little Bug?" Scarlett urged softly, turning the amulet over again.

"That night when the bad man had me. And you were there and Cassius and Nuri and the other girl," Tula said, tears pooling in her eyes. "They took me away and put me in a room. I was sitting on the floor, in the corner, and found a hole in the wall. It was in there. It looked like the one you always wear."

"It was hidden?" Scarlett asked.

"I took it," she cried, her lower lip trembling. "I know it wasn't good, Scarlett. But I was looking at it, and the man came back, and I didn't want to get in trouble."

"Shh, Little Bug," Scarlett soothed, pulling the child into her arms. "I am not upset with you."

Sorin watched the scene playing out in front of him. Watched a queen sitting on a stone floor comforting an orphan. He dropped down beside them, his hand coming to Scarlett's back.

"Can we make a trade, Tula?" he asked, and the little girl pulled back from Scarlett's shoulder, tear stains on her cheeks.

"Wh-what kind of trade?" she sniffled.

"If Scarlett and I made you a new, special necklace, could we trade you for that one?"

Her eyes brightened at that thought. "You can do that?"

"If that sounds like a good trade to you?" Sorin replied with a wink.

Tula nodded her head enthusiastically, sitting back on her heels expectantly.

Sorin formed a small flame in his palm, no bigger than a coin, then he made it take the shape of a heart. Scarlett's hand came up over his, and water magic flowed into his flames, freezing the fire as it wove amongst it. In the center of the heart, she put a white flame before encasing the entire thing in hoarfrost crystal, leaving it cool to the touch.

"Does it meet your approval?" Sorin asked when they'd finished, holding it out for Tula's inspection.

"I love it!" she cried, in a pitch Sorin was sure only little girls could hit. Scarlett reached over and lifted the chain from around Tula's neck. She placed the pendant in her little hands as she said, "Thank you for this, Tula."

Tula was staring at the pendant with wonder. She looked up at Rayner. "Did you see my new necklace?"

He chuckled. "I did. It is beautiful. How about we go find a chain to put it on so you do not lose it?"

"I have to go to a meeting, Tula, but I will come see you later tonight. Okay?" Scarlett asked, her attention fixed on the amulet in her hand.

But Tula was already tugging on Rayner's hand and leading him away. "I need to show Marion and Cilla my new necklace," she was telling him.

"Let's go somewhere else, Love," Sorin said, touching her elbow and pulling her from her thoughts.

Without a word, she grabbed his hand and pulled him through a rip in the world. He found himself standing in their private chambers at his Fiera Palace. She had already dropped his hand and was making her way to the large dressing room. He followed and when he entered, he found her holding her own spirit amulet. The amulet Eliné had given her. A circle with a crescent sitting on its side atop it, hung from the chain. It was Saylah's symbol, and it appeared to be the same black material as the one they'd just traded Tula for. It hung from a chain that looked identical to Tula's as well.

"The keys have always been trying to get home," she murmured. She looked up at him, and he couldn't read her expression, but he felt a tentative hope emanating down the bond. "The keys have always been trying to get home," she repeated a little louder, as if that explained everything.

"I am going to need a little more than that, Love," he said, coming to her side and taking her amulet from her, turning it over in his hand.

"Juliette and the man in my dreams have both said that to me," she said. "The keys have always been trying to get home. When I first saw the Oracle, when I first learned of the keys, she told me a child of each possesses them on a chain of wind-kissed stone."

"A child of each what?" Sorin asked, reaching for Tula's amulet as well, holding the two side-by-side.

"That I don't know yet, but it cannot be a coincidence that Ashtine recognized Tula's as skystone. I bet if she had seen mine before, she would have said it sooner, but I haven't worn it since our bonding," Scarlett said, beginning to pace in the dressing room, her hand combing through her hair.

"But the Oracle said they were on a chain of wind-kissed stone. Wouldn't that lead one to believe the key would be on the chain?" Sorin asked. He still wasn't convinced these were chains of skystone. They were just too . . . dull.

Her hand shot out and snatched her necklace from his grasp. She ran her fingers along the amulet, holding it up to the light. The amulet seemed to absorb the light, as if it were sucking it into itself. "That son of a bitch," she muttered under her breath. She met his gaze once more as she said, "The amulets are nightstone."

"Nightstone?" Sorin repeated in confusion. "Nightstone is not a thing."

His confusion only intensified as Scarlett dropped to the floor, her head tipping back and laughter spilling from her lips. "He never gave me a rock. He was showing me I already had it." Then she lifted the amulet to her lips and spoke to it. "Something like this, you asshole? Speaking into a rock?"

"Scarlett . . . Are you feeling all right?" Sorin ventured carefully, but it certainly seemed as if she'd gone mad.

"Fantastic," she replied, getting her laughter under control. "We found the first two keys."

"I understand why you seem to think that, but I do not think we should jump to any conclusions," Sorin started.

But she had already pushed back to her feet, throwing her arms around his neck and pressing her lips to his. Any argument he'd been about to make flew from his mind, as he tilted her head back and deepened the kiss. He herded her towards the wall, his hands on her hips as he walked her backwards. Her hands slid down his shoulders, down his arms, her nails digging into his forearms as he moved his lips to her neck, brushing her hair out of the way. A breathy moan escaped her lips, and he couldn't help but smile with smug satisfaction against her skin at the sound.

Gods, he had missed that sound.

He had missed having her close. Missed the taste of her. Her scent.

But the sounds she made when she came for him?

Yeah, those topped the list of things he'd missed most. He craved those sounds like he craved air in his lungs.

But before he could do anything about hearing those sounds again, a fire message appeared by his head.

Then another. And another.

He growled in frustration, reaching up and plucking the messages from the flames.

"They are all from Cyrus, stating they are waiting for us."

"Glad to know he is still a busybody," Scarlett muttered breathlessly, her cheeks flushed.

"We really should go and clear the air with them before we meet with Talwyn tomorrow," Sorin replied, shoving down every ounce of desire and forcing his feet to take a step back from her.

She sighed heavily, bending down to retrieve the amulets from where they'd been dropped to the floor. She pocketed them before meeting his eyes once more. The lightness that had been in them moments ago was gone. "They will forgive me eventually, right?"

He reached out and cupped her cheek. "Yes, Love. They likely already do."

"Do you?"

"Yes," he answered.

"Really?" she asked skeptically. "Because you're still blocking me out most of the time."

"Forgiveness does not equal trust," he replied, running his thumb along her cheekbone. "But that will come in time. Give me time, Scarlett."

Her lips pressed into a thin line, but she nodded once before stepping from his touch. "I need to grab a couple books from the library chamber and then we can go back."

Sorin nodded and sent a quick reply to Cyrus, letting him know they'd be back within the hour, before he followed Scarlett out of the dressing room. The guards and help all bowed as they passed them in the halls, welcoming Scarlett home. She smiled at them all, greeting most by name, but her smiles didn't reach her eyes. Not like they had moments ago when she was showing her magic to Tula or laughing on the floor of their dressing room.

She didn't say anything as they made the trek through the library shelves, into the dusty passages, and down the secret stairwell to the chamber below. She lit the various candles and torches around the room with a flick of her fingers, and Sorin couldn't help but smile softly at her casual use of her gifts. Mere months ago, she'd been terrified of them. Refused to use them unless supervised. And now?

Now she threw flames, froze fire, and created with shadows as if it were part of her. Just as it was always intended to be.

She was rifling through books on the table, muttering to herself, when she glanced at him as if she sensed his stare. "What?" she asked, dropping a pile of books back onto the table and blowing a piece of hair out of her face.

"Nothing," he answered, coming to her side. "What are we looking for?"

"There were two books down here. One was about Avonleyan customs. I didn't look into it much as I was more concerned with the wards and the war than learning about the Avonleyan people," she explained, beginning to look through another stack.

"And the other book?" he asked, looking through a stack of books near him. He wouldn't be of much help though. He couldn't read the Avonleyan language, so he wouldn't know if he stumbled across the book or not.

She cast him a quick glance before quickly averting her eyes back to her task. "A book on Blood Magic."

He stilled. "Scarlett," he said, her name a warning.

"Alaric knows how to use it, Sorin. Maybe Mikale does too. And Lord Tyndell," she said, moving to yet another stack of books. "It would be stupid to not learn as much as we can about it."

"You intend to simply study it or practice it?" he asked pointedly.

She stilled for a fraction of a second before continuing her search. When she didn't answer him, though, he said tightly, "Scarlett, tell me you are not planning to practice more Blood Magic."

"Well, since we're doing this whole not-keeping-things-from-each-other thing . . ." She trailed off, moving to a bookcase.

"For fuck's sake, Scarlett," Sorin seethed. "You cannot be serious."

"Look at you using your big boy words," she taunted, smirking at him in that infuriating way she knew would make him see red.

He crossed the chamber to her in three long strides. She had turned her back to him again, running her fingers along the spines of the books on a shelf. She gasped when he gripped her arm, spinning her and pressing her back to the shelves behind her.

"You will tell me before you enact any of those Marks, Scarlett. We will discuss it and be in agreement before you do it," he said, low and even. It was taking everything in him to not lose his temper. She pursed her lips, looking everywhere but at him. "Scarlett," he growled.

"I cannot promise that, Sorin," she finally said. "If we are in the midst of a fight and I need to use one, I cannot stop and ask your permission."

"Blood Magic should not be used at all, but if you are going to insist on using it, it should certainly not be used without care and meticulous thought," he argued. "Gods, Scarlett, did you learn nothing at all from this?"

"Stop speaking to me like I am a child, Sorin," she spat back. "I understand your concern here—"

"You clearly do not," he said, releasing her and pushing back off the bookshelf. "Find your books so we can go."

"So now you are going to throw a temper tantrum? Delightful," she muttered, turning back to the bookcase.

He said nothing. He just stalked to the doorway and waited for her. She would glance at him every once in a while, but she never held his gaze for longer than a second. After several more minutes, she finally found the two books she'd been looking for and came to his side.

Clutching the books to her chest, she looked up at him. "We can discuss this more, Sorin. We can come to an agreement, but I need you to be on my side when we meet with the others again. I need you."

He cupped the nape of her neck and hauled her to his lips, pressing a hard kiss to her mouth. "I am yours, and you are mine. It is always you and me. Always together."

"Okay," she breathed onto his lips, relief sparking down the bond.

A few minutes later, they had climbed the steps and stepped through a fire portal back to the Black Halls. Scarlett had sent the books off with a shadow panther, and they were once again sitting at a table with his Court, Briar, and Sawyer. No one was speaking, although Rayner and Sawyer seemed far less hostile. Briar had never carried the same anger the rest of them had, regarding her actions. Cyrus was sitting rigidly in his seat, and Eliza had her arms crossed, her grey eyes hard.

Scarlett took a deep breath beside him before she said, "So, what else do you guys want to know?"

Eliza snorted with derision. "I think the better question is what else do you need to tell us?"

"I am fairly certain Sorin and I found two of the seven Avonleyan keys," Scarlett said casually, and Sorin tipped his head back in exasperation.

"For the love of Anala, Scarlett," he muttered, knowing exactly what was coming as Eliza spoke.

"So now you are keeping secrets from us too?" she demanded, her furious gaze landing on him.

Scarlett held up her hand before things escalated further. "To be fair, we just found them after we had eaten lunch. Rayner was there, although I hadn't pieced it all together yet at that point."

Briar barked a laugh from where he sat. "Always with the dramatics, Sunshine," he teased.

She threw him a quick grin before turning back to the others and quickly filling them in on what she believed to be the keys.

"I am still not convinced the chains are skystone," Sorin said when she had finished speaking. "And there is no way to know if the amulets are indeed the keys without involving Talwyn. So the question is, are we wanting to tell her our suspicions, or do we wait until we are sure and have found the other keys?"

"Ashtine can confirm if they are skystone or not," Briar said.

"With Nasima?" Scarlett asked, rolling white flames between her fingers as she contemplated the decisions before them.

"Likely not," Briar said, his features darkening. "But she can take them to the Shira Cliffs. She can enter the places where skystone is found. In that sacred space, her own power should be able to recognize the skystone."

Scarlett nodded. "Let's wait until that is confirmed before saying anything to Talwyn. I think our main concern, after Tarek, needs to be the Contessa," she said. "I am assuming the Summit did not happen?"

Briar shook his head. "No. From my understanding, they were still waiting for a response from the Contessa. The High Witch also made it very clear she would not attend unless you were present."

"And the Beta was with us," Rayner added.

Scarlett nodded again. "Is it normal for the Contessa to take this long to respond?"

"She is reclusive, but no," Sorin supplied. "This is unusual."

"We can get Talwyn and Azrael's input on that tomorrow," she said after a moment. "I do not want Cassius brought up tomorrow or the fact that he is half-Avonleyan."

That had everyone's eyes snapping back to her.

"Explain," Cyrus bit out. The first and only word he'd spoken since they'd reconvened.

"It is why your blood is helping him heal," she said. "Avonleyans need Fae to heal and replenish their magic."

"And you?" Sawyer asked.

"I am full-blooded Avonleyan." The entire room fell silent.

"That explains your shadows and white flames," Briar said, more to himself than the room.

"Yes," Scarlett answered.

"You want this kept from Talwyn?" Rayner asked.

"I want Cassius kept out of all discussions for the time being," Scarlett clarified. "As for my own heritage, Sorin and I discussed that this morning and think it would be best if we told Talwyn, rather than her learning it some other way."

The rest of the day was spent in further discussion of the meeting with Talwyn tomorrow, Scarlett revealing what she did and did not know of the Maraan Lords, the wards, everything really. They had dinner served in that council room, and when the sun had long since set, Sorin finally ordered a halt to the meeting. She was exhausted, and he knew she'd want to check in on Cassius again before she would allow herself to sleep.

When they did finally retire to the queen's chambers, she was asleep when he emerged from the bathing room after washing up. He pulled the quilt up higher and over her shoulder before he moved to an armchair by the fire. He would go to bed soon enough, but Scarlett was not the only one who had taken books from the chamber in the Fiera Palace.

While they had been searching, he had found some of her notes and books and sent them to a pocket between the realms. He was determined to learn the Avonleyan language. He was determined to figure out this Source thing for her. So he settled in, her notes and translations on the table beside him, and began.

CHAPTER 25
CALLAN

Callan was slumped in his chair on the dais at the front of the ballroom. His chin in his hand and leaning to the side on the armrest, he sighed as he looked out over the preening nobility.

This was his engagement ball. Somehow, his mother had put this together in a matter of days. His betrothal to Tava had been announced four days ago, and here they were.

"Sit up, Callan," his mother chided, leaning across his father's empty throne. His sister was seated on her other side, and there was an empty seat for Tava to his right. She would be arriving at any moment.

His eyes slid to his father, who was off to the side conversing with several Lords and nobles from neighboring towns. Mikale and Veda were nearby, whispering amongst themselves, and all Callan had thought about these last few days was how incredibly idiotic this whole thing was. All of them— Mikale, Veda, Lord Tyndell, Tava, Drake, himself— pretending they didn't know exactly what was going on here. All of them skirting around the issue that this was all about Scarlett and some dark purpose the Maraan Lords seemed to have, that required Veda to be seated on a throne. All of them speaking in riddles and nuances to keep his father oblivious to everything.

"He will be better when Lady Tava arrives," Eva quipped from their mother's side, her hands resting in the lap of her rose pink gown, ever the princess in training.

"I should certainly hope so," Queen Meredith replied curtly, her disapproval of his current mood and behavior clear.

"Of course he will," Eva said, her smile wide and genuine. "How can a person not smile when they see the one they love?"

Love.

To be a child and still be that naïve. To believe she will one day marry for love rather than the far more inevitable scenario of being given to a neighboring kingdom or noble household to strengthen alliances or secure deals.

The large entrance doors being opened drew his attention, and before he knew what he was doing, Callan was standing and striding towards the Tyndells, who had just arrived.

"See, Mother," he heard Eva saying, but he didn't hear any more of their conversation as he skirted around the various people milling about.

Tava was on her father's arm. She looked beautiful in a dress of cerulean blue that brought out her ocean blue eyes and that hugged her slim figure, cinching at the waist before falling to the floor. Her golden hair was pinned half up. The rest had been curled and hung around her shoulders.

He reached for her hand as soon as he stood before them, bringing the back of it to his lips and pressing a soft kiss to her skin. "Tava," he breathed, "you look stunning."

Tava dipped into a small curtsey, her hand still in his. "Thank you, Callan," she murmured, her cheeks turning pink. He was certain that was not part of the ruse.

"May I steal her from you, Lord Tyndell?" Callan asked, his eyes still fixed on Tava.

"It appears you already have," came the Lord's gruff response; and that had his gaze snapping to the Lord's.

"Father," Tava chided lightly, pulling her hand from Callan's and laying it on her father's arm. "He is not stealing me from you."

He patted her hand, a tight smile forming on his face, his square jaw rigid. "That is how it feels, my dear. I am still adjusting to all of this. It seems to have come about so quickly. Neither your brother nor I knew you were interested in anyone, let alone the Crown Prince."

"You are unhappy with the arrangement?" Tava asked, her brows arching.

He patted her hand again. "This is not the place," he said, taking her hand and passing it back to Callan. "Go enjoy yourself. This event is for you and the Crown Prince, after all."

And the way he said those last words had Callan immediately on edge. His voice had dropped into a smooth growl that had Callan pulling Tava protectively into his side. Drake, who had been standing on Tava's other side, seemed to have noticed too. His eyes had narrowed slightly on his father as the man began making his way towards the king.

"Do not let her out of your sight tonight," Drake said, his voice low and full of worry.

"I do not intend to," Callan answered, his arm sliding around her waist. "She is not Scarlett, Callan," Drake hissed, having taken the liberty to stop with formalities as soon as he'd learned of this agreement between him and Tava. "She does not have daggers strapped beneath her skirts."

"Thank the gods for that," Callan muttered.

"I will be watching too," Drake said.

Tava was smiling brightly as Callan began leading her into the room, Drake staying close to her side. She looked every bit the excited fiancé. "You need to keep an eye on Mikale and Father, Drake," she said casually. "They are acting strangely this evening."

"I can do that while keeping an eye on you as well," Drake countered.

"How are they acting strangely?" Callan asked. And how would she know? They had just arrived. She hadn't even spoken to Mikale yet.

"Mikale and Veda are keeping their distance from the others," Tava replied. "And Father seems to be making a deliberate effort to make it clear they are not seen conversing much. The king's Inner Circle is almost always together at these types of events."

Callan looked to the king again, where Lord Tyndell and Lord Lairwood were congregated with him along with a few other Lords. It was odd that Mikale wasn't with them. He tended to be by his father's side or at his side. He hadn't made any effort to even greet Callan this evening.

Callan had just assumed it was because he was still upset about the turn of events with this engagement.

"Do what you must, Drake," Tava said. Then, looking up at Callan, she added, "We need to dance. People are watching our every move. *They* are watching our every move."

Callan plastered a smile on his features, drawing Tava to him when they reached the dance floor; other couples quickly moving to give them space. He began leading her through dance steps, and after a few moments, she said, "You are tense tonight."

"It seems that is my general state of being as of late," he answered, his eyes darting around the room.

"Ignore them, Callan," she said softly. "Pretend it is just another ball. Another celebration. Being in front of a crowd has never seemed to bother you before."

"There was not a constant sense of danger before," he countered, bringing his eyes back to hers, finding them bright with amusement.

"You are the Crown Prince," she mused. "You have personal guards *because* there is always potential danger."

"You are supposedly becoming a princess," he said. "Maybe you should be given a guard."

"If I were truly to become one, I would maybe agree with you," she teased.

"Actually, I think it would be a good idea," he said, pulling her into him a little more.

Tava scoffed. "I do not need a personal guard. I have Drake."

"And when Drake is not around?"

"Callan, I do not think it is necessary," Tava replied, realizing he was serious.

Callan glanced around at the hall again. At the way Veda was watching their every move. At the way Mikale still had not joined his father and the other Lords.

"I think it is quite necessary," Callan finally said. She opened her mouth to speak, but he shook his head and continued. "It is the least I can do, Tava. You have placed yourself in danger for Windonelle. I can certainly provide you with a measure of protection. Besides, as has already been stated, it would be expected for the soon-to-be-princess to have some sort of guard with her at all times."

Tava shot him a frank look. "Callan—"

"May we cut in for dances with the happy couple?"

Callan and Tava both turned to find Mikale and Veda standing there expectantly. Where the hell were Sloan and Finn? Why hadn't they intercepted them?

"You two lovebirds have danced the last three songs together," Veda said sweetly. "Surely you can bear to be apart for one dance, no?"

Had it really been three dances?

He glanced down at Tava, who gave him a small smile as she said, "Of course. It would be a pleasure."

She disentangled herself from Callan's arms where they still held her and placed her hand into Mikale's outstretched one. Callan's jaw was tight as he watched Mikale lead her away to the other side of the dance floor.

"You clearly are not as smitten with her as you were with your secret lover," Veda said tauntingly, stepping into him and placing her hand on his shoulder.

"What is that supposed to mean?" Callan gritted out as he took her hand in his and fell into the dance movements by memory alone.

"I mean that when your *secret lover* would deign to make appearances, your eyes never left her. You certainly never danced with anyone else while she was here," Veda all but sneered. "Yet here you are, dancing with me instead of the woman you supposedly love."

"Supposedly? What would you know of love?" he bit back.

"Far more than you would think," Veda answered. "I have watched many people succumb to the weakness of love."

"Weakness?" he repeated. "If you find love to be a weakness, I do not think you know anything of it at all."

"No? You have never found yourself suffering unfairly because of love?" Veda asked, her head tilting to the side.

Callan pressed his tongue to his cheek, his eyes darting to where Tava and Mikale were dancing. She was smiling politely at him, but her posture was stiff and rigid.

"That is what I thought," Veda said when he did not reply. "*Love* makes people do uncharacteristic things."

"Or maybe it just draws out the best parts of a person," Callan countered.

"Is that what she did for you?"

"I did not realize we were discussing her so openly now," Callan ground out.

"Would you rather discuss this sham of a relationship you have with Lady Tava?" Veda asked with a cruel tilt of her lips.

"I will remind you that I am the Crown Prince, and she is to be my wife, Lady Veda. You will give her the same respect you give me. Although that currently is none, so I will insist you give her more respect than you are giving me," Callan said, his voice filled with dangerous softness.

Veda's dark eyes widened slightly at his fierce tone, but before she could reply, Tava was at his side. "I am so sorry to interrupt, but I was hoping to get some air," she said, placing a hand on his arm. "Callan?"

"Of course," he replied, immediately releasing Veda and taking Tava's hand in his.

"It is funny," Veda said, stepping away from them. "He always sought to keep them from this life of royalty, despite what he is. Despite what they are. Yet they are finding their way to thrones anyway."

Callan didn't say anything in reply as he led Tava to a side exit reserved for the royal family. Finn was already there, pushing the door open for them.

"Where have you two been?" Callan hissed under his breath when he walked past him.

"We tried to intercept them," Finn answered, the door clicking shut behind him. "They are crafty."

"I want you guarding Tava from now on," Callan said, spinning around and pointing his finger at him. "Sloan can stay with me."

"Cal," Finn sighed, his fingers running along his brows. "Let's talk to your father. We will get someone to guard Lady Tava. He won't be happy if you go down to one guard."

"I do not give a fuck what he wants," Callan spat. "He is already getting everything he wants at this point. Do not fight me on this, Finn."

"All right," Finn said, sounding resigned. "Do you want me to come with you, or stay here and guard this door?"

"Just . . . stay here," Callan said, turning his back on him and leading Tava down to another door that would lead to a hall.

"Where are we going, Callan?" Tava asked softly beside him when they'd entered the hallway.

"You said you needed some air," he replied, glancing down at her briefly.

"I did, but it was because I could tell *you* needed a moment," she answered.

He pushed open a door and gestured for her to go through. "Are you always this selfless?" he asked, stepping in after her. He'd led her to a small conservatory with several large windows. It was far too cold to actually go out and get some air, but he thought this to be the best alternative for her.

"What?" she asked, glancing over at him from where she'd stopped before one of the windows.

"You interrupted my dance with Veda because you saw I needed a moment. You agreed to this scheme for the people of this kingdom. You did much for Scarlett after . . . everything," he answered, coming to her side. "All incredibly selfless things."

"Or it is simply kindness," she said with a shrug.

"Kindness and selflessness could be considered semantics, you know."

Tava laughed softly. "I suppose they could be."

A comfortable silence fell between them, and she ran her fingers along the leaves of a large fern.

"Veda does not believe us," he finally sighed, running his hand along his jaw.

"I never expected them to," Tava answered.

"Do you not find this somewhat ridiculous?"

She smiled serenely up at him. "You will need to be a little more specific."

"All of this," he said, his arm sweeping out in an encompassing gesture. "The fact that we are pretending to be in a relationship to appease my father. And for what? To keep him from learning of Mikale and Veda and your father? Why are we all speaking in riddles and acting as though we all do not know exactly what the other is hiding and seeking?"

Tava's head tilted slightly to the side as she studied him. She'd picked a small purple flower and was twirling the stem of it between her fingers. "You wish to fight back?"

"What? No," Callan started.

"Hmm," Tava mused, bringing the flower to her nose and sniffing. "It sounds to me like you want to."

Her ocean blue eyes were watching him curiously, waiting for his next words. And he realized she was right. He *did* want to strike back at them, at *someone*, for forcing them into this. For coming after his people. For coming after him.

"What if I did? Want to fight back?" he asked slowly.

Her lips tilted up a little more. "I would say you are the Crown Prince. Who is going to stop you?"

"And you?"

"What of me?"

"Do you wish to fight back? Against what your father is pushing? Against what they are trying to do to the children of the Black Syndicate?"

Tava stepped towards him and reached up, tucking the flower along a pocket of his tunic. "I have fought back every day since you left for the Fire Court, Callan," she replied, her voice quiet and fierce. "I snuck out of my house in the dead of night to meet with Death's Shadow. I paid for food and clothing to be left in pre-arranged places and made sure they found their way to those who needed them. I passed information I heard in passing to Scarlett, to Sorin, to Cassius. All of it to fight back. All of it to fight for those who deserve something better than what they were dealt in life."

She looked up at him, her fingers resting against his chest where they had smoothed fabric down around the flower stem. "I have sat among the highest of our society and those that society wishes didn't exist. They all deserve to be fought for, Callan. We deserve rulers who care for us as mortals. Not magical beings whose first priority will always be their own."

"So selfless," he murmured.

Then she pushed up on her toes, her lips pressing to his. He was so surprised, he didn't move at first, but as her small fists clenched the front of his tunic, he found his own arms coming up and pulling her closer, deepening the kiss. She tasted like pure sunlight, and it was so stark and different from the last person he'd kissed. It was almost a shock to his senses, and it was one he didn't entirely mind. Entirely unexpected, but something he found himself welcoming.

The door banged open, and it had Tava jumping in his arms as they both spun towards the door. Her lips popped open in shock, and then she was burying her face in his chest, her cheeks flaring bright red, as his eyes landed on Veda Lairwood. Her mouth was hanging open in shock, and her dark eyes were alight with rage.

"Veda," Callan ground out, his hold on Tava tightening. Where the hell were Sloan and Finn? "Can we help you with something?"

"I—" She cleared her throat, her hands smoothing down her pale green dress.

"We will return to the grand hall in a moment," Callan said darkly, a clear dismissal.

"Of course," Veda said tightly, turning on her heel, the door snicking shut behind her.

Tava pulled back from his chest, a sly smile on her lips.

"You knew she would come looking for us?" Callan asked, realization dawning.

"Call it a hunch," she said with a wink, taking a step back.

"You were waiting for her?" He didn't know if he should feel sheepish for reading into that kiss or impressed by her cleverness that never ceased to amaze him.

"I was," Tava said, reaching to smooth his tunic once more. "I hope I did not overstep with my actions."

"You didn't," he answered quickly.

She cleared her throat slightly as she stepped back again. "Are you ready to go back?"

"Not particularly," he muttered, and Tava laughed under her breath as he took her hand and began leading her from the conservatory and back to the grand hall.

"You are failing to see the opportunity that has been presented to us," she said.

"What opportunity?"

"Events like this are notorious for the highest in society showing off in public. They speak of things, Callan. They boast of deals made, affairs had, knowledge they shouldn't know," she said with an air of knowing. "You can learn very interesting things if you simply place yourself in the right place at the right time."

"You know," Callan mused, pulling open the door to the side room and ushering her through, "you truly are quite the cunning little fox."

She huffed a breath of laughter. "I am nothing special."

"I think we will need to disagree on that," he replied as they stepped through the adjacent door and back into the ballroom. "So what do you suggest we do, little fox?"

Tava elbowed him in the ribs with another breath of laughter. "Let's go greet people. Mingle. It will admittedly be harder to blend into the background when I am standing beside the prince though," she said, her hand going to her throat and fiddling with her amulet.

"Where do you want to start?"

"We need to be positioned in places where we can hear multiple conversations at once," Tava answered, her eyes scanning the room. "You are the important one here. You keep them engaged in conversation, and I will see what else I can hear around us."

"So eavesdropping is indeed something you have made a habit," he teased, leaning down to speak in her ear so she could hear him over the din of the hall.

"Always be listening, Callan," she replied, a wry smile pulling at the corner of her lips. "You never know what you will hear."

CHAPTER 26
SCARLETT

Scarlett took a deep breath before she stepped into the private training pits on the sprawling grounds of the Black Halls. They were located on cliffs that overlooked the sea to the south, and the sea air calmed her nerves some.

They were meeting with Talwyn, Azrael, and Ashtine this afternoon. She had awoken to Sorin demanding to know all the places Mikale had touched her while she'd been held captive, and he'd taken his time replacing those touches with his own and then some. When they had finally dressed, she had checked in on Cassius, who was still asleep with no change, and ate a small breakfast with the children in the great hall.

Eliza's ire had finally started relenting towards the end of the day last night. There was still distrust there, but she had at least stopped snapping at Scarlett every time she spoke to her. Scarlett considered that a win.

Now, though . . . Now she needed to face the male working off a temper with the general in the sparring ring.

Cyrus had said all but a handful of words the entire afternoon and evening. He wouldn't even look at Scarlett, and when Sorin had insisted they end things for the day, Cyrus had stood and left without a backward glance.

Eliza spotted her first and quickly ended the match they were engaged in. Cyrus took one look at Scarlett, then crossed to the far side of the pit, drinking from a waterskin. Eliza made her way to Scarlett, her eyes taking in her training gear, the sword strapped to her back.

"You are here for him?" she asked, crossing her arms.

"I am," Scarlett answered. "You and I are . . . okay?"

Eliza pushed her tongue to her cheek. "Not entirely, but we're certainly better off than you currently are with him."

"I will fix it. With you. With him," Scarlett said, her eyes darting to the Fire Court Second.

"You damn well better," Eliza retorted, sheathing her sword before grabbing her things and stalking from the pit.

Scarlett slowly made her way over to Cyrus, who was now sitting on the bench, staring straight ahead. She lowered down beside him, her elbows coming to rest on her knees.

"Hi, Darling," she said softly.

"Do *not* 'hi, Darling' me," he hissed at her.

She gave an exaggerated sigh. "Let's take this to the sparring ring then."

His lip curled up as he finally met her gaze. "That would not be a good idea right now."

"Well, you are clearly refusing to speak with me, so it appears that is our only other option at the moment," Scarlett said.

"Or you could just fuck off," Cyrus spat.

She rolled her eyes. "These godsdamn Fae temper tantrums." She pushed to her feet. "Get your ass in the ring."

"No," Cyrus snarled.

"No?" she questioned, her head tilting slightly to the side.

"I know it is not a word you are accustomed to hearing," he bit out. Scarlett gritted her teeth at the jab. "If you can verbally spar with me, you can certainly spar with me with a sword. Get in the fucking ring, Cyrus."

"No, Scarlett," he snarled back.

"Okay, have it your way," she said with a wicked smirk, slowly beginning to back away from him, holding her hands up in a placating gesture.

His golden eyes narrowed on her, and when she was several feet back . . . she blasted him with ice cold water from both hands.

She was already racing for the ring when his bellow of rage reached her ears. A shield of thin shadows swirled around her, and she saw him stalking towards her, his hair and clothing already dry from the flames licking up and down his body. She sent some of her shadows slithering towards him as she taunted, "Show me your darkness, and I'll show you mine."

Cyrus's lip curled up in a snarl, and he drew a sword from flames, the same wreathing down the blade. Scarlett pulled the Spirit Sword from her back, her white flames encompassing it.

"Are you going to hide behind your shadows, *Darling?*"

"I do not hide from anything, asshole," she bit back, her shadows dissipating.

Their blades met, and they were both thrown backwards from the blast that radiated from their power colliding. Neither of them were putting much effort into tampering down their magic.

Scarlett was back on her feet in an instant and saw Cyrus had done the same. They were slowly circling each other, and golden eyes locked on silver ones. "I am sorry, Cyrus," Scarlett said, making sure she spoke loud enough for him to hear.

His response was lunging at her. She brought her blade up to meet his, and she leapt back from him, anticipating he would do the same, but he did not. He advanced, and Scarlett had to duck to avoid his next swing. She popped back up, spinning to the side, and caught his next strike at the last second, their magic flaring and exploding from them again and sending her flying.

She managed to keep her grip on her sword and roll back to her feet, finding Cyrus standing a few feet away and waiting for her, already in an offensive position. Movement caught her eye, and she saw Sorin leaning against the stone archway of the entrance to the private pits, his ankles crossed. His arms were folded over his broad chest, but he made no move to intervene. He just jerked his chin in Cyrus's direction, telling her to get back in there.

Scarlett gritted her teeth, prowling forward. Their blades met again.

And again. And again.

Flames and sparks and embers flew from every strike.

"Cyrus," she said between breaths as he advanced, fire flaring in his golden irises. "I cannot go into a meeting with Talwyn with you not speaking to me. I am sorry. I am so fucking sorry. I will do whatever you require of me to prove it to you, but I need you, Cyrus. I need you as surely as I need Sorin. I need you as much as I need Cassius. You are my family—"

She wasn't prepared for the power that he amplified down his sword when it met her blade this time. She went flying through the air yet again, but this time she landed on her back, the air forced from her lungs. She coughed, trying to catch her breath, biting down on the groan of pain that flared up her spine. Her sword was a few feet away, but as she reached for it, a booted foot settled on her wrist. She looked up into Cyrus's face, his own sword discarded. He didn't put his full weight on her arm, but he made it clear he would not allow her to get her weapon.

She heard Sorin call to him in warning, and Cyrus flipped him off over his shoulder as he came closer and dropped into a crouch beside her head, his hands hanging loosely between his knees.

"I grew up on the streets. Not in Solembra, but in a port city on the west coast called Aelyndee. I actually hate being at the Black Halls, so close to the sea," he said, his tone cold and grave. The little air Scarlett had been able to get down caught in her throat. She knew Cyrus had been an orphan, had grown up poor, but he had never spoken of it. Not to her, at least.

"My mother left me and my father as soon as I was weaned from her breast," he continued. "My father was killed when he was trying to steal a loaf of bread from the market for me. I was two and hadn't eaten in three days. My first memories are of an aching belly, rife with hunger, and hiding in the back of my father's cart while I heard him beg for mercy, saying he was just trying to feed his boy."

Scarlett couldn't move. She hardly dared to breathe. Cyrus was staring off into the distance, out at the sea.

"Vagrants would take me in from time to time when I was younger, but as I got older, by the age of six, no one wanted to be burdened with me. I worked at the docks when I could. I stole when I couldn't. I was beaten up by other boys as often as I was doing the beating.

"One day, when I was eleven, I was on the run. I had stolen, of all fucking things, a loaf of bread and had almost gotten caught, just like my father had. Another boy whistled at me from a second-story window, and in seconds I had managed to climb a drainpipe and slip inside. I heard the market guards rush by a few seconds later. I shared that loaf of bread with that boy. His name was Merrik, and from that day on, we were inseparable. You can steal a lot more shit when you have someone causing a distraction, and we took turns being the decoy. You can steal even more when you learn to play on people's weaknesses. You can take what you want when you learn that desperate people will do desperate things when shoved into a corner. We were a team. We found a place by the docks, and we made it our home. He was the first friend I ever had. The first person I ever loved. Eventually, he was my first everything. He was the only family I needed.

"Until he decided he could handle a job on his own. It was seven years later. We were still young, even by mortal standards, but we'd both grown into our power, learned to wield our flames together. As best as we could without formal instruction, anyway. We had learned of a wealthy merchant from the capital who was going to be touring the town and had spent the last few days plotting out the best ways to rob him. But Merrik had gotten a tip that he was going to be arriving early, that very afternoon to be exact. He ended up trailing the carriage of the Fae merchant to the docks, and when the merchant was touring a ship, he made the last-second decision to rob him right then, rather than wait for me.

"I was out doing another job. It was a standard job. One we did every month, collecting on a few of our . . . investments. He knew where to find me. He could have come and gotten me. We could have robbed that merchant blind together with very little effort, but he decided he didn't have time to run it by me first. He didn't have time to come find me, to make sure all the details were covered. He got caught. They shackled weights to his ankles and threw him from the end of the docks. After they beat him within an inch of his life, of course. Because we were nothing, after all. Just urchins that had run wild on the streets and now were thieves and criminals."

Scarlett swallowed back the tears burning the back of her eyes, the pain in her spine completely forgotten.

"I learned of his fate from another boy later that night. I packed up our little home, leaving all of his things behind, and left Aelyndee that same night. I trusted no one. For years. Decades. Until an Ash Rider intercepted me pick-pocketing coin in a tavern in a no-name town at the base of the Fiera Mountains. I later learned he'd been watching me for several months. The Fire Court Royal had been receiving complaints from all over the Court of coin and other valuables mysteriously going missing. The Fire Prince had handed the task over to his Ash Rider. Rayner, being the nosy bastard that he is, had his various spies search into my past, when he figured out that I was the one single-handedly stealing from all these people as I wandered around the Court, never knowing a home. There wasn't much to find out about me, but what was there, he found it. I was introduced to Sorin, later Thia, and, you know the rest. But do you know what runs through my mind to this day, Scarlett?" he asked, finally bringing his eyes back to hers.

She shook her head, not trusting herself to speak.

"If Merrik had just come and found me, if he had waited, if he had run his plan by me, I would have seen the holes. We would have altered the plans and pocketed a fuck ton of coin. If he had just *fucking said something*, everything could have been different.

"I don't live in the past. I don't wallow in regrets or linger on what could have been. But the family that I have lost in my life, barring my mother, if you can even call her that, their losses could have all been avoided if someone had just fucking said something. If my father had set his pride aside, and explained how he needed food for his starving son to others on the streets, someone would have fed his child. If Merrik had waited, found me, and told me about his change of plans, we would have done the job together and survived. If Thia hadn't been as stubborn as you are, if she would have used her godsdamn head and *said something* to Sorin instead of thinking she could handle a clan of Night Children largely on her own and agreeing to his insane plan, my soul would still be whole.

"I do not give the term 'family' to people lightly. Not after Merrik. In fact, only a handful of others have managed to obtain such a status in my life, but I gave it to you. The moment you looked up at me and said 'hi' when I called you Darling. And all I could think while you were gone, is that if you would have *said something*, everything could have been different."

"I am sorry, Cyrus," Scarlett whispered from where she lay in the dirt. Her heart was breaking.

So much loss. So much hurt.

He'd been alone, a broken little boy. He'd found love, then lost it. Then he'd been alone again, still just as broken. He'd wandered, looking for a home, until home had found him. Where he found so much love. Where he'd only survived the loss of his truest love because of the love of the rest of them.

"Do you know why I am the Fire Court Second, Scarlett?" he asked. When she shook her head again, he looked away, back out at the sea once more. "It is not because I am the most-skilled warrior or because I have some vast knowledge of politics. I have learned both of those skills, yes, but I am the Fire Court Second because I know what desperation does to a person. I know a desperate man will do whatever he must to feed his family. I know that a desperate general will make rash decisions when he is on the brink of losing a war. I know a desperate king will choose his throne over his people the vast majority of the time. I know wealthy businessmen will make illegal deals to keep their riches. I know people in poverty will do the same. I know how to think like the desperate and exploit those weaknesses, because that's what I did. For decades. I can anticipate how people will react, and Sorin gave me a place to use those skills to help people rather than exploit them. Our Court works together— utilizing my shrewdness, Eliza's battle strategies, Rayner's gathered intelligence, and Sorin's power and title."

His eyes came back to hers, the flames in them having banked long ago while he had been speaking. "We are a family. We choose each other. We claim each other. We challenge each other, push each other, listen to each other. But it only works because we trust each other. And when we do not do those things? That is when we break. That is when unnecessary tragedy is allowed to bloom."

"I trust you, Cyrus," Scarlett whispered. "I do. I trust all of you."

"Do you, Darling?" he asked, and Scarlett held in the sob of relief when he called her that. "Do you trust Sorin and Briar when they offer you advice on ruling? Do you trust Rayner to gather necessary information for you? Do you trust Eliza to devise battle plans? Do you trust me enough to strategize with me and include me in your insanely brilliant plans? We are not trying to tell you what to do, Scarlett. We simply want to be beside you while you do it. Because we are a family."

Scarlett pushed herself up out of the dirt and flung her arms around Cyrus's neck, his arms coming around her just as tightly.

"We were all alone at some point, Scarlett," he said into her hair. "All of us have experienced being only able to depend on oneself. We have all had to learn to trust others, to let ourselves depend on others. But you are a queen. You need to get there faster than we did."

She nodded into his neck. "I understand," she whispered.

He held her tightly for another few moments and then he said, "Do we need to find Beatrix to heal you after I threw you across the pit?"

She lurched back, finding a smirk on his lips. "I'm already healing, jackass. Perks of being Avonleyan, when my power is fully replenished."

Cyrus pushed to his feet, helping Scarlett to her own. He retrieved her sword for her before going to gather his things. Sorin was already striding toward her. "You need to start training to fight with your magic, now that you can control it."

"You think?" Scarlett drawled. "Cyrus just single-handedly kicked my ass."

"Are you feeling okay? Are you feeling weak?" he asked, reaching to take the sword she'd sheathed and unbuckled from her back.

She sighed heavily. "Stop being so fussy."

"Never, Love," he said with a wink, pressing a quick kiss to her brow.

Cyrus joined them, and they walked back to the Halls, trekking up the stairs to the queen's wing.

"I need to go give blood to Cassius," Cyrus said when they were nearing the upper levels.

"Thank you for doing this for him, Cyrus," Scarlett said.

Cyrus leaned down and pressed a kiss to her cheek. "Welcome back, Darling."

Scarlett and Sorin went to their chambers, and Scarlett bathed quickly before dressing in charcoal grey pants and a black tunic. They took a small lunch in their room, and before she knew it, it was time to go meet with Talwyn, Azrael, and Ashtine.

CHAPTER 27
TALWYN

"Stop pacing, Talwyn," Azrael said from where he sat at the desk in her chambers at the White Halls. He didn't even look up from the reports and correspondence he was going over. Everything that had come in while he'd been in the mortal lands.

He'd slept for over a day, finally waking late last evening. The first words out of his mouth had been, "Tell me what happened with Ashtine and Stellan." Not that Talwyn had expected anything else. His focus was always singular, always her best moves for their Courts, for her throne.

She didn't pause her pacing in front of the window as she retorted, "This meeting has me anxious."

"Clearly," he grunted. Talwyn bit down on a retort until he added, "You should be more anxious about your relations with Princess Ashtine and the Shifters."

She sent a whip of wind in his direction, blowing the papers from the desk and sending them fluttering to the floor.

He slowly dragged his gaze to hers. "Very queenly of you, Talwyn."

"Fuck off, Azrael."

He didn't bother to respond. Just set a letter aside and began reading through the next.

She'd tried to keep herself busy while he'd slept. She'd gone to Stellan to let him know that Arianna was back, then took him to the Black Halls. She didn't hang around long to see how that reunion went. She'd never admit it to anyone, but she didn't want to see Scarlett until Azrael could be with her. If Tarek were indeed alive . . .

So rather than risk running into her and Sorin when Stellan found Arianna, she'd come back to the White Halls. She'd sent a message to Ashtine asking if she was free. Her reply had asked if it was urgent, and when Talwyn had said no, Ashtine had told her she was not available at the moment.

Which was just great.

She'd gone through reports, read that same correspondence Azrael was currently poring over, but none of it had distracted her enough to keep her mind from Tarek. She was trying to be prepared for every outcome. Trying to anticipate how she would react to each and every way that conversation could go. Trying to make sure her emotions would stay in check, her features neutral, her magic under control.

"I swear to Silas, Talwyn, you are going to wear a path right through that rug," Azrael said, finally setting the various letters and reports down and pushing to his feet.

"Well?" she demanded, gesturing to the stack of papers, her feet continuing that same path.

"Once we hear what the Western Courts have to say today, we can move forward from there," Azrael replied, folding his arms across his chest.

He'd filled her in on the little he'd learned while on that mission with Sorin and his Court, but she still didn't know where these Maraan Lords had come from or what they wanted with Scarlett. She was powerful, yes, but that couldn't be everything.

"Are you ready?"

Talwyn finally paused, glancing over her shoulder at Azrael. "Of course I am ready," she snapped.

His brown eyes studied her for a long moment, and she held his stare, daring him to push this any further right now.

He finally sighed, saying only, "Let's go," before reaching for her hand and letting her Travel them to the Black Halls.

They were met by Briar and Ashtine, and Talwyn bit her tongue at finding the princess once again here before her. They were escorted to one of the main floor council rooms. It was one of the bigger meeting rooms and far more formal than she had come to expect from Scarlett.

They followed Briar and Ashtine into the room, and her eyes landed on her cousin standing at one end of the room with Sorin and Cyrus. They were speaking softly amongst themselves, but at the sound of their entrance, they all stopped and turned to her. Scarlett immediately made her way to them, her eyes fixed on Azrael, who watched her warily.

"Talwyn," she said cordially, glancing at her quickly before returning her attention to the Earth Prince. "Prince Azrael, I owe you my gratitude and a debt," she said, inclining her head slightly. "Thank you for getting everyone out. I am told that doing so pushed your power to the edge of its limits. Have you recovered all right?"

"I have," Azrael said slowly, clearly as wary of her formalities as Talwyn was.

"That is good to hear. We have much to discuss," she said, gesturing towards the table where the Fire and Water Courts had taken their seats. Scarlett went back to Sorin, and they both made their way to the table, Scarlett taking the seat at the head of it with Sorin to her right. Briar sat at her left.

Talwyn made her way to the other end of the long, polished table.

When she'd taken her seat, a tense silence settled over the room.

Which her cousin broke with the unconventional flare she'd begun to become accustomed to.

"So what would you like to know first?" Scarlett asked, sitting back casually in her chair.

"What would you like to tell me first?" Talwyn countered.

"I have quite the list today," she replied, propping her head onto her hand. "But I want to make sure all of your questions are answered before we move on to my list of topics."

"Fine," Talwyn said tightly. "Why don't you tell me what the hell you were doing at the border of the Earth Court."

"Aiding you, of course. There was a clan of Night Children there," Scarlett drawled. And before Talwyn could say anything, she added with a wry grin and wink, "You're welcome, by the way."

A gust of wind blew through the room, and Talwyn clamped down on her magic while Scarlett just poured herself a glass of water, taking a sip, before she met Talwyn's eyes again.

"As was previously stated to your consort, we did not request aid," Azrael said from her right.

"And when were you planning to arrive to stop the advance into the Night Child territory?" Scarlett asked, setting her water glass down.

"Why would they want to go there?" Talwyn demanded, her thoughts of Tarek momentarily forgotten at the mention of mortals and rogue Night Children trying to enter that territory.

She sat rigidly still while Scarlett told them of her theories and what she overheard while at the border.

Before she had single-handedly taken almost all of them out with her power.

"They were waiting for me?" Talwyn asked when Scarlett fell silent.

Scarlett glanced at Sorin quickly before she said, "Yes, but before we speak of that, I need to know if you've heard from the Contessa. Did she ever respond about attending the Summit?"

"The Summit was obviously postponed," Talwyn replied.

"Obviously," Scarlett said, rolling her eyes. "But did she ever respond? Has anyone heard anything from her?"

"The Contessa is very private," Ashtine said.

"So I've heard, but no one else is concerned that we have not heard from her?" Scarlett asked, glancing at her own Courts. "From what I heard, their goal was to get to her. I think we need to at least send someone in to investigate." Her silver eyes shifted to the Ash Rider. "Rayner?"

"I have had people trying to look into it since you brought it up yesterday, but they have not found anything yet," he answered, his tone conveying just how unhappy he was with that.

"What is required to go there? What . . . *protocols* need to be followed?" She turned, batting her lashes at Sorin. Clearly they'd discussed this matter, and as he held her gaze, Talwyn could only assume they were communicating with their twin flame bond.

Which brought Tarek back to the forefront of Talwyn's mind.

"So we will send a small company to the Night Children to speak with the Contessa," Talwyn said impatiently. "Now tell me why they were waiting for me."

Scarlett went still, her hands falling to the arms of her chair. She seemed almost . . . nervous? She'd never seen her cousin so unsure before.

Scarlett pushed out a long breath of air before she said, "They were waiting for you to arrive before they proceeded to try to enter the territory. Apparently, they had deemed the Earth Court a safer passage than the Witch Kingdoms."

Azrael snorted a huff of amusement beside her, and Talwyn had to agree. The Witches were cruel and ruthless, but Azrael's Court was . . . arguably worse, especially if she would have joined them in a fight.

Scarlett sucked on a tooth before she said, "They said they were prepared to handle you and your magic."

Talwyn said nothing. Just stared at her cousin, waiting for her to go on. Scarlett blew out another breath as she said, "They have more than just Night Children aiding them. They have at least one Fae. He was the one who detained me when my power was depleted to the point that I could not fight back . . . And he claims to know you."

Talwyn did not move. She did not allow any of the panic and dread she was feeling to cross her features. Just stared and waited.

"It is Tarek Ordos, isn't it?" Azrael asked grimly, putting Talwyn out of the misery of waiting for her cousin to get to the damn point.

Scarlett's eyes widened as she looked at the Earth Prince. "How do you know that?"

"I didn't," Azrael replied. "But as I told Talwyn when I returned, I had my suspicions. His voice was very familiar when I heard him speak in the Black Syndicate."

Sorin was shaking his head. "He hardly spoke when you were present. As I have told Scarlett, the odds of it being Ordos are nearly impossible."

"He was my Third for over a century, Aditya. Well before he was thought to be the queen's twin flame," Azrael retorted, and Talwyn somehow managed to stiffen further. It was amazing her spine hadn't snapped at this point.

"You honestly think it could be the same Fae?" Sorin asked, and Talwyn could hear the clear doubt in his tone. "I was there that day they died. I saw them being—" He paused, glancing at Cyrus then to Talwyn, before saying, "There is no way any of them survived that."

"And as *I* have told Sorin," Scarlett cut in, "the way he spoke, the things he appears to know, makes it hard for me to believe it is anyone other than Tarek Ordos."

"What did he say that makes you believe that?" Talwyn asked, finally finding it in her to say something. Her voice was even. Controlled. Cold.

"When I was still weakened after the fight at the border, he told me he'd been waiting for you," Scarlett said, her eyes settling back on Talwyn's. There was a softness there, a pitying look. "He said he knew how to handle you."

"That means nothing," Talwyn said. "That confirms nothing."

"Then he told me we were almost family. That he was the . . ." Scarlett paused again, looking at Azrael, before saying, "He said he was the rightful heir of the Earth Court and that he was your twin flame."

"Again, that confirms nothing," Talwyn said. "And the fact that he believes he should be ruling over the Earth Court makes me even less inclined to believe such a thing. Tarek never once hinted at that."

Scarlett sighed in clear exasperation. "How exactly would you lot like me to prove this to you? Shall I go back to Baylorin, track him down, and drag him back here for you to confirm his identity?"

The fires in the hearths at either end of the room flared as Sorin's head whipped to his wife. "Do not even think about going back there right now," he snarled.

Scarlett rolled her eyes at him before smiling sweetly, clearly saying something to him down their bond again.

"I have to agree with Sorin on this," Talwyn said. "I cannot believe that Tarek has been stuck in the mortal lands for the last decade without finding some way to notify me that he was still alive."

Scarlett grimaced slightly as she ventured cautiously, "I do not think 'stuck there' is how I would describe his situation."

"Explain," Talwyn demanded.

"He has taken a Blood Mark of loyalty to Alaric. He has bound himself to him," Scarlett said.

"*If* it is somehow Tarek Ordos, then he was forced into that," Talwyn snapped.

"Blood Marks cannot be forced on you," Scarlett said softly. "Not that one, anyway. It must be accepted by the choice of the bearer, or Alaric would have forced it upon me."

"Few can do Blood Magic that powerful," Azrael said. "The Avonleyans and the Maraans," Scarlett agreed. "And the Sorceress," Ashtine supplied.

"The who?" Scarlett asked, her head tilting to the side as her attention slid to Ashtine.

"The Sorceress in the Water Prison beneath these halls,"

Ashtine lilted. "Prince Briar can get you in," she added, gesturing to the Water Prince down the table.

"Sorin?" she asked, turning to the Fire Prince.

"Later, Scarlett," Sorin replied tightly. "I will tell you of her later."

"What, exactly, is it that these Maraan Lords want from you?" asked Azrael.

"They want me to find the keys to enter Avonleya so that Alaric can have revenge and then, I would assume, rule here and there," Scarlett answered, sipping at her water again.

"Do you think they are powerful enough to take on the Avonleyans?" Azrael asked.

Scarlett shrugged. "It does not matter if I think they are powerful enough. They clearly think they are. They tried before, did they not?"

"And nearly succeeded before the Avonleyans fled back to their continent, leaving those they'd recruited for help to fend for themselves," Talwyn snarled bitterly.

Scarlett seemed to mull this over, tapping her nails on the table. "That is one way of looking at it, I suppose."

"What is another?" Talwyn asked from between clenched teeth.

"They went back to guard whatever it is that the Maraans want on that continent," she answered.

"Which is?"

Scarlett shrugged. "That is something I have been trying to figure out for months."

"Do you think they were waiting to detain Talwyn for the same purpose?" Azrael asked.

"Possibly. It would make shifting the keys back to their original state easier to already have her, I suppose," Scarlett mused, clearly contemplating a number of things as she stared out a window to the right.

"Possibly?" Talwyn questioned. "Is that not why they wanted you?"

"Partly," she answered.

"Partly," Talwyn deadpanned. "By all means, please explain the other part."

"They want my bloodline," Scarlett answered, bringing her focus back to the table.

"Eliné's bloodline? Why?"

Scarlett shook her head. "Not Eliné's. My Avonleayn bloodline."

Azrael's head whipped to Scarlett. "You have Avonleyan blood?"

"Yes."

"How much?" he demanded.

"Apparently all of it," she answered casually, her head coming to rest on her hand again.

"You are full-blooded Avonleyan?" Azrael asked.

"Yes," she confirmed. "Although, my heritage has now changed twice in less than a year, so who really knows at this point?" She lounged back in her seat, looking thoughtful. "Maybe I will be an actual goddess by this time next year."

"A goddess who got thrown across a training pit a few hours ago?" Cyrus mused with an arched brow. "I think not."

Scarlett stuck her tongue out at him with a scowl and a glare.

"You are pure-blooded Avonleyan?" Talwyn repeated, her blood seeming to have frozen in her veins.

"Yes," Scarlett answered.

Talwyn looked to Ashtine. "How long have you known?"

Ashtine held her stare as she said, "I learned of her heritage at the same moment you did."

"Bullshit," Talwyn spat. "You have been found with them, before my arrivals, more times than not these past weeks. Not to mention the winds—"

"As I have repeatedly reported to you, your Majesty," Ashtine interjected, her usual lilt turning cold and lethal, "the winds no longer speak to me and stopped whispering of Avonleya weeks ago."

"How much does my bloodline truly matter?" Scarlett drawled.

"It matters," Talwyn bit back, dragging her eyes back to her cousin. No, wait. *Not* her cousin. "Because if you are not Fae, if you are not Eliné's heir, then you have no claim to the throne of the Western Courts." The entire room went still. Briar and Sorin were glancing at each other. Their Courts exchanging glances as well. Had none of these idiots thought of this?

Scarlett's silver eyes were fixed on Talwyn as she said with controlled calm, "Come again?"

"I said," Talwyn replied, enunciating her words sardonically, "that if you do not carry Eliné's bloodline, then you are not the heir to her throne, and thus have no right to rule over *Fae*."

"I may not carry her blood in my veins," Scarlett said, her tone going lethal, "but her gifts were transferred into my blood." In emphasis, she raised a hand, letting orange flames spring to life while shards of ice spun around them. "Blood Magic was used to do so."

"That does not give you a right to her throne," Talwyn spat.

Celeste help her if she was going to let an *Avonleyan* have the throne of the Western Courts. It was not an option. Because an Avonleyan certainly would not aid her in her vendetta against her own people.

And yet she was the only one who could find the fucking keys.

A saccharine smile spread across Scarlett's face as she fidgeted with the flames and ice still conjured in her hand. "Correct me if I'm wrong, because I am not entirely well-versed in Fae customs and politics yet, but it is my understanding that the most powerful of an element claims the throne. It is why the prince sitting to your right holds his throne, and the Fae in the mortal lands is so disgruntled." Talwyn's lip curled up as Scarlett continued. Her face had gone cruel, and her tone had turned vicious. "Eliné's gifts make me the most powerful being with fire and water magic. If someone wants my throne, they shall have to fight me for it." Shadows suddenly flitted amongst the ice shards, and the flames turned blindingly white. "But I will not lose," she added with a wicked grin.

"Maybe we need to take a little break," Sorin ventured, clearly trying to ease the tension in the room. Maybe recognizing his wife was about to lose control. Maybe recognizing so was Talwyn.

"A wise idea," Azrael chimed in, pushing to his feet. "Ashtine. Talwyn. The White Halls?"

As he spoke, an earth portal appeared to their left. Talwyn got to her feet, but before she had taken a step, Scarlett spoke once more. She was watching the earth portal spin, not even bothering to look at Talwyn when she spoke to her.

"Tell me, your Majesty, which of the subjects we spoke of today concerns you the most? My newly discovered bloodline, your possibly still-living twin flame, or the potentially missing Contessa?"

"All of them concern me, along with the missing keys and these Maraan Lords," Talwyn replied, bracing her hands on the table as she leaned towards the queen, Scarlett finally dragging her eyes to meet her stare.

"Which would you prefer we deal with first?"

"I would prefer it if a full-blooded *Fae Queen* sat across from me at this table to discuss these matters with me since they directly affect those the Avonleyans fucked over," Talwyn spat.

Scarlett's head tilted to the side. "Just to be clear, your biggest issue with this is not that I am not Fae. It is that I have Avonleyan blood, yes?"

"Yes," Talwyn seethed.

Scarlett casually got to her feet, stretching her arms above her head and yawning widely, as if they were not in the middle of a heated discussion, and Talwyn wasn't about to make the wood table beneath her hands explode. "Perhaps you should discuss your Second's bloodline and where he got those Traveling powers from then . . . And why he is using an earth portal instead of Traveling right now."

Talwyn's head whipped to Azrael. "What the fuck is she talking about?"

Azrael, though, was glaring daggers at Scarlett.

"That's why he thinks he is owed the Earth Court, isn't it?" Scarlett asked, holding the Earth Prince's stare. "For the same reason Queen Talwyn believes I should not hold my throne."

"We are not the same," Azrael replied, his tone so full of violence that the entirety of the Water and Fire Courts were on their feet, and Sorin was pulling Scarlett into his side.

"You know," Scarlett said, a slight smirk lifting one side of her lips, "I'm thinking you will need more than a 'little break.' Why don't we reconvene in a few days?"

Azrael took a step towards her, but he froze when two shadow panthers took shape in front of him, eyes blazing with white flames. Scarlett freed herself from Sorin's hold and took a few steps towards Azrael, her shadow panthers prowling back and forth before her. "You know I am right, Prince Luan. You know that the Fae aiding Alaric is the same Tarek Ordos that was your Third. He did not die in that ambush a decade ago."

Azrael said nothing, a muscle feathering in his jaw as he ground his teeth together.

"You need to convince her that I am not an enemy here," Scarlett added.

"She already believes you to be an enemy," Azrael retorted. "And now, thanks to you, she will think the same of me, despite my loyalty to her since she assumed the throne."

"I will be your best chance at defeating them, at keeping these Courts from falling into their hands. You know this," Scarlett countered.

"And had you kept your godsdamn mouth shut, I could have helped her see that," Azrael snarled. "Now you could have very well just fucked us all over."

And Talwyn didn't know what to think at this point. Because she knew, she just *knew*, deep down, that what Scarlett was saying was true. Tarek was alive. Tarek had been in the mortal kingdoms this entire time. An entire fucking decade and had never contacted her. Never tried to reach her. Let her believe he was dead. Let her grieve. Let her feel abandoned and alone. Again.

And now Azrael had been lying to her. For years. Had never told her that he had Avonleyan blood. Had never informed her that his family had taken the Royal seat from Tarek's family. Neither of them had ever said a godsdamn word about it.

Lightning skittered from her hands, her feet, bouncing along the stone floor of the room and had Azrael spinning to face her.

"Talwyn, get it under control," he ordered.

He had moved in front of her, gripping her shoulders as wind tore through the space. She could see Ashtine in her periphery, working to control the gusts, and Prince Briar had moved to her side.

"Talwyn!" Azrael barked.

"Get her out of here, Luan," Sorin barked, and then Azrael was shoving her roughly through the earth portal, and she found herself in Xylon Forest.

"Talwyn," Azrael sighed, running a hand down his face.

"Say it," she hissed, her fists clenching and unclenching at her sides. She could feel energy crackling along her knuckles, and the earth was shaking beneath their feet.

"When you calm down, we will talk about this," Azrael countered, his hand falling to his side. He'd planted his feet, clearly ready for a fight.

"Say it!" she all but screamed at him. Her breathing was ragged, her chest heaving. Her entire body was trembling, her spine almost aching from the intensity of it. "Are you like her?"

"No," he answered. "I am not full-blooded Avonleyan, Talwyn. My grandfather on my father's side was a quarter Avonleyan. I am far more Fae than I am Avonleyan."

"You never thought to say anything?" she demanded. "It is a long and complicated history, Talwyn—"

"Did you ever plan on actually helping me get into Avonleya?" she asked, cutting him off before he could try to give her some pathetic excuse for keeping this from her.

"Yes," he answered tightly.

She barked a laugh of disbelief. "Let me rephrase that: Did you ever plan on actually helping me get *revenge* against Avonleya?"

Azrael didn't say anything, glancing away from her for a split second, but that was all the confirmation she needed. She took a step back from him, the branches on the surrounding trees bowing under her wind gusts. When Azrael's eyes came back to her, they widened in shock before he said, "Fuck."

And then Talwyn was somehow looking up at him, and a howl in the distance had her ears perking up.

Wait. Her ears perking up?

She dipped her chin to find black, clawed paws on the ground, and when she brought her eyes back to Azrael, a message was disappearing amongst a swirl of sand and leaves. "Stay calm, Talwyn," he said, trying to sound soothing, but Azrael did soothing about as well as a wolf would soothe a deer. An earth portal opened to his right. "Go through. We need to go to Stellan."

She opened her mouth to tell him she wasn't going anywhere with him right now, but all that came from her was a snarl. And not a Fae snarl, but a canine snarl of fury. The snapping of twigs had her swinging her head to the side, where she found Maliq stepping from the trees. She was almost eye-level with him.

"Talwyn," Azrael ground out, "I do not know how to help you with this. I cannot walk you through shifting back. We need to go to Stellan. I sent him a message that we were coming."

Maliq nuzzled into her side, and Talwyn found herself taking another step back from Azrael.

"Do not do this, Talwyn," Azrael said, and she could swear that there was actual panic entering his eyes. "You need to learn to control this, especially with the things we are currently facing."

If she could, she would have laughed at him. Instead, a huff of some sort came from her. She wasn't going anywhere with him. These last few weeks had been pure hell. She'd fought with Ashtine, certainly lost her friendship somehow. Her relationship with the Shifters was already strained, and he wanted to take her there to ask for help? That could hardly go over well. She'd faced these weeks alone, without Azrael, only to learn that not only is Tarek likely alive and had chosen to abandon her, but the only person she had confided everything in had betrayed her. And she honestly couldn't decide whose betrayal was worse: Tarek's or Azrael's.

Both shredded her.

Both made her chest feel like it had been cracked open, the little that was left of her heart after the loss of her parents, after Eliné, after Sorin, being left to shrivel into nothing and be tossed away on her own winds.

More howling pierced the air, and Maliq took a step back towards the trees, as if waiting to see what she was going to do. She looked between the wolf and Azrael.

"Talwyn." She was certain she'd never seen him look so somber. "Please, Talwyn. Go through the portal."

She held his stare a moment longer before she turned back to Maliq, rubbing up beside him and pulling them both through a rip in the air, somehow knowing how to access that particular power in this form. She brought them to the northern part of the Xylon Forest, and minutes later, wolves slunk from the trees to greet them.

Her wolves. Her pack.

The only creatures who had never left her alone.

CHAPTER 28
SCARLETT

Scarlett emerged from the bathing room in the queen's private chambers after taking a long, hot bath. The day had been exhausting— physically, emotionally, mentally. All of it.

After Azrael had hauled Talwyn from the Black Halls, Briar and Ashtine had gone to the Water Court along with Briar's Inner Court. Scarlett and Sorin had enjoyed a dinner with their family in the private wing, and her only request had been that there was no talk of her time in Baylorin or any of the issues they were currently facing. She'd wanted a somewhat normal night, and by the end of the evening, she'd almost felt completely relaxed.

Almost.

"I haven't seen Nuri since I've been here," she said, running a brush through her wet hair.

Sorin glanced at her over the back of the cream-colored sofa he sat on across the room. Her hair was instantly dry. "She has been busy looking after the children," he replied, his attention going back to whatever he was looking at. "But you have seen her since we've been here. A few times."

"She did not come here with us," Scarlett argued, setting the brush on a side table. She had one of Sorin's shirts on. With it reaching nearly to her knees, she hadn't bothered with anything else.

"She checked on Cassius a few times," Sorin said, his focus fixed on, well, not on her. She had no idea what he was doing. "She was there when you needed to feed. To help you, since she feeds the same way."

"I do not *feed*," Scarlett scoffed. "Gods, you make me sound like a prized horse or hound or some other animal."

He looked back at her, clearly trying to fight a smile as he said, "You were pretty feral at that time. An animal is probably an accurate description."

She shot him a dry look while also flipping him her middle finger.

He chuckled, turning back to whatever had him so occupied. "Speaking of that . . . You have used a fair amount of your Avonleyan magic since then."

"And?" she asked, trying to keep the annoyance from his incessant worrying about this from her tone.

"Your eyes aren't as bright. They are a pale blue," he added.

"And?"

She heard him sigh before he said, "Perhaps you should drink what I left for you by the desk."

Scarlett turned slowly to find a small glass of red liquid. Endearment and disgust immediately warred inside of her. The mere fact that he cared enough to notice the little tells, to do this for her just in case, knowing she was not a fan of the whole drinking blood thing . . . But also, that was a small glass of blood sitting there. She did not think she would ever get used to the idea of needing something like that to fill her magic.

"I am not drinking that," Scarlett scowled.

"You need to keep your power reserves filled until we figure out another way, Scarlett," Sorin replied. She heard the page of a book turn and finally realized he was reading.

Scarlett shook her head. "No. It's . . . weird."

"Would you prefer it fresh from my arm, then?" He didn't look at her, but she could hear the teasing in his voice. "Or some other place?"

She grabbed a nearby pillow from the bed and threw it at his head.

A low laugh came from him as she made her way over to where he sat, leaving the blood behind and leaning over the back of the sofa. "What are you doing?"

"Research," he grunted.

"Regarding?"

He slowly brought his eyes to hers. "Isn't this an interesting turn of events? *You* asking what *I* am researching for a change," he teased.

"You're such an ass," she retorted, rolling her eyes and reaching to smack his shoulder, but he caught her wrist.

"I still have that list of names you call me, you know," he said, before tugging on her arm and hauling her over the back of the sofa. She fell onto the cushions beside him, laughter tumbling from her lips. She pushed herself up to sit beside him, reaching for the book in his lap.

"This is written in the Avonleyan language," she said, running her fingers along a page.

"I am aware," he replied, turning into her when she pulled the book into her own lap.

"How can you read it?"

"I can't. Not well anyway." He nodded towards the side table where a small stack of papers sat. "That is why I have your translation notes."

"You took them when we were in Solembra yesterday?"

"Mhmm," he hummed as she skimmed the page.

"Why?"

"A few reasons, but the main one is to help you figure out this Source issue," he answered.

"I've been looking through these books for months, Sorin. I don't remember ever coming across the mention of a Source."

"I had to start somewhere," he said with a shrug. "If anything, it will allow me to learn the language a little more to help narrow down books in the future."

She turned the page of the ancient text. This was a book about Avonleyan history and politics. Things she didn't understand, involving people and places she couldn't properly translate.

"What other books did you bring?"

"Hmm?" Sorin asked, and sounded so distracted that Scarlett brought her eyes back to his once more.

"What other books did you bring?" she repeated.

"Books?" She stared at him, part in confusion and part in concern, as he slowly leaned forward to speak into her ear. "Sorry, Love, but you are aware you are not wearing pants, right?"

She rolled her eyes. "I thought we were going to bed, not researching things in ancient books."

Sorin sat back a bit, arching a brow. A half smile was playing on the corner of his mouth. "So to clarify, you were coming to bed without pants?"

She reached for the pillow beside her and smacked him in the face with it again. "For the record, the nightclothes I usually wear to bed do not include pants, and they tend to leave far more on show than your shirt."

He sighed dramatically, his fingers beginning to draw small circles on her bare knee. "That is a valid point, I suppose. I have missed those nightclothes."

"Funny," she quipped, her eyes going back to the text. "You'd become so quick to remove them, I assumed they no longer held your interest."

A pinch to her inner thigh had her hissing as he muttered, "There's that tongue again."

His fingers continued painting idle circles on her knee as he peered over her shoulder. These pages were all discussing the various cities in Avonleya and the responsibilities of the Lords and Ladies who presided over them. She had yet to come across a map of the kingdom, though. In her months of research and countless books, even the descriptions of the lands were vague.

"What does this part say?" Sorin asked, pointing to a spot in the middle of the opposite page. "I recognize a few words— king, power, Mark."

She skimmed the section quickly. "It is speaking of taking a Mark of loyalty to the king, of pledging one's power to him. I would assume like Alaric wanted me to do."

Sorin's fingers paused on her skin for just a moment at the mention of Alaric. "Did the Avonleyan Kings require such a thing?"

Scarlett turned the page as she skimmed the text a little more. "I can't say for sure," she murmured. She pointed at a word. "This means willingly, but this word here means drawing from or forcefully taken. But it doesn't appear to say anything about if the ruling parties required it or from whom."

"How did you figure out Azrael had Avonleyan blood?" Sorin asked.

Scarlett's eyes flew to his. "I didn't know until today. Until that very moment. I wasn't keeping it from you. And even then, it was more of a hunch than being certain."

His fingers squeezed her knee gently, his golden eyes softening. "I believe you, Love. I wasn't accusing you."

She nodded, brushing her fingers along the pages of the book. "I found it odd that he created a portal rather than just Traveling with Talwyn. And then I remembered Alaric saying the Traveling gift came from the Avonleyans."

"All the Fae gifts came from the Avonleyans," Sorin said.

"Yes, but Alaric also told me that the Maraans could Travel as well. That they were among the only bloodlines who could do so."

"But some of the Fae *can* Travel," Sorin countered.

Scarlett closed the book, turning slightly to face him better on the sofa. "How many, Sorin? You said yourself it is incredibly rare. Other than the Fae Queens, who were gifted the ability by the Avonleyans alongside their elemental gifts, what other Fae Travelers have you known? Or even heard of, for that matter? Outside of the Luan bloodline."

Sorin was quiet, clearly contemplating her argument.

"It is also why Tarek thinks his family should still rule the Earth Court. Just like Talwyn doesn't think I should have my throne because I do not possess Fae blood, Tarek believes the Luans have an unfair advantage for the Royal seat because their Avonleyan blood makes them more powerful."

"Do you think he is half-Avonleyan like Cassius?" Sorin asked.

Scarlett shrugged. "I don't know. Like I said, it was just a guess to begin with. I am assuming his power reserves for Traveling haven't refilled yet. That's why he was using a portal instead of Traveling."

"So he needs to feed?" Sorin asked.

Scarlett made a face. "Stop saying that."

He smirked at her. "How would you like me to refer to it?"

"Just . . . don't refer to it at all."

Sorin gave her a frank stare as he said, "We cannot just ignore it, Scarlett. You need to keep your power replenished. You need to be prepared for whatever they might try next."

"What I need to do is train to fight using my powers and weapons. I need to be able to use them at the same time seamlessly. Cyrus kicked my ass because I had to either focus on controlling my magic or my sword," Scarlett grumbled.

"And if you are going to be training that intensely with your gifts, you need to keep them replenished," Sorin said pointedly.

"Then we best figure out this Source thing," she said blandly.

"Agreed," Sorin said, "but first I would like to revisit this no pants dilemma."

"It's not a dilem—"

But her words cut off when he gripped under her knee and tugged, pulling her down onto her back on the sofa. He was leaning over her a heartbeat later. "It *is* a dilemma," he countered. "You are asking me to focus on other things— Avonleya, training, *Luan*." He said his name with a sneering curl of his lip.

"Tarek said you do not even know all the reasons there is conflict between your two Courts. That you are just carrying on animosity—"

"There you go again," Sorin sighed, cutting her off again, "asking me to focus on something other than the fact that you are not wearing pants."

She smiled coyly at him as she casually said, "Or underthings."

Sorin's eyes darkened as his pupils instantly dilated, and a feral growl rumbled from his chest. He moved so godsdamn fast, she didn't register it until she felt his tongue licking up her center, flicking that sensitive bundle of nerves when he reached it.

"Gods," she gasped, her fingers digging into the sofa cushion.

"Not quite, Love," he said with a satisfied smirk, looking up at her from his place between her thighs. He brought his mouth to the crease of her left thigh, slowly trailing kisses along it. "Tell me. Did you still want to discuss the feud between the Fire and Earth Courts?"

"Ass," she breathed as he moved to the other thigh.

Canines scraped and nipped. "You are reusing names. You need to get more creative."

She pulled her foot up, preparing to show him just how creative she could be, but he caught her ankle with a dark chuckle, throwing her leg over his shoulder. Before she could say anything, his tongue went up her center again, and her hand was slipping into raven-black locks, pulling him closer. She felt him chuckle again, the sound vibrating against her flesh as his tongue continued to taste her, making her writhe against him. A hand came up to her torso, holding her in place, and a curse fell from her lips as he brought her to the edge of pleasure again and again, but never let her go over.

"Sorin," she growled when he again pulled her back right as she reached that tipping point.

"Yes, my Love," he murmured, the rumble of his voice against her holding her right at that precipice.

Her answer was her fingers tightening in his hair and tugging his mouth forcefully against her.

His mouth closed around those nerves, sucking it between his teeth at the same time he finally slipped two fingers inside her, curling them to hit that perfect spot. He had her wound so tightly by now, her head fell back immediately as release raced up her spine, her back arching and pressing her even harder against his mouth where his tongue never stopped, stroking and licking her through it all.

As she fell lax against the sofa, he gave her a taunting smile, his lips swollen and glossy as they curved up. He lowered her leg from his shoulder, and his fingers trailed slowly along her now-slick thighs, that small sensation almost too much after what he'd just put her through. As his fingers climbed higher, his body followed. His shirt was pushed up as he moved along her body, those lips trailing his hands.

"New pants dilemma," she gasped, sucking in a breath when he exposed her breasts to the air.

"Oh?" he asked, rolling a nipple between his thumb and forefinger and making her arch off the sofa again.

"You're still wearing yours," she rasped, fingers already reaching for the buttons.

A rough laugh left him, and he pressed a kiss to her other breast, before pushing off of her and quickly taking care of the new dilemma. Instead of climbing back onto the sofa, he came to a stop beside it. His eyes raked over her with predatory hunger. Scarlett didn't have it in her to move. She was still trying to catch her breath, which wasn't exactly easy with him standing beside her.

Without any clothing on.

His fingers trailed lightly from her hairline down to her lips, where he brushed a thumb across her bottom one. "What shall I do with you tonight, my Love?" he murmured, his wandering eyes now fixed on her rapidly rising and falling chest.

"I don't know," she managed to get out. "You're the one with all that *experience*."

His eyes snapped back to hers, and she bit her lip, trying to keep the taunting smile from forming. "You and this godsdamn tongue."

Then he was hauling her into a sitting position, pulling his shirt over her head and tossing it to the floor. His hands landed on her hips, forcing her up onto her knees and turning her to face the back of the sofa. Her knees sank into the cushions further when he was suddenly kneeling behind her. The coarse hairs on his legs felt rough against her own bare legs, and she sucked in another sharp breath when she felt him digging into her back.

"So interested in these *experiences*," he breathed into her ear. His fingers were skating up her sides, gliding along her ribs then back down to her hips. "If you want me to set something up with Arianna, you only need to say the word."

"And *Jamahl*," she drawled.

One of those trailing hands shot to her breast, tweaking a nipple hard enough to make her hiss and bat his hand away.

"What would you do with two males worshiping you, my Love?" And the gravel in his tone had her clenching her thighs together as her core pulsed.

She managed to hold in the whimper threatening to escape her as she rasped, "You could scarcely handle Arianna touching my arm. I doubt you would fare well with more than that."

"True," he conceded, his lips brushing over the spot just below her ear. "I could maybe be persuaded to worship you beside another at some point, but not anytime in the near future." Feather-light kisses continued down her neck and had her dropping her head back against his shoulder. "I suppose that leaves all the worshipping to me."

"I suppose it does," she agreed.

His hands came to her shoulders, brushing down the length of her arms until they closed around her own hands. He brought them to the back of the sofa, then he whispered into her ear, "Do not let go."

She felt his canines scrape down her throat again until they met the juncture where her neck met her shoulder, and he clamped down, drawing a cry from her. Her hips bucked back into him as she jerked forward at the unexpected hurt. But his tongue was already lapping at it, soothing the pain away as her fingers curled into the back of the sofa.

"I have noticed, Princess, that you only tend to follow orders at the same moments your manners seem to make those rare appearances," he said casually.

"I swear to Saylah, Sorin—"

But before she could finish any type of threat, he thrust into her and a moan of pleasure came out instead.

"You were saying?" he crooned into her ear.

All thoughts were driven from her mind as he slammed back into her harder. She couldn't have said anything even if she'd wanted to. Words weren't a thing she could focus on when all of her attention was on the feel of him filling her, his fingers digging into her hips as he drove into her over and over again. Each thrust pressed her deeper into the back of the sofa. His ragged breathing filled her ears, mixing with the sound of skin against skin.

One of his hands slid across her torso until two of his fingers slid between her folds and began pressing tight circles to her center. Her breath caught in her throat, and she started to bring one of her hands back to loop around his neck, to feel him. Before her fingers had even finished unfurling though, his fingers, his entire body, stilled against her. "Do not let go," he growled, a single thrust of his hips drawing another moan from her.

"Sorin," she groaned.

"Say my name like *that* all you like, Love, but do not let go," he rasped, his voice near guttural as his fingers began moving again too, those circles faster and tighter. Everything in her was tightening, release shimmering at the base of her spine. His other hand moved to her back, pressing down and forcing her forward, her back arching and ass pressing back into him even more.

A feral growl left him when she felt him send his flames to brush along her shadows. Then she couldn't breathe at all as that pleasure washed over her. Devoured her. There wasn't room for anything but this. For them. For what they were.

He pressed down with those two fingers, sending her careening over the edge once more, and his name indeed fell from her lips again. His own movements became choppy and erratic, faster and somehow harder, until she felt him pulsing inside her as he found his own release.

She collapsed against the back of the sofa, and he fell forward on top of her. She could feel his heaving chest against her back. Her fingers were still tightly curled around the back of the sofa, and she slowly released her grip as she gulped down air.

Neither of them moved for several minutes until he peeled himself off of her with a groan. Scarlett sank down onto the cushions, rolling onto her back and pushing hair out of her face.

"I'm sleeping here tonight."

"The fuck you are."

"I'm too tired to walk to the bed," she whined.

"It is times like these I find it hard to believe you are Death's Maiden," he muttered, arms sliding beneath her back and knees. She was scooped up in a fluid motion, her head falling against his chest.

"It's your fault I can't move."

"You're welcome, but I think it is your fault for creating the no pants dilemma."

"Oh my gods," she muttered. "Careful, Sorin, or your ego won't fit in the bed with us."

He gently lay her on the bed as he said softly into her ear, "Aren't you grateful to be benefiting from all those *experiences?*"

"I hate you," she grumbled, rolling onto her side.

"The sounds you were making a few minutes ago would suggest otherwise," he replied, pulling the blankets up and over her.

"I'm going to sleep now."

"Good night, Love."

"We were quite patient with you before, my pet."

Scarlett was standing on the balcony of the queen's chambers in the Black Halls staring out across the sea. But at the sound of his voice, she spun, taking a step back.

"What are you doing here?"

A slow, cruel smile spread over Mikale's lips as he took another step towards her. "He sent me to deliver a message."

As he advanced, she retreated until she was bumping up against the balcony railing. "I am surprised to see you still live considering I escaped you . . . again," she replied, forcing herself to keep her breathing steady.

This is a dream, she reminded herself over and over. He can't hurt me here.

Mikale flashed his teeth at her verbal jab before seeming to leash his temper. "I am not here to listen to your smart mouth," he said sharply.

"Then you probably should not have come," she retorted, her spine straightening.

His smile became one of knowing, as he came closer. "I forget how young you are sometimes," he mused. "Always seeing things so black and white. Right and wrong." He came to a stop directly in front of her, reaching up and twirling a strand of her hair around his finger. "Light and dark."

Scarlett slapped his hand away, her hair tugging sharply at the action, and he chuckled lightly as he stepped back from her. "You will understand why I am still breathing soon enough, but as I said, I was sent to deliver a message."

"What a good little errand boy you are," Scarlett cooed.

"Careful, my pet, no one has won our game yet," he retorted sharply.

"I am no longer worried about such things," she answered, lifting a hand so shadows writhed in her palm.

Mikale sucked in a breath, but instead of a flash of fear in his dark eyes, it was . . . desire?

"Such beautiful darkness," he said, his eyes fixed on the shadows she wielded. His head tilted to the side as he continued, "You know, when they first appeared all those months ago in my house, I did not know what they were. I am considerably younger than the other Lords. I knew what was inside of you, but having never seen it . . . Well, you can understand my wariness." He stepped closer again, regaining the distance that had been put between them. "We only ever desired to help you learn to control it."

"Somehow I doubt that," she deadpanned.

His dark eyes slid to her, and that knowing smile pulled at his lips again. "As I was saying, we've been so patient with you."

"I was unaware I was being vexing."

Mikale's jaw clenched as he swallowed down some sort of retort. There was a note of restraint in his voice as he continued. "He's been patient, but as he told you, his patience is growing thin. He even attempted to make peace with you by denying me access to your body, and you threw it back in his face."

Scarlett couldn't help the laugh of disbelief that burst from her. "Oh yes," she drawled, "how ungrateful of me. He wouldn't let you take from me, but your hands were allowed to roam. I was still chained to a fucking wall. Still denied food, water. Still forced to watch him torture and nearly kill Cassius."

Mikale's hand came up again, and she raised her own, her shadows striking for him as quickly as asps.

But they dissipated before they came close. She tried to summon them again. Tried to summon her flames. Something. Anything. But she couldn't. Somehow, in this dream world, Mikale had managed to cut her off from them. Had given her a false sense of security.

Her heart leapt to her throat as his fingers skated down her cheek. She was leaning back, away from him, but that meant she was also leaning back over the balcony railing. This may be a dream, but that was still a drop to death below her, and she didn't want to test if her death in this twisted dream world would result in her death in the real one.

"What he is going to do to you when you return," Mikale mused to himself, clearly getting lost in his thoughts. He stepped further into her, her back arching more as she tried to keep distance between them. One of his arms looped around her waist, holding her in place as he brought his face inches from hers. His hot breath fanned over her cheek when he spoke again. "When you return, you will be so broken, you will beg to take that Blood Mark."

"Cassius lives," she managed to rasp out.

Mikale shrugged his shoulders slightly. "For now." His fingers flexed where they held her waist, and he forced her back over that railing even farther, her feet coming up so she was balancing on her tiptoes. "But if you think that was the last time he will willingly give his life to keep you from breaking, you are sorely mistaken. That is the life he is cursed with as your Guardian. Eventually, he will not survive it."

One of her feet slipped, and a gasp escaped her as she fought for purchase on the balcony floor. Her bare foot trying to catch on anything. Mikale only laughed, his other hand coming up to grip her jaw and force her eyes to his.

"That is his message for you, my pet," he said, nothing but dark amusement staring back at her. "Eventually, everyone you love will give their lives for you. That is their curse for knowing you, for choosing to follow you. You will be the cause of their death."

Tears stung at the back of her eyes, and she swallowed, willing them back. She tried to shake her head in denial, but Mikale's grip on her jaw only tightened, becoming bruising.

"How selfish of you to allow them to give up their existence so you can live," he continued, his tone becoming soft.

"I would never ask that of them," she rasped, her feet completely off the ground now as Mikale held her balanced over that balcony railing.

"Oh, my pet," he crooned with mock sympathy, "you won't have to. That is their curse for knowing you, remember?"

CHAPTER 29
SORIN

Sorin slowly rose out of the depths of slumber.
Until he reached for her to find her side of the bed cold.
He jolted upright. It was rare he did not feel her wake. Rarer still that he did not feel her get out of bed.

"Scarlett?" he called into the dark room. A glance at the windows told him it was not even dawn yet. He threw back the blankets and quickly pulled on a pair of pants. He could feel her. She wasn't far.

Scarlett . . . he sent down their bond.

He hadn't used it much. Hadn't let her use it much either. It wasn't out of spite. It wasn't out of some twisted desire to teach her a lesson of some sort. But it was about protecting these Courts. It was about forcing her to speak to him, talk with him about her thoughts and plans, rather than assuming he knew them because of the bond. It was about getting her comfortable recognizing and voicing her emotions rather than forcing them down or trying to ignore them all together. It was about making her *ask* others, ask *him*, what he is thinking, what he is feeling.

He didn't know how else to get her to start trusting him. To start trusting the others. He didn't know how else to get her used to asking for help, how to get her comfortable asking for input and how others felt about things. She'd been doing everything alone for so damn long. She hadn't depended on others so thoroughly since Juliette and Nuri, and they'd been raised together. Trained together to the point of being able to know each other's thoughts and next moves on instinct alone. But that had become fractured with Juliette's death, had been on rocky ground before that even, and he wasn't sure what the dynamic between the three would be now.

And then there was Cassius. Perhaps the one person she did trust implicitly, without question or thought. Someone she'd only seen once since leaving Baylorin until she had to watch him be tortured nearly to death in front of her.

Don't burn things to the ground in a fit, Sorin. I'm fine. I'm on the beach.

He was already pulling a lightweight tunic over his head and opening a fire portal as he replied, *How long have you been down there?*

No response came, and when he turned his focus to her emotions, he couldn't separate them all. They were a swirling storm in her soul. He stepped onto the sand, immediately spotting her sitting a ways down the beach, letting sand sift between her fingers as she stared out across the sea. Within a minute, he was lowering to sit beside her while she scooped up another handful of granules. Her hair was swaying gently in the breeze off the water, and her shadows were freely floating around her as if she'd let them out to breathe.

After several moments of silence, he asked softly, "How long have you been down here?"

She shrugged. "A few hours, maybe?"

Sorin nodded, biting down on the frustration of her sitting on a deserted beach by herself for hours. Not frustration at her, not entirely anyway. More frustration with himself for not seeing this coming. For not feeling her get out of the godsdamn bed. For not being here for her these last few hours.

She'd done such things a few times in Solembra, going off by herself and wandering along the Tana River or disappearing to various rooms of the palace to be alone. Always on the hard days, when she was so lost in her grief, her guilt, her soul.

She hadn't spoken much of what was done to her these past few weeks. She'd been chained to a wall, given little food and water, watched Cassius be used against her . . .

Then again, he hadn't given her much time to tell him either. They'd had to deal with Cassius, then her own power. Then he'd been unable to hold back his own anger at the whole situation, at *her*, before she'd had to face the same wrath from the others when he had no idea what she was processing, what she'd experienced at the hands of her former master.

He sighed heavily. "I am sorry, Scarlett."

She was reaching for another handful of sand, but she stilled at his words. "What could you possibly have to be sorry for?"

"For not giving you a chance to breathe before our discussions about your actions. For not giving you time to process before forcing you to—"

She held up a hand to stop him, and the words died on his lips. She said nothing for nearly a full minute, and he was about to speak again when she said, "You do not have anything to apologize for, Sorin. Your feelings regarding my choices are valid. What I made you go through . . . I needed to hear those things. From you. From the others."

"Yes, but not as soon as you woke. Not when you were dealing with Cassius. Not without knowing what you had endured, what you were processing after your time with Alaric. To be honest, Scarlett, I was no better than Callan when you woke in Solembra," Sorin said, his gaze fixing on the horizon that was just starting to see the first hints of the coming dawn.

She didn't say anything in response to that for several minutes, resuming her sand sifting. The sound of the waves gently rolling to the shore was the only thing disturbing the silence, and her eyes drifted closed. He still couldn't sort through everything she was feeling, although he was trying to avoid reading her emotions the way it was, wanting her to voice them.

"Actions have consequences, Sorin," she finally said. "I am not exempt from that. I could even say the consequences are greater for me now because of who I am, the role I am in. You cannot shield me from the consequences of my actions."

"No, I cannot, but I should be your reprieve from those consequences. I should be the place for you to breathe," Sorin countered.

"And you are," she said, finally turning to look at him. "You are that for me, Sorin, but that does not mean you are not affected. That does not mean that you are not allowed to voice those same feelings if you have them."

"I should have waited."

"No. Things needed to be said. We needed to have things out

in the open between us before I met with the others. I know that's why you did it. I understand why you insisted on that conversation when you did. It needed to happen, and when we did meet with the others, you were that place for me to breathe. I knew that no matter what the others threw at me, you were still with me. You were still in my corner."

"I will always be in your corner, Scarlett," Sorin said softly, getting lost in her eyes.

"I know, Sorin," she replied quietly. "I know that I could set the world on fire simply because I wanted to, and you would still claim me. You would still stand beside me. You would still be mine."

She gave him a soft, almost sad, smile before she dropped down onto her back in the sand, her eyes going to the sky that was beginning to lighten.

"Do you ever wonder what the stars do when we cannot see them?" she asked.

Sorin stilled at such an odd question, glancing down at her before he moved to his back beside her.

"I suppose I have never thought about such a thing," he answered.

She'd interlaced her fingers, stacking them on her stomach, watching the stars fade as the light began to overtake the darkness.

When she didn't say anything after a few moments, he asked, "What drew you to the sea in the dead of night?"

"I think best by the water, and I've come to prefer the dark over the light. I am more comfortable in it," she murmured.

He stacked his own hands on his stomach. "I know these things, Love, but what thoughts called you to them tonight?"

"I couldn't sleep. Nightmares."

He started a little, his head turning from the sky to her. "You had nightmares last night?"

She nodded.

"Gods, Scarlett, I am—"

"Do not apologize to me, Sorin. I did not wake screaming. I did not wake unable to breathe. I did not wake thinking I was somewhere else," she said, her shadows brushing along her skin as though they were soothing her.

And he never thought he would be jealous of floating darkness, but here he was, wishing he was one of her shadows so that he could soothe whatever was threatening her stars. But there was no way to force trust. He knew this better than anyone. He could nudge her towards it. He could make not trusting him difficult. But just as he couldn't make himself entirely trust her right now, he couldn't force her to entirely trust him either.

"Mikale was in my dream," she whispered, snapping him from his thoughts.

"As in you were dreaming of the past, or . . ."

"The latter," she answered. "He was controlling my dream. He took my magic from me there. I couldn't access it."

"Scarlett, why didn't you wake me?" he asked, his voice low, trying to hide the disappointment he was feeling.

"He didn't . . . I mean, he touched me, but not like that. He held me over a balcony railing—"

She paused at the low snarl that rippled from his chest.

She gave him a side-long glance before she cleared her throat and continued, "He said he was delivering a message from Alaric."

"And the message?" Sorin gritted out. When she didn't answer for several minutes, he prompted again, his tone softer, "What was the message, Scarlett?"

He heard her swallow, and he rolled onto his side, propping himself on an elbow so he could look down at her. Tears were pooling in her eyes, and he cupped her cheek, turning her head to look at him. When her eyes met his, he could finally make out everything she was feeling, could see those emotions looking back at him.

Dread.

Guilt.

Heartache.

"What did he do to you, my Love?" he whispered.

"He told me that Cassius would die because of me."

"But Cassius lives. He will wake any day."

She swallowed again, her eyes darting away from him. "Yes, but he is my Guardian. He will be driven to risk his life for mine, at any cost."

"He chose that, Scarlett. He *chose* to be your Guardian. That was his choice," Sorin argued gently.

Her eyes flashed back to his, anger flashing in their depths. "When he was *ten*, Sorin. He was a child. He didn't know what he was committing to, what was being asked of him. We were both children."

Sorin opened his mouth to say something, but what was there to say to that? She was right. He didn't know how the Guardian bond came to be, what was all involved in that. Scarlett had only mentioned her dream in the middle of other discussions, and it was not the most pressing matter at the time.

His hand slipped from her cheek as her gaze went back to the sky, the last star winking out as the sun crested the horizon, spreading its light and warmth over the beach.

"Alaric's message was that eventually Cassius, everyone I love, will give their lives for me. That is their curse for being in my life, for choosing to be in my corner."

"Scarlett," Sorin said quietly, his tone ringing with pain as he felt her guilt down the bond.

"He's not wrong, Sorin. Look at the people already caught up in this mess simply because they are a part of my life— Cassius, Callan, Tava, Juliette, those innocent children. He's not wrong," she whispered.

Games. She always spoke of how the Assassin Lord liked to play games, and he was playing one now. This was how he controlled her. This was how he broke her. Every fucking time. Planting these thoughts, then watching them grow and overtake every part of her being like a godsdamn weed in a garden, choking out all the things that could provide nourishment. This was why he never bothered with physical torture when she was chained to his dungeon study wall. His attacks were all mental, all emotional. They cut deeper than any blade would. He wormed his way into every thought, every relationship she had, and did this shit because he knew where the cracks in her armor were. He knew which spots were weakest, which parts would crumble with just the right amount of pressure.

And he didn't know what to say to her. He didn't know what words would make it better, or how to argue against the fact that the people in her life would give their lives for her, because they would. Without a second thought, his Court, Briar's Court, Cassius, all of them would give their lives to save hers.

But not one of them would look at it as a curse.

He could tell her that until he was blue in the face, and it wouldn't matter. Not right now. So instead he said what he always said to her on the hard days.

"You are my necessity, Scarlett."

"And by you being mine, I feel as though I am leading you to slaughter, along with everyone else who follows us," she answered, barely audible.

Silence settled around them, the sky growing brighter as the sun rose higher. He settled back onto his back in the sand and reached over, taking her hand in his, squeezing her fingers gently, wishing he could take the weight of her world from her shoulders, yet knowing she would never let him.

"You are not alone in this, Scarlett," he said, watching a gull soar overhead.

"Maybe I should be," she answered.

And that was his tipping point. Those four words had him pushing back up onto his elbow and forcing her gaze to his once more. "Do not let him do this to you, Scarlett. Do not give him this kind of power over you. You say he is no longer your master? Then do not let him be."

"He's in my head, Sorin," she whispered, tears slipping down her cheeks. "For years, he's said things, guided me to think a certain way, feel certain things. I can't get him out. He's so loud."

"Then let me be louder, Love," Sorin replied. "When he is all-consuming, come to me, and let me be more. Let me consume you so there is nothing left for him to have."

"I do not deserve you," she rasped, more tears sliding down her face.

"You deserve every star and more," he replied. "Every star in the dark, forgotten parts of the sky, you deserve each and every one of them. What you do not deserve is to have some fucking bastard tell you that your mere existence is a curse on those who know you, who *choose* to be in your life. What you do not deserve, Scarlett, is to think you are undeserving of having people love you, care for you. What you do not deserve is thinking you are better off alone."

A small sob escaped her lips and had him bringing his face closer to hers so that their noses were almost touching.

"The thing is, Scarlett, even if you wanted to be alone, that is no longer an option because I will always come for you, always find you, and always remind you who you do belong to."

"I am yours," she whispered, her breath a whisper across his lips.

"You are *mine*," he confirmed. "So if anyone gets to consume you, Scarlett, it will be me. And if that is my curse, I will cross the Veil the luckiest son of a bitch to have ever walked this world, and then I will hunt you down in the After to consume you all over again."

Something escaped her that was a cross between a laugh and a sob, and his lips met hers to capture the sound. He pulled away after a few seconds, settling back down on his back, her hand still wrapped in his.

Some time later, two sets of boots stopped above them, a head of coppery-red hair and one of dark chestnut hair peering down at them.

"You missed breakfast, Darling," Cyrus drawled to Scarlett, his hair falling into his golden eyes. "I thought for sure you were lying dead somewhere."

Scarlett rolled her eyes, releasing Sorin's hand and pushing herself up into a sitting position. "I am clearly not. Did you bring me something to eat?"

Sorin was on his feet a moment later, reaching down to pull her up as Cyrus arched a brow at her. "Am I supposed to wait on you hand and foot?"

"I am your queen," she shot back, brushing sand off the back of her pants.

"That I thought was dead," Cyrus countered. "Why would I bring a dead queen food?"

"For the love of Anala. Why must you always speak?" Eliza grumbled, handing over a folded cloth that was indeed wrapped around a few biscuits, keeping them warm. "Rayner told us you were down here," she explained.

Cyrus smirked, handing over a couple of pears he was carrying, and Scarlett snatched one out of his grip, immediately biting into it.

"See, this is why I thought you were dead. You always eat like you're a starving wildcat, so I could not fathom how you could miss breakfast," Cyrus teased drolly.

Scarlett flipped him her middle finger, taking another bite of her pear. "What *are* you two doing down here?" Eliza asked, glancing between Scarlett and Sorin.

"Pondering what the stars do when we cannot see them," Scarlett sighed, her gaze going back out over the sea as she ate her fruit.

Eliza and Cyrus both glanced at Sorin, concern and confusion in their eyes, but Sorin shook his head, telling them to leave it, his mouth pressing into a thin line.

"Luan sent a note," Cyrus said after a moment of silence, extending a piece of parchment to Sorin. "Said they needed to postpone our meeting a few days."

"It does not say why," Sorin remarked, reading over the words.

"Is that odd? For her to not explain herself to you?" Scarlett asked, tossing her pear core into the sea before starting on her biscuit.

"I suppose not," Sorin admitted, incinerating the note and letting the ashes flit away on the breeze. "It is odd, however, that she is postponing this meeting. She was pretty livid when she left yesterday."

Scarlett hummed an acknowledgement, still staring out across the water.

"I found it odd they didn't specify another day and time," Cyrus said, his arms folding across his chest.

Eliza let out an annoyed huff. "Apparently, she still thinks we must drop whatever we are doing when she decides it is convenient for her to meet."

"I suppose we will deal with it when we need to. We have other things we need to focus on in the meantime," Sorin replied.

"The Contessa?" Eliza asked, one of her brows arching. She'd been itching to go to the Night Child territory since Scarlett had brought it up. Apparently it had been too long since she'd gotten to shed a little blood, despite having done so days ago in Baylorin.

"That is one of them, yes," Sorin said. He turned back to Scarlett. "Are you ready, Love?"

She'd finished off her biscuit and had her arms wrapped around herself, her hands running along her upper arms as if trying to warm herself. Her shadows seemed to have thickened.

"Do you think the stars are cursed to be stuck in the sky?" she mused, and her words had Cyrus and Eliza looking back at him with the same concern that had been there moments ago.

"No, Scarlett," Sorin answered. "I do not think the stars are cursed to have to stay in the darkness when they love it there."

"Maybe they only love it because they do not think they can leave," she said thoughtfully.

"Maybe they love it so much they have never felt the need to seek anything else. Maybe they have looked down from where they reside in the night and found that there is nothing that compares, that their curse is anything but," he challenged. Then he closed the space between them, tilting her chin up with his finger and forcing her to look at him. "Maybe the darkness needs to accept the fact that the stars do not want to go anywhere. And maybe the darkness needs to tell the demons that haunt it, that the stars have already staked their claim and there is nothing left for them to have."

Her eyes fell closed, a small shudder wracking her frame. When she reopened them, there was some semblance of clarity there, as if the noise in her soul had finally quieted, finally stilled.

"Are you ready to go back?" Sorin asked quietly. "Yes," she whispered.

"Why do I feel like we just witnessed an entire conversation with Ashtine?" Cyrus cut in. "I swear to Anala, Scarlett, if you start speaking like her . . ."

Scarlett pushed past Sorin, beginning to make her way back to the Black Halls, but she paused by Cyrus, the hint of a wry smile pulling at the corner of her lips. She reached up and patted his cheek patronizingly as she said, "Don't worry, Darling. The winds don't speak to me, only the stars. And they're awfully annoying most of the time, so I tend to just ignore them."

Sorin barked a laugh at the look of bewilderment on Cyrus's face as she continued past him, and Eliza fell into step beside her, the two females speaking in low voices to one another.

"Did you really understand what she was saying?" Cyrus asked, when Sorin came to his side.

"She was saying you are annoying," he answered with a slight snigger. At his blank look, Sorin clarified, "We are her stars. She is struggling with us willingly choosing to follow her. To face these threats, this danger, with her."

Cyrus was quiet for a moment before he asked, "Is she all right now? After speaking with you?"

"No, she is not," Sorin admitted.

Cyrus cut him a quick glance before his eyes continued to track the females as they climbed a sandy dune. "What do we need to do?"

"I don't know," Sorin answered, pushing a hand through his hair. "She is not the same as when she left. She is different. In so many ways."

"Has she spoken much of what she experienced? What they did to her?"

Sorin shook his head, and they began to follow the same path Scarlett and Eliza were on ahead of them. "She needs Cassius to wake up. He knows parts of her I do not, things the Assassin Lord would target." He watched as Scarlett let out a small laugh at something Eliza was saying, but her shadows didn't lessen. He sighed heavily. "She needs Cassius to wake up."

CHAPTER 30
CALLAN

Callan sat in his private sitting room, a glass of liquor dangling from his fingertips. It had been a long day of council meetings.

He'd sat in that stuffy meeting room for hours, listening to his father's Lords debate everything from the docks to the cost of crops to the increasing "problem" of the beggars on the streets. He'd refrained from doing much speaking, still trying to get caught up on everything that had transpired while he'd been off "vacationing for the last few months" as his father liked to say. There was also the fact that every time he attempted to contribute, the look his father gave him told him to keep his mouth shut. So he'd sat and listened to the Lords prattle on, making notes on things he'd someday change when he was the one sitting at the head of that table.

But he was also watching the Lords, marking their mannerisms, their facial expressions. Noting the little tells of when they disagreed but didn't say so, or when they were pleased with a decision. The things Tava had been teaching him to pay attention to.

He watched how Lord Cardington shuffled his papers, trying to hide his excitement, when there was talk of taking land from farmers in the north so that the kingdom could provide more food for the underprivileged. The Lord would directly profit from such an operation, seeing as one of his businesses transported the majority of the food to and from the capital. Of course, the annexation of the land would be for the better of all of Windonelle, and surely the current owners would easily find other employment and ways to provide for their families. Or so the Lord had said in a bid to convince the others. Nothing had been officially decided and decreed, but the Lord seemed confident enough.

He watched Duke Travers clench his jaw almost imperceptibly when the king dismissed his concerns of tension with Toreall as soon as Lord Tyndell said there was nothing to worry about. Everyone else moved on to the next topic, but Callan saw the glare the duke sent Lord Tyndell, the man's brown eyes seeming to darken with malice.

And he watched Lord Friswith hide the smirk that said he saw the duke's glare, too.

Tava had been utterly brilliant at the engagement ball. While Callan had made small talk with the various nobility, Tava had maintained her shy demeanor, ever the timid and docile Lady. She greeted everyone he introduced her to, danced with a few of them here and there, but he never let her out of his sight. And when he would be on the dance floor with her, she would tell him of things she'd overheard and what to watch for with certain Lords, particularly his father's Inner Circle.

Ever the little fox in the chicken coop.

Which is how she had heard her father speaking in a low voice with Lord Friswith of a rising threat to the west and things they needed to do to begin preparing for that threat. She heard him whisper of how he planned to bring it to the king's attention at an upcoming council meeting and was asking for the Lord's support in the matter. Since there was nothing but water to the west of Windonelle, he was obviously referencing Avonleya, and, in turn, Scarlett and the Fae. A servant had stepped in to offer Callan and Tava wine at that moment, and by the time they'd moved on, her father and Lord Friswith had moved out of earshot.

A quick knock on the door pulled Callan from his thoughts as a voice called from the other side, "Callan? It's me."

Tava?

He glanced at the clock above the fireplace. It was nearly midnight.

What was she doing here?

Before he could answer, the door was pushed open, and Finn came in, throwing him an exasperated look as Tava followed.

"You should have waited for him to answer," she was chastising Finn.

"I told you, his night guard said he was in here. It's fine," Finn sighed.

Tava huffed, letting the door snick shut behind her.

"What are you two doing here at this hour?" Callan asked, glancing back and forth between them.

"We need to talk about this guard thing, Callan," Tava said, removing the cloak she was wearing and tossing it over a chair.

"Oh?" Callan asked, arching a brow and glancing at Finn.

Finn rolled his eyes, moving to the liquor cart and pouring himself a finger of whiskey.

"Yes," Tava was saying, her hands coming to her hips. She had on black pants and a black tunic, and her hair was braided down her back. The boots she was wearing came nearly to her knees, and Callan found himself trying to recall if he had ever seen her in anything other than a dress.

"He is everywhere. All the time. If Drake isn't there, then Finn is," Tava groused.

Callan cocked his head to the side as he watched the Lady begin to pace. He'd definitely never seen her this riled, and he wasn't entirely sure what to make of it.

"He is your personal guard, Tava," Callan said slowly. "It is expected of him to be there all the time. That is his job."

"Then make it not his job," she snapped.

Callan glanced at Finn again, and he sighed. "She has tried to sneak from the manor the last three nights and is frustrated she is not as stealthy as she thinks she is."

Callan's brows shot up. "Why are you leaving the manor at this hour of the night?"

"I have things to tend to," she said with a wave of her hand.

"Such as?" Callan pressed.

"Just . . . things, Callan. Things I cannot have a royal guard following me around for."

"Before I address that incredibly vague statement, I would like to clarify that you are trying to sneak out of the manor and evade your personal guard to go somewhere alone in the middle of the night?" Callan asked, setting his empty liquor glass on the table beside him.

"No! I mean . . ." She paused, biting her bottom lip for a moment before saying, "I know how this sounds . . ."

"Do you?" Callan asked. "Because it sounds like you are sneaking off to do scandalous things, Lady Tyndell."

Her cheeks went bright red as she tried to sputter a response, and Callan hid the teasing smile tilting the corner of his lips behind his thumb, as he watched her grow more and more flustered.

Until the thought occurred to him that maybe she *did* have someone else. He was just a ruse after all, so it wouldn't be inconceivable for her to have someone else. But if she did, he clearly wasn't of nobility.

"Tava," Callan said, pushing to his feet. "Do you . . . Are you trying to go see someone?"

Somehow her cheeks reddened even more as her hand came up to cover her face. "No, Callan," she said, clear frustration in her voice. "I am trying to go see someone, but not in that way. I do not have some secret lover."

The relief that flooded through him took him by surprise, but he said, "If you did, I would understand, but I would also need to know. We cannot have any more people knowing about this—"

"I am not having some scandalous affair, Callan," Tava cut in.

"It would not really be an affair so to speak," Callan mused.

"Stop," Tava said, holding up her hand. "I have some tonics and elixirs I deliver to some of the poorer districts, along with food and clothing. I have not been able to do so for several days now, due to our circumstances and now him," she said with a jerk of her chin towards Finn.

"Hold on a minute. Are you saying you go to the slums by yourself at night to deliver these things?" Callan demanded.

"I have been doing so for nearly two years, Callan," she replied.

"By yourself?" he repeated.

"Not right away, no," she answered. "Scarlett would go, and she started taking me with her—"

"So *she* took you out to the slums with her?" he demanded, rage instantly seeping into his tone.

"I *asked* to go with her, Callan," Tava shot back. "And when she became so wrapped up in the Black Syndicate orphans and everything with you and Sorin . . . I couldn't let those people go forgotten again, so I started making sure the tonics the High Healer got to me were delivered to those who needed them. I started making sure that orphans outside of the Black Syndicate were getting food and clothing, too. As much as I can anyway. Because they matter just as much as the children Scarlett is trying to save."

Her face was red for an entirely different reason now. Now it was tinted with fury, and Callan didn't know what to say in response as she continued.

"But I am not her. Clearly. I cannot even get out of my godsdamn home the ways she took me so many times. I do not know that I am making much of a difference, but the little difference I was making is now being diminished because I cannot get there with Finn blocking my way." Silence rang loudly in the room, and Callan ran his hand along his jaw, unsure of where to start with all of this. For one, he was positive he had never heard such language from her lips. He glanced at Finn, who was sipping his liquor and looking back and forth between them with interest.

"You have anything to say to this?" Callan asked him.

"Nope," Finn answered, settling back into the sofa where he'd taken a seat. "This is your fake fiancé. I will let you deal with it."

"There is nothing to deal with," Tava cut in, her tone already calmer. "I just need you to stay here while I go deliver these things."

"Does Drake know you do this?" Callan asked, watching her carefully.

Her lips pursed, and her eyes darted to the fire that was slowly dying out in the hearth. "No. He has other things to worry about."

"Tava, the slums are nearly as dangerous as the Black Syndicate," Callan ventured.

She scoffed at him. "They are not, Callan. They are not even close to the same. The Black Syndicate is full of crime lords, mercenaries, and drug peddlers. The slums are full of people who are forgotten because they are sick or poor or alone, with no one to care of their existence."

"Even if that is the case, it is dangerous now," Callan said, trying a different tactic. "People know we are betrothed. Some will see you as a ticket to a ransom reward for your return." She opened her mouth to argue, but before she could, he continued, "And I do not speak of the poor in the slums. I speak of those wanting to move up in society and willing to hire out the aforementioned mercenaries and thieves to make that happen."

Tava sucked on a tooth as she contemplated his words, before she sighed heavily and sank into the chair her cloak was draped over. And for the first time, she let it show how much this whole arrangement was wearing on her. Scarcely a week had passed, but the life he lived was already taking its toll, was already draining light from her.

"Finn, can you give us a few minutes, please?"

"Of course," Finn said, dropping his now empty glass back on the liquor cart. "I'll be back in an hour."

Callan nodded and waited until the door had closed behind him before turning back to Tava. Her chin was propped in her hand as she watched the small fire, her other hand running her spirit amulet back and forth on its ivory chain.

"Tava, do you need out of this arrangement?" he asked, getting straight to the point.

Her eyes widened slightly as her gaze landed on to his. "No, Callan. I am sorry if I made you think that."

"Please do not apologize to me. My life, the things expected of me, the dangers I deal with, and that you now deal with by merely being associated with me, are not trivial things, Tava. They would be a weight on anyone's shoulders, especially when you have not grown up being expected to carry them," Callan replied.

"I was raised in this society just as you were," she argued.

"Yes, but being raised noble and being raised royal are still two very different things, Tava. More than that, if a lady's family is hoping to marry her into a royal status, her upbringing is also different from what you experienced."

"I understand that," she sighed again. "But no, I do not need an out. I was unprepared for this whole personal guard thing interfering with my dealings in the slums, but I will figure something out."

"I am not asking you not to go there, Tava, but let Finn come with you. Or Drake. Or me."

"You cannot come. Neither can Finn. Even Drake would be a stretch," she replied, her eyes going back to the fire.

"Why?"

"Because you are the crown. Finn is a royal guard, and Drake is nobility and a Commander," she replied, as if the reasoning were obvious.

"You are nobility," he pointed out dryly.

"Yes, but for a long time, I accompanied Scarlett on trips. They came to know and trust me because of her."

"So because *she* does not take me there, they will not trust me?" he retorted bitterly.

Tava glanced at him, looking him up and down quickly, before pushing to her feet and reaching for her cloak. "No, they will not trust you because you are the crown."

"They do not trust the king?"

Some kind of hollow laugh passed her lips. "No, Callan, they do not trust the crown. They do not trust the ruler who seems to have forgotten them, who does not care if they have food, shelter, clothing. They do not trust the people who sneer at them when they ask for help to feed their children who have not had full bellies in months."

Callan stepped back at the viciousness of her words. She had her cloak back on now and was heading for the door.

"Where are you going?"

"There are a few families in particular there who need these tonics. They are sick and have not had them for several days. I need to get them there somehow," Tava answered, reaching for the door handle, but Callan was already there, holding the door shut.

"Let me come with you."

"I just told you why you cannot, Callan."

"I cannot let you go there by yourself, Tava. Not any more."

"So what do you propose I do?"

"I can cover myself, keep my face hidden. They do not need to know I am the Crown Prince. Finn can do the same."

"That will never work," Tava said, shaking her head. "It is your only option, Tava."

She held his stare for a long moment before finally accepting that he would not relent on this. "Fine," she sighed, waving a hand at him to get his cloak.

He never took his eyes off of her, fearing she would slip out the door without him if he did.

He'd experienced that enough in his life.

Within minutes they had tracked down Finn, and Callan filled him in on the plan. The castle halls were quiet during the late hour, and the few guards they did pass didn't question anything. When they were outside in the brisk winter air, Callan turned to make his way to the stables, but Tava grabbed his arm, shaking her head.

"We walk. They will immediately know you are nobility if you arrive on horseback or in a carriage."

He nodded his understanding, his hands shoved deep into his cloak. "How do you get the tonics?" he asked quietly.

"The High Healer used to deliver them with Scarlett's tonic. When that was no longer needed, Cassius would get them to me.

Now she leaves them in a prearranged location, and I pick them up during the day under the guise of errands."

It took them nearly an hour to get to the slums on foot, most of the hour spent in silence. Each district they went through became progressively more run down. The air became more stale. The puddles he was stepping in were definitely not melted snow, and the faces leering out of doorways had him wondering how Tava thought it was in any way safe to travel these streets at night alone.

She finally turned and began walking towards a small shack. He couldn't call it a house. It was hardly standing. There were a few boards over windows, but not enough to keep the elements out. The roof was sagging in on one side, and the front steps had long since rotted away. The door Tava was reaching for wasn't even properly latched shut. It likely couldn't close properly anymore, he supposed.

"Maybe we should let Finn go first," Callan whispered, grabbing Tava's other arm and pulling her to a halt.

"She is an old woman that can hardly stand. I assure you we are safe," Tava replied quietly before shrugging out of his grip and pushing through the door.

"Tava? Is that you?"

The voice was crackled with age, raspy and somewhat slurred. "It is, Helen," Tava replied, her voice impossibly gentle.

Callan tracked her in the dark as she moved to a small table and pulled a match from her pocket, lighting a candle and illuminating the room. An old woman was indeed huddled in a corner, threadbare blankets wrapped around her frail body. Her thin, white hair was poking out the sides of a hat, and her shivering was visible even in the shadows.

"Who are they?" Helen rasped, eyeing him and Finn as if she could see their faces beneath their hoods.

"They are friends," Tava said, kneeling before the old woman. "I don't trust 'em," the old woman spat.

"You did not trust me at first either, remember?" Helen grunted in response.

"Have you been able to get up and move around?"

"Been three days," Helen said. "Chloe brought me food and water."

"I am sorry I was not able to get here sooner," Tava said, her voice carrying a hint of guilt that Callan felt in his own soul. He had been the one keeping her from coming.

Tava pulled two vials from her cloak pocket, uncorking one and bringing it to the woman's lips. She drank the entire thing down, shifting a little when it was gone.

"I have another. You can take it in the morning. It should keep you comfortable until I can get you more," Tava said, tucking the other vial into Helen's gnarled hand before readjusting the blankets over her. "I will try to bring more blankets, too."

"I'm fine. There are others who need the blankets more than I do," Helen said, tucking her hand back under the scraps of fabric.

"I can only assume you have already given away too many of your own, Helen. I will bring you another as soon as I can," Tava replied. "Do you need anything else before I go?"

"Blow the light out, child," Helen said, leaning her head back against the wall, her eyes falling shut. "I won't get over there anytime soon."

"Of course, Helen," Tava said, pushing to her feet.

"Ivan fell off the wagon again," Helen called out. "Last I heard, he was in that alley by the Burchards' hovel."

Tava sighed heavily. "Thank you, Helen. I will get him."

"Stay safe, Child."

Tava blew the candle out before pushing past Callan and Finn and stepping back out into the winter chill.

Finn was pulling the door shut as much as he could behind them, as Tava pulled her hood back up, shoving her hands into her cloak.

"She will . . ." Callan swallowed thickly as he felt Tava's gaze settle on him beneath her hood. "She cannot be warm enough," he tried again. "What is her tonic for?"

"She has a condition that causes her joints to stiffen and become painful, sometimes making mobility nearly impossible," Tava replied tightly. "The tonic offers enough relief from the pain that she can at least move around, which helps ease the discomfort even more." She paused for a moment before adding, "Although with this cold, I doubt even the tonics will be enough to ease that right now."

She led the way back to the street, passing more of the same types of shacks these people called their homes. Callan had never been this deep in the slums. He had certainly never come here as a child. The slums were full of lazy men and women who would rather fall into a liquor bottle than make an honest living. Fathers who abandoned their families, and mothers who regretted having children. That's what he'd been told, taught to believe, and while he hadn't entirely believed such things as he got older, he could admit there was still some sort of stigma attached to the place and its people. His parents would lose their minds if they knew he was in the slums of Baylorin with only Finn as a guard.

They would likely faint if they knew his betrothed was kneeling before them.

A few minutes later, Tava turned down an alleyway. There were a handful of barrels alight and several people gathered around them, trying to soak in the warmth. Most of them didn't even acknowledge their presence as they passed. A few looked at them, and, although they could not see him beneath his hood, Callan could see them, illuminated by the flames. Gaunt faces, weathered by age and the elements. Hopeless eyes. Defeated souls.

Tava strode purposefully along until they were nearly at the end of the alley where a man was sitting against the brick wall. His eyes were half-closed, and Callan was fairly certain that was vomit down the front of the coat he was wearing. He had a scraggly beard, and the shoes he was wearing had holes in the toes.

Tava pushed her hood back, going to kneel once more, and Callan couldn't keep himself from grabbing her elbow to stop her. She looked back at him over her shoulder as she said, "You insisted on coming with me, and I compromised on that front. But I will not allow you to keep me from helping these people."

Callan opened and closed his mouth, having nothing really to say to that as she jerked her elbow from his grip.

"We're here if anything happens," Finn murmured from his other side, his eyes keenly watching the alley and the people in it.

"Ivan," Tava said quietly, shaking the man's shoulders. "Ivan, can you hear me?"

"Is that you, angel?" the man slurred.

"The angel is not here tonight," she answered softly. "Just her helper." "Nah," the man slurred again. "You were always the angel. She was just the shadows you traveled in."

Tava laughed softly. "If you say so, Ivan. Let's get you up and over to Mary Ellen's."

"Gah," he grumbled. "She ain't gonna let me back in that place."

"Of course she will," Tava said, looping his arm around her slender shoulders, and before he realized he was moving, Callan was coming to the man's other side.

"This ain't no angel," Ivan slurred as Callan looped his other arm around his own shoulders.

"Maybe it is," Tava argued. "He is helping you, is he not?"

"Fuck, angel. The shadows helped me, too, but that didn't make her no angel." A hiccup escaped him as they got Ivan on his feet.

"Let me take him. You lead the way," Finn said, coming to relieve Tava.

Tava let him and began leading them back down the alley. There were whispers as they passed by this time, and a few even started following them. Tava didn't seem concerned, but Callan sure as hell was. These people may not know the Crown Prince was among them, but he was certain at least a few of them had to know that Tava was now engaged to him. News had to reach even this corner of the slums, didn't it?

It took ten minutes to get to their next destination. This building seemed to be in better repair than any of the others they had passed. It was two stories and had a wrap-around porch, although a number of the boards were rotted, and Tava stepped carefully as she made her way to the door.

"Hey, angel," Ivan slurred again while they waited for someone to answer the bell she had rung, when she pulled a string near the door.

"Yes, Ivan?" she asked pleasantly.

"Didn't I hear you was getting married?"

Tava's spine stiffened, and she pulled her cloak tighter around herself. "I do not know. Did you hear that?"

"Pretty sure. Is it true?"

Tava cleared her throat. "Yes, Ivan. I will soon be married."

Ivan whistled low under his breath. "That's one lucky son of a bitch. You take such good care o' me. I can jus' imagine how good you take of 'em."

"That is enough, Ivan," Tava said firmly as the door opened.

A formidable looking woman stood there in a long, cotton nightgown. Her face was illuminated by a candle, and Callan could just make out the streaks of grey in her light brown hair. Her brown eyes skipped from Tava to Ivan and back again before she sighed and stepped to the side.

"I was wondering when I would see him again," the woman said, as Tava stepped past her and motioned for Callan and Finn to enter.

"How are you, Mary Ellen?" Tava asked when the woman shut the door behind her.

"I'd be better if I was still sleeping," she grumbled.

"I am sure that is the case. Helen told me he has found his way into the alcohol again," Tava replied.

"It ain't my fault," Ivan said, while he was lowered to a sagging sofa against a wall. "I jus' miss my Alice so much. She was the only thing that could keep my demons away."

"I know, Ivan," Tava said quietly. "Do you need anything else before we go?" she asked, turning to Mary Ellen.

"No, dear. I got him from here," the woman answered. "Go get some rest. You look exhausted." Tava's cheeks flushed slightly at the words, as Mary Ellen added, "You can't do the work the two of you were doing together by yourself, dear. Even though you are certainly attempting it."

"I will be fine, Mary Ellen. If I cannot return with food and blankets myself, I will make sure that some finds its way here," Tava answered. She turned to leave before pausing and looking back over her shoulder. "How is William?"

Mary Ellen's face went taut. "He did not make it."

"When?" Tava asked quietly.

"Two days ago."

Tava nodded once, then went to the door without another word. They made their way back to the street in silence, Callan and Finn flanking her.

"I have one more stop to make. To drop off a tonic," Tava said.

"All right," Callan agreed. They walked in silence a few more minutes before Callan asked, "Who was Alice?"

"Ivan's daughter," Tava answered curtly.

"She . . . died?"

"Yes."

"How?"

"Ivan was arrested in the markets. They said he was trying to steal. He swears he wasn't. Either way, he was held in the stocks for a week. No one knew where he'd hidden Alice while he'd gone out to try to find her food. By the time they found her, she had died from dehydration," Tava answered. "She was four."

Callan nearly tripped over his feet, but before he could say anything more, a figure rushed out in front of them.

"You!" the man cried, reaching for Tava's hand. "You are the one they talk about. You help them!"

The man's eyes were frantic, and he seemed half-crazed, but Finn had already stepped in front of Tava, blocking the man's access to her. Callan was pulling her into his side.

"Relax. He just needs help," Tava said quietly, nudging Finn to the side.

"It's you, right? The one he calls the angel?"

"Are you speaking of Ivan?" Tava asked.

"Yeah, that's him. He said you can help my son," the man cried. "These the shadows?"

"No. She is not here, but I can try to help. What do you need?"

"Can you come see him?"

Tava shook her head. "I'm sorry. I am not a healer, but if you tell me what is wrong, I can see if they can help and bring—"

"No, you need to come see him. He's only a lil' boy. Please!"

"All right," Tava said, taking a step towards the man.

The man tensed as Finn and Callan began to follow. "Ivan said not to trust anyone else. Only the angel."

"It is all right. They are with me," Tava said soothingly.

The man shook his head. "No. Just you."

Tava glanced over her shoulder at him, and Callan shook his head. There was no way they were going to let her go off by herself with this man.

Tava bit her lip, turning back to the man. "I am sorry, but if they cannot come, I cannot help."

"He said you would help," the man said, a hint of rage bleeding into his plea.

"And I want to help," Tava replied. "If you can just tell me what is wrong with him."

"I need you to come see," he insisted.

"If the shadow was with her, would she be allowed to come?" Finn asked from where he still stood between the man and Tava.

"I only trust the angel," the man ground out.

"Just let me go see—" Tava started.

"No," Finn said, before Callan could say it himself.

"You said you would help me, not hinder me," Tava said harshly.

"I am helping," Finn replied, his voice low. "Something is off here, Lady Tava. Not one other person has insisted on it only being you."

"They do not trust outsiders," she argued.

"You need to come with me," the man said, his anger growing. "My kid needs you."

"She is not going with you alone. If he needs help that badly, you will let us accompany her," Finn said calmly.

"She said only her," the man insisted.

"She? Who is she?" Finn asked, his hand dropping casually to his side, within reach of his weapons.

Tava had caught the slip though as well, her entire body stiffening as she pressed into Callan's side.

"I mean Ivan," the man said, stumbling over his words. "He said only her."

"Who sent you to retrieve her?" Callan demanded.

The man's face morphed into ire, his lip curling up into a sneer. "It don't matter. It will be reported back that the prince's whore was seen here with other men."

Finn had the man's coat fisted in his hand in the next heartbeat, a dagger at his throat. "I will not ask again: who sent you to retrieve her?"

"Fuck, man!" the man cried, as Finn dragged him down a side street and pressed him up against a wall.

"Who?" Finn demanded, throwing his elbow up and knocking the man's head back against the bricks.

A startled cry escaped Tava, her hand clamping over her mouth.

"A woman," the man bit out. "She gave Ivan liquor and me coin. Said when she came here, to get her to the laundry place and she'd take care of things from there."

"What did she look like?" Finn asked, his dagger pressing into the man's throat and a bead of blood welling.

"She wore a hood like you fuckers!" the man spat. "I don't know. I need the money. I got mouths to feed. She said she'd come with me if I told her I needed help. That my kid needed help."

"Let him go," Tava said, her voice hardly a whisper.

"Tava," Callan started.

"Let him go," she said again, louder this time.

"He tried to—"

"I know what he tried to do," Tava interrupted. "But he didn't succeed. Release him. He was only trying to feed his family."

Callan could feel Finn's eyes on him, waiting for his orders, and he jerked his chin. Finn stepped away, placing himself between them and the man.

"Get the fuck out of here," Finn snarled. "And report back to whomever you are working, for that if anyone attempts to abduct her again, they will answer to the Crown."

"The fucking crown," the man snarled, spitting at their feet. "Like any one of us here gives a fuck about the Crown. They won't do anything unless it will add to their fucking coffers." He started off down the alley, heading back for the main street, but he paused as he neared them. "You can bet we don't need your help any more either, *angel*," he drawled, pointing his finger at Tava. "You can just go be with your prince and stay the fuck outta here."

Callan's grip on her tightened as the man disappeared around the corner.

"Are you all right?" he asked, looking down at her and trying to see her face beneath the hood.

"Can we go please?" she whispered.

Callan nodded, keeping her close as Finn led them down the street and out of the slums. She was trembling beside him, and he knew it wasn't from the cold. There were no passing carriages at this time of night, so they were forced to walk the hour back to the castle.

"Do you want me to take Lady Tava home?" Finn asked when they reached the castle gates.

He glanced down at her, her arms crossed over her chest and still shaking.

"No. Send a note to the Tyndells letting them know she is here. Tell them we had an early breakfast together or something, and that you escorted her," Callan answered.

"Done," Finn replied, as they made their way to a side entrance that would lead directly to the wing Callan's private chambers were in.

When they reached the landing of his floor, Finn bid them goodnight and headed for his own chambers down the hall, and Callan let Tava into his rooms. He pulled her cloak from around her, getting her settled on the sofa before attempting to get the fire going in the grate. It came back to life a little, enough to give off a small amount of heat. He poured them each a finger of whiskey before he grabbed a blanket, wrapping it around her shoulders and handing her a glass. Then he took a seat on the other end of the sofa.

"Tava, are you all right?" he asked gently.

"I should really go home," she said softly. "My father and Drake will be worried."

"I already have messages en route to them."

"My father will not be pleased to hear I spent the night with you."

"You stayed in another room because we wanted to have a quiet breakfast together this morning. He can talk to me if he has any questions," Callan replied simply. "Finn and the night guard are our witnesses if needed."

Tava nodded, silence falling around them again for several minutes before she said, "You knew this was a possibility."

"You said yourself a few nights ago that I have personal guards because there is always danger," he said. "It comes with the royal title. We also have some prominent enemies right now."

Tava nodded once. "I should have seen it coming. It was stupid not to. I just didn't think I would matter that much in the great scheme of things."

Callan cocked his head. "You did not think that becoming royalty would matter in the great scheme of things?"

"I mean, I knew it would, but *I* have never been that important," she replied with a sigh, sipping on the liquor. "I have always been in the background, more of an afterthought."

"You are anything but an afterthought, Tava," Callan argued.

She glanced at him and gave him a small, knowing smile. "You rarely spoke to me before everything with Scarlett, Callan. Even when you dined in my home, I was formally greeted and then I sat quietly at the table. I am not complaining or seeking pity. I prefer to be in the background. You hear more there. However, I did not anticipate it affecting the people I was trying to help."

"You are more worried about those who tried to aid in your abduction, than you are about the people who are actually trying to kidnap you?" Callan asked, a brow arching.

"I have people who care enough about me that my disappearance would be felt. My father. Drake. A few others. They would look for me, fight for me," Tava answered. "Those people . . . Most of them do not have that. If one of them disappeared, few would notice and even less would care."

"So incredibly selfless," Callan murmured, watching the light of the flame flicker over her features.

"I am not selfless, Callan," Tava replied, pulling the blanket tighter around her shoulders. "I simply care about the ones the kings and queens of this world forgot about. That is not being selfless. That is being a decent human being."

They both got lost in their own thoughts after that, sipping on their drinks and letting their nerves settle. He'd never realized that Scarlett's aid had gone beyond the Black Syndicate, although it shouldn't surprise him. At that point in time, her priorities were those who could not help themselves.

Now her priorities appeared to be her new subjects and how they would be affected by the Maraan Lords. They hadn't heard much from the Fae, and he was fine with that. They could stay in their Courts, and he would help his own people.

"She never told me," he said into the quiet. "She never told me of anything other than the orphans in the Black Syndicate."

"Why would she?" Tava asked. She'd removed her boots, tucking her feet beneath her.

"She was seeking my help."

"And how long did it take for them to come to you?" Tava asked. "How many avenues did they try before they took the one that led to you?"

When Callan had nothing to say to that, she said, "You were their last resort, Callan. She was one of them, not one of you. She was one of the forgotten."

"She was raised by an Assassin Lord," Callan argued defensively.

Tava scoffed. "Yes, what a lovely childhood. Being given over to a master and taught to take life. What child wouldn't want to grow up in such conditions?"

"You are incredibly candid when we are alone," Callan muttered.

"And you are incredibly naïve to think she would have told you anything of her world when the Crown has proven time and again that they do not care," Tava shot back.

"She could have tried," he argued. "I told her that I wanted to take care of the people within our own borders while my father and his council seeks more land. I told her this was where my focus lies."

"And yet you have done nothing to prove such a thing," Tava replied. "You say she could have tried? So could you, Callan. Before tonight, had you ever been to the slums? Before tonight, had you ever cared for someone who could not take care of themselves? Before tonight, had you ever seen them as actual people? Tried to understand their world? The struggles they face? Why they face them? Do you even care now?"

There was so much passion and fierceness in her voice that Callan sat up straighter at it, marveled at it.

"How were you raised in this world and yet somehow not succumb to the fallacies of nobility?" he asked, leaning towards her.

"You see things when you are in the background, Callan. You see all the things the rest of the world tries to ignore," she answered softly.

"Can you show them to me?"

Her eyes finally met his at the question, and as she studied him, he felt as if she were studying his soul, trying to decide if he was worthy of such a thing.

She sighed. "Not any more. Not after tonight. I am no longer welcome in their world. More than that, I fear they will be used again to try to get to me and that is not fair to them."

"So we eliminate the threat," Callan said.

"We do not even know who the threat is."

"Little fox, I think we both know who was behind what happened tonight."

"Stop calling me that," she said on a breath of laughter.

"It fits you so well, though," he replied with a grin.

"You really think it was Veda?"

"I'd bet my crown on it."

"How incredibly elitist of you," she mocked.

"We will deal with this threat, Lady Tava," Callan said. "Then you can bring me into your world, and show me the ones you keep company with in the background."

"Deal, your Highness," she replied, holding her nearly empty glass out to him.

He knocked his own against it in agreement, and found himself wondering how anyone could think of Lady Tava Tyndell as an afterthought.

CHAPTER 31
TALWYN

She smelled him before she heard him. The scent of fir and soil. Another ever-changing scent was on the winds, too.

A Shifter.

Stellan specifically.

She was curled in the middle of a couple other wolves. A head rested on her hip. Her own head was lying on Maliq's neck. She'd been in her wolf form for nearly three days now. They'd run under the moon. They'd drank from streams. The other wolves had hunted, but she couldn't bring herself to eat raw meat from a fresh kill, not even as a wolf. She relished the idea of staying in this form forever. Of not having to go back and face the shit-storm that had exploded before her.

Tarek. Azrael.

The Avonleyans.

But she did need to eat.

She sat up, shaking her powerful limbs out. Her ears flattened to her head as she spotted Azrael sitting against the trunk of a giant tree. A mountain cat with olive green eyes sat rigidly beside him. Stellan always preferred feline forms whenever possible. A tawny-colored wolf lay at his feet.

She planted her paws, staring down the Earth Prince, a low growl in her throat.

"Talwyn, you have had time," Azrael said. "It is time to come home and face this."

She didn't do anything. Didn't move. It's not like she could say anything in response, even if she wanted to.

There was a flash of gold light, and Stellan stood beside Azrael.

He was shirtless, but wore the same lightweight pants he often sported in Siofra. She couldn't help but wonder where his clothes went when he shifted. Would she have clothes when she figured out how to shift back?

Ilyas was instantly on his feet before Stellan, and the Alpha ran a hand down his back as he said, "Come with us, your Majesty. Arianna and Sariah are waiting for you. We will help you hone your gift."

She still didn't move, and the rest of her pack had woken, moving restlessly behind her. She glanced back to Maliq watching her, his jade green eyes seeming to await her decision.

"You must be getting hungry," Stellan said casually. "If you do not want to shift back, then at least let us teach you how to hunt so you can eat."

Azrael sighed, getting to his feet. An earth portal appeared to his left. "Let's go, Talwyn." When she still refused to move a muscle, he said,

"You need explanations to accept this, and I will tell you what I know. Afterwards, if you want to come back to the wolves, I will not follow."

With a huff, she finally found it in her to move, taking a few steps to the portal. A flare of soft green light in her periphery had her glancing back to find Maliq gone.

Talwyn stepped through the earth portal directly into a sand cave of some sort. There were solid pillars throughout the structure, and in the center stood a jaguar and a tiger. As the portal closed behind the males, a sharp cry had her looking to the ceiling where a red-tailed hawk was flying. It dove for the ground, shifting and landing mid-stride. Arianna went straight to her brother, the beads in her long hair clinking as she moved.

"Took you long enough," she said in her sultry tone.

"Not now, Arianna," Stellan replied, then let out a yelp when she sent energy skittering across the sand to his feet. "Really?" he said in agitation.

"We are still fighting, Stellan," she said airily. "This does not change that." Stellan rolled his eyes at his sister, turning to look down at Talwyn, but before he could say anything, Arianna said, "Get out. You and Ilyas go get her some food. Sariah and I will get started."

Talwyn sat, watching the siblings. Arianna didn't even bother to see if her orders were followed. She clearly just expected them to be. She'd always admired the Beta from afar. The female couldn't care less what anyone else thought of her. She was fierce and commanding, expecting obedience and fighting for what she wanted, even if she fought by herself. And while she may currently be fighting with the Alpha, the siblings were a force to reckon with.

Which is why she wanted them on her side when she came for Avonleya.

"I am not leaving," Azrael snarled, his threat clear in his tone if Arianna should try to force him, which had the Alpha snarling his own warning at him.

Stellan and Ilyas left the sand cave, and Arianna leveled her gaze on Talwyn. "I cannot say I am surprised you shifted into a wolf," she mused, slowly circling Talwyn. "You have Maliq as your spirit animal. You are bonded to Celeste, and your mother's other form was a wolf."

At the mention of her mother, Talwyn was on her feet.

"I am going to assume you only have one other form like Queen Henna did, which is why Sariah is here. How I shift is different from how others with only one form shift."

At her name, Sariah slunk forward, only coming to a stop when she was nose-to-nose with Talwyn.

"But," Arianna continued, "you can shift energy, matter, ether, which is something most Shifters cannot do. So go to that place, your Majesty. However you shift energy at will, go there."

There was another flash of light, and Sariah was kneeling before her, the female's face as close as it had been in her feline form. "There is a thread," she said softly. "It connects your animal form to your Fae form. Look for it. Hunt for it in your soul."

Talwyn let out a huff. She'd done this before. She'd known she should be able to shift her form. It was in her blood. It was in her being as her mother's daughter. She'd spent a ridiculous amount of time searching her well of power for something that could help her shift her form, but had never been successful. For years she'd done so with no success.

"It is there," Arianna said softly, as though she had read her thoughts. Talwyn felt her hand run along her side. "You think it is not, but it is the thread back to yourself."

"It hides because you are in pain," Sariah added. "It is hidden because you do not wish to find it."

"But you must," Arianna said, her hand continuing to glide along the fur of Talwyn's wolf form. "Most of us shift for the first time due to some sort of fear or trauma. For me, it was when my father died. I stayed in the form of a small fox for nearly a week. Stellan shifted for the first time after he made his first kill with a sword."

Sariah had shifted back into her jaguar form, sprawling out on her side on the sandy floor, as if settling in for a long wait.

Jamahl had shifted into his human form and had his arms wrapped around his Beta's waist from behind. Arianna had stopped petting Talwyn, reaching up to loop a hand behind his neck as she studied her a bit more.

"This will take many hours, possibly days, Prince," she commented, addressing Azrael, who was standing off to the side, his arms crossed and looking pissy as always. Talwyn bared her teeth at him when he met her gaze. Arianna glanced between the two before she ventured, "Perhaps you should go, Prince. You will make this more difficult."

"As I have already said, I am not going anywhere. She will shift and leave before giving me a chance to speak," he replied, his stare fixed on Talwyn.

He wasn't wrong. That had been her plan.

Talwyn plopped down on her achingly empty belly, her head coming to rest between her paws. She closed her eyes, looking into that well in her soul. She dug beneath the winds and the breezes, the flowers and the soil. She let everything fade away around her. She drowned out the voices of the others. But there was no thread. Nothing that would pull her back to her Fae form.

She didn't know how long she lay there before the smell of braised meat reached her nose. Her eyes snapped open, her mouth watering.

But she went still when she found Azrael holding the platter of food, everyone else having disappeared.

"We need to talk," Azrael ground out. "Or rather, you need to listen while I speak. Perhaps you being stuck in your wolf form is for the best right now."

Talwyn snarled at him, snapping her teeth, but he didn't acknowledge the action. He simply set the platter of food down on the ground before he slid down the wall of the sand cave. He rested his forearms on his bent knees, clasping his hands loosely in front of him.

"My grandfather was born in Avonleya. He came over during the Great War. He was a warrior in one of their armies, a commander. As I told you, he was a quarter Avonleyan. Fae used to reside over there and lived among the Avonleyans. Whether or not they still do, I cannot say. There are so many different versions of history now, it is hard to say what is truth.

"I never met my grandfather. He met my grandmother here. A powerful, earth-wielding Fae female. He'd been stationed in the Earth Court for most of his time as a commander from what I was told. My father was born during the war, and it was when things were beginning to turn in the favor of Deimas and Esmeray that my grandfather decided to take the Royal seat of the Earth Court. My father was young. Too young to understand the politics. Our bloodline was always strong in earth magic, but because of the Avonleyan power in his blood, my grandfather easily defeated the sitting prince. Why he found the middle of a war to be a good time for such political upheaval, I do not know, but he won and became the Earth Prince."

Talwyn didn't acknowledge Azrael as he spoke. She just ate the steaming beef and chicken that had been prepared for her. But she was listening, hanging on to every word.

"My grandfather prized power, presumably because he would have been considered less powerful in Avonleya due to his heritage. I cannot say for sure, but based on the fact that he immediately set out to find the most powerful earth female for my father to marry, I can say it is a safe bet, especially as my father was obsessed with the same. One can only assume he was raised in such a manner. It is why an arrangement was made between my father and Eliza's father, before either of us was even conceived. I was born a century before her, but my father waited to see if her family would produce a female."

She looked up at him at that. She had known, of course, that Eliza had been promised to him. She didn't know all the details, only that her power had manifested as fire rather than earth, and her father had disowned her. But not before Marking her to be unable to bear children, to carry on the fire magic in her veins. He killed her mother before leaving Eliza in the Fire Court.

Azrael seemed to sense where her thoughts had gone, because

he said, "I tried to find her. When I learned what her father had done to her, I tried to find her. It had never mattered to me. Marriage was . . ." He paused, as if trying to find the right wording. "It was a political alliance. That is how I was raised to view marriage and relationships. Any relationship worth putting time into was for alliances only. Marriage was for producing powerful heirs to maintain our control of the Court. Beyond that?" He shrugged. "But I was not outraged to learn of her magic. She certainly did not deserve what her father did to her. By the time I had tracked her down, she had already been found by the Fire Court, further straining relations that had been tense my entire life."

Talwyn had stopped eating. She didn't look at him, but it made sense, she supposed. His focus had always been on what was best for their Courts, what was best for her throne. This wasn't new information. It was just an explanation as to why.

And had absolutely nothing to do with him not telling her of his Avonleyan bloodline.

"That is getting off topic, though," Azrael continued. "My father and mother were killed by Esmeray before everything with Eliza happened. Sorin and I may have ascended to our thrones at the same time, but I still had a century on him. I had been working at my father's side for decades. The power transition was nothing for me. Not like it was for the other Royals."

He spoke so casually about it all. Talwyn wanted to ask if he'd even grieved the death of his parents. Had he felt anything at all?

"My father's Inner Court became my Inner Court. I knew them all well by this point, and when my father's Third faded and crossed the Veil, it was only natural that his son took his place. That is how Tarek Ordos became my Third. I knew that his family used to occupy my throne. I knew that it was his family my grandfather had challenged and bested. When he won, the Ordos family became part of his Inner Court. Resentment at that time would only be natural, but they served my grandfather and father loyally. I did not realize that such resentment still simmered centuries later. I never anticipated that such a need for revenge would cause him to seek an even higher seat of power, but looking back on it now, it all makes sense."

Her eyes narrowed and a low growl escaped her at what he was implying— that Tarek had sought her out because of her claim to the throne and not because he was her twin flame.

"If Tarek would challenge me now, he would still lose," Azrael said, apparently not noticing her growl or choosing to ignore her. Probably the latter. "My Avonleyan blood will always give me a slight advantage, but it is blood I did not even know I possessed until I was well into my second century of life. My father told me that when the Avonleyans fell back, my grandfather did not want it known that he was descended from there, even if only a fraction of our bloodline could be traced back. Documents were altered. People were sworn to secrecy. Oath Marks were given, and eventually, it was forgotten. Traveling was thought to be a rare gift like the Ash Riders and the Wind Walkers. Although, knowing the things I know now, I would venture to guess those are Avonelyan gifts in some way or another as well."

Talwyn had sat, watching him as he spoke, trying to absorb and process everything he was telling her. Still waiting for him to get to the part about why he had never told her.

"I did not think it mattered. Not anymore," he said. "In fact, I rarely thought of the fact that I carry Avonleyan blood in my veins. Not until the day you told me of your plans for revenge. I had been your Second for only a few years when you confided that in me, what you and Ashtine dreamed of one day achieving. I thought of telling you then, but I could not tell if you were serious or if it was just that— a dream.

"Until the day you arrived in my chambers after Tarek had been attacked, when we thought he had died. When Sorin became so lost to his own failure and Cyrus's grief . . ." Azrael trailed off, clearly reining in his dislike for the Fire Prince. And even though she was furious with him, even though she felt a level of betrayal she hadn't felt since that day with Sorin, something in her empty chest squeezed slightly at seeing him so angry on her behalf. He ground his teeth together, his jaw clenching, and it took several seconds before he was able to go on.

"You slept in my chambers that night, and when you woke, there were no tears. There was no grief or sorrow. Only fury and revenge stared back at me as you said, 'We have work to do, Prince.' And I knew. In that moment, I knew that if I ever told you of my heritage, you would never be able to see beyond it. You woke with a renewed craving for what you felt was justice. You woke wanting to hurt those you felt were responsible for the pain you were refusing to acknowledge, and I didn't . . . I didn't know how to help you through that, Talwyn." He met her gaze, and Talwyn almost lurched back from him. His eyes looked haunted, almost desperate for something. He looked at her as if she could give him whatever it was he was seeking, and she had no idea what he wanted from her. "I still do not know how to help you see that your anger is misplaced.

That going after an entire kingdom, a kingdom you will likely fall to, will not make you feel better. Will not atone for the death of your parents. The death of Tarek. The betrayal of Sorin. I do not know how to help you understand that giving your life for this will accomplish nothing but leave your kingdom with an heirless throne."

Talwyn opened her mouth to argue, before remembering she couldn't speak.

Azrael got to his feet, looking down at her from his towering height. "I know you feel outnumbered, Talwyn. I know you feel as though Ashtine and I have turned against you by pulling out of this quest for vengeance. I hope that you see that is not the case, before you do something incredibly foolish. But, for the sake of your appearance, I would suggest that you and I at least appear to still be aligned in our goals. When the time comes to make hard choices, if we still do not agree, I will walk away. I will let you go, if that is what you desire."

He turned then, walking out of the cave, and leaving her standing alone.

He was wrong. Her anger was not misplaced. It was targeted right at the people who caused all of this.

She began pacing back and forth in the cave, everything he'd told her running through her mind. None of it excused him. None of it was a valid reason for not telling her what ran through his veins. If he was right, the same ran through Ashtine's veins as well. Did she know? Was she keeping the same secret from her? A growl rippled from her at that thought.

Of course she felt outnumbered. Because she was. The two people she thought would stand beside her through anything, had all but told her they would stand against her if forced to choose. Ashtine may have chosen her over the winds, but the princess also resented her for it. And Azrael?

I will walk away. I will let you go if that is what you desire.

She didn't need anyone to fight for her. She didn't need anyone at all. Would it be nice? Perhaps, but the Fates had obviously decided she didn't deserve such a thing.

She needed no one. Not Sorin.

Not Tarek. Not Ashtine. Not Azrael.

No. All she needed was the head of the Avonleyan king lying at her feet while the kingdom burned to nothing around her.

Because Azrael was wrong.

Tasting that justice, achieving that revenge, would change everything. She didn't care what happened to the kingdom after she was done with it. There wouldn't be anything left to rule over anyway. There wouldn't be anyone left to use her people for their own gain, just to abandon them.

As that calm, fury-filled clarity settled over her, she saw that glimmering thread in her soul. It wove among her winds and flowers, the ether buzzing around it. She grabbed hold of it, tugging until she felt her body changing, morphing, shifting.

Until she stood on two feet, dressed in the same clothing she had been wearing at the meeting with Scarlett.

She needed to pay the Queen of the Western Courts a visit. It was time to find these keys.

It was time to finally end this for good.

CHAPTER 32
SORIN

"This isn't working," Scarlett sighed, sheathing her sword down her back and brushing back stray hair that had escaped from her braid.

They had been out in the training pits all morning, as they had been every morning for the last week. They spent the morning hours here. They spent their afternoons in various meetings with various people, and they spent their evenings researching until they couldn't keep their eyes open or until other . . . *distractions* arose.

Scarlett had thrown herself completely into learning to fight with her magic and weapons in tandem, as she did with everything she set out to learn. And while she needed to learn to do so seamlessly, she was clearly frustrated that it wasn't coming more naturally to her.

Sorin sheathed his own blade, closing the distance between them. "You are not going to master this in a few days, Scarlett. It is no different from how you trained to harness your power. You are still learning to do that, in addition to trying to fight with it."

"I understand that, but you're going easy on me. I don't need you to do that," she argued, her hands coming to her hips. "In fact, I need you to do the opposite."

"Of course he is," a male voice drawled from the stone archway, and they turned to find Cyrus leaning against it. He pushed off the stones, coming toward them. "He's not going to attack you, Darling. You're his twin flame."

"That is not why," Sorin replied, reaching over to adjust a strap on the leathers she was wearing. The High Witch had gotten her another witch-suit along with the lighter-weight witch-leathers she preferred over Fae leathers or mortal armor.

She batted his hands away in frustration. "Then what, exactly, is the reason?"

"The reason, Princess, is that I do not want you tapping into your shadows and white flames as much, because you refuse to—"

"If you say *feed*, I am going to knock you on your ass," she warned.

"Mmm," he hummed. "My favorite kind of threats: empty ones."

He caught the fist that came swinging for his face a moment later, Cyrus chuckling beside them.

"And you say I throw temper tantrums," Sorin teased.

Scarlett snatched her wrist back and stuck her tongue out at him.

And if that didn't make him start envisioning all the other uses she'd found for that tongue lately . . .

Scarlett smirked at him as if she knew exactly where his thoughts had gone, and she likely did, considering his mental shields had been slipping more and more these last few days.

"You'll never learn a thing if you are constantly stopping to do *that*," came Eliza's annoyed voice as she came into the pit.

"I'm not going to learn anything because he's too afraid to push me," Scarlett retorted.

"As I have already stated, I am not afraid to push you. I am far more worried about the fact that you refuse to acknowledge the need to *feed*," he replied, watching the ire ignite in her eyes at the word. They were still silvery-blue, but muted and dull. She may refuse to acknowledge it, but she'd used her shadows plenty this last week. If she didn't do something about it, icy blue eyes would look back at him soon. She'd still be able to access her Avonleyan gifts, but they wouldn't be nearly as powerful as they could be. As they should be at all times really, now that they knew what they were dealing with.

She took a step away from him, and when he moved to regain that distance, his foot slipped out from under him, and he ended up on his ass, on a layer of ice beneath his feet. Cyrus and Eliza were roaring with laughter, and Scarlett leaned down over him with a wicked glint in her eyes.

"Tell me about empty threats again," she purred.

His hand snapped out to pull her down with him, but she leapt back with a fiendish laugh, sending those very shadows he was so damn worried about raking sensuously down his face, his neck, his torso. It was as though her own fucking fingers were dragging lower and lower.

"It's no wonder you aren't getting anywhere if this is how you spend your *training hours*," Cyrus said. "Although, I shouldn't really be surprised considering the things I walked in on during your magic training in Solembra."

Scarlett sent him a droll look, throwing him a vulgar gesture.

Sorin had managed to get back to his feet, melting the ice beneath him, as Eliza said, "He is always going to go easy on you. He physically cannot intentionally hurt you. It would go against the twin flame bond."

"He didn't go easy on me when he was training me in Baylorin," Scarlett grumbled.

"That's because he was trying to deny his feelings for you and thought torturing you would help," came a voice from the far shadows of the pit. A voice of silk and honey. And Scarlett whirled towards it.

Nuri appeared from a shadowed corner of the pit, and Scarlett was racing towards her. The two females embraced each other, their grips fierce. Nuri was clad in her usual black, gloves in place, but her hood was down, letting Sorin see her eyes close as she held Scarlett close.

"Where the fuck have you been?" Scarlett hissed at the female.

"Here and there," Nuri answered, neither of them willing to be the first to release the other.

She had asked Sorin about her every day. And every day his answer had been the same: Nuri had been busy tending to the children, making trips to the markets for necessities for them. But even he had been surprised the female hadn't carved out some amount of time to come see Scarlett. He was told she'd checked in on her, on Cassius too. But somehow the two females always managed to miss each other.

"I know what 'here and there' means," Scarlett replied softly.

"It is fine, Sister," Nuri answered, finally pulling back, a half-smile tugging at the corner of her lips. She took a step back, drawing her scimitars from where they always sat at her sides. A wicked glint entered her eyes that Sorin recognized all too well. "Shall we?"

Scarlett drew the sword from her back, then pulled a long knife from her belt.

"None of your fancy magic tricks, Sister," Nuri said, pointing one of her scimitars at her.

"No biting, *Sister*," Scarlett crooned back.

The two had already begun circling each other, their eyes assessing the other's movements, watching for weaknesses that may have arisen since they last sparred.

"No coddling from your underlings," Nuri countered, with a nod of her head in the direction of Sorin, Eliza, and Cyrus.

"I did not realize you needed so many rules in place to best me," Scarlett taunted.

At her words, Nuri bared her teeth, her fangs absent, as she shot forward with the speed of her kind, but Scarlett was ready for it, meeting her blade with her own.

"Are we going to let this go?" Cyrus asked, his eyes on the females.

"I dare you to try and interfere with *that*," Eliza replied, her grey eyes bright with excitement at watching two of the Wraiths of Death spar.

Sorin crossed his arms, leaning back against the stone wall of the pit. They'd made their way over here, trying to give the females space as they'd reconnected. Every primal instinct in him was roaring at him to go fight for her, but considering he'd seen Scarlett pin the female to the ground with a dagger through the forearm, he wasn't inclined to intervene at this particular moment.

"She can handle it," Sorin finally said, a soft smile lifting his lips as he watched her duck to avoid a blow, before landing a clean kick to Nuri's side and causing the Night Child to curse.

"She's leaving her right side unguarded too long," Cyrus murmured.

"I noticed," Sorin said, having caught the same small mistake Cyrus was referencing. "If Nuri doesn't capitalize on it, I will the next time we spar."

Cyrus snorted a laugh. "She's not wrong, you know. You're going too easy on her. You need to push her, Sorin. Mikale won't go easy. Alaric won't—"

"I am well aware of what they will do to her," Sorin snarled, embers flickering in his vision. She'd told him a little more over the last few days. Things that had been said to her while she was chained to a wall. Things that had been done to her when she was growing up, when she had been training to become Death's Maiden. But not enough. Not enough for him to know her the way Cassius would. The way maybe even the Night Child she was currently sparring with would. In time, he would learn all those stories, but time was not a luxury they currently had.

He lurched forward as Nuri's blade skimmed across Scarlett's shoulder. If it weren't for the leathers she was wearing, it would have been a deep slice into her skin. Cyrus's hand clamped onto his shoulder, reminding him that this was a sparring match between friends.

"These are new!" Scarlett hissed in outrage, lunging forward.

"Obviously," Nuri drawled, dancing backwards from her attack. "They need to be scuffed up a little."

A soft snarl came from Scarlett as she attacked again, but she didn't let up this time. She came for her again and again, forcing Nuri to block and retreat. And when the Night Child tried to dodge her next strike, Scarlett's knife snagged on the collar of her tunic.

Nuri dropped one of her scimitars, reaching for a dagger instead, as Scarlett suddenly said, "I yield." Her weapons hit the ground, and Sorin was running because Nuri didn't have time to slow her attack. Her dagger was still coming down, and Scarlett was stepping into the blow.

"What the fuck is she doing?" Cyrus ground out, keeping pace beside him, but they wouldn't be fast enough.

They were both raising their hands to use flames to stop what was about to happen, but shadows latched onto Nuri's wrist, halting the dagger a mere inch from piercing Scarlett's throat. Scarlett just reached up, brushing the dagger aside as though it were an annoying insect. Nuri had started laughing like the insane female she was, and Scarlett was reaching towards her.

Sorin opened his mouth to yell, to rage, to say *something*, but nothing came out, because what the fuck had she been thinking? He didn't even know where to start.

Another raging female didn't seem to have that problem, though. Eliza pushed between him and Cyrus, gripping Scarlett's arm and spinning her around. "Have you lost your godsdamn mind?"

"I'm fine," Scarlett said distractedly, trying to turn back to Nuri, who had managed to stop laughing like a godsdamn maniac. She was watching Scarlett with curiosity, but Eliza wasn't done.

"You are clearly not fucking fine," Eliza snapped. "You nearly had a dagger shoved into your throat."

"But I didn't," she replied, her eyes fixed on Nuri.

"Scarlett," Sorin ground out from between his teeth.

She shrugged out of Eliza's grip, turning back to fully face Nuri. Her hand came up to wrap around a necklace that had slipped out when Scarlett's sword had snagged on the female's collar.

A spirit amulet.

On a white chain with silver running through it.

"You have had this for years," Scarlett murmured to herself.

"Yes. Since it was gifted to me by Alaric," Nuri said, watching Scarlett as carefully as the rest of them were now.

Scarlett's eyes flew to hers. "Alaric gave you this?"

"Yes, when I was a child. I was ecstatic because it was like yours and Juliette's," Nuri replied.

Scarlett's eyes went wide at that, and she turned, dropping to her knees and beginning to write in the dirt.

"Not this again," Cyrus muttered.

Sorin lowered to his knees beside her, relieved to find her writing words in the dirt instead of Marks.

On one side she had listed out various bloodlines: Shifters, Night Children, Fae, Witches, Mortals, Avonleyans. Across from that were names: Tula, Nuri, ?, Juliette, ?, Me.

"A child of each possesses them on a chain of wind-kissed stone," Sorin muttered.

Scarlett looked up at him, her eyes bright with excitement. "They have always been trying to get home."

"They have always been trying to get to you," he said. He could hear the tentative awe in his tone.

"Alaric didn't even know what he had," she whispered, before a laugh of disbelief slipped from her lips. "I was around nearly all of them for years. *Years.* So was he, and he had no godsdamn idea."

"Are you saying our amulets are some of these keys?" Nuri demanded from where she still stood. Eliza and Cyrus were looking on, shock on their features.

"Yes," Scarlett answered, glancing up at her before going back to the list. "If you'd been around these last few days, you'd know of my suspicions."

"I have been around. Taking care of the children while you've been playing all-important queen," Nuri bit back.

A snarl had Sorin's lip curling up, and Cyrus had taken a step towards Nuri. One look at her face, and Sorin knew she was only half-joking. Nuri just gave him a taunting grin.

Scarlett ignored the verbal jab though, her attention completely returned to her list. "I had one. Tula had one and is a full-blooded Shifter. Juliette had the Witch key, and Nuri possess the Night Child one. That leaves a mortal key and Fae key, but that is only six bloodlines. There are seven keys. What could the other be?"

"Maraan?" Sorin supplied.

"I cannot imagine Eliné would have entrusted a key to a Maraan. That would be a little counterproductive," she mused, sitting back on her heels.

Nuri had walked around them, stopping beside the writing. "Tula had one of these?"

"Yes," Scarlett answered. Sorin could tell by her tone she was only half-listening, lost in thought like she often got when she was working something out. "She found it hidden in the Lairwood House the night she was held captive."

"The night Juliette died?" Nuri clarified.

Scarlett's eyes flashed to hers before quickly darting away once more. "Yes."

"So where is Juliette's now?" Nuri asked. "She must have been wearing it that night, and Sybil never got to see her body . . ."

Scarlett's eyes closed, and she tried to hide the slight grimace, but he saw it. He saw that it still cut deep, even though Juliette was, for all intents and purposes, still alive.

Scarlett . . .

Her eyes opened, locking on his. *I'm fine,* came down the bond. Then she cleared her throat before she said, her voice quiet, "I do not know. My best guess would be somewhere in the Lairwood House? We need to find out what Mikale did with her body after that night."

"And the other two?" Cyrus asked. Sorin glanced up to find his Second had gone to the same place his wife had, trying to work out a puzzle with the answer just out of reach.

"I need to think on them," Scarlett answered, pushing to her feet. "The others were all close. I've been around them for years."

Sorin had gotten to his own feet. He was about to ask if she had any ideas, when a loud roar had them all reaching for weapons. The sound shook the pit, small pebbles shaking loose from the stone archway. Sorin was reaching for Scarlett, pulling her into his side, while Cyrus and Eliza closed in around them. Even Nuri had moved to their back, her fangs snapping out.

Another loud roar pierced the air, and shadows were swirling around them all, shields of flames joining them.

"What is that?" Scarlett murmured, her eyes darting around, searching for the source as intently as the rest of them.

"I do not know," Sorin answered. "Nothing should be able to get in here. Not with the wards around the Black Halls."

Another shadow fell over them that had them all looking towards the sky, where the sun was being blotted out by something massive gliding on black wings. It banked, clearly circling around to come back to them, and Sorin was pulling Scarlett in tighter.

"Is that . . ." Scarlett asked, the shock on her face matching what Sorin was feeling.

"That is not possible," Cyrus muttered, but he had lowered his weapons, just as Sorin and Eliza had.

The ground shuddered around them when a huge, scaled body landed on the ground several feet away from them. Sorin gripped Scarlett's waist, steadying her as she stumbled at the rocking of the earth beneath their feet.

There was a snort and huff that had smoke furling from the giant reptile's nostrils. Its vertical pupils were surrounded by glowing yellow irises, and they were fixed on them. It had to be at least twenty feet long, and the creature tucked its wings to its side as its barbed tail thumped the ground behind him.

"It's a dragon," Scarlett breathed.

"It is Ranvir," Sorin corrected quietly.

"You know the dragon?" Scarlett asked, looking up at him.

"He is Sargon's spirit animal. His brother, Ejder, is Arius's," Sorin replied.

"Why is he here?" Scarlett asked, disentangling herself from his grasp, her head tilting as she studied the dragon before them.

"My best guess is that he is here for Cassius," Sorin answered.

Scarlett's gaze swung back to him. "You think he is Cassius's spirit animal?"

Sorin shrugged, the others standing in shocked silence around them. "It will not surprise me if he is."

Scarlett's gaze went back to the reptile. His deep green scales glinted in the sun, and it huffed again. She took a step forward, but Sorin gripped her arm, halting her.

"What are you doing?"

"I'm going to say hello," she answered, looking back at him.

"You are not touching a dragon, Scarlett," Sorin replied, giving her an incredulous look.

She looked back to Ranvir. He was watching her intently, and he lowered his head slightly, as if inviting her to pet him. "I think he'd like it," she said to Sorin, trying to tug her arm from his grip. "Maybe he would take me flying."

"By the gods," Sorin swore. "No, Love. You are not riding a spirit animal."

"But I've ridden Rinji," she argued.

"Yes, but Rinji is Luan's spirit animal, and he was with us." "So if Cassius is with me, I can ride Ranvir?"

"He is not here for Cassius. Not in the way you are thinking," came the High Witch's stern voice. They turned to find her standing several paces behind them, her lips thinned as she looked upon the dragon before them.

"How do you know?" Scarlett asked, her gaze returning to the dragon, who was watching them all carefully.

"Bonding takes place in Shira Forest, not here," Hazel replied, finally moving forward. "But Ranvir is already bonded to another. Unless he has passed, Ranvir is not here for a bonding ritual. However, his business here is likely Cassius."

Scarlett tried to take a step forward again, but Sorin's hand tightened on her arm. She shot him a glare over her shoulder.

"He will not hurt the queen, Prince," the High Witch said. "He knows who she is. He knows whose blood runs in her veins."

"And whose blood is that?" Sorin asked tightly at the same time that Scarlett asked, "What business does he have with Cassius?"

The High Witch seemed to glare at the dragon before she met Scarlett's gaze. "Ranvir is here on behalf of the one he is bonded to."

"And who is that?" Scarlett pressed.

The High Witch's lips pursed once more before she answered, "Cassius's father."

"What?" Scarlett demanded, jerking free of Sorin's hold and closing the distance between herself and the High Witch. Eliza and

Cyrus tensed beside him, clearly still as leery of the High Witch as Sorin was, despite what she said about being close with Eliné.

"Cassius's father was unaware of his existence. Ranvir's arrival would tell me that is no longer the case. Since he cannot come here himself, he sent his pet."

Sorin choked down the laugh at her referring to a giant dragon that belonged to the god of courage and war as a pet.

Scarlett started to say something else, but she stopped short, as if suddenly realizing something. "Why are you down here? You haven't left Cassius's side since we arrived."

For the first time Sorin could ever remember, a small smile lifted on the High Witch's lips. "I came to find you. He is waking."

Scarlett went preternaturally still. For a few brief seconds, it seemed she did not even breathe, but those seconds gave Sorin time to reach her side where he barely caught her hand before she Traveled from the pits.

CHAPTER 33
SCARLETT

Scarlett sat cross-legged on the bed beside Cassius, holding his hand in hers. He still hadn't opened his eyes, but his body shifted slightly every once in a while. Small groans would escape him whenever he did.

Hazel had not returned, giving them privacy for when he did wake. She was grateful for that; although she knew it must be agony for the High Witch not to be in here right now. Sorin was here, though, keeping her company until he woke. Not letting her get lost in her own thoughts.

Mikale hadn't been back in her dreams since that night when she couldn't fall back to sleep and Sorin had found her on the beach. And even with Sorin sitting on a chair that he'd dragged over beside the bed, all she could think about was how many times would she have to do this? How many times would she be sitting beside Cassius, waiting for him to wake up, because he'd tied his life to her own when he was ten years old? How many times before he didn't wake up?

"Stop," Sorin ordered softly, pulling her from those spiraling thoughts.

"Maybe we can find a way to reverse the Guardian Mark in the books we're looking through," she mused, brushing her thumb along the back of Cassius's hand and fighting off the exhaustion already trying to settle over her. It wasn't even midday yet.

"Maybe we should wait until he is awake to see if he even wants to do such a thing," Sorin countered. "I think you should let him have that choice."

"Of course it will be his choice," Scarlett said. "But if he wants an out, I want it to be ready for him."

"And if he does not want an out? If he chooses to stay bonded to you as your Guardian, will you let him? Or will you try and talk him out of it? As you have continually tried to talk us out of our own choices to stay by your side since you have returned?"

"That's . . ." She paused, pursing her lips before she finished. "That's not fair of you to say."

"What is not fair, Scarlett, is for you to want to make your own choices, for you to want the freedom of that for everyone, but then for you to not accept the choices others make," Sorin replied.

Her gaze fell to her hand locked around Cassius's. "I don't want to talk about this right now," she said softly.

Sorin tsked under his breath, muttering, "Of course you don't."

She tried to hide the flicker of hurt that went down the bond at his words, but he hadn't taught her how to shield against that yet. Either he hadn't had time or hadn't wanted to. She wasn't entirely sure which one.

"I didn't—"

"Don't try to take it back now, Sorin. You did mean it."

"You are right," he conceded. "I did, but I could have worded it differently."

"You don't need to tiptoe around me. I can handle when you need to say things to me."

"It is not that I think I need to tiptoe around you," he said. "I know you can handle far more than most can. I often forget how young you truly are when I think of how much you have faced in your short life. But as I have previously said, I want to be your reprieve from the weights of your world. I do not wish to add to them."

"That is not always an option," she shot back.

"Obviously," he replied. "But when the option is available, I wish to take it, rather than add to the burdens you are already trying to carry because you refuse to let others help."

"No tiptoeing there, hmm?" she muttered.

A low groan from Cassius had her attention shifting back to him before Sorin said anything in reply. Fingers curled around her own, squeezing slightly, and her heart stuttered as the hope that he was finally waking grew in her chest. His eyelids were fluttering, his mouth parting, and a few seconds later, a garbled, "Seastar?" came from his mouth.

Tears were instantly on her cheeks as she pushed up onto her knees to lean over him. "I'm here, Cass," she whispered, trying to get her tears under control.

It took another minute before his eyes opened fully, his good eye darting around the room before settling on her. And the world seemed to still as they just looked at each other. Then Scarlett was laughing through her tears, and a smile was lifting up on Cassius's lips as she was lurching forward and into his arms. She tried to be careful of where his injuries had been, but he pulled her close, his face burrowing into her hair.

"You held on, Seastar," he whispered.

"So did you," she answered into his chest.

Rustling behind her had her pulling back to look up at Sorin. He merely bent over her and pressed a quick kiss to her temple before he said, "I will let you two have some time. Let me know if you need anything."

She smiled up at him with gratitude. He wasn't even out the door yet when she was crawling under the blankets and settling into Cassius's side, his arm wrapping tightly around her and holding her close.

"Tell me what happened," he rasped, his throat dry from lack of use. "Let me get you some water," Scarlett said, trying to pull away from him, but his grip only tightened around her. "In a moment. Just . . . In a moment."

"Okay," she whispered, relaxing back into him.

The minutes ticked by as they sat in silence, soaking in each other's presence. She soaked in all of it— the unlabored rise and fall of his chest, the steady beat of his heart, the warmth of his body against hers.

"I thought I was going to lose you," she finally breathed.

"I did not think I would ever lay eyes on you again on this side of the Veil," he admitted. "I suppose eye would be a better word choice."

Scarlett tilted her head up to look at his eyes. One chocolate brown eye looked back at her, while the other was milky white and cloudy, the brown color so dull it was hardly visible. "I'm sorry," she whispered.

"If that is the only permanent injury I am left with after all of that, I will not complain, Seastar," he replied, squeezing her gently.

"I do not know which injuries are permanent and which will still heal yet. Your eye is permanent, yes, because of the blade used according to Hazel, but the others . . . She will know better than I will," Scarlett replied, reaching up and running her fingers down the side of his face.

"Is Hazel a healer?" Cassius asked, shifting slightly.

Scarlett bit her lip before clearing her throat. "Hazel is a Witch. The High Witch. She is, for all intents and purposes, the queen of the Witches. And yes, she is a Healer. She actually trained Eliné."

"She trained your mother?"

"Eliné is not my mother," Scarlett answered. Then she took a deep breath before she added, "But Hazel is yours."

"This High Witch is . . . my mother?" Cassius repeated.

Scarlett nodded. "She has not left your side since I brought you here."

"And here is?" he asked, looking around the room.

"The Black Halls. I guess you could say it's my palace or castle or whatever. It's at the southern part of the continent. At the mouth of the Tykese River," she replied, fiddling with a loose thread on the blanket.

"This is not where Sorin brought me before?"

"No. That was his palace in Solembra. In the Fire Court."

She felt him nod, and she glanced back up at him. "What are you thinking?"

He let loose a long breath, grimacing as he adjusted his body again. "I don't even know where to begin to be honest. Just tell me . . . how you found her. Start there."

Scarlett got up to get him water as she told him of Hazel, how they'd worked out who he was, and who he was to Hazel. She told him of the brief history Hazel had shared and how Eliné had apparently helped get him out of the Witch Kingdoms to save him.

"And my father?" Cassius asked when she finished speaking.

"Hazel has hinted at who he is, but she's about as helpful as Juliette is sometimes," Scarlett grumbled.

Cassius stiffened. "Juliette?"

And then Scarlett was telling him of how she had died but hadn't died fully, of how she didn't completely understand it, but that Juliette was now the Oracle that spoke in prophecies and riddles that were absolutely no help whatsoever.

"I don't know what to say to any of this," Cassius finally said. While she'd been speaking, she had helped him sit up, propping pillows against the headboard of the bed, and now she sat cross-legged beside him once more, holding a glass of water and making him take sips every once in a while.

"There is so much more, Cassius. So much to tell you, but it's...a lot to take in. And, if you're okay with it, I know Hazel would really like to see you," Scarlett said, biting her lip as she watched him carefully. She would never force this if he wasn't ready.

"The woman saved my life and hasn't left my side in days. I suppose I owe her a thank you at the very least," he said, but there was a touch of bitterness to his tone.

"Cass, you owe her nothing," Scarlett said gently. "If you are not ready to meet her, then she will not enter this room without your permission."

"I understand why she had Eliné take me away, but also . . . If she is this High Witch . . . She couldn't order my safety? And why didn't Eliné ever say anything? About any of this?" Cassius said.

"I don't know," Scarlett admitted. "I've found so many answers since coming here, but I've also gained even more questions."

"You've gotten tattoos since coming here, too," he said, nodding towards her left hand.

She smiled softly at the Mark that ran down her thumb and first two fingers. "Tattoos. A crown. A husband," she said casually with a slight shrug. "Nothing too exciting."

"I heard," Cassius said with a knowing smirk.

"Yes," she said with an exaggerated sigh, "the Prick of Fire himself."

"Gods, I hope you call him that to his face," Cassius said with a chuckle that had him immediately grimacing.

"Not yet," she mused. "But he did recently challenge me to come up with more creative names to call him." He motioned her closer, and she nestled back into his side, slipping her legs under the blankets.

"I will meet Hazel in a bit," he finally said when she was settled. "I just need a little time to adjust to everything."

"You should eat something."

"Are you going to feed me, Seastar?" he teased.

"No," she groused, poking him in the rib. He hissed at her as she said, "But I know a prince who will bring food up here."

"Aditya waiting on me?" Cassius mused.

"Mhmm," she hummed.

"That is something I wouldn't mind seeing."

And a half hour later, Sorin was coming into the room, a tray of food floating along on a flame next to him, keeping it warm. The door clicked shut behind him, and he lowered it to a small table off to the side.

"How are you feeling, Cassius?" he asked, immediately beginning to fill a plate.

"I've been better," Cassius answered. "But you got her out. That's all that matters."

"That is certainly not all that matters," Scarlett cut in.

Sorin made his way to the bed, two plates in his hands. He passed one to Cassius before handing one to Scarlett. "You need to eat too, Love."

Scarlett rolled her eyes but took a bite of the sandwich on her plate while giving him a sarcastic smile.

Sorin gave her an unimpressed smirk before he said, "You should also *feed*."

"Godsdammit, Sorin," Scarlett snapped, throwing the sandwich at him.

Sorin laughed at her, swatting the food aside before it smacked him in his face. It landed with a dull plop on the floor. "Maybe your Guardian can convince you if I cannot."

Cassius was looking back and forth between them, a mixture of confusion and amusement on his features.

"You're a prick. You've just been waiting to get in here to say something about this, haven't you?" Scarlett seethed.

He just offered her another mocking smile that told her he was not even a little sorry.

"Something you need to fill me in on, Seastar?" Cassius asked, taking a bite of his sandwich.

"It can wait," she replied with a pointed look at Sorin.

"Can it though?" Sorin asked. "Your eyes are almost back to blue."

"I have blue eyes, Sorin."

"When your power reserves are full, you do not."

Cassius set his sandwich down. "I think you need to fill me in."

"No. I am not going to sit here and let the two of you gang up on me about this," she huffed.

Sorin shrugged. "You can tell him, or I will."

"Sorin," she snarled.

"Scarlett," he parroted.

Stop this, she seethed down the bond. *Stop this, and I will . . . figure something out tonight.*

Sorin arched a brow. *Not good enough, Princess.*

She narrowed her eyes. *If we don't figure something out, I will . . . feed.* Her lip curled up in disgust at the very thought of doing this.

"I'm not sure what I am witnessing, but it's awkward," Cassius said, continuing to glance between them.

Scarlett waved a hand in dismissal. "It's our bond. We can speak to each other in our minds."

"That's weird *and* awkward," Cassius replied.

"Even if that part of our argument is settled, Cassius still needs to know about feeding, Scarlett," Sorin said pointedly. "He will be directly affected by such a thing in more ways than one."

"I am aware, Sorin," she sighed in annoyance. "I would have gotten around to it eventually."

"Now seems as good a time as any."

"And here I thought Cyrus was the busybody of the family," she grumbled under her breath. She ignored Sorin's droll glare, turning back to Cassius. "The things we need to discuss . . . They're big, Cass. If you need to rest for a while, I understand."

"I'm fine, Scarlett. Sorin appears insistent."

"That's because he is an overbearing ass, but it *can* wait if you need to rest."

Cassius rested his head back against the pillows, his eyes drifting closed. "Speak, Scarlett."

She scowled at him, but let the order slide, considering he'd just woken up from nearly dying.

"You asked about your father," she started.

That had his eyes opening again, and his head snapping back up. "You said he was hinted at but did not know him."

"I don't," she said quickly, "but I know where he is from. According to Hazel, he is from the same place my parents are—Avonleya."

Cassius didn't say anything. He just stared at her, not moving. Not even blinking.

"Cassius?" she ventured.

"You are saying that . . . my father is Avonleyan? That your parents . . . That *you* are Avonleyan?"

"Yes," she answered. "My mother was not Eliné."

"Who are your parents?"

"I don't know. I just know they are Avonleyan. From what I've been told by various people anyway."

Sorin had moved wordlessly back to the chair he'd previously occupied, casually watching everything play out.

And obviously making sure she didn't omit anything.

Scarlett cleared her throat. "The thing that Mother Hen here is worried about, is that Avonleyans depend on Fae to keep their magic reserves fueled. The Fae refill their power like mortals recharge— through rest and food. The Avonleyans do so via the Fae. By feeding off of their magic."

"And you are refusing to do this? To feed to keep your power levels full?"

"Yes," Sorin cut in.

"*No*," Scarlett growled, shooting him a glare. He arched a brow. "I mean, yes, but because I do not need to right now."

"You mean you do not want to," Sorin supplied.

"No, Sorin, that is not what I mean," she retorted.

Cassius glanced between the two again before his gaze settled on Sorin. "Say what she isn't, Aditya."

Scarlett crossed her arms in a huff.

"She needs to find a Source to draw from, but we do not know what that means. Until we figure it out, the only way to feed to keep her power fully replenished is to drink from a Fae. Like the Night Children do," Sorin explained.

"Ah," was Cassius's reply.

"That is all you have to say?" Sorin asked, both brows arching this time.

"I can understand how that would be . . ."

"Gross? Disgusting? Repugnant?" Scarlett supplied.

"No one asked for a vocabulary lesson, Scarlett," Sorin said.

"No one asked for your opinion on this matter, yet here we are."

Sorin sighed, running a hand down his face. "Listen," he said, addressing Cassius once more. "We are facing enemies we know nothing about. Her shadows and her white flames are Avonleyan gifts and are her greatest advantage in a battle. She needs to keep her power reserves full at all times, even if that means feeding like a Night Child until we figure out this Source issue."

"I agree with you," Cassius said.

"I do appreciate you two speaking of me like I am not in the room," Scarlett cut in.

Sorin ignored her. "If she does not, if she lets herself get too weak, she will start drawing power from you which will impede your ability to protect her."

"Sorin!" Scarlett cried.

Sorin leaned forward in his chair. "Everything is getting laid out here, Scarlett. This will not be like the border where you withhold information until you have everything figured out. Furthermore, all of this directly affects Cassius. He deserves to know."

"You could be more tactful about it," she muttered.

Sorin sat back. "He is a Commander in an army. I assure you, he prefers bluntness over tactfulness."

"He speaks truth, Seastar. You know this," Cassius said. "Why will you draw power from me?"

Scarlett filled him in on the Guardian Mark, how they got it, and what it meant for him. When she finished with the details, she added, "You made this choice as a child, Cass. If it is something you no longer want, we will find a way to sever it."

"Why would I no longer want it?"

"Because it requires you to keep me safe at all costs. To put my well-being above all others, above your own life."

"How is that any different from the last fifteen years?"

"Because it was not your choice."

"Of course it was," Cassius said, picking up a piece of cheese and taking a bite.

She shook her head. "Maybe it feels like it was, but it was this Guardian link all this time. Driving you to protect me."

"I disagree. I think this Guardian thing simply made my job . . . easier," Cassius said, popping the rest of the cheese into his mouth. "It certainly clears up a lot of things."

"It is a job that was forced on you," she argued.

"Doesn't sound like it. From what you told me, I wanted this."

"Of course it sounded exciting as a *child*, Cassius. You didn't understand—"

"I didn't understand that I was tying my life to that of a child I already fiercely protected? I didn't understand that I was being asked to give my life for yours should it ever be asked? Even though I was already willing to do just that? Even as a *child*?"

Tears were pooling in her eyes, and Scarlett blinked them back, looking down at her hands. "You were forced into this, Cassius," she said, her voice little more than a whisper. "You didn't want to drink from that chalice, and they made you."

"Would you like to do the entire thing again so you will know I am choosing to become your Guardian of my own free will, then?"

Her head flew up, her gaze meeting his. His face was hard, completely serious.

"You and I have always been more, Scarlett," he said, his features softening. "We have always been more than friends. We have always been more than family. Even as children, even before this Mark, we were more."

"We are soulmates," she said, a tear slipping free. "Our fates have always been intertwined."

"Then I fail to see why we are having this discussion," he said, settling back into the pillows once more.

She opened her mouth to argue further, but Sorin cut her off.

"He prefers the darkness, Scarlett. Let him stay in it," he said gently. "Let us stay in your darkness."

"Okay," she breathed. "Okay."

"You're sure you are ready?" Scarlett asked from her spot near the window in Cassius's room. He was coming out of the bathing room, Sorin nearby in case he needed help. Yesterday Cassius had leaned on him every time he'd needed to walk. Today Cassius was insisting on doing everything himself.

Hazel had given Scarlett instructions on tonics to take to make sure he continued to heal, and Cyrus had delivered a small glass of blood for him. Scarlett had turned away while he'd drank that down.

As for her deal to "figure something out" with Sorin . . . She'd conveniently fallen asleep before such a discussion could be had, but she knew he hadn't forgotten. She knew he'd be bringing it up again, likely at the most inconvenient time.

"Yes, Scarlett," Cassius sighed, pausing by an armchair and gripping the back. His breathing was heavy.

"You should let Sorin help you."

"You should feed," Cassius shot back.

"You should fuck off," Scarlett parroted.

Sorin chuckled, stepping forward and letting Cassius throw an arm around his shoulders. "Do not worry, Cassius. She will feed by the end of the day. I swear it."

"You can both fuck all the way off," she muttered, going to the bed and adjusting sheets and pillows before Cassius was lowering back onto the mattress.

He had just gotten settled when there was a sharp knock on the door.

Scarlett glanced at Cassius. He swallowed thickly before nodding his head.

Sorin opened the door, and the High Witch entered, stopping just over the threshold. Her sharp, angular features were tight, but her violet eyes were bright when they landed on Cassius. She had stopped wearing her witchsuit after the first few days here, opting instead for fitted black pants and black tunics. Her brown hair was pulled back in a tight braid that ran down her back. She stood rigidly, her hands at her sides.

Cassius had gone utterly still where he sat in the bed, and Scarlett had to wonder if he was even breathing.

"You good, Cass?" she asked quietly, reaching over and squeezing his hand.

The action seemed to jar something in him, and he pushed out a long breath before nodding mutely.

Scarlett cleared her throat. "This is Hazel Hecate, the High Witch."

"You are my mother?" Cassius asked. She was sure no one else could hear it, but she heard the slight tremor in his voice.

"I am," Hazel said.

"You . . . had me sent away."

A slight wince crossed her features, but it was gone just as quickly. "For your protection, yes," Hazel confirmed.

"And my father?"

"You look like him," Hazel said. That was a hint of longing in her voice, her eyes drinking in all of Cassius's features. "You sound like him too."

Scarlett squeezed his hand again. "He . . . Does he know?"

"He did not know of your existence until you were brought here, out of the enchantments that surround the mortal kingdoms. They veiled you in a way, but bringing you here alerted him. He sent Ranvir to confirm," Hazel answered.

"Then why didn't he send Ranvir when Cassius was in Solembra?" Scarlett asked.

Hazel glanced briefly in her direction. "When was that?"

"Months ago. He was there for a few hours."

"Then likely not long enough for him to sense his blood across such a distance," Hazel replied.

"Where is he?" Cassius asked.

"I would assume in Avonleya. If he were outside those wards, he would have come for you himself."

Scarlett heard Cassius suck in a sharp breath. "He would have come if he'd known?"

"He cannot. Just as the others cannot leave that land, but yes, Cassius. If he could have come to you, he would have," Hazel answered.

"And you?"

"I have wondered about you every day since you left my arms. I have waited for this day for twenty-five years. I could not be more proud of how you have survived, of the person you have become."

"No thanks to you," he replied bitterly.

"Correct," she agreed. "I can take no credit for anything you are, other than for your immense gifts."

"Because that is what the Witches place value on, right?"

Hazel was quiet for several long moments. "Yes. Witches value power above all else, like most magic-wielders of this world."

"That is how you were able to justify abandoning a baby to the mortal kingdoms?"

"I will not apologize for saving your life."

"Will you apologize for anything?"

Scarlett was about to intervene, but Sorin noticed because he spoke down their bond.

Let this play out, Scarlett.

I did not anticipate Cassius reacting this way. He's always so . . . calm and collected. With you maybe, Sorin replied. *He can be just as big of a prick as any of us, and his feelings on this are valid.*

I'm not saying they aren't, but—

"Do I wish things could have been different? I do," Hazel was saying.

"You are the High Witch. You could have decreed such a thing," Cassius retorted.

"Things are never that simple, Cassius," Hazel replied. "Your own queen can attest to that."

"You didn't even try," Cassius spat.

"What do you think I did while I carried you in my womb?" Hazel demanded.

Cassius fell silent, his tongue pressing into his cheek, and a thick tension settled over the room.

"So . . . Hazel needs to check some of your injuries," Scarlett said when things started to become far too awkward.

Cassius nodded, and Hazel came to his side.

"The one on your leg. How is it feeling?" she asked, pulling the blankets back.

"Like there is still a dagger in it," Cassius grunted.

"I was afraid of that." Her hand hovered over the spot he'd been stabbed by both Veda and Alaric. Faint white light began emanating, and Cassius started at the magic.

"Can I do that?" he asked after another bout of silence.

"More than likely, yes," Hazel answered. "When Avonleyan bloodlines cross with another magical bloodline, the offspring will have gifts from both. However, the more dominant power will be stronger."

"You were more powerful than my father?"

Hazel glanced at him briefly before focusing back on her magic. "It depends on what kind of power you value. In terms of healing and spell-weaving, yes."

"What are the other gifts of the Avoneleyans?" Scarlett asked. She'd climbed onto the bed, sitting beside Cassius, Sorin having taken a seat in his chair.

"We are unable to speak of them," she replied. "To speak of what we know."

"Convenient," Cassius muttered.

"It sounds similar to how we are unable to speak of the Fae Royals in the mortal kingdoms," Sorin chimed in.

"Similar, yes," Hazel agreed. "They wanted their secrets kept. This was how they went about it."

"So it is more than the Bargain Mark on your arm?" Scarlett asked.

"Yes. The Bargain Mark was from your mother and relates to you specifically," she answered. The light faded from her palm, and she turned her attention to Cassius's side where he'd nearly bled out. "You need to find a Source. You both do."

"So I've been told," Scarlett muttered.

"Why would I need a Source?" Cassius asked. "I've never exhibited magic like Scarlett."

"The queen is different," Hazel answered. "But you are still half-Avonleyan. You will have at least one of your father's gifts, likely more, and will need full power reserves to utilize them. In addition, your Ward will draw on those power reserves if her life is in danger."

Cassius looked to Scarlett, and she nodded in confirmation.

"How does this Source thing work?" Scarlett asked at the same time that Cassius asked, "What were my father's gifts?"

"Are," Hazel corrected. "What *are* your father's gifts. If Ranvir appeared, he still lives. Those are both excellent questions, and you would do well to find the answers."

"Helpful as always," Scarlett muttered.

"Can you tell me his name?" Cassius asked.

Hazel pulled her hand from his side. Her fingers curled slightly at her sides, and her lips pursed. She exhaled sharply before she said, "Tybalt. Your father's name is Tybalt."

"And my parents?" Scarlett asked.

Hazel shook her head. "I cannot speak of them."

The small kernel of hope that had sprung to life in her chest wilted, and she didn't know why she'd even let it form. Cassius reached for her hand at the same moment she felt Sorin's fingers brush along her lower back.

"Your eye will be permanent," Hazel said, her gaze searching Cassius's face.

"Scarlett told me."

"The wound from your side will take the longest to heal completely. You will need to continue to take Fae blood until you find a Source," she continued. "And your leg will never completely heal, but it will get better. Your magic will stabilize it, however, when you use your magic too much, it will ache and could become a problem."

"Thank you, Hazel," Scarlett said.

"We should go prepare for tonight," Sorin said softly.

"What is tonight?" Cassius asked.

"We are going to visit Callan," Scarlett said. "We need his help to find another one of the keys."

This morning, she'd met with the others and Nuri to discuss the keys. They still had no idea where the Fae or mortal keys were, let alone the missing bloodline. But they knew where the Witch key had last been seen, so they could at least start with that one. The problem was that its last known whereabouts were inside the Lairwood Estate which was warded against her and the Fae. They wouldn't be able to get in undetected, and if it had been discovered and Alaric now had it, she couldn't risk going to the Black Syndicate right now.

"I'm coming with you," Cassius said, immediately throwing back the blankets.

"No, Cass," she said, grabbing his arm to keep in bed. "You cannot even walk to and from the bathing room by yourself. You cannot travel with us to the mortal lands."

"What if you need me?"

"What I need is for you to heal completely before attempting to protect me," Scarlett chided.

"She speaks truth," Hazel said. "Pushing yourself will delay the healing and keep you down longer. I know the Guardian bond is driving you to protect her, but you will not be much help right now."

"You are very blunt," Cassius muttered.

"Feelings and emotions have no place in such decisions," Hazel replied.

"Did you think the same thing when you sent me away?" he asked.

Scarlett had been climbing off the bed and getting to her feet, but she stilled at his words.

"Yes," Hazel answered. "It was the only way I could let you go, and it is the only way I survived the last twenty-five years."

"Yet you are here now. Because what? It is the best *decision*?"

"Because a young queen reminded me that hope is for the dreamers, and while I will not ask for your forgiveness or apologize for my choices, I do dream of knowing my son."

CHAPTER 34
CALLAN

Callan pushed the door shut to his bedroom, not really caring if it latched or not. He'd told his night guard that only Tava was allowed into his suite, but he doubted she'd show up tonight.

He'd only seen her for a few brief moments over the last few days. His mother had been keeping her busy with wedding preparations, and when she wasn't with the queen, her father seemed to be monopolizing her time. Callan didn't particularly like that, considering he was in league with Mikale and Veda, but Drake promised he was keeping an eye on her.

He unbuckled the weapons belt he had around his waist, before toeing off his boots.

"Hello, Callan."

Callan swore as he whirled towards the hearth.

She stood there, the shadows of the crackling fire dancing around her. Then again, maybe they were her shadows. She was clad in black. Just like she'd always been all those nights ago. Weapons in place. Hood up. A silver braid snaking over her shoulder. Toying with a dagger in her hand.

He just stared at her for a long moment, and she stared back from beneath that hood, waiting for him to make the first move apparently.

"You need to stop sneaking in here," he said lamely.

She idly spun the tip of her dagger against her fingertip. "I no longer need to sneak in, Prince."

"I suppose you wouldn't," Callan agreed, his tone tight. "What are you doing here?"

"While I do not need to sneak into the castle, there are other places I do need to get into, that have wards to keep me out," she said. She slid the dagger into . . . wherever she hid all those godsdamn weapons of hers. She crossed her arms and leaned a hip against the wall. "Seems a little backward to me that the castle doesn't have wards at this point, but I digress. It did make this little meeting easier."

"What are you doing here?" he repeated.

"We are in need of your assistance."

"We?"

"You did not think I would let her travel alone, did you?"

Callan whirled again at the dark voice that spoke from the shadows behind him. Sorin stepped into view, a wicked, sensuous smile on his features as he looked Callan up and down once with disinterest.

"Don't be a prick, Sorin," Scarlett sighed, pulling her hood back.

"I have done nothing."

"Look," Scarlett said, drawing Callan's attention back to her. "There is something I need, and we have reason to believe Mikale has it."

"And?" Callan asked.

"*And* there are wards around the Lairwood Estate so I cannot Travel onto the property."

Callan crossed his arms. "I fail to see how this affects me or my people."

"You cannot be serious," Scarlett replied. When Callan just stared stoically at her, she said, "Callan, they . . . They want your throne."

"And we are taking care of that," he answered. "As I told you before, we do not want or need your help."

A knock on the main door had them all going still before it opened a crack, and Tava slipped through along with Drake.

"We came as quickly as we could," Tava said, rushing into the bedroom.

"How did you—" He turned to glare at Scarlett. "You gave her a warning, but not me?"

"I didn't know how amicable you would be," Scarlett replied. "Apparently, it was the right choice."

"What is this about?" Drake asked, pushing the bedroom door closed behind him.

"As I was just telling Callan, we need help retrieving something I believe is at the Lairwood Estate," Scarlett answered.

"What is it?" Tava asked, moving to Callan's side.

"A spirit amulet," Scarlett answered. "It was Juliette's. She would have been wearing it the night she died. We were never given her body. We do not know what Mikale did with it."

"Sybil does not have her personal effects?" Tava asked, reaching up and unbuttoning her cloak. Callan reached for it as she removed it from her shoulders.

"I don't know. If it's not at the Lairwood Estate somewhere, my next guess would be Alaric has it. Maybe he gave it back to Sybil. But I am unable to Travel into the Lairwood Estate, and it would be unwise for me to enter the Black Syndicate right now," Scarlett said.

"Again, I fail to see how this affects me or my people," Callan cut in coldly.

"We believe the amulets to be keys that will enable us to enter Avonleya. Alaric is also trying to get into Avonleya," Scarlett answered.

"And?" Callan said.

Scarlett huffed a sigh of frustration as Sorin silently came to her side. "They've already infiltrated your kingdom, Callan. We do not know what they want, but I can only assume it is nothing good, considering they went to war centuries ago over whatever it is," she said.

"Maybe whatever they are after is not something Avonleya should possess alone or at all," Callan countered.

"Callan." All she said was his name, clearly not knowing what else to say to that.

Delicate fingers landed on his arm, and he found Tava looking up at him. "You said you wished to fight back," she said, her eyes searching his. "Here is a way to do that. Help Sorin and Scarlett find something Mikale and my father clearly want."

He glanced back at Scarlett and Sorin, trying not to roll his eyes at their perfection as they stood there, side-by-side.

"You do not know what they want?"

"Not yet, no," Scarlett answered.

"Will you share the answer when you figure it out?" Scarlett looked up at Sorin, who only shrugged slightly.

"If it will not needlessly endanger anyone, yes," she answered.

"The secrets you keep tend to needlessly endanger everyone," Callan retorted.

Sorin's hands slid into his pockets. "This will be your only warning, Mortal Prince. Speak to her like that again, and her secrets will be the least of your worries." Flames flickered in his eyes, embers seeming to flit amongst his hair.

"How will we know if we find it?" Drake cut in, stepping closer to his sister.

Scarlett reached into a pocket and pulled a necklace out. A black stone spirit amulet hung from an ivory chain.

"The chain will be ivory with silver in it, and the amulet itself will be black."

"You just described an amulet you can buy from any peddler on the street corners," Callan said.

"Whose symbol will be on it?" Tava asked, her fingers reaching for her own necklace and sliding Falein's amulet along the chain.

When Scarlett didn't reply, Callan glanced back at her to find she'd gone still. Her eyes were narrowed on Tava's hand. "Where did you get your necklace, Tava?"

Tava froze next to him. "What?"

"Your spirit amulet? Where did you get it?"

Tava looked at her brother before glancing quickly at Callan. "I found it in a box of what I assumed were my mother's things. Years ago."

Scarlett took a step forward, her hand outstretched. "May I see it?" Tava hesitated before reaching up and unclasping the necklace, placing it in Scarlett's palm. She held it up, studying the jewelry intently.

"She has mixed blood, Scarlett," Sorin was saying.

"I am aware, but if it was her mother's, it could be the mortal key..."

"We would need to take it to the Shira Cliffs with the others," Sorin replied.

"Tomorrow. We should take them all tomorrow after the meeting with Talwyn."

"We are still in the room," Callan cut in dryly.

"Tava, can I take this? I think it may be one of them," Scarlett said, ignoring Callan.

"One of what, exactly?" Tava asked.

"One of seven keys that were hidden by Eliné. Together, they can unlock the wards to Avonleya," she answered. "I believe we have already found three, and if this is another..."

"How can you be sure?" Drake asked.

"I can't," Scarlett said. "Not until I take them to the Wind Court and Princess Ashtine confirms the chains are, in fact, windstone."

"Why do you think my mother would have had one of these keys?" Tava asked, her eyes fixed on the necklace Scarlett still held aloft.

"Because one of each was hidden with a child of each bloodline on the continent. If this was your mother's, it could be the mortal key," Scarlett answered.

"But why would she have it?" Tava pressed.

Scarlett seemed to be debating how to answer. "The best way I can explain it, is that the keys have been trying to get back to me. How the current owners have come into them have all seemed like weird coincidences to be honest, but I am finding they are anything but coincidence."

"Say we find an amulet at the Lairwood Estate," Drake cut in. "How will we know if it is the one you seek?"

"I suppose you won't," Scarlett admitted. "Just bring me any amulet you find with Reselda's symbol."

"And how are we supposed to contact you?" Callan asked.

"Amaré will come to you every evening at this time," Sorin replied. "If you have found something, give him a note to bring to us. If not, you can send him on his way."

"But you have that vial if anything urgent arises," Scarlett added.

He did still have it. Despite everything in him wanting to get rid of the thing, smashing it would only summon her here. That was the last thing he wanted, yet here she stood anyway.

"I know you think you are handling things, Callan," Scarlett said, her tone softening slightly, "but I assure you they are ten steps ahead of you."

"And you do not think they are ahead of you?"

"After being held captive by them for weeks, I know they are," she replied. "That is what terrifies me most. That is what steals my sleep at night. That is why I am here."

"What are we supposed to do? Invite ourselves over for dinner?" Callan asked, pacing on the rug in his sitting room.

Scarlett and Sorin had left minutes ago, disappearing into thin air. She'd given the Tyndells an update on Cassius and the orphans, and she'd listened to any information Tava had for them. Callan hadn't said much after the discussion of the amulets, but he'd listened.

And he'd watched.

Scarlett had seemed tired. Exhausted. He could see it in her eyes. She held herself with the grace of a queen, but her darkness still lingered, even though her shadows never made an appearance. Sorin was discreet, but Callan caught the quick glances he sent her way. The slight tightening of his lips at whatever he saw when he looked at her. And while Sorin's marriage band still adorned his finger, Scarlett's did not. They might resemble perfection on the outside, but something was off.

"You are the Crown Prince. It is not as if they could refuse," Drake replied from where he'd taken a seat at one end of the sofa.

"They would be too suspicious," Tava said, bringing Callan a glass of liquor before taking another to her brother.

"I would be more concerned with where we are even supposed to begin looking if we get in," Drake said with a nod of thanks to Tava as she perched on the arm of the sofa next to him.

"Juliette was killed in the cells beneath the house," Tava said thoughtfully. "If it came loose while they moved her body, it could be anywhere. Anyone could have found it and pocketed it."

"This will be like trying to find a black cat in the dark," Callan said.

"Difficult but not impossible," Tava replied. "The cat's eyes would give it away."

Drake huffed a laugh. "Only you Tava," he murmured.

"I think instead of focusing on getting into the Lairwood Estate, we need to draw Mikale and Veda out so someone can go in and look," Tava continued, ignoring the teasing comment of her brother. Her hand came to her throat, her fingers dragging across her skin, searching for the amulet that had hung there for years.

Callan ran a hand along his jaw, mulling that over. "Mikale would be easy enough. We could plan a hunting outing, but how do we draw out Veda and somehow get away to go into the Estate?"

"I could go in myself—"

"Absolutely not," Drake said before Callan could say the same.

"Then perhaps we wait for an opportunity to present itself," Tava said.

"I would prefer to get this over and done with so we no longer need to deal with them," Callan grumbled.

"Bitterness does not suit you, Prince," Tava commented, taking her brother's glass and swallowing a sip of his liquor.

"Tava," Drake chided.

"It is fine," Callan said with a dismissive wave of his hand. "She is to be my wife after all. She should be able to speak openly."

"When did it stop being a ruse?" Drake asked, his brow arching.

"It didn't," Tava replied, handing the glass back to him.

Drake looked back and forth between Callan and Tava. "We should go, Tava," he said after several beats of awkward silence.

"I need to visit with Callan for a bit," she replied.

"And how are you to get home?"

"I will make sure she gets home safely," Callan said, staring at Tava over his glass as he took another sip. He'd be lying if he said he didn't want to visit with her, even if only for a few minutes. She kept him sane these days, especially in their private moments. She didn't spare his feelings or mind her manners. She was like the queen that had left a little bit ago if he were being honest, albeit much less . . . dark.

"I can wait if I need to," Drake said, pushing to his feet and setting his empty glass on a side table.

"I will be fine, Drake. I will send word. Father is gone on business again anyway. No one will know I was gone," Tava reassured him.

He bent and pressed a light kiss to her cheek. "Be safe, Tava."

"Always," she said with a soft smile, reaching over and squeezing his hand.

"Prince," Drake said with a quick bow.

"Thank you, Drake," Callan replied, motioning dismissal with his glass.

Tava slid into Drake's vacated seat when the chamber door clicked shut behind him. She held Callan's gaze, her head tilted slightly to the side as if she were searching him for something.

"So, little fox, what did we need to discuss?" Callan asked, taking another sip from his nearly empty glass.

A half-smile tugged at her lips, her head coming to rest on her hand where she had her elbow propped on the arm of the sofa. "You know that even once we accomplish this task, you will not be rid of them, do you not?"

"What would we need them for?"

Her lips tipped up again in a knowing smile. "Scarlett is not one you simply forget."

"And if I want to forget her?"

"There's that bitterness again, Prince."

He scowled at her. "Stop calling me that."

She just shrugged at him, and Callan had to fight back the smile that tried to form on his lips at how casual the Lady had become with him.

"I am simply saying that once Scarlett claims you as one of her own, there is no going back. She will forever see you as hers. Not as a lover," she added quickly when he opened his mouth to argue. "But as someone she would give her life to protect. She will always worry about your wellbeing, Callan."

"I am not her subject. I am not her responsibility."

"No. You are so much more. She would consider you family," Tava replied.

Callan could only scoff at that.

Her pale brow arched. "You think I do not know what I am speaking of? You shared a bed with her for more than a year, Callan. And while she may have kept secrets, you cannot tell me she did not make it clear that she would risk her life for those she loves."

"I am not one of them any more," he answered.

Tava tsked under her breath. "Then you have clearly gone blind and deaf, because if you knew where to look and truly listened when she spoke, you would know that is not true."

He gritted his teeth at the response.

"I think what irritates you most is the fact that she does still care so deeply for you, even if it's not how you envisioned," Tava said, her eyes seeming to watch him carefully. "But to be quite frank, and all of your history aside, you would be stupid to alienate yourself from someone so powerful."

"And why is that?"

"Obviously because should you ever need her assistance to protect *your people*, it would be best to be on good terms with those who can literally set the world on fire," she answered. "It is about more than you and her and what you may or may not have been. It is about your kingdom, and if you cannot set your bitterness aside for your people, then you are not the king I thought you were becoming."

"If Drake could hear you speaking to me now," Callan muttered.

"I am to be your wife after all," she replied with a wry smile.

He mulled over some of what she said for a few moments before he asked, "You lived with her for over a year. Did you ever question who or what she was?"

"I knew who she was. I knew the night Cassius brought her to us."

"And you were fine with that? With bringing Death's Maiden into your home?"

"I trust Drake, and he trusts Cassius. And if you had seen her that night . . . In the days and months that followed that night . . ." She swallowed, again absent-mindedly reaching for the spirit amulet that was no longer there. "She may as well have been a spirit of the After."

Callan took another sip of his drink, trying not to think about what had happened that night. What had changed everything.

His own would-be Hand-to-the-King.

Memories of Scarlett asking about Mikale that night surged to the forefront of his mind. How they'd argued on the paths in the gardens. How he'd already known then, before everything happened with Mikale, that she'd already started pulling away from him. How he'd desperately clung to some idealistic vision he'd formed of the two of them ruling over Windonelle together.

"Were you two close while she lived with you?"

Tava seemed to contemplate this for a minute before she shrugged slightly. "We became friends of a sort, but I would not say we were particularly close."

"Yet you still knew more of her life than I did, and we'd shared a bed for over a year before she came to your home."

"I never asked her to be something she's not," Tava replied. "Just as I have never asked the people in the slums to be something they are not. No one should have to change to feel worthy of someone else."

"She changed me," he countered.

"But did she ask you to change, Callan?"

"No, but that doesn't negate the fact."

"Hmm," she hummed.

And that sound. It always came right before she said something that was going to make him reevaluate everything. Some profound statement was about to come from her mouth, and she wouldn't even realize it.

"Do you regret any of the changes that were not forced upon you? Because if you do, then you are, of course, free to go back to how things were. No one is stopping you."

He swirled his glass, the few remaining ice cubes clinking lightly against the sides. He didn't regret how Scarlett had started to open his eyes to those on the streets. He didn't regret rising to the ways she had challenged him, challenged his ways of thinking. He didn't regret trying to help her and innocent children. He supposed as the months had worn on, though, his motivations had shifted from trying to help to trying to gain her favor. How else could he explain missing the ones only Tava seemed to remember? How else could he explain being willing to leave his people to save his own life, when he knew there were threats lurking in the shadows of his streets?

He could blame Scarlett all he liked, but she had told him, said so many times, that his fate did not reside in her darkness. He was the one who had insisted she was wrong. He was the one who had refused to accept her life in the shadows. He was the one who had hoped he could change her in the ways she had changed him. And maybe he had changed her in some ways, just not in the ways he had wanted.

No, the only changes he regretted were the bitterness and animosity that had started growing in his chest, taking root and spreading like a godsdamn wasting disease. The bitterness and the disease were one and the same if he really thought about it. Both ate away at a person until there was nothing but a shell left. One killed the body, the other destroyed the soul.

He'd been so lost in thought, he hadn't heard Tava get up and grab her cloak from his bedroom. She re-emerged now, her fingers working the buttons as she walked. He was on his feet and moving toward her in the next heartbeat. "It is late."

She gave him a half-smile, one of her brows arching in amusement. "That is why I am leaving."

"Stay. Please."

The grin slowly faded. "I cannot stay, Callan."

"It can be just like before. We can say we wanted to have breakfast because we have been unable to spend much time together lately. You can sleep in the bed again. I will stay out here," he said, gesturing toward the sofa where he had slept after their visit to the slums.

Tava bit her lower lip, uncertainty entering her eyes. "I do not think it is a good idea, Callan."

"And why is that, little fox?" he asked, reaching out and brushing her hair back over her shoulder.

Her eyes fell to the floor. "Because there are times I think you forget this is indeed a ruse, and I do not wish to make you think that is the case."

Callan stiffened. "I apologize if I have made you feel uncomfortable, Tava."

"You haven't," she said quickly. "Truth be told, I enjoy conversing with you. I enjoy these late night visits and honest conversations. I find the small talk of Court to be quite pointless and talking about things that actually matter is a breath of fresh air. Something I only had with Drake, Cassius, and Scarlett until now."

"And you think I forget this is a ruse at times because . . . ?"

She met his gaze, that damn bottom lip between her teeth again. "I know how to read people, Callan. You know this."

"And if I swear I only ask you to stay because I also enjoy our conversations? That I enjoy your candidness and find your honesty refreshing? That I value the *friendship* that has formed because of this ruse?"

She shifted on her feet, her eyes staring into his intently. He had to work not to fidget under her scrutiny. He felt as though she were somehow reading his soul. He *had* grown incredibly comfortable with her, but that was a necessity in and of itself. If they were going to make others believe this was a real relationship, they had to be comfortable around one another. They needed to appear to have inside secrets, to share coy smiles, to be seeking to spend time together.

She finally said, "I cannot replace her, Callan."

He took a step back at her words. He opened his mouth but closed it again, unable to speak because nothing would come to him.

"It may not be intentional, but I am constantly compared to her. By you. By Drake. It is in the little things. Drake reminding you that I do not have daggers strapped beneath my skirts. I see it in your eyes when I speak or when you get lost in thought."

"She has nothing to do with this. With us. With . . . any of it."

A sad, knowing smile formed on her lips. "I should go."

She turned to leave, and he reached out and grabbed her arm. "Tava."

"I will think on ways to get into the Lairwood Estate. Perhaps we can meet at some point tomorrow and see if we have come up with anything," she said.

He shook his head. "No. Stay, and we can discuss them over breakfast." He could tell by the set of her features she was still going to say no. "I have meetings all day tomorrow. It is nearly impossible for us to meet these days."

"Yes," she agreed. "I think that has been orchestrated."

Callan's brows arched. "By Mikale?"

"By him. By my father. For what purpose? I do not yet know."

"Then stay and let's discuss it."

"And if I am caught in here at such hours of the night?"

He couldn't help the smile that tugged this time. "It would probably help the ruse if such a thing occurred."

A laugh came from Tava that only made him smile more. He almost had her convinced.

"I suppose that is a fair point," she conceded.

Callan slowly released her arm, his hand dropping to his side. "So you will stay?"

"I will stay."

CHAPTER 35
SCARLETT

"I don't know how to work this out," Scarlett said when they stepped from the air into their rooms at the Black Halls. "Is Tava's key the mortal key, or is she the unknown bloodline?"

"We likely will not know until we find the other keys, I imagine," Sorin answered, reaching over and undoing the clasps on her cloak before slipping it off her shoulders.

She pulled a dagger from the sheath on her thigh and began idly flipping it as she mused, "It would be helpful to know so we knew where to focus our search."

"Or we could focus on the Fae key, the one we know is still missing, and see if the last one finds its way to you as the rest seem to be doing," Sorin countered, swiping the dagger when she flipped it into the air again. She was about to protest, but he pressed a glass of wine into her hand with a wink.

She took a sip before she said, "You don't happen to have a spirit amulet lying around, do you, Prince?"

A low chuckle rumbled from him. "I do not."

She huffed a dramatic sigh, taking another sip of wine, and a comfortable silence settled over the room. Sorin had disappeared into the dressing room when she called out to him, "You said there were libraries here."

His voice floated out to her from the adjoining room. "There are."

"Can you take me to them?"

"Perhaps we should explore that tomorrow."

"Why?" She glanced at the delicate clock by the bedside. "It's still early. Unless your ancient ass is tired?"

"Careful, Love . . ."

She smiled to herself, taking another sip of wine before she set the glass down and began removing weapons. They hadn't been sure what they would encounter at the Baylorin castle. She was hoping that by Traveling directly to Callan's rooms they would come and go without detection. And while that was how it had played out, she would never underestimate Mikale or Alaric again. So they had gone in with more weapons than likely necessary and her Semiria ring on Sorin's finger.

"If you won't take me to the library, I will just have to hunt it down myself. I'm sure some of the help would be happy to point me in the right direction," she called to him, shucking off her jacket. What was he doing in there?

"I never said I wouldn't take you there. I simply said tomorrow would be better."

"Tomorrow we are meeting with Talwyn," she argued.

"In the afternoon. We have all morning."

"We train in the mornings."

"Perhaps we should take tomorrow morning off."

"Stop saying *perhaps*."

Another faint chuckle was her response.

"Seriously, Sorin. I want to see if there are any books on Avonleya there."

"And we will. Tomorrow."

She gritted her teeth in frustration, inhaling deeply through her nose before she said tightly, "And you think this is your call why?"

"Because, Love, we have something else to take care of tonight."

"Which is what? Because if you're about to suggest sex, you can take that thought and shove—"

She was reaching for her wine glass again when the scent that hit her made her still. It was luscious and metallic and . . . all-consuming. Her shadows rose unbidden, reaching out from her in tendrils, and embers white as starlight danced on the edges of her vision. She slowly turned in the direction her shadows were stretching, to find Sorin leaning casually against the doorway of the dressing room, her dagger in his hand with blood dripping off the tip. There was a thin cut on the opposite forearm, a steady trickle of crimson seeping from it.

"What are you doing?" she rasped, forcing her eyes to move from the blood to his face.

"We are meeting with Talwyn tomorrow," he replied. "But even if we were not, your magic needs to be refilled, Scarlett. You have avoided this long enough."

"I have avoided nothing," she hissed. "I think I would know my power reserves, my strength, my *body*, better than you."

"We will leave the argument about who knows your body better for another time," he said with a flash of a smirk, "but you need to do this, Scarlett. I understand it is not ideal, but—"

"Not *ideal*?" she scoffed. "While that is certainly true, it is not the point."

He arched a brow, waiting for her to go on.

"The *point* is that I do not need to do that right now, and if and when I do need to, it will be my call, not yours."

"Why do you refuse this, Scarlett? If this were Cassius you would be forcing Cyrus's blood down his throat, which you have actually done by the way," Sorin replied.

"To save his life," she cried. "I should hope if I were unconscious with a foot across the Veil you would do the same."

"I am trying to prevent that from ever happening," he retorted.

"This is not your call to make," Scarlett snarled.

"So I am supposed to . . . what? Watch you weaken? Watch your power drop more each day? Knowing I literally carry the answer in my veins?" Sorin asked, stalking forward. "And what happens when we go to the mortal kingdoms and things do not play out like they did today? What happens when we are required to fight, and you are not at your strongest? What happens when you are taken from me again because you refused this?"

"This is not your call to make," she repeated.

The thin cut on his arm was already beginning to knit itself back together, and his grip tightened on the handle of her dagger.

"You recognize that if you do not do this, you will continue to weaken? You will begin to draw power and strength from Cassius, slowing his healing?" Sorin demanded.

Scarlett looked away from him, sucking on a tooth.

She felt his hand cup her cheek, a thumb brush along her cheekbone. "Talk to me, Love," he said softly. "There has to be more to this than you simply not wanting to drink blood."

"There isn't," she ground out.

"You are lying."

"Can you just trust that I will know if and when I need to do this?"

"No, I cannot. Not without a reason," he replied. "And if you continue to refuse, I will no longer train with you. I will order the others to stop as well, even though an order will not be necessary. They all agree with me, and so would Cassius if I asked him."

"I am their queen," she said incredulously.

"And I am their prince and king," he said simply, his hand slipping from her face.

"Sorin! I need to train!"

"It will be utterly pointless if you are not training with all of your power, Scarlett. It will be useless if you do not have any power to wield," he shot back.

"Gods, I truly do hate you sometimes."

"I know, Love," he said, bending and pressing a light kiss to her cheek. "Let me know when you have changed your mind."

She pushed him away from her, stalking to the door. He didn't say anything to stop her, and she was fine with that. She didn't particularly want to see his face right now.

She wasn't sure where her feet were taking her, but she also wasn't surprised when she found herself on the beach, staring out across the sea. The stars were muted tonight, clouds casting them in shadows, and the half-moon was lost among them too.

Sorin wasn't wrong. She was weakening. She could swear all of her power reserves were draining far faster than they ever had before. Not just her shadows and white flames, but her fire and ice too. How often had she used her magic in the Fire Court when she was trying to master it? She still had never weakened this quickly. She was exhausted every night when she climbed into bed. And sure, maybe all the evening activities with Sorin kept her up later than was really necessary, but there had been a few nights where she'd gotten ten hours of sleep or more and was still dragging by the end of the day. Of course Sorin had noticed. She was honestly surprised it'd taken him this long to confront her about it. She'd known it was coming. She was the one who'd turned it into an argument because she was on edge. She was tired and worried and that made her agitated and difficult. More difficult than usual anyway.

I sent you someone.

She sighed. She really just wanted some time by herself to figure all of this out, and if he'd sent Cassius down here when he could barely stand on his leg . . .

"And so the sea calls to those who understand her song." She turned to find a water portal snapping shut behind Briar. "Hello, Sunshine."

She snickered. "I do believe you are the only one who comments on the little light I possess before my darkness."

"An occasional reminder that the light does, in fact, exist alongside the darkness, does not seem like a bad thing," he replied, coming to a stop beside her. His hands slid into the pockets of his pants. His hair had grown longer. It was past his shoulders now.

After several minutes of silence, she said, "Sorin says you think I can breathe under water."

"You can," he confirmed.

"How?" she demanded, turning to look up at him.

"You control the water element, Sunshine. You can simply will it to part and create air pockets," he answered with a shrug.

"Just like that, hmm?" she mused sarcastically.

"It will take practice, of course, like anything does." He paused. "It will also require the use of your gifts, which will not be possible if your power reserves are not adequately filled."

Scarlett rolled her eyes. "If that is what you wish to discuss, you can take your leave."

"I have no desire to discuss it," Briar said dismissively. "Simply stating a fact."

"Mhmm."

Waves rolled to the shore, the sound soothing her soul as she stood in the night.

"Could you show me to the library here?"

"I could."

"Will you?"

"What is it you are looking for?"

"What am I not looking for at this point?" she said with a huff. "Information on the Maraans. The Avonleyans. Figuring out what a Source is. The keys."

"Ah."

"So will you? Show me where they are?"

"I don't see why not," he replied. "However, I think you would have better luck in the libraries of the Wind Court. They are much more extensive."

Her gaze flew back to his. "Why would you just bring this up now?"

"Why would a young queen refuse to keep her magic fully replenished? Mysteries of the universes, I suppose," he mused.

"Funny," Scarlett deadpanned.

Briar merely shrugged.

"Will Ashtine let me visit them?"

"I may be able to persuade her."

Scarlett snorted a laugh. "I bet, Prince." Another bout of silence before she asked, "Why is Nasima not with Ashtine?"

Briar visibly stiffened. Even in the night she could see his features darken, his twinkling eyes harden. "Because she chose Talwyn over the winds," he finally gritted out.

"What does that even mean?"

"The winds favor Avonleya. You have an idea of how Talwyn feels about the kingdom. She became upset with Ashtine when the winds stopped whispering of the kingdom across the sea. Ashtine has kept Talwyn's secrets, so I do not entirely know what has been said or done, but her loyalty was called into question. When she chose to stand by Talwyn, the winds stopped speaking to her all together. Nasima left, and she finds it very difficult to walk among them."

She wasn't sure what to say to that. She could feel the aggression rolling off of Briar. "You do not agree with her choice?"

"No. I have tried to convince her to reconsider, but in the end, it is her choice to make." He paused, then added, "Just as it is yours to allow yourself to weaken, I suppose."

"Where is she now?"

"At her Wind Citadel in the Shira Cliffs. She is . . . not well."

Scarlett nodded. "At least you are accepting of her choices," she grumbled.

"Understanding and accepting are two very different things," Briar said. "But that argument aside, she has given me reasons for her choices, to help me understand. We have discussed them as much as we can. The bigger issue is that her duty to Queen Talwyn prohibits her from being able to give me detailed explanations. Something that is not a hindrance for you and Sorin. He seeks to trust you."

"It is my own fault he does not," she replied quietly.

"Yes," he agreed, never one to say something simply to try and make her feel better or assuage her guilt. "But it is also in your power to rebuild such a thing."

"Such a thing takes time."

"It does, but refusing to start somewhere will only make it take longer."

"I often forget you are as old as Sorin," Scarlett replied. "Then you speak like an ancient sage, and I remember you are the same age."

"For the record, Sorin is older by three seasons."

A laugh bubbled up from Scarlett's throat. "And Sawyer?"

"I am older than him by nearly seven decades."

Scarlett nodded, folding her arms in front of her, her gaze settling on the water once more.

"None of us wish to make decisions for you, Scarlett," Briar said after another beat of silence. "We only wish to understand why you make them the way you do."

"I think even if I gave him a reason, he would not find it a valid one," she replied.

"Perhaps," Briar conceded. "But again, understanding and accepting are two very different things." When she didn't say anything in response, he said, "I will let you listen to the sea, Sunshine. I just wanted to make sure you did not need to be pulled from the river."

"Thank you, Briar."

"Send word if you need anything."

She nodded, and a moment later, she heard the sound of his water portal.

Sometime later, when she finally turned to head back to the Black Halls, she spotted Sorin sitting atop a small dune a ways up the beach. He stood when she started in his direction, meeting her halfway.

"How long have you been down here?" Scarlett asked when he reached to tuck her hair behind her ear.

"Since Briar left."

"Just sitting there?"

"Mhmm."

"That's kind of creepy."

He flicked her nose. "You are the queen. More than that, you were recently held captive. If you honestly think someone does not have eyes on you at all times, you are sorely mistaken."

"Not creepy at all," she said.

A quick smile graced his lips. "How are you?"

"Tired."

"Sleep in tomorrow. Then I will take you to the library," he said, taking her hand and opening a fire portal.

"You're really not going to train with me?" she asked, letting him lead her through.

"Not until your power well is filled, no. And neither will anyone else," he added.

"Maybe I will just train by myself then," she bit back.

"I cannot stop that, but I will choose not to partake in it."

She released his hand and silently made her way to the dressing room. She pulled her boots off and stripped off her tunic and pants before pulling on one of his shirts. When she re-emerged, he was sitting on the sofa, studying texts and comparing them to her translation notes.

She sighed loudly. "If you put it in a cup, like Cyrus does for Cassius, I will drink it. But I won't . . . Not directly from you. I don't like the loss of control that comes with that."

Sorin slowly set the book on the low table before him. "Is that what this has all been about, Scarlett? You are afraid of losing control? Do you even remember when you fed last time?"

"Don't say *fed*," she groused, her nose scrunching in disgust.

"Do you refuse this because you are afraid of losing control?" he repeated.

"No. Not entirely anyway," she replied, moving to the bed and sitting cross-legged.

"Care to expand on that?"

"Not particularly."

He gave her a pointed look from where he still sat on the sofa, angled to face her over the back of it.

She blew out a long breath. "I lived years without any control over my own choices and decisions. I do not like that this forces me to do something that I find abhorrent."

It was not entirely lost on her that she found drinking blood to be more abhorrent than taking life for payment. She tried not to let her thoughts linger on what that said about her.

"You never seemed upset about Nuri having to do so."

"I suppose not," she agreed, fiddling with a crease on the blanket.

"It is no different than your body requiring food or water, Scarlett," he added. "Do you feel as though those things control you?"

"No," she replied. "Although the necessity is rather a nuisance at times."

He huffed a laugh under his breath. "Only you would find eating a nuisance."

"Think about all the other things one could accomplish if you didn't need to eat, sleep, or even use the bathing room."

Sorin blinked at her. "I can honestly say, in all my years, I have never contemplated such a thing."

Scarlett shrugged, her eyes dropping back to her lap. "Anyway, if you put it in a glass . . ."

"I have offered a glass before, and you still refused."

"As I have already said, I find all of this . . . I am not a Night Child. I do not like the idea of doing this, and having it forced upon me makes me want to resist it even more."

"Fair enough."

"That's it? After all of this, that's all you have to say."

Sorin shrugged. "I understand why you have been resisting this so adamantly. I can also only assume the Avonleyans outlawed it and found an alternative for a reason." He stood, crossing the distance to her. He planted his hands on either side of her on the bed, the mattress dipping under his extra weight. He leaned forward, nearly nose-to-nose with her. "I swear to you we will find another way, Scarlett, but until then, you need to do this. I need you to be at your strongest. I need your magic to protect you. I need you able to fight when required. *I need you*. And if you are ever taken from me again, I cannot promise I will not burn everything and everyone to the ground until I find you. It will not matter if they are enemy or innocent, friend or family. It will not matter if the entire world is nothing but ash by the time I get to you. None of it will matter because my need for you is all-consuming."

She cupped his face in her hands. "Thank you for loving me like the stars love the night, Sorin."

His forehead fell forward, resting against hers. "All the way through the darkness, Love."

CHAPTER 36
TALWYN

"Who is that?" Talwyn demanded when she entered the council room at the Black Halls.

Azrael was at her side, but today was the first day she'd seen him since Siofra. They had conversed by earth messages, nothing more. When she'd arrived at the gates of the Black Halls a few minutes ago, he had been waiting for her. He'd looked her over carefully before asking if anything needed to be discussed before they entered.

She'd spent the last few days alone. Ashtine rarely left her Citadel as of late and only when absolutely necessary. She was here now, though, standing near the far wall conversing quietly with Prince Briar. She recognized Death's Shadow. She'd been pointed out when Azrael had arrived with all the children a few weeks ago. There was a Witch standing among them, although not one she recognized, and sitting at the table was a male with brown hair that reached past his shoulders. One eye was a deep brown. The other was hidden behind a silver patch. Scarlett was sitting on the table next to him, her feet swinging. She was leaning in close, speaking quietly with the male. Sorin was with his Court nearby, clearly comfortable with his wife speaking so intimately with the male.

"That is Cassius," Azrael answered. "I am surprised he lives. He was nearly in the After when we retrieved Scarlett."

"But who is he to her?"

"He is a Witch. We sought him out as soon as we arrived. He created powerful wards around several places in the Windonelle capital."

"Then what is he doing here if he works for the Maraan Lords?"

"He is important to Scarlett," Azrael replied.

"That does not mean he should be *here*," Talwyn retorted.

"Since these are my halls and not yours," Scarlett suddenly quipped, "that is not your call to make." She turned to look at Talwyn, her lips curved into a wicked smile. "Welcome back, your Majesty."

"These meetings are for the Royals and their Courts. Not childhood friends," Talwyn said, moving forward to take a seat at the other end of the table.

"He is part of my Court," Scarlett answered with a shrug, hopping down from the table. She threw a wink at the male before moving to take her seat.

"A Witch is part of your Court? That is not how things are done," Talwyn replied tightly.

That wicked smile only curved up more. "I am sure you've come to realize I am rather unconventional. And seeing as I am not Fae, but Avonleyan, it only seemed fitting to have a half-Avonleyan in my Court." She reached for a pitcher of water, but Cyrus was already pouring her a glass. "Of course, seeing as you have your own Second with Avonleyan blood in his veins, you can understand where I am coming from."

Talwyn's fingers dug into the table from where she'd placed them both flat on the table before her. How the fuck were there Avonleyans popping up everywhere all of the sudden?

"Is he your Second then?" Talwyn asked through gritted teeth.

"No. That is still my husband . . . The king," she added with a nod at Sorin, who had taken his seat beside her.

"Your Third?"

"That is Briar."

"Then what is he doing here?"

"Cassius is the Hand to the Queen," Sorin cut in before Scarlett could reply.

"Any other questions you need answered before we move on to my agenda this afternoon?" Scarlett asked.

"Why don't you start, and we will go from there," Talwyn managed to grit out, sitting back in her chair. She took a deep breath, getting herself under control. There was no way she was going to let this meeting end like the last one. No way anyone was going to see her as anything other than the Fae Queen they'd known for decades.

Scarlett stood, pulling four objects from her pocket. Three she plunked down onto the table, the fourth she tossed to Prince Briar.

"Pass that down to Princess Ashtine if you would please, Prince."

Talwyn watched him pass a necklace, a spirit amulet from the looks of it, down the table until Ashtine's Second, Ermir, placed it into her hands.

"You found another?" Ashtine asked, taking the necklace. Her eyes lifted to Scarlett, surprise and question filling them.

"I have found two others," Scarlett answered, gesturing to the three items that rested in front of her.

"Interesting," Ashtine murmured, her attention returning to the necklace.

"Why are we playing with spirit amulets?" Talwyn asked.

Scarlett had sat back casually in her chair, her eyes settling onto Talwyn. And Talwyn braced herself, because she could tell by the look in her eyes that what she was about to say was going to tip her back over an edge.

"I believe they are four of the Avonleyan Keys."

Talwyn blinked slowly at her. That was the only movement she made as she stared back at Scarlett. She could feel Azrael watching her.

"Why do you believe these to be the keys?" Azrael asked for her.

"I have my reasons and theories, but so far, they are proving to be accurate," Scarlett answered.

"How long have you had these?" Talwyn demanded.

"Depends on which one you're referencing," Scarlett replied too sweetly.

"Why am I only learning about them now?" Talwyn tried again.

"I had debated telling you during our last little meeting, but then you threw one of the best Fae temper tantrums I've seen yet," Scarlett replied. She turned to Sorin, her head propping on her fist. "Did you take notes on how to improve your next one, Prince?"

Sawyer choked on his water down the table as he suppressed a laugh.

Sorin released a long-suffering sigh, his fingers running along his brows. "Perhaps now is not the best time for your delightful, yet insulting, sarcasm, Love."

"*Perhaps* you should stop saying perhaps," she muttered back, rolling her eyes.

Sorin's lips twitched, but he turned back to face Talwyn. "We just began theorizing about them after we returned, when we stumbled upon one by sheer luck. We are not even sure they are the actual keys. We need Ashtine to take them to the Shira Cliffs to confirm they are skystone first."

"They are skystone," Ashtine lilted softly from beside Talwyn. "But you may come see for yourself if you require tangible proof."

The princess looked exhausted. She'd lost weight, and her eyes were muted. Even her hair seemed more dull, her skin ghostly pale. She moved to pass the amulet back to Scarlett, but Talwyn held out her hand for it. Ashtine passed it to her instead, giving her a wary look.

"Do you have any ideas as to where the other three are?" Talwyn asked, studying the amulet. The chain did seem to be skystone. It just lacked skystone's brightness. The amulet attached to it though, this one being Falein's symbol, was the darkest stone she'd ever seen.

"One of them, yes. The other two, no," Scarlett answered. "I do, however, know a Fae will be in possession of one of them."

"Why?" Talwyn asked.

She continued to study the amulet while Scarlett gave a brief explanation of what the Oracle had said to her.

"There could be a hundred ways to interpret the Oracle's words," Talwyn said when Scarlett finished speaking. "She is hardly helpful on the best of days."

"Rude," drifted an icy voice from a shadowy corner on the far side of the room. Azrael and Talwyn both spun quickly towards the source to find Death's Shadow and the Witch standing there, both in black and both blending in with the darkness around them.

"Who are you, and why are you here?" Talwyn demanded.

"Talwyn," Ashtine said quietly, "she is the Oracle of whom you speak."

The Witch tilted her head slightly, her red-brown hair swaying with the movement.

Talwyn worked hard to change the tone of her voice from annoyance to respect. "I apologize," she said tightly, bowing her head. "I did not realize you had left your cave."

"I came to check in on an old friend," the Oracle replied, her eyes darting to Cassius.

Talwyn didn't know how to respond to that. The Oracle was centuries old . . .

"I replaced the previous Oracle upon my mortal death," the Oracle supplied, sensing her confusion. "Before that, though, I was called Death Incarnate by some."

Talwyn started, the amulet clattering to the table. "You were a Wraith of Death." Her eyes darted from her, to the Night Child smiling like a maniac in the shadows, to Scarlett, who was smirking like a damn cat where she still sat casually in her seat. "You all . . . All of you are here."

"Allow me to introduce you to my *childhood friends*," Scarlett purred. "I am told you know Death's Shadow, although we call her Nuri," she continued, nodding towards the dark corner. "You have just met Juliette— a Witch, the Oracle, and the niece of the High Witch." Her gaze then shifted to Cassius. "As for this one, he trained us at the Fellowship in the Black Syndicate and was one of my personal tutors."

Talwyn schooled her features back into neutrality, pushing down the shock at learning who all these people truly were . . . and at having not only an Avonleyan on the Western Courts throne, but a godsdamn Wraith of Death.

"And why, exactly, are they all here?" Talwyn asked tightly.

"Because we need to find the Contessa, and they are going into the Night Child territory with me," Scarlett answered.

⁂

They spent the rest of the meeting planning the mission into the Night Child territory that was to happen in three days. All the Courts were sending in extra spies to see if the Contessa's whereabouts could be pinpointed. Talwyn had to admit she was getting worried though. No one's spies had seen or heard from the Contessa in months. All had been quiet on the Night Child front. It wasn't uncommon not to hear from her, but *someone* inside her lands always knew how to get in touch with her.

She'd wanted to take one of the amulets with her to see if she could shift the shape of them. Scarlett had said the amulets themselves were something called nightstone, but, of course, she'd refused to let her leave with even one of the things. She said once they had confirmed they were the actual keys and had found the other three, they could start working on shifting them. It wasn't as if she could argue with her. They were equals, no matter how much it disgusted Talwyn that an Avonleyan sat on a Fae throne.

Talwyn was walking down the path to the main gates so she could Travel home, when the sound of footsteps behind her had her tensing. A moment later, he spoke.

"So this is how we are going to do this now? I am your Second, Talwyn. We need to speak outside of formal meetings."

"Do we?" Talwyn asked. "I seem to learn more during these formal meetings than outside of them these days."

Azrael apparently chose to ignore the verbal bait. "You need someone, Talwyn. Ashtine is . . . not herself. And even if she were . . . You need someone."

"That someone is not you."

"Who else do you have left? You have pushed everyone else away," he countered.

"Thank you for pointing out how utterly alone I am."

"Talwyn," he growled, his hand closing around her elbow and tugging her to a stop.

Her eyes fell to his hand before slowly dragging to his eyes.

"Your foul moods do not scare me. They never have," he said, his fingers remaining wrapped around her arm.

"Then perhaps you have gotten *too* close, Prince," she bit out.

Azrael's brow arched. "So expecting to have conversations with you is too much to ask, but being between your legs is fine?"

She bared her teeth at him, tugging her arm, but he held firm, stepping into her further.

"It is my job as your Second to challenge you and provide counsel," he said, his voice dropping low.

"Then maybe I need to re-evaluate who I keep in my Inner Court," she spat back.

"This is all over a bloodline that does not matter."

"I wager Tarek, if he is truly alive, would disagree with that statement."

"Talwyn," Azrael growled again in frustration.

"Release me. I have things to tend to," she said, her tone becoming dangerous.

"You are saying all this, these past decades of loyalty, mean nothing? These decades of— It is all nothing to you?"

"You were good for distractions," she sneered. "Unless you are here for that, you are dismissed."

Azrael flashed his teeth at her in a feral grin. "If you need a hate-fuck, all you need to do is ask, your Majesty."

"Release me," she ordered again, her voice nothing more than a lethal whisper.

His hand left her flesh this time, and when he took a step back from her, something tightened in her chest. "I will see you in three days when we go into the Night Child territory. Send a message if you need something before then."

She left him standing on the path, and the moment she crossed the gates she Traveled to the woods in Windonelle where she'd once tracked down Sorin. She'd been working with Stellan and Arianna every day since Azrael and Stellan had come to collect her in the forest. She was able to shift back and forth fairly easily now, but she could not entirely control when she shifted yet. And with everything going on, she found it harder to control her magic. It took more focus, more energy.

But when she stepped into the mortal kingdom, her ring on her finger, she shifted on command. Paws hit the dirt, and her ears cocked forward, listening to everything around her. She slowly began padding along the woods. Her nose went to the ground, trying to pick up a familiar scent.

She'd gone to the spot where Scarlett had been taken by those Night Children. Azrael had mentioned scenting something familiar there. They had thought there was a traitor in the Earth Court. She hadn't been able to find the scent when she'd gone there though. It had been so hidden to begin with that it was long gone when she had tried to find it.

But she'd recognize Tarek's scent anywhere. She just wanted to see if she could find it. She *needed* to know if he was really here, if he'd been here this entire time.

She followed the woods as far as she could, until she reached the outskirts of the capital, where she sat and watched, trying to figure out what her next move should be, when footsteps had her ears perking and head tilting as she listened. These were silent footsteps, softer than mortals tended to move. A hunter, perhaps?

She slunk along some trees, keeping to the brush to stay hidden. The scent of moonlight and night hit her as she drew closer, but it was muted. It should be much stronger if they were this close.

"How much longer are we going to wait?" one of the vampyres hissed, and a moment later, they came into view.

There was a small clan of around twenty Night Children all gathered around a small make-shift campsite. There was a little fire in the center of it, but they all kept their distance, apparently preferring to freeze rather than risk touching the flames.

"They keep making promises that it will be soon, yet we still sit here, shunned from our own lands and not allowed into theirs," another said. This one a female.

"If they manage to keep their promises, it will be worth it," said another.

"Do you have reason to believe the promises made to you will not be kept?"

Talwyn stilled at that voice. She knew that voice.

Had spent countless hours with the owner of that voice.

She tipped her nose to the air, trying to scent him, but there was nothing. None of his forest and soil scent that used to soothe her. Not a hint.

A figure in all black stepped into view across from her. His attire matched what she'd seen Death's Shadow moving about in at the Black Halls. He had a hood up, obscuring his face from view. She was standing before she realized she'd moved, and forced herself to still once more as the figure stepped to the center of the vampyre clan.

The Night Children had fallen silent, many bowing to the male. Two, though, were glaring back at him. One was the female that had been grousing about broken promises.

"We were supposed to be in that territory months ago," the female said, her chin lifting.

"And as you are well aware, factors we were not anticipating pushed back our timeline. But not for much longer," the male answered.

His very voice was calling to her, making it nearly impossible to keep her paws planted while she listened.

"It is taking too long," the female vampyre replied.

"Patience, my friend."

"What do you know of patience?" sneered the first male who had spoken.

The figure's head turned slowly to him, and the vampyre's throat worked as he swallowed, taking a small step back. "I know more about patience than you can even begin to imagine." He took a step towards the Night Child. "The things playing out now have been in the works for decades, centuries. Do not whine to me about your pathetic wait of a few years."

"We simply wish to be welcomed back into our homeland," one of the vampyres said, her head still bowed, eyes on the ground.

"As do I," the hooded male said coldly.

Talwyn sucked in a breath, but in her wolf form it came out as more of a huff. It wasn't loud, but the hooded male's head tilted to the side slightly.

"Your whining aside, I did not come here to coddle and soothe away your worries," he said. "I came here to relay information."

"Which is what?" the first vampyre asked.

"We will be preoccupied for the next few days. You are to stay out of the city, away from any mortals. If he learns you have decided not to heed these orders, the next mission you are sent on will be facing *her*."

"We would never survive her," one of the vampyres with his head still bowed said. "She slaughtered our kin without any aid. If she is back with her twin flame—"

"Then I suppose you will need to control yourselves."

There were murmurs of agreement from the Night Children before the hooded man told them he would return in a few days when their business had been taken care of. He turned to leave the way he had come, and Talwyn backed into the brush behind her. She moved as fast as she dared to try to trail him. She was still unable to pick up any scent from him.

Talwyn paused when she came to a denser part of the forest. The trees above were so thick that it blocked out the setting sun, a thin layer of darkness settling into place. She strained her hearing, trying to pick up something, anything. But if it was truly *him*, he would move with the grace of the Fae.

The rustle of brush nearby had her swinging her head to the left, her eyes piercing easily through the darkness. He stepped into view from between two trees, walking to the place where the path he'd been following split into two. He stopped, tipping his head back as though he were trying to see the sky through the trees.

What was he doing?

Talwyn sat, watching him carefully, debating her best options to keep following him. She was hoping he'd remove his hood. She just wanted to see his face, wanted to confirm it was really him.

"A little longer, Moonflower. A little longer, and I will be home where I belong."

Talwyn's blood froze. Her breath caught in her chest. She couldn't have sucked in air if she'd wanted to. She couldn't move to follow him as he took the path to the right and continued on to wherever he was heading.

Moonflower.

That was the name he had given her one night while they'd sat under the full moon in a secluded oasis in the Earth Court.

It was him. He was here.

And whatever he was doing, it was keeping him from her.

CHAPTER 37
SORIN

"It's freezing here," Scarlett groused.

Sorin hid his smile, reaching over and sending a flood of heat through her. She stuffed her hands deeper into the fur-lined cloak she was wearing. The winds swirled around them, snow flurried with it, and her hair fluttered around her face. She wasn't wrong. The Wind Court was always, well, windy. The winds tended to shift from breezy to gale storm depending on the princess's mood, and with Ashtine's demeanor lately, the winds whipping about weren't a surprise.

They stood before a stone bridge that stretched across a cavern leading to Ashtine's Citadel. The domes of the various towers of her fortress reached into the clouds. The Citadel sat atop the highest cliffs. Only the cliffs where skystone could be found towered higher. Those same cliffs could also only be reached by the winding steps located in the back courtyard of the Citadel.

Sorin pressed a hand to the small of Scarlett's back, guiding her forward. "It will be warmer inside."

She grumbled something under her breath that Sorin couldn't make out, even with his Fae hearing. She had woken in a mood, and he hadn't quite worked out if it was simply an off day or if something was bothering her.

Nothing else was said, and when the main doors were pulled open, they were greeted not by Princess Ashtine but by Briar. It was still a shock for Sorin to think of him with the princess. Ashtine was just so . . . Ashtine.

"Good morning, Sunshine," Briar greeted warmly when Scarlett pulled back her hood.

"Morning," she replied, far more subdued than normal. Well, it used to be unusual. This mood and state were starting to become more commonplace, and he wasn't quite sure what to make of it yet.

Briar's eyes darted to Sorin in question, but he could only shrug as he watched Scarlett taking in the great foyer.

"Ashtine will be along shortly. Did you eat this morning?" Briar asked.

"Mhmm," Scarlett murmured, moving to look at a large painting along the wall.

"You had a pear," Sorin said, his tone conveying exactly what he thought of that "breakfast." It wasn't enough for a mortal, let alone a magic-wielder who needed food for their power reserves.

"I'm fine," she replied dismissively.

"Scarlett."

She waved him off, moving on to another painting.

True to her word, she'd drunk a small cup of his blood a few nights ago. She hadn't requested more since, and he didn't want to push her on this again. Not unless he needed to, but he also couldn't wrap his mind around *why* she wouldn't want to keep her power wells fully replenished at all times. Not with everything that was going on. Not with everything she had just been through. If they had known, if her Avonleyan powers had been at full-strength, she would have been better prepared for that fight at the border. Yet she still resisted.

"That is a portrait of Sefarina."

They all turned to the lilting voice when Princess Ashtine entered the foyer.

"What someone thinks she looks like?" Scarlett asked, her head tilting as she studied the painting of the wind goddess. She had hair like moonlight, white and silver— much like Ashtine's— and sky-blue eyes with winds that seemed to swirl in them. How someone could paint wind Sorin didn't know, but the artist had managed it. A long, silver gown flowed around her ample curves, and the woman appeared to be floating, her bare feet an inch above the clouds painted beneath her.

"One of her preferred forms, perhaps," Ashtine agreed.

Scarlett turned from the painting to face her. "Thank you for allowing me to come here this morning."

"You brought the amulets?"

"I did," Scarlett answered, patting a pocket on her cloak. "Briar also mentioned you have extensive libraries here. I was hoping to look through them."

"The keys first," Ashtine answered. "Then we can discuss the libraries."

Briar fell into step beside her, keeping space between them. Apparently their relationship was a secret from all except their Inner Courts. Did Ashtine's Inner Court even know? Should they ever take their affairs public, the two Courts would likely not be happy. The Royals taking an official partner outside of their own Courts would be nothing short of a scandal. Such politics among the Courts were the reason Eliza now resided in the Fire Court. Any heirs produced would favor one power or the other, not both, leaving one Court essentially heirless.

He glanced side-long at his wife while they followed behind. Her hands were shoved back in the folds of her cloak, as if even inside she had not escaped the winter chill.

Are you all right?

She looked at him quickly before fixing her eyes ahead once more. *I am fine.*

You do not not seem fine . . .

Her lips pressed into a thin line. *I am just tired.*

His brows rose at that. She had slept soundly all night. He had no doubt about that. She had been asleep well before he had climbed into bed beside her. He had continued combing through her translation notes and trying to read the books they'd brought from Solembra. How she had learned and mastered the language so quickly was beyond him. It was incredibly complicated. That aside, he had only slept a few hours himself, and he woke before her. She hadn't moved from where he'd pulled her into his chest.

Before he could decide what to say in response, they'd reached doors that would lead out to the Citadel courtyards. Scarlett was already pulling her hood back over head, sighing slightly when the winds blew snow inside the moment the doors were opened. Maybe she just really did not like the cold, and it had put her in a foul mood. They hadn't even known each other a year. There was still plenty to learn, he supposed.

Her head tipped back as she beheld the winding stairs along the steep cliffside that Ashtine and Briar were leading the way to.

"Can we not portal to the top?" she asked. "Or Travel? I can Travel us up there."

"Sorry, Sunshine," Briar said, looking back over his shoulder with a quick grin. "It is warded against portals."

Scarlett opened her mouth to speak, but Ashtine said first, "And Traveling."

The princess began climbing the narrow steps, Briar right behind her. The steps weren't wide enough to walk side-by-side. Sorin ushered Scarlett forward behind the Water Prince and began climbing behind her.

"This trek could take the place of training today," he said to her lightly.

"Sure," she replied.

He reached forward, grabbing her hand, and she paused, looking back at him. Shadows flitted across dull, silvery-blue irises. This was more than the cold weather.

"Do you need to talk about something, Love?" Even a step above him she didn't reach his full height. She still had to tilt her head back slightly to look into his face.

"Not that I am aware of," she answered. "Unless there is something you need to talk about? In which case, I ask that we do so when we are not freezing our asses off."

"Is this delightful mood solely because you are cold?" he asked, sending another wave of heat into her. "You have magic to stay warm, you know."

"I am well-aware of what my magic is capable of," she snapped in reply.

His brows flew up at her sharp tone.

"I apologize," she sighed. "As I said, I am tired."

"Did you have dreams last night?" he asked cautiously.

"No."

"You are feeling all right?"

"You already asked me that today."

"But I do not believe your answer, so I feel the need to ask again," he countered.

She squeezed his fingers still wrapped around her hand before she let go and turned back to continue up the stairs. It was a fifteen minute climb until they finally reached the top. Ashtine sent a small whirlwind through an archway, and the arch glowed faintly, recognizing her magic and lowering any wards to allow them to pass.

"It is beautiful up here," Scarlett said softly, pushing her hood back.

The winds were calm and still in this space. They had climbed through clouds when they neared the top, and he had watched Scarlett trail her fingers through them before quickly shoving her hand back into her cloak. Then he'd heard her grumble something about how she should have brought her fur-lined gloves.

"Not quite the song of the sea but serene nonetheless," Briar said, tossing a wink at Ashtine.

A slight smile graced the princess's lips, and Sorin recognized Briar doing the same thing he was trying to do— anything that would lighten the mood of the one he loved.

Ashtine turned to Scarlett, gesturing to her pocket. "The amulets." Scarlett pulled the four necklaces from her cloak, placing them in Ashtine's palm. She crossed to a small rocky platform in the center of the space. An altar, Sorin realized. He'd only been here once, and it was before he ruled a Court. He'd come with Briar on a tour of sorts. All the heirs to the Courts had been given tours of the other territories.

Scarlett followed Ashtine, watching the chains carefully. "What are they supposed to do?"

"The silver in the chains should be moving," the Wind Princess murmured. "There is something wrong."

Sorin shot a look at Briar before he said cautiously, "Maybe it is not skystone after all."

"It has to be," Scarlett said, a slight desperation ringing in her tone that had Sorin moving to her side and placing a hand on her shoulder.

"It is skystone," Ashtine said.

Sorin tried again. "I understand why you think that, but—"

"It is!" she said sharply, and Sorin's eyes widened. He had never heard the princess speak in something other than her signature mystical lilt.

"What could be wrong?" Scarlett asked.

"It is not the skystone. It is me," Ashtine whispered, eyes fixed on the amulets.

"Try to call Nasima, Ashtine," Briar said softly.

"She will not answer. She does not heed my summons anymore." The princess struck out, slapping the amulets from the altar and sending them flying to the ground. "Nothing is right anymore.

Down is up, and left is right. Black is white, and the winds flee from my mere presence." Her small hand slammed down onto the altar, and a blast of wind erupted from it, the rock shuddering beneath the impact. Her chest was heaving, and the winds she'd created seemed to swirl about the Courtyard as if they were seeking a way out but could not find it.

Sorin had tugged Scarlett back and into his chest, a thin shield of flame surrounding them. She had buried her face in his chest at the wind explosion, and she peeked out now, but Sorin's hold on her did not lessen. Every part of him was on high alert.

He watched the Wind Princess warily as Briar slowly reached for her. Both of her hands were braced on the stone, her head bowed. Sorin knew she had not been herself. Briar had told him what had happened. Or the little that he knew anyway. Sorin had not realized it was this bad. That Ashtine, the quirky princess who spoke in lilting riddles and oddities, had descended into . . . this.

"Come here, my dear," Briar said softly, and when Ashtine lifted her head, tears were coursing down her face.

"I cannot survive this, my heart. I cannot live without them," she cried softly.

"I know, Ashtine. I know." He pulled her into his chest, meeting Sorin's gaze as the princess cried into his cloak.

Scarlett began squirming, trying to work her way out of Sorin's grip, but he still refused to ease up.

"You're being a mother hen," she muttered.

"Did you not just see that?" he demanded in a hushed whisper.

"She is hurting, Sorin. She is not going to hurt me."

"Not on purpose maybe."

With a sigh, she created a swirl of shadows that cloaked her. They hovered close to her body and moved as though they were dark scales on her skin. "She will not touch me," Scarlett said.

"When did you . . ." Sorin trailed off, not quite sure what to say or think as he looked at his wife. She could be Saylah herself. "When did you learn to do that?"

"I was told to master my Avonleyan magic. I have been doing so," she answered, glancing back to Briar and Ashtine. The prince was murmuring softly into her ear.

"But when?" Sorin asked again. She was rarely out of his sight since returning.

"I came across some things during our research," Scarlett answered, watching the other Royals.

Sorin stilled at her words. "What other things have you learned?"

"Nothing exciting."

"Scarlett..."

Her gaze came back to his. "I am keeping nothing I have learned from you," she hissed, those shadows swimming across her eyes again.

What is wrong? he pressed down the bond, but a wall of shadows slammed down along that mental bridge, and he took a physical step back from her.

"When did you learn how to do *that*?" he demanded, his tone no longer hushed.

"There is something wrong," Ashtine said, her head lifting from Briar's chest.

"It is okay, Ashtine," Scarlett said gently, ignoring him and taking a step toward her. "I believe you. I believe that these are skystone. I do not need proof. I never did."

Ashtine shook her head. "Not that. You are . . . You are different. You are not the same as when you left."

Scarlett stooped to scoop up the amulets from the ground. "I suppose I am not."

Ashtine extracted herself from Briar, coming to stand before the queen as she stood. Sorin tensed at her closeness after such a burst of uncontrolled power, but he forced himself to remain where he stood. For an entire minute, no one said anything, and the two females simply stared at one another.

"The turmoil in my soul is a fraction of the tempest that plagues your own," Ashtine murmured.

Scarlett said nothing.

"I will take you to the libraries," Ashtine said then, stepping back from Scarlett. "There is one chamber in particular I think you will find of special interest."

She turned and made her way to the archway, Briar moving to follow. Sorin caught his eye, and the Water Prince understood the silent words he conveyed: they would catch up in a moment.

Sorin stepped into Scarlett's path when she began to move towards the archway.

"Out with it," Sorin demanded, folding his arms across his chest. "With what?"

"With what has you in this mood. What Ashtine was referencing. Where you learned to block the bond like that."

"You have been blocking me out whenever you please since I returned. It only seemed fitting that I be able to do the same when it suited me," she retorted.

"Fair enough," he conceded, and her mouth gaped open in obvious shock at his agreement. "But where did you learn it?"

"A book."

His eyes narrowed. "The same one you learned that from?" he asked, with a jerk of his chin towards what he could only call shadow armor.

"*Perhaps*," she said with a sardonic curl of her lips.

"Why are you so insistent on picking a fight with me today?"

"Because you keep asking me annoying questions."

"For fuck's sake," Sorin said, raking a hand through his hair. "I am trying here, Scarlett. I need you to meet me halfway."

"I am tired, Sorin."

"You should be more than rested. You slept soundly for hours. Are you feeling unwell?"

"My soul is tired. I mean, yes. I am physically tired as well, which is concerning and something I want to discuss with you, but I mean my soul is tired. I am *tired*. This, all of this," she continued, gesturing widely with her hand and sighing deeply. "Today my responsibilities are just weighing on me. I am not trying to be a pain in your ass. Not any more than usual anyway."

He huffed a soft laugh, reaching over to pull her hood up for her. "Let's go to the libraries, and when we return to the Black Halls, we take the rest of the day off. We can go to Solembra if you want. Or the mountain chalet. The Water Court and sit next to the sea in the sun and warmth. Whatever you need."

She smiled weakly up at him. "We cannot afford to take time off right now, Sorin."

"We cannot afford not to. Not if days like today are going to be the result."

"Let's see how long this takes before we plan the rest of our day," she said, stepping around him and making her way to the steps.

"I am not going to give up on this, Scarlett."

"I do not doubt that," she murmured, pulling an amulet from her pocket and studying it as she crossed under the archway.

He followed, feeling the wards snap back into place once he

cleared the archway, and they made their way back down to the Citadel.

"Do you have any idea where the Fae key might be?" Scarlett asked Ashtine while they were led through underground passageways beneath the Citadel. They'd shed their fur-lined cloaks above, and he'd gotten Scarlett to eat the small sandwiches that were awaiting them when they returned. Briar and Ashtine had gone back to putting distance between themselves, and now Ashtine was escorting them to the libraries.

Each Court had a library, as did the White Halls and Black Halls, but none of them compared to that of the Wind Court. Their libraries were housed in catacombs beneath the Citadel, spanning the entirety of the structure and beyond. Sorin had no idea how big the libraries truly were, only that they were extensive and the Wind Court was extremely protective of the tomes they contained. Visitors were always escorted, never allowed to roam alone, and several areas were closed to outsiders.

"I have many ideas. Will any of them be helpful to you? Likely not," Ashtine replied, her usual lilt and oddness having returned. "But I suspect they will find their way to you as the others have."

Scarlett nodded. She pulled an amulet from her pocket again as they walked, her own this time. She ran her fingers over Saylah's symbol, goddess of shadows and night. "Any idea who the final bloodline might be? The six bloodlines of this continent are covered."

"That you know of," Ashtine said.

Sorin and Briar were walking behind the females, but they were listening to every word. Briar met Sorin's quick glance at Ashtine's words.

Scarlett seemed to weigh how to respond, clearly remembering that speaking with the Wind Princess could be difficult. "You have said my powers walked this world before. Did you know I was Avonleyan when you met me?"

"No. I am not a Seer."

"But you are very knowledgeable."

"Only when the winds speak through me."

"Do you regret your choice?"

"Scarlett," Sorin warned, but Briar shook his head, apparently wanting to hear the answer.

Ashtine was quiet for so long Sorin didn't think she was going to respond.

"Queen Talwyn is unaccustomed to loyalty given freely. She does not understand the idea of someone willingly choosing her above others. Not without some kind of cost to her. No one has ever done so before."

Guilt barreled into Sorin at those words. Scarlett obviously felt it too, glancing back over her shoulder at him, her eyes wide in alarm.

"Queen Talwyn does not understand unconditional love," Ashtine continued, drawing Scarlett's attention back to her. "To answer your inquiry, no. I do not regret choosing my queen, my friend, over my gifts. I do not regret being able to show her that unconditional love exists in this world, even for her. The cost for me has been extreme, something I would only bear for one other person. As for your previous question," she said, her tone making it clear any discussion about Talwyn was over. She reached for the amulet Scarlett was still fiddling with. "Many bloodlines have walked this world at some point or another. How many remain is unknown even to the winds, but I would start beneath the Black Halls."

"You mentioned this before," Scarlett said, and dread pooled in Sorin's gut. With everything else going on, he had also forgotten Ashtine's brief mention of what, *who*, exactly resided beneath the Black Halls. His hand instantly brushed over where the Bargain Mark was on his skin. Briar gave him a pointed look, saying he remembered the last time they were beneath those Halls too.

"Something about a sorceress," Scarlett was saying.

"*The* Sorceress," Ashtine corrected. "Yes, she resides in the prison beneath your Halls."

"And she is in this prison because . . . ?"

"Yes, Sorin, please explain who exactly the Sorceress is to your wife," Briar chimed in, and Sorin shot him a dark glare.

"The Sorceress was captured by Queen Eliné and Queen Henna during the war. She is said to be not of this world. No one knows where she came from, but her powers were stripped from her. Half of her gifts were used to create the Witch bloodline. Her other gifts were bestowed upon those who are now the Shifters," Sorin explained.

"Why would you not mention her sooner?" Scarlett asked. "Ashtine is right. She could be the final bloodline."

"She does not have an amulet, Scarlett. Her cell is bare. She is incredibly dangerous."

"How so, if she no longer has her gifts?"

"She still has her knowledge. She can still practice Blood Magic if she gets access to blood," Sorin said darkly.

"Perhaps her knowledge would be helpful," Scarlett tossed back over her shoulder, continuing to follow Ashtine.

"Everything has a cost with her. Answers to questions will be no different, and her prices are steep," Sorin replied.

"Your husband would know," Briar cut in.

Scarlett seemed to miss a step, but she kept walking. "Sorin?" A clear demand for an explanation.

He glared at Briar again. "She is how I found you in Baylorin after we fought. When you Traveled and could not get home."

"She was your work around?"

"Yes."

"And the cost?"

"I made a bargain with her."

"What did you barter with?"

"The blood of a god."

Scarlett stiffened, but she kept walking. "How do you plan to attain such a thing?"

"I don't," Sorin answered.

"It seems unwise to break a bargain with this Sorceress."

"I will not be breaking it. She said if I did not find such a thing before my death, my bargain would be fulfilled. I have not looked very hard," he said.

Scarlett glanced back at him once more but only said, "We need to go see her."

"Prince Briar is the only one who can grant such access," Ashtine lilted.

She handed the amulet she still held back to Scarlett as they came to a stop in front of a set of towering white doors. He had been to the Wind Court libraries before, but he'd never entered through these doors. A guard was stationed on either side, and when Sorin reached out a hand to touch the doors, spears blocked his access.

"Touching without permission is rude, Prince," Scarlett chided.

"Says the queen whose manners only appear when—"

"Sorin!" Scarlett exclaimed, her cheeks flushing.

He smirked tauntingly, arching a brow at her and latching on to this small piece of normalcy between them.

You are an ass, she sent down the bond.

Sorin only chuckled softly, looking at Ashtine. "These doors are skystone."

"Yes," the princess replied. "Only the Royal family and priestesses have been in this section of the catacombs."

"You think the books I need are in there?" Scarlett asked, turning back to the doors with renewed interest.

"Perhaps," Ashtine replied simply. "But that is not why I brought you here."

Ashtine nodded to the guards who immediately stepped aside, one grabbing a handle and pulling the door open for them to pass. They crossed the threshold, and Scarlett audibly gasped. Sorin nearly did the same.

Everything beyond the doors was skystone. The shelves. The tables. Even the godsdamn floor was skystone. A few priestesses moved among the stacks, bowing when Ashtine passed. Scarlett was moving towards a shelf as though she were being drawn to it by some force she couldn't control.

Touching without permission is rude, he taunted down the bond.

She flipped him off over her shoulder, not bothering to look back at him.

Her fingers glided along book spines. Ashtine stood back, her hands clasped in front of her, a small smile on her face as she watched Scarlett move along the books. "I am afraid those books will likely not provide the answers you seek."

"How do you know where everything is?"

"Ashtine spent much of her childhood among these catacombs," Briar answered. "She likely knows them better than the priestesses who serve here."

"Why do priestesses serve in a library?" Scarlett asked.

"They are priestesses of Falein," Briar replied, referring to the goddess of wisdom and cleverness.

"Ah," was Scarlett's reply. She moved to another shelf. "I could spend months in here."

"Unfortunately for you, you only have the day," Sorin teased. "And we do have pressing matters, Love."

"I know," she sighed, looking longingly at the books before making her way reluctantly back to where the rest of them stood waiting for her.

"There are texts on Avonleya in here," Ashtine said. "However, before I take to you their location, there is another place I wish for you to see."

"Lead the way," Scarlett murmured, her eyes bouncing around the space.

Sorin grabbed her hand, leading her forward. She nearly tripped on her own feet.

"You still need to watch where you are going, Love," he said in amusement.

"I trust you not to lead me astray," she replied, tipping her head back to the ceiling. Various depictions of the gods had been hand-painted there over the years.

He followed Ashtine, towing Scarlett along behind him, and the princess led them down several hallways that seemed to slowly bring them deeper below ground. When she turned another corner, Sorin stilled. Scarlett ran into his back.

"Gods, Sorin," she grunted, bouncing off of him, but then she stilled, too.

At the end of the corridor they'd just entered was a set of black doors, so dark they seemed to swallow any light.

Scarlett released his hand, taking another step forward. "Is that . . . nightstone?"

"I have never been beyond those doors," Ashtine said. "Although I tried many times as a child."

"Who has?" Scarlett asked, moving past her.

"No one that I have ever met," the princess answered. "We cannot unlock the doors."

Scarlett froze. "Then how are we to enter?"

"You believe what you carry in your pocket to be a key, do you not?" Ashtine asked.

"But I would need Talwyn to change its shape."

"There is not a lock on these doors, your Majesty," Ashtine said, gesturing to the doors. "I do believe the key lies in your blood, just as it draws the Avonleyan keys to you."

"What am I supposed to do?"

"A shadow or white flame should suffice," Ashtine said with an encouraging smile.

Scarlett looked up at Sorin.

Go ahead, Love.

She swallowed before wreathing her hand in shadows and laying her palm on one of the doors. Silver light flared beneath it, and there was an audible click. She pushed, and the door slowly opened. She went to take a step in, but Sorin was beside her in the next breath, grabbing her elbow.

"Let me go in first," he said, pushing the door open farther, a ball of flame appearing above their heads.

Scarlett rolled her eyes. "She just said no one has been beyond these doors in centuries. Do you think someone has been *living* in there?"

"No one has been beyond these doors in centuries. That is the entire point here," Sorin retorted, pushing past her and peering into the darkness beyond the door. The flames illuminated a long, rectangular chamber. Shelves full of books ran the length of both sides.

White flames raced past him along the skystone floor, running the entire length of the room and reflecting off of it. The room illuminated, and he looked back at Scarlett, who gave him a simpering smile. "You were taking too long."

"These books are not in any language I have ever seen," came Ashtine's voice from where she'd drifted over to one of the bookshelves.

Scarlett moved next to her, pulling one from the shelf. "This is similar to the Avonleyan language, but slightly different. Some of these words though . . ." She ran her finger along some text. "Some of these words will be the same."

Briar had moved farther down the chamber along the trail of flames Scarlett had let linger to keep the space lit in a low light. "Any guesses as to why there is a mirror at the end of this chamber?"

Ashtine's head snapped up. "A what?"

He pointed to the end of the chamber where the room was indeed reflected back to them. The mirror was the size of a large door, starting at the floor and reaching perhaps a foot taller than Sorin.

"It is a mirror gate," Ashtine breathed.

"What is that?" Scarlett asked, returning the book to the shelf, her attention now also on the mirror.

"There have long been legends of the mirror gates. They are said to be doors between the kingdoms," Ashtine replied, making her way towards the mirror.

"So every kingdom would have one?" Scarlett asked, following her. "In theory. Knowledge of them was long lost. Only brief mentions in old scrolls," Ashtine said.

As they neared the mirror, they could see the symbols of the gods were carved faintly into the skystone around it. Scarlett reached into her pocket, drawing out one of the amulets, holding it up beside the symbols. A messy knot, black as night, beside the same carved into stone blindingly white. Temural, god of the wild and untamed.

"Where do you think it leads?" Scarlett asked, leaning in to study the symbols more, her breath coasting over the amulet.

"Home, Lady of Darkness. It will lead you home," came an answering voice, and Sorin was snatching Scarlett back from the mirror in the next heartbeat.

Standing in the mirror, looking back at them, was a tall, broad man. He was as muscled as any Fae warrior. His silver hair reached past his shoulders, arched ears barely visible, and his silver eyes matched Scarlett's when her power was at full strength. The male barely glanced at the rest of them, his focus on Scarlett, who was staring back with wide eyes.

Shock was flooding him down the bond, but there was no fear. No terror. And the shock was quickly morphing into something else. Her shadow armor covered her skin as she forced Sorin to release her, and she stepped towards the mirror.

"Time for explanations, Lord of Night."

CHAPTER 38
SCARLETT

He was inside the fucking mirror, staring back at her. A faint smile of amusement played across his lips as he surveyed her.

"I have been waiting a long time for you to discover one of these mirrors," the beautiful man said, adjusting the sleeve of the black jacket he wore.

"Why?"

"They do not require magic to operate, unlike when I seek you out in your dreams," he answered.

"You have just been . . . what? Standing in front of a mirror for months on end waiting for me to appear?" she asked, tilting her head. "That seems like a rather dull use of your time."

The man chuckled. "You spoke to me through the stone."

She glanced down at the amulet she still held in her hand, Temural's symbol hanging from the chain.

"You were serious about that?"

"Why would I lie about it?"

"I just thought you were being an ass."

"Scarlett," came Sorin's tentative voice from behind her. "Is this . . .?"

"The man I see in my dreams? Yes," she answered. "He is bonded to Altaria."

"Who are you?" Sorin demanded, stepping to her side.

A dark smile curved up on the man's lips. "Someone who does not answer to you, Prince of Flames."

"Perhaps not, but you entering my wife's dreams is a problem," Sorin said darkly.

"Is it?"

A growl rippled from Sorin, and Scarlett sighed. "Stop acting like an overprotective animal. He's never once threatened me or attempted to hurt me."

"That is not in the least bit comforting," Sorin retorted. "Are there more mirrors?" came Ashtine's lilt.

Scarlett glanced back to find Briar standing before her, hand raised and a dagger of ice grasped in it.

"There are, your Highness," the man answered. "Before you inquire, I cannot reveal the locations. They can only be found by those who already know where they are."

"That's convenient," Scarlett muttered.

"Did you not find one?" he asked.

"By accident," she drawled.

"Or by fate," the man said with a shrug.

"*Fate*," she spat.

His head cocked to the side as he took her in, studying her. "You do not believe in the Fates?"

"Does it matter?"

"Not really. The Fates do not care if you believe in them or not."

Scarlett clucked her tongue, crossing her arms, and glared back at him. "So what? I can come to where you are through this mirror?"

"No. It is not a literal gate. It is a *mirror*," the man drawled.

"That is called a mirror *gate*," Scarlett retorted, really not in the mood to argue with him over semantics.

She had woken with a headache. She was exhausted. She hadn't been lying when she'd told Sorin that. It didn't seem to matter how much sleep she got lately. She never felt fully rested. Even more so, she never felt like her power wells stayed full. She had been trying to conserve her magic the last two days, just to test a theory, but they seemed to slowly drain whether she released her gifts or not. She had no idea what to make of it.

The man shrugged again. "Fair enough, but no, it is not a door of any sort. I know some legends claim such a thing, but they are simply mirrors between different kingdoms. Nothing more. It is more of a communication method."

"Great," Scarlett muttered. "What message do you need to deliver this time?"

The man was silent, appearing to study her closer. "You are . . . unwell."

"You don't say?" she bit back. His brows rose at her address. "Since our last little rendezvous, I have found four of the seven keys you instructed me to find. I still do not know where the lock is, and I have been practicing with my gifts. What more do you want from me? Because I do not have much left to give."

"I know that a lot is being asked of you," he started, his tone softening.

"Then stop asking!" she cried.

She felt Sorin reach for her down the bond, to try to comfort her, soothe her, but she shoved him out. She didn't want comfort right now. She wanted answers. For once, *just once*, she wanted some straight answers. No riddles. No guessing games. Just a fucking answer.

The entire room had fallen silent at her outburst, but her eyes remained fixed on the man in the mirror.

The man who had found her in her dreams.

"What are you leading me towards?" she whispered.

"Your destiny, Lady of Darkness. I am leading you towards your destiny."

"And if I do not want it?"

"You sentence this world to a fate worse than death."

"There is no one else?"

"I did not even know there was you until your gifts called to me. Until then, there was no hope. Learning of your existence gave an entire kingdom hope. Gave a world that does not even know they need it, hope," he answered. He moved as if to step towards her, before remembering he stood before a mirror.

"A siren's call draws unexpected attention," Scarlett murmured.

"Indeed."

"You are a Seer?"

"I am a dreamer."

"Hope is for the dreamers," she said softly.

Scarlett pushed her hair back out of her face, her tunic bunching as she did. She felt the cool air of the catacombs along the bare skin of her midriff as she blew out a breath. Her arm dropped to her side.

"Well, that explains a lot," the man muttered. Then louder he asked, "Have you found a Source?"

"I don't know what that means," she replied, exasperated by this entire conversation.

"How have you replenished your shadows?"

"The only way I know how," she answered, dropping down to sit on the floor.

"Can you tell us what a Source is? Or how to find one?" Sorin asked. "We have been researching but have found nothing on the matter."

The man nodded, understanding seeming to dawn in his silver gaze. His eyes shifted back to Scarlett where she sat on the floor. "You have a Guardian, yes? Ranvir reported that you do."

"You know Ranvir?"

"I do. That is not important right now. You have a Guardian, yes?"

"I do. Cassius."

"Cassius?"

"That is my Guardian's name."

"We did not know his name," he murmured. A faint smile lifted on his lips before saying louder, "You obviously have a book of Blood Magic, yes? That is where you found the other Mark to block your bonds?"

"Yes," she said, ignoring the way Sorin stiffened at the mention of Blood Magic.

"As soon as we are done here, you need to get that book and go straight to your Guardian. Show him the Mark right above your hip. As your Guardian, he will need to nullify it," the man instructed.

"Mark above my hip?" She lifted her tunic slightly, seeing only bare skin.

"It was clever magic, but your Guardian will be able to see it," the man said gravely. "You will find many things much easier when it is taken care of. Until then, do not touch your power unless absolutely necessary. None of it."

"Why?" she demanded, pushing back to her feet.

"That is a draining Mark. You have been exhausted lately, no? Your power wanes more quickly? You have been on edge? Yes?"

"That is why? Because he . . . Alaric placed a Mark on me?" The man nodded, his lips pressed into a taut line.

"The headaches?"

"From your Avonleyan gifts draining. The headaches are the first sign of needing your Source."

"Thank you," she whispered, tears of utter relief welling in her eyes.

She reached out, laying her palm against the glass.

He brought his hand to hers. Her hand looked tiny against his reflection. "When night and darkness meet, when dreams and stars collide, when ashes meld with shadows, you will find me waiting."

⁂

They had stayed only another hour after the man had disappeared from the mirror gate. Scarlett had known better than to ask if she could borrow any of the books from that chamber, known Ashtine would decline. But the princess had said she would be happy to escort her to the chamber whenever Scarlett wished, so she had left that for another day.

Now she raced for the door the moment she stepped through the fire portal Sorin had created. He'd brought them to their rooms in the Black Halls, and Scarlett was in the hallway before Sorin had even closed the portal.

She burst through Cassius's door without knocking. Cassius shot up from the chair he'd been sitting in. Cyrus, Eliza, and Rayner did the same. She didn't take the time to think about what they might all be doing in here. She was already pulling her tunic over her head, leaving just the band around her breasts.

Cassius and Cyrus had both been coming towards her, but Cyrus faltered as she dropped the tunic to the floor. Cassius, however, was unfazed by her utter lack of propriety as always.

"What is wrong?" he demanded, taking her shoulders and leaning back to inspect her.

"What Marks do you see, Cassius?"

Sorin had taken his time following, the door just now clicking shut behind him. He noted her shirt on the floor, but said nothing, leaning back against the door, crossing his arms.

"Sorin?" Cyrus asked, but the prince just shook his head before nodding to Cassius to answer her question.

"Like your twin flame Mark?" Cassius asked, his eyes dropping to her left hand.

"Yes, but more like this," Scarlett answered. "Do you see this Mark?" She lifted her right arm, exposing her forearm.

"The three stars and triangle there? Of course I see them," Cassius answered. "Why?"

Sorin pushed off the door at that. "You can see them?" Cassius looked over at him. "I take it that is of significance."

"No one else can see them, Cass," Scarlett breathed. "Which others can you see?"

"This one," he answered, brushing two fingers along her collarbone. "Yes," Scarlett nodded. She twisted to show him her back. "And there?" His calloused fingers skimmed over the Guardian Mark along the base of her spine.

"You have that one, too," she said softly, twisting back around. "More," she urged. "Do you see any more?"

Cassius took a small step back to see her better, before reaching out with one finger and swiping it above her left hip. "This one."

At his words, Scarlett summoned her shadows, shaping them into a panther who carried the book she'd kept most guarded. She took it from the panther's maw, the shadows immediately dissipating. Her headache had only increased throughout the day. There was a throbbing behind her eyes, and she felt like she could sleep for days.

"Find it in here," she said, shoving the book at Cassius. "Find that Mark and show it to me."

Cassius studied her a moment longer, before moving back to the chair he'd been sitting in and beginning to thumb through the book. Scarlett made her way to the sofa, plopping down on her back and closing her eyes.

"So . . . who is filling us in here?" Cyrus asked.

Scarlett felt him lift her feet, settling them into his lap. A second later, Sorin was lifting her into a sitting position. He slipped her tunic back over her head before lowering her down onto a pillow against his legs.

"I met the man who visits Scarlett in her dreams," Sorin answered.

Scarlett only half-listened, letting Sorin handle explaining everything they'd learned in the Wind Court today. Sorin's fingers were moving soothingly along her hairline as they discussed the man, the keys, her. She didn't offer anything to the conversation. No input. No insights.

They were going to find the Contessa in two days. All she really cared about at this point was being able to hold her own and preserve her power levels so she could use them when needed. It was the main reason she had asked Nuri and Juliette to join her. It wasn't that she didn't think they couldn't handle it, but if she wasn't at full strength, they'd need more. She needed people she could work with seamlessly. There was really only Nuri and Juliette for that.

"Here," Cassius said almost an hour later. "It is this one."

Scarlett had nearly fallen asleep while they'd sat there, but she about fell off the sofa when she tried to get up too quickly at Cassius's words.

"Easy, Love," Sorin murmured, saving her from face-planting on the floor.

She moved, making room beside her so Cassius could sit, and she found herself squished between him and Sorin.

"It is this one," Cassius repeated, pointing to a Mark that looked like a triangle with a line through it. It vaguely reminded Scarlet of a bell. "But I can't read this."

Scarlett pulled the book into her lap. "This is a draining Mark, just like he said."

Sorin was looking over her shoulder. "What does this part say?" he asked, pointing at a small description beneath the Mark.

Scarlett skimmed the passage quickly. "It has various uses, but all of them revolve around essentially draining something of its power. It can be done slowly or quickly, depending on how it is drawn. It explains why I've been so tired. Why my power has felt off."

"And you did not say anything sooner because?" Sorin asked tightly.

"Because I thought it was just everything going on, everything we are dealing with. Maybe my body adjusting to Avonleyan gifts," Scarlett answered, continuing to skim the page. "I was just beginning to question it more."

Sorin didn't reply, and she didn't have it in her to care if he felt slighted right now. Not with the headache and the exhaustion. None of them had experience with Avonleyan gifts. None of them knew if what she'd been experiencing would have been considered abnormal.

"I don't understand how he hid it from me," Scarlett went on. "I know why all of you cannot see it, but I should be able to . . ."

"Forget that," Cyrus cut in. "How do we reverse it?"

"I'm looking, Darling," Scarlett retorted. She turned a few

more pages. "Why are you all in here anyway?" She felt a tense sort of silence settle over the room. Without looking up, she said, "Say it."

"My spies reported movements of the mortal armies in Toreall and Rydeon," Rayner said quietly.

"To the Earth Court border?" Scarlett asked, turning another page. "A portion of them, yes," Rayner confirmed. "But there is a greater number going north and south in Rydeon."

Scarlett glanced at the Ash Rider. "To our borders?"

"It would appear so," he agreed.

"Hmm," she hummed, her attention returning to the book.

"This is the part where you fill us in on your thoughts, Darling," Cyrus said from down the sofa.

"It would appear they are preparing an attack of some sorts," she replied.

"Our Courts and the Earth Court?" Eliza cut in. "What of the Wind Court?"

"Talwyn is still a key player in all of this," Scarlett said, her focus remaining on the spell book in her lap. "If they can sway her, the Wind and Earth Courts will likely follow."

"What of Windonelle's forces?" Cassius asked, settling back into the sofa and stretching an arm along the back behind her. "None of them are moving?"

"Not that we have seen," Rayner replied.

"They are waiting for me," Scarlett said simply. "And for this thing with Callan and Tava to play out."

"Waiting for you to what?"

"She was the closely guarded weapon," Eliza supplied. "She still is one."

"It would be stupid to center their plans around her," Sorin argued. "They cannot be doing that."

"Alaric is always ten steps ahead," Scarlett muttered.

"But he also trained you to think the same way," Cyrus countered. "Which is how you always seem to figure all this shit out before the rest of us. This is the part where you *say something*."

"I have no insights to share right now, Cyrus," Scarlett said. "The mortal kings are puppets. I haven't figured out how he is controlling them yet." She turned another page and stilled. "Cass."

Cassius and Sorin both leaned forward.

"Tell me what I'm looking at, Seastar," Cassius said.

"This Mark will nullify the draining Mark, but it can only be done by the Guardian of the person afflicted," Scarlett replied.

"What do I need to do?" Cassius asked.

"You need to use your blood to draw this Mark atop the draining Mark, but it needs to be precise, Cass. Perfectly drawn. Start practicing," she said, nodding towards a small desk along the wall.

"Yes, your Majesty," he teased.

She stuck her tongue out at him as he rose from the sofa, making his way to the desk to grab some paper and charcoal. He still had a limp when he moved, but he was adjusting to only seeing with one eye fairly well.

"When you do it, though, the draining Mark will resist," Scarlett said, continuing to translate the text.

"What does that mean?" Sorin asked.

"It will drain as much of my power as it can before it's nullified. He will feel a strong urge to stop when the Guardian link senses he is harming rather than protecting. I might start trying to pull from Cassius."

"That won't be an issue. I'm here for him," Cyrus chimed in. "I can be ready."

"And I am here for you," Sorin added. "This will be fine."

"Come, Scarlett. Tell me what needs to be changed," Cassius called from the desk.

"No," she said immediately when she saw what he'd drawn. "This line isn't straight enough. This angle needs to be sharper. This part smaller," she added, pointing to various parts of the Mark he'd drawn.

"What happens if it's not perfect?" Cassius asked, beginning to draw again.

"I do not wish to find out."

She made Cassius redraw the Mark for the next twenty minutes, and when it was perfect, she made him draw it ten more times exactly the same way.

She pushed out a long breath as she laid back onto the sofa, pulling the tunic up to just below her breasts. Cassius was kneeling on the floor beside her. Her head rested in Sorin's lap, and everyone else was gathered around them.

"This isn't awkward at all," she muttered under her breath.

"We're one big, happy family, Darling. It's fine," Cyrus replied with a wink.

"Whatever."

"Ready?" Cassius asked, a knife poised and ready to slash along his palm.

"Whenever you are."

A moment later, his finger was tracing along her hip, a warm, sticky substance running along her flesh.

"You doing okay, Love?" Sorin murmured. "So far . . ."

Cassius's finger left her skin, but when it returned a second later and began drawing once more, the ache in her head intensified. A pounding began in her skull, and she squeezed her eyes shut against it.

"Love . . ."

"I'm fine. Keep going, Cass," she ordered when she felt him pause.

His finger left again, presumably to dip into more of his blood, and when the third line of the Mark began, she felt as if flames and ice were being dragged from her very being. Burning cold flooded her veins, and she gritted her teeth, her shadows surging in a bid to protect her.

"Seastar," Cassius gasped, his finger stalling. "I feel you—"

"Keep going, Cassius," she panted through her teeth.

The pressure in her head was making bright spots dance behind her closed lids. Or maybe that was her own white embers. Her back arched off the sofa when Cassius's finger began moving again. She heard him suck in a sharp breath when her shadows reached for him, latched onto his arms, trying to protect her but also tugging at his own gifts.

"Scarlett," he gasped.

"I know," she panted. "Focus. It must be perfect."

"Get cups," she heard Sorin bark at someone. "They are going to need blood when this is done."

His hands were on her shoulders, keeping her pinned to the sofa. Someone was holding her legs down. She assumed it was Cyrus. "This is the last of it, Love," Sorin was saying.

"By the gods," Eliza muttered. "Sorin . . . Her tears are red."

"It is Blood Magic, Eliza," Sorin snapped. "I do not know what else you expected."

Scarlett felt it then. Blood trickling from her nose, her ears, her eyes. She could feel her shadows digging into Cassius, trying to drag his hand away. All of her strength went into holding back her magic, trying to convince it to let this happen.

"There," she heard Cassius pant at the same moment the burning in her body stopped, but now . . .

Now the pain in her head was excruciating. She was exhausted. Her power reserves hadn't felt this low since she'd fought at the Earth Court border.

"Scarlett. Look at me, Love," Sorin said cautiously. She felt him wiping the blood from her cheeks, beneath her nose. "Open your eyes."

"She's still drawing from me," Cassius rasped. "She's too weak to stop it."

"We're working on it," Eliza replied tightly.

The scent of blood hit her senses then, and she lurched up. Cassius was leaning against the sofa, his head hanging between his bent knees. Cyrus had a gash along his arm, blood trickling into a cup that Eliza was holding beneath it. Her nostrils flared, and she lunged forward, but an arm snaked around her waist.

"No, Love," Sorin whispered soothingly into her ear. "One more minute."

Her head whipped to him. His arm was bleeding into a glass that Rayner held. She wasn't waiting. Not another second. Her power wells physically ached from the emptiness, and she was desperate to relieve any of the throbbing in her skull.

Scarlett twisted in his arm, grabbing his bleeding one and pulling it to her lips. She sucked hard on the gash, and she heard Sorin hiss, but her magic sighed deeply in relief. Her entire body relaxed as he pulled her against him, keeping his arm in place at her mouth. Her shadows flowed around her like a mist, white embers drifting among them. It had never felt like this. Her magic felt . . . energized. Charged in a way she couldn't describe. The power coursing through her with every pull from Sorin was enthralling, all-consuming. His flames feeding her shadows. Her focus was on needing more of that feeling. More and more and more.

"Enough, Scarlett," she heard him say after some time, attempting to pull his arm away.

She moaned in protest, but hands were pulling her away from him. "You have to force it, Rayner," Sorin said.

A hand gripped her jaw, making her release Sorin, and the moment she did, she was pulled back into his chest. Sorin held her there, stroking her hair, not letting her move.

"Relax, Love. Rest," he murmured.

She melted against him, exhaustion settling into her limbs. Her fire and ice were still depleted, but the power thrumming in her veins? Gods, it was exquisite. Was this what it was supposed to be like all the time? When she found a Source, would this be a constant?

"Sleep," Sorin murmured again, his hand beginning to run up and down her spine.

And Scarlett let the darkness have her.

CHAPTER 39
CALLAN

"We will be gone for the next month," Lord Tyndell was saying to the other Lords gathered for the daily council meeting.

Callan sat to his father's left, idly leafing through reports before him.

"Are you leaving that general you spoke so highly of in charge in your absence?" his father was asking. "Renwell? Was that his name? You have not mentioned him in quite some time."

"I am afraid he returned to his homeland," Lord Tyndell replied smoothly. "We held on to him as long as we could, and he certainly trained your High Force impeccably."

"Shame," his father grunted. "Who replaced him?"

"Mikale took over while the Crown Prince was . . . on his leave," the Lord replied, a sly smile on his lips when he glanced to Callan. "Now one of the High Force soldiers was promoted."

"What of your son?" the king asked. "You still do not want to train him to take your place? He would be valuable in times such as these."

The Lord's face hardened. "Drake is not cut out for this."

"And why is that?" Callan asked, settling back in his chair. All attention swiveled to him, but he kept his eyes fixed on the Lord, waiting for his response.

"Drake will be better served as a Lord of this Court. Inter-Court matters would suit him better," the Lord replied.

"You do not believe you could properly prepare him as your successor?" Callan pushed.

"This is not something that needs to be decided right now," the king cut in. "We have other matters to discuss."

"We do," Callan agreed. He pulled a report from the stack and laid it on top of the others. "What do you know of Rydeon and Toreall moving their forces around to the Fae borders?"

Lord Tyndell and Mikale tensed. They both recovered quickly, but Callan caught it.

When Amaré had arrived to see if there was anything to report about this amulet they were supposed to be looking for, he'd had a message in his beak. It was from Cassius, and somehow the fact that it had come from him and not Scarlett or Sorin didn't make him feel quite so . . . bitter as Tava liked to put it. It was petty. He knew it was, but he really wanted little to do with them at this point. What was in that report, though . . . What did these other kingdoms know that they didn't?

"What is this?" the king demanded, reaching over and taking the report from the pile. "Where did you get this?"

"You have made it clear I was to begin taking my responsibilities more seriously," Callan replied calmly. "I have connections in the other kingdoms. People I have met while . . . How did you put it, Lord Tyndell? While I was *on leave?*"

"Who?" Lord Tyndell gritted out from between his teeth.

"Who is not important," Callan replied, though he was certain the Lord knew exactly who his connections were.

"It is if those are false reports," the Lord countered.

"I do not believe they are, but I do think it is something that should be looked into either way. We do not want to be caught unprepared and look like fools," Callan said, returning his gaze to his father.

"What do you know of this, Balam?" the king asked tightly, his eyes skimming the report.

"We have heard nothing of the sort, your Majesty," the Lord replied. "But it is something we can certainly look into on our travels this month. We are going to Toreall after all. We can set something up with Rydeon as well."

"I want updates as soon as possible," the king said, placing the report on the table. "Do we need to be preparing for something, Balam?"

"We are always prepared, your Majesty. You know this," the Lord answered.

"Take Mikale with you," Callan said.

"What?" Mikale interjected from down the table.

"I would like to be kept up-to-date on this matter. To make sure my sources remain reliable. What better way than to have my to-be closest advisor there to be my eyes and ears himself?" Callan asked.

"I am sure Lord Tyndell's reports will be more than sufficient," Mikale said, his eyes fixed on the Lord across the table.

"No, I like this idea," the king cut in.

"But, your Majesty—"

"My son is finally taking an interest in matters," the king said, cutting Mikale off. "This will be good for both of you."

"Yes, your Majesty," Mikale replied. Callan could tell those words tasted like poison on his lips.

But it had worked. Mikale would be gone for a month or more.

It had been Tava's idea. She had been there when Amaré had arrived with the letter from Cassius. It was Drake who had created the "report" based on Cassius's letter. They knew Lord Tyndell wouldn't be able to outright deny anything. It would only take messengers to confirm the other two mortal kingdoms were indeed moving forces around. They had made Lord Tyndell look inept and gotten Mikale out of the kingdom, essentially killing two birds with one stone.

Now they only needed to worry about Veda.

A quick rap on his chamber doors told him it was Finn, and a second later, Tava was entering the room with Finn and Sloan behind her. She was dressed in pants and a tunic. She wore those boots that went nearly to her knees, and her hair was braided in a plait down her back.

"What are you doing here at this hour?" Callan asked Sloan. He was his guard all day, but the night guards took over when Callan retired for the evening.

"Your betrothed has an agenda tonight," Sloan said, nodding his head in Tava's direction.

"It is not an agenda," she said with a smile at him. "I call it an opportunity."

"Call it what you want, Lady Tyndell. It's dangerous as shit after what I was told happened last time," Sloan countered.

"What is this about, Tava?" Callan asked from where he'd been sitting near the hearth.

"I just learned that Veda has taken an extended leave, since her brother will be gone for the next several weeks," she said, her smile widening.

Lord Tyndell and Mikale had left the day prior, and they had been working on how they could get into the Lairwood Estate with him gone. Veda leaving as well was a stroke of pure luck.

"You want to go to the Lairwood house tonight?" Callan asked in surprise.

Tava shook her head, moving to sit on the edge of the sofa. "I learned she was leaving from the High Healer. This is an opportunity for me to go back to the poor districts and deliver some items."

"You want to go to the slums tonight?" Callan asked, his brows flying up.

"Yes. It is the perfect time," she said excitedly.

Callan glanced at Finn and Sloan. The former looked wary. The latter had his arms crossed, with a look that said this was absolutely not going to happen.

"Tava," Callan started carefully. "After our last escapade there, I really do not think this is a good idea. Not until things have calmed down."

"Veda is not going to be here," Tava repeated.

"I understand that, but we do not know for sure it was Veda behind your attempted abduction. She is just our best guess."

"They depend on me for things, Callan."

"And you are still getting them necessities, Tava," Callan countered. They had discussed it a few times, how she found other ways to make sure they were getting blankets, food, tonics.

"And they did tell you not to come back, Lady Tava," Finn interjected. "I do not think Lady Veda would need to be our only worry there any more."

"That was one man," Tava argued. "What of Helen? Of Mary Ellen? Of the families who were not involved in any of that? Who are simply trying to survive?"

"I am not trying to imply they do not matter," Callan said, attempting to reason with her. This was so unlike her. She was always so logical and astute. Granted, he had only truly come to know her these last several weeks. But they'd spent enough time together in those weeks, he felt like he could say he knew her fairly well.

"Then what are you trying to say?" she demanded, her voice beginning to rise.

"That it is not your responsibility," Callan answered, his own voice rising. "Someone is trying to kidnap you, Tava! How can you have such little regard for your own wellbeing?"

Tava stared back at him, her eyes hard. It was so silent in the room, all Callan could hear was the quiet ticking of the clock. The silence seemed to stretch on and on before Tava cleared her throat, clasping her hands in her lap. "Have I ever told you how much I love hot summer days?"

Confusion had his brows knitting together at the sudden change in subject, but it was mere seconds before realization dawned on him.

This was what was going to drive to her to seek an end to their arrangement?

"Tava," Callan said, rising and taking a step towards her. "Let's talk about this."

"You have said quite enough, Callan," she said calmly, her throat working to contain her emotions as she got to her feet.

"Tava, please. It is too dangerous for you to go there, even if we do end this ruse. It will take time for news to spread, and even then . . ."

And even then she might not ever be able to take up the things she had been doing. The people there knew she was engaged to the Crown. They knew she was nobility, willing to get into bed with the people who chose to turn a blind eye to their plights. That was his fault. That was something she had sacrificed for him.

"You say it is not my responsibility," Tava said suddenly. "Then whose is it, Callan? Yours? The king's? What makes my wellbeing so much more important than any of theirs? Simply because of who I was born to? Someone needs to care, Callan."

"And who is to care about you?" he countered. "Who is to care that you are putting yourself at risk when there are other ways to serve them?"

"No one questions when Scarlett wants to swing a sword and sneak around in the night, but when I do it to *help* people and not kill them, my wellbeing suddenly becomes more important?"

"You are not her," Callan said.

"Thank the gods for that," Sloan muttered under his breath.

Callan gripped her shoulders. "You are not her, Tava," he repeated. "You have said so yourself. And that recklessness? That inability to let anyone take care of her? That is not something to covet. Those are qualities you should not strive for. Being unable to let anyone in? That is not something you want."

"You know nothing of what I want," Tava all but spat back at him.

"Then tell me," he said. "Tell me what you want, Tava."

"I want to matter, Callan!" she cried, two tears slipping free. "I want to matter not because of my bloodline, not because I can produce heirs. I want to make a difference for someone, not because they did something to earn it, but because they deserve it simply by being alive. Because while I did not grow up among them, I still know what it is to be forgotten. I still know what it is to be left in the background. Do I know what it is like to go hungry? To not have shelter? To be poor? No. Do I know what it is to move unseen among others like a spirit? Yes."

"Tava," Callan breathed, pulling her into his chest and his arms wrapping around her. His chin rested atop her head, and he felt her small hands fist in his shirt at his sides.

After several minutes of holding her, she pushed back, swiping at her cheeks with her fingers. "Please, Callan. Veda is gone. Can we go this last time? Then we can find other ways to help them, but this last time . . . Please."

"I still do not think it is a good idea," he said gently.

Her shoulders sagged, and he knew she wouldn't defy him on this. It was too ingrained in her. She would fall into line, obey the order of a man, of her Crown Prince.

And he hated it.

He hated that she would give in, simply because she had been taught that men were superior and that her place was above commoners but below royalty. He hated that anyone would feel that way, but seeing *her* hurting because of it, caused something in his chest to tighten.

He exhaled sharply through his nose. "One time, Tava. This is the last time we do this. We go in disguised and discreet, and tomorrow you and I will discuss ways to help them here and in other cities in the kingdom."

She met his gaze, a tentative hope entering her eyes. "You mean that?"

"I still do not think it is a good idea," he said again.

"It is a stupid idea," Sloan cut in, but Finn was already gathering cloaks and extra weapons.

"We take horses until we are a few blocks away," Finn said, as they left Callan's chambers and began making their way down to the grounds. "We are not walking an hour back here if things do not go well. Which I am expecting they will not, by the way."

"It is a few tonics and blankets," Tava said softly, her hands deep in the pockets of her cloak. She wouldn't look at any of them, and Callan could read her well enough by this point to know she was feeling guilty.

The woman was feeling guilty for wanting to help those who could not help themselves.

How utterly ridiculous was that?

Sloan brought out Callan's black stallion first, and Callan turned to Tava. "Do you want to ride with me or with Finn?"

"You. If that is all right," she answered, her eyes fixed on the ground.

He gestured to her to come forward, and he helped her into the saddle before he swung up behind her. Once they were both situated and Finn and Sloan were atop their horses, they made their way to the pickup location the High Healer had sent to Tava.

"Have you ever met the High Healer?" he asked Tava.

She shook her head. "No. Messengers always delivered Scarlett's tonics. When we would go to the poor neighborhoods, Scarlett always had what we needed. When she was gone, the High Healer reached out to me, and it became what it is now."

"The High Healer reached out to you? Why?"

She shrugged against his chest. "She must have known I often helped Scarlett, I suppose."

Neither of them spoke again until after they had retrieved the two small bags of supplies that Sloan and Finn now had attached to their saddles. He had so much he wanted to say to her. He didn't want her to think her compassion was a fault. He didn't want her to think he was upset that she wanted to help these people. She was right. It should be him demanding this. It should be him wanting to know why his father didn't do more. And he certainly did not want her to feel as if she didn't matter.

When they were a few blocks from the slums, they left the horses with Finn. Callan and Sloan each had a bag looped over an arm, Tava walking between them. All was quiet when they turned onto the street. Much quieter than it had been when they had come here last time. They made their way to Helen's shack first, and Tava quickly made her way up the walk and through the decrepit door.

"Helen?" she called out.

"Tava?" came the old woman's raspy voice.

Tava quickly lit a candle before moving to the woman's side.

She was in the same corner she'd been sitting in last time, huddled under scraps of fabric.

"What are you doing here, Child?" Helen asked, her eyes seeming to widen some.

"I brought you tonics and blankets," Tava answered, motioning Callan to come forward with the bag he carried. "I am sorry I could not come sooner."

"You wasn't suppose to come," the woman said, her head shaking slightly.

"What do you mean?" Tava asked, digging through the bag until she found the vials she was looking for.

The old woman looked up at Callan like she could see his face beneath the hood.

"They will be waiting for her when you leave this house," she rasped. Tava stilled, her fingers on the cork of the vial.

"Who will be?" Sloan demanded, stepping forward.

Helen stiffened. "What you keep bringing strangers here for, Tava? He was not with you last time."

"They are helping me," Tava said. "Who will be waiting for me, Helen?"

"You wasn't suppose to come," Helen said again, reaching a shaky hand out to take the vial Tava was extending to her.

"We need to go," Sloan said, and Callan saw his hands shift beneath his cloak, reaching for weapons.

"Give me some blankets," Tava said instead, pointing at the bag Sloan still had on his shoulder.

Sloan swore under his breath, but passed the bag to Callan. He pulled two small, wool blankets from the bag, handing them to Tava, who tucked them carefully around Helen.

"Can I get you anything else before we leave?" she asked the old woman.

"You need to get outta here," the woman said, grasping Tava's hands between her own. "You get outta here and go where it's safe. Don't come back."

Tava pulled a hand free and patted Helen's arm. "Do not worry about me, Helen. That is why I brought them with me," she said with a wink and nod at Callan and Sloan.

"They won't matter, Child. They wants you," the woman said somberly as Tava pushed to her feet. Callan immediately reached a hand out to help her up.

"I think we should go, Tava," Callan said while they made their way back to the front door. Tava had left three more vials of the tonic on the small table beside the candle and was pulling on her gloves. He reached over and pulled her hood up for her.

"We are going," Sloan cut in, his tone daring either of them to argue with him.

"Let's just take the rest of these things to Mary Ellen and—"

She stopped speaking as they stepped out the door and found a group of twenty men standing before them. Some held torches, illuminating the space. Others held pipes. Clubs. Knives.

Sloan stepped in front of both of them, and Callan was pulling Tava into him, his hand going to the short sword at his waist.

"Hey there, angel," one man near the front of the group said. Callan recognized him as the same man who had tried to get her to follow him the last time they were here. "We was hoping you'd show up tonight. They said you would."

"Who is 'they'?" Callan asked.

"Ain't no business of yours, is it?" the man sneered. "In fact, I'll make you two a deal. You give us her, and we let you walk outta here."

"I am afraid that is not an option tonight," Callan answered, his arm tightening around Tava.

"What is going to happen," Sloan cut in, his tone dark and commanding, "is you lot are going to let us walk out of here. No one is going to do anything stupid, and we will all go on about our business."

A few of the men in the group chuckled, and the entire mob seemed to lurch forward.

"Nah," the man, apparently the leader, said. "That ain't what's going to happen at all. See, we will be getting quite a bit o' coin if we bring the angel to them."

"We will give you more coin to let us leave without a problem," Callan countered, taking a step back when the crowd moved closer again.

The man scoffed. "Angel," he chided, shaking his head, "you bringing more high society shit in here? Ain't enough to be better than us by marrying a prince?"

"I am not better than any of you," Tava replied, and Callan was rather impressed by the confidence in her voice. There was no quavering, no note of fear. "And neither are they. We only want to help."

"You want to help us, *angel?*" the man sneered.

"I do," Tava insisted, undeterred by the man's tone.

"Then let us turn you over to be used for whatever purposes they want," he sneered again. "That's the only way a noble whore like yourself could be of any use to us lowlifes in the slums."

"Watch your mouth," Callan snapped, and the entire crowd broke out into laughter.

"You know she's gonna marry the prince, right?" the man asked. "Don't get in the way of this over a piece you won't be able to touch any more soon anyway."

Sloan had drawn his sword as the crowd had moved closer. "Who wants her?" he asked.

"Don't care," the man shrugged. "Alls I know is I'm gonna get enough coin to feed my family for a year when I drag her outta here," he continued, pointing the knife he held at Tava.

"You are not going to touch her," Callan snarled.

"That's where you're wrong," the man sneered. "She's coming with us, and maybe we'll even break her in a lil' more before her prince gets her."

"Maybe her prince won't even want her any more after we're done," another man chimed.

"Wouldn't that be poetic, angel?" the first man said, moving closer again. "You thinkin' you're better than us, only to be tossed out by your prince?"

Tava was beginning to tremble beside him, but her voice was steady when she said, "I have never thought I was better than any of you."

"See, I used to think that, angel," the man said, tapping the hilt of his knife against his chin. "Then you went and got engaged to the godsdamn Crown Prince. You ain't any better than them, and you'll forget about us, just like they did. You jus' come here to make yerself feel better. You ain't ever cared."

"That is not true," Tava insisted.

The man shrugged again. "I don't really care if it is or not, and we're done talking. Come down here like a good bitch, and we'll go easy on ya."

"I have already stated you are not going to touch her," Callan said, pulling his short sword from its scabbard.

"Unless you got the royal guard here with ya, you ain't gonna stop us," the man sneered.

"How convenient," Sloan said, his tone low and deadly as he pulled back his hood. "That is exactly who is with them."

The crowd all stumbled back a step. The man's eyes flew back to Tava, wrath and fury blazing in them. "You brought the motherfuckin' royal guard here?"

"It's only one," a man yelled from the back. "We can handle one." Callan looked down at Tava, and she was already shaking her head.

He could see the pleading in her eyes, begging him not to do what he was about to, but there was really no other way out of this.

"I am sorry, Tava," he murmured, before releasing his arm from around her and pulling back his hood. There were audible gasps and curse words muttered. He was recognizable enough, even in torchlight. "If any of you lay a finger on any of us, know that we have more royal guards waiting for our return. There will be no hesitation if they need to come for us."

Hatred emanated from the mob before him, and the man who had been speaking spat at their feet. He pointed his knife at Tava again. "If you ever come back here again, *angel*, we will kill you. Get the fuck out."

The crowd slowly backed away, giving them space to move down the walkway. Sloan kept himself positioned between Callan and Tava and the crowd, but the men didn't move to attack or pursue them. They didn't know it was only Finn waiting for them to return, and apparently, they didn't want to risk bringing more of the royal guard into the slums. Callan had Tava's hand gripped firmly in his, and his grip didn't loosen, not even when Finn and the horses came into sight.

"What happened?" Finn asked, instantly drawing his weapon when he saw their hoods down and swords out.

"It was a fucking trap," Sloan growled, reaching for the reins of his horse.

"Are you all right?" Finn asked, his gaze swinging to Callan and Tava.

"We are fine," Callan replied, reaching to help Tava onto the horse.

"Let's just get out of here."

Within seconds, they were mounted and had the horses moving down the streets at a quick pace. Callan didn't breathe easier until they were back in the Elite District, and he didn't want to think about what kind of prince that made him. That he didn't feel safe among his own people. No, he didn't have it in him to contemplate that tonight.

"Please take me home," Tava said quietly. The first words she'd uttered since leaving the slums.

"If that is what you wish," Callan said.

A few minutes later, he was helping her dismount and walking her to her front door. It was locked, as one would expect it to be at this hour of the night. He was about to ask if there was another door they should try, but Tava brought her gloved hand up, banging on the door.

"Drake!" she called, something cracking in her voice. She was banging her fist again. "Drake! Let me in!"

She kept banging on the door, until it was yanked open, Drake standing there shirtless, in loose pants, and barefoot. "Tava? What are you—"

Tava said nothing, pushing past her brother and moving inside and up the grand staircase before disappearing down the hall.

Drake turned to Callan. "What happened?" he demanded. He looked furious. Protective. Ready to defend his sister against whatever threats were plaguing her.

Callan pulled his gloves off, placing them in a pocket of his cloak. "Will you allow me to speak with her?"

"No," Drake said immediately. "Not until you tell me what has happened. Is she hurt? Is she all right?"

"She is not hurt," Callan reassured him. "We had . . . an unexpected night."

"Explain," Drake snarled.

"I cannot," Callan replied. "Not without betraying her confidence, which I am unwilling to do."

"I did not even know she was gone," Drake said, carving a hand through his golden hair. "I got in late. Her door was closed. I assumed she was asleep. No one said anything."

"Your previous resident taught her many ways to leave this house unnoticed," Callan said.

Drake sighed. "Of course she did."

"May I go speak with her, please? If not, I will wait in the sitting room until she comes down."

Drake studied him for a moment, his stare nearly as piercing as his sister's. "Third door down on the right," he finally said, nodding towards the stairs.

"Thank you, Drake," Callan said, clapping him on the shoulder when he stepped past him and headed up the stairs. When he came to her door, he knocked softly.

"I do not wish to speak right now, Drake," Tava called out, a slight quaver in her voice.

"It is me, Tava. May I come in?"

Silence came from the other side of the door and stretched on and on before the door finally opened. She still wore the pants and tunic, but she'd removed her boots. Her hair was unbound and loose around her shoulders.

"May I come in?" Callan repeated.

"Of course, your Highness," she said, stepping to the side so he could enter.

Callan stiffened at the formality. That was not how this conversation was going to go.

He pushed the door shut behind him, watching Tava drift over to a window. He looked around the room, slightly shocked to find various clothing strewn about. Books and papers were scattered across a low-lying table. It made sense, he supposed. This was perhaps the one place she was not required to be perfect and proper. The one place she *could* be messy and chaotic.

"What can I do for you?" Tava asked, drawing his attention back to her. She had her hands clasped loosely in front of her, back straight.

"First off, we are not going to do this," Callan said, gesturing between them. "This formal shit is not what we do any more."

"Make no mistake, your Highness," Tava said coldly, "if you were not the Crown Prince, I would not have let you in tonight."

"You let me in because you felt like you had to?"

"Who am I to deny a Crown Prince?"

The words clanged through him. When they'd been said to him before, they had been teasing and mocking from the lips of a brash assassin. But Tava . . . She meant them.

"You truly believe that? That you are beneath me simply because of my title?" Callan asked.

"Is it right? No. Is it the reality of our world? Yes," Tava answered.

"Outside maybe," Callan countered. "But not when it is just us, Tava. Not when we are alone."

"Why should that make any difference, Callan?" she cried. "Why is it that outside these walls, I am nothing but a woman who is expected to act a certain way, speak a certain way? I am expected to accept my place? Be given to whomever will benefit from my bloodline the most? Spread my legs and produce heirs to further this entire broken system? Why is it that I have the ability to help those at the bottom and even they do not want my help? What good is all of *this* if I can do nothing with it?" She picked up a porcelain teacup from a small side table, hurling it at the wall. It shattered, shards flying in every direction as she sank down along the wall behind her. Her face fell into her hands, golden hair falling around her.

Callan unclasped his cloak, pulling it off and draping it across a chair, before he slowly moved towards her. He lowered himself to his knees before reaching tentatively for her wrists, pulling them gently from her face. Tears streaked down her face, and he found himself wiping them away.

"Little fox," he sighed, maneuvering so he sat next to her against the wall. He kept one hand clasped in his, and her head fell against his shoulder. "You have done more good than you could possibly imagine, even if you cannot see it."

"How, Callan? They will not even allow me to serve them any more," she said through her tears.

"Perhaps not directly, but because of you, because you took me there and showed me a side of my kingdom I did not want to see, they are no longer forgotten," he answered gently. "We will make sure of that, Tava. You have my word."

"There are so many more. Just like them. Not only here in Baylorin, Callan, but all over Windonelle. In Rydeon. Toreall." She swallowed thickly. "How can no one else care?"

"So incredibly selfless," he murmured, reaching over and brushing hair back off of her forehead.

"I have said before, I am not selfless. I simply care," Tava replied. Then she added, in a whisper so soft Callan almost didn't hear it, "Sometimes I wish I did not."

"Do not say that, Tava. You are the standard by which everyone should be measured. Your level of caring is what I strive for. Without you, I would be engaged to a Maraan Lady, and I still do not even know what that means," Callan said.

"And yet she has somehow still destroyed something I have worked years to build," she said, and Callan reached over to brush tears away once more.

His fingers ran along her jaw, pausing to cup her chin and tipping her face up to him. "What you are doing matters, Tava. What you are doing is making a difference. You may not see it. You may feel like it is futile, but I promise your actions are being felt in a ripple effect. And if you have made a difference in even one person's life, would you not consider it worth it?"

"Yes," she breathed.

"Then know that you have made a difference in mine."

Her eyes fell closed, and he released her chin, letting her head fall back to his shoulder. He rested his cheek against her hair. After several minutes, she said, "You tried to tell me this would happen. I feel incredibly foolish that I insisted on going."

"Do not feel foolish, Tava."

"You were right, you know. I may have been raised as nobility, but it is still very different from being royalty."

Callan tensed beside her. "Do you still wish to call off our arrangement?"

"No, Callan," she said softly. "I do not wish for that at all."

Relief flooded through him, and he felt his entire body relax at her words. "Tava?"

"Yes?"

"I see you, Tava. I just . . . want you to know that I see you. You are not in my background. You are not a spirit that blends in. I see you. I apologize that it took this long to do so."

Tava had stilled beside him. After several seconds of silence she asked quietly, "Is this still a ruse, Callan?"

Always to the point. Always so observant. And if he were being honest, this hadn't been a ruse for weeks now. Maybe Eliza had been right when she had told him Scarlett had been an obstacle preventing him from moving forward. Maybe with her gone, he could see what had been right in front of him for years. She was just as brilliant as Scarlett. She was more compassionate, more caring, and instead of luring him into shadows, Tava called him to the light.

"No, little fox," he finally answered. "I do not think it is." He waited for her to reply, and when she didn't say anything, he said, "I do believe you figured out it stopped being a ruse well before I did."

"I do not wish to be a replacement for her, Callan," she said softly. "I do not wish to be some consolation prize. That is worse than not being seen."

Callan straightened, turning to face her. He took her face in his hands. "Please do not think that."

"You loved her, Callan," Tava replied, her eyes filled with a sad sort of acceptance.

"But I do not any more. Perhaps I never did."

"You followed her to the Fire Court."

Callan shook his head, refusing to accept that Scarlett was going to ruin this for him too. "She once said to me that I was in love with the idea of her, and I think she was right. She challenged me. She started to make me think differently. She started to open my eyes, but you? Tava, *you* took the blindfold off. You showed me the things she would only tell me about. *You* showed me what I could be, what I *should* be."

Tava swallowed thickly before reaching up and removing his hands from her face. "I think you should go, Callan. It has been a long night. Emotions are high. We can talk tomorrow if you wish."

"I wish to speak with you every day, Tava. I wish to never go a day without speaking to you again." Her cheeks flushed slightly, but she started to push to her feet. Callan quickly got to his own so he could help her up. When she went to pull away from him again, he squeezed her fingers, halting her. "I am not saying I am in love with you, Tava. Do not think I have simply thrown myself into something new to avoid whatever it was Scarlett and I were."

"Then what are you saying, Callan?"

"I am saying I want to try. I want to try making this ruse real and see where it goes," he answered, stepping into her, her head tilting back to look at him. "You do not need to decide right this moment," he went on when she hesitated. "You have dealt with enough tonight. When you decide, let me know. Yes?"

"Callan, I . . ." Her eyes darted to the side for a moment before settling back on him. "I was not expecting this. This was not part of the plan."

"Maybe the plan was shit from the beginning," he said, and Tava huffed a laugh. His eyes dipped to her mouth at the sound.

"Perhaps it was, your Highness," she conceded. "I will consider it."

CHAPTER 40
SORIN

"Somehow I pictured working with the Wraiths of Death to be different," Cyrus said from atop his mare beside Sorin.

"I am somehow not surprised," Sorin replied.

"Tell me again why we are going in on horseback instead of using your super fancy disappearing and reappearing trick," Nuri was saying from atop a brown and black spotted horse.

"Because I can only use that if I know where I'm going. We don't know where the Contessa is," Scarlett bit back, her black horse huffing and pawing at the ground in agitation. "And before you ask, we're not using portals because the Contessa does not know we are coming. We do not wish to create another unnecessary conflict by showing up unannounced and uninvited."

"And tell me again why Juliette isn't using her super special vision to just see where we need to go?" Nuri drawled like she was bored out of her skull.

"Because it doesn't work that way," Juliette returned icily.

"The point is, we're doing it this way to lessen the chances of everyone dying," Scarlett cut in.

"Can Juliette even die? She's technically already dead," Nuri said, casually adjusting the gloves on her hands.

Scarlett tensed, but before Sorin could open his mouth to say something, Juliette said, "Stop being a bitch."

Nuri sighed dramatically. "And tell me why we're waiting for the fire prick to give the go ahead?"

Scarlett leaned forward to pat her horse's neck when he stomped a hoof in the dirt again. "Letting him make decisions makes him feel important."

Cyrus barked a laugh, and Sorin cleared his throat loudly. Scarlett peered over her shoulder, fluttering her lashes innocently at him. Her eyes were bright. They hadn't dimmed at all since Cassius had nullified that draining Mark on her skin. And her power... Holy gods. Training with her the last few days had been nothing short of fascinating. Godsdamn terrifying, but utterly fascinating.

She'd slept for nearly an entire day after that Mark had been taken care of, and when she'd awakened, she'd looked fully rested for the first time since he'd brought her back from Baylorin. She was more like her old self, still different, but her energy, her strength, her gifts? All of it was stronger. All of it was greater. He pitied anyone she may have to fight on this journey. She still struggled with using her magic and sword together fluidly, but as long as she had access to her magic, it wouldn't matter. Not against Night Children.

Luan and Talwyn sat atop their horses several feet away from the rest of their group. Things seemed tense between those two, despite their attempts to hide it. Words exchanged between them were clipped and to the point. Like she spoke to everyone else actually. So maybe there wasn't anything going on and it was simply Talwyn being Talwyn.

Eliza had gone back to the Fire Court to get their own forces prepared for whatever might come of the mortal armies gathering at their borders. Scarlett had asked Briar to oversee things at the Black Halls until they returned. Sawyer was readying things in the Water Court. Cassius had been forced to stay behind, still not recovered enough for a trip like this. Now they sat waiting at the border between the Earth Court and Night Child territory for word from Rayner, who was scouting inside the Night Court for the best direction to head first. The plan was simple: Find the Contessa, warn her of the coming threat, and figure out the best way to prepare for it. Complicatedly simple, he supposed.

A fire message appeared amid a swirl of ashes near Sorin's head, and he plucked the note from the center. Talwyn and Azrael were watching him and were already moving closer.

"Rayner says we should try her northern villa first," Sorin said. "He will let us know if he gets a better lead."

"Talwyn and I take the lead?" Luan asked.

"Yes," Sorin confirmed. "Those three stay in the middle unless we need to fight, but I am hoping the Night Children won't disturb all of us in a group. Cyrus and I will follow last."

"Agreed," Talwyn said coolly. "Two queens among them should stay their hands, not to mention you three."

Without another word, Talwyn and Luan moved to the front of their company. They coaxed the horses through a sand portal that Luan created, taking them to the northernmost part of the Earth Court so they could cross the border as close to the Contessa's villa as possible. Apparently, he still hadn't recovered enough magic to Travel far, and not with all of them in tow. As long as they were able to maintain a decent pace, they should reach the villa by sundown though.

It was a few hours later, when Sorin was listening to the three females ahead of him bicker about one thing or another. He didn't know what Luan and Talwyn were making of the exchanges between the Wraiths of Death, but Sorin was thoroughly enjoying it. To think that these three were among some of the most feared. If people only knew what they argued about. Currently, it was about a pair of twins that Juliette and Nuri had slept with, but they couldn't agree on when that had occurred.

"That was not the time we took out those three smugglers," Juliette said. "We used poison for them."

"Your point?" Nuri asked from the Witch's left.

"I bedded that guy from the show the smugglers were traveling with," Juliette replied, like that cleared up everything.

Nuri was about to argue, but Scarlett cut in from Juliette's other side. "No, she's right. The night you two fucked those twins, you both had blood all over your clothes from cutting up the targets in the basement of that warehouse."

"Wait. Was that the time we arranged body parts into a message?" Nuri asked.

"Mhmm," Scarlett answered. "That's why we were so filthy. It was a long message. Lots of parts needed. I wanted to go home and bathe, but you two insisted on fucking first."

"We have *needs*," Nuri half-drawled, half-whined.

"Clearly bloodlust has more than one meaning for you," Scarlett quipped.

"Bitch," Nuri muttered.

The females all started laughing before moving onto another

memory. "Holy fuck," Cyrus muttered. "Eliza is going to be so pissed she is missing this."

"Maybe let's not tell her we heard the Wraiths recounting all their tales."

"I think if she heard the things they're recounting, she would be incredibly disappointed," Cyrus supplied. "They've spent more time discussing men than actual jobs."

"The men were far more entertaining than the jobs," Nuri called back to them.

"Depends on the job," Juliette objected. "The guy from the night Scarlett made the target choke on his own flesh . . . Let's just say watching the man choke was more fulfilling than anything I've ever experienced in bed."

"Now *that* target I remember," Nuri said. "Very creative that night, Sister."

"It seemed fitting for someone who was keeping eleven young women in his basement and 'lending them out' as he put it," Scarlett said with a shrug.

"Wait, so he choked on his . . ." Cyrus trailed off under his breath.

"I am thinking so," Sorin supplied.

"Oh, it was more than that," Nuri said, cackling with manic delight. "Fingers. Eyeballs. His actual ba—"

"I got it," Cyrus said, cutting her off and wincing.

Such a vicious thing, Sorin shot down the bond.

My only regret is that I couldn't make him suffer longer. Her voice was dark and cold as it echoed in his mind. *But we had another engagement to be at, so he was blessed with only six hours.*

Gods, I love you.

She looked back at him from her horse, and he could clearly see the look she shot him. His blood heated at the sight of it.

"Calm down," Cyrus muttered. "I am not going to ride beside you smelling *that* all day."

Scarlett snorted a laugh as she fell back into conversation with Nuri and Juliette.

"This is good for her," Cyrus said after a time.

"It is," Sorin agreed. "A small sense of normalcy in the midst of whatever this is."

"Are we going to do anything about the Night Child that has been following us since we entered the territory?"

"I am assuming he is reporting back to the Contessa. Until he proves otherwise, we will let him be," Sorin answered. "Nuri has seen him. So have Luan and Talwyn."

Sorin had scented him a few minutes after they'd crossed, and he caught flashes of movement in the trees along the road they traveled. He knew the Night Child ahead of them had immediately marked him as well, and Luan and Talwyn were as trained as he and Cyrus were. If Juliette or Scarlett had noticed him, they hadn't given any indication, and Sorin was content to let her have this time to not worry about anything.

Twilight was just settling over the land when they crested a small hill and looked down on a sprawling villa below. A high stone wall surrounded the property with iron gates at the entrance. The place looked deserted. There were no guards at those gates, no movement beyond them.

"Do not tell me we just traveled all day to spend the night on the ground," Scarlett grumbled when Sorin brought his horse to a stop beside her.

"We knew she might not be here," he replied, tossing her a pear. They'd stopped to eat several hours ago, but they had all agreed to push through dinner and eat when they arrived at the villa.

She caught the pear and took a bite as she mused, "Any chance we could still sleep in there rather than in the dirt?"

"You want to break into the Contessa's villa?" Cyrus asked in amusement.

"No," she admonished. "I want to see if someone is home and ask if we can sleep in a comfortable bed." She took another bite of the pear. "Then if no one is home, yes, I want to break in."

Cyrus laughed, sliding down from his horse. They were going to walk the remaining distance and let the horses start to cool down. Cyrus took Scarlett's reins from her when she dismounted, and Sorin slid to the ground as well.

"Do you mean to tell me you never slept on the ground when traveling for all your jobs with the Wraiths?" Cyrus asked.

"Rarely," Scarlett said, her eyes scanning the countryside. "My sisters always found beds."

"So I heard," Cyrus said. "And you?"

Scarlett shrugged as she said with a wink, "I broke into villas." Then she sauntered over to join Nuri and Juliette.

"Rosalyn is not here," Talwyn said.

Sorin turned to face her and Luan making their way over, Luan leading both of their horses.

"It does appear to be deserted," Sorin replied, looking over the villa below.

"No other word from Rayner?" she asked.

Sorin shook his head. "Nothing from your people?"

"There has been no sign of her since we started actively looking," Luan answered grimly.

"Do we really have no idea when the Contessa was last seen?" Cyrus asked.

"She's so damn secretive. It's not uncommon to not hear from her for a decade or more."

"Valid point," Sorin conceded.

"What are they doing?" Talwyn asked, and Sorin followed her gaze to the Wraiths, who were striding down the hill, leaving their horses, and the rest of them, behind.

Because of course they were.

Scarlett, Sorin growled down the bond.

I'm tired, Sorin. And hungry. Let's get this over with.

"For fuck's sake," he muttered.

"She's not stopping, is she?" Cyrus asked as Sorin began following the three females ahead of them.

"No, she is not," he sighed, grabbing another horse to lead along with his own.

"She is going to get us all killed one day," Luan grumbled.

"Not likely. She will pull some plan out of her ass and end up saving the godsdamn day," Cyrus said.

Sorin glanced side-long at Talwyn. She'd been noticeably quiet. She wasn't one to chatter, but she also wasn't one to sit back and let others take the lead like she had all day. A silent Talwyn was almost more harrowing than the three females stalking down the hill.

Almost.

The Wraiths reached the gates, which were clearly locked. No one came to greet them. No one moved anywhere beyond them. Then all the Fae paused as they watched them move to the wall, hands trailing along stones.

"What are they—" Cyrus started, but stopped when they seemed to find what they were looking for.

And all three of them scaled that wall like godsdamned cats, disappearing over the top into the darkening shadows of night.

"Fuck," Sorin grunted, breaking into a run. He'd thought they'd at least wait for them when they found the gates locked. In hindsight, he had no idea why he'd assumed such a thing.

"How did they climb this?" Luan asked when they all reached the wall, examining the spot where they had climbed. He ran his hand along the smooth stones. "There is nothing to use for purchase here."

"You are aware the Contessa does not take kindly to trespassers, are you not?" came a smooth voice from behind them. The Fae all stilled, slowly turning to face the Night Child standing behind them.

He had dark blond hair that curled around his ears. His blue eyes were bright, even in the growing darkness, and his pale skin reflected the little light left. His hands were in the pockets of his tailored pants, his head tilted slightly to the side as he surveyed them. A dangerous, pointed smile was on his lips.

Auberon Isra.

The Contessa's Second.

She had no one else. No one else was needed.

"Auberon," Luan said casually, stepping in front of Talwyn. "We have been trying to reach the Contessa for quite some time now."

"And so you have sent . . ." He glanced at the wall as though he could see who had scaled it to the other side. "The Wraiths of Death to find her? Have they turned from assassins to bounty hunters?"

"Is there a reward for finding the Contessa?" Cyrus countered.

"Who said she was missing?" Auberon asked, his hair ruffling in the night breeze.

"Enough of this," Talwyn cut in. "Is the Contessa here? And if not, where can we find her?"

Auberon's blue eyes swept over them once more. "She is not here, your Majesty."

"And the second part of that question?" Talwyn demanded.

"She wishes not to be disturbed."

"I am afraid this is a matter of urgency," Sorin insisted.

Auberon looked him over once more before saying simply,

"Come." He turned and began walking towards the gates. "Unless you would prefer to scale the wall like your companions."

"The horses?" Cyrus asked.

"There are stables," Auberon replied, producing a silver key from his pocket and unlocking the gates.

Wards zipped along his skin when Sorin entered the gates, two horses in tow. Auberon was pointing them to the stables when he hissed, fangs snapping out. The Fae all turned to find a dagger at his throat and a shadow at his back.

Death's Shadow.

"One of my own kind," she purred. "Perhaps an actual challenge for once."

"Who are you?" Auberon hissed again.

Nuri clicked her tongue. "Fire prick?"

"Release him," Sorin sighed. "He is helping."

"Who is he?"

Scarlett stepped from shadows to their left, and Juliette dropped down from the gods-knew-where.

"Eliza is going to be so pissed she is missing this," Cyrus murmured again beneath his breath.

"Auberon Isra," Sorin said to Scarlett when she came to his side. "He serves the Contessa. Auberon, meet my wife, Scarlett Semiria, Queen of the Western Courts."

Auberon's eyes widened slightly in surprise. "We did not hear news of a new queen here."

"Then it appears we have much to discuss," Scarlett replied, jerking her chin towards the villa.

Nuri stepped away, disappearing among shadows before somehow reappearing by Scarlett's side a moment later. Cyrus cursed under his breath.

Auberon led them all into a sitting room in the villa, and when they had all taken seats on various chairs and sofas, Talwyn asked, "Where is Rosalyn?"

"In hiding," Auberon answered casually from his chair.

"Hiding?" Luan questioned.

Auberon nodded. "She became . . . concerned months ago. She went into hiding then."

"Why not send for aid?" Luan asked.

"Rosalyn has controlled this territory without aid for centuries," Auberon answered coldly.

"And yet now she is in hiding," Talwyn retorted. "Where is she? We have matters to discuss."

"Discuss them with me," Auberon replied.

"No," Talwyn bit out.

"He does not know where she is," Scarlett said nonchalantly from beside Sorin on the sofa. She pushed to her feet, unclasping her cloak and removing it from her shoulders. She looped it over her arm. "Is there food here? I am famished."

"Of course I know where my Contessa is," Auberon snapped before quickly regaining his composure.

"Such lies," Nuri crooned from where she leaned against a wall, one foot propped behind her and flipping one of her knives. "You have been trailing us since we crossed the border, hoping we would lead you to her."

"*You* were following us?" Sorin asked, his brow arching in surprise.

The Night Child pressed his tongue to his cheek, glaring at Nuri.

"He waited to approach until it was just you four," Scarlett said, stretching her arms above her head. "Kitchen?"

"You three scaled that wall so he would come out?" Luan asked.

Scarlett seemed to mull this over. "It seemed easier than dragging him from the trees. Although to be fair, Nuri did make a compelling argument for doing so."

Nuri smiled that grin that made Sorin fairly certain she was half mad. "Anyway... Food?"

She didn't wait any longer. Nuri and Juliette peeled away from the wall, and the three of them wandered away down a hall, chatting idly about what kind of food they hoped to find.

"She is . . . unconventional," Auberon commented, watching her go. "You have no idea," Talwyn muttered. "You do not know where Rosalyn is hiding?"

"No," Auberon answered tightly. "I have been unable to find her for months."

"Who else knows?" Cyrus asked soberly.

"No one."

Sorin blinked at him. "You have kept this a secret for months?"

"She is reclusive enough that no one seeing her for months is nothing new," Auberon replied. "She once did not make a public appearance for eight years. Only showed herself to take care of a small clan who believed her to be dead and were planning to try to take over her leadership."

"I can find her."

They all looked to the doorway where Scarlett stood, a sandwich in hand. Where had she found that so quickly?

"How exactly?" Talwyn asked tightly.

With a wicked grin, a shadow panther appeared, a book in its large maw.

And Sorin knew exactly where this was going before she held up the book of Blood Magic spells.

"No," Sorin snarled at the same time Luan barked, "Fucking hell."

"I thought you said they didn't get along," Nuri said, sauntering past Scarlett back into the room. She had a glass in her hand, and when she raised it toward Auberon, Sorin was fairly certain he knew what it contained. "I helped myself," Death's Shadow said with a wink.

Scarlett's nose wrinkled at her. "Drink that somewhere I cannot see you please."

Nuri arched an amused brow at her. Clasping the sandwich between her teeth to free a hand, Scarlett flipped her off in return.

And then Juliette was there, handing Scarlett something else that she slipped into a pocket before Sorin could make out what it was.

Then Death Incarnate took the sandwich from Scarlett's teeth.

The queen growled. Literally growled like a feral cat at Juliette. "Give that back," she said around the food in her mouth.

"It was *mine* to begin with," Juliette retorted, taking a big bite. "Get your own."

"I am a queen."

"I am the Oracle. Oracle trumps queen," Juliette said with a shrug.

"You are truly the Wraiths of Death?" Auberon said, his mouth slightly agape as he watched the females bicker.

"How did you three ever actually accomplish anything?" Cyrus asked, settling an arm along the back of the sofa.

"Careful, Darling," Scarlett crooned. "You really do not want to know the answer to that."

"I really kind of do," he challenged.

And Sorin could swear three sets of female eyes darkened.

"You want to use Blood Magic to find the Contessa?" Talwyn said after a moment of tense silence.

"Unless you have a better idea," Scarlett replied, crossing her arms and leaning against the doorframe.

Talwyn's lips pursed, her eyes narrowing.

"We should check in with Rayner. See if he has any updated information," Sorin said.

"Her Second hasn't been able to find her for months, Sorin," Scarlett said. "What makes you think Rayner is going to find her?"

"We are not using Blood Magic, Scarlett." She said nothing.

"Scarlett."

"Sorin," she parroted.

"Sometimes they throw down when they argue," he heard Nuri muttering gleefully to Juliette. "If they do, my money is on Scarlett."

"Fifty gold marks on Sorin," Juliette replied.

"Deal."

"By the gods," Luan muttered from his chair. "This is a godsdamn spectacle. How are you three possibly the Wraiths of Death?"

"You'll find out tomorrow when we track down the Contessa," Scarlett said, pushing off the doorway. "Which room can I sleep in, Auberon?"

Auberon glanced at the Fae.

"We are not using Blood Magic to do this, Scarlett," Sorin said, working to keep his tone calm as he pushed to his feet.

"Fine, fine. *We* do not have to do anything," she said with a dismissive wave of her hand.

Let's take a walk, he gritted out down the bond.

I'm good. Thanks.

A fire portal appeared directly to her left, and Sorin began stalking towards her.

"Let us know who wins so we know who has to pay up," Nuri called after him while he waited for Scarlett to go through. She huffed a dramatic sigh before making a big show of stepping through the portal.

"What?" she demanded, turning to face him under the cloudy night sky near the stables. She wrapped her arms tightly around herself. It wasn't the winter chill of Solembra, but the night was still cool.

"You know what," Sorin retorted. "We are *not* using Blood Magic."

"I do not have the time to spend traipsing all over this territory, Sorin. This needs to be taken care of. Preferably tomorrow," she argued.

"And what happens when there are other consequences from the Blood Magic? What happens when you do not understand the costs? *Again*."

"We do not have the time to spend on this, Sorin," she insisted.

"How do you figure that?" he demanded. "We have heard nothing from Alaric or Mikale or Lord Tyndell since we came for you."

"Exactly!" she cried. She ran her hands through her hair. "We have heard nothing except that there are forces being moved around. They are *moving*, Sorin. They want the Contessa. They are coming for her, and it is my fear that they already have her. Alaric is a patient man, but when he strikes? He will be everywhere. He will be here. He will be at home. He will be in every court, in every territory."

"He cannot be, Scarlett—"

"He *can* be, Sorin. He is already moving pieces into place. Can't you see? He will be everywhere, and we are not prepared. We will have to pick which lands to save and which to surrender," she insisted.

"We have allies in every territory, every Court, Scarlett. He will not simply march in and overtake us all," Sorin said, trying to soothe the hysteria he could see in her eyes.

She shook her head, tipping her face up to the stars. "You do not know him," she whispered. She brought her eyes back to his, and tears glimmered in the little light of the moon. "I need you to trust me, Sorin. I know you do not. I know it is a lot to ask of you after everything, but I *need* you to trust me on this. Please."

He could only stare at her. Raw and real. Those were the emotions in her eyes, flooding down the bond.

"It is not that I do not trust you, Scarlett," he said slowly. "It is that I do not trust Blood Magic."

"Blood Magic is not inherently bad, Sorin," she replied. "It is how it is used. One could say the same for darkness." At her words, she lifted a palm, shadows pooling there before reaching for him and brushing down his arm.

"Blood Magic is unpredictable," he countered, his flames rising up to meet her shadows.

She stepped into him. "It is a tracking Mark. That is all," Scarlett said, her palms settling on his chest, sliding up and over his shoulders.

One of his arms snaked around her waist, tugging her further into him. "You are not going to distract me from this conversation with your hands, Love."

"No?"

"No."

"I think they could be just as distracting as my tongue."

"I know they can be," he gritted out, "but this conversation needs to happen first."

She pushed out a heavy breath, stepping back. "I have been studying this Mark since I found it when searching for the nullifying Mark that day."

"Why didn't you say anything sooner?"

"I did," she answered. "To Rayner. We needed someone close to the Contessa to be able to use it. I asked Rayner who this would be, and he told me of Auberon. So I told Rayner to pick a location, then find Auberon and conveniently reveal our plans where he would hear of them."

Sorin started. "Rayner sent us to the northern villa because . . ."

"Because that was the location Auberon was closest to so he would be able to catch up with us the fastest," Scarlett confirmed. "I wanted him to find us, follow us. I didn't know if it would work, so Rayner is also looking for the Contessa, but . . ." She shrugged.

Sorin could only blink at her.

Scarlett cleared her throat. "The Mark will require Auberon's blood, and he will need to draw it."

"Night Children cannot do Blood Magic," Sorin said quickly.

"I know. He will need to draw it in his blood, then my blood will be splashed across it to activate it. It will be connected to him, though. He is the one who will learn where she is, and then I am hoping we can portal there," Scarlett explained.

Sorin slid his hand into her hair, tipping her head back. "What is the cost?"

"My magic," she answered. "The Mark depends on my magic, so it will drain my reserves until Auberon learns her location. I will need to . . . feed before we go to her."

"That cost does not seem very steep," he said with a frown.

"It could be, depending on what one is trying to find," she

answered. "Or if one did not have a way to replenish their magic well right away."

He lowered his mouth, brushing his lips against hers. "I am ready for that distraction now," he murmured onto them.

He felt her lips curve against his own before the familiar sensation of Traveling tugged at him.

"Apparently she won," Nuri said wryly. "Pay up."

Sorin pulled back, giving Scarlett an unimpressed glare. "Really? You took us back here."

"They wanted to know who won," she said, sucking her lower lip between her teeth as she started to back away from him.

"Up the stairs, end of the hall, last door on the right," Cyrus said from the sofa where he now sipped on a glass of amber liquor. "And you're wrong, Death's Shadow. I'm fairly certain Sorin is about to win."

He wasn't wrong, as Sorin followed his queen out of the sitting room and up the stairs. She threw him a coy look over her shoulder before she pushed through the door of the room they'd been assigned. She turned to face him when he'd shut the door behind him.

She was slowly removing weapons, her eyes never leaving his. "Tell me, king of mother hens, what kind of distraction would you prefer this night?"

He shot her an unimpressed glare at her newest name, and she smirked lightly at him. He began to prowl towards her, but stilled when he felt her shadows rake down his arms, his chest, his torso. She was removing her boots now, her movements casual as her shadows continued their torturous descent.

She stood upright again, kicking her boots to the side before sliding her tunic over her head, standing before him in just her pants and the band around her breasts. She slowly made her way towards him, hips swaying, and his eyes roaming where they willed.

"Nothing to say?" she crooned, and he cursed when those shadows caressed his cock through his pants. She huffed a laugh, beginning to circle him. Her actual fingers dragged along the back of his shoulders.

"You are as wicked as you are vicious," he gritted out.

"Mmm," she hummed, coming to a stop in front of him. "You did not answer me, prince of fussiness."

He went to reach for her, to silence that godsdamn tongue, when her shadows ran down his length again; and he stumbled, letting out a groan as she danced back a few steps, biting her lower lip, her eyes glittering with sinful promises.

"Come here," he said in a low command, tracking her movements when she slowly began circling him again, staying out of his reach.

"You asked for a distraction," she mocked. "Are you not thoroughly distracted?"

But then she was gasping at the flames brushing along her own body. He was on her a moment later, his hands landing on her hips and fingers immediately beginning to roam over her exposed flesh.

"Teasing is not the type of distraction I had in mind," he breathed into her ear, goosebumps erupting along her skin under his fingertips.

"You never specified what kind of distraction you were looking for," she replied breathlessly.

A low chuckle rumbled through him, and he made quick work of the band around her breasts. "In my experience, the less clothing, the better the distraction," he said, fingers drifting to the buttons of her pants.

"You do have more *experience*, I suppose," she said with a dramatic sigh.

"Mmm," he hummed, pushing her pants over her hips, her undergarments with them. "Arianna and Jamahl would not be an option tonight, but I am sure there is a male or two downstairs who would be more than willing to join us."

"What?" she started, her hands landing on his shoulder when she stumbled while stepping out of her pants at his words.

"You just seem very jealous of my *experiences*, my Love," he continued, shoving her pants aside with his foot.

"How do you always manage to turn this around so that *I* am the one being teased?" she whined, with a pout forming on her lips.

He leaned in to whisper, "experience," and his hands found her hips once more. He began walking her backwards towards the desk that was in the room.

She scoffed, rolling her eyes. "And why am I always naked while you always remain fully clothed?"

"I excel at distracting," he replied, lifting her up and setting her bare ass on the desk. She scoffed again. He arched a brow. "You do not believe me?" he asked. "How else did I get you naked, sitting atop a desk with your beautiful breasts in my mouth, Princess?"

"My breasts are not—"

He moved before she finished speaking, his mouth closing around a peaked tip and sucking hard. She moaned, her back arching beautifully, as her hands landed on the desk behind her. He slid his hands down her thighs to her knees, pushing them wider and stepping further into her. His mouth moved to her other breast before his tongue was tasting her neck, and her head fell back, another breathy moan escaping her.

He pressed a kiss below her ear before he said in a guttural tone, "Do not move."

"What?" Her head snapped up.

His hands were still on her knees, and his fingers flexed in emphasis when he repeated, "Do not move, my Love," before stepping away from her a few feet.

She gaped at him, and he lazily slipped his tunic over his head, hiding his smirk. But she hadn't moved. Not an inch. Her hands were still braced behind her, her chest thrust forward, and those luscious breasts on full display. Her legs were still spread wide, giving him a view he was certain he could spend the entirety of the afterlife staring at.

"I am supposed to be distracting you," she said petulantly, her eyes watching him intently when he stooped down to unbuckle his boots.

"And you are doing a wonderful job, my Love," he replied when he stood back up, toeing the boots off. "I assure you, the only thing I am thinking about right now is sinking my cock between those pretty thighs you have spread open so nicely for me. I am completely and utterly distracted."

This time, he didn't hide his smirk when her cheeks flushed. He watched her eyes dip to where his fingers were at the buttons of his pants. Watched her throat work as he slipped them off. Watched the tremor go through her body when he started making his way back over to her. Her head tipped back so she could look into his face, her lips parting, and tongue darting out, swiping along her bottom lip.

"What are you waiting for then?" she rasped, her voice low and throaty in a way that had his cock twitching against her.

"For your manners to make those rare appearances."

"Sorin." He was pretty sure she'd meant that to be a reprimand, but it came out as a plea, a note of desperation in her tone.

"Or begging," he said. "That works, too."

Before she could spout off with whatever was surely to come from her mouth next, he was gripping her hips and yanking her forward onto his length. He groaned at the same time her breath caught, and he captured her lips with his mouth. Her arms looped around his neck, fingers twining in the hair at the base of it. Her legs wrapped around his waist, heels digging into his back and pushing him further into her as she rocked against him.

And when a hand dropped down to grip the edge of the desk, the nails of her other hand dug into the nape of his neck; and one of his hands slipped over her mouth to stifle the sound of her coming. Not that it really mattered. It was no secret what they had been coming up here to do. Cyrus had made certain of that, forever a busybody. But even if he hadn't announced it, the sound of the desk hitting the wall with every thrust into her, certainly told them everything they needed to know.

Her forehead was against his shoulder, his hand moving up and down her back as they both worked to steady their breathing after he'd followed her over the edge of pleasure. She'd unwound her legs, letting them dangle over the edge of the desk, one hand resting on his chest over his racing heart.

"One of these days," she rasped, "it will be me with the upper hand in these distractions."

"Everyone should have goals," he replied, a breath of laughter coming from his lips when her other hand pinched his thigh sharply.

He didn't bother to tell her that she already had the upper hand in every way. He didn't bother to tell her that all she had to do was say the word, and he'd be on his knees before her. He didn't bother to tell her that she already held all the power. That he would crawl through every darkness, every flame, and every shadow to worship her in every way possible.

He didn't say any of that. Instead, he tipped her mouth up to his, brushing his lips lightly against hers. Then he was scooping her up and carrying her to the bed, where he made sure she was sleeping deeply before he let himself follow her even into the depths of slumber.

CHAPTER 41
SCARLETT

"I think you've got it," Scarlett said, studying Auberon's latest drawing of the Mark they were going to be using. "Are you ready?"

The vampyre met her gaze, his blue eyes bright. She didn't miss how they dipped briefly to her throat. Neither did Sorin, and he shifted subtly closer to her. "How will this work exactly?"

"I have no idea," Scarlett said with a shrug. "I suppose we are about to find out."

They were outside on a terrace of the villa. The sun was shining brightly, and she breathed the fresh air deep into her lungs. She rolled her shoulders, stretching out her neck as they moved to the dirt beyond the stone patio. Shaking her arms out, she glanced at Juliette and Nuri who were sitting along the low terrace wall. Scarlett had no idea what they were going to find when they figured out where the Contessa was, but the dread coiling in the pit of her stomach told her it wasn't going to be anything good.

"You good, Love?" Sorin asked, coming to her side.

"Mhmm," she hummed, pushing down the unease. He had already filled a small glass with his blood, Cyrus now holding that cup ready and waiting for her.

Auberon dropped to his knees in the dirt, a knife in hand, and Scarlett knelt opposite him. The four Fae gathered around them. Azrael hadn't been particularly happy about this development, but Talwyn had been surprisingly amenable to the idea, agreeing that they needed to find the Contessa as quickly as possible.

Auberon cut a gash along his palm, dipping his finger in and beginning to draw the Mark she'd made him practice for the last hour. When he was done, Sorin handed her a dagger, and she quickly dragged it down her forearm, letting her blood spill over it. She didn't know how much of her blood it would take, but the moment the first drop hit the Mark, she felt a tug at her shadows. White flames raced along the Mark, tracing every line and angle as her blood dripped onto it. Shadows filled her vision and twined around her arms.

"Anything?" she heard Sorin grit out to Auberon.

"Nothing," the vampyre replied.

"Focus," Scarlett hissed from between her teeth. "The magic will show you. Focus on it."

"You are beginning to heal, Love," Sorin said softly. She felt him lower to the ground beside her.

"Then reopen the wound," she ordered. She'd dropped the dagger at some point. Her shadows were beginning to strain, as if suddenly realizing they were being used and pulled from her.

"Perhaps we should re-evaluate—"

"No coddling, fire prick," Nuri chided, and Scarlett turned her head to find Nuri kneeling beside her other side. In less than a second, she pulled a knife from her boot and sliced along Scarlett's forearm again, moving it back over the Mark. "Focus on the Contessa," she ordered Auberon.

Scarlett's breathing was ragged as her magic was forced to give more and more. White embers were sparking in her vision among the shadows, and she was fairly certain she was going to pass out when Auberon said, "Got it."

Nuri released Scarlett's arm, and she fell against Sorin's chest. He was already lifting a glass to her lips, and she couldn't help the grimace as she swallowed the coppery-tasting liquid. Her magic sighed in relief, already refilling with each gulp from the glass. She drained the entire thing, and when Sorin tipped the glass up, his voice came down the bond.

Do you need more?

No. Her voice sounded breathless even down the bond. *I just need a minute to recoup before we go.*

You swear it?

I know that I need to be at full strength right now, Sorin.

He pressed a kiss to her temple, and Scarlett tuned back into the conversation happening around them.

"The riverfront property? You are sure," Talwyn was asking.

"Positive," Auberon confirmed. "What are we waiting for?"

"She needs a minute," Sorin replied, his voice low and lethal, daring anyone to challenge him.

"Is she all right?" Cyrus asked.

"I'm fine, Darling," Scarlett said. "Do you have any water?"

A minute later, he was handing her a glass, and she downed the entire thing, trying to get the taste of blood out of her mouth. "Can we portal there?" she asked, passing the glass back to Cyrus.

"I can Travel us," Talwyn said. "I know where we are going."

Scarlett nodded, pushing off of Sorin and sitting up. When her head finally stopped spinning, Sorin helped her to her feet. He swung her cloak around her shoulders, clasping the clips for her.

"You are sure about this?" he murmured, reaching to pull her hood up.

"Do we have a choice?"

"You always have a choice, Scarlett," he said, his hands cupping her face.

"Then my choice is to help the Contessa," she said with a weak smile.

He brushed a quick kiss to her lips. "Then let's go, my Queen."

She felt her cheeks flush slightly as she turned to the others. "It would be best to take us in some place farther away," she said to Talwyn. "Then we can see what we are dealing with rather than landing at the front door."

"Agreed," Azrael said, his arms crossed over his chest.

"I will take us in a few miles north," Talwyn replied.

"We evaluate and make a plan before anyone goes ahead. Can we all agree on that?" Sorin asked, command ringing in his tone as he leveled his gaze on Scarlett, Nuri, and Juliette.

"You act like we run into dangerous places without thinking," Nuri scoffed. "We always know what we are doing."

"Are we in agreement?" Sorin asked again.

Scarlett patted his arm with a sympathetic smile, while Nuri gave him a feral grin.

"Let's go, your Majesty," Scarlett said, reaching for Talwyn's hand.

A moment later, they were standing upstream of a river. She reached up, sending off a message among her shadows, something she'd taught herself to do, just as she'd taught herself mental shields. The shadow messages let Eliza, Rayner, and Briar know where they were, on the off chance they would need back-up. Briar could have help here fairly quickly, and Rayner was around somewhere. Her gaze fell on a sprawling estate along the river a little over two miles off. It was larger than the villa they had stayed in last night. Tall, white pillars were visible even from this distance, and a veranda ran around the entire second story of the building.

"You have not checked here before?" Scarlett asked Auberon, scanning the estate.

"Of course I have. Multiple times," Auberon retorted. "But the Contessa has a network of underground passages connecting her homes. She moves about unseen if she so chooses."

"Then why have you not monitored these tunnels?" Talwyn demanded.

"Because they are warded so that only the Contessa can access them," Auberon gritted out.

"That seems incredibly irresponsible in the case of an emergency," Scarlett mused, tilting her head as she studied the estate more.

"Obviously," Auberon muttered under his breath.

"You are seeing what I am seeing, yes?" Juliette asked, coming to her side.

"I am," Scarlett confirmed. "Nuri?"

"Yes. I will go up. You two do your usual?"

"No," Sorin snarled, stepping into their path. "Explain."

Juliette and Nuri moved away a few steps, giving her room to deal with the Fae.

"I need you to trust me on this, Sorin."

"I need you to include us on this, Scarlett," he countered.

Scarlett glanced back at the estate before looking back at him. "It is not that I do not trust you," she replied. "It is that I have worked with them for years. Did you just witness our thirty second conversation? We already knew what each saw and were thinking. We already have a plan that does not need to be explained to each other. When we are down there, we will know how each will react." Sorin tried to interject, but Scarlett raised a hand to stop him. "I know that someday, I will have that with all of you. Years from now, I will fit with your Court the way I fit with them now. But that day is not today. That time is not now. It is why I wanted them with us for this task."

"You have been planning to exclude us this entire time?" Cyrus demanded.

Scarlett shook her head. "No. I am not excluding you. I am simply asking that you let us go first."

"You are a *queen*," Azrael sneered, as if that was argument enough.

Scarlett supposed it probably was. Who in their right mind would let the queen of two Fae Courts scout an obviously dangerous property for foul play?

"Do not allow this, Sorin," Talwyn interjected. "Or this will end like it did for Thia."

Scarlett whirled on her. "Do not try and make him feel guilty about that," she spat, her finger pointed at the Fae Queen. "*That* has nothing to do with this. This is different in every way, and he does not *allow* me to do anything."

She turned back to Sorin. "I will be able to communicate with you through the bond. If anything feels wrong, I will Travel us out immediately and we regroup."

"This entire thing feels wrong," Cyrus muttered.

Scarlett ignored Cyrus, holding Sorin's gaze. Golden eyes searched her own. "You feel well enough? Your power reserves are full enough?"

"Yes."

An arm looped around her waist, tugging her roughly forward, and she tilted her head back to be able to see his face. "You do not block the bond. Not even a little bit. And no Blood Magic."

Scarlett swallowed, nodding once. He lowered his mouth to hers, the kiss full of his worry about this entire scenario.

"I do not like this," he breathed onto her lips, so low she barely heard him.

"I know," she whispered back. "I will be fine. I promise."

With another quick brush of lips, he released her, and she stepped back. "Once we are inside, I will let you know. Then send Auberon in to help us find the Contessa. The rest of you search the grounds."

She didn't wait for confirmation, turning and striding to Nuri and Juliette. In unison, the three of them pulled up their hoods. Black stains against the bright early spring day. They wouldn't be staying in the light, though. They had already spotted the shadowy valley down the hillside that would take them almost the entire way to the estate.

"It has been so long since we started a fire," Nuri mused when the three of them began stalking forward.

"We are not burning anything today," Scarlett replied.

"At least I hope not," Juliette added.

"Eliza is going to be so pissed," Scarlett heard Cyrus mutter.

They moved soundlessly through the valley, Scarlett using her shadows to veil them even more, and when they reached a small copse around the property, they darted among them, disappearing into the trees. Nuri veered off, climbing an oak to the right. Juliette and Scarlett continued forward and waited on the edge of the copse. When Nuri did not reappear after a few minutes, they prowled forward. Nuri was either waiting for them or in trouble. She only came back if they needed to re-evaluate. Unless she'd been detained. Which had only happened once.

Or twice.

"See you on the other side, Sister," Juliette said, a wild grin filling her face, and Scarlett couldn't help but grin back. Because as wrong as it was to be a killer, to be trained to execute judgment for those who believed themselves gods, she had missed prowling through the night and the shadows with her sisters.

Juliette went to the left. Scarlett went to the right. They would each come in from separate sides of the gate. Nuri would find them eventually.

Scarlett kept close to the wall, her back pressed to it, her breathing steady.

You split up? Sorin demanded, his voice ringing with disbelief and disapproval in her head. *Where the fuck is Nuri?*

Already over the wall, Scarlett answered. *We will reunite shortly.*

Why are you not together?

So that we're not all caught at once, obviously, Scarlett said. *If one of us is caught unawares, there are two others to assist.*

She ran her hands along the wall. It was smoother than the one around the villa had been. There had at least been cracks in that stone wall to provide the smallest amount of grip to climb up. There was nothing on this one. It was as smooth as marble, which was rather inconvenient.

Glancing behind her, the trees were perhaps a hundred feet away. That could be enough room, she supposed. It would have to be. Slipping into the trees, she pulled her hood back and unhooked her cloak, tossing it to the side. She didn't want to risk it getting caught on anything.

Scarlett . . . What are you doing?

It should work, she replied.

Scarlett!

She didn't let herself think about it, though. She took off running, throwing white flames in front of her, followed by ice to wrap around that fire, freezing it. She leapt, over and over, making the flames higher and higher. Steps up. One. Two. Three. She felt them shatter under the impact of her feet, leaving no room for hesitation, as she kept building flames higher and higher.

Her hands grasped the ledge of the wall, and she hoisted herself up. Dropping to the other side, she landed in a crouch, pulling a dagger from her boot, ready to throw it, stab someone with it. Whatever was needed really.

But all was quiet on this side of the wall. And there was Nuri, lounging against the rail along the top of the veranda. She pointed to the right, and Scarlett saw the trellis. In a matter of minutes, she'd crossed the yard and climbed to the balcony, striding to Nuri's side.

"Juliette?" she asked, taking a moment to catch her breath.

"Here," she answered, dropping down from the eaves of the roof.

"The front door?" Scarlett asked, turning to Nuri.

"All doors are securely locked. Warded, too, if I had to guess," she replied.

"So just this window, then?"

They all turned to the window before them. They'd seen it from the hillside where the Fae were waiting. The slightest flutter of a curtain. The window was cracked open the smallest amount. If it hadn't been for that slight movement, they never would have known. Either someone had moved it inside, or a passing breeze had ruffled it. Either way, it meant someone was inside or the window was a way in.

"Ready?" Juliette asked.

Nuri and Scarlett nodded, and they moved forward. Juliette pulled her short sword, wedging the blade into the crack and pushing down, creating the leverage to lift the window just enough for them to squeeze in. Nuri quickly pushed the window back into place once they were inside.

We're fine, she sent down the bond to Sorin. *Juliette will be out in a minute to unlock the front gates for you.*

You made steps. Out of fire.

Scarlett snorted softly in laughter, Nuri and Juliette glancing over at her. *Is that admiration I hear, Prince?*

"Quit flirting," Nuri chided.

"How many times did I have to put up with you two flirting and sneaking off on jobs?" Scarlett whispered back.

"She makes a valid point," Juliette said.

They stepped from what was obviously a bedroom out into a hallway.

Doors lined either side, all of them closed.

"We need Auberon. He'll know where these tunnels are," Scarlett said.

"I'll get the gates," Juliette answered.

She peeled away, heading for the stairs. She'd find the keys easily enough. People always kept them in the same places. Nuri and Scarlett began checking the rooms along the hallway. She didn't expect to find anything, but they could at least clear them before Auberon got here.

"Will you stay in Avonleya when you go there?" Nuri asked casually, opening another door.

Scarlett paused, her hand hovering over a door handle. "That is random."

"I am assuming when you find the keys, you will go there. That is your homeland," she replied, poking her head into the room she was checking.

"I cannot imagine I will. I hold a throne here. I have responsibilities," Scarlett said, eyes scanning her own room.

"That did not stop you from leaving the Syndicate."

"*You* aided Sorin in taking me from there," Scarlett retorted, clamping down on the surge of irritation.

"Yes, but I thought you'd come back," Nuri said, her tone the same.

Casual and relaxed, as though they were discussing books. "I came for the children, did I not?"

"Only because Alaric took you."

Scarlett pulled her door closed sharper than she'd intended. The snap of it echoing down the deserted hall. "Just because I did not plan for the way it happened does not mean I was not planning to return. We were planning to leave, to come for you and Cassius and the others, two days from the day everything happened."

Nuri didn't say anything, moving to the next room.

"I was trying, Nuri. I was drowning and trying to stay afloat and trying to get back to . . . I was trying," Scarlett said.

"It was only a question," Nuri said, closing the final door as they came to the end of the hall.

But it was never 'only a question' with Nuri.

They were descending the stairs, when Auberon came rushing through the front doors. "The Witch is searching the grounds with the Fae. This way."

He led them through a grand room, an elegant dining room, and into a decent sized study. But the moment the study doors opened, they all froze. Sitting behind a gleaming oak desk was a woman, who if it wasn't for the dirt covering her skin and in her hair, would surely be stunning. She had golden hair beneath the dirt and mud from what Scarlett could tell. Her skin was pale, and she was thin. Far too thin. She wore a thin red dress that clung to her. A gag was in her mouth between dry and bloodless lips, and her amber eyes had a reddish tint to them. They widened with dread when they entered, chains securing her to the chair.

Shirastone chains.

"Your grace," Auberon cried, rushing forward to his Contessa's side. He hissed when he touched the chains, jerking back. Nuri and Scarlett moved to come to her side as well, but a deep voice came from the left.

"Scarlett, my dear. I have been looking forward to seeing you again."

Scarlett pulled the spirit sword that was sheathed down her back, her shadow armor slithering into place atop the Witch-leathers she was wearing.

"And you have mastered more of your darkness. Delightful," Lord Tyndell said, clapping his hands as if this indeed excited him.

"Help Auberon with the Contessa," she said to Nuri. "I will take care of this."

Nuri didn't ask questions, just rushed to the Contessa, who was screaming around her gag.

"How did you find her?" Scarlett asked.

Lord Tyndell made a show of seeming to consider her question before finally saying, "Your Court has spies. So does ours."

"Like Tarek?" Scarlett countered.

"He has been a valuable asset, yes," he agreed.

He took a step forward, and Scarlett raised her sword, leveling it with his chest. Her shadows writhed into panthers before her, and white flames sparked off the blade.

Lord Tyndell's smile only grew.

"Do not take another step," Scarlett said, her voice soft venom. "Nuri, get them out of here."

"Working on it," Nuri hissed back.

Lord Tyndell clasped his hands behind his back, making no move to try to keep the Contessa for his own.

"Who is here with you?" Scarlett demanded.

"They are keeping your . . . associates busy at the moment." Dread flooded her veins like ice water.

Sorin?

Scarlett. What is wrong?

She swallowed thickly, glancing at Nuri and Auberon. The latter was trying to loosen the gag from the Contessa's mouth, but it was apparently kept in place with magic. Nuri was struggling with the chains.

We found the Contessa. She's . . . Lord Tyndell is here.

Get out of there, Scarlett. Now.

But she couldn't leave the others.

"You will find Traveling ineffective inside the estate," Lord Tyndell said as if he'd read her mind.

"Fuck this," Nuri suddenly said. "Grab the chair, Auberon. We'll figure out the chains after we're out of here."

Scarlett was completely fine with that idea. She kept her sword trained on Lord Tyndell while Nuri and Auberon hauled the chair across the study and out the door. Scarlett slowly started backing towards the door to follow.

"Leaving so soon?" Lord Tyndell asked. "I would love the opportunity to catch up with you, my dear."

"I do not plan on leaving without killing you first," Scarlett retorted, her shadow panthers prowling forward.

"Is that so? But what of your sister?"

"What?"

A muffled scream had her head whipping to the side to find Juliette bound and gagged in the corner of the room. Where had she come from?

Scarlett? Nuri is out here. Where are you?

I can't Travel, Sorin. Juliette is here—

Juliette is out here with us.

What?

Juliette is out here with us, Scarlett. I am coming for you.

She slowly dragged her gaze back to Lord Tyndell, her lip peeling back into a sneer at the realization that he had somehow slipped into her mind and altered her reality. "I am going to kill you," she hissed, her panthers moving forward again. Flames rose at her fingertips, and she took a step towards the Lord.

"He will be so pleased to know your powers have grown," Lord Tyndell said.

The illusion of Juliette screamed again, and Scarlett tried to block out the sound. Until the doors burst open, and Sorin ran through, Cyrus on his heels. Relief tumbled through her, but she didn't stop her advance.

"I would give you a message to deliver to him, but the dead cannot speak," she replied.

Lord Tyndell chuckled merrily. "Always so quick-witted. It truly made for the most entertaining dinners."

Scarlett? Where are you?

What do you . . . She glanced back over her shoulder where Sorin and Cyrus were flanking her, swords drawn, faces merciless. *Where are you?*

Trying to get inside this fucking house, but there are . . . I do not know what we are fighting, but I am coming.

I need to block you out, Sorin.

What? No! Don't you dare, Scarlett.

I have to. I love you like the stars love the night.

Scarlett—

But she slammed shadows around her, strengthening her shadow armor and putting up a mental shield. Shadows and flames and ice. All of it thickening and climbing higher, blocking out everyone and everything. She could feel Sorin banging against it, but as those shadows slid into place, Lord Tyndell disappeared from before her eyes along with Juliette's cries and Sorin and Cyrus at her back.

Lord Tyndell was here. She was certain of that. But where he was playing these games from she did not know. Sending her panthers before her, she crept out of the study and back through what appeared to be an empty house. She kept her mental shield firmly locked in place. Even a crack and Lord Tyndell would be inside her head again. As she drew near the front of the estate, the sounds of swords clanging and shouting reached her. She raced for the front door.

And then skidded to a halt on the front porch.

There was . . . a small army here. Skilled soldiers. The High Force?

"Up, Scarlett! Look up!" Sorin was bellowing from somewhere.

Her eyes scanned the yard, looking for him as she moved to the edge of the front porch and looked up at the sky from beneath the veranda.

Where men with wings flew.

"What the actual fuck?" Scarlett whispered, stepping out from under the veranda.

Were those feathers on the wings?

There were ten of them from what she could see, dodging fire as Sorin and Cyrus shot flaming arrows at them.

More sounds of fighting came from beyond the front gates. She could only assume Talwyn and Azrael fought there. Auberon was fighting with twin short swords off to one side, and Juliette was . . .?

Where were Nuri and Juliette?

"Scarlett!" Cyrus cried.

As if in slow motion, Scarlett looked his way just as one of the flying men dove at her. She ducked, feeling soft wings brush her back. The ground shook when he landed nearby, and she stood upright once more.

The man advanced, a shirastone dagger in one hand. He was huge. Easily taller than Sorin and more muscled. He wore a sleeveless grey tunic and grey pants that matched the grey of his wings, and some kind of lightweight armor over top of everything. She cocked her head, studying how he moved.

"Not the time to admire the pretty muscles, Darling," Cyrus panted, suddenly at her side. He nocked another arrow, sending it flying at the advancing man, but the man caught it by the shaft, just as she'd seen Sorin do.

"What are they?" Scarlett asked, raising a hand and letting shadows begin to pool there.

"Don't really give a fuck right now," Cyrus replied, another arrow already nocked and being released at one of the men still airborne. "You going to help out at all or just stand here?"

Scarlett rolled her eyes, snapping her shadows out from her like a whip and wrapping them tightly around the winged-man's neck. He paused, grabbing at his throat, his fingers closing around black mist.

A smile curled onto Scarlett's lips, and she winked at him when the man's eyes widened, fixating on her. He cocked his arm back to throw his dagger, but another whip of shadows wrapped around his wrist, halting his movement.

"They did not tell us one of you were here," the man gasped out.

"Surprise," Scarlett purred, stalking forward.

"Scarlett," Cyrus warned.

The shadows around the man's throat squeezed tighter, but he didn't show any sign of panic. Signs of strangulation, yes, but no terror and unease. These beings were warriors, impeccably trained to not show weakness and to face death fearlessly.

She was mere feet from him when a scream pierced the air.

A scream she knew in her bones.

"Where is Juliette?" Scarlett demanded, turning to Cyrus.

He shook his head, arrow after arrow flying from his bow. One look at his quiver told her he would be switching to a sword soon.

White flames sprang from her fingertips and landed directly on the man's feathery wings. A bellow of rage and pain left the man then. A second later, her sword was slashing across his throat, blood spraying her face and neck.

She left Cyrus to finish him, racing towards the sound of the scream. Rounding the corner, the scream pierced the air again, and she looked up to find Juliette being hauled through the sky by one of the winged men. Her arm hung at an odd angle, and there was blood dripping down her temple.

"Scarlett," Sorin panted, appearing at her side. "I couldn't get to her fast enough."

"I got her," Scarlett replied, sheathing her sword down her back. She pulled a small vial from her pocket, throwing it to the ground and stomping on it. A wisp of violet smoke wafted up before dissipating on the breeze. "Cover me."

"What are you—"

But she was already running, her shadows converging before her. They twisted and writhed.

Four legs. A long, spiked tail. A snout. Scales. Wings.

And right before that shadow dragon went for the sky, Scarlett was leaping to its back. She didn't know how it worked. She wasn't about to question how shadows could hold her. She suspected they could only do so because it *was* her. With a flick of her wrist, she fashioned a bridle of sorts out of white flames, clinging to the reins as the dragon shot straight up, racing after the man who had Juliette. She knew more winged men chased her.

She knew Sorin's arrows found their marks when they bellowed in agony.

The ones that he missed, her shadow dragon did not, orange flames spewing from its mouth.

The man holding Juliette looked back, his eyes widening. Juliette twisted, taking advantage of his moment of shock, and then she was falling, plummeting towards the ground. Scarlett snapped cords of shadows for her, wrapping around her torso, but her power was waning. It was taking too much to keep this shadow dragon corporal. Could Juliette die again? Scarlett didn't know, but she had prepared for this possibility.

And as an eagle's screech reached her ears, Scarlett's entire body heaved a sigh of relief as a blur shot by her. Wings tucked in tight, diving straight for where Juliette was hanging from nothing but swirling darkness. Scarlett may have been sitting atop a dragon of shadows, but she still stared in complete wonder at the half-lion, half-eagle beast the High Witch sat atop as it hovered beside Juliette. Sleek golden fur ran along its back half, a tail with a tuft of hair at the end helping it maintain balance.

Feathered wings of the same color swept out from both sides, before fur shifted to feathers of ivory and paws became taloned feet at its front half.

The Witches actually flew on griffins. Scarlett let out a breath of laughter.

The griffin was taking Juliette gently between its talons, and since Juliette didn't seem at all panicked, she'd clearly been around the griffins before. Hazel looked back at Scarlett, nodding once before the griffin rose to the sky and flew from that battle still raging below.

Right. Battle.

With a tug on the reins, the shadow dragon shifted and began making its way back to the ground.

She leapt from its back, landing on her feet next to Sorin, who was shoving his sword through the gut of one of the winged males before pulling the sword back and slicing through his neck and setting his wings on fire. Then he whirled to Scarlett, who was sucking the last of her shadows into herself. No more shadow armor. No more shielding with it. She needed to conserve that power from here on out.

Which also left her more vulnerable to Lord Tyndell. He had to still be here somewhere.

"You are utterly reckless, utterly stupid, and utterly brilliant," Sorin seethed, his free hand snapping out and grasping the front of her leathers, tugging her into him. His mouth slammed onto hers, his tongue forcing its way in. The kiss ended as quickly as it had started and well before Scarlett could get over her surprise.

Sorin pulled back, already throwing a dagger over her shoulder, and she glanced back to see it sink into the thigh of . . . a Night Child.

"Really? Now there are vampyres here? Fantastic," she said with a slight whine.

She and Sorin pivoted so they were back-to-back. She'd unsheathed her sword, her other hand holding a long knife that Sorin had tossed to her.

"Why hasn't Auberon called them off?" Scarlett demanded, meeting the blade of one of the Night Children, her foot planting into its gut to shove him back.

"I do believe these particular Night Children have defected from the Contessa," Sorin replied, another knife leaving his hand.

"Where are Nuri and the Contessa?" The same vampyre came at her again, and she let him get close enough that his fangs grazed her arm before her knife went into the side of his head.

"Stop playing," Sorin growled, his eyes dipping to the shallow wound on her arm.

"It's a scratch," she shot back. "Where is Nuri?"

"Auberon told her of some place to take the Contessa. She said she would get in contact with us when Rosalyn was safe," Sorin replied. "Why was Hazel here?"

"To get Juliette obviously," Scarlett retorted. Three Night Children were converging on her. One look back told her four more were coming for Sorin.

And she was so, *so* done with this shit.

She threw her weapons to the ground and spun, grabbing Sorin's arm. Before he could react, she was shoving up his sleeve and her canines were piercing his forearm. She took three big swallows, enough to feel her reserves swell the smallest amount, before she released him. His eyes were wide, but the shock quickly became understanding, those golden irises flickering flames.

Collars of white flames appeared around every Night Child she could see, shadows slithering up their bodies before going up their noses and down their throats. No room for screams. Shadows shaped like eagles were soaring for the three remaining winged men. They were back-flapping, trying to get out of range, but they weren't going anywhere. When the shadows caught up with them, they shifted to flames. Feathers caught alight and then they were plummeting to the ground, where Cyrus and Sorin were waiting, swords wreathed in flames severing heads.

"Behind you," Cyrus yelled, and she spun to find a Night Child less than ten feet away. Water sprang from her palm, freezing on contact with the vampyre. She let the ice encase him, freezing him solid. She'd let one of the males take care of him from there.

"Talwyn and Azrael?" she panted.

"Still outside the gates," Sorin answered. "We need to go before more show up."

"We cannot leave them here," she said, sinking to her knees to give her trembling legs a break, trying to catch her breath.

"Luan will make sure she gets out," Sorin said, sending flames to the man she'd encased in ice. He stood over her, his eyes scanning every direction, watching for more threats. "We need to go."

"Is that who I think it is?" Cyrus asked suddenly, and Scarlett lifted her head. Her gaze followed Cyrus's to a section of the perimeter wall where the air seemed to be shimmering slightly.

Where Lord Tyndell stood staring back at her.

And beside him a figure, his face hidden by his cloak and hood. Alaric.

"Motherfucker," Sorin snarled, gripping her arm and hauling her to her feet. A fire portal sprang to life beside them. "We are going, Scarlett."

Lord Tyndell only smiled at her before both him and Alaric disappeared into the air.

CHAPTER 42
TALWYN

"What are these things?" Talwyn ground out, her winds swirling. The gusts were making it hard for the winged males to get airborne and kept them on the ground. Forcing them to fight with blades was about the only advantage she and Azrael had at this point. They were unnaturally strong, easily breaking through the thick vines she and the Earth Prince conjured to try to contain them. They seemed wary of her lightning, but she could not wield that continuously or for long periods of time. Coupled with keeping her winds strong enough, Azrael was doing most of the actual fighting.

They had come out of nowhere, seeming to plummet from the sky, the earth shuddering beneath them when they landed. They had yelled at Cyrus and Sorin to go ahead and find Scarlett when the Oracle had unlocked the gates. There were only six of these winged men, but six was more than enough.

"No idea," Azrael grunted, his sword clashing with the serrated blade of one of the men. "I can only assume they are guarding the Contessa."

If there were winged men trying to keep them from her, she was either in danger, or she was allying against the Courts. Either way it spelled absolute shit for them.

Shouting and cursing from beyond the estate wall filled the air. They must be encountering the same enemies.

Azrael managed to swipe his blade across the stomach of one of them. The man hardly flinched but struck with his own blade, Azrael barely avoiding the hit when he leapt back.

"We need to get out of here," Azrael gritted out, tracking all the men.

"And leave the others?" She cracked her whip of lightning, wrapping it around the sword of one of the men who had surged towards her. The energy flowed down the blade and into the man's body. He jolted, his body tensing and jaw clenching, and while he could not move, Azrael was slicing at the wings down his back. One feathered wing fell to the dirt, the man howling in pain and rage, blood spurting from the wound on his back. The next swipe of Azrael's sword was across the male's throat.

"That was luck," Azrael breathed, falling back to Talwyn's side as two more men approached, violence written on their features.

"It is the only way we have found to best them," Talwyn answered, shifting her winds to swirl around them as a shield rather than keep the men at bay. The action, however, let them get airborne.

The two Fae looked up, watching the winged men soar above them, arrows beginning to bounce off her air shield. Azrael was right. They needed to get the hell out of here.

Just as Talwyn was about to grab Azrael and Travel out, the assault of arrows halted, the men flying up and over the wall to whatever was happening beyond. She looked at Azrael, her shield dissolving, and they both began moving to the gates. If they could fight with the others, perhaps they could figure out an easier way to defeat the threat.

Until a figure in black stepped from the gates and into their path.

Talwyn and Azrael both stilled, and Talwyn's chest constricted completely when the man pulled back his hood. Black hair, straight and disheveled, swept across his brow, contrasting against dark, golden skin. Pale green eyes peered back at them, relief shifting across his features.

"Thank Silas," he cried, rushing towards them. "I have been looking everywhere for you."

Azrael had stepped in front of Talwyn, his sword raised. But Talwyn couldn't speak.

Not as Tarek Ordos stopped mere feet in front of them.

He bowed low, a subject before his queen, before he straightened and looked straight into her soul.

"Talwyn," he said softly.

A snarl emanated from Azrael. "Do not speak to her."

Hearing them both speak pulled her out of whatever state she had fallen into. She felt her features shift, harden. Her eyes narrowed on Tarek, and his own dropped back to the ground, head bowed once more. When she took a step towards him, fingers grazed her arm as though they would try to stop her.

She met Azrael's gaze impassively. "I do not need anyone to protect me," she sneered.

He seemed to search her eyes before his chin dipped minutely. "You do not," he agreed, his arm dropping to his side.

Talwyn crossed the distance between them and Tarek, and he lifted his head once more. She knew what he saw when he looked at her. Her features were emotionless. Her mouth was a tight line. Her back was straight, her chin raised.

He saw the Fae Queen everyone had seen for decades.

Her bracelet began unwinding from her wrist. She shouldn't be using the Shifter magic. Not after depleting so much of it fighting those winged men, but she couldn't let him see that she was even slightly weakened.

"Talwyn," he started, but her hand lifted, her fingers slowly curling into a fist.

Slowly cutting off his air supply.

His green eyes widened for a moment before some sort of resolve seemed to fill them. He raised his palms before him, and he slowly lowered to his knees, dropping his chin in submission. He did not squirm as she withheld his oxygen. He did not beg. He took her fury as she just stared down at him.

And when she reached out and placed a single finger under his chin and raised his face to look up at her, he met her stare, his blue-tinged lips pursing slightly.

She released his air, and he sucked in a few deep breaths while she held his chin up. His eyes never left hers. "Speak."

"It was all for you," he replied, his voice raspy.

Her head tilted to the side, but she said nothing. She'd learned long ago that most would reveal their secrets without much prompting, if they thought she already knew.

"I was taken captive," he went on, his voice low. "After the mission to find Queen Eliné failed. The others thought I was dead like Thia. I woke in the cells of the Black Syndicate. It was death, or be smart about survival. It was show my hand, or keep my cards close until I could get back to you."

Talwyn's gaze dropped to his left hand where a twin flame Mark had once stood against his bronze skin. It was gone now, just like her own. A piece of his soul lost among the worlds. Destined to be as incomplete as she was.

Never whole. Forever fractured.

"Stand," she said, her hand dropping to her side, and she took a step back from him.

He did so slowly and made no comment when vines appeared around his wrists before jerking them behind his back. Azrael came to her side.

"Where do you want to take him?" he asked. "The Halls or the Alcazar?"

"The Halls," Talwyn answered coldly. She wanted her own turf, her own space. A place completely under her control.

Azrael nodded, an earth portal springing to life to their left. He gripped Tarek by the bicep, ready to escort him through. With one last calculating look at her twin flame, Talwyn turned and stepped through.

"What is your plan here, Talwyn?" Azrael asked.

Tarek was down in a holding cell at the White Halls, and they had gone up to the private wing. Azrael had stalked off to his own chambers to bathe and wash off the blood and gore from battle. She had done the same.

She hadn't said a single word to either of them. Azrael had known what she'd wanted done without having to ask. He didn't need to. They had been this tandem unit for years.

And then he'd fucked everything up.

Talwyn strode from the dressing room in fresh clothing, sliding a dagger into a thigh sheath. She eyed her Second, who stood in a long-sleeve tunic and pants near the window, arms crossed.

"You summoned Ashtine?"

"I was waiting," he replied. "Until you told me what you wanted." Talwyn snorted a breath of disbelief, and his eyes narrowed on her. "Say what you need to say, Talwyn," Azrael bit out. "You and I both detest pretty words to avoid hurting feelings."

"Feelings have no place here," Talwyn snapped.

Azrael's brow arched. "No? You have no emotional attachment to the male down in your holding cells? Feelings are not playing any role in how this entire situation is being handled? Come now, Talwyn," he scoffed.

"You are the one who taught me not to let my emotions cloud my judgment," she retorted.

"Yes, but I also tried to teach you that in order to do so, you must first deal with those emotions. Obviously I failed."

Talwyn didn't say anything as she drew a wind message in the air, sending it off to Ashtine.

"What is your plan?" Azrael asked again. He had crossed the room to her and raised a hand as if he were going to reach for her, before apparently reconsidering and dropping it down to his side once more.

"When Ashtine gets here, we can speak with Tarek in one of the underground studies," Talwyn replied.

"In one of the studies?" Azrael repeated incredulously. "Why are we not speaking to him through his cell bars?"

"Why would we?"

"Because he has been working with our enemies, Talwyn."

"There has been no concrete proof of that," she countered. She hadn't told him that she'd seen Tarek speaking with those Night Children in Baylorin days before they'd gone to find the Contessa.

She hadn't told anyone about that.

"He aided in the capture of Scarlett," Azrael said. "So she says."

Azrael was silent for a long moment before he said, "So much for emotions not having any place here."

Talwyn opened her mouth to snap a reply, but a wind portal appeared, Ashtine stepping through a moment later. Talwyn couldn't remember the last time she'd seen the princess use a portal instead of walking among the winds.

"You summoned me?" she asked curtly, but she sounded exhausted. If the dark circles under her eyes were any indicator, she was.

Talwyn swallowed uncertainly before she said, "Yes. Tarek is here. In the cells. We are going to speak with him."

Ashtine blinked at her. "Queen Scarlett spoke the truth, then? That he lives and is working with the Maraan Lords?"

"He lives," Talwyn replied. "Whether or not he is working with the Maraan Lords remains to be seen."

"Why would she lie about that?" Ashtine asked, her head tilting to the side slightly. Silver hair slipped over her shoulder. Her eyes looked distant.

"She lies about everything else," Talwyn said.

"Such as?" Ashtine pressed.

"The fact that she is Avonleyan," Talwyn spat.

"She did not lie about that. She told you the first time she saw you after learning of her heritage herself."

Talwyn's fists clenched at her side. "The amulets then."

"You left that meeting," Ashtine said. "She said she planned to tell you, but you left."

Talwyn scoffed. "She wasn't going to tell me anything."

"Hmm," was all Ashtine hummed before gesturing for Talwyn to lead the way.

The trek down to the cells was silent, save for their footfalls echoing around them. They stopped outside Tarek's cell, a unit coming to a collective halt. Azrael on her right. Ashtine on her left, just as it had been for decades. Tarek looked up from where he sat against the wall, his elbows resting on bent knees.

"Look at you, Moonflower," he said softly, meeting her eyes. "Still unapologetically the only one that matters in the room."

"Get up," she said, turning her back on him and leaving Azrael to lead him to the study down the hall. She went straight to the large desk, settling into the chair behind it. Ashtine moved gracefully to a chair off to the side, and Azrael all but threw Tarek into a hard chair across from the desk, before moving to Talwyn's side.

She stared at Tarek, her eyes hard and unforgiving. She looked like a female about to unleash wrath, but she said nothing. Not to intimidate, but because she didn't know what to say. Tarek's head cocked slightly as he stared back at her. The corner of his lips twitched as though he knew she was conflicted, but that was the only tell he gave. She finally jerked her chin at him, and Azrael understood the message to take over and ask the questions.

"Were you involved in the capture and detainment of Queen Scarlett?" Azrael asked.

Tarek's eyes remained fixed on Talwyn when he answered. "I was." She forced herself to stay still. She did not blink. She did not flinch, despite wanting to lurch forward at the admission.

"Explain," Azrael growled.

Tarek settled back into his chair. His wrists had been secured by shirastone shackles when they had arrived, and the chains clinked as he let his hands fall to his lap. "I could not very well let her go and blow my cover, could I?"

"You are suggesting you infiltrated mortals?" Ashtine asked, her back straight and poised as always.

"Either Queen Scarlett is keeping things from you if you believe I was working with mortals, or you are fishing for information, your Highness," Tarek replied coolly, glancing at the princess.

"Watch it, Ordos," Azrael snarled. "You said you were taken captive. Now you are saying you infiltrated their forces. Which is it?"

Talwyn shifted, setting her elbow on the armrest and resting her chin on her hand, watching Tarek. He leaned forward, eyes searing into hers as if he were speaking solely to her. "I would have never left you willingly, Talwyn. You have to know that." When her only reply was a slow blink, he sat back slightly. "I *was* taken captive. When the Night Children realized they had not killed me, they took me to the ones they were working for— the Assassin Lord and Lord Tyndell, the leader of King Theodore's armies."

"Mikale Lairwood?" Ashtine asked.

Tarek nodded. "He is one of them as well, but he is new to his position. The others outrank him."

"Others?" Ashtine asked airily. "Only Alaric and Balam?"

Tarek blinked at her. "I was unaware you were on a first name basis with them."

"You have not been gone long enough to forget how Princess Ashtine speaks," Talwyn said coolly. "It is rather unforgettable." The sound of her voice had Tarek's head whipping back to her. "Answer the question. Are there more besides those three?"

He looked to Azrael, then glanced once more at Ashtine, before saying, "Let me speak to you alone, Talwyn."

Azrael huffed a laugh of disbelief as Talwyn said, "No."

"Please," Tarek said. "There are . . . things you should know."

"That is why we are here," she answered without an ounce of warmth.

"It involves Avonleya. Your plans. The Courts . . ."

Tarek trailed off, glancing pointedly at Azrael.

"You speak of his Avonleyan lineage?" Talwyn asked.

Tarek started slightly. "You know?"

"I do."

"For how long?"

Talwyn arched a brow. "Does it matter?"

Tarek pressed his tongue to his cheek. A thick silence hung in the air for several minutes while they all waited for him to continue speaking. Finally, he said, "I have information to share, things to explain, but I will only do so with you alone."

"Then you can fuck off back to a cell," Azrael spat.

"I was unaware you spoke for the queen now," Tarek replied snidely.

"You were my Third, Ordos," Azrael said, his palms slamming onto the desk as he leaned forward. "The queen is not the only one you betrayed here."

"Do not speak to me of betrayal," Tarek sneered, his lip curling slightly in disgust. "Sins of the fathers and all that. Not to mention whose bed my *twin flame* has been sharing since I have been gone."

"You no longer bear such a Marking. Neither of you do," Ashtine lilted. "That would lead one to believe you are not twin flames."

"We were obviously unable to complete the Trials in time," Tarek drawled.

Ashtine only hummed in contemplation.

"Whose bed I have been sharing should be the least of your concerns here," Talwyn cut in coldly. "You have let me believe you were *dead* for an entire decade. If I chose to fuck others in those years, you really have no say in the matter."

Tarek clenched his jaw but wisely said nothing else, his head dropping forward.

"On that note, you let me believe you were dead for *ten years*," she reiterated. "Why would I believe anything you have to say to me?"

Tarek slowly raised his eyes back to hers. "Because I know you, Talwyn. I know what you desire. I know what you seek. If I had any choice in the matter, I would have found a way to inform you I survived. Everything I have done these last ten years was to not only get back to you, but to help you achieve what you so desperately want."

"And what is that?" Azrael sneered.

"Revenge," Tarek purred.

Talwyn sat up straighter, her hand dropping to the armrest. "Go on."

"The Maraan Lords and your own endeavors are aligned, my queen," Tarek said, his entire attention focused on Talwyn. "The war that was fought centuries ago did not cease. It simply paused."

"Avonleya ran and left behind their allies," Talwyn said.

"Indeed they did," Tarek agreed. "And they should pay for not only that, but everything they have taken and kept from this continent."

"What do you mean taken and kept?"

His gaze slid to Azrael. "They took kingdoms that do not belong to them." His stare shifted to Ashtine. "They possess gifts that make them superior in every way and use them to force others beneath them." His eyes resettled on Talwyn. "They took parents from children, children from parents, and they keep others out to protect what never should have entered our world. What endangers our entire realm. That is why the Maraans came in the first place, Talwyn. They did not come to ignite a war. They came to retrieve what started the war to begin with. What sought sanctuary here and instead brought bloodshed. Your revenge is justified. Let me help you obtain it."

"You are wrong," Ashtine cut in, her tone edged. Talwyn looked at her to find her glaring back at Tarek, papers fluttering lightly nearby.

"Wrong about what?" he asked.

"About all of it. Revenge being justified. The Avonleyans. Everything," she replied.

"Then please. Correct me," Tarek said, gesturing with his bound hands for her to speak.

She turned pleading eyes to Talwyn. "The winds would not lie to me, Talwyn. You know this."

"You have said the winds abandoned you," Talwyn said icily.

"They have. Because I chose loyalty to you over them. Because you are against them."

"The Avonleyans?" Talwyn sneered. "Not too long ago you were against them, too. Or have you forgotten?"

Ashtine shook her head, the air around her becoming more intense. "I have not forgotten, but you have forgotten whom we come from. Who granted us our gifts."

"I was not born to serve the Avonleyans," Talwyn snarled.

"No," Ashtine agreed, "you were not, but they are not who blessed the Fae or the Witches or the Shifters. If you are angry with someone, it should not be with the Avonleyans. Their kingdom is as innocent as your own."

"Bullshit," Tarek spat, but a vine was quickly winding around his throat, silencing him. Talwyn glanced at Azrael, who was glaring at Tarek.

"Who should I be angry with then, Ashtine?" Talwyn asked, turning back to the princess.

"Must you be angry with someone? Can you not see that the Maraans are just as destructive as you believe the Avonleyans to be? They sacrifice *children*, Talwyn. Innocent children to achieve their ends," Ashtine cried. "If you side with them, you are simply trading a make-believe villain for a real one. Only you will serve the latter."

Ashtine stood then, a wind portal appearing to her right. "You are leaving?" Talwyn asked, jolting to her feet.

"I am tired," Ashtine conceded. "And I have already debated the merits of this with you more times than I can count. I have sacrificed much to prove my loyalty, and still you push for more. I have nothing left to give."

With that, the Wind Princess stepped from the study.

"Release him," Talwyn said to Azrael, her voice monotone, as she lowered back to her seat.

The vines disappeared from Tarek's throat, and he sucked down air, glaring with so much malice at Azrael, Talwyn could practically reach out and touch it.

"Tell me, Tarek," she said, "how did you manage to hide such distaste for your prince for so long?"

"I am very patient, Talwyn. You know this," he replied. "It took time and patience to gain the trust of the Assassin Lord, to learn the secrets I now know."

"Apparently ten whole years," she gritted out.

"Speak with me privately, Talwyn," Tarek urged. "Without your Second and Third here to whisper in your ear."

"So that you can do the whispering?" Azrael cut in. "I think not. A snake does not shed its skin so easily."

"Says the male who has hidden his true bloodline," Tarek retorted. He had a point. They both had points.

"Leave us," she said to Azrael. Before he could argue, she continued, "I will speak with him and then with you."

"That is a terrible idea," Azrael said. He took her chair, spinning it to face him. His hands landed on the armrests, his face stopping inches in front of hers. "He knows how to manipulate you, Talwyn." His voice was low, intense. "He knows what words to say, what emotions to play on."

"So do you," she replied coldly, holding his eye.

"The difference, Talwyn, is that I would never do so. I have always been—"

"Honest?" she laughed. "Try again, Prince."

A muscle feathered in his jaw. "I have never told you things just because it is what you want to hear. I am not afraid to challenge you. I am not afraid to hurt your feelings. This is *emotional*, Talwyn. You have an entire kingdom depending on you. You *need* someone else here."

"That someone is no longer you."

"Fuck, Talwyn," he said, pushing off the chair and stepping back from her. His hands ran through his hair in frustration before he turned back to her once more. "You think I am the dishonest one here? You think you cannot trust me? That I am the one who will manipulate you?" His arm flung out, finger pointing at Tarek. "Make sure you ask him about that twin flame bond during your little chat. Because that Mark does not just disappear. You are smart enough to know that."

"We could not finish the Trials," she started to argue.

His hands landed on the armrests again. "In the years you had that Mark, it never grew. You never completed even *one* Trial. That is not because you did not have time. Deep down, you know why that Mark no longer graces your skin. Something never felt quite right about it. You have seen a true twin flame bond. Twice. You know that what Ordos convinced you that you had with him was nothing compared to what you have seen Cyrus and Aditya find. Hiding from a truth is just as *dishonest* as keeping truth hidden."

Without another word, he left the study, the door slamming closed behind him.

The silence was so loud in the room it was deafening, and it hung there, thick and heavy. Talwyn stared at the wall she now faced since Azrael had spun her chair. No one else would dare do such a thing, because no one else would ever dare call her out. Not like that. Only ever him. The one who had never left her alone. She knew he would come back if she asked. She knew he would—

"Talwyn." Tarek's familiar voice cut through her thoughts. "Let me come to you. Take these off and let me . . . He is wrong. Everything he just said is wrong."

But she didn't know that it was. Deep down, she didn't fear that Azrael might be right. She feared that she already knew he was.

She pulled a key from her pocket and strode towards Tarek. As she turned the lock, a manacle falling free, she said, "Tell me everything."

CHAPTER 43
SCARLETT

Scarlett sat outside on a bench in one of the courtyards of the Black Halls. Many of the children were running, playing with balls, and just generally enjoying the sunshine after having been stuck inside warehouses and secret hideaways for months, if not years. Add the balmy weather here, versus the winter chill that plagued Baylorin, and the children were thrilled.

She had a book in her lap. She'd been trying to find information on these winged men they'd fought two days ago. Sorin had carried her through a fire portal, and she'd almost immediately passed out. Apparently they had gotten her to drink some of Sorin's blood at some point, because when she'd woken this morning after sleeping straight through the prior day, her power reserves were no longer empty. They weren't completely full, but she didn't feel completely drained either.

The sun had been streaming in the windows, and she'd woken to an empty bed. The sofa in her room had not been empty, however. Cassius sat, apparently holding vigil until she either woke or Sorin returned. He'd informed her that Sorin had gone with Cyrus and Eliza to the Fire Court to check on some things and make sure their forces were primed and ready to face what was coming. She wasn't completely sure what that meant, but as soon as Sorin returned, she was sure she'd find out. She also wanted to know what they'd heard from Talwyn and Prince Azrael.

"What's this one about, Seastar?" Cassius asked when she paused the turning of her pages to skim the text. He sat beside her, his arm stretched along the back of the bench.

She sighed. "Nothing helpful. The word 'wings' caught my eye, but it's speaking of different types of wings, not the beings that bear them."

She began turning the pages again. Cassius was idly flipping through the pages of the book on Blood Magic. Not that he could read it well, but he was studying the Marks intently, trying to learn what he could. Hazel was still checking in with him daily. Sometimes he would ask her questions, other days he was stonily silent while she tended to him. The wound in his side was almost completely healed, and his leg was likely as good as it was going to get. She still taught him how to make an herbal compress to apply to the wound while he slept, hoping it would encourage more healing.

"This Mark matches the one on your arm," he said, tapping on a page of the book. She glanced over to find the three stars below an inverted triangle. She propped her arm beside it, comparing the two. "What is it for?" he asked.

Scarlett sat up straighter, pulling the book towards herself. "It's how he woke my Avonleyan magic," she murmured, her eyes flying over the words.

"Who?"

"The man in my dream. The Lord of Night or whatever," she said, growing more excited the more she read. "He gave me this Mark in one of my dreams. It wasn't until after that, my magic started getting out of control."

Cassius was shaking his head. "No, Scarlett. Your tonic was keeping it suppressed."

"The fire and water maybe," she countered. "But when did the shadows start showing up, Cass? Think about it."

"I . . . Perhaps you are right, but how did he do this in a dream?"

"It is connected to his own magic somehow," she answered. "But do you know what this means?" When he stared back at her in confusion, she said, "This is why you've never exhibited your father's gifts. They haven't been awakened."

"You think that if you give me this Mark, I will start . . ." He blew out a long breath, running his hand through his hair. "I think you are right, Seastar."

She jumped to her feet, gathering both books to her chest. "Let's go somewhere else. I don't want the children witnessing Blood Magic."

"Right now?" he asked, arching a brow.

"Now seems as good a time as any. The sooner it starts manifesting, the sooner you can begin learning to control it," she answered, striding for the opening across the courtyard.

Cassius fell into step beside her, and she led them down the rocky paths along the dunes and to the beach. When they came to a section far from the Halls, she knelt, flipping back to the page with the Mark. Cassius knelt beside her, watching as she began practicing the Mark in the sand. It wasn't nearly as complicated as some of the other ones. It would require mixing his blood with the blood of one whose gifts were already awakened. "What do you think my father's gifts are?" Cassius wondered aloud while she worked.

"I don't know, Cass," she answered softly. "How are you and Hazel getting on?"

"She is . . . formidable, yet I think she is trying."

"She is," Scarlett confirmed. "She cares deeply for you. When she learned that I knew you . . . She cares, Cass."

"I know. I just cannot reconcile that fact with the knowledge that she sent me to grow up on the streets. Alone."

"You were not alone," Scarlett countered, erasing the Mark in the sand and drawing again. But she understood what he meant. She had felt alone in Baylorin, despite having him and Nuri and Juliette.

"She did not know that was how things would turn out, Scarlett. She had no idea what would happen to me. She did not know if I lived or if I died before I saw my first year of life completed," Cassius countered, a hard edge slipping into his voice.

"That is a fair point, but . . ." Scarlett trailed off, studying the Mark she'd just drawn for errors before wiping it away and drawing again.

"But?" Cassius prompted.

"The Oracle had given her a prophecy as to when you could return. That would give her reason to believe that you would live, Cassius. That would give her hope." When Cassius didn't say anything, she went on. "And despite the circumstances you were dealt, you not only lived, you thrived. Was your childhood one of dreams? Of course not. Nor was mine. Nor was Juliette's or Nuri's. I cannot imagine any of us would have chosen to be trained in how to take life. Well, maybe Nuri," she added with a slight frown, again wiping away the Mark in the sand. "My point is, despite how you were raised and what you were trained to do, you are still kind. You are still compassionate. You are loyal to a fault. You are still someone I am honored to call a friend, and I do not deserve to call you my Guardian, but I am so grateful I can."

"Seastar," he said, fondness clear in his tone.

Scarlett sat back on her heels, meeting his eye. "You owe her nothing, Cassius. If you wish to never speak to her, never get to know her. If you wish to have nothing to do with her, I will support your decision. But I also think you should give her a chance. I think you will find when you are with her, in her element, she becomes much more approachable. She only wishes to know you."

A half-smile curled onto Cassius's mouth. "When did our roles reverse, Seastar? Usually I am the one giving the advice."

"When you spend so much time around ancient, immortal Fae who speak like sages, it's bound to rub off at some point, I suppose," she said. "I have this down. Are you ready?"

"Ready if you are," he replied, rolling back the sleeve of his tunic.

Scarlett pulled the dagger she had sheathed at her thigh and cut a gash along her palm before handing it to Cassius. He cut his own palm, tipping it to allow his blood to mix with hers. She mixed them in her hand just as she remembered the man doing in that dream, then began drawing with the tip of her finger onto Cassius's skin.

She was starting on the second star when a furious growl sounded behind her.

"What the fuck are you doing?"

"Um, Seastar . . ." Cassius said, his eyes wide, staring over her shoulder.

She said nothing. Just threw up a wall of flames and shadows behind her to keep Sorin and whoever was with him back.

Scarlett! That same growl came down their bond, and she slammed a wall of shadows around her mind, too. She'd deal with that in a moment. She didn't know what would happen if a Blood Mark went unfinished, but she didn't really want to find out.

Dipping her finger back into the blood, she finished the Mark. It flared brightly before fading to silvery-white against Cassius's tanned skin. She dropped all her shields when she finished, and Cassius drew his arm back to study the Mark.

"What now?" Cassius asked.

"We wait," Scarlett answered simply.

"And the brooding Fae at your back?" he asked in amusement.

"I have found it best to let him throw his temper tantrum before we discuss things."

A snicker told her Cyrus was with him, and a glance over her shoulder found Eliza and Rayner there as well. They looked wary, but Sorin was livid. Flames flared in his eyes. Embers were floating among his black strands, and his hands were curled into tight fists at his side.

"Well? Go on, Prince," she said, leaning back on her hands and waiting for his tirade.

"Sometimes I cannot decide if you are brave or stupid," Eliza commented, her eyes darting from her to Sorin and back.

"Sometimes I question the same thing," Scarlett replied nonchalantly with a shrug.

"You were doing Blood Magic," Sorin cut it, his voice lethally calm.

"I was," she agreed.

"Without a discussion first."

"I discussed it with Cassius."

His answer was another growl.

"Gods, you're like an animal," she sighed, pushing to her feet and moving to stand in front of him. Reaching up, she took his face in her hands. "Sorin, that Mark is nothing bad. The Mark I gave him matches the one on my arm. It will awaken his Avonleyan magic."

The flames in his eyes slowly banked. His breathing slowly returned to normal. "How can you be sure?"

"Because despite what you seem to think, not all Blood Magic is bad," she answered, running a thumb along his cheek. "I will not deny that Blood Magic can be incredibly dangerous, obviously, but so can your own magic until you understand it and learn to control it. Just as I was taught the Fae were the enemy, you were taught falsehoods about Blood Magic."

"You truly believe that?" Eliza asked curiously.

Her hands slowly slid from Sorin's face. "I do," she answered, facing her friend. "When used properly, it is just as valuable as a spell a Witch casts or the gifts we all use."

Cyrus was running a hand along his jaw. "She makes a valid point, Sorin. Look at everything that has come to light in the last few months that we knew nothing about. She's full-blooded Avonleyan for fuck's sake. We thought they were all locked away across the sea, and yet here she stands. And the son of the High Witch stands beside her, Avonleyan blood running in his veins too."

"On the way to the Fire Court when this all began, you said to me that history depends on which book you are reading. This is no different," Scarlett said, stooping down to pick up the books from the sand, passing them to Cassius. "Darkness is feared because you cannot see where it leads. Blood Magic is the same. But I would venture to guess there are stars to be found within it, too."

Sorin swallowed thickly. He reached for her, pulling her back into his chest, his hands settling on her waist. "All I can think of, all that fills my head when I see you doing Blood Magic, is you being taken from me." His brow fell against hers. "I cannot unsee that Mark in the dirt. Your blood splashed across it. Your ring floating on shadows..."

"I know, Sorin," she murmured, her hands resting against his chest. "That is not happening again. I swear to you I do not use those spells, those Marks, unless I am certain I understand all the costs. Never again like before. I promise."

His eyes fell closed, and he inhaled deeply. "Do we need to leave or...?" Cyrus asked.

Scarlett pulled back, shooting a stream of water into his face from her palm as she shifted her attention to Rayner. "Do you have news from Nuri?"

Rayner nodded, his grey eyes swirling. "She said the Contessa is still well, but it is not safe to bring her out yet."

Scarlett nodded. As long as Nuri was with the Contessa, Scarlett wasn't worried about Alaric getting near her. And if these tunnels were as hard to enter as Auberon claimed, Nuri should be able to keep her hidden as long as necessary.

She turned back to Sorin. "Lunch?"

"Who fed you when we were not around, Darling?" Cyrus asked, a fire portal opening to the left. Scarlett stuck her tongue out at him as they all filed through and stepped into one of the private dining areas of the Halls, a lunch spread already set and waiting for them.

She looked up at Sorin, batting her lashes knowing he was the one who had made sure this would be waiting for them. "You really do love me, don't you?"

"Perhaps," he agreed.

"Or he does not wish to deal with you when you are ravenous," Cyrus interjected. "I'm sure it is one of the two."

"Considering he has put up with you for the last how many decades, I'm delightful by comparison," Scarlett retorted, making her way towards the food.

"Darling, you literally growl if someone gets in the way of your food."

"The males in this room, save for Cassius, literally growl all the damn time," she replied without looking up from the plate she was filling.

"Stop speaking, Cyrus," Eliza cut in before Cyrus could say anything more in response.

"Eliza, dear, are you feeling left out?" Cyrus teased.

"No, but I only seem to acquire a headache when you open your mouth," she retorted.

Scarlett snorted a laugh, giving a taunting smirk to Cyrus.

"Why do I feel like I am refereeing children?" Sorin drawled from down the table.

"The actual children in these Halls are better behaved," Rayner grumbled, pulling out a chair for Scarlett as she approached the dining table.

"Rayner!" Scarlett cried with glee. "Did you just join in the bantering?"

"We should declare this day a holiday to memorialize the moment," Cyrus called from the food spread.

"Can I do that?" Scarlett asked.

"You are the queen. I don't see why not," Cyrus replied.

"We should get cake to celebrate," Scarlett mused.

"For the love of Anala," Eliza muttered, plopping into a seat at the table.

Scarlett laughed, feeling a lightness in her chest she hadn't felt in days. Sorin sank into the seat beside her a moment later, leaning over and pressing a light kiss to her cheek.

What was that for?

You slept for two days, Love. You are lucky that is the only place I am kissing at this moment.

I wouldn't exactly call that luck . . .

Scarlett watched as his pupils instantly dilated, followed by swift glances from the rest of the Fae at the table.

Cyrus cleared his throat from across the table where he sat next to Cassius. "Care to share how Hazel showed up at the River Estate, Darling?"

Scarlett scowled at him. There went the lightheartedness she'd felt moments ago.

She took a bite of cheese before she said, "She came when I summoned her."

"You summoned the High Witch," Cyrus repeated dubiously. "In the middle of that fight."

"Obviously."

"How?"

Scarlett sighed, setting down the bread she'd been about to take a bite of. "Bringing Juliette with us was a risk. She is the Oracle, after all. She may have died a mortal death, but I am assuming she can die a more permanent one. And I do not wish to know what would happen if the Oracle died before being replaced or whatever happens with that. I had Hazel brew up a potion that would signal her if she was needed to come in and get Juliette."

"But how did she know where we were?" Sorin asked.

"I sent her a message when Talwyn Traveled us upstream from the manor. The same time I let Rayner and Eliza know where we were."

"But she cannot cross the wards without an escort," Eliza cut in.

Scarlett reached for her glass of water. "I *may have* taken Hazel across the wards right before we entered the Night Children territory. How she got the griffin across, though, I have no idea." She turned to face Sorin. "So much better than broomsticks, by the way."

Sorin stared back at her, unimpressed.

"And you felt the need to leave us uninformed yet again because . . . ?" Cyrus asked, settling back in his chair, drumming his fingers on the table. His food forgotten before him.

Scarlett rolled her eyes. "I was not leaving you uninformed," she replied. "You were all busy preparing things in the Fire Court, communicating with Talwyn and Prince Azrael. These were matters I could handle myself, and I did. If you lot think I am going to run every small detail and decision past you, you are in for a rude awakening."

Scarlett glanced at Cassius, who was trying to keep a smile from forming on his lips. When he couldn't fight it, he snatched up his glass of water, hiding the smile behind it.

"This is not funny, Cass," she snapped at him.

"Watching them try to figure out how your mind works is rather entertaining, Seastar. I haven't figured it out in fifteen years," he said with a wink. "Speaking of which . . ."

"No one was speaking of years, Cassius," she said pointedly.

"Twenty of them is a pretty big deal, Seastar."

"Shut up, Cassius."

"Scarlett . . . When is your birthday?" Sorin asked slowly from beside her, clearly catching on.

"It does not matter."

"Cassius?"

"It is in three days," Cass replied.

"Shut. Up," she snarled, throwing her bread at him.

"You were seriously not going to tell me it was your birthday?" Sorin demanded.

Scarlett picked up her fork, pushing vegetables around on her plate. "I have not celebrated my birthday since my mo— Since Eliné died."

That had not stopped Nuri and Juliette and Cassius from attempting to celebrate it. But Eliné had always made the day so incredibly special. She'd take the day off from healing, and they would spend the entire day together. With her birthday being on the tail-end of winter, it was usually chilly and dreary outside, but that never stopped Eliné from waking her up before the sun rose with hotcakes smothered in rich syrup and topped with fresh whipped cream and strawberries. Then they would bundle up and spend the entire day on the beach if the weather permitted. Eliné would build a fire, and they would roast meats and treats all day long. She would read her books, build in the sand, and tell her stories of all sorts of imaginary kingdoms and people. Although, Scarlett had to wonder now if they were all that imaginary. When the sun would start to set, they would lie on their backs on the blankets Eliné would always bring. More would be piled on top of them to keep the winter chill out, and they would watch the stars come out.

There had only been one year that Scarlett could remember the weather being so terrible they could not go to the beach. It had been her last birthday before Eliné had been killed, and, of all people, Alaric had been the one to make that day special.

By giving her her very first dagger. To a godsdamn eight-year-old.

Granted, it had come with chocolate cake, hot cocoa, and the only time she had been allowed into his private quarters. He had a partially-covered balcony off of his bedroom, and he had let them sit there and watch the stars come out that night. Even then, he had been subtly planting those tiny nuggets in her mind— that he would take care of her, provide for her, save her.

Scarlett tossed her fork down, no longer hungry. The table had fallen silent while she'd slipped into memories.

"Scarlett," Cassius started.

"Don't." She pushed away from the table, moving towards the double doors that led out to the balcony. Reaching the railing, she leaned on her arms, breathing in the sea air. She closed her eyes, her hair blowing across her face.

She felt someone settle beside her. Not Sorin. She would know if it was him.

"Your birthday should be celebrated, Seastar," Cassius said gently. "I did not bring it up to drag up old memories."

"You know why it is just another day to me, Cassius," she said, turning to look at him. "You know why, and you still chose to bring it up. In front of so many people."

"Because they love you, Scarlett. They would want to share in your birthday. They can create new memories to replace the ones that bleed every time they are scratched open."

Her head fell against his shoulder. "Eliné and Alaric always seemed so . . . close. Do you think she knew?"

"That he was the son of Deimas and Esmeray? I cannot imagine she did."

"Why there? Why would she bring me to the Black Syndicate? To an Assassin Lord of all people? She could have hidden me away anywhere."

"I don't know," he replied, his cheek pressing against her hair.

"There had to be a reason that they chose there. Nothing was left to chance. Nothing was done without planning. Even you and I."

"Maybe that's why you were brought to Baylorin. Because I was already there," Cassius supplied.

"Perhaps."

The sound of rushing water had them both turning to see Briar stepping from a water portal. He stilled when he saw them.

"I apologize if I am interrupting."

"You aren't," Scarlett said, pushing off the railing and going to him.

"You are sure about this?" Briar asked, pulling open one of the doors for her.

"I am." The Fae around the table all turned to her, but her eyes landed on her twin flame's. "Have you finished eating, Prince? We have a date with a Sorceress."

"Do not get near her cell," Sorin was saying as they traversed the halls. "Offer her nothing. Give her nothing."

Briar seemed to choke down a laugh. "The irony of this moment," he muttered.

Sorin glared at him over Scarlett's head where she walked between the two princes. Cassius was at her back. Briar had portaled them into the Underwater Prison, and the feeling of her magic being forced quiet when they had crossed wards was unsettling. They had explained before coming here that their magic would be inaccessible, but actually experiencing it had summoned memories of being chained to walls, her gifts just out of reach.

After several minutes, they stopped at the top of a small staircase. Sorin gripped her shoulders, turning her to face him. "She is not from this world, Scarlett. She will say things that will make you question yourself, what you know. She is—"

"She is cunning and conniving and will do and say whatever she can to get out of there," Briar cut in harshly. "There is a reason we rarely speak with her."

Scarlett peered curiously down the dark stairwell once more. It might be all kinds of wrong, but she was genuinely intrigued at this point.

They quietly descended the steps and when they reached the bottom, the area illuminated by several lit braziers along the wall opposite her cell, she was standing just on the other side of her bars. They had told her the bars were made of shirastone. Apparently all the cells here were. There were small windows through which Scarlett could see the mer on guard outside her cell down here, sea water and sea creatures drifting by.

But Scarlett's attention was fixed on the woman standing still as a statue on the other side of those bars. Jet black hair hung to her waist, stark against her pale skin and beige shift. Bright violet eyes that seemed to radiate stared back at her, and the smile that was on her lips was nothing short of serpentine.

"I told you I would call in my debt when I was ready, Prince of Fire," the Sorceress said, her eyes still fixed on Scarlett. Her head tilted to the side. "Although I suppose it is King of the Western Courts now, is it not?"

The blood of a god. That is what Sorin had agreed to give her should he ever find such a thing.

"I am not here to discuss my bargain with you," Sorin replied coolly, his hand coming to the small of Scarlett's back.

"No," the Sorceress agreed, drifting closer to the bars. "You have come to make a new bargain."

"There will be no bargains made this day," Briar cut in sharply.

The Sorceress's violet stare shot to him. "Prince of Water and Ice." Her nostrils flared as she seemed to sniff the air, her smile curving upwards even more. "You smell of the winds." Her eyes drifted to Cassius, and they seemed to widen slightly. "You, however, smell of other worlds."

Scarlett stepped forward at that, drawing the Sorceress's gaze back to her. "What world do you come from?"

"Release me from this cell, and I will show you."

"Not happening," Sorin said flatly.

The Sorceress drifted away, moving about her sparse space. She dragged her hand along the stone walls of her cell. If her nails weren't broken and cracked to nothing, Scarlett imagined the sound would have been horrific. "Do you like stories, Lady of Darkness?"

Scarlett lurched forward, Sorin's hand latching onto her arm and stopping her from coming any closer to the cell bars. "How do you know that title?"

"I know a great number of things," she answered, her lips turning down in a slight pout. "Is that not why you are here?"

"What is your name?"

"In this world? The Sorceress."

"And in other worlds?"

The Sorceress shrugged a bony shoulder. "Depends on the world." She moved closer to the bars once more, seeming to glide in front of them. "You smell like her."

"Like who?"

"You never answered me. Do you like stories?"

"Only if they are true," Scarlett answered.

"Truth is a matter of perspective, don't you think?" the Sorceress countered. "Would you like to hear one about beginnings and endings, or one about two sisters?"

"What is the cost?" Sorin demanded before Scarlett could answer. Briar stood stoically on her other side, arms crossed and features impossible to read.

The Sorceress's lips curled up. "I shall give her one at no cost. The other . . . We can negotiate if she wishes to hear it."

"I would rather you just answer some questions," Scarlett replied, trying to shrug off Sorin's grip, but he held firm.

"Do not be rude," the Sorceress chided lightly. "A story first and then we can discuss a cost for the answers you seek."

Scarlett sighed. "Fine. Which story would be more beneficial to hear?"

"Who am I to decide such a thing?"

"Beginnings and endings," Cassius said from behind Scarlett. She glanced back at him, but his entire focus was on the Sorceress before them. She turned back to the Sorceress and nodded for her to go ahead.

"In all things there must be balance," she began. "Beginnings and endings. Light and dark. Fire and shadows."

Scarlett stepped back into Sorin as the Sorceress went on.

"The worlds are no different. Beings emerged from the Chaos to create such a thing."

"You speak of the gods?" Scarlett asked.

"Do not interrupt the story," the Sorceress snapped, her tone so vicious, it had Sorin wrapping an arm around her waist and tugging her back farther from the cell. "They went to various parts of the stars, setting up their own kingdoms, maintaining balance. The Firsts created the Lessers, and from them the various worlds grew and prospered. Some grew faster than others. Some worlds were favored more than others."

"The beginning," Scarlett breathed.

"He was one of the Firsts."

"He?" Scarlett asked, moving closer to her once more.

"There were six Firsts, but Beginning and Ending each have their roles to play. They became the most powerful, working together to keep the balance. Beginning created. Ending judged."

"You speak of life and death," Scarlett said quietly.

The Sorceress's hands shot out, grasping the bars of the cell. She didn't seem to notice the shirastone biting into her skin. "Stop interrupting, *Lady*."

She stepped back from the bars, moving to the wall and dragging her hand along it once more. "With the aid of the other Firsts and Lessers, new beings were created and scattered among the worlds, but some were created and kept close. Some were loyal to Beginning. Some were loyal to Ending. But over time, Beginning began to crave something more. He had always favored her, always desired her."

"He loved someone?" Scarlett asked, drifting closer still to the cell, ignoring Sorin's low warning.

"What is love?" the Sorceress countered with a small shrug, not seeming to mind this particular interruption. Her slim hands gripped the cell bars once more. "He *wanted*, but she did not, for she had already bound herself to another. Had already created with him, keeping their true heritage a secret. When he learned of this, rage consumed him. He summoned those loyal to him, waged war against the other. And so the balance tipped."

"She had bound herself to death?" Scarlett asked. "You speak of Arius and Serafina. And their children, Temural and Saylah."

"Chaos descended on the worlds they ruled. Some worlds were ended. Some were abandoned. Some were forgotten."

"What of this world?" Scarlett demanded. "What of the world we live in?"

"Some worlds became sanctuaries," the Sorceress whispered.

"How do you know these things? Who are you?"

The Sorceress stepped back from the bars. "The other story comes at a cost, Lady."

Scarlett's nose scrunched in confusion. "The story of two sisters is about you?"

The Sorceress only smiled back at her.

Huffing a sigh of frustration, Scarlett pulled her spirit amulet from her pocket. "What do you know of this?"

"Of what? The skystone? The nightstone? The goddess of that symbol? Or the key?"

Scarlett's lips pursed, unsure of how to respond to that, knowing that any answer she sought would require a price to be paid. The Sorceress's head tilted slightly as she studied Scarlett. Scarlett cleared her throat. "I have several questions. I will not negotiate a price for each answer."

"You will not negotiate a price at all," Sorin cut in, stepping to her side.

"But she must," the Sorceress replied, her tone shifting, becoming like the hiss of a snake. "She requires what I have."

"Knowledge can be found in other places," Sorin ground out.

"Yes, but the final key cannot."

Scarlett felt her world shift beneath her as Sorin said, "You lie."

"Did I not tell you the last time you were here that Eliné and Henna came to visit me?"

"And you denied them aid," Sorin retorted.

"I did not," the Sorceress disagreed. "They refused to pay my price, but it was you who assumed that was all they asked of me."

"Why would Eliné entrust a key to you?" Cassius interjected from where he stood against the wall.

"What are you doing on this side of the Edria Sea?" the Sorceress asked, curiosity filling her violet eyes.

Scarlett sighed in exasperation. "What is the price? For the key you possess and the answer to five questions. Beyond your freedom. That is not an option."

"You shall find anything is an option if the need is great enough," the Sorceress said.

"She cannot possibly have the key, Scarlett. Where would she even keep it hidden?" Sorin cut in.

Scarlett turned to him. "We are not going to find out if you keep interrupting my negotiations with a Sorceress from another world," Scarlett bit back.

"You are fascinating," the Sorceress mused. "So much like him."

"Like who?" Scarlett demanded.

"Keys and locks. Locks and keys," the Sorceress said in an eerily sing-song voice, backing away from the bars. "But you only need one lock. One lock, seven keys." Her violet eyes scanned over everyone on the other side of the bars before settling back onto Scarlett. "Of course, keys can open more than one lock, and some keys and locks do not go together at all."

"You know where the lock is?" Scarlett asked, trying to track the Sorceress's erratic movements.

But the Sorceress dropped to the floor of her cell, beginning to draw Marks in the dust there. Scarlett stepped closer, watching carefully.

"What is she writing?" Sorin asked softly.

Scarlett shook her head. "I am not sure yet. I don't know them well enough to say for sure without that book."

The Sorceress's head flew up. "What book?"

Scarlett's eyes widened before a smile slowly began to curve up her lips. She pressed her palm to Sorin's chest, pushing him back so it was just her and Sorceress.

"I will tell you of the book I speak of, for the answer to one of my questions," Scarlett purred softly.

The Sorceress's features shifted, fury filling her eyes. She lurched forward, grasping the bars and seeming to crawl up them as she drew herself to her feet. She was slightly taller than Scarlett, and when she was standing, she pressed her face to the bars as well. "This is not a game, Lady of Darkness."

"No games," Scarlett agreed. "Information in exchange for knowledge."

The Sorceress hissed at her.

Scarlett gripped the bars, right below the Sorceress's hands, bringing her face inches from the female's. She heard all the males behind her shift closer, heard Sorin's reprimand down the bond, but she ignored it. "Men with wings. We fought them a few days ago. What do you know of them?" Scarlett asked, ignoring the Sorceress's shift in demeanor.

The Sorceress's brows arched in surprise. "The seraphs are here? Beyond the Lords?"

"I cannot answer that without knowing what the seraphs are," Scarlett drawled sarcastically.

The Sorceress's eyes flashed. "If they were feathered wings, they were likely seraphs, summoned by their kin, the Maraans. What book?"

"It is a book of Blood Marks and spells," Scarlett replied. "The Maraan Lords do not have wings."

"The highest of the seraphs, the Maraans, were gifted the ability to banish their wings when desired, like the beings that created them," the Sorceress replied impatiently. "Where is this book?"

"In my possession," Scarlett answered. "Where is my key?"

"In my possession," the Sorceress snarled. "I will trade it for that book."

"No."

The Sorceress threw herself back from the bars, beginning to prowl around her cell. Fingers gripped her hair, pulling at the lank, black strands. Scarlett hadn't moved, but when the Sorceress whirled on her, flying for the bars with her teeth bared, Scarlett lurched back. Sorin's arm was already looping around her waist, jerking her back against him, while a sword was leveled at the Sorceress's throat.

"Where did you find it?" the Sorceress demanded.

"You are saying Alaric is one of these seraphs? And Mikale? Lord Tyndell? What of his children?"

"The seraphs cannot have offspring here. New seraphs can only be born in one world with the aid of—" The Sorceress hissed, her lips pressing together.

"Go on," Scarlett crooned, drifting closer once more.

"The key for my book," the Sorceress bit out.

"*Your* book?"

"It was stolen from me," she spat.

"And now it is mine," Scarlett replied casually, moving along the cell, dragging her hand along the shirastone bars. "Seraphs cannot be born here, but what of half-seraphs?"

The Sorceress's hands fisted at her sides. "There can be no such thing."

Scarlett paused. "But Lord Tyndell has two children."

"They cannot carry seraph blood."

That didn't make any sense, but Scarlett didn't have time to ponder why Lord Tyndell would keep two mortal children and raise them as his own.

"How did these seraphs get here?" Scarlett asked.

"Enough," the Sorceress hissed. "I will tell you no more. Not without payment."

"Fair enough," Scarlett conceded. Before anyone could utter another word, Scarlett had a dagger slashing across her palm. She shoved her hand through the bars of the cell, her blood dripping onto the Marks the Sorceress had drawn.

"No!" the Sorceress wailed, dropping to the ground and trying to wipe the Marks away, but all she managed to do was smear Scarlett's blood across the ground.

"What are you doing?" Sorin demanded, yanking Scarlett's hand back out of the bars.

"Cass, search for a Mark," Scarlett called out, her gaze dropping to the floor, searching. Only he would be able to see it besides her.

"What kind of—"

Scarlett looked up when Cassius sucked in a breath. She followed his gaze to the wall at the end of the room where a faint Mark was shimmering in the torchlight.

"Clever of you," she remarked to the Sorceress, drawing her dagger once more. She cut her palm again, dipping a finger into her blood. She began to draw a new Mark over the shimmering one.

"You would not have known of it if you did not have my book," the Sorceress cried, still on her knees on the ground. "I cannot use this now," she wailed, dragging blood and dirt stained hands down her face, blood smearing across her cheeks. "You have ruined everything. I have nothing any more. No more debts to call in. Nothing."

Scarlett stepped back when she finished the Mark she was drawing. It flared slightly before fading, and Scarlett tentatively touched her fingertips to the stone. When they met no resistance, she pressed her hand into the compartment that had been concealed with an illusion Mark. Withdrawing it, she held a necklace in her hands, the symbol of Serafina, goddess of dreams and stars, carved of nightstone hanging from a chain of white.

"Thank you for your help," Scarlett said, pocketing the amulet.

The Sorceress grabbed the bars, dragging herself forward. "Achaz sent his deadliest seraphs here to hunt them down. He will wipe you all from the face of this world and all the others, and he will make them watch while he does it. He will reward me for being faithful, and when I have retrieved my book, I will bring you back from the After to drain your blood again myself," she hissed.

Scarlett slowly lowered to a crouch before the Sorceress, so that she stared directly into violet eyes. "I do not know who Achaz is, but I am going to kill every single one of the seraphs he has sent here. I have already started," she said in a deadly soft tone. "And if he comes for me himself when I am done, I will kill him too."

"You cannot kill him. He cannot die," the Sorceress spat back.

A smile as chilling as death itself tilted up on Scarlett's lips. She grasped the Sorceress's hands over top of the shirastone bars, squeezing so the stone bit into the female's skin even more. She hissed, but Scarlett did not release her, bringing her face right up to the Sorceress's. "Then he can live on as ashes beneath my feet."

Scarlett pushed off the bars. She strode for the stairs, the three males falling into place behind her.

"You are not a goddess," the Sorceress called after her. "You cannot stop this."

Scarlett paused at the base of the stairs, glancing back over her shoulder. "Perhaps a goddess cannot stop this, but a Lady of Darkness can."

The Sorceress was left shrieking on her knees as Scarlett climbed the stairs, the Sorceress's screams echoing off the walls.

CHAPTER 44
SORIN

Sorin looked down at his wife. She was sleeping beside him, entirely bare, silver hair mussed and fanned around her against the dark bedding, and looking thoroughly and utterly sated.

Which had been the plan.

Scarlett had Traveled them straight from the Underwater Prison to the Wind Court. Princess Ashtine had been waiting in the grand foyer as though she'd been expecting them. Maybe she had been. Maybe Scarlett had sent her a message when she'd arranged that escapade with Briar. Scarlett had asked to go to the chamber behind the nightstone doors, and when Ashtine had led them there, Scarlett had spent the next half hour trying to call that man to appear in the mirror gate. He hadn't seen her like that in . . . Well, not since she'd been a whirlwind of wrath when he'd told her he'd known she was royalty and kept it from her.

But that had been rage roiling off of her in waves when he did not appear. He hadn't needed their bond to feel it. Apparently, neither had Briar or Cassius. They'd all hung back, watching as she became more and more agitated. Her voice had risen from annoyed to screams of frustration, but when she had thrown that amulet she'd manipulated from the Sorceress across the godsdamn room, Sorin had finally stepped in.

Or he'd tried to at least.

She'd brushed him off, ignored his questions, both the ones he'd spoken aloud and the ones he'd tried to ask down their bond. Cassius had shot him a look telling him to let her be, and while he'd hated it, he'd complied. She'd then proceeded to pull books off the shelves, leafing through them before tossing them aside. And seeing her handle ancient books like that was what had pushed Princess Ashtine over the edge.

In a hard voice he rarely heard from the Wind Princess, she'd informed his queen in no uncertain terms that should she throw one more item in that chamber, she would not be returning to the catacombs beneath her Citadel.

Scarlett had apologized in a hushed tone before lowering to her knees and scouring the books on the lower shelves with much more care. After three hours of seemingly nothing, she had risen and walked from that chamber without a godsdamn word.

And all he could think about for much of that time, was how he had just watched her go head-to-head with the Sorceress and come away the victor.

But she was also obsessing over something, or many things he supposed, the Sorceress had said. Something that was said was driving her to utter madness, but when they'd arrived back at the Black Halls, he didn't have it in him to press her about what she was figuring out. Not when she went straight into the bathing chamber and shut the door behind her. When she emerged later with wet hair, he could tell she'd gone to that place though. That place where other voices threatened her stars, so he'd spent the next hour reminding her of who she belonged to. The clarity in her eyes as she drifted off to sleep had been worth putting off the conversation of what had set her on edge.

He bent, brushing a soft kiss to her temple. A small murmur was his only answer, and he pulled the blankets up over her shoulder before he slipped from the bed. He shoved his legs into some pants, not bothering to button them, and made his way to the sofa in front of the hearth. He pulled her notes and translations to him once again, running his hand down his face.

They'd had little time to speak privately since she'd woken this morning, after sleeping for nearly two days. Cyrus's questions about the High Witch were the first and only thing she'd spoken about in regards to the fight at the Contessa's river front estate, and he had so many questions to ask her.

And these seraphs the Sorceress had mentioned? They were one of the biggest things they needed to figure out, but that wasn't what he was looking for tonight. No, tonight he'd be looking for the same thing he'd been looking for since he got her back.

She'd used so much of her power during that battle, and they'd only gotten her to drink a few sips of his blood before she'd fallen into one of those deep sleeps that would restore her fire and water gifts. She hadn't asked for more when she'd seen him, and he knew better than to push that right now, despite her eyes being more bluish-silver than the bright silver he'd begun to grow accustomed to. So here he sat, rifling through books he could hardly decipher, trying to find the answer.

Three days later, Sorin woke to a cold bed, just as he had every morning since their visit to the Sorceress. He wasn't concerned as he slid from the sheets, splashed cold water on his face, and dressed in casual pants and a tunic for the day. He knew where he'd find her. Down on the beach where she had been the last two mornings. Cassius would be there, watching over her.

She'd been only half-present these last few days. She would train in the mornings, and then go straight to that chamber in the Wind Court right after lunch. There she would stay until Sorin would remind her that eating and sleeping were necessary. She'd pack up her notes with a small, wary smile and let him lead her from the Citadel catacombs, where they'd meet up with the others for a quiet dinner. They'd fill her in on various happenings in the Courts. She'd make any necessary decisions and update them on some of her own findings. They tried not to push her to share more, trying to find a balance between letting her figure out how to trust and depend on them, while also allowing her to make her own way as queen. She'd go back to their rooms and bury herself in books again, falling asleep on the sofa with a book in her lap and rising before the sun was fully up.

He'd left small glasses of his blood for her, and they'd be emptied when he checked, so he knew she was drinking them, but her eyes weren't as bright. Not since that trip to the Sorceress. Maybe, he'd realized, she hadn't come away the victor after all.

Sorin stepped from a fire portal onto the beach, walking a few feet to come to a stop beside Cassius. Scarlett was walking barefoot through the surf as it rolled onto the sand, shadows trailing in her wake.

Neither male said anything for several minutes before Cassius broke the silence.

"Don't say anything about it. Tell the others."

Sorin's eyes were fixed on his wife as he asked, "What is the Guardian bond like for you?"

Cassius glanced at him. "What?"

"What can you feel from her? I can feel her emotions, feel her presence, speak down our bond into her mind. Can you do any of that?" Sorin clarified, sliding his hands into his pockets.

"No," Cassius said. "None of those things. I guess I can kind of sense her presence. Not like I've witnessed between you two, but a smaller-scale version of that part maybe? But I can feel when she is hurt physically. When we are training and she takes a hit, I feel that. And I can feel when her power reserves are getting too low if it begins to become a threat to her wellbeing. It feels like a pull on my very soul when she draws from me."

Sorin didn't say anything. Just nodded in acknowledgment. Several more minutes of silence passed between them, the sun climbing higher.

"I have not seen her like this in a very long time," Cassius said quietly, once again breaking that silence.

"She struggles with things Alaric has whispered into her ear for years," Sorin answered.

Cassius nodded knowingly. "Yes, but this is . . . not that."

At that, Sorin turned to look at him. "What do you mean?"

"This is . . ." He pushed out a long breath, running a hand through his brown hair. He'd cut it shorter a few days ago. It was shaggy, curling around his ears. "This is the calm before the storm, Sorin." Cassius turned his entire body to face him. "I know you all wish she shared more, included you more on her scheming and planning, and while I agree that she does need to do that, you also need to let her . . . be *her*, Sorin. That brilliant, wicked, cunning thing you fell in love with? Let her be that."

Sorin stiffened. "I do not wish to change her, Cassius," he said defensively. "I never have. I just need her to recognize she is not alone, that she does not need to face this alone. That she has others she can trust."

"I know that. And I know that she can be brash and reckless and so godsdamn infuriating. But I also know that as soon as everything clicks into place for whatever she is working out, she will bring you all in. I see it at our nightly dinners. I see it when she lets you read through her notes while she pores over books. She's trying to include you all, but you know as well as I do that she's the one who is going to figure this out. We can try to help, but honestly, the best thing you can do to help her right now is let her build up that storm. Because when she unleashes it?" Cassius shook his head, as if he couldn't find the words to finish his thoughts.

"When she unleashes it, there will be nothing left but ashes in her wake," Sorin finished for him.

"I want to show you something," Sorin said softly into her ear when they rose from the table after dinner that night. His Court knew what he had planned. He'd asked some of the staff to clean and prepare the room the day he'd found out what day this was.

Her head tilted quizzically to the side. "I hate to tell you this, Prince, but I've already seen everything you have to offer."

He flicked her nose, nipping at her earlobe when he murmured, "You really have not, Love." He felt the small tremor run down her body, saw her limbs tense slightly at his tone, and he grinned against her skin. "Will you let me show you?"

She nodded slightly, and he brought his hand to her lower back, ushering her from the room. Cyrus caught his eye over the top of her head, sending him a knowing wink. When they were out of the dining room and walking down a quiet hall, he said, "Have I told you lately how absolutely stunning you are?"

She'd changed before dinner into a simple dress. It was a rose pink color and was so godsdamn *feminine*. He couldn't remember the last time he'd seen her in a dress. He was certain he'd never seen her in pink of all colors, and it was so . . . unexpected. It had a wide neckline and scooped down the back, cinching at her waist before flowing to the floor. He had nearly stopped breathing when she'd emerged from the dressing room to head down to dinner with the others.

"Mmm," she hummed now, "you may have mentioned it a time or two this evening."

A time or two was an understatement. She'd pinned her hair up, exposing the column of her neck. Dinner had, admittedly, been the last thing on his mind at that point. He'd hardly tasted the fish and vegetables that had been prepared.

"You act as if you've never seen me in a dress before," she continued, her tone teasing. "You seem to have forgotten that dress from the pier."

"Love, I could never forget *that* dress."

She cast him a side-long glance, a soft smile gracing her lips. His fingers flexed slightly where they still rested on the small of her back.

"Where are we going?" she asked.

"I know you have not had much time to explore the Halls with everything going on," he replied. "But this room? You should definitely know of this room."

She tsked softly under her breath. "You know how I feel about surprises, Sorin."

"You will like this one. I promise."

She pursed her lips slightly but didn't argue further. Which he found oddly disappointing.

"I have missed you these past days," he said softly, guiding her around a corner.

Her nose wrinkled, brow bunching. "I have been with you almost every hour of the day."

"Physically yes, but . . ."

"Ah," she said quietly. She lifted a hand, trailing her fingertips along the wall. "I . . ." She sighed heavily. "I do not know what you are asking of me here, Sorin."

"I am asking nothing," he answered, motioning for her to descend a small set of stairs. "Just making an observation. Creating an opening."

A quick lift of lips before that small smile vanished from her mouth. "I have tried to . . ." She swallowed thickly before trying again. "I have tried to explain, to keep you all updated, but I do not understand what I am trying to find. How am I to explain something I do not understand?"

Sorin kept his posture relaxed, but inside he was sitting up straight. She was actually speaking to him about this. Had it really been this simple all along? Get her alone and just . . . ask? He was so used to her keeping secrets that it had honestly never occurred to him that she just didn't know *how* to tell him, how to include him.

"What did the Sorceress say to you that led to all of this?" he asked gently, hoping he'd chosen the right words. She was his twin flame. This conversation shouldn't be this hard, this complicated.

"She said many things," she answered quietly. "So many things."

"Tell me one."

"This thing with the keys and the lock. How they may not go together."

"She was just trying to gain the upper hand, Scarlett."

"I don't think she was, Sorin. I don't think—"

She stopped short when he pushed open a door, ushering her through. The fire was burning steadily in the hearth, casting a warm glow around the room. A few candles had been strategically placed to add enough light to see by, but not brighten the room too much. A plush sofa sat in front of the hearth, and two wing-backed chairs were off to the side, a small table between them. A drink cart was on the back wall. But none of that was what had caused Scarlett to pause just over the threshold of the small lounge. No, that was caused by the piano in the center of the room. Black and gleaming, it had clearly been cleaned and polished. The bench was cushioned for comfort, and the keys were uncovered, waiting for her.

He wasn't entirely sure she was breathing when he nudged her farther into the room so he could shut the door behind them. He brought his hands to her shoulders as he leaned in and whispered, "Go play, Love."

Her fingers were resting delicately on her throat when she said, "I did not know there was a piano here."

"I figured as much," Sorin said, stepping around her to move to the drink cart. He nodded at the instrument again. "Go play, Love," he repeated.

"I really should be going through more books," she said quietly, but her feet moved forward as if she couldn't help it. Her fingers brushed along the tops of the keys.

"You can take one night off, Scarlett," he answered, ice clinking into his glass. "As you may recall, I once told you it is just as important to take the time to look at the stars. Or in this case, play the piano."

Her lips twitched, and she looked up to meet his gaze. "You arranged this for me?"

"The piano has always been here. I used to play it every once in a while when Eliné lived here, but I made sure it was cleaned and tuned for you, yes," he said, taking a sip of the liquor he'd poured.

He slid a hand into his pocket, watching her eyes fall back to the piano.

"I have never played on one this grand before."

"You are a queen, my Love."

"That is what they say," she murmured, finally sliding onto the bench. For a moment, he hadn't been sure she was going to sit. Her fingers curled slightly over the keys, her foot hovering over a foot pedal.

And then she played.

Sorin moved to one of the chairs, his glass dangling from his fingertips as he watched her fall into the music she created. Her body swayed with each chord, breathing in each note.

For nearly two hours she played, before he pushed to his feet and moved behind her. His finger traced the scoop of the back of her dress. Still her fingers didn't miss a note. Not until he bent to whisper in her ear, "Happy Birthday, my Love."

Her fingers tripped over themselves, the music distorted by the mistaken keys. She scowled at him. "You just ruined this by making it a birthday present."

"So much animosity over the day you entered this world," he quipped.

"You know that is not why. I assume you spoke with Cassius about it," she replied, her eyes dropping back to the keys.

"You may have denied your family the ability to celebrate you, but will you really deny my desire to worship you?" he asked, his fingers moving to skate up the side of her neck.

"If you're going to consider it a *birthday gift*, then yes. I will deny you," she bit back, her eyes coming back to his.

"But I have so much to give to you tonight," he continued, ignoring her slight outburst. His other hand dipped into his pocket.

She rolled her eyes. "On this day I do not want anything from anyone," she replied, turning back to the piano, but she stilled when he pulled his hand from his pocket and held the object he'd been carrying around with him all day before her eyes, pinched between his thumb and forefinger.

"Sorin," she whispered, her voice catching.

A gold band. A diamond in the center with two smaller rubies flanking it.

"You never once asked of it," he said softly. He leaned forward, his chest pressing gently against her back as he reached for her hand.

"I trusted you to return it when you were ready," she answered, her voice hushed while she watched him slide the ring onto her finger. "After what I put you through . . . I did not have the right to ask for it back."

"My love," he sighed, his lips pressing a tender kiss to her cheek. She leaned back against his chest, studying the band back on her finger where it belonged. "I have more to give you."

"I need nothing else, Sorin."

"I disagree," he murmured onto her skin. His hands slid along her sides, down to her hips before he whispered into her ear once more. "You need a Source."

"What?" she demanded, her entire body twisting to face him. Her eyes were wide as she stared back at him.

"I discovered what a Source is," he answered, bringing a hand up to cup her cheek. "And I found you one."

"When? How?" she sputtered, clamoring over the bench to stand.

Sorin chuckled. "You are not the only one capable of working things out."

"I know that," she admonished with a frown. "When did you figure this out?"

"Two nights ago."

"And you are just informing me now?"

"It seemed like a good birthday gift," he replied with a slight shrug. "You are incredibly hard to buy for, outside of things that kill people."

"Sorin!" she snapped. He just winked at her.

"Gods," she snapped again, her fingers coming up to rub her temples. "I've been drinking blood for two days longer than I needed to be."

"One day," he corrected. "You have not had any today."

"Semantics," she grumbled.

He grabbed her hand, bringing it to his mouth, where he pressed a kiss to the back of it. "Come with me, Love."

He led her from the piano lounge and while they were making their way down the various corridors, she asked, "What is it? A Source?"

"Someone for you to draw power from, to restore your Avonleyan gifts."

"Which is what?"

"Not what," he replied. "Who."

"Who?"

"Yes, who. You know Avonleyans depend on Fae to feed their magic."

"How is this any different than drinking blood?"

"Because a Mark is given. The Mark, when activated, allows you to draw the magic that feeds your gifts directly from your Source, rather than drinking it from their blood," Sorin explained. "I suspect it will be similar to how you draw from Cassius when needed."

"Why can't Cassius just be my Source then?"

"Because he is a last resort. You only draw from him if you are in danger. Additionally, there is the fact that he is not Fae. He will not feed your magic properly," Sorin answered. "Drawing from him is like using a dressing to cover a wound until it can be properly cared for."

He'd finally found the text in a book he'd gone to Solembra to hunt down. The book had been referenced briefly in passing in one of the other books he'd been painstakingly translating, and, against all hope, he'd gone back to that chamber in the Fiera Palace and went through a dozen shelves before finally finding it. Whether it was luck or an act of the Fates, he didn't care. He'd found it.

He'd brought it back to the Black Halls, where he'd stayed up most of the night translating the chapter on Sources. They had been created when the Avonleyans began having trouble controlling themselves when feeding. Although, in the book, they were not called Avonleyans but Legacy. The Fae were beginning to be treated more as a commodity to be used when and however the Legacy wished. They had been on a path that would lead to glorified slavery, Sorin had realized as he'd read through the material. Many of the gods became angered, proclaiming that the Fae had been created to keep the balance, a check against the power of the Legacy. Feeding off their blood became forbidden, and a Mark had been created to bind a single Fae to a Legacy.

If that hadn't been interesting enough, he had also learned another tidbit of information about the Night Children. It was common knowledge among magic wielders that the Night Children had descended from the Avonleyans. What was not known was that they had been cursed by Arius himself for refusing to take Sources and choosing to continue feeding as they do now. As punishment, Arius stripped them of their Avonleyan gifts and cursed them to weaken in sunlight and be driven by their bloodlust.

God of Endings indeed, if the Sorceress was to be believed.

Sorin pushed open the door to the queen's chambers, stepping aside to let Scarlett enter first. She turned to him as soon as he followed her through, her eyes brighter than they had been in days.

"Show me," she said, practically bouncing on her toes in excitement.

Sorin huffed out a laugh, motioning to the sofa where all the books and papers were scattered about on the low-lying table. He grabbed the book, opening it to the pages he had marked before handing it to her. While she immediately started reading through it, he poured her a glass of wine from the bottle he'd had sent up after dinner. She murmured a thanks, not even looking up to take the glass, too engrossed in her reading. He took a seat beside her, slowly beginning to remove the pins from her hair. Soft curls fell along her shoulders, and when he had them all down, he began twining one around his finger.

"This is . . ." she finally said, worrying her lower lip. "This is a lot to ask of a Fae." She looked up at him. "This is a lifelong commitment. Once the Mark is given, it cannot be removed."

"That was my understanding as well," he agreed.

"You said you found me a Source?"

"I did."

"Do they truly understand what that means?"

"They do."

Her eyes narrowed in suspicion. "Who is it?" The corner of his mouth lifted into a half-smile.

"No," she said decidedly, lurching back from him.

He only arched a brow at her, waiting for her tirade. He'd known she would object to this. He was also prepared with his own arguments.

"You cannot be serious, Sorin," she said when he remained silent. "You cannot be my Source."

"And why is that?"

"Because you are the Fire Prince for one," she said, her tone ringing with disbelief.

"You are incredibly powerful, Scarlett. It would make sense for your Source to be powerful as well. You will draw more magic to refill your own," he countered.

"You are the king, Sorin! If my power is depleted, it would be stupid to draw from you and weaken us both. Think of having to do that in the middle of a battle," she argued.

"You mean how you fed from me in the middle of the fight with the seraphs and Night Children? That seemed to work out pretty well," he replied with a nonchalant shrug.

"Sorin, this is serious! Don't act so cavalier about it!"

"It is very serious," he agreed. "That is why I have been searching for the answer for weeks for you."

"And this is your solution? For *you* to become my Source? That is utterly absurd."

Sorin barked a laugh.

"And so not funny!" she cried, smacking his shoulder.

"Scarlett, you and your antics are the definition of absurd," he replied calmly, snatching her wrist when she drew back to hit him again. "May I speak now?"

She huffed, pulling her wrist out of his grasp and crossing her arms.

She threw herself back against the sofa, looking away from him.

"And you say *I* throw temper tantrums," he tsked. She flipped him off with a glare.

He picked up the glass of wine she'd set on the table, pressing it back into her hand as he said, "Aside from the fact that I have, for all intents and purposes, been your Source since you returned, you are correct. It is a lot to ask of a Fae. It is a bond built on mutual trust. The Avonleyan puts their trust in their Source to be available at all times. They must become vulnerable and honest about their needs and weaknesses. The Source, on the other hand, must trust the Avonleyan not to take advantage of them. Not to drain their power reserves unnecessarily. It is a balance, Scarlett. It is a balance that will only work with trust and honesty."

Scarlett had gone still, the wine glass frozen halfway to her lips. She slowly lowered it back down. "It still seems incredibly idiotic to bind the two ruling parties in such a way. Even more so for you. You rule both as a prince and a king. If something were to happen to me—"

"As has already been stated, repeatedly I might add, I do not wish to rule without you at my side. I do not wish to live without you at my side. If you leave this world, I will follow, whether I am your Source or not."

Scarlett set the wine glass carefully back onto the table, reaching for the book that had been shoved to the side during their argument. She tapped one of the pages with her nail a couple times, mulling something over. "You are sure?" she finally asked. "I could ask Eliza if power is your argument. Or Cyrus. Or Sawyer."

"I will, admittedly, become uncontrollably jealous if you create this sort of relationship with someone else," he said.

She scoffed. "Your Fae possessiveness is the least of my worries here, Prince."

His hand shot out, lightly gripping her chin between his thumb and forefinger. He brought his face close to hers. "As has also already been stated, you are mine, Scarlett. Mine to claim. Mine to consume. So perhaps my *Fae possessiveness* should be a little more of a concern for you."

"So fussy," she murmured, her fingers coming up and brushing along his jaw.

He pressed a kiss to her lips before releasing her chin. "So we are in agreement?"

She bit her lip again, glancing back down at the text. "Okay," she finally breathed. "Okay."

For the next several hours, Scarlett studied that book. Sorin was fairly certain she had it memorized by this point, but she refused to go through with the Mark until it was perfect. It was well into the night when she finally said, "Are you ready?"

"When you are, Princess."

She took a deep breath, rolling her shoulders back and stretching out her neck. The same mannerisms she did before going into a fight. The same things he'd watched her do when they were trying to get out of the Fellowship.

"Are you preparing for battle?" Sorin teased, watching her stand to collect a dagger from across the room.

She looked back over her shoulder. "You are the one so concerned about Blood Magic," she retorted. "I am surprised you are not fretting like the mother hen you are."

"Careful, Love," he warned, his eyes narrowing.

He tracked her every step as she sauntered back to him. She was still in that dress, and he straightened when she hiked up the sides before straddling his hips and lowering onto his lap. Her empty hand came up, fingers gliding through his hair. His hands landed on her backside, squeezing gently and tugging her closer.

"You are sure about this, Sorin?"

"Yes, Scarlett. It will be an honor to be such a thing for you," he said.

"You do not need to do this. I will not hold it against you if—"

He brought a hand up, pressing a finger to her lips. "You are mine, Scarlett, and I am yours. In every possible way."

She held his stare for a moment longer before nodding once. "Where do you want the Mark?" she asked, her voice little more than a whisper.

"From what I read, it needs to be easily accessible," he answered, having put quite a bit of thought into this. "I was thinking my forearm."

Scarlett considered for a moment before agreeing, leaning back slightly and reaching for his right arm. Her fingers ran along his skin, and he fought back the shiver that her touch always elicited. She raised the dagger, slicing a long, thin gash down his forearm, before setting it aside and dipping her finger into the welling blood. She began to trace a Mark along his flesh. He wasn't watching her finger move, though. Sorin's eyes were fixed on Scarlett's face as she took such care, her brow scrunched in concentration.

When she had finished the Mark, she sat up, reaching for the dagger once more. She met his eyes, the question she sent down their bond evident in her own.

Are you sure? Last chance . . .

Sorin took the dagger from her hand himself then, and when she shifted her palm face up, he made the cut himself. She leaned forward, brushing her lips across his in the lightest of kisses, before she brought her cut hand down on top of the open wound in his forearm, over the Mark she'd just painstakingly traced onto him.

He had experienced his power mixing with Scarlett's before. He had felt the euphoria of it when it had come together while he had driven into her body. But this? This was rawer. Rougher. So pleasurable it *hurt*.

He felt his flames rise up in a bid to protect him, fighting against the shadows and white flames she was forcing into him. His fire seemed to sense what was happening, and her magic bore down on the embers, forcing them into submission. The pleasure turned into real pain then, as their magic fought for dominance in his very soul.

He hissed between his teeth, his entire body tensing. Scarlett's fingers were digging into his arm as she held onto him, refusing to break the connection. If she did, they would have to restart the entire process.

Sorin was panting when her white flames began to win out. Burning raced through his veins. He'd never felt the pain of a burn. Not with fire literally running through his blood, but he felt it now. And gods, it was excruciating.

"I'm sorry," Scarlett was saying, tears slipping down her cheeks as she gritted her teeth. The sight of her crying for him made his chest ache more. And that pain? That was worse than the stars seeming to explode under his skin. Her shadows wound around his fire, still struggling to fight against her.

A cord of flaming orange seemed to vibrate up out of his skin beneath her palm, at the same moment a cord of black did the same from hers. They wrapped around each other, intertwining until they were so tangled together they couldn't be separated. The cord flared bright silver before it settled back into them.

Scarlett released his arm, gasping, and Sorin collapsed back against the sofa. Her hands came up, framing his face. "Are you all right?" she asked, fingers smoothing down his cheeks.

"Fine, Love," he muttered, his eyes falling closed. "Just give me a moment to catch my breath."

Now that the searing burning had subsided, he didn't feel . . . anything. No different than he had before. A little weaker maybe, as though he'd been training heavily with his power and needed to sleep to refill his reserves. He really did just need to catch his breath.

When he opened his eyes, she was staring at him, studying him anxiously, but her eyes were bright silver. They were practically glowing, like they got when she'd lost control and wouldn't stop drinking directly from him.

"How do *you* feel?" he asked, reaching up and brushing back the hair that had fallen into her face.

"I feel fine," she said quickly. "I am not the one who just became a Source of power."

"It worked then?"

"Yes, Sorin, it worked. Are you all right?" she said impatiently.

His hand wrapped around the nape of her neck, pulling her mouth to his. She instantly melted against him, and he wasted no time pushing his tongue into her mouth. Her soft whimper vibrated against his lips, and he was shoving that dress up the rest of the way. She pulled it over her head for him, just as impatient, before her hands slid beneath his tunic, skimming his sides when she slipped it over his head.

She leaned in to bring her lips back to his, but he halted her, his fingers coming up to brush against her collarbone where a silvery Mark was visible. He heard her suck in a sharp breath when he reached for her arm. Three stars and an inverted triangle. Right there where she had once asked if he could see a Mark. The same place the Source Mark sat on his arm.

"You can see them," she breathed.

His hands fell to her hips, and he rotated her until he found the Guardian Mark on her back. He traced it with a fingertip, goosebumps erupting along her skin when she shuddered slightly.

"I can," he said in awe. "I can see them all. It must be because..."

"Because you're my Source," she agreed. "You need to be able to see if there are any threats to my power. Just like Cassius."

"Do you think I will be able to see his too?" he wondered, unable to pull his eyes from the Marks she had always insisted were there.

She shrugged slightly. "I suppose we will find out tomorrow. Or rather, later today." She looked over her shoulder at him, a slight frown tugging on her lips. "Gods, it's nearly dawn. I'm sleeping until lunch."

He chuckled softly. "Good plan, Princess. I have one more gift to give you anyway."

Her eyes narrowed as he spun her back in his lap to face him. Her bare chest brushed against his. His hands instantly rose to her breasts, thumbs brushing over peaked nipples.

"I need nothing else, Sorin. Only you," she replied, her lips finding his once more. He let her take control of the kiss, her mouth moving softly against his while his hands explored flesh he knew as well as his own. But he'd never get enough of this, of her, of feeling her beneath his fingertips. Her hands slid down his chest, her fingers tracing along the ridges of his muscles until they reached his pants. She deftly undid the buttons before rising and removing her undergarments while he quickly lost his own pants.

She slowly climbed back on top of him, her hands sliding back into his hair while his slid down her ribs onto her waist. His thumbs were making idle swipes on her hips as she straddled him once more, holding herself just above him. He could feel her heat on the head of his cock. His fingers flexed into her skin as she dragged herself across him, her lips curving up in a smirk.

His head tipped back on the sofa, his eyes falling closed when she did it again. "It is amusing, you know," he mused.

"What is?" she asked, her movements stilling.

"That you think you are in control here," he said.

"What?"

Before she could say anything else, his hands gripped her hips tightly and yanked her down onto him. She let out a gasp that quickly became a moan. His lips began trailing down her throat, her collarbone, over that Mark he could see, down to her breasts.

"It is even more amusing that you thought you could tease me without any retaliation," he murmured onto her flesh, right before his mouth closed around a nipple. She sucked in a breath, arching into him, but when she tried to move against him, his fingers dug in even more, keeping her still.

"It's my birthday," she whined when he moved his mouth to her other breast.

He snorted a laugh. "First of all, that was yesterday," he replied, one hand sliding around to grip her ass. "Second, you refused to let anyone even mention such a thing. How contriving of you to use it as an excuse now."

"Sorin," she pouted when she tried to move again, but he held her firmly, fully impaled on him.

His mouth trailed back up to her throat where his tongue had her writhing against him despite his efforts to hold her still. She pressed her forehead into his, her breaths short and sharp feathering across his lips.

"My name on your lips will forever be my weakness, Love," he rasped, his hold loosening to let her rock her hips against him. A moan of relief left her as she did it again. The hand that had been holding her hip snaked in between them, his thumb dipping in to rub against her center.

His tongue darted out, gliding across her bottom lip. It was all she needed to bring her mouth back to his. Her hands were braced on his shoulders, her nails digging in when his hands moved back to her hips and began guiding her movements. Between her tongue in his mouth and being buried deep inside her, he let himself get lost in all she was, all they were.

When she murmured "more" onto his lips, it was all she needed to say. He stood, bringing her with him, never once breaking their kiss. He walked them over to the bed, where he gently laid her on her back. Her legs stayed wrapped around his waist where he still stood at the edge of the bed bent over her. Her arms had looped around his neck, and now she slowly unwound them, her hands sliding to his chest.

"You make my entire world a better place, Sorin," she whispered.

"You have said you do not want a world without me in it, but I will simply not survive in a world where there is not a you and me."

"There will never be such a thing, Scarlett," he said, brushing kisses across her brow.

"I know," she breathed, her back arching when he started moving inside her again, withdrawing slowly and dragging himself against her inner walls. "I just . . . You always ask if I am all right, but you, Sorin? As long as you are with me, I will always be all right. Your touch eases my fears, and your kisses are every star in my darkness."

"Love," he breathed, but her finger came to rest against his lips, and she shook her head slightly.

"You've brought me back. Every time," she swallowed thickly, and he could see thin pools of silver glimmering in her eyes. "I need you to know that the world, *my* world, is a better place since you came along."

A soft smile lifted his lips, and he pressed them lightly to hers. Then he did as he had promised in the piano lounge.

He worshipped her.

CHAPTER 45
CALLAN

"I received confirmation this afternoon from Lord Lairwood that Veda is still out of the city," Tava said when she swept into the conservatory that evening. Her cheeks and nose were red from the last cold snap that had spread over the city that day. They always got one last cold spell right before spring truly arrived.

Callan was instantly striding for her, taking the gloves she had pulled from her hands. She pulled her hood back as he ushered her towards the small hearth in the corner where she immediately began warming her hands.

"And Lord Lairwood will be dining with my father tonight," Callan said from her side.

"This is going to work," Tava said as though she were trying to convince herself.

"Promise you will stay with one of us the entire time," Callan said. She glanced up at him. "I promise, Callan," she replied softly.

He nodded, resisting the urge to reach up and run his knuckles along her cheek.

It had been a week since the disaster that had happened in the slums, since she had agreed to consider trying to make this more than some act.

He had asked her to let him know when she'd made her decision, but as of this moment, she still hadn't even hinted at it. She continued on with the ruse— meeting with his mother, making wedding preparations, making public appearances with him.

He shoved all those thoughts aside when Sloan and Finn entered the room, cloaks on and weapons in place. With all the Lairwoods out, they were going to the estate tonight. Drake would be getting them in, pretending he was stopping to get something for the Lord on his way to the castle, and then they would search. They were each taking a floor. Finn was taking the main, Sloan the basement, Drake the second floor, and he was taking the top floor. Tava would join one of them.

"Take any spirit amulet you happen to come across," Tava said, taking the gloves back from Callan. "It does not matter what it looks like. If you find one, pocket it. We will leave it up to Scarlett to determine what she needs."

"Remind me why we are doing the work of thieves," Sloan grumbled. "We need to start somewhere," Tava said, unfazed by his sour attitude.

"Clear as many rooms as you can in the time frame."

They had agreed to two hours. Even that would be pushing it. Finn had pushed for only an hour, but they had argued that was barely enough time to get started.

"If you get any feelings of unease, anything at all, you leave," Finn cut in, looking pointedly at Callan.

"Understood," Callan agreed, swinging his cloak over his shoulders as Tava pulled her hood up.

They exited out the side door of the conservatory, leaving tracks in the slushy snow that had fallen. He had weapons strapped to his waist, and even Tava had a dagger down her boot. She had surprised him when she'd said Scarlett had shown her some basic maneuvers with the weapon. Nothing fancy, but she knew how to hold it and how to angle it if needed.

They had decided to forego the carriage in case they needed to make a quick escape. He wasn't too worried about that. He was the Crown Prince. It was unlikely he would be questioned, and if he was . . . Well, he was the Crown Prince. It wouldn't much matter if Lord Lairwood himself discovered him snooping through his home.

He helped Tava onto his horse before swinging up behind her, pulling her back into the cradle of his hips. She relaxed back against his chest, his arm wrapping around her middle.

"I have a dress fitting tomorrow," she said softly, her hands holding onto the pommel of the saddle while the horses made their way down the streets.

"Oh?" he asked, keeping his own voice low.

"It is an odd feeling. To be selecting a wedding dress for a fake wedding."

"That is an understandable way to feel about it," he agreed.

The supposed wedding was still six months away, to be held in early fall. Even if she agreed to try to make something work between them, he still wouldn't want a wedding that soon. He wanted time to get to know her, really get to know her. He wanted those secret meet-ups, the stolen moments, the peaceful afternoons of just being together.

She cleared her throat, shifting slightly against him. "I know you are likely anxious for an answer from me," she said cautiously.

And *that* had him straightening behind her, listening intently, but he said nothing. Just waited.

"Nothing would really change," she was saying. "At least not publicly. It would still need to be believed that we have really fallen in love. But the private moments would be . . ."

She trailed off, uncertainty sounding in her voice.

"They would be real," he finished for her. "But even then, nothing needs to change, Tava. I do not want you to change. Be just as candid. Be just as compassionate. I want to see it all."

"That is unnerving," she murmured under her breath, but he heard it and huffed out a low chuckle.

He bent down so he could speak into her ear. "Is that an agreement, then? To end the ruse and make it real, little fox?"

He knew if he could see her face, her cheeks would be tinged pink with a blush.

"I suppose it is," she agreed quietly.

Callan couldn't help the grin that spread across his face as they continued to follow Finn's horse in front of them. Sloan trailed behind, keeping them in the middle. And for just a moment, he let himself imagine it. Let himself imagine building something with someone who wouldn't slip out before the sun rose. Someone who he wouldn't have to meet in secret or with masks on. Someone who he wouldn't have to hide in the shadows but who he could be seen with in the light.

Minutes later, they were passing the gates to the Lairwood Estate. The guards had been notified by Drake they were coming. What lie he had told them, Callan had no idea, but they didn't question anything when he helped Tava down from his horse. Sloan told them to keep the horses out, that this would not be a long visit.

Hopefully that would be the case.

They went around to a side entrance where Drake was waiting. Tava was ushered through first, and he immediately reached up to push back his sister's hood. "You all right?" he asked her tightly.

"I am fine, Drake," she said, patting his cheek lovingly. "I do not like that you are a part of this."

"Need I remind you that *you* made me a part of this the night Cassius brought a Wraith of Death through our servant's entrance?" she asked, a brow arching as she pulled her gloves off and stuffed them in her cloak pockets.

"No, you do not need to remind me of that," Drake scowled, his focus turning to Callan and the others. "Most of the staff have retired for the evening. But even still, be discreet."

"We all know what to do," Sloan said. "Let's get on with it."

No one said anything as they all made their way into the house. Drake and Callan turned to the stairs, Tava following. When they reached the second floor, Drake turned to his sister.

"Come, Tava," he said, motioning for her to follow him down the hall. "I will go with Callan," she said, turning to continue climbing the stairs.

"Tava—"

"I have her," Callan said, cutting him off. "Do not worry. She will not leave my sight."

Drake pressed his lips together, clearly unhappy with how this was going.

"We do not have time to debate this, Drake," Tava said, moving up the steps. "Go."

Drake watched her for another few seconds before turning and heading to the first room. Callan could swear he heard him muttering under his breath something about "get rid of the assassin and still have a mouthy woman bossing me around."

Callan quickly caught up to Tava, and as he fell into step beside her, he reached for her hand. He felt her stiffen slightly before allowing her fingers to intertwine with his.

After inspecting the first three rooms, it quickly became apparent this portion of the floor was guest rooms.

"I cannot imagine it would have gotten shoved into a guest room," Tava said when they moved to the room across the hall from one they had just searched.

"What if they did not keep it at all?" Callan said.

"That is a possibility," Tava conceded. "But again, we need to start somewhere. Scarlett was adamant about finding it."

She moved to the nightstand beside the bed, pulling open drawers and quickly rifling through sparse contents. Callan did the same in the small armoire. There really were not any other places to look through, so they made their way back out to the hall.

"There was another set of stairs," Tava mused in a hushed tone when they came upon a bathing room.

"What?" Callan asked, opening the cabinet doors above the sink.

"Off to the side of the main stairs," Tava said, crouching down to look through drawers. "There was a small staircase. I think we should go back and see where it leads. Honestly, searching a guest wing is likely pointless."

"All right." He had to agree with her logic on this. If the Lairwoods thought the amulet was worth something, it wouldn't be hidden here. It would be kept somewhere safe. And if they'd thought it was just a piece of junk, they would have tossed it, and this entire escapade was a waste of time.

He led Tava back to the main staircase, and she pointed to a small stone archway off to the side. There was indeed a narrow staircase that seemed to spiral upwards.

He went first, her hand once again clasped in his. The staircase wound up, and Callan began to wonder how much longer it would go on when they finally reached the top landing. There was a single door at the top that was slightly ajar. But as they drew closer, Callan saw it was ajar because it could no longer latch. The handle appeared to be . . . melted.

"Oh my gods," Tava whispered, sucking in a breath. A hand came to her mouth, her eyes widening.

"What is it?" he asked, his body tensing in alarm.

"This is where he kept her," she whispered.

"What?"

"Scarlett," Tava said, taking a tentative step forward. "This is where Mikale kept her before Sorin . . . He did that." She pointed to the melted door handle.

Call it curiosity, but he found himself moving forward. He carefully pushed the door open, the hinges creaking slightly, and they both stilled.

The room was small and sparse. An uncomfortable-looking bed took up much of the space. There was a small bath off to the side. A dresser and armoire stood on one wall. A nightstand was on either side of the bed. There was one small window to the right, but there was nowhere to go this high up.

Tava stepped farther into the room. "We . . ." She trailed off, seemingly to collect herself before trying again. "We may as well check the room since we are up here," she whispered, as if speaking would alert spirits they were here.

Callan couldn't blame her. This room felt haunted. Like the shadows that followed Scarlett were born here.

Tava moved to the nightstands while Callan made his way to the dresser.

Gods, even the air in here was stifling. It wasn't warm by any means. There weren't even ashes in the darkened hearth. The room was drafty and cold, but the air was . . . heavy with whatever had happened in here.

"Callan," Tava called softly. Her tone had him shoving the empty drawer he was looking through shut and moving to her side. But before he'd reached her, a cold voice had them both spinning towards the bathing room.

"Somehow I am not surprised that it is you two that have found this room."

Veda Lairwood stood in the doorway. She was in a black dress, her hair unbound and loose around her shoulders. But the two long knives she held in her hands had Callan shoving Tava behind him and drawing his short sword.

"What are you doing here?" he demanded, not knowing what else to say because what *was* she doing here? She was supposed to be gone, out of the city.

"What am *I* doing here?" Veda asked, a sharp laugh escaping her. "I live here, your Highness. Your turn."

She leaned casually against the bathing room doorway, appearing to wait for his answer. When he didn't say anything, she shrugged, apparently unconcerned.

"We knew, you know," she said. "We knew you were searching for something. We just didn't know what. It was clever though. Getting Mikale sent on that tour to Toreall. Getting two of us out of the way in one shot." A chilling smile curled up on her lips. "Of course, it also paved the way for this perfect little trap."

"What do you want?" Callan demanded, trying to slowly move himself and Tava towards the door.

Her head cocked to the side. "What I have always wanted, Callan. To be your queen."

"Why?"

Her brows flew up. "Why does any noble lady wish to be a queen?"

"You are not a noble lady," he countered.

"Rude," Veda pouted, taking a step into the room. "I am more of a noble lady than that one you are hiding behind you. Where I am from, I may as well be a princess."

"Then go back," Callan bit out.

Veda scoffed. "We do not wish to go back. We were promised this world once our task is completed."

"Then why is it so important to be my queen?" Callan pressed, trying to keep her talking as they inched closer to the door.

Veda sighed heavily. "It is simply easier with one of us on the throne, but you two certainly managed to ruin that, didn't you? He was very unhappy with this little development."

"He? Mikale?"

"Mikale," Veda scoffed. "My brother is not who we answer to."

"The Assassin Lord then?"

The flicker of surprise that passed over her face was gone as quickly as it appeared. "You learned much in your time away."

"I learned enough," he answered.

They were halfway to the door when Veda moved in a blur of motion. She suddenly stood in front of the only exit, tsking softly under breath. "One of you is not leaving this room alive, Crown Prince. We both know who that is."

"You will not touch her," he snarled, raising his short sword.

"It is almost as if you truly love her," Veda mocked.

He could feel Tava beginning to tremble behind him. She was pressed into his back, the movement of her chest telling him just how quickly she was breathing.

"It is funny," Veda said thoughtfully. "All of this, our entire reason for being here, is because of love. The fact she is even able to stand behind you is because of love. I tried to warn you not to succumb to such weakness. Look what it has led to."

Callan had no idea what she was referencing, but she didn't seem to notice.

"What is even more ironic is that we tried so many ways to get our hands on her, and you have delivered her to us yourself," Veda continued. She shrugged indifferently. "Saved me some coin, I suppose."

"You pretended to leave so that Tava would go back to the slums?" Callan asked.

"It seemed the easiest place to secure her," Veda replied. Then her face hardened. "It wasn't as if Balam would harm her, and it is not as if we could do anything here. You have her under constant watch, but I knew she slipped from that manor. I knew she crept to the slums most nights. The Wraith taught her many things, but she is still mortal. She does not have the grace of magic-wielders."

"Mortal?" Tava asked, peeking out from around Callan. "My father is not mortal."

"Half-mortal then," Veda said dismissively. "Either way, you are more mortal than not." She took a step towards them, herding them back against a wall.

And Callan had no idea what to do. No idea how to save her, how to get Tava out. He had one ace in his pocket, but it was quickly becoming his only shot.

"Do you know how we become of age in my world?" Veda asked. When neither Callan nor Tava spoke, she continued. "We secure our power. By taking it from another."

"You . . . steal someone's gifts?" Tava asked. Her trembling had seemed to lessen, and she moved a little more to Callan's side.

Veda appeared to mull this over before she said, "Can you really steal something from someone who is dead?"

"Oh my gods," Tava whispered.

"It is quite the ordeal," Veda went on. "The more powerful the magic we come to possess, the greater honor we receive. Naturally, we seek to overpower the strongest being we can."

"That is where the Maraans get their magic?" Tava asked.

"I had, of course, wanted to take a Conjurer or a Summoner, but that is a nearly impossible task. They are closely guarded in my world, so I had to settle. I would not have been allowed to accompany Mikale if I did not complete my rite."

"What . . . What gifts did you steal?" Tava asked, her voice a mere whisper.

Veda's chilling smile grew. "I am so glad you asked, Lady Tyndell. We do not use our gifts much here. We have been ordered to keep them a secret so that they do not learn of our abilities.

However, seeing as you are not going to walk out of this room, I do not see the harm. And I have grown quite tiresome of this cat-and-mouse game."

With a flick of her wrist, Tava was pulled from Callan's side by . . . nothing. There were no vines like he'd seen earth-wielders use. There was no gust of wind to suggest wind magic. No fire. No shadows like Scarlett used. There was nothing.

Tava's scream as she flew across the room, and into Veda's hold, had Callan reaching into his pocket without thinking.

"For choosing her over me, I think I shall let you watch her die, Prince," Veda crooned softly, one of her knives pressing against Tava's throat.

Before she had finished speaking, Callan had thrown that vial Scarlett had given him the last time he'd spoken to her in Solembra. He was crushing it beneath his boot, watching the black smoke— no, the black shadows— swirl up from the vial.

And then he was holding his breath, praying to any god that would listen that she would get here in time.

CHAPTER 46
SCARLETT

"Are the ships prepared to set sail at a moment's notice?" Scarlett asked no one in particular. She was sitting on the floor at a low table in one of the various lounges in the Black Halls. She'd grown tired of meeting in the formal rooms with long tables and uncomfortable chairs. She sat with her back against Sorin's legs where he sat on the sofa behind her. The amulets were spread out before her. The book of Blood Magic, that apparently belonged to the Sorceress, was open beside her as she studied it.

"They are. Ours and Briar's," Cyrus answered from across the room where he was playing a round of billiards with Cassius. He cursed then, and Scarlett glanced up to see Cassius sink the final two balls. "Is it part of your training in the Black Syndicate to learn how to run a fucking table?" he grumbled, slapping coin into Cassius's waiting palm.

"You are just really, really bad at it," Scarlett said, returning her attention to the amulets. "But our coin purses appreciate that about you."

She didn't hear his mumbled response, but she had a good idea of what he said.

"Any word from Briar about the Wind Court?" she asked, again to no one in particular.

"He stopped by this morning while you were training," Eliza replied.

She was sprawled across an armchair, book in hand. "Said Ashtine has moved forces into various locations. Prepared if needed."

"Good."

She could taste it on the air. Something was coming. The

entire land seemed to have stopped breathing these last few days. Everyone was waiting for the one thing that would set chaos into motion. She was trying to be prepared for every angle without spreading their resources too thin. She didn't know where Talwyn would fall. They hadn't heard from her in days, only Azrael giving vague updates, if one could even call them that. Ashtine had told Briar that Tarek had been brought to the White Halls, but nothing more than that. And that . . .

That did not bode well for any of them. Scarlett knew how Tarek could speak and spin pretty words. Talwyn was as stubborn and as unforgiving as a Witch, but Scarlett didn't know how that would translate when emotions became involved.

Nuri was still hidden away with the Contessa. Her updates reported rogue Night Children in the territory. Scarlett had spent the entirety of an afternoon convincing Hazel to bring aid to the Contessa and her land if needed. She hadn't been happy about it, but had finally relented.

And the Shifters? She and Sorin had gone to meet with them the day after her birthday. The siblings were . . . interesting. She couldn't tell if the meeting had gone well or not. Sorin insisted it had, that they would side with her, but she wasn't so sure. Stellan was definitely still upset that she had taken this long to formally greet him, whatever that meant. Arianna was welcoming, her warm, olive eyes tracking their every movement, while Jamahl massaged her neck and shoulders. Would the Beta be enough, though? Not if there ended up being a fight about whom to support between her and her brother.

Scarlett sighed heavily, tossing the amulet of Serafina onto the table. She tipped her head back into Sorin's lap, closing her eyes. She was tired of waiting. She was ready for whatever was to come, whether that be a trap, a grand reveal from Alaric, war . . .

She knew that sounded awful, that wishing for bloodshed to just happen already likely made her a terrible person, but she'd come to terms with that long ago.

Fingers brushing feather-light along her now exposed throat drew her from her thoughts.

Flames brushing against her shadows had her subtly clenching her thighs together.

"Ready for bed, Love?" came a whispered breath in her ear.

Her eyes fluttered open to find Sorin leaning over her, eyes glowing with hunger. She caught his hand in hers. His left hand, where his twin flame Mark now wound around his ring finger beneath his marriage band. Apparently becoming her Source had fulfilled his portion of the Sacrifice Trial. Now they were just waiting on her to do the same, so their bond could be Anointed.

Which was fine.

What was a bit more pressure weighing on her, right?

Before she could reply to his proposition, Rayner's low voice cut through the room. "Scarlett, what are those?"

Scarlett and Sorin both shifted their focus to the Ash Rider, and Scarlett followed his gaze.

To where shadows were shimmering like mist in the corner of the room.

"Shit," Scarlett muttered, lurching to her feet. With a thought, her shadows coated her like a second skin, thick as armor. She slid the amulets into her pocket, unwilling to leave them in the hands of anyone else. She was pulling the spirit sword from the air and grabbing any other weapons she could find, including two daggers right off Cyrus's body. "Sorin! Weapons! I need you with me," she barked in command. "Rayner, you too. In case we need to send word back. The rest of you, be ready."

"What is going on?" Sorin demanded, already strapping on the weapons Eliza was handing him. Flames were receding, leaving his fighting leathers in their place.

In less than two minutes, she was striding towards that shadowy mist.

Sorin and Rayner falling into place beside her.

"Callan needs me," was her only reply before she stepped into the shadows.

CHAPTER 47
CALLAN

"Stop! Stop!" Callan was bellowing over the sounds of Tava's screams while Veda slowly dug one of her knives deeper in the gash she had sliced along Tava's collarbone. "Stop! We can come to an agreement!"

Veda sneered at him. "The agreement has already been made. This is the payment."

"Really, Veda? You could at least play with someone who likes the same games as you," came an arrogant voice of shadows.

Veda froze, and Callan whirled.

Scarlett stood there, flanked by her king and Ash Rider. Shadows coated her skin, and her eyes were bright silver.

"You always were quite the coward," Scarlett tsked, moving forward with the grace of a feline. She was casual, as though she hadn't just shown up to fight with a being from another world.

"What are you doing here?" Veda all but screeched.

Scarlett nodded in Callan's direction with a wink at him. "Someone told me you weren't playing nice." Then her entire face went dark and cold. Her voice was that of death when she spoke again. "And you have come after what is mine."

Words Tava had said to him weeks ago filtered back to him.

Once Scarlett claims you as one of her own, there is no going back.

He had never been more grateful that she was claiming Tava, that she had apparently claimed her long before this night.

"What is yours?" Veda sneered. "You cannot have everything, Scarlett. It is selfish of you."

Scarlett tilted her head to the side. "Let Tava go."

Veda's response was to dig the knife deeper into Tava's skin, another scream piercing the room.

Scarlett seemed to pause, as if listening to something. Their bond, Callan realized, glancing at Sorin. They could communicate through their bond.

"I heard screaming—" Drake stopped short where he burst into the room. "Tava," he breathed. His gaze swiveled to Scarlett and Sorin.

"Hello, Drake," Scarlett said with a sigh. "There is a ... situation."

"So use some fire magic and fucking fix it," Drake snapped, his eyes going back to his sister in desperation that Callan was feeling in his soul.

"They cannot," Veda said with a smirk. "The grounds are warded against Fae magic."

Something sparked in Scarlett's eyes at that, although what, Callan couldn't even begin to fathom. He had called her here to help and things seemed to have gone from bad to worse. Sorin wordlessly passed her the two daggers he pulled from his belt while he leaned over and said something into Rayner's ear. Rayner only nodded before crossing his arms and leaning casually against the wall.

"Release Tava," Scarlett said again. "And if you even think of letting a blade touch her skin again, it will be one of the last things you do."

"I have the upper hand here, Scarlett," Veda sneered again. "You are in no position to make demands."

A dagger was flying across the room before Callan could blink. Tava let out a small scream, but it left her unscathed, grazing Veda's cheek before embedding in the wall behind her.

The Lady gasped, her fingers coming up to touch the cut. Her shock gave Tava the opportunity she needed to wrench herself away, stumbling as she went. Callan was already pulling her into his arms before Drake even had a chance to reach for her.

"I am so sorry, Tava," Callan murmured, clutching her tightly to his chest.

"Do not apologize," she whispered, her hands fisting in his shirt. "Let's just focus on getting out of here alive."

"That is more like it," Scarlett was saying, stretching her neck from side to side. "Now, Veda, if you want to play ..." She brought her arm back, the second dagger poised to fly.

"Wait!" Veda screeched again, her hand coming up.

Scarlett's head cocked quizzically, her eyes studying at her own hand. "That's ... interesting." Her eyes slid back to Veda. "Someone has a secret." When Veda's lips pursed, her hand still in the air before her, Scarlett said, "Tell me, Lady Veda, what are the gifts of a Maraan? Or should I say a *seraph*?"

"How do you know that term?" Veda demanded, her face draining of color.

"I had a little chat with a Sorceress," Scarlett said, wrenching her hand out of the air. It seemed as if it took effort to do so, and when she did, Veda almost appeared to shrink back.

"A Sorceress?" Veda asked meekly.

"That is what she calls herself here," Scarlett said impatiently. "Not important. What *is* important is how I am going to kill you this night."

Shadows rippled around Scarlett, shifting and writhing, but before they could form into anything, Callan gasped as wings erupted from Veda's back. They were feathered and gold, and he could not even begin to comprehend what he was seeing.

Scarlett, however, had apparently seen such a thing before.

"You have got to be fucking kidding me," Scarlett cursed, sounding more annoyed than anything. "Here?"

Then the window behind them was shattering. Callan was shielding Tava with his body. They had all thrown themselves to the floor, covering their heads.

All but Veda.

Who was leaping from the window and into the sky.

"Where the fuck does she think she's going?" Scarlett muttered, instantly on her feet and prowling to the window.

"We will find her, Scarlett," Sorin said, trying to calm the queen.

"I will not lose her," she snarled, before leaping onto the window ledge, glass crunching under her boots. "If they won't make the first move, then I will." Then she stepped off the edge, falling straight down.

"Scarlett!" Tava cried, lurching for the window. Her hands landed on the ledge, blood instantly welling from shards of broken glass cutting into her skin. Callan moved to pull her back, but suddenly she was stumbling back into him.

As a huge dragon made entirely of shadows shot towards the sky. A queen of darkness and shadows and ashes on its back, illuminated only by the light of the full moon.

He could just make out Veda flapping away from the house, climbing higher into the night sky.

"Godsdammit," Sorin muttered, pushing past them all and running for the stairs. They all ran after him, sounding like a herd of horses as they all raced down the stairs. Tava's hand was gripped in his when they cleared the narrow spiral staircase and started down the main steps.

"Finn and Sloan," Tava gasped, her eyes frantically searching while they ran.

"We're here," Finn said when they made it to the main floor.

"What the hell is going on?" Sloan demanded, a sword already drawn. His eyes widened when he spotted Sorin and Rayner. "What are *they* doing here?"

The Fae said nothing. They just raced through the main doors, everyone on their heels.

"There," Rayner said, pointing to the sky.

The moon was so bright they could see everything. No one said a word. No one could.

Well, none of the mortals anyway.

"She is going to be the death of me," Sorin muttered. "We cannot even fucking help her. The wards are stifling our magic." He cursed again, looking like he wanted to punch something.

Or burn something to the ground, Callan supposed.

"Her shadows will keep her safe," Rayner said passively, his eyes fixed on the sky.

Sorin didn't say anything in response.

They all watched as the shadow dragon finally caught up to Veda.

They all watched as Scarlett appeared to be repositioning, as Veda looked back over her shoulder and screamed.

Because that was Scarlett leaping from her shadows and onto Veda's back. That was moonlight glinting off a sword as it came down. That was a golden wing sliced clean off, falling to the ground. That was blood, appearing black in the night, raining down from the female in the sky, sprinkling onto their skin as they began to fall, Veda unable to keep them aloft with only one wing.

"She is utterly insane," Drake murmured in shock and disbelief.

The blade was glinting again, slicing off the other wing, and then they were both plummeting to the ground. Veda's screams were piercing the night.

The closer they free fell, the more they could make out Veda's cries. "You will kill us both, you crazy bitch!"

The drops of blood landing on the faces of those watching were getting bigger, no longer sprinkles of red, but none of them could look away.

The shadow dragon appeared below them, catching Scarlett, but Scarlett shoved Veda away from her.

The Maraan Lady screamed again, only to have bands of white flames appear around her torso, halting her sharply a few feet above the ground. The Lady jerked, another cry falling from her lips. Scarlett leapt gracefully to the ground a moment later, the shadow dragon dissipating into the night. The flames disappeared then, Veda thumping to ground directly onto her back, another scream of agony coming from the female.

Scarlett reached over her shoulder, slowly pulling the sword from her back where she had somehow managed to sheath it during that free fall. Her face was splattered with blood, more red than the ivory color of her skin. None of them had moved, not even the Fae.

"Oh, Veda," Scarlett tsked, lifting one leg to the other side of the prone female, straddling her so she now stood directly over her. "Haven't you learned yet?"

"Learned what?" Veda coughed out, more blood spraying from her mouth.

"A Lady of Darkness cannot die," Scarlett purred. Then her head cocked to the side. "Maraan Lords can though. I have killed one before. Can Maraan Ladies be killed the same way? I will admit, I am *dying* to find out."

"She is terrifying," Tava whispered in a hushed voice, pressing into Callan's side.

"You have no idea, little fox," Callan murmured, his arm sliding around her waist.

"That sword is not shirastone," Veda rasped. She appeared to be trying to push herself up with her hands, but they just slipped on the grass, slick with her own blood that was pouring from her back.

"Hmm," Scarlett mused, seeming to study the blade. "That is true." Then she lifted her head, her eyes meeting Veda's once more. "But the seraphs I burned to death seemed pretty dead when I finished with them." At her words, blinding white flames ignited down the blade of the sword, lighting up the entire yard. Callan had to look away, shielding his face while his eyes adjusted. Tava had buried her face in his chest, and when he turned back to see what was happening, his hand came up to keep her face there. He covered her ears, trying to drown out Veda's screams.

"Do not look, Tava," he said hoarsely, his throat thick as he watched Death's Maiden plunge that sword into Veda's thigh.

"That is for Cassius," Scarlett said, her voice so lethal, Callan found himself dragging Tava away from her a few steps.

But as horrifying as this was to witness, he couldn't say he was sorry. Not when they had tried to force his hand in a marriage to this *thing* writhing on the ground. Not when they had fucked with his life so godsdamn much, forcing him to flee for his life. And not with what came from Scarlett's mouth next.

The sword sliced across Veda's clavicle, dragging deep. "That is for Tava."

A hand was cut clean off just above the wrist, flying a foot away, more blood spraying as she said, "That is for thinking you ever had any right to touch Callan."

Veda's cries and shrieks were incoherent now. Garbled words gasped in pain as the torture continued.

The sword was slicing through her stomach. "That is for thinking you could fuck with me."

The last swipe came across the female's throat. Scarlett dropped the sword to the ground beside her as she bent low, her face inches from Veda's where blood seeped from her neck. Scarlett's voice was eerily soft, but they all heard her. "And that is for thinking you could ever win."

She stepped back then, and as she did, flames of bluest wildfire started at Veda's feet, quickly crawling up her body. But no more screams came from her. Somehow Callan knew that Scarlett had stood over her, making sure the life faded from her eyes before she had moved away.

Sorin moved then, dragging a dagger down his own forearm as he approached his wife. He took her hand, slicing a gash across her palm before placing it atop the wound he'd cut into his flesh. Scarlett scarcely seemed to notice, her eyes fixed on Veda's body while it became nothing but ash.

Tava shifted, and Callan lowered his hands from her ears as she peeked out, watching Sorin and Scarlett. Rayner had moved, picking up Scarlett's sword and wiping the blade on his pants in an attempt to clean it somewhat.

Sorin's other hand came to Scarlett's chin, tilting her face up to his, and Scarlett's eyes flicked to him. The blood on her face seemed to glisten in the moonlight. "You are so fucking beautiful," Sorin said. "But please stop riding the godsdamn shadow dragon."

A smirk curled onto Scarlett's lips. "Take me home and give me something else to ride then, Prince."

A second later, Sorin was slamming his mouth onto hers, her hand still clasped to his forearm, and the other came up to grip the back of his neck.

"Oh my gods," Tava gasped, her hand flying to her mouth as she averted her gaze. Callan glanced down and could see her blush in the glow of the body burning before them.

But before anyone could say anything else, a cool voice cut through the night.

"I am hurt, your Majesty. You did not invite me to the fun." Everyone stiffened, turning to the trees where two figures emerged.

One cloaked and hooded. One on four paws with jade green eyes that glowed in the night.

Queen Talwyn's wolves were here.

CHAPTER 48
SCARLETT

Sorin leaned over, whispering something to Rayner, who disappeared a moment later among the ashes of Veda's burning corpse. The woman's blood was still splattered across her face. The rush of the kill still coursed through her veins.

And that kill?

It had been one of the most satisfying deaths she had ever bestowed. She hadn't felt that much satisfaction after a death since... Lord Winston, perhaps? Or maybe the night she had made that man renting out young girls choke on his own body parts?

She could only imagine what it would feel like to kill Mikale. Lord Tyndell.

Alaric.

But now another male who needed to die stood before them, a giant wolf at his side.

"How rude of you not to extend an invitation," Tarek continued. "You have hurt my tender feelings."

"Allow me to demonstrate just how much I can hurt you," Scarlett sneered, taking a step towards him, but Sorin was holding her back. His fingers curled around her elbow.

"Now, now," Tarek chided. "We both know you could not do much right now. Fae gifts are suppressed within these wards, and you have not taken enough from your Source to refill what it took to put on that spectacular display of violence."

"I still have a sword," Scarlett sneered, Sorin passing the spirit sword to her. Rayner had handed it to him while Sorin was whispering orders.

"Ah, yes. That could be a problem, but..."

"Fuck," she heard Sloan mutter as more figures prowled out of the shadows.

Night Children. Dozens of them.

Remind me why you just sent Rayner off on an adventure, Scarlett shot down the bond to Sorin.

He went to get reinforcements.

Who?

Luan.

Azrael?

That made sense, she supposed. He was the only one who could Travel. If he had finally regained the ability that is.

They had pivoted, their backs to each other, as they monitored the Night Children closing in. Fangs appeared and hands reached for Tava and Callan.

"Stop," Tarek said casually, and all the Night Children froze.

"Since when do you command vampyres?" Scarlett asked.

"Since the Contessa pledged loyalty to the Assassin Lord," Tarek replied.

"What?" Scarlett said, unable to keep the shock from her voice.

The Contessa was still with Nuri. There was no way they had gotten to her. Absolutely none.

"I am going to need you and your entourage to come with me, your Majesty," Tarek continued. "There are some people who simply cannot wait to see you again."

"We are going to go nowhere with you," Sorin retorted.

"But I really think you are going to want to be there to see the new king take his throne," Tarek countered.

"What are you talking about?" Callan demanded.

He was still holding Tava to his side. Drake, Finn, and Sloan had closed ranks around them.

"And you, Crown Prince? You are definitely going to want to come with me to say your goodbyes."

⁂

They all filed silently into the castle, having had no choice but to let this play out. It was that or watch the mortals be slaughtered in front of her. Tarek had forced her and Sorin apart, not allowing her to continue drawing from him to refill her power. She now walked beside Tarek, the wolf at his side. Sorin was in the middle of the company, ten Night Children escorting him.

They spoke down their bond though. There was nothing Tarek could do to stop that. They'd discussed possible escape plans, ways to fight their way out, but with this many vampyres surrounding them? There was no way to do so without risking the lives of Callan, Tava, and the others.

But Sorin had also informed her of another little problem. Only it wasn't a 'little' problem in the slightest.

Talwyn is the wolf, he'd told her while they'd passed silently through the Elite District.

Obviously it is one of her wolves.

No, Love. Talwyn is the wolf. She has shifted.

She can do that?

Apparently, she can now. I would recognize her eyes anywhere. And Queen Henna could shift. Into a wolf.

Scarlett did not even want to entertain what it meant that Talwyn was here, with Tarek, escorting them to the castle. It obviously couldn't mean anything good for them and wasn't that just fantastic.

Tarek led them to the throne room, where he took Scarlett to the foot of the dais. The others were herded off to the side.

"I thought there'd be a bigger welcoming party," Scarlett drawled, looking dramatically around the room.

"They will be here momentarily," Tarek said, a hand gliding down Talwyn's fur. "But to be sure we are not interrupted by anything unnecessary . . ." He crossed to Sorin and held out his hand. "I will take that ring from you."

Sorin pressed his tongue to his cheek before slipping it off his finger and slamming it into his palm. Tarek immediately slid it onto his own digit, sighing deeply as his magic clearly sprang to life. "You have no idea how long I have waited for this moment," Tarek murmured.

"I would venture to guess it has been around ten years," Sorin said. "Oh no, Prince of Fire. Far longer," Tarek replied, turning his back on him and moving back to the dais. He sat down on the edge, seeming to get comfortable, stretching his legs out in front of him. Talwyn moved to sit at his side. "This is going to be quite the show," he quipped. "And I am so delighted to have a front-row seat."

Footsteps echoed a moment before the double doors of the throne room were opened and Mikale Lairwood came strolling through. He paused a moment, looking around at everyone gathered.

"You are supposed to be gone with my father," Tava said, shock and fear in her voice.

Mikale nodded in acknowledgement. "And I was," he agreed. "But apparently your allies failed to inform you that some of the Maraans can Travel. It takes but a heartbeat to cross the continent."

Callan's gaze swung to Scarlett. "Is that true?" he demanded.

"I . . . Alaric can Travel. He is the only one I know that can for sure," she admitted. "But I didn't know your plans hinged on them being gone. I would have told you, Callan. I would have—"

But he just turned away from her, shifting more to block Tava from view.

"Anyway," Mikale went on, striding forward, "when I was alerted that some special visitors had crossed the wards of my property, we came straight home." He stopped in front of Scarlett, glancing over his shoulder at Sorin as he reached out to finger a strand of her hair. Sorin went rigid, a hand sliding to the sword at his waist.

"Don't," Tarek said as though he was bored, vines immediately snaking along Sorin's wrists before yanking them behind his back.

Mikale's gaze settled back onto Scarlett, a cruel smirk pulling on his lips. "What happened to me seeing my death the next time you saw my face, my pet?"

Scarlett tilted her head, pretending to contemplate his question. "Did I say *your* death? I meant your sister's." Her voice went icy with the words.

He went still. "You lie."

"I really don't," she simpered. "The Crown Prince was there. So was Tarek. They all saw it," she added, gesturing in Callan's direction.

Mikale glanced at Callan, who gave one nod of his head from where he stood shielding Tava behind him. Then he looked to Tarek who merely shrugged.

Mikale's head swung back to her, his eyes going pitch black. "You little cunt."

Her hand came over her heart in mock dismay. "My Lord! Such foul language in front of a *Lady*."

"When he gives you back to me, you are going to regret every bit of that smart mouth," Mikale snarled, raising a hand as if he were going to strike her, but Scarlett just smiled, a shadow panther forming beside her. It probably wasn't the smartest move to touch that magic right now, but she had a godsdamn point to make.

"There it is," came Lord Tyndell's voice when he entered the room with a hooded man at his side. Hood or not, Scarlett recognized Alaric. Lord Tyndell clapped his hands together. "Look at that beautiful darkness."

They were all here. All the Lords, and trailing behind them, all bound and gagged, was the royal family— King Theodore, Queen Meredith, and Princess Eva. Callan lurched forward but halted just as abruptly, clearly torn between leaving Tava's side and going to his family.

Sloan and Finn didn't hesitate in the slightest, though, both rushing forward, swords drawn.

Alaric merely raised a hand, and both of them froze. Literally froze, as if they were unable to move at all.

At the display of power, Scarlett sucked her shadows back into herself. This was suddenly not the time nor place to make a point. She was going to need every drop of power to get them all out of here alive.

But then Alaric was closing his fist, and Finn and Sloan were crumpling to the ground as though they had been hit on the back of the head. And they were not moving. Their chests were not rising.

"What did you do?" Scarlett demanded, her voice a harsh whisper as she moved towards them.

"Do not move, Death's Maiden," Alaric said, reaching up and pulling back his hood, revealing his face to the room.

"Oh, my pet," Mikale crooned mercilessly. "Did I not tell you that you have yet to experience his power?"

"What did he do?" she repeated, her eyes fixed on the unmoving guards.

Mikale leaned in to whisper into her ear. "He squeezed their hearts until they burst."

"No!" Scarlett cried. Her head swung to Callan, who was staring in shock at his guards, his closest friends, dead on the floor. "Callan, I am so sorry. Callan, I—"

Mikale pulled back, a dark laugh coming from him. "There's that curse I spoke of. Simply because they knew you. How many more will you allow to die because you refuse to submit?"

"Do not listen to anything he says, Scarlett," Sorin was suddenly yelling to her. "Do you hear me? You are not a curse on anyone. Their deaths are not your fault."

But they were. Mikale was right. All because they knew her. All because they were wrapped up in whatever this was. All because—

"Enough of this." Alaric finally spoke, his cold, calculating voice cutting through everything, despite the fact he spoke at a normal volume. His gaze raked over Callan and Tava. The latter had silent tears tracking down her face as she clutched Callan's hand, staring at Sloan and Finn on the ground. "Where is Veda?"

Rage surged through Scarlett, hot and fierce. "She's the one with the golden wings, right?" Scarlett sneered at him.

Alaric blinked slowly at her. "Yes."

"Dead," Scarlett spat. Then she looked directly at Mikale. "I chased her into the sky, cut those wings from her back, sliced her up, and then let her burn until there was nothing but ashes. Not shirastone, but it seems to have done the trick."

"That is unfortunate," Lord Tyndell tsked. "Veda was one of our most powerful females." He looked at Alaric. "They will not send another. Not again."

"Pity," Scarlett drawled.

"It is," the Lord agreed. "For now we have no choice but to put another on the throne."

"Your own daughter stands to take the throne," Drake suddenly cut in. "Why were you all so adamant about Veda being on it? What does it even matter?"

"There is so much you do not understand, Drake," Lord Tyndell said. Scarlett could swear his tone had almost softened a touch, but that couldn't be. They were not his actual children. "You were never meant to be involved in any of this."

"Veda being in the position of queen would have simply made this transition smoother," Alaric said. "Like it was in the other kingdoms."

"The other . . ." Callan trailed off, seeming to snap out of some kind of daze. "Rydeon and Toreall?"

"Those transitions were quiet, happening naturally. Much like this one would have been if certain assets had been kept under control." Alaric's piercing stare settled on Mikale, whose hands clenched at his sides.

Scarlett winced in mock sympathy. "How many times have I evaded you now? You might need two hands to count."

Mikale opened his mouth to say something in response, but Alaric was already speaking once more. "The plan to take this throne has been in place for decades, and sometimes those plans must be altered," he said, moving to stand behind the king. The royal family had all been forced to their knees, Queen Meredith trembling beside her husband. Princess Eva's face was pressed into her mother's side, her small body shaking violently, and all Scarlett could see was Tula trying to cling to Juliette.

Moving as fast as a Night Child, Alaric had a dagger dragging across King Theodore's throat. Queen Meredith screamed, but it was cut short when the same dagger slashed across her neck next.

"No!" Callan bellowed, releasing his hold on Tava and lurching towards his parents. "Spare her! I beg of you! Let Eva live!"

"A Solgard heir cannot remain alive," Alaric said casually, already closing a fist around the princess's light brown hair. The little girl screamed around the gag in her mouth as he jerked her head up.

"Please! No!" Callan was yelling, trying to get to her, but Mikale and Lord Tyndell were holding him back. Drake was clutching tightly to Tava. Sorin was still bound by the vines, unable to move with Tarek holding his leash.

"Stop!" Scarlett cried, shadows leaping from her and creating a shield around Eva. "Alaric, stop!"

The dagger halted, unable to pierce her shield, and she grunted at the effort to keep it in place.

"Stop!" she panted.

Alaric shrugged, sliding the dagger into his belt. "You will not be able to hold that shield in place forever, my Wraith. By all means, please drain that power. You are far more amenable when weakened."

He strode for the dais, stepping up and settling back onto the king's throne.

"That is not yours," Scarlett snarled. "Callan still lives."

"For now," Alaric agreed, propping his head on a fist to apparently wait her out.

"So this is what? All for you to become the king?"

A slow smile lifted on his lips. "You know what is required of you for that information, Scarlett."

"Never," she sneered.

He sighed heavily. "Did you bring the keys?"

"Did I . . . What?" she asked, thrown by the sudden change in subject.

"The keys. I assume you have found them all by this point. It is why I allowed you to be retrieved all those weeks ago."

"Allowed me to be . . . You did not *allow* me to escape."

"I knew they were coming for you that night," Alaric replied, his dark eyes studying her.

"Impossible," Sorin snarled.

He arched a brow, looking at the Fire Prince. "I knew you would come for her at some point. You are all under this delusion that she is yours."

"She is mine," Sorin growled, jerking against his binds.

"She has never been yours," Alaric said sharply, and Scarlett couldn't help but wonder why he wasn't using that power he possessed against any of them. He could easily control them all with a flick of his wrist if what he'd done to Finn and Sloan was any indication. Why had he not just done that to the king and queen? Or Princess Eva?

"How did you know?" Scarlett asked, swallowing thickly, trying to hide the tremor working its way through her limbs. Tarek was right. She hadn't drawn nearly enough from Sorin to be expending this much of her power. She still had fire and water, but she needed to save something, anything. "How did you know they were coming that night?"

"The Contessa told me," Alaric said simply.

"The Contessa?" Scarlett repeated. "How would she have known?"

"I suppose that was not her title at that time," Alaric mused, relaxing back against the throne. "No, that didn't become her title until *you* delivered the former Contessa directly into her hands."

"What?"

"Imagine our surprise when you walked out of Dresden Forest a few months ago. We were planning to go in for her ourselves, but you figured that out, didn't you?" Alaric said, an almost fond smile filling his face. "So damn clever. Just like I taught you to be. So our plans were altered. It was for the better, to be honest. We had no idea where Rosalyn had hidden herself away. So I let you escape and sent one of my own with you, knowing you would stop at nothing until you found her. To keep her from me."

"No," Scarlett whispered, her knees threatening to give out. Not from her waning power, but because of what he was insinuating . . .

"Oh, yes, Scarlett," Alaric said, pushing to his feet and stepping off the dais to stand in front of her. His hand came up, cupping her cheek. "You found her, then sent her off with the one who now holds her place."

At his words, his hand slipped from her cheek, and Nuri stepped from the shadows. Her hood was down, her eyes were bleak as they stared back at her. Slowly, she raised her hand. There were no gloves in place this night. Nothing to hide the Blood Mark in the center of her palm. The Mark that matched the one on Tarek's palm.

"Oh, Nuri," Scarlett whispered, her heart breaking with agony and betrayal as she looked at her sister standing beside her master.

"You were . . ," Nuri swallowed, looking away from her. "He agreed to leave the children alone if I agreed to the Mark. You were taking too long to come back. I didn't . . . You were taking too long."

She'd been playing them all along. She would disappear for hours, days even, when at the Black Halls. How many days was it before Scarlett had even seen her when they'd arrived there? She'd always been in her hood and gloves, but Scarlett had never suspected a thing. She was Death's Shadow and a Night Child. She needed to be protected from the sun. She . . .

She was in the perfect position to do exactly what she'd done. What she'd felt she'd needed to do.

This had always been about the children for her. Always. The forgotten orphans on the streets that no one seemed to care about. That were being used, slaughtered, and discarded.

"Do not look at her with such pity," Alaric soothed, slowly beginning to circle her. "She was raised for this role. Trained for it. Just as you were. Nuri just accepted what was always intended to be her place."

But Scarlett couldn't look away from Nuri, who refused to meet her gaze again. She had killed the Contessa. She now controlled the Night Children, and Alaric controlled her. The violent, vicious, uncontrollable Night Children were now controlled by someone just as volatile. Conditioned to take on this role since Alaric had snatched her off the streets, always knowing what she was.

Breathe, Love, came down the bond. *Hold that shield. Protect Callan's sister. There is much you cannot control right now, but you can control that.*

I can't, Sorin. Not much longer . . .

Rayner will be here soon. Help will be here soon. Hold on, Scarlett. You can do this. Breathe. In and out.

She gritted her teeth, reinforcing that shield around Eva. Callan was still being held by Lord Tyndell and Mikale, but now Tarek was pushing to his feet. Before Scarlett could do anything, Alaric was gripping her arms, holding them in place behind her back. He spoke softly into her ear. "Do not struggle, my Wraith, or I kill Prince Callan next."

She nodded her understanding, and Tarek began patting down her torso, her hips, until he reached the pockets of her pants. His hand slipped inside, and he pulled out the amulets.

"There are only six," he said to Alaric.

A flash of light, and Talwyn stood before them in her usual attire. "I have the last one," she said, her voice monotone and cold. She wouldn't look at any of them.

"You do not," Scarlett corrected.

"I possess one of them," Talwyn insisted.

"You did," Scarlett replied listlessly. "An amulet of Celeste, right?" She nodded at the amulets Tarck held in his hand.

Talwyn stalked forward, fingering through them until she found hers. "How?" she demanded.

"Juliette lifted it from your pack the evening we stayed at the Contessa's northern villa. When we went to the kitchen to get food. She replaced it with a fake. You are bonded to Maliq. I took a chance on you having Celeste's amulet," Scarlett answered. "I guessed you knew its whereabouts after you learned of them at our meeting. I figured you'd keep it close after discovering I was searching for them so diligently." She shrugged. "I was right."

Alaric chuckled behind her, releasing her arms. "Finally putting that cleverness to use. I bet you even know where the final key is, don't you?"

"Fuck off," she spat at him.

Which earned her a quick fist to the gut.

Sorin roared with rage behind her but was quickly choking as vines wrapped around his throat, squeezing tight.

Scarlett snarled, throwing a ball of flame at Tarek, who barely managed to avoid it, but the distraction cost her, and her shield fell around Princess Eva. Alaric was already drawing the dagger from his belt, striding towards the girl, and Scarlett started when she saw the blade. Up close, she could see it wasn't just any blade but one as dark as night itself.

He possessed a dagger of nightstone.

"No!" she screamed, grappling with the dregs of her shadows, trying to get a shield around Eva, but then the air was shifting. There was the deafening sound of some kind of explosion, and black flames of some sort seemed to radiate out from her.

But they weren't from her.

They were from her Guardian who stood beside her, having stepped from the air.

And he wasn't alone.

Ashtine, Briar, and Azrael were with him.

The entirety of the Fae Royals now stood in this room. "Briar! The girl!" Scarlett cried.

But their gifts didn't work here. Not in the mortal lands. And even if they could, they didn't possess Semiria rings to overcome the wards. That was the only way she figured Tarek and Talwyn were accessing their gifts.

Everything was happening so fast. Too fast. Scarlett couldn't keep track.

Alaric was already striding for Eva once more as Cassius's arm looped around Scarlett's waist when her knees buckled under the strain of her power. She began drawing from him, the Guardian link sensing the threats against her, and she leaned against Cassius, throwing an ice shield around Eva.

But Alaric switched directions, heading for Callan, his hand raising.

Callan winced, clutching at his chest.

"No!" Tava screamed. "No! Callan!" Drake had his arms wrapped tightly around her, holding her back as she strained, kicking and thrashing, trying to get to Callan.

Sorin had managed to get his sword and a knife free when Tarek and Talwyn had been thrown across the room by Cassius's power. He was fighting his way to her, cutting away the vines that kept reappearing. But that was lightning at Talwyn's fingertips.

Azrael was yelling at her, trying to get her attention over the chaos of the room. Briar had twin swords raised, Ashtine at his side with blades that were curved into a sickle shape. Mikale and Lord Tyndell were drawing near them with their own blades.

And death. It hovered. She could feel it all around them. She'd bestowed it enough to know when it had come to stake a claim.

And tonight it would feast.

Sorin, I love you, she sent down the bond. *Find me in the After. In the places between the stars.*

No! He shouted down the bond, and Scarlett watched as he swung that sword again and again.

She watched as a bolt of energy from Talwyn's hand hit him straight in the chest.

She watched as he staggered once before dropping to his knees. His eyes found hers.

And the pain in her chest.

Oh gods. Alaric had to be squeezing her heart because the pain in her chest was pure agony. She couldn't draw a breath, but somehow she was screaming. Her lungs wouldn't expand, but that was sheer anguish pouring from her lips.

There was pressure around her waist, her ribs. Arms wrapped tightly around her, lifting her off her feet and tugging her back against a hard chest, keeping her from going to him. Someone was speaking into her ear, but she couldn't hear what they were saying. Because he was dying. And she was dying. Her soul was dying.

You do not feel your soul ripping apart the way I did at her death if half of it is not being torn away from you.

That was what Cyrus had said to her, when he'd spoken of Thia dying.

But this? This was not half of her soul being torn away from her. This was her entire being shattering into nothing.

Love . . . His voice filtered down the bond, breathless and raspy. *I would still choose to stay in the darkness . . . Even now.*

"Sorin!" Her scream ripped through the room, piercing and full of despair. A vortex of fire and ice and shadows burst from her, swirling around her and Cassius as she lost control of everything.

CHAPTER 49
CALLAN

Scarlett's screams pierced the air, but the ones coming from Tava were just as agonizing.

Because she was screaming his name as the Assassin Lord tightened the phantom grip on his heart, squeezing tighter and tighter.

He'd failed in all the ways that mattered. He'd failed to protect his mother.

He'd failed to protect his sister. He'd failed to protect his people. He'd failed to protect her.

There was no way any of them were leaving here alive. The Fae were useless without their gifts. Sure, they could fight better than any human soldier, but that did little when the people they were fighting *could* access their gifts.

When the Fae Queen could bring the Prince of Fire to his knees with a single bolt of energy from her very palm.

When the male beside her could strangle with vines.

When Mikale and the Lord could apparently sprout wings from their backs and do the gods knew what.

When the Assassin Lord before him could squeeze the very life from him simply by raising his hand.

He was already on his knees, having dropped to them almost immediately when his chest had begun constricting. Now he lurched forward onto his hands, his back bowing.

Light was flashing in his vision, and he knew the air he managed to suck into his lungs would be the last breath he took.

Except it wasn't.

The pressure in his chest was suddenly gone. His vision cleared, landing on his sister who was shrieking where she sat on the floor, still bound and gagged. He crawled to her, not letting himself look at the carnage going on around him. He pulled the gag from her mouth, clamping a hand over it.

"You need to stop screaming, Eva," he rasped. "Stop."

She nodded, her entire body trembling, and he pulled her into his side. Only then did he look up and take in what was transpiring. There was a . . . whirlwind of fire and ice and shadows. That was the only way he could describe it. It swirled around Scarlett, where she was thrashing and screaming, her face tilted to the ceiling as her pain and grief poured out of her. Cassius had her clasped to his chest, holding her head to his shoulder so she didn't snap her godsdamn neck.

Sorin was on the ground, not moving, a red bird flying above him. Amaré.

It slowly registered then that there was a horse with water for a mane. A silver hawk.

A stag.

A panther.

There were spirit animals here. That had been the light flashing when he thought he'd been about to die.

The Fae were all panting. Briar and a petite female, with hair as silver as Scarlett's, had made their way to Tava and Drake, now guarding them. Prince Azrael was before Talwyn and the other male.

The Assassin Lord, Lord Tyndell, and Mikale were all retreating a few steps as the panther stalked forward.

"You tell her I am coming. Tell her I will find her and deliver her to him. I will deliver all of you to him," the Assassin Lord spat at the panther.

The panther snarled, massive teeth bared, just as ashes swirled, and Rayner appeared. He looked around the room, taking it all in. His eyes widened when they landed on Sorin, lying unmoving where he'd fallen.

He quickly made his way to the swirling mass that was Scarlett, but Callan couldn't hear what he was yelling over Scarlett's screams. She was going to blow-out her vocal cords.

"Come, Prince."

Callan looked up. He hadn't seen Briar make his way over to him while the panther was keeping the Maraan Lords busy.

"We are getting out of here."

"How?" Callan rasped, standing and scooping Eva up into his arms, settling her on his hip. She wrapped her small arms around his neck, burying her face into his shoulder. He followed Briar over to the Tyndells. "Scarlett cannot possibly Travel."

"She cannot," Briar agreed. "But we are hoping her Guardian can. If Scarlett has not siphoned too much of his power."

"Prince Azrael?" Callan asked.

Briar paused, his gaze snagging on the prince and Fae Queen for a moment before he said, "I do not think he will be leaving with us, and he does not have a ring to access his magic. We took tonics in hopes of being able to access our gifts here. That is why we are not feeling the effects we normally do upon entering the mortal lands. But there are wards—"

"Callan!" Tava cried when they neared, Drake easing his grip to allow her to come to him. He shifted Eva so he could loop an arm around Tava, pressing a kiss to the crown of her head. "I didn't think . . ." She trailed off, her voice breaking.

"Me either," Callan replied grimly.

"Cassius will try and get her calm enough for us to get near him," Rayner said, coming up beside them all. "Everyone needs to be touching. We will have seconds, if that."

Tava clutched onto Callan's arm, reaching back with her other hand to grab Drake's. Rayner was already lowering himself beside Sorin, his hand resting on the prince's shoulder.

"I cannot go," the petite female was saying to Briar.

"Ashtine, you cannot stay," Briar argued. "This is the start of war!"

"I pledged my loyalty to Talwyn," she said softly.

"Before all of this!" There was panic in Briar's voice, pleading.

"She needs to know that someone chose her for her," Asthine replied, her hand coming up, fingers gently grazing the Water Prince's jaw.

"You understand that we will be on opposing sides now? Do you recognize what you are doing?" Briar insisted, his hands coming up to frame her face.

"I do," Ashtine replied, two tears slipping down her cheeks. "Take care of Nasima for me."

"This is killing you," Briar said, so much anguish in his voice. "This will kill you."

"Then I shall once more be able to walk among the winds," she answered sadly, her thumb brushing along Briar's cheekbone.

"Ashtine." Her name was a plea and a cry on the Water Prince's lips as he brought his mouth to hers.

Callan looked away then, already feeling like he had intruded on a truly intimate moment.

A goodbye that was just as heart-wrenching as the one pouring from Scarlett's lungs.

"Drayce," Rayner said, his deep voice soft but urgent. "He is coming."

"Be well, my heart," Ashtine said softly, pulling away from Briar.

The Water Prince's eyes stayed on her as he walked backwards, stretching a hand out behind him to take Rayner's, who was reaching for him. Drake placed a hand on Briar's shoulder, and a few seconds later, Cassius stood before them.

"We will bring him with us, Seastar. I promise. Just for a few seconds." However he reached her, Callan didn't know, but there was the briefest of reprieves from her magic. Or maybe it simply gave out. He didn't know how long she could expend power like that.

But as he felt the now familiar tug of Traveling, he found himself wishing he could bring the bodies of his parents with, too.

Of Finn. Of Sloan.

Of his entire world that had just turned to ash.

CHAPTER 50
TALWYN

Talwyn watched as the spirit animals disappeared in flashes of light once Scarlett was gone, with nearly everyone else.

All the spirit animals but Rinji that is.

The stag stood stoically at Azrael's side, watchful and waiting.

It wasn't lost on her that Maliq had not shown up. Another abandonment that sliced away at her soul.

What was left of it after killing Sorin anyway.

It didn't seem real. It had all seemed to happen in slow motion. The chaos of battle around them. Sorin fighting his way to Scarlett, slashing through earth magic with such ferocity that Talwyn knew nothing would keep him from reaching her. He shouldn't have been able to fight magic without his ring. Even trained as a Fae warrior, he shouldn't have been able to break through the vines they sent to bind him. But the rage, the desperation, the need to protect his twin flame at all costs had driven him forward. He would have found a way to burn the world to the ground to get to her. Nothing would have kept him from reaching his twin flame.

Nothing but death.

She hadn't realized what she'd done until it was over. Until he was falling to his knees. Until Scarlett had started screaming. Until Azrael had met her eyes. His brown eyes were full, not of accusation, but sympathy.

Because she had not planned that. That was not supposed to happen. And she couldn't stop seeing Sorin drop to his knees. She couldn't stop hearing Scarlett's screams. Couldn't keep memories of hide-and-seek and frozen cream and the name 'Little Whirlwind' from her mind.

"I have been trying to reach you for days," Azrael said, pulling her from memories she could not hide from. He still held twin swords in his hands at his sides. "You locked me out of the Halls. Of . . . everywhere."

"I told you that you were no longer the person I could depend on," she retorted coldly, pushing down every emotion trying to war inside of her. Letting the numbness settle in.

"And he is?" Azrael demanded, a jerk of his chin at Tarek. "The one who let you believe he was dead for an entire decade? The one who left you? Broke your heart? Abandoned you? Lied to you about—"

"Let's not speak of who has lied to whom here," Talwyn sneered, cutting him off.

"He is using you, Talwyn," Azrael insisted. "You have to know that."

"The Prince speaks truth," came Ashtine's lilt when she appeared at Azrael's side.

Talwyn blinked in surprise. "You are still here."

"I told you my loyalty resides with you," she replied.

"But . . . you do not agree with this war."

"I do not agree with your choices," Ashtine agreed. "But my friendship with you does not rely upon conditions."

And Talwyn was unsure of how to answer that, because every relationship in her life had been built on conditions, hers or someone else's. A relationship was built with her out of necessity. Eliné and Sorin had taken her in because she needed to be trained to rule. Relationships with the other rulers had been built for the purpose of building alliances and loyalty. And Azrael? Well, out of a mutual need. She needed a Second, and he was the Earth Prince. She was under no illusion that he would have given her the time of day had she not been a queen.

"They got away!" the youngest of the Lords was bellowing, raging across the room where Shirina had nearly backed them into a corner. He whirled on who Talwyn now knew was the Assassin Lord of the Black Syndicate, Alaric. Tarek had introduced them when she had Traveled them here three days ago. "You cannot tell me this was part of your plan," the young Lord was snarling, his finger pointed at Alaric in accusation.

"Calm down," Alaric said coldly. "We still have the keys."

Talwyn looked down at Tarek's hand where the six amulets were indeed still clasped tightly in his fist. Fury at Scarlett having stolen from her flooded through her veins. She had known immediately where the Fae key was, as soon as Scarlett had explained the amulets to her. It had been her mother's, passed down to Talwyn with the Semiria ring. She never wore the thing, not one to need useless embellishments. It was why Ashtine had never seen it, would not have known that Talwyn possessed it.

"We are still missing one," the young Lord retorted.

"Scarlett will bring it to us," Alaric said, clearly not worried in the slightest. "And until she does, Queen Talwyn can begin working on how to shift them into their original states. This is not a setback."

"Not a setback?" the Lord snarled. "How many times will you let her go until you keep her?"

"You mean how long until I will allow you to fuck her again?" Alaric asked, his brow arching. "That is what you are really asking, is it not?" The young Lord bristled as Alaric stepped closer to him, his tone going lethal. "Do not forget whom you serve here, Mikale, and in case you need the reminder, it is not the cunt of what belongs to me."

The Lord's eyes dropped to the ground.

"He mourns his sister," the older Lord said, stepping forward. "He forgets his place."

"Then he would do well to remember it, or he will join her," Alaric said coldly. He turned towards a shadowed corner of the room. "As for *you*. You will fight with us next time, *Contessa*."

"You cannot honestly expect me to fight her, Alaric," Death's Shadow drawled, and Talwyn couldn't hide the surprise at how she spoke to her master. Although, it shouldn't really shock her, considering how Scarlett spoke to him herself. "Did you want me to kill her? You know that cannot happen."

"Of course I do not want her dead. Part of the reason for your existence these past years has been to keep the girl alive," Alaric said. "But when Fae Royalty stand against us again, I expect you to do what you were trained to do."

Nuri scoffed. "And the spirit animals? I suppose you wanted me to stand against them as well?"

The Assassin Lord's face seemed to darken, his eyes narrowing on the Night Child. "I will take care of them myself." He turned to face the older Lord. "What do you make of Cassius's powers? How did we not know of them?"

"I have never learned who his father is," the Lord answered. "Only that his mother is the High Witch."

"Yes, yes," Alaric said in annoyance. "We have known that for years. Sybil keeps us well informed on the Witch front. I am surprised she does not know, however."

"She would not keep such information from us," the Lord replied. "For her sake, I hope not. But he can Travel."

"So he must have Avonleyan blood," the Lord finished for him.

"Sepharina?" Alaric mused.

The Lord shook his head. "That was not wind magic."

Alaric grunted in annoyance before his gaze settled back on Talwyn and the others. "Think on it, Balam," he said to the Lord. "We can discuss it later. Get Mikale out of my sight."

"Of course," Balam said with a small bow of his head before turning and striding from the throne room, Mikale following him out.

"Sorry about that, your Majesty," Alaric said as he approached. A pleased smile filled his features. One that Talwyn was sure few saw. "Inner Court matters. Something I am sure you can relate to." His gaze swept over Azrael and Ashtine before settling on Tarek. "We have much to go over, Tarek. Finish up here, get someone to clean this place up, and meet us in the Syndicate."

Tarek nodded in understanding, and Alaric swept from the room, the heavy doors clanging shut behind him. The bodies of the king and queen and Callan's two guards were still on the ground. She had known the king and queen were not to survive this night. She had not known he had planned to kill Callan and his younger sister as well. Details she would be discussing in length with Tarek when this matter with Azrael and Ashtine was taken care of.

Ashtine cleared her throat. "While I have made the choice to remain loyal to *you*, Talwyn, that loyalty is separate from my Court's loyalty to the Eastern Fae Queen."

"What?" Talwyn demanded, whirling on the princess.

"I have no desire to be here while you discuss ways to desecrate what has been created in this land, even if much of it has been built upon falsehoods." She looked up at Azrael. "Will you take me home, please?"

A muscle feathered in Azrael's jaw. "Yes, but I need to speak with Talwyn first."

"Understood," Ashtine replied. "I will wait at the main gates with Rinji."

After she and the stag had left the room, Azrael turned back to Talwyn. "Speak with me. Alone."

"There is a private room behind the dais," Tarek said, nodding to the thrones. "Go there while I get this mess taken care of."

Azrael didn't wait, stalking towards the indicated area. He pushed through a door, turning to face her as she followed him through. His arms were folded across his broad chest, watching her as she shut the door behind them.

"What?" she bit out.

"That is all you have to say?" he asked dryly. "What do you want me to say, Prince Luan?"

"Prince Luan," he scoffed.

Talwyn clenched her jaw before she gritted out, "He says he does not wish to challenge you for your Court."

"Of course, he doesn't, Talwyn," Azrael retorted. "One, he knows he would lose that fight. Two, why would he fight for a Court, when he has a clear path to a throne to rule over two? More if these Maraan pricks get their way."

"They do not want to rule the Courts," Talwyn shot back.

"No, they will let you believe you are ruling them, just as they have let the mortal kings believe they have been ruling in the human lands for centuries. Events of tonight clearly prove otherwise."

A heavy silence fell in the room. "How did you find me?"

"The Ash Rider came for me. Aditya sent him. Said you were in wolf form with Tarek, that you needed me. He was clearly mistaken."

Talwyn had to work to keep the surprise from her features, to keep her mask in place. He had come simply because he had thought she had needed him? No questions? Just dropped everything and came to her?

"Back in Siofra," he said suddenly, "when I was telling you of my heritage, I told you that when my parents had been killed and I had assumed the throne, nothing had really changed for me. And that was true. I ran the Earth Court. I worked with Eliné on various matters for the kingdom, but everything I did was always for the betterment of the Earth Court."

He paused for so long that Talwyn wondered if that was all he had to say, and what it mattered. She didn't care. Not any more.

But when he spoke again, there was a pointed deliberation to his tone. "Everything stayed the same until the day a young queen showed up at my home, having just been bonded to a spirit animal, and not knowing a single fucking thing about what to do with her throne. That day, everything changed."

"I do not know what you are trying to say, but spit it out, Az," Talwyn snapped.

"Dammit, Talwyn. *You* changed everything. Until that day, relationships were for political alliances, for producing powerful heirs, for making sure the Earth Court remained profitable. Until that day. Until you. Until you literally appeared out of thin air and turned my entire world upside down. I did not know how to react. I did not know how to let in those feelings, but that day? The purpose of a relationship took on a different meaning for me. And over the years, as I watched you grow into the queen you were always meant to be, love took on a different meaning for me, too."

Talwyn found herself pressing her back to the door, having lurched back from what he appeared to be saying.

"I should have . . . told you sooner. All of it. Everything. Maybe things would be different, but I didn't know how. I was too much of a . . . coward," he was saying. His jaw was sharp, his eyes pinned on her. She couldn't hold his gaze, her eyes darting around the room, trying to focus on anything but him. "But I know what love looks like Talwyn. And so do you. You saw it today when Aditya was fighting with everything he had to get to Scarlett. You saw it when Cyrus lost his fucking mind when Thia died. If you'd open your godsdamn eyes, you'd see it between Ashtine and Briar." Talwyn's gaze flew to his at that. "And you and I both know that is not what you have with Tarek."

That had her pushing off the door, stalking towards him, fury coursing through her. "You know *nothing* of what I have with Tarek," she seethed, her finger poking him hard in the chest, a gust of wind pushing into him and making him stumble back a step.

But instead of responding to that, Azrael said, "You will have to pick a side, Talwyn. You have to know that."

"Do I?" Talwyn countered. "I could give two fucks less about the Maraan Lords and what they want in Avonleya. As long as that kingdom falls and becomes rubble at my feet, Alaric and the others can have whatever they want there. They are a means to an end. They are the ones being used here, not me."

A laugh of utter disbelief came from Azrael. "At least acknowledge you are purposefully putting on blinders here, Talwyn. You are putting your Courts, your people, those you are duty bound to protect, at risk for what? Revenge you think you are owed? When will it be enough? What do you want?"

"I want it all!" she screamed. "I am owed my revenge! I have lost everything because of them and what they started! If anyone has been used here, it is our people. Good enough to fight a war for them, but not good enough to be protected when they ran back and hid behind their wards. Good enough to be chosen until someone better came along, and then abandoned as if they were nothing."

Something softened in his eyes. "Talwyn," he murmured.

But she was done talking. She was done listening. She was done with him. She was done with all of this. "Aiding the Maraans in this, secures the safety of my Courts. If you cannot see that, then I am not the naïve one here."

"They will be used to fight a war that is not theirs, just as you accuse the Avonleyans of doing," Azrael countered.

"They will not. I will not allow that to happen. I have given everything for these Courts. Everything," she hissed. "I will be damned if an Avonelyan thinks she can come in here and take what I have dedicated my entire life to."

Azrael was shaking his head, a hand carving through his dark hair.

Then he was prowling towards her, taking her chin between his thumb and forefinger, forcing her to meet his gaze.

"I want to make one thing very clear, Talwyn," he said. "I am not walking away because I want to. I am not letting you go because I do not care. I am letting you go because you refuse to let anyone fight for you. You refuse to even entertain the idea that someone could want you for you. That someone would see the value of *who* you are. I see everything you cannot see. And Tarek? He does not see you, Talwyn. He sees a path to a throne. He has not watched you grow into the queen you are today. He left you willingly, not because you forced him to walk away. He willingly abandoned you. But know that when I walk away from you tonight, it kills me to do so."

"You are no different," she whispered, her voice harsh and intending to wound. "You have conditions for what we are."

"The only condition I have is that you choose me, too, Talwyn," he answered, his voice gruff and low. "I do not believe this was all for nothing, so know that on the days and nights you feel alone, when you find yourself standing among the destruction you have brought about, I will be out there. We are not done, you and I, and I will come for you as soon as you let me do so."

He dropped her chin, taking a step back from her. "But I cannot stand by and watch you lead our people to their death."

Talwyn hadn't moved. Her face was still tilted up, her lips pressed into a thin line. She said nothing until she heard his hand on the door, beginning to pull it open. Then she found herself spinning towards him.

"They plan to invade the Courts," she said, her tone firm and monotone. "I will let them cross the wards."

Azrael stilled. He stared straight ahead, his eyes fixed on the door in front of him. "I will tell the others. Drayce and Adit— The Fire Court."

"I know," she said, the numbness she'd felt when her power had slammed into Sorin's chest returning.

Numbness because she would not allow herself to feel the crater it had left in her soul.

This was no place for feelings and emotions.

"How you are feeling right now? About exacting your revenge against Sorin?" Azrael said, as if he could see her fractured soul. "You are glimpsing your future, Talwyn. That feeling is all your future holds if you stay on this path."

Then he was gone, the door banging shut behind him.

"How is it coming along?"

Tarek's hand brushed the back of her neck before she felt him coast his lips along her flesh.

It had been a week since the king and queen of Windonelle had been murdered. It had been a week since Prince Callan and Princess Eva had fled for their lives. Lord Lairwood, Hand to the King, was next in line to take the throne according to royal charters, all neatly orchestrated over the centuries by Alaric and Balam Tyndell themselves. Of course, Lord Lairwood was also conveniently murdered that night, leaving the path to the throne open for none other than Mikale Lairwood himself. Talwyn had also learned that Mikale and his sister were not Lord Lairwood's flesh and blood.

Balam had used the strange powers he had to alter people's reality, and made the Lord believe them to be his children.

Alaric had been right. It would have been a much smoother transition if Callan had married Veda. She knew now the plan had been to eventually kill Callan, when enough time had passed, and then Veda would have called on her brother to take the throne after claiming she didn't know the first thing about ruling a kingdom. There would be bumps and resistance with how things had actually played out.

But Alaric had taken care of that, too.

Everything had been pinned and blamed on the Faè. Well, not all the Fae. Specifically the "treacherous Fire Court" to the North with the aid of the Water Court to the South. But humans being mortal, they were wary of all the Courts, her own included, despite it being declared the Fae Queen of the Eastern Courts was on their side. Despite it being announced that she had killed the Fire Prince in revenge for killing their king and queen. The humans had been too distrustful of the Fae for far too long, though, taught to believe that all their troubles stemmed from them because of the Great War.

Because of Avonleya.

She sat at a desk in a suite at the Baylorin castle, the amulets spread out before her. Alaric did not want them to leave the mortal lands, so she was stuck working on trying to shift their form here, rather than taking them back to the White Halls. Tarek had stayed with her every night, gone during the days to do whatever tasks were assigned to him. She was included in many meetings, but she knew there were others being held without her.

She did the same in her own kingdom after all, having meetings long into the night with Azrael and Ashtine after the other Royals had departed.

Not that she had to worry about that any more. She had learned that the winged men she and Azrael had fought were called seraphs, and there were more of them. So many more than she'd have ever guessed. And those rips in the planes she'd been taken to at one time with Scarlett? That was how they were getting them into this world. Through some combination of Blood Magic and Maraan gifts.

They had these rips in every mortal kingdom. Several rips, actually. They had them in the Night Child lands. Their next focus was the Fae Courts. Talwyn had agreed to let them in on the condition that none of her innocent people would be hurt in any of the Courts. Alaric himself had reassured her that this was solely to force Scarlett's hand to get them into Avonleya. They were building an army to bring against Avonleya and he had promised she would see the Aonvelyan king's head at her feet, and that was all she cared about.

"This nightstone is different," she replied, Tarek's fingers skating across her cheek while he stood behind her. "I have shifted matter and energy plenty of times, but this is denser. Harder. More resistant."

"You can do it," Tarek said softly, fingers dragging down her throat, across her collarbone. "Your mother would not have left the task to you if she did not believe you could accomplish it."

"What are you doing here in the morning?" she asked. He was generally gone before she woke, only returning for a midday meal with her before they both went to meet with the Lords and be briefed on any new developments.

"I had nothing to tend to this morning, so I thought I would check in on you," Tarek replied, reaching past her to pick up one of the amulets.

Some . . . *thing* fluttered in her chest at his words, but his next ones had it dying just as quickly.

"What do you plan to do with the Courts?"

"What do you mean what do I plan to do with them? I will rule them. As I have the last several decades," she replied sharply, her attention going back to the amulets. She picked up her own, holding the cool metal in her palm. It never warmed. No matter how long she held it. It was always cool to the touch.

"Yes, but you are down a few Royals now," Tarek said casually. Too casually.

Talwyn stiffened, but he continued speaking, not seeming to notice. "When we enter the Fire and Water Courts, Alaric will not let the Royals live if they refuse to side with us. Then again, I guess we only need to worry about Drayce," he mused, apparently simply thinking out loud at this point. "I know you do not wish to see an Avonleyan ruling over them, and Alaric will not let Scarlett remain in her role. He has . . . other plans for her."

"Such as?" Talwyn asked, trying to keep the annoyance from her tone but failing.

"He will not share that with you unless you choose the Blood Bond."

She had been offered this Blood Bond three times now. This thing that bound Tarek and Death's Shadow to the Maraans. Alaric specifically. She was told it would offer the ultimate protection. Unconditional loyalty that goes both ways. That was how Tarek described it, but she still wasn't convinced. It seemed too . . . convenient. It was wrapped up too pretty. She'd learned long ago that anything good and beautiful in her life wouldn't stick around for long. The Fates did not find her worthy enough to gift her anything that valuable. Pretty things always came at a cost. It was just a matter of figuring out how big the cost would be.

It was never worth it.

Ignoring his comment about the Blood Bond for now, Talwyn said, "Alaric told me no innocents will be harmed in this."

"Do you honestly believe Prince Drayce will willingly allow us into his Court? That Cyrus and Eliza and Rayner will not fight against us? They cannot stay in their positions, Talwyn."

She let the amulet she was holding plunk down onto the desk, leaning back rigidly in her chair and looking up at him. "So this is why you are truly here? To learn about my plans for the Courts?"

Tarek shrugged. "It is something that needs to be discussed. Now seemed as good a time as any."

Talwyn's jaw was clenched so tightly it hurt. "The Courts are mine to worry about. No one else's."

"No one is trying to take them from you, Moonflower," he said softly. "But we do need to know what to expect so we are all on the same page."

"They will be offered the choice of aligning with us or abdicating," she said.

"Talwyn, Alaric will not let them live if they do not join our cause."

"That is not his choice to make."

"He will not risk letting them live to start up a secret rebellion. To find ways to work against him and thwart his efforts. He has waited too long. There will be no room for mercy. Not any more," Tarek said.

"They are my Courts, not his," Talwyn said again, pushing to her feet so she no longer needed to look up at him. Annoyingly,

Azrael's words chose that moment to emerge at the forefront of her thoughts.

They will let you believe you are ruling them, just as they have let mortal kings believe they have been ruling in the human lands for centuries.

"If the Water and Fire Courts will not fall in line, Ashtine can handle matters in the Water Court until we can take the time to find a new Royal properly. Ermir will watch over the Wind Court in her absence, and I will handle the Fire Court personally," she finally said, her voice as icy as a bitter wind.

"And the Earth Court?" Tarek asked, his head tilting to the side as he watched her.

"What of it?"

Tarek scoffed. "Luan clearly does not side with you, Talwyn. He cannot be left in his position."

"And I suppose *you* want it? Is that truly what this has all been about? You taking back the Earth Court?"

Tarek's brow arched. "Someone has been talking. Was it the false queen or the false prince?"

"How I learned of it is none of your concern. Answer the question," she demanded.

Tarek's hands shot out, snatching her waist and dragging her into him. His nose was nearly touching hers and when he next spoke, she could feel his breath on her lips. "My sole focus these last ten years has been you, Talwyn. Always you. What was best for you, your Courts, and the revenge you deserve to take. I do not care about petty rivalries among the Courts nor who is sitting on a throne, as long as you are the queen of it all."

"And as long as you are at my side, right?" She'd meant it to come out cold and sharp, but there was an edge of something else in her tone that made it sound almost broken.

Because everything had a cost, and she was just now figuring out what the cost of his love was likely to be.

"Do you not wish me to be at your side?" Tarek asked, his hands on her hips beginning to roam. "We are twin flames, Talwyn."

"Are we?"

His movements stopped, and he leaned back to see her face better. "You doubt us? What we are? What we have?"

"There is a lot that does not add up, Tarek," she retorted. "A lot that does not make sense."

Tarek's arms dropped to his side, and he pushed away from her, stalking to the middle of the room. Then he was spinning back to face her. "You let them whisper lies. Like snakes in the grass, they have planted seeds to destroy what we have. When I have spent the last ten years sacrificing *everything*. For you."

"Do not act as if I have not sacrificed just as much for you," Talwyn sneered in reply. "And I did not ask you to sacrifice anything for me."

"Of course not," Tarek said with a roll of his eyes. "You would never lower yourself enough to let someone do something for you."

"No," she said, taking a few steps to him, then halting. "I know that sacrifices are never given freely. There is always a cost, and I do not like to have debts hanging over my head."

Tarek stilled, seeming to consider this, before he closed the distance between them and took her hand. "And if the only payment I ask is your heart, Talwyn?"

The corner of her mouth curled up into a sardonic half-smile. "I know that notion is too pretty to be true," she replied. "And even if it were not, there is nothing left of my heart to give to you. That cost was paid long ago."

CHAPTER 51
SCARLETT

Scarlett sat at a desk, her feet propped on top, ankles crossed. She leaned back, her hands clenching around the ends of the armrests so tightly it hurt. But that was good. It grounded her. Kept her in this place. Kept her focused.

She glanced down, seeing her bare skin. Her bare left hand.

No dark mark against her skin, swirling down around her fingers. No diamond and ruby ring on her finger.

Her eyes flicked to the wall where she'd been chained for weeks, searching for anything to take her mind off of him. Of how he'd sank to his knees, then to the floor. Of Cassius holding her tightly in that throne room.

Of the utter insanity that had encompassed her. That she could barely keep at bay now.

No. This was not the time to think of that day three weeks ago. So she focused on the spot where she'd sat chained to a wall, forcing herself to breathe in and out.

In and out. In and out.

And she waited.

But not for long.

The door banged open, a hooded figure stalking in. He came up short when he saw her sitting there. Slowly, he raised his hands, pulling back his hood. Black eyes bored into hers.

"Death's Maiden," Alaric said casually. "It is about time you came home."

"Is it?" Scarlett asked, her head tilting to the side.

Alaric nonchalantly removed his cloak, draping it over the sofa against the wall where Tarek had often sat, observing her.

"You could have at least left a few of them alive on your way in, though."

Scarlett shrugged. She'd left a trail for him to follow. Every assassin, every Night Child, every seraph she had come upon as she slowly strolled along the streets of the Black Syndicate, onto the grounds of the Fellowship, and through the halls down to his dungeon study had met their death. Some by fire until they were ash. Some by drowning on dry land. Some by shadows. Some by blades.

All by wrath.

"I am assuming you brought me the final key?" he asked when she didn't reply.

Scarlett reached into a pocket, pulling out Juliette's amulet, Reselda's symbol hanging from the chain of skystone. She spun it around on her finger. "This one?"

Alaric only nodded his head once, hands sliding into his pockets. "Has Queen Talwyn learned to shift them yet?"

"She has."

"Impressive," Scarlett quipped. "I thought it would take her longer."

"Three weeks was too long the way it was," Alaric retorted, a slight bite to his tone.

Scarlett tsked under her breath. "Someone is growing impatient."

"I made it very clear I was out of patience."

"And time."

When Alaric just stared back at her unblinkingly, she dropped her booted feet to the ground. She planted her elbows on his desk, resting her chin on her hand as she asked sweetly, "Is Achaz out of patience too?"

He stilled. "How do you know that name?"

"It seems you left out quite a bit of history when providing my education," she said, spinning the amulet around her finger again.

"You were told what you needed to know to fulfill your purpose," he replied coolly.

Scarlett hummed in response.

"I will admit that while I am not surprised to see you here, I am surprised to see you so . . . collected," Alaric said cautiously, as if she were an explosive substance that could go off at any moment.

He wasn't wrong.

The images that used to flash through her mind had been replaced. They were no longer Veda stabbing Cassius. Nuri bleeding out. An old office. Plunging a dagger into Juliette's heart.

It was him fighting his way to her.

Him swearing there would be no more goodbyes. A bolt of energy hitting his chest.

Him staggering before dropping to his knees. His golden eyes finding hers, slowly dimming. *I would still choose to stay in the darkness.*

And screaming.

So much screaming.

Her eyes dipped to her bare left hand once more before refocusing on Alaric. He was watching her carefully, taking in all her little tells that he knew so well.

She cleared her throat, placing the amulet on the desk before her. She couldn't lose it here.

Not now. Not yet. Soon.

"You are really going to do this?" she asked. "You are really going to be no better than your parents and start a war? Over what? What exactly is it you want with Avonleya?"

"My dear child," Alaric said, a cruel smile tilting up his lips just the slightest amount. "The war never ceased. This war has been raging for centuries. Perhaps longer than this world has even existed. They brought war to this world. Did you forget? We were sent to retrieve what they guard."

"We? You speak as if you were not born here." Her eyes widened as the Sorceress's words replayed in her head. "You weren't born here. You came through the rips. Was Esmeray even your mother?"

"No," Alaric answered.

"But Deimas was your father?"

Alaric's blank stare was answer enough. Yes, he was.

"Were they killed here?"

"Esmeray was."

"And Deimas?"

"He suffered the consequences of his failure."

"Consequences you are about to face? That is why you are out of time," Scarlett clarified.

Alaric's lips pursed slightly. "Sometimes I think it was a mistake to train you as my prodigy."

She tossed him a saccharine smile. "I suppose you live and learn."

"I suppose we do."

He moved forward then, sinking into one of the chairs before his own desk. How many times had Scarlett sat in that very chair? Discussing jobs and targets. Juliette in the other chair. Nuri lurking in the shadows.

Her heart tugged at the thought of Nuri.

Not now, she chided herself, forcing her attention back to Alaric as he reclined in the chair.

"So what now, Death's Maiden?" Alaric asked, bringing up a leg and crossing his ankle over his knee. He was the portrait of arrogant ease.

Scarlett hummed again in contemplation. "Now I am going to make your life a living hell."

"Is that so?"

"Mhmm," she replied. "The beauty of it is that you won't even know it has happened until it is too late." She smiled then. A thing of horror and malice. "For the most part anyway."

Alaric smiled, his hands resting on his bent knee. "You really think you can beat me, Scarlett? I made you what you are. I created you."

"You did," she agreed, standing then and moving to his alcohol cart. She poured herself a knuckle's length of liquor, swirling it around the glass. "And I want you to remember that when you are standing among the ashes of everything I've burned to the ground. You taught me everything I know. You taught me what weaknesses to expose. You taught me how to find cracks and make them chasms." She knocked back the entire glass of alcohol. "I am already inside, Alaric," she purred.

"Because I allowed you in," he replied coolly, his smile slipping a little.

"Then I suppose you have allowed everything that is about to happen."

The two stared at each other. Master and student.

Maraan and Avonleyan. Torturer and tortured.

"You have seen what I can do, Scarlett," he finally said, his voice low and lethal. "Do not think I will hesitate for one second to make you suffer. To take everything from you until you remember that I *own you*."

She let her glass plunk onto the alcohol cart before she began strolling for the door. "You have already taken everything from me, Alaric. There is nothing left for you to own. But you?" She paused in the doorway, looking back over her shoulder. She took in his stiffened posture. The way his eyes had narrowed slightly on her. "It appears you have everything to lose."

"Do not step one foot out that door, Scarlett Monrhoe," he hissed, rising smoothly to his feet.

"Aditya," she sneered. "My name is Queen Scarlett Aditya. And I take orders from no one."

She pulled the door shut behind her as she walked through the dungeon halls of the Fellowship for the final time. She dragged her fingers along the cool stone walls while flipping the dagger she'd taken from his study.

A nightstone dagger.

As she approached the stairs leading up to his private wing, the guards at the bottom lurched into action.

But she had already struck, their blood freezing instantly in their veins. She knew Alaric was letting her walk away. She knew his arrogance would keep him from chasing after her, forcing her to stay. He thought he would eventually win this game.

He was wrong.

He had taught her much of what she knew. He had created Death's Maiden.

But he had not created a Lady of Darkness.

With a smile lifting the corners of her mouth, she turned down the hall to his private quarters. Rooms she had only entered one other time. With a twitch of her fingers, white flames blasted the doors open. It was the only room she hadn't been to yet, having wandered all the other halls before she'd made her way to the dungeon study to wait for him.

She'd kept herself hidden from his wards until then. The Sorceress's book had all sorts of interesting Marks hidden within its pages. The cost? Being hidden to her Guardian as well within the wards. Cassius was waiting for her outside the Fellowship grounds. She'd refused to let anyone else come with her. No one else knew the streets of the Black Syndicate as well as they did. No one else would know what to watch for.

Who to watch for.

Scarlett walked past Alaric's giant four-poster bed, dragging the nightstone dagger along the mattress, before sending another blast of flames at the balcony doors.

She was leaning against the railing when Alaric finally tracked her down.

"You claim you want to leave, yet you keep waiting for me," he said smugly, his hands in pockets once more as he leaned against the doorjamb.

"I just really want to see your face when you realize just how far underneath your skin I am," she answered, her shadows beginning to converge behind her, twisting and writhing.

His mask of casual indifference faltered at her words. "What are you talking about?"

"It is rather poetic, isn't it?" she replied, climbing up onto the balcony railing, balancing precariously. "I wished for death that day, you know. That day. The days after. Even now at times. Feeling him ripped away from me. Just feeling . . ."

Him fighting his way to her. Him swearing there would be no more goodbyes. A bolt of energy—

Alaric lurched forward, his voice cutting through her downward spiral. "Get down from there, Scarlett. Now."

"I would start checking all those cracks," she replied. Flinging her arms out to the side, she free fell backwards.

"No!"

She heard Alaric's cry of panic as she hit the back of her shadow dragon. She sat up, turning to look down at Alaric's enraged face as her dragon flapped its wings, keeping her airborne.

Then she let out all that fury and grief and brokenness and *power* she'd been storing up for three entire weeks.

She yanked on the invisible thread within her soul that she had slowly unspooled across the entirety of the Fellowship as she'd walked the halls.

And she smiled darkly as white flames erupted everywhere, and Alaric's face went slack with shock.

It took him a few seconds to recover before wings ripped from his back, black and feathered. He shot to the sky with a roar of rage, but the orange flames that spewed from her shadow dragon's mouth had him staying back several feet.

She'd been banking on his ability to snuff out life with his fist being useless against her. From the fact that he hadn't even tried to use it, she appeared to be correct.

"You will pay for this!" he bellowed, his beloved Fellowship burning around him. "Enjoy your freedom, Scarlett *Monrhoe*. This is the last time I will let you walk away from me."

"You created this nightmare, Alaric," she replied, loud enough for him to hear. "You won't wake up from it until I allow it, and then it will only be for me to kill you myself."

Before he could say another word, her dragon was flapping up. She flew in a tight circle, swooping low enough for her to grab Cassius's outstretched arm when they glided past where he was hidden on a rooftop.

"You burned it down," Cassius said, looking back over his shoulder at the building that had been their home for so many years. She hadn't told anyone of that part of her plan. It was nearly ashes now, her white flames consuming it within minutes.

"That was just the beginning. Soon the entire world will be on fire," Scarlett replied, the dragon climbing higher into the sky.

Towards the stars that chose the darkness and the ashes in the voids between them.

CHAPTER 52
ALARIC

That fucking girl.
That fucking girl.
It was all Alaric could think as he flew towards the castle. He landed on an upper terrace, banishing his wings as he stormed through the doors and into the council room. Rage flooded through him, hot and acidic.

She was going to pay for all of this. She thought she knew what suffering was? She thought losing her twin flame was as bad as it could get?

She was going to learn exactly what it meant to be in a nightmare. "Get the Fae Queen," he snarled at Mikale, who had shot to his feet at his entrance.

"What happened?" Mikale demanded.

"She burned the entire fucking Fellowship to the ground," Alaric ground out. A servant entered the room carrying a tray of food, and he immediately gripped the young woman's heart in his power, squeezing and squeezing until there was nothing left.

She'd figured it out, too quickly, that he wasn't able to use his power on her. She likely didn't know why yet, but he knew she'd figure it out soon enough. And when she did, his task would get that much harder to complete.

And now she knew he was on a timeline and that his time was running out.

"Fuck!" he bellowed, snatching up anything he could get his hands on and hurling them around the space. Books. Papers. Dishes. Decor. Furniture. By the time he could see through the haze of red that had clouded his vision, the council room was destroyed. The servant's dead body was on the floor amid spilled food and beverages and debris.

Scarlett may have taken his strong hold, but that arrogant child had forgotten about the last key. She thought she'd been so damn sneaky taking that nightstone dagger from his desk, but in her haste to leave with it, she'd left the last key sitting there.

He had them all.

All seven of the Avonleyan keys.

He would have Talwyn shift them to their true form, and then he would hunt Scarlett down. She would take that fucking Blood Bond, and she would let him into Avonleya. He would not fail like his father had. He would succeed, and this world would be his to rule, his to own. Far from Achaz. Free of the duties required of him as a Maraan Prince.

That would be his reward for completing this task.

Nuri emerged from the shadows of the room, a maniacal smile on her face. "She is going to destroy you."

"Shut your fucking mouth," Alaric snarled, his hand snapping towards her. Nuri's hands grasped at her chest, a strangled cry rising up her throat, but that smile never left her face.

"Alaric." Balam's smooth, calming voice floated through the room. "We need her alive."

"Where is the Fae Queen?" Alaric demanded, releasing his adopted daughter. She bared her fangs at him as she recovered from his power coiling around her heart. He ignored her. She couldn't hurt him. Not since she took that Blood Bond to save those children.

He'd tried to rip that out of her. That heart that *cared* too much. He'd tried to drive it out of all three of them. Instead, they'd bonded. Latched onto each other. Became something truly horrific.

And something so much easier to manipulate. Until the day Juliette had died.

Sybil had not realized just how much of the gift of sight her daughter had. That Juliette had seen what needed to happen.

Scarlett thought Mikale and Veda had orchestrated the events of that night. And they had to an extent.

But so had Juliette.

"Talwyn is tending to matters in the Courts," Tarek supplied.

"Trying to instill order since we went in and took over the Fire and Water Courts."

"And she let the Royals and the Inner Courts go," Alaric said sharply, his power slipping around Tarek's heart now. "Did you not understand your task?"

"I did, my Lord," Tarek wheezed out. "The Fae Queen must be handled carefully. You know this. Be too forceful with her and she will leave our side." He sucked in a rattling breath. "They fled. Including Luan. Only Princess Ashtine remains. The other Royals have disappeared."

"But they still live," Alaric sneered.

"Not all of them," Mikale cut in with a sadistic grin. He looked at Tarek. "Seeing your queen take him out was truly beautiful. I was so glad I was there to witness it."

"You idiot," Alaric said, releasing Tarek from his power's hold. "It is precisely because of that act that we are in this mess."

"So she burned your little clubhouse down," Mikale said, rolling his eyes. "Does it really matter that much?"

"That *clubhouse* mattered more than the life of you and your sister combined," Alaric said. Mikale's mouth snapped shut, his jaw tightening as he bit his tongue on whatever he was about to say.

Smart move.

Alaric turned to Balam. "Take Tarek and get the Fae Queen. We have the final key. I want them shifted. Today."

Scarlett thought she would best him? That she would take him down? Make him suffer?

She was a weapon that he had created. And he wanted his property back.

He had spent the entire afternoon and evening reconstructing the map before him. The original had been destroyed in that fire she had set, consumed by her white flames.

Starfire.

Nothing could withstand it.

He'd had to combine his own power with that of Balam and Mikale to recreate this map. It showed the entirety of the continent, along with the rifts they'd created to allow more seraphs through. When he went to Avonleya with Scarlett in tow, he would have an army at his back. An army that would actually stand a chance against the power of the Avonleyans and what they had locked away within their lands.

His father had been foolish to think he could defeat them with wits. Thinking he could sneak in, control the Fae Queens through their sister. Manipulation of emotions and relationships could only get one so far. Alaric's own Wraiths of Death had proved that much.

Black pillars shimmered like mist where the rifts were, seraphs guarding each of them. Five in each of the mortal kingdoms. Three in the Night Children territory. They'd opened one in each of the Courts since they'd entered, but more would be coming. Tarek was right. They needed to be careful with Talwyn. She couldn't know he was taking Fae children from her Courts to open these rifts. She wouldn't understand the necessity of their sacrifice. Then again, she was so blinded by her need for vengeance, maybe she would.

They had been debating whether to go into the Shifter territory or the Witch Kingdoms next. Both were unpleasant. The Witches were just plain ruthless, and the Shifter siblings were cunning and dangerous. There were arguments to be made on both sides as to which one to pursue first. For now, he was content to leave them contained behind the wards that bound them to their lands.

They had moved to a different council room within the Baylorin castle after his temper had destroyed the previous one. Talwyn was in a corner working with the keys, Tarek monitoring her progress. She had not been particularly amenable to being summoned here on such short notice.

"You are changing the plans, then?" Balam asked quietly, studying the map. "You want to go to Avonleya before we have strongholds in the other two territories? Is that wise?"

"I think it would be unwise to delay anything once we have secured Scarlett once more. She can be given no more opportunities to escape again. When we have her, we move in," Alaric replied, his fingers drumming on the table.

"I believe it would be just as unwise to alter the plans that we have been carefully putting into place for centuries," Balam countered.

"You just want those mortal children back in your possession for only the gods know why," Alaric retorted, his fingers drumming again.

"I would not expect you to understand," Balam replied calmly.

"It is done."

They both turned at the sound of Talwyn's voice. She was standing, the skystone chains hanging from her hand. Amulets of the traitor gods no longer hung from them but seven nightstone keys. The tops of the keys still held the shape of the gods' symbols, but they tapered down to long points, two pointed prongs sticking out on either side like thorns.

Alaric stood, slowly walking towards her, taking in this surreal moment. How long had he waited to find these keys? How much had gone into orchestrating the events that had led up to this? How many years of making sure the right people were in the right place at the right time? All leading up to this moment and the ones to come.

He reached out, feeling the cool stone against his palm as he took the keys from the Fae Queen. He squeezed them in his fist, feeling the pointed prongs break skin. He didn't care. He finally held them in his hand.

They vibrated slightly against his palm, a tingling sensation shooting up his arm. Pure power held within them. He hadn't expected that. He'd thought they'd need Scarlett's power to activate the keys. But maybe not . . .

He turned to say something about it to Balam, but stilled.

Balam's eyes were fixed on the map. And Alaric could see why, as the shimmering pillars that represented the rifts slowly began to disappear. One by one, they winked out.

"What is happening?" Mikale asked from where he'd been sitting, quietly brooding for the last three hours.

"It appears all of our rifts are closing," Balam said, his black eyes lifting to meet Alaric's.

Without another word, they both Traveled to the closest rift. Two seraph sentries snapped to attention at their appearance, but they ignored them as they approached the rip. It was by a pond in a secluded clearing just north of the castle. Or it was supposed to be.

"The Night Children lands. The one by the river estate," Alaric said, Traveling in the next heartbeat.

They both stepped from the air within seconds of each other, staring at the spot along the estate wall where they had let the seraphs in to fight Scarlett and the Royals when they'd found the Contessa.

The rift was gone. Vanished. As if it had been closed up and sealed. "How is this possible?" Balam asked, anger edging into his voice.

"I do not know," Alaric ground out through gritted teeth. "Toreall. The one where they captured Scarlett."

Balam nodded, and moments later they were standing beside the trees of the Dresden Forest, just on the other side of the Earth Court.

That rift was gone too.

But the cry of an eagle had them both turning to the sky. Not an eagle. A griffin. Three of them.

"How the fuck are they out of the wards?" Alaric seethed, watching as the griffins flew closer and closer.

Balam said nothing, his eyes fixed on the approaching beasts and riders.

The High Witch and two of her sentries.

The ground shuddered beneath Alaric's feet when the griffins landed, their massive wings folding against their sides.

"Queen Scarlett Aditya has a message for you," the High Witch said, her tone hard and unforgiving, while her sentries eyed him and Balam with distaste.

"And what is that?" Alaric gritted out from between his teeth.

"Remember that she is already inside." The High Witch lifted her chin a little higher then, her griffin's wings already stretching back out and preparing to take off. "And that keys can open more than one lock, and some keys and locks do not go together at all."

With that, the High Witch was flying back to the skies, her sentries right behind her, turning and heading back to their lands. Alaric slowly looked down at the keys he still held in his hand.

He felt Balam's hand land on his shoulder before he Traveled them back to the council room in the castle.

"She played you like a fucking fool," Balam sneered as soon as they stepped from the air.

He snatched the keys from his hands, holding them before his face. He studied them for only a few seconds before throwing them onto the table. One look at the enchanted map told Alaric that every single rift that had been created over the last decade had been closed.

"What has happened?" Talwyn demanded, stepping to the table and picking up one of the keys, turning it over in her hand.

"She closed them all," Alaric murmured under his breath, unable to believe she had pulled this off. That she had indeed played him. She hadn't left that amulet by accident. She had wanted him to have it. Wanted him to have all of them. Wanted him to have Talwyn shift them into the keys.

Because she had altered them. These keys weren't going to get him into Avonleya.

He moved forward, picking up a key himself. Mikale did the same.

And Tarek.

He could see it then. The tiny Blood Mark at the top of the key, where the god's symbol still held its form. This one was Falein's, goddess of cleverness and wisdom.

How fitting.

"She not only closed all the godsdamn rifts, she sealed the realms," Balam bellowed. He spun, pointing an accusing finger at Alaric. "How many times did I tell you to quit playing with her? How many times did I tell you to keep her locked up? You insisted you had her under control. That she answered to you and only you, despite her proving time and again you have never owned that girl."

Balam swiped up another key. The points at the end pricked his skin, blood immediately welling. This key was Temural's, god of the wild and untamed. The god the Shifters tended to worship.

"Not only did she just prevent us from opening more rifts to bring in more forces, she lowered the wards keeping the Witches and Shifters contained. In one fell swoop, she just changed everything." He tossed the key back down on the table.

He stalked for the door, pausing beside Alaric. "You deserve every ounce of wrath Achaz will bring down upon your head for this."

Then Balam was storming out of the council room.

Silence fell in the room, but it was soon interrupted by slow, psychotic laughter. The laughter grew and grew. Alaric turned to face Nuri Halloway.

"Nothing about this is funny, you insane bloodsucker," Mikale snapped, chucking the key he was holding at her. She didn't even flinch when it cut a gash along her temple. "You are bound to us. If we go down, you go down with us."

"Oh, I always knew I would burn beside you for what I did," Nuri replied through her laughter.

"Then why the fuck are you laughing?" Mikale demanded.

"Because it is funny," she replied, as if this were the most obvious thing in the world.

"How?" he asked incredulously.

Her honey-colored eyes slid to Alaric. "Because you created a weapon to start and end a war, and in the end, it will only serve to destroy you."

Alaric's fist tightened around the key he still held. He could feel it cutting deeper and deeper into his skin as his fist clenched tighter and tighter, blood beginning to drip to the floor at his feet.

If Scarlett wanted a war, then she had just started one.

THE VOIDS BETWEEN THE STARS

He was looking for her.
    For shadows.
    For darkness.
For home.
He would not stop until he found her.
You promised . . .
He could hear her.
No goodbyes . . .
Could hear her crying.
Always be a you and me . . .
Could hear her screaming.
He had to find her. She needed him. She was hurting. She was drowning. She was alone in her darkness.

"You cannot be here."

He appeared then, seeming to shimmer before him, as though he weren't really there at all. He'd only seen this man once before. But he knew who it was.

A Lord of Night.

"You cannot be here," he repeated.

"Who are you?" That didn't sound like his voice. He looked down, but there was nothing to see. No arms, legs, body. Maybe those weren't needed in the spaces between stars.

"She is coming for you. You need to heed her call."

"Who are you?" He repeated, not sure how he was even speaking.

You promised . . .

"You should not be interfering with this."

This voice was feminine— ethereal and cold. A moment later, a female appeared beside the Lord of Night. She was stunning, her hair silver and flowing down past her navel. A crown of white flames as bright as starlight sat upon her head. Thick kohl lined her eyes, dark red on her lips. She wore a black, nearly sheer, gown, and around her shoulders sat a white python, stark against her bronze skin.

Serafina, goddess of dreams and stars.

No goodbyes . . .

The Lord of Night bowed his head. "I was sent by her."

"My daughter should not be interfering with this," Serafina replied, the snake gliding along her shoulders, down her arms, around her torso.

"We have little choice. It is interfere or choose death." The Lord of Night would not lift his head.

He knew he should probably look away. He was not worthy to look upon a goddess. But he was unsure how to do so without having an actual body.

Always be a you and me . . .

"That is not your place, nor is it hers. She knows this," Serafina said.

"With all due respect, my Lady, she seeks to protect what is hers. Something I am sure you understand," the Lord of Night replied.

"You think I do not know who you are, Cethin Sutara?" Serafina asked coldly.

The Lord of Night said nothing.

The goddess's eyes shifted to him, to whatever form he was here. "A Fae of Fire. This is who she places her hope on?"

"Without him, his other half will not survive. She will break. She will . . . come for him in another way," the Lord of Night replied.

You promised . . .

Her screams were growing fainter. She was getting farther away.

He was going to lose her.

No goodbyes . . .

Serafina's piercing silver eyes seemed to roam over his absent body.

What she saw, he did not know.

"Does my daughter believe the two of you can save them?"

"Yes," the Lord of Night answered.

Serafina fell silent again.

Always be a you and me . . .

"And my daughter . . . Saylah will . . . ?" she finally asked, trailing off.

"Will leave our world once she is sure it is safe to do so. When she is certain they will not seek her there again," said the Lord of Night.

"Do not walk in dreams this side of the Veil again," Serafina said coldly. "I will not stay Arius's judgment twice, even if you are our blood."

"Understood, my Lady. Thank you for your grace," the Lord of Night replied.

Serafina fell quiet, raising an arm so the snake could coil around it, moving back to her shoulders.

You promised . . .

He needed to go. He needed to get back to her.

Serafina's silver gaze settled back on him. "Go home, Son of Fire. Anala will find it interesting Amaré has chosen a full-blooded Fae." She studied him a moment longer.

Home.

Home was darkness and shadows and ashes.

"Tell your sister the Mark works both ways," Serafina said, turning back to the Lord of Night.

The Lord's head snapped up at that. Silver eyes met mirrors of their own.

"The Source Mark?"

"Yes," Serafina replied. "It is a secret of Arius, well-kept for many reasons. Arius will come for you himself if you reveal it to anyone else and will kill anyone else you tell. There will be a cost for this."

"I will gladly pay it," the Lord of Night said without any hesitation.

"You are not who will pay this price," Serafina said, her eyes moving back to where he stood without a physical body, before returning to the Lord of Night. "You know of the melding Mark?"

"Yes, but I cannot leave my lands."

"That is not my problem to solve, Cethin Sutara, but make your move quickly. Soon the Veil will close for him, and this will no longer be an option. Even now Arius comes for him."

She looked away from the Lord of Night and back at him one

final time. "She is shadows and stars, wildness and darkness. Follow them home."

Then the goddess was gone. So was the Lord of Night. *No goodbyes...*

Shadows brushed down flesh he could not see.

Always be a you and me... A white ember appeared. *You promised...*

Then another.

No goodbyes...

Another ember, flaring brighter than the stars.

Always be a you and me.

A NOTE FROM THE AUTHOR

Here we are! The end of another book. Writing *Lady of Ashes* was a different experience from the first two. *Darkness* and *Shadows* were already written when I published the first book last September. That was not the case with *Lady of Ashes*. This was my first time writing an entire book with people knowing it was coming and highly anticipating it. The pressure was overwhelming at times, and every day the fact that you all love and want more of Scarlett and crew is beyond surreal to me.

Lots happened in *Lady of Ashes*. Some things you probably didn't like. (I swear to Saylah what happened to Sorin was never planned! The characters do their own thing and tell their story. I sobbed when I finished that chapter. I will never forget messaging my alpha readers and saying, "I have no idea what the fuck just happened!" But remember, hope is for the dreamers. And book four is already started!) Anyway, the point is, my characters aren't perfect. I wanted you to see their flaws— from Sorin being a complete ass when Scarlett was being held captive, to Scarlett unnecessarily taunting Talwyn at inappropriate times, to Callan's bitterness and Talwyn's abandonment issues. Because life is messy, and none of us are perfect. Trusting people is hard. Admitting you were wrong is hard. Letting people in is hard. Growing as a person is hard. And none of that happens overnight. So Sorin and Scarlett, Callan and Talwyn— they're messy. They make wrong choices. They face hard decisions. They face harder consequences, and like Briar tells Scarlett, understanding and accepting are two very different things.

We make choices in life. Some are good. Some are bad. Some affect others positively, some negatively. We can't go back, only forward, so we lift our chins and face the future. We fix what we can, apologize for what we can't, and do whatever is necessary to make things right. But know this: You are worthy of good things, no matter what mistakes you made in the past. You deserve every star in the sky. Don't let anyone ever tell you otherwise.

XX~ Melissa

Scarlett's next book will be out soon, but until then, I want to keep in touch! I get messages from you guys every day, and they fill my cup more than you could ever know. I would love for you to join my little nook on Facebook at Melissa's Dragon Cave. To stay up-to-date on release dates, new series, and more, be sure and sign up for the newsletter, too!

One more thing: Your reviews on Amazon and Goodreads are HUGE for me as an author. I'd be forever grateful if you could go over to one (or both!) of them and leave a short review of *Lady of Ashes* to help Scarlett's story reach others. Word of mouth is an author's best friend and much appreciated. Shouts from rooftops are great, too.

Instagram: @melissa_k_roehrich
TikTok: @authormelissakroehrich
Facebook: Melissa K. Roehrich
Facebook Reader Group: Melissa's Dragon Cave
Website: www.melissakroehrich.com

ACKNOWLEDGMENTS

Thank you to my readers for falling in love with Scarlett, Sorin, and everyone in their world from the very beginning. Your comments, messages, and excitement for more filled my cup so much. Writing and publishing are hard, and those sweet words always come at the perfect time to remind me that it is all worth it in the end.

To my book besties: Sara Abel, Brittney Irvin, and Tracey Goodson. Where to even start? Thank you for being my ride-or-dies. Thank you for your unending support and encouragement. Thank you for letting me ramble and talk through things. Thank you for reading the roughest and messiest of drafts and then re-reading them when I make them better. Thank you for making me laugh on the daily. Thank you for getting excited about fictional men I create in my head and claiming them, based on name alone. Thank you for every single damn thing you do. (Except the incessant spicy jokes. You can all take those and shove them where not even Arius can follow.)

A big thank you to Megan Visger, Ashton Taylor, and Diane Dyk for being amazing as my final sets of eyes. Seriously, these books are nothing without you, and I am eternally grateful for you. Thank you to my ARC/Street Team. My dream was a team that was so much more than just an ARC/review exchange, and you guys have done just that. I cherish each of you and am humbled you choose to stay on my team.

Thank you to the Melissa's Nook and Posse reader's group. Your excitement over these books makes writing them that much more enjoyable. I love sharing snippets and watching your theories unfold. I love the beautiful thing that group is becoming, and I am so humbled you choose to stick around.

And finally, my husband— Thank you for doing the laundry. Thank you for cleaning the house when I'm coming up on deadlines. Thank you for being an amazing father to our boys. Thank you for chasing dreams and going on adventures. Thank you for loving me like the stars love the night— all the way through the darkness.

CAPTIVATED BY LADY OF DARKNESS? JOIN SCARLETT AS THE STORY CONTINUES...

Book 1: Lady of Darkness
Owned by a ruthless Assassin Lord, Scarlett Monrhoe and her two sisters have been trained since they were children to torture and take life. They are the most feared trio on the continent, but they are also wild and unpredictable.

Book 2: Lady of Shadows
Whisked away to the Fire Court, Scarlett Monrhoe finds herself in the hands of the man who killed her mother. The Prince of Fire. Thrust amongst the Fae court she loathes, she is at their mercy. She doesn't know what plans he has for her, but she has plans of her own. She just hasn't decided how thoroughly she wants to break him yet.

Book 3: Lady of Ashes
Scarlett Semiria knew the cost of her actions the day she sacrificed everything to keep her family, her Courts, and her twin flame safe. At least she thought she did. When she discovers the cost was more than she could have ever anticipated, she finds herself once again forced to choose between saving innocents or saving the ones she loves. But this choice might just leave her so broken, even the stars won't be able to bring her back.

Book 4: Lady of Embers
When they met her, she was a whirlwind of shadows and darkness. Standing among the ashes of betrayal and grief, now she is a tempest of rage and malice. Queen Scarlett Aditya will hunt them all down, one by one, and make them pay. Starting with the one who took her brightest star from her.

Book 5: Lady of Starfire
Scarlett Sutara Aditya has finally learned the full cost to save her world and correct mistakes that are not hers, but she refuses to accept the fate that has been decided for her. Making demands of her own, she fights for her twin flame, her family, and the realm that balances on her destiny. She has always played games by her own rules, but this time, winning might cost her everything.

ONE PLACE. MANY STORIES

Bold, innovative and
empowering publishing.

FOLLOW US ON:

@HQStories